"They will cheer far louder for you, I think, than they ever will for my own sons.

They will cheer far louder even than they do for me, their rightful lord, to whom they owe so much." It seemed that Orso's smile slipped, and his face looked tired, and sad, and worn without it. "They will cheer, in fact, a little too loudly for my taste."

There was the barest flash of movement at the corner of her eye, enough to make her bring up her hand on an instinct.

The wire hissed taut around it, snatching it up under her chin, crushing it chokingly tight against her throat.

Benna started forwards. "Mon—" Metal glinted as Prince Ario stabbed him in the neck. He missed his throat, caught him just under the ear.

Orso carefully stepped back as blood speckled the tiles with red. Foscar's mouth fell open, wine glass dropping from his hand, shattering on the floor.

Praise for
Best Served Cold

"A satisfyingly brutal fantasy quest. *Best Served Cold*? Modern fantasy doesn't get much hotter than this."   —Dave Bradley, *SFX*

Praise for
The Heroes

"Abercrombie never glosses over a moment of the madness, passion, and horror of war, nor the tribulations that turn ordinary people into the titular heroes."   —*Publishers Weekly* (starred review)

"Brilliant."   —*Guardian*

"Reminiscent of . . . Jim Butcher's Codex Alera novels in terms of scope and military action, this will appeal particularly to military fantasy buffs."
                    —*Library Journal*

"Magnificent, richly entertaining."   —*Time* magazine

"*The Heroes* is as irresistibly inviting as a bowl of pistachios. After that first taste, you're going to find it almost impossible to stop until it's all gone."
                    —*Philadelphia Inquirer*

"It's violent and full of treachery and horror, but it's delivered with Abercrombie's signature dark humor and a hint of cynicism."
                    —*Sci Fi* magazine

"This has been my favorite read of the past year and I cannot recommend *The Heroes* highly enough."   —*Grasping for the Wind*

"The book is gloriously funny. It's like an epic fantasy version of *All Quiet on the Western Front* spiked with some of the irreverence of Altman's *M*A*S*H*. The human tragedy has plenty of comedy to go around."   —*SFF Net*

"A blast to read."   —*SF Site*

"Though I have loved the books before, for me this is Joe's highlight to date. This is an evolution from, and a distillation of, all that was great in his previous books...The man just keeps getting better and better. Damn him!"

—SFFWorld.com

Praise for

The Blade Itself

"Abercrombie has written the finest epic fantasy trilogy in recent memory. He's one writer that no one should miss."

—Junot Diaz

"There are great characters, sparky dialogue, an action-packed plot, and from the very first words ('The End') and an opening scene that is literally a cliffhanger, you know you are in for a cheeky, vivid, exhilarating ride."

—Starburst

"Delightfully twisted and evil."

—Guardian

"An admirably hard, fast and unpretentious read."

—SFX

"Abercrombie kicks off his series masterfully with a heroic fantasy without conventional heroes...Their dialogue is full of cynicism and wit, their lives full of intrigue, battles and magic."

—RT Book Reviews

"If you're fond of bloodless, turgid fantasy with characters as thin as newspaper and as boring as plaster saints, Joe Abercrombie is really going to ruin your day. A long career for this guy would be a gift to our genre."

—Scott Lynch, author of The Lies of Locke Lamora

"In addition to excellent characterizations and fascinating world-building, Abercrombie also writes the best fight scenes I have read in ages. I'm glad the whole package is good, but I could happily recommend The Blade Itself for the fight scenes alone."

—SF Site

"Joe Abercrombie's *The Blade Itself* is sure to delight readers tired of the predictable machinations of standard fantasies...An author to watch."

—bn.com

Praise for
Before They Are Hanged

"Dark, deeply ironic and full of character gems that will appeal to your cynical side, *Before They Are Hanged* is as brilliant as its predecessor."

—*SFRevu*

"*Before They Are Hanged* is an excellent sequel from an author writing compelling, character-driven, adult fantasy, for readers who want to be entertained as well as challenged."

—SFFWorld.com

"This grim and vivid sequel to 2007's *The Blade Itself* transcends its middle volume status, keeping the reader engaged with complicated plotting and intriguing character development."

—*Publishers Weekly*

Praise for
Last Argument of Kings

"You should always end with the best. Wow them in the final act, make the last chorus a belter, build to a climax and them get them on their feet applauding when the curtain falls. *Last Argument of Kings* is the textbook example of this theory in practice."

—*SFX*

"A seminal work of modern fantasy."

—*SFRevu*

"Abercrombie is headed for superstar status."

—Jeff VanderMeer

By Joe Abercrombie

THE FIRST LAW TRILOGY

The Blade Itself
Before They Are Hanged
Last Argument of Kings

Best Served Cold

The Heroes

Red Country

THE SHATTERED SEA TRILOGY

Half a King
Half the World
Half a War

BEST
SERVED COLD

JOE ABERCROMBIE

www.orbitbooks.net

Orbit
Hachette Book Group
1290 Avenue of the Americas, New York, NY 10104
www.OrbitBooks.net

Printed in the United States of America

LSC-C

Originally published in hardcover by Orbit.

First Trade Edition: July 2012
10   9

Orbit is an imprint of Hachette Book Group, Inc.
The Orbit name and logo are trademarks of Little, Brown Book Group Limited.

The Hachette Speakers Bureau provides a wide range of authors for speaking events. To find out more, go to www.hachettespeakersbureau.com or call (866) 376-6591.

The publisher is not responsible for websites (or their content) that are not owned by the publisher.

Library of Congress Control Number: 2012932678

ISBN 978-0-316-19835-6 (pbk.)

For Grace
One day you will read this
And be slightly worried

Benna Murcatto
Saves a Life

The sunrise was the colour of bad blood. It leaked out of the east and stained the dark sky red, marked the scraps of cloud with stolen gold. Underneath it the road twisted up the mountainside towards the fortress of Fontezarmo—a cluster of sharp towers, ash-black against the wounded heavens. The sunrise was red, black and gold.

The colours of their profession.

"You look especially beautiful this morning, Monza."

She sighed, as if that was an accident. As if she hadn't spent an hour preening herself before the mirror. "Facts are facts. Stating them isn't a gift. You only prove you're not blind." She yawned, stretched in her saddle, made him wait a moment longer. "But I'll hear more."

He noisily cleared his throat and held up one hand, a bad actor preparing for his grand speech. "Your hair is like to . . . a veil of shimmering sable!"

"You pompous cock. What was it yesterday? A curtain of midnight. I liked that better, it had some poetry to it. Bad poetry, but still."

"Shit." He squinted up at the clouds. "Your eyes, then, gleam like piercing sapphires, beyond price!"

"I've got stones in my face, now?"

"Lips like rose petals?"

She spat at him, but he was ready and dodged it, the phlegm clearing his horse and falling on the dry stones beside the track. "That's to make your roses grow, arsehole. You can do better."

1

"Harder every day," he muttered. "That jewel I bought looks wonderful well on you."

She held up her right hand to admire it, a ruby the size of an almond, catching the first glimmers of sunlight and glistening like an open wound. "I've had worse gifts."

"It matches your fiery temper."

She snorted. "And my bloody reputation."

"Piss on your reputation! Nothing but idiots' chatter! You're a dream. A vision. You look like…" He snapped his fingers. "The very Goddess of War!"

"Goddess, eh?"

"Of War. You like it?"

"It'll do. If you can kiss Duke Orso's arse half so well, we might even get a bonus."

Benna puckered his lips at her. "I love nothing more of a morning than a faceful of his Excellency's rich, round buttocks. They taste like…power."

Hooves crunched on the dusty track, saddles creaked and harnesses rattled. The road turned back on itself, and again. The rest of the world dropped away below them. The eastern sky bled out from red to butchered pink. The river crept slowly into view, winding through the autumn woods in the base of the steep valley. Glittering like an army on the march, flowing swift and merciless towards the sea. Towards Talins.

"I'm waiting," he said.

"For what?"

"My share of the compliments, of course."

"If your head swells any further it'll fucking burst." She twitched her silken cuffs up. "And I don't want your brains on my new shirt."

"Stabbed!" Benna clutched one hand to his chest. "Right here! Is this how you repay my years of devotion, you heartless bitch?"

"How dare *you* presume to be devoted to *me*, peasant? You're like a tick devoted to a tiger!"

"Tiger? Hah! When they compare you to an animal they usually pick a snake."

"Better than a maggot."

"Whore."

"Coward."

"Murderer."

She could hardly deny that one. Silence settled on them again. A bird trilled from a thirsty tree beside the road.

Benna's horse drew gradually up beside hers, and ever so gently he murmured, "You look especially beautiful this morning, Monza."

That brought a smile to the corner of her mouth. The corner he couldn't see. "Well. Facts are facts."

She spurred round one more steep bend, and the outermost wall of the citadel thrust up ahead of them. A narrow bridge crossed a dizzy ravine to the gatehouse, water sparkling as it fell away beneath. At the far end an archway yawned, welcoming as a grave.

"They've strengthened the walls since last year," muttered Benna. "I wouldn't fancy trying to storm the place."

"Don't pretend you'd have the guts to climb the ladder."

"I wouldn't fancy telling someone else to storm the place."

"Don't pretend you'd have the guts to give the orders."

"I wouldn't fancy watching you tell someone else to storm the place."

"No." She leaned gingerly from her saddle and frowned down at the plummeting drop on her left. Then she peered up at the sheer wall on her right, battlements a jagged black edge against the brightening sky. "It's almost as if Orso's worried someone might try to kill him."

"He's got enemies?" breathed Benna, eyes round as saucers with mock amazement.

"Only half of Styria."

"Then...we've got enemies?"

"More than half of Styria."

"But I've tried so hard to be popular..." They trotted between two dour-faced soldiers, spears and steel caps polished to a murderous glint. Hoofbeats echoed in the darkness of the long tunnel, sloping gradually upwards. "You have that look, now."

"What look?"

"No more fun today."

"Huh." She felt the familiar frown gripping her face. "You can afford to smile. You're the good one."

It was a different world beyond the gates, air heavy with lavender, shining green after the grey mountainside. A world of close-clipped lawns, of hedges tortured into wondrous shapes, of fountains throwing up glittering

3

spray. Grim guardsmen, the black cross of Talins stitched into their white surcoats, spoiled the mood at every doorway.

"Monza…"

"Yes?"

"Let's make this the last season on campaign," Benna wheedled. "The last summer in the dust. Let's find something more comfortable to do. Now, while we're young."

"What about the Thousand Swords? Closer to ten thousand now, all looking to us for orders."

"They can look elsewhere. They joined us for plunder and we've given them plenty. They've no loyalty beyond their own profit."

She had to admit the Thousand Swords had never represented the best of mankind, or even the best of mercenaries. Most of them were a step above the criminal. Most of the rest were a step below. But that wasn't the point. "You have to stick at something in your life," she grunted.

"I don't see why."

"That's you all over. One more season and Visserine will fall, and Rogont will surrender, and the League of Eight will be just a bad memory. Orso can crown himself King of Styria, and we can melt away and be forgotten."

"We deserve to be remembered. We could have our own city. You could be the noble Duchess Monzcarro of…wherever—"

"And you the fearless Duke Benna?" She laughed at that. "You stupid arse. You can scarcely govern your own bowels without my help. War's a dark enough trade, I draw the line at politics. Orso crowned, then we retire."

Benna sighed. "I thought we were mercenaries. Cosca never stuck to an employer like this."

"I'm not Cosca. And anyway, it's not wise to say no to the Lord of Talins."

"You just love to fight."

"No. I love to win. Just one more season, then we can see the world. Visit the Old Empire. Tour the Thousand Isles. Sail to Adua and stand in the shadow of the House of the Maker. Everything we talked about." Benna pouted, just as he always did when he didn't get his way. He pouted, but he never said no. It scratched at her, sometimes, that she always had to make the choices. "Since we've clearly only got one pair of balls between us, don't you ever feel the need to borrow them yourself?"

"They look better on you. Besides, you've got all the brains. It's best they stay together."

"What do you get from the deal?"

Benna grinned at her. "The winning smile."

"Smile, then. For one more season." She swung down from her saddle, jerked her sword belt straight, tossed the reins at the groom and strode for the inner gatehouse. Benna had to hurry to catch up, getting tangled with his own sword on the way. For a man who earned his living from war, he'd always been an embarrassment where weapons were concerned.

The inner courtyard was split into wide terraces at the summit of the mountain, planted with exotic palms and even more heavily guarded than the outer. An ancient column said to come from the palace of Scarpius stood tall in the centre, casting a shimmering reflection in a round pool teeming with silvery fish. The immensity of glass, bronze and marble that was Duke Orso's palace towered around it on three sides like a monstrous cat with a mouse between its paws. Since the spring they'd built a vast new wing along the northern wall, its festoons of decorative stonework still half-shrouded in scaffolding.

"They've been building," she said.

"Of course. How could Prince Ario manage with only ten halls for his shoes?"

"A man can't be fashionable these days without at least twenty rooms of footwear."

Benna frowned down at his own gold-buckled boots. "I've no more than thirty pairs all told. I feel my shortcomings most keenly."

"As do we all," she muttered. A half-finished set of statues stood along the roofline. Duke Orso giving alms to the poor. Duke Orso gifting knowledge to the ignorant. Duke Orso shielding the weak from harm.

"I'm surprised he hasn't got one of the whole of Styria tonguing his arse," whispered Benna in her ear.

She pointed to a partly chiselled block of marble. "That's next."

"Benna!"

Count Foscar, Orso's younger son, rushed around the pool like an eager puppy, shoes crunching on fresh-raked gravel, freckled face all lit up. He'd made an ill-advised attempt at a beard since Monza had last seen him but the sprinkling of sandy hairs only made him look more boyish. He might have inherited all the honesty in his family, but the looks had gone else-

5

where. Benna grinned, threw one arm around Foscar's shoulders and ruffled his hair. An insult from anyone else, from Benna it was effortlessly charming. He had a knack of making people happy that always seemed like magic to Monza. Her talents lay in the opposite direction.

"Your father here yet?" she asked.

"Yes, and my brother too. They're with their banker."

"How's his mood?"

"Good, so far as I can tell, but you know my father. Still, he's never angry with you two, is he? You always bring good news. You bring good news today, yes?"

"Shall I tell him, Monza, or—"

"Borletta's fallen. Cantain's dead."

Foscar didn't celebrate. He hadn't his father's appetite for corpses. "Cantain was a good man."

That was a long way from the point, as far as Monza could see. "He was your father's enemy."

"A man you could respect, though. There are precious few of them left in Styria. He's really dead?"

Benna blew out his cheeks. "Well, his head's off, and spiked above the gates, so unless you know one hell of a physician..."

They passed through a high archway, the hall beyond dim and echoing as an emperor's tomb, light filtering down in dusty columns and pooling on the marble floor. Suits of old armour stood gleaming to silent attention, antique weapons clutched in steel fists. The sharp clicking of boot heels snapped from the walls as a man in a dark uniform paced towards them.

"Shit," Benna hissed in her ear. "That reptile Ganmark's here."

"Leave it be."

"There's no way that cold-blooded bastard's as good with a sword as they say—"

"He is."

"If I was half a man, I'd—"

"You're not. So leave it be."

General Ganmark's face was strangely soft, his moustaches limp, his pale grey eyes always watery, lending him a look of perpetual sadness. The rumour was he'd been thrown out of the Union army for a sexual indiscretion involving another officer, and crossed the sea to find a more broad-minded master. The breadth of Duke Orso's mind was infinite where his servants were concerned, provided they were effective. She and Benna were proof enough of that.

Ganmark nodded stiffly to Monza. "General Murcatto." He nodded stiffly to Benna. "General Murcatto. Count Foscar, you are keeping to your exercises, I hope?"

"Sparring every day."

"Then we will make a swordsman of you yet."

Benna snorted. "That, or a bore."

"Either one would be something," droned Ganmark in his clipped Union accent. "A man without discipline is no better than a dog. A soldier without discipline is no better than a corpse. Worse, in fact. A corpse is no threat to his comrades."

Benna opened his mouth but Monza talked over him. He could make an arse of himself later, if he pleased. "How was your season?"

"I played my part, keeping your flanks free of Rogont and his Osprians."

"Stalling the Duke of Delay?" Benna smirked. "Quite the challenge."

"No more than a supporting role. A comic turn in a great tragedy, but one appreciated by the audience, I hope."

The echoes of their footsteps swelled as they passed through another archway and into the towering rotunda at the heart of the palace. The curving walls were vast panels of sculpture showing scenes from antiquity. Wars between demons and magi, and other such rubbish. High above, the great dome was frescoed with seven winged women against a stormy sky — armed, armoured and angry-looking. The Fates, bringing destinies to earth. Aropella's greatest work. She'd heard it had taken him eight years to finish. Monza never got over how tiny, weak, utterly insignificant this space made her feel. That was the point of it.

The four of them climbed a sweeping staircase, wide enough for twice as many to walk abreast. "And where have your comic talents taken you?" she asked Ganmark.

"Fire and murder, to the gates of Puranti and back."

Benna curled his lip. "Any actual fighting?"

"Why ever would I do that? Have you not read your Stolicus? 'An animal fights his way to victory—'"

"'A general marches there,'" Monza finished for him. "Did you raise many laughs?"

"Not for the enemy, I suppose. Precious few for anyone, but that is war."

"I find time to chuckle," threw in Benna.

"Some men laugh easily. It makes them winning dinner companions." Ganmark's soft eyes moved across to Monza's. "I note you are not smiling."

"I will. Once the League of Eight are finished and Orso is King of Styria. Then we can all hang up our swords."

"In my experience swords do not hang comfortably from hooks. They have a habit of finding their way back into one's hands."

"I daresay Orso will keep you on," said Benna. "Even if it's only to polish the tiles."

Ganmark did not give so much as a sharp breath. "Then his Excellency will have the cleanest floors in all of Styria."

A pair of high doors faced the top of the stairs, gleaming with inlaid wood, carved with lions' faces. A thick-set man paced up and down before them like a loyal old hound before his master's bedchamber. Faithful Carpi, the longest-serving captain in the Thousand Swords, the scars of a hundred engagements marked out on his broad, weathered, honest face.

"Faithful!" Benna seized the old mercenary's big slab of a hand. "Climbing a mountain, at your age? Shouldn't you be in a brothel somewhere?"

"If only." Carpi shrugged. "But his Excellency sent for me."

"And you, being an obedient sort... obeyed."

"That's why they call me Faithful."

"How did you leave things in Borletta?" asked Monza.

"Quiet. Most of the men are quartered outside the walls with Andiche and Victus. Best if they don't set fire to the place, I thought. I left some of the more reliable ones in Cantain's palace with Sesaria watching over them. Old-timers, like me, from back in Cosca's day. Seasoned men, not prone to impulsiveness."

Benna chuckled. "Slow thinkers, you mean?"

"Slow but steady. We get there in the end."

"Going in, then?" Foscar set his shoulder to one of the doors and heaved it open. Ganmark and Faithful followed. Monza paused a moment on the threshold, trying to find her hardest face. She looked up and saw Benna smiling at her. Without thinking, she found herself smiling back. She leaned and whispered in his ear.

"I love you."

"Of course you do." He stepped through the doorway, and she followed.

Duke Orso's private study was a marble hall the size of a market square. Lofty windows marched in bold procession along one side, standing open, a keen breeze washing through and making the vivid hangings twitch and rustle. Beyond them a long terrace seemed to hang in empty air, overlooking the steepest drop from the mountain's summit.

The opposite wall was covered with towering panels, painted by the foremost artists of Styria, displaying the great battles of history. The victories of Stolicus, of Harod the Great, of Farans and Verturio, all preserved in sweeping oils. The message that Orso was the latest in a line of royal winners was hard to miss, even though his great-grandfather had been a usurper, and a common criminal besides.

The largest painting of them all faced the door, ten strides high at the least. Who else but Grand Duke Orso? He was seated upon a rearing charger, his shining sword raised high, his piercing eye fixed on the far horizon, urging his men to victory at the Battle of Etrea. The painter seemed to have been unaware that Orso hadn't come within fifty miles of the fighting.

But then fine lies beat tedious truths every time, as he had often told her.

The Duke of Talins himself sat crabbed over a desk, wielding a pen rather than a sword. A tall, gaunt, hook-nosed man stood at his elbow, staring down as keenly as a vulture waiting for thirsty travellers to die. A great shape lurked near them, in the shadows against the wall. Gobba, Orso's bodyguard, fat-necked as a great hog. Prince Ario, the duke's eldest son and heir, lounged in a gilded chair nearer at hand. He had one leg crossed over the other, a wine glass dangling carelessly, a bland smile balanced on his blandly handsome face.

"I found these beggars wandering the grounds," called Foscar, "and thought I'd commend them to your charity, Father!"

"Charity?" Orso's sharp voice echoed around the cavernous room. "I am not a great admirer of the stuff. Make yourselves comfortable, my friends, I will be with you shortly."

"If it isn't the Butcher of Caprile," murmured Ario, "and her little Benna too."

"Your Highness. You look well." Monza thought he looked an indolent cock, but kept it to herself.

"You too, as ever. If all soldiers looked as you did, I might even be

9

tempted to go on campaign myself. A new bauble?" Ario waved his own jewel-encrusted hand limply towards the ruby on Monza's finger.

"Just what was to hand when I was dressing."

"I wish I'd been there. Wine?"

"Just after dawn?"

He glanced heavy-lidded towards the windows. "Still last night as far as I'm concerned." As if staying up late was a heroic achievement.

"I will." Benna was already pouring himself a glass, never to be out-done as far as showing off went. Most likely he'd be drunk within the hour and embarrass himself, but Monza was tired of playing his mother. She strolled past the monumental fireplace held up by carven figures of Juvens and Kanedias, and towards Orso's desk.

"Sign here, and here, and here," the gaunt man was saying, one bony finger hovering over the documents.

"You know Mauthis, do you?" Orso gave a sour glance in his direction. "My leash-holder."

"Always your humble servant, your Excellency. The Banking House of Valint and Balk agrees to this further loan for the period of one year, after which they regret they must charge interest."

Orso snorted. "As the plague regrets the dead, I'll be bound." He scratched out a parting swirl on the last signature and tossed down his pen. "Everyone must kneel to someone, eh? Make sure you extend to your superiors my infinite gratitude for their indulgence."

"I shall do so." Mauthis collected up the documents. "That concludes our business, your Excellency. I must leave at once if I mean to catch the evening tide for Westport—"

"No. Stay a while longer. We have one other matter to discuss."

Mauthis' dead eyes moved towards Monza, then back to Orso. "As your Excellency desires."

The duke rose smoothly from his desk. "To happier business, then. You do bring happy news, eh, Monzcarro?"

"I do, your Excellency."

"Ah, whatever would I do without you?" There was a trace of iron grey in his black hair since she'd seen him last, perhaps some deeper lines at the corners of his eyes, but his air of complete command was impressive as ever. He leaned forwards and kissed her on both cheeks, then whispered in her ear, "Ganmark can lead soldiers well enough, but for a man who sucks cocks he hasn't the slightest sense of humour. Come, tell me of your victories in the open air." He left one arm draped around her shoulders and guided her, past the sneering Prince Ario, through the open windows onto the high terrace.

The sun was climbing now, and the bright world was full of colour. The blood had drained from the sky and left it a vivid blue, white clouds crawling high above. Below, at the very bottom of a dizzy drop, the river wound through the wooded valley, autumn leaves pale green, burned orange, faded yellow, angry red, light glinting silver on fast-flowing water. To the east, the forest crumbled away into a patchwork of fields — squares of fallow green, rich black earth, golden crop. Further still and the river met the grey sea, branching out in a wide delta choked with islands. Monza could just make out the suggestion of tiny towers there, buildings, bridges, walls. Great Talins, no bigger than her thumbnail.

She narrowed her eyes against the stiff breeze, pushed some stray hair out of her face. "I never tire of this view."

"How could you? It's why I built this damn place. Here I can keep one eye always on my subjects, as a watchful parent should upon his children. Just to make sure they don't hurt themselves while they play, you understand."

"Your people are lucky to have such a just and caring father," she lied smoothly.

"Just and caring." Orso frowned thoughtfully towards the distant sea. "Do you think that is how history will remember me?"

Monza thought it incredibly unlikely. "What did Bialoveld say? 'History is written by the victors.'"

The duke squeezed her shoulder. "All this, and well read into the bargain. Ario is ambitious enough, but he has no insight. I'd be surprised if he could read to the end of a signpost in one sitting. All he cares about is whoring. And shoes. My daughter Terez, meanwhile, weeps most bitterly because I married her to a king. I swear, if I had offered great Euz as the groom she would have whined for a husband better fitting her station." He gave a heavy sigh. "None of my children understand me. My great-grandfather was a mercenary, you know. A fact I do not like to advertise." Though he told her every other time they met. "A man who never shed a tear in his life, and wore on his feet whatever was to hand. A low-born fighting man, who seized power in Talins by the sharpness of his mind and sword together." More by blunt ruthlessness and brutality, the way Monza had heard the tale. "We are from the same stock, you and I. We have made ourselves, out of nothing."

Orso had been born to the wealthiest dukedom in Styria and never done a hard day's work in his life, but Monza bit her tongue. "You do me too much honour, your Excellency."

"Less than you deserve. Now tell me of Borletta."

"You heard about the battle on the High Bank?"

"I heard you scattered the League of Eight's army, just as you did at Sweet Pines! Ganmark says Duke Salier had three times your number!"

"Numbers are a hindrance if they're lazy, ill-prepared and led by idiots. An army of farmers from Borletta, cobblers from Affoia, glass-blowers from Visserine. Amateurs. They camped by the river, thinking we were far away, scarcely posted guards. We came up through the woods at night and caught them at sunrise, not even in their armour."

"I can see Salier now, the fat pig, waddling from his bed to run!"

"Faithful led the charge. We broke them quickly, captured their supplies."

"Turned the golden cornfields crimson, I was told."

"They hardly even fought. Ten times as many drowned trying to swim the river as died fighting. More than four thousand prisoners. Some ransoms were paid, some not, some men were hanged."

"And few tears shed, eh, Monza?"

"Not by me. If they were so keen to live, they could've surrendered."

"As they did at Caprile?"

She stared straight back into Orso's black eyes. "Just as they did at Caprile."

"Borletta is besieged, then?"

"Fallen already."

The duke's face lit up like a boy's on his birthday. "Fallen? Cantain surrendered?"

"When his people heard of Salier's defeat, they lost hope."

"And people without hope are a dangerous crowd, even in a republic."

"Especially in a republic. A mob dragged Cantain from the palace, hanged him from the highest tower, opened the gates and threw themselves on the mercy of the Thousand Swords."

"Hah! Slaughtered by the very people he laboured to keep free. There's the gratitude of the common man, eh, Monza? Cantain should have taken my money when I offered. It would have been cheaper for both of us."

"The people are falling over themselves to become your subjects. I've given orders they should be spared, where possible."

"Mercy, eh?"

"Mercy and cowardice are the same," she snapped out. "But you want their land, not their lives, no? Dead men can't obey."

Orso smiled. "Why can my sons not mark my lessons as you have? I entirely approve. Hang only the leaders. And Cantain's head above the gates. Nothing encourages obedience like a good example."

"Already rotting, with those of his sons."

"Fine work!" The Lord of Talins clapped his hands, as though he never heard such pleasing music as the news of rotting heads. "What of the takings?"

The accounts were Benna's business, and he came forwards now, sliding a folded paper from his chest pocket. "The city was scoured, your Excellency. Every building stripped, every floor dug up, every person searched. The usual rules apply, according to our terms of engagement. Quarter for the man that finds it, quarter for his captain, quarter for the generals," and he bowed low, unfolding the paper and offering it out, "and quarter for our noble employer."

Orso's smile broadened as his eyes scanned down the figures. "My blessing on the Rule of Quarters! Enough to keep you both in my service a little longer." He stepped between Monza and Benna, placed a gentle hand on each of their shoulders and led them back through the open windows. Towards the round table of black marble in the centre of the room, and the great map spread out upon it. Ganmark, Ario and Faithful had already gathered there. Gobba still lurked in the shadows, thick arms folded across his chest. "What of our one-time friends and now our bitter enemies, the treacherous citizens of Visserine?"

"The fields round the city are burned up to the gates, almost." Monza scattered carnage across the countryside with a few waves of her finger. "Farmers driven off, livestock slaughtered. It'll be a lean winter for fat Duke Salier, and a leaner spring."

"He will have to rely on the noble Duke Rogont and his Osprians," said Ganmark, with the faintest of smiles.

Prince Ario snickered. "Much talk blows down from Ospria, always, but little help."

"Visserine is poised to drop into your lap next year, your Excellency."

"And with it the heart is torn from the League of Eight."

"The crown of Styria will be yours."

The mention of crowns teased Orso's smile still wider. "And we have you to thank, Monzcarro. I do not forget that."

"Not only me."

"Curse your modesty. Benna has played his part, and our good friend General Ganmark, and Faithful too, but no one could deny this is your work. Your commitment, your single-mindedness, your swiftness to act! You shall have a great triumph, just as the heroes of ancient Aulcus did. You shall ride through the streets of Talins and my people will shower you with flower petals in honour of your many victories." Benna was grinning, but Monza couldn't join him. She'd never had much taste for congratulations. "They will cheer far louder for you, I think, than they ever will for my own sons. They will cheer far louder even than they do for me, their rightful lord, to whom they owe so much." It seemed that Orso's smile slipped, and his face looked tired, and sad, and worn without it. "They will cheer, in fact, a little too loudly for my taste."

There was the barest flash of movement at the corner of her eye, enough to make her bring up her hand on an instinct.

The wire hissed taut around it, snatching it up under her chin, crushing it chokingly tight against her throat.

Benna started forwards. "Mon—" Metal glinted as Prince Ario stabbed him in the neck. He missed his throat, caught him just under the ear.

Orso carefully stepped back as blood speckled the tiles with red. Foscar's mouth fell open, wine glass dropping from his hand, shattering on the floor.

Monza tried to scream, but only spluttered through her half-shut windpipe, made a sound like a honking pig. She fished at the hilt of her dagger with her free hand but someone caught her wrist, held it fast. Faithful Carpi, pressed up tight against her left side.

"Sorry," he muttered in her ear, pulling her sword from its scabbard and flinging it clattering across the room.

Benna stumbled, gurgling red drool, one hand clutched to the side of his face, black blood leaking out between white fingers. His other hand

14

fumbled for his sword while Ario watched him, frozen. He drew a clumsy foot of steel before General Ganmark stepped up and stabbed him, smoothly and precisely — once, twice, three times. The thin blade slid in and out of Benna's body, the only sound the soft breath from his gaping mouth. Blood shot across the floor in long streaks, began to leak out into his white shirt in dark circles. He tottered forwards, tripped over his own feet and crashed down, half-drawn sword scraping against the marble underneath him.

Monza strained, every muscle trembling, but she was held helpless as a fly in honey. She heard Gobba grunting with effort in her ear, his stubbly face rubbing against her cheek, his great body warm against her back. She felt the wire cut slowly into the sides of her neck, deep into the side of her hand, caught fast against her throat. She felt the blood running down her forearm, into the collar of her shirt.

One of Benna's hands crawled across the floor, reaching out for her. He lifted himself an inch or two, veins bulging from his neck. Ganmark leaned forwards and calmly ran him through the heart from behind. Benna quivered for a moment, then sagged down and was still, pale cheek smeared with red. Dark blood crept out from under him, worked its way along the cracks between the tiles.

"Well." Ganmark leaned down and wiped his sword on the back of Benna's shirt. "That's that."

Mauthis watched, frowning. Slightly puzzled, slightly irritated, slightly bored. As though examining a set of figures that wouldn't quite add.

Orso gestured at the body. "Get rid of that, Ario."

"Me?" The prince's lip curled.

"Yes, you. And you can help him, Foscar. The two of you must learn what needs to be done to keep our family in power."

"No!" Foscar stumbled away. "I'll have no part of this!" He turned and ran from the room, his boots slapping against the marble floor.

"That boy is soft as syrup," muttered Orso at his back. "Ganmark, help him."

Monza's bulging eyes followed them as they dragged Benna's corpse out through the doors to the terrace, Ganmark grim and careful at the head end, Ario cursing as he daintily took one boot, the other smearing a red trail after them. They heaved Benna up onto the balustrade and rolled him off. Like that he was gone.

"Ah!" squawked Ario, waving one hand. "Damn it! You scratched me!"

Ganmark stared back at him. "I apologise, your Highness. Murder can be a painful business."

The prince looked around for something to wipe his bloody hands on. He reached for the rich hangings beside the window.

"Not there!" snapped Orso. "That's Kantic silk, at fifty scales a piece!"

"Where, then?"

"Find something else, or leave them red! Sometimes I wonder if your mother told the truth about your paternity, boy." Ario wiped his hands sulkily on the front of his shirt while Monza stared, face burning from lack of air. Orso frowned over at her, a blurred black figure through the wet in her eyes, the hair tangled across her face. "Is she still alive? Whatever are you about, Gobba?"

"Fucking wire's caught on her hand," hissed the bodyguard.

"Find another way to be done with her, then, lackwit."

"I'll do it." Faithful pulled the dagger from her belt, still pinning her wrist with his other hand. "I really am sorry."

"Just get to it!" growled Gobba.

The blade went back, steel glinting in a shaft of light. Monza stomped down on Gobba's foot with all the strength she had left. The bodyguard grunted, grip slipping on the wire, and she dragged it away from her neck, growling, twisting hard as Carpi stabbed at her.

The blade went well wide of the mark, slid in under her bottom rib. Cold metal, but it felt burning hot, a line of fire from her stomach to her back. It slid right through and the point pricked Gobba's gut.

"Gah!" He let go the wire and Monza whooped in air, started shrieking mindlessly, lashed at him with her elbow and sent him staggering. Faithful was caught off guard, fumbled the knife as he pulled it out of her and sent it spinning across the floor. She kicked at him, missed his groin and caught his hip, bent him over. She snatched at a dagger on his belt, pulled it from its sheath, but her cut hand was clumsy and he caught her wrist before she could ram the blade into him. They wrestled with it, teeth bared, gasping spit in each other's faces, lurching back and forth, their hands sticky with her blood.

"Kill her!"

There was a crunch and her head was full of light. The floor cracked against her skull, slapped her in the back. She spat blood, mad screams guttering to a long drawn croak, clawing at the smooth floor with her nails.

"Fucking bitch!" The heel of Gobba's big boot cracked down on her right hand and sent pain lancing up her forearm, tore a sick gasp from her. His boot crunched again across her knuckles, then her fingers, then her wrist. At the same time Faithful's foot was thudding into her ribs, over and over, making her cough and shudder. Her shattered hand twisted, turned sideways on. Gobba's heel crashed down and crushed it flat into the cold marble with a splintering of bone. She flopped back, hardly able to breathe, the room turning over, history's painted winners grinning down.

"You stabbed me, you dumb old bastard! You stabbed me!"

"You're hardly even cut, fathead! You should've kept a hold on her!"

"I should stab the useless pair of you!" hissed Orso's voice. "Just get it done!"

Gobba's great fist came down, dragged Monza up by her throat. She tried to grab at him with her left hand but all her strength had leaked out through the hole in her side, the cuts in her neck. Her clumsy fingertips only smeared red traces across his stubbly face. Her arm was dragged away, twisted sharply behind her back.

"Where's Hermon's gold?" came Gobba's rough voice. "Eh, Murcatto? What did you do with the gold?"

Monza forced her head up. "Lick my arse, cocksucker." Not clever, perhaps, but from the heart.

"There never was any gold!" snapped Faithful. "I told you that, pig!"

"There's this much." One by one, Gobba twisted the battered rings from her dangling fingers, already bloating, turning angry purple, bent and shapeless as rotten sausages. "Good stone, that," he said, peering at the ruby. "Seems a waste of decent flesh, though. Why not give me a moment with her? A moment's all it would take."

Prince Ario tittered. "Speed isn't always something to be proud of."

"For pity's sake!" Orso's voice. "We're not animals. Off the terrace and let us be done. I am late for breakfast."

She felt herself dragged, head lolling. Sunlight stabbed at her. She was lifted, limp boots scraping on stone. Blue sky turning. Up onto the balustrade. The breath scraped at her nose, shuddered in her chest. She twisted, kicked. Her body, struggling vainly to stay alive.

"Let me make sure of her." Ganmark's voice.

"How sure do we need to be?" Blurry through the bloody hair across her eyes she saw Orso's lined face. "I hope you understand. My great-grandfather was a mercenary. A low-born fighting man, who seized power by the sharp-ness of his mind and sword together. I cannot allow another mercenary to seize power in Talins."

She meant to spit in his face, but all she did was blow bloody drool down her own chin. "Fuck yourse—"

Then she was flying.

Her torn shirt billowed and flapped against her tingling skin. She turned over, and over, and the world tumbled around her. Blue sky with shreds of cloud, black towers at the mountain top, grey rock face rushing past, yellow-green trees and sparkling river, blue sky with shreds of cloud, and again, and again, faster, and faster.

Cold wind ripped at her hair, roared in her ears, whistled between her teeth along with her terrified breath. She could see each tree, now, each branch, each leaf. They surged up towards her. She opened her mouth to scream—

Twigs snatched, grabbed, lashed at her. A broken branch knocked her spinning. Wood cracked and tore around her as she plunged down, down, and crashed into the mountainside. Her legs splintered under her plum-meting weight, her shoulder broke apart against firm earth. But rather than dashing her brains out on the rocks, she only shattered her jaw against her brother's bloody chest, his mangled body wedged against the base of a tree.

Which was how Benna Murcatto saved his sister's life.

She bounced from the corpse, three-quarters senseless, and down the steep mountainside, over and over, flailing like a broken doll. Rocks, and roots, and hard earth clubbed, punched, crushed her, as if she was battered apart with a hundred hammers.

She tore through a patch of bushes, thorns whipping and clutching. She rolled, and rolled, down the sloping earth in a cloud of dirt and leaves. She tumbled over a tree root, crumpled on a mossy rock. She slid slowly to a stop, on her back, and was still.

"Huuuurrrrhhh..."

Stones clattered down around her, sticks and gravel. Dust slowly settled. She heard wind, creaking in the branches, crackling in the leaves. Or her own breath, creaking and crackling in her broken throat. The sun flickered through black trees, jabbing at one eye. The other was dark. Flies buzzed, zipping and swimming in the warm morning air. She was down with the waste from Orso's kitchens. Sprawled out helpless in the midst of the rotten vegetables, and the cooking slime, and the stinking offal left over from the last month's magnificent meals. Tossed out with the rubbish.

"Huuurrhhh…"

A jagged, mindless sound. She was embarrassed by it, almost, but couldn't stop making it. Animal horror. Mad despair. The groan of the dead, in hell. Her eye darted desperately around. She saw the wreck of her right hand, a shapeless, purple glove with a bloody gash in the side. One finger trembled slightly. Its tip brushed against torn skin on her elbow. The forearm was folded in half, a broken-off twig of grey bone sticking through bloody silk. It didn't look real. Like a cheap theatre prop.

"Huurrhhh…"

The fear had hold of her now, swelling with every breath. She couldn't move her head. She couldn't move her tongue in her mouth. She could feel the pain, gnawing at the edge of her mind. A terrible mass, pressing up against her, crushing every part of her, worse, and worse, and worse.

"Huurhh…uurh…"

Benna was dead. A streak of wet ran from her flickering eye and she felt it trickle slowly down her cheek. Why was she not dead? How could she not be dead?

Soon, please. Before the pain got any worse. Please, let it be soon.

"Uurh…uh…uh."

Please, death.

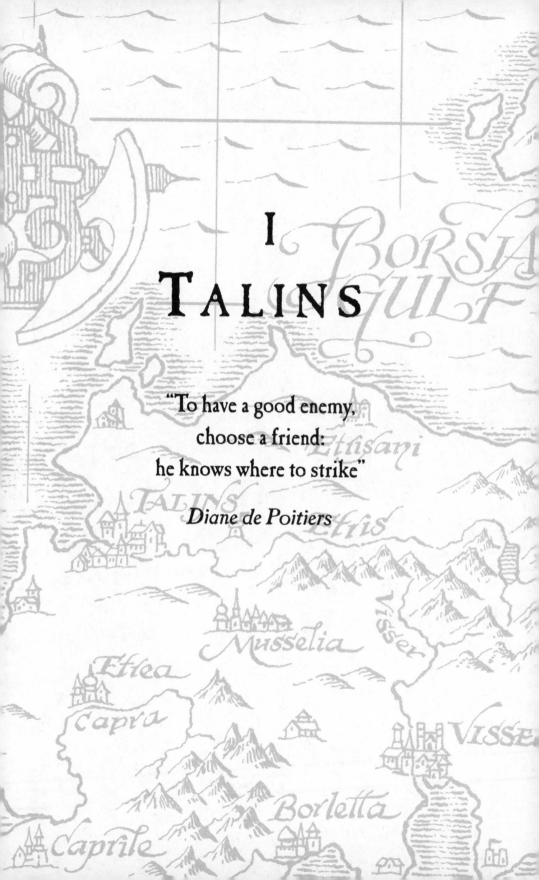

I
TALINS

"To have a good enemy,
choose a friend:
he knows where to strike"

Diane de Poitiers

*J*appo Murcatto never said why he had such a good sword, but he knew well how to use it. Since his son was by five years his younger child and sickly too, from a tender age he passed on the skill to his daughter. Monzcarro had been her father's mother's name, in the days when her family had pretended at nobility. Her own mother had not cared for it in the least, but since she had died giving birth to Benna that scarcely mattered.

Those were peaceful years in Styria, which were as rare as gold. At ploughing time Monza would hurry behind her father while the blade scraped through the dirt, weeding any big stones from the fresh black earth and throwing them into the wood. At reaping time she would hurry behind her father while his scythe-blade flashed, gathering the cut stalks into sheaves.

"Monza," he would say, smiling down at her, "what would I do without you?"

She helped with the threshing and tossed the seed, split logs and drew water. She cooked, swept, washed, carried, milked the goat. Her hands were always raw from some kind of work. Her brother did what he could, but he was small, and ill, and could do little. Those were hard years, but they were happy ones.

When Monza was fourteen, Jappo Murcatto caught the fever. She and Benna watched him cough, and sweat, and wither. One night her father seized Monza by her wrist, and stared at her with bright eyes.

"Tomorrow, break the ground in the upper field, or the wheat won't rise in time. Plant all you can." He touched her cheek. "It's not fair that it should fall to you, but your brother is so small. Watch over him." And he was dead.

Benna cried, and cried, but Monza's eyes stayed dry. She was thinking about the seed that needing planting, and how she would do it. That night Benna was

23

too scared to sleep alone, and so they slept together in her narrow bed, and held each other for comfort. They had no one else now.

The next morning, in the darkness, Monza dragged her father's corpse from the house, through the woods behind and rolled it into the river. Not because she had no love in her, but because she had no time to bury him.

By sunrise she was breaking the ground in the upper field.

Land of Opportunity

Irst thing Shivers noticed as the boat wallowed in towards the wharves, it was nothing like as warm as he'd been expecting. He'd heard the sun always shone in Styria. Like a nice bath, all year round. If Shivers had been offered a bath like this he'd have stayed dirty, and probably had a few sharp words to say besides. Talins huddled under grey skies, clouds bulging, a keen breeze off the sea, cold rain speckling his cheek from time to time and reminding him of home. And not in a good way. Still, he was set on looking at the sunny side of the case. Probably just a shitty day was all. You get 'em everywhere.

There surely was a seedy look about the place, though, as the sailors scuttled to make the boat fast to the dock. Brick buildings lined the grey sweep of the bay, narrow windowed, all squashed in together, roofs slumping, paint peeling, cracked-up render stained with salt, green with moss, black with mould. Down near the slimy cobbles the walls were plastered over with big papers, slapped up at all angles, ripped and pasted over each other, torn edges fluttering. Faces on them, and words printed. Warnings, maybe, but Shivers weren't much of a reader. Specially not in Styrian. Speaking the language was going to be enough of a challenge.

The waterfront crawled with people, and not many looked happy. Or healthy. Or rich. There was quite the smell. Or to be more precise, a proper reek. Rotten salt fish, old corpses, coal smoke and overflowing latrine pits rolled up together. If this was the home of the grand new man he was hoping to become, Shivers had to admit to being more'n a touch disappointed. For the briefest moment he thought about paying over most of what he had left for a trip straight back home to the North on the next tide. But he shook it off. He was done with war, done with leading men to death, done with killing and all that went along with it. He was set on being a better man. He was going to do the right thing, and this was where he was going to do it.

"Right, then." He gave the nearest sailor a cheery nod. "Off I go." He got no more'n a grunt in return, but his brother used to tell him it was what you gave out that made a man, not what you got back. So he grinned like he'd got a merry send-off, strode down the clattering gangplank and into his brave new life in Styria.

He'd scarcely taken a dozen paces, staring up at looming buildings on one side, swaying masts on the other, before someone barged into him and near knocked him sideways.

"My apologies," Shivers said in Styrian, keeping things civilised. "Didn't see you there, friend." The man kept going, didn't even turn. That prickled some at Shivers' pride. He had plenty of it still, the one thing his father had left him. He hadn't lived through seven years of battles, skirmishes, waking with snow on his blanket, shit food and worse singing so he could come down here and get shouldered.

But being a bastard was crime and punishment both. Let go of it, his brother would've told him. Shivers was meant to be looking on the sunny side. So he took a turn away from the docks, down a wide road and into the city. Past a clutch of beggars on blankets, waving stumps and withered limbs. Through a square where a great statue stood of a frowning man, pointing off to nowhere. Shivers didn't have a clue who he was meant to be, but he looked pretty damn pleased with himself. The smell of cooking wafted up, made Shivers' guts grumble. Drew him over to some kind of stall where they had sticks of meat over a fire in a can.

"One o' them," said Shivers, pointing. Didn't seem much else needed saying, so he kept it simple. Less chance of mistakes. When the cook told him the price he near choked on his tongue. Would've got him a whole sheep in the North, maybe even a breeding pair. The meat was half fat and the rest gristle. Didn't taste near so good as it had smelled, but by that point it weren't much surprise. It seemed most things in Styria weren't quite as advertised.

The rain had started up stronger now, flitting down into Shivers' eyes as he ate. Not much compared to storms he'd laughed through in the North, but enough to damp his mood a touch, make him wonder where the hell he'd rest his head tonight. It trickled from mossy eaves and broken gutters, turned the cobbles dark, made the people hunch and curse. He came from the close buildings and onto a wide river bank, all built up and fenced in with stone. He paused a moment, wondering which way to go.

The city went on far as he could see, bridges upstream and down, buildings on the far bank even bigger than on this side — towers, domes, roofs, going on and on, half-shrouded and turned dreamy grey by the rain. More torn papers flapping in the breeze, letters daubed over 'em too with bright coloured paint, streaks running down to the cobbled street. Letters high as a man in places. Shivers peered over at one set, trying to make some sense of it.

Another shoulder caught him, right in the ribs, made him grunt. This time he whipped round snarling, little meat stick clutched in his fist like he might've clutched a blade. Then he took a breath. Weren't all that long ago Shivers had let the Bloody-Nine go free. He remembered that morning like it was yesterday, the snow outside the windows, the knife in his hand, the rattle as he'd let it fall. He'd let the man who killed his brother live, passed up revenge, all so he could be a better man. Step away from blood. Stepping away from a loose shoulder in a crowd was nothing to sing about.

He forced half a smile back on and walked the other way, up onto the bridge. Silly thing like the knock of a shoulder could leave you cursing for days, and he didn't want to poison his new beginning 'fore it even got begun. Statues stood on either side, staring off above the water, monsters of white stone streaky with bird droppings. People flooded past, one kind of river flowing over the other. People of every type and colour. So many he felt like nothing in the midst of 'em. Bound to have a few shoulders catch you in a place like this.

Something brushed his arm. Before he knew it he'd grabbed someone round the neck, was bending him back over the parapet twenty strides above the churning water, gripping his throat like he was strangling a chicken. "Knock me, you bastard?" he snarled in Northern. "I'll cut your fucking eyes out!"

He was a little man, and he looked bloody scared. Might've been a head shorter'n Shivers, and not much more than half his weight. Getting over the first red flush of rage, Shivers realised this poor fool had barely even touched him. No malice in it. How come he could shrug off big wrongs then lose his temper over nothing? He'd always been his own worst enemy.

"Sorry, friend," he said in Styrian, and meaning it too. He let the man slither down, brushed the crumpled front of his coat with a clumsy hand. "Real sorry about that. Little…what do you call it…mistake is all. Sorry. Do you want…" Shivers found he was offering the stick, one last shred of fatty meat still clinging to it. The man stared. Shivers winced. 'Course he didn't want that. Shivers hardly wanted it himself. "Sorry…" The man turned and dashed off into the crowd, looking once over his shoulder, scared, like he'd just survived being attacked by a madman. Maybe he had. Shivers stood on the bridge, frowned down at that brown water churning past. Same sort of water they had in the North, it had to be said.

Seemed being a better man might be harder work than he'd thought.

The Bone-Thief

When her eyes opened, she saw bones.

Bones long and short, thick and thin, white, yellow, brown. Covering the peeling wall from floor to ceiling. Hundreds of them. Nailed up in patterns, a madman's mosaic. Her eyes rolled down, sore and sticky. A tongue of fire flickered in a sooty hearth. On the mantelpiece above, skulls grinned emptily at her, neatly stacked three high.

Human bones, then. Monza felt her skin turn icy cold.

She tried to sit up. The vague sense of numb stiffness flared into pain so suddenly she nearly puked. The darkened room lurched, blurred. She was held fast, lying on something hard. Her mind was full of mud, she couldn't remember how she'd got here.

Her head rolled sideways and she saw a table. On the table was a metal tray. On the tray was a careful arrangement of instruments. Pincers, pliers, needles and scissors. A small but very businesslike saw. A dozen knives at least, all shapes and sizes. Her widening eyes darted over their polished blades — curved, straight, jagged edges cruel and eager in the firelight. A surgeon's tools?

Or a torturer's?

"Benna?" Her voice was a ghostly squeak. Her tongue, her gums, her throat, the passages in her nose, all raw as skinned meat. She tried to move again, could scarcely lift her head. Even that much effort sent a groaning stab through her neck and into her shoulder, set off a dull pulsing up her legs, down her right arm, through her ribs. The pain brought fear with it, the fear brought pain. Her breath quickened, shuddering and wheezing through her sore nostrils.

Click, click.

She froze, silence prickling at her ears. Then a scraping, a key in a lock. Frantically now she squirmed, pain bursting in every joint, ripping at every muscle, blood battering behind her eyes, thick tongue wedged into her teeth to stop herself screaming. A door creaked open and banged shut. Footsteps on bare boards, hardly making a sound, but each one still a jab of fear in her throat. A shadow reached out across the floor — a huge shape, twisted, monstrous. Her eyes strained to the corners, nothing she could do but wait for the worst.

A figure came through the doorway, walked straight past her and over to a tall cupboard. A man no more than average height, in fact, with short fair hair. The misshapen shadow was caused by a canvas sack over one shoulder. He hummed tunelessly to himself as he emptied it, placing each item carefully on its proper shelf, then turning it back and forth until it faced precisely into the room.

If he was a monster, he seemed an everyday sort of one, with an eye for the details.

He swung the doors gently shut, folded his empty bag once, twice, and slid it under the cupboard. He took off his stained coat and hung it from a hook, brushed it down with a brisk hand, turned and stopped dead. A pale, lean face. Not old, but deeply lined, with harsh cheekbones and eyes hungry bright in bruised sockets.

They stared at each other for a moment, both seeming equally shocked. Then his colourless lips twitched into a sickly smile.

"You are awake!"

"Who are you?" A terrified scratch in her dried-up throat.

"My name is not important." He spoke with the trace of a Union accent. "Suffice it to say I am a student of the physical sciences."

"A healer?"

"Among other things. As you may have gathered, I am an enthusiast, chiefly, for bones. Which is why I am so glad that you…fell into my life." He grinned again, but it was like the skulls' grins, never touching his eyes.

"How did…" She had to wrestle with the words, jaw stiff as rusted hinges. It was like trying to talk with a turd in her mouth, and hardly better tasting. "How did I get here?"

"I need bodies for my work. They are sometimes to be found where I found you. But I have never before found one still alive. I would judge you to be a spectacularly lucky woman." He seemed to think about it for a moment. "It would have been luckier still if you had not fallen in the first place but ... since you did —"

"Where's my 'rother? Where's Benna?"

"Benna?"

Memory flooded back in a blinding instant. Blood pumping from between her brother's clutching fingers. The long blade sliding through his chest while she watched, helpless. His slack face, smeared with red.

She gave a croaking scream, bucked and twisted. Agony flashed up every limb and made her squirm the more, shudder, retch, but she was held fast. Her host watched her struggle, waxy face empty as a blank page. She sagged back, spitting and moaning as the pain grew worse and worse, gripping her like a giant vise, steadily tightened.

"Anger solves nothing."

All she could do was growl, snatched breaths slurping through her gritted teeth.

"I imagine you are in some pain, now." He pulled open a drawer in the cupboard and took out a long pipe, bowl stained black. "I would try to get used to it, if you can." He stooped and fished a hot coal from the fire with a set of tongs. "I fear that pain will come to be your constant companion."

The worn mouthpiece loomed at her. She'd seen husk-smokers often enough, sprawling like corpses, withered to useless husks themselves, caring for nothing but the next pipe. Husk was like mercy. A thing for the weak. For the cowardly.

He smiled his dead-man's smile again. "This will help."

Enough pain makes a coward of anyone.

The smoke burned at her lungs and made her sore ribs shake, each choke sending new shocks to the tips of her fingers. She groaned, face screwing up, struggling again, but more weakly, now. One more cough, and she lay limp. The edge was gone from the pain. The edge was gone from the fear and the panic. Everything slowly melted. Soft, warm, comfortable. Someone made a long, low moan. Her, maybe. She felt a tear run down the side of her face.

"More?" This time she held the smoke as it bit, blew it tickling out in a shimmering plume. Her breath came slower, and slower, the surging of blood in her head calmed to a gentle lapping.

"More?" The voice washed over her like waves on the smooth beach.

The bones were blurred now, glistening in haloes of warm light. The coals in the grate were precious jewels, sparkling every colour. There was barely any pain, and what there was didn't matter. Nothing did. Her eyes flickered pleasantly, then even more pleasantly drifted shut. Mosaic patterns danced and shifted on the insides of her eyelids. She floated on a warm sea, honey sweet...

Back with us?" His face flickered into focus, hanging limp and white as a flag of surrender. "I was worried, I confess. I never expected you to wake, but now that you have, it would be a shame if—"

"Benna?" Monza's head was still floating. She grunted, tried to work one ankle, and the grinding ache brought the truth back, crushed her face into a hopeless grimace.

"Still sore? Perhaps I have a way to lift your spirits." He rubbed his long hands together. "The stitches are all out, now."

"How long did I sleep?"

"A few hours."

"Before that?"

"Just over twelve weeks." She stared back, numb. "Through the autumn, and into winter, and the new year will soon come. A fine time for new beginnings. That you have woken at all is nothing short of miraculous. Your injuries were...well, I think you will be pleased with my work. I know I am."

He slid a greasy cushion from under the bench and propped her head up, handling her as carelessly as a butcher handles meat, bringing her chin forwards so she could look down at herself. So there was no choice but to. Her body was a lumpy outline under a coarse grey blanket, three leather belts across chest, hips and ankles.

"The straps are for your own protection, to prevent you rolling from the bench while you slept." He hacked out a sudden chuckle. "We wouldn't want you breaking anything, would we? Ha...ha! Wouldn't want to break anything." He unbuckled the last of the belts, took the blanket between thumb and forefinger while she stared down, desperate to know, and desperate not to know at once.

He whipped it away like a showman displaying his prize exhibit.

She hardly recognised her own body. Stark naked, gaunt and withered as a beggar's, pale skin stretched tight over ugly knobbles of bone, stained all over with great black, brown, purple, yellow blooms of bruise. Her eyes darted over her own wasted flesh, steadily widening as she struggled to take it in. She was slit all over with red lines. Dark and angry, edged with raised pink flesh, stippled with the dots of pulled stitches. There were four, one above the other, following the curves of her hollow ribs on one side. More angled across her hips, down her legs, her right arm, her left foot.

She'd started to tremble. This butchered carcass couldn't be her body. Her breath hissed through her rattling teeth, and the blotched and shrivelled ribcage heaved in time. "Uh…" she grunted. "Uh…"

"I know! Impressive, eh?" He leaned forwards over her, following the ladder of red marks on her chest with sharp movements of his hand. "The ribs here and the breastbone were quite shattered. It was necessary to make incisions to repair them, you understand, and to work on the lung. I kept the cutting to the minimum, but you can see that the damage—"

"Uh…"

"The left hip I am especially pleased with." Pointing out a crimson zig-zag from the corner of her hollow stomach down to the inside of her withered leg, surrounded on both sides by trails of red dots. "The thighbone, here, unfortunately broke into itself." He clicked his tongue and poked a finger into his clenched fist. "Shortening the leg by a fraction, but, as luck would have it, your other shin was shattered, and I was able to remove the tiniest section of bone to make up the difference." He frowned as he pushed her knees together, then watched them roll apart, feet flopping hopelessly outwards. "One knee slightly higher than the other, and you won't stand quite so tall but, considering—"

"Uh…"

"Set, now." He grinned as he squeezed gently at her shrivelled legs from the tops of her thighs down to her knobbly ankles. She watched him touching her, like a cook kneading at a plucked chicken, and hardly felt it. "All quite set, and the screws removed. A wonder, believe me. If the doubters at the academy could see this now they wouldn't be laughing. If my old master could see this, even he—"

"Uh…" She slowly raised her right hand. Or the trembling mockery of a hand that dangled from the end of her arm. The palm was bent, shrunken, a great ugly scar where Gobba's wire had cut into the side. The fingers were crooked as tree roots, squashed together, the little one sticking out at a strange angle. Her breath hissed through gritted teeth as she tried to make a fist. The fingers scarcely moved, but the pain still shot up her arm and made bile burn the back of her throat.

"The best I could do. Small bones, you see, badly damaged, and the tendons of the little finger were quite severed." Her host seemed disappointed. "A shock, of course. The marks will fade...somewhat. But really, considering the fall...well, here." The mouthpiece of the husk-pipe came towards her and she sucked on it greedily. Clung to it with her teeth as if it was her only hope. It was.

He tore a tiny piece from the corner of the loaf, the kind you might feed birds with. Monza watched him do it, mouth filling with sour spit. Hunger or sickness, there wasn't much difference. She took it dumbly, lifted it to her lips, so weak that her left hand trembled with the effort, forced it between her teeth and down her throat.

Like swallowing broken glass.

"Slowly," he murmured, "very slowly, you have eaten nothing but milk and sugar-water since you fell."

The bread caught in her craw and she retched, gut clamping up tight around the knife-wound Faithful had given her.

"Here." He slid his hand round her skull, gentle but firm, lifted her head and tipped a bottle of water to her lips. She swallowed, and again, then her eyes flicked towards his fingers. She could feel unfamiliar lumps there, down the side of her head. "I was forced to remove several pieces of your skull. I replaced them with coins."

"Coins?"

"Would you rather I had left your brains exposed? Gold does not rust. Gold does not rot. An expensive treatment, of course, but if you had died, I could always have recouped my investment, and since you have not, well...I consider it money well spent. Your scalp will feel somewhat lumpy, but your hair will grow back. Such beautiful hair you have. Black as midnight."

He let her head fall gently back against the bench and his hand lingered there. A soft touch. Almost a caress.

"Normally I am a taciturn man. Too much time spent alone, perhaps." He flashed his corpse-smile at her. "But I find you...bring out the best in me. The mother of my children is the same. You remind me of her, in a way."

Monza half-smiled back, but in her gut she felt a creeping of disgust. It mingled with the sickness she was feeling every so often, now. That sweating need.

She swallowed. "Could I—"

"Of course." He was already holding the pipe out to her.

Close it."

"It won't close!" she hissed, three of the fingers just curling, the little one still sticking out straight, or as close to straight as it ever came. She remembered how nimble-fingered she used to be, how sure, and quick, and the frustration and the fury were sharper even than the pain. "They won't close!"

"For weeks you have been lying here. I did not mend you so you could smoke husk and do nothing. Try harder."

"Do you want to fucking try?"

"Very well." His hand closed relentlessly around hers and forced the bent fingers into a crunching fist. Her eyes bulged from her head, breath whistling too fast for her to scream.

"I doubt you understand how much I am helping you." He squeezed tighter and tighter. "One cannot grow without pain. One cannot improve without it. Suffering drives us to achieve great things." The fingers of her good hand plucked and scrabbled uselessly at his fist. "Love is a fine cushion to rest upon, but only hate can make you a better person. There." He let go of her and she sagged back, whimpering, watched her trembling fingers come gradually halfway open, scars standing out purple.

She wanted to kill him. She wanted to shriek every curse she knew. But she needed him too badly. So she held her tongue, sobbed, gasped, ground her teeth, smacked the back of her head against the bench.

"Now, close your hand." She stared into his face, empty as a fresh-dug grave. "Now, or I must do it for you."

She growled with the effort, whole arm throbbing to the shoulder. Gradually, the fingers inched closed, the little one still sticking straight. "There, you fucker!" She shook her numb, knobbly, twisted fist under his nose. "There!"

"Was that so hard?" He held the pipe out to her and she snatched it from him. "You need not thank me."

* * *

And we will see if you can take the—"

She squealed, knees buckling, would have fallen if he hadn't caught her.

"Still?" He frowned. "You should be able to walk. The bones are knitted. Pain, of course, but…perhaps a fragment within one of the joints, still. Where does it hurt?"

"Everywhere!" she snarled at him.

"I trust this is not simply your stubbornness. I would hate to open the wounds in your legs again unnecessarily." He hooked one arm under her knees and lifted her without much effort back onto the bench. "I must go for a while."

She clutched at him. "You'll be back soon?"

"Very soon."

His footsteps vanished down the corridor. She heard the front door click shut, the sound of the key scraping in the lock.

"Son of a fucking whore." And she swung her legs down from the bench. She winced as her feet touched the floor, bared her teeth as she straightened up, growled softly as she let go of the bench and stood on her own feet.

It hurt like hell, and it felt good.

She took a long breath, gathered herself and began to waddle towards the far side of the room, pains shooting through her ankles, knees, hips, into her back, arms held out wide for balance. She made it to the cupboard and clung to its corner, slid open the drawer. The pipe lay inside, a jar of bubbly green glass beside it with some black lumps of husk in the bottom. How she wanted it. Her mouth was dry, her palms sticky with sick need. She slapped the drawer closed and hobbled back to the bench. Everything was still pierced with cold aches, but she was getting stronger each day. Soon she'd be ready. But not yet.

Patience is the parent of success, Stolicus wrote.

Across the room, and back, growling through her clenched teeth. Across the room and back, lurching and grimacing. Across the room and back, whimpering, wobbling, spitting. She leaned against the bench, long enough to get her breath.

Across the room and back again.

*   *   *

The mirror had a crack across it, but she wished it had been far more broken.

Your hair is like a curtain of midnight!

Shaved off down the left side of her head, grown back to a scabby stubble. The rest hung lank, tangled and greasy as old seaweed.

Your eyes gleam like piercing sapphires, beyond price!

Yellow, bloodshot, lashes gummed to clumps, rimmed red-raw in sockets purple-black with pain.

Lips like rose petals?

Cracked, parched, peeling grey with yellow scum gathered at the corners. There were three long scabs across her sucked-in cheek, sore brown against waxy white.

You look especially beautiful this morning, Monza . . .

On each side of her neck, withered down to a bundle of pale cords, the red scars left by Gobba's wire. She looked like a woman just dead of the plague. She looked scarcely better than the skulls stacked on the mantelpiece.

Beyond the mirror, her host was smiling. "What did I tell you? You look well."

The very Goddess of War!

"I look a fucking carnival curiosity!" she sneered, and the ruined crone in the mirror sneered back at her.

"Better than when I found you. You should learn to look on the happy side of the case." He tossed the mirror down, stood and pulled on his coat. "I must leave you for the time being, but I will be back, as I always am. Continue working the hand, but keep your strength. Later I must cut into your legs and establish the cause of your difficulty in standing."

She forced a sickly smile onto her face. "Yes. I see."

"Good. Soon, then." He threw his canvas bag over his shoulder. His footsteps creaked down the corridor, the lock closed. She counted slowly to ten.

Off the bench and she snatched up a pair of needles and a knife from the tray. She limped to the cupboard, ripped open the drawer, stuffed the pipe into the pocket of the borrowed trousers hanging from her hip bones, the jar with it. She lurched down the hall, boards creaking under bare feet. Into the bedroom, grimacing as she fished the old boots from under the bed, grunting as she pulled them on.

Out into the corridor again, her breath hissing with effort, and pain, and fear. She knelt down by the front door, or at least lowered herself by creaking degrees until her burning knees were on the boards. It was a long time since she'd worked a lock. She fished and stabbed with the needles, twisted hand fumbling.

"Turn, you bastard. Turn."

Luckily the lock wasn't good. The tumblers caught, turned with a satisfying clatter. She grabbed the knob and hauled the door open.

Night, and a hard one. Cold rain lashed an overgrown yard, rank weeds edged with the slightest glimmer of moonlight, crumbling walls slick with wet. Beyond a leaning fence bare trees rose up, darkness gathered under their branches. A rough night for an invalid to be out of doors. But the chill wind whipping at her face, the clean air in her mouth, felt almost like being alive again. Better to freeze free than spend another moment with the bones. She ducked out into the rain, hobbled across the garden, nettles snatching at her. Into the trees, between their glistening trunks, and she struck away from the track and didn't look back.

Up a long slope, bent double, good hand dragging at the muddy ground, pulling her on. She grunted at each slipping footfall, every muscle screeching at her. Black rain dripped from black branches, pattered on fallen leaves, crept through her hair and plastered it across her face, crept through her stolen clothes and stuck them to her sore skin.

"One more step."

She had to make some distance from the bench, and the knives, and that slack, white, empty face. That face, and the one in the mirror.

"One more step ... one more step ... one more step."

The black ground lurched past, her hand trailing against the wet mud, the tree roots. She followed her father as he pushed the plough, long ago, hand trailing through the turned earth for stones.

What would I do without you?

She knelt in the cold woods beside Cosca, waiting for the ambush, her nose full of that damp, crisp smell of trees, her heart bursting with fear and excitement.

You have a devil in you.

She thought of whatever she needed to so she could keep going, memories rushing on ahead of her clumsy boots.

Off the terrace and let us be done.

She stopped, stood bent over, shuddering smoky breaths into the wet night. No idea how far she'd come, where she'd started, where she was going. For now, it hardly mattered.

She wedged her back against a slimy tree-trunk, prised at her belt buckle with her good hand, shoved at it with the side of the other one. It took her a teeth-gritted age to finally get the damn thing open. At least she didn't have to pull her trousers down. They sagged off her bony arse and down her scarred legs under their own weight. She paused a moment, wondering how she'd get them back up.

One battle at a time, Stolicus wrote.

She grabbed a low branch, slick with rain, lowered herself under it, right hand cradled against her wet shirt, bare knees trembling.

"Come on," she hissed, trying to make her knotted bladder unclench. "If you need to go, just go. Just go. Just—"

She grunted with relief, piss spattering into the mud along with the rain, trickling down the hillside. Her right leg was burning worse than ever, wasted muscles quivering. She winced as she tried to move her hand down the branch, shift her weight to her other leg. In a sick instant one foot flew out from under her and she went over backwards, breath whooping in, reason all blotted out by the dizzy memory of falling. She bit her tongue as her head cracked down in the mud, slid a stride or two, flailed to a stop in a wet hollow full of rotting leaves. She lay in the tapping rain, trousers tangled round her ankles, and wept.

It was a low moment, no doubt of that.

She bawled like a baby. Helpless, heedless, desperate. Her sobs racked her, choked her, made her mangled body shake. She didn't know the last time she'd cried. Never, maybe. Benna had done the weeping for both of them. Now all the pain and fear of a dozen black years and more came leaking out of her screwed-up face. She lay in the mud, and tortured herself with everything she'd lost.

Benna was dead, and everything good in her was dead with him. The way they made each other laugh. That understanding that comes from a life together, gone. He'd been home, family, friend and more, all killed at once. All snuffed out carelessly as a cheap candle. Her hand was ruined. She held the aching, mocking remnant of it to her chest. The way she used to draw a sword, use a pen, firmly shake a hand, all crushed under Gobba's boot. The way she used to walk, run, ride, all scattered broken down

39

the mountainside under Orso's balcony. Her place in the world, ten years' work, built with her own sweat and blood, struggled for, sweated for, vanished like smoke. All she'd worked for, hoped for, dreamed of.

Dead.

She worked her belt back up, dead leaves dragged up with it, and fumbled it shut. A few last sobs, then she snorted snot down, wiped the rest from under her nose on her cold hand. The life she'd had was gone. The woman she'd been was gone. What they'd broken could never be mended.

But there was no point weeping about it now.

She knelt in the mud, shivering in the darkness, silent. These things weren't just gone, they'd been stolen from her. Her brother wasn't just dead, he'd been murdered. Slaughtered like an animal. She forced her twisted fingers closed until they made a trembling fist.

"I'll kill them."

She made herself see their faces, one by one. Gobba, the fat hog, lounging in the shadows. *A waste of decent flesh.* Her face twitched as she saw his boot stomp down across her hand, felt the bones splinter. Mauthis, the banker, his cold eyes staring down at her brother's corpse. Inconvenienced. Faithful Carpi. A man who'd walked beside her, eaten beside her, fought beside her, year upon year. *I really am sorry.* She saw his arm go back, ready to stab her through, felt the wound niggling at her side, pressed at it through her wet shirt, dug her fingers into it back and front until it burned like fury.

"I'll kill them."

Ganmark. She saw his soft, tired face. Flinched as his sword punched through Benna's body. *That's that.* Prince Ario, lounging in his chair, wine glass dangling. His knife cut Benna's neck open, blood bubbling between his fingers. She made herself see each detail, remember each word said. Foscar, too. *I'll have no part of this.* But that changed nothing.

"I'll kill them all."

And Orso, last. Orso, who she'd fought for, struggled for, killed for. Grand Duke Orso, Lord of Talins, who'd turned on them over a rumour. Murdered her brother, left her broken for nothing. For a fear they'd steal his place. Her jaw ached, her teeth were clenched so hard. She felt his fatherly hand on her shoulder and her shivering flesh crawled. She saw his smile, heard his voice echoing in her pounding skull.

What would I do without you?

Seven men.

She dragged herself up, chewing at her sore lip, and lurched off through the dark trees, water trickling from her sodden hair and down her face. The pain gnawed through her legs, her sides, her hand, her skull, but she bit down hard and forced herself on.

"I'll kill them...I'll kill them...I'll kill them..."

It hardly needed to be said. She was done with crying.

The old track was grown over, almost past recognition. Branches thrashed at Monza's aching body. Brambles snatched at her burning legs. She crept through a gap in the overgrown hedgerow and frowned down at the place where she'd been born. She wished she'd been able to make the stubborn soil bear a crop as well as it bloomed thorn and nettle now. The upper field was a patch of dead scrub. The lower was a mass of briar. The remains of the mean farmhouse peered sadly over from the edge of the woods, and she peered sadly back.

It seemed that time had given both of them a kicking.

She squatted, gritting her teeth as her withered muscles stretched around her crooked bones, listening to a few birds cawing at the sinking sun, watching the wind twitch the wild grass and snatch at the nettles. Until she was sure the place was every bit as abandoned as it looked. Then she gently worked the life back into her battered legs and limped for the buildings. The house where her father died was a tumbled-down shell and a rotted beam or two, its outline so small it was hard to believe she could ever have lived there. She, and her father, and Benna too. She turned her head and spat into the dry dirt. She hadn't come here for bitter-sweet remembrances.

She'd come for revenge.

The shovel was where she'd left it two winters ago, blade still bright under some rubbish in the corner of the roofless barn. Thirty strides into the trees. Hard to imagine how easily she'd taken those long, smooth, laughing steps as she waddled through the weeds, spade dragging behind her. Into the quiet woods, wincing at every footfall, broken patterns of sunlight dancing across the fallen leaves as the evening wore down.

Thirty strides. She hacked the brambles away with the edge of the shovel, finally managed to drag the rotten tree-trunk to one side and began to dig. It would've been some task with both her hands and both her legs. As she was now, it was a groaning, sweating, teeth-grinding ordeal. But

Monza had never been one to give up halfway, whatever the costs. *You have a devil in you*, Cosca used to tell her, and he'd been right. He'd learned it the hard way.

Night was coming on when she heard the hollow clomp of metal against wood. She scraped the last soil away, prised the iron ring from the dirt with broken fingernails. She strained, growled, stolen clothes stuck cold to her scarred skin. The trapdoor came open with a squealing of metal and a black hole beckoned, a ladder half-seen in the darkness.

She worked her way down, painstakingly slow since she'd no interest in breaking any more bones. She fumbled in the black until she found the shelf, wrestled with the flint in her bad joke of a hand and finally got the lamp lit. Light flared out weakly around the vaulted cellar, glittering along the metal edges of Benna's precautions, sitting safe, just as they'd left them.

He always had liked to plan ahead.

Keys hung from a row of rusted hooks. Keys to empty buildings, scattered across Styria. Places to hide. A rack along the left-hand wall bristled with blades, long and short. She opened a chest beside it. Clothes, carefully folded, never worn. She doubted they'd even fit her wasted body now. She reached out to touch one of Benna's shirts, remembering him picking out the silk for it, caught sight of her own right hand in the lamplight. She snatched up a pair of gloves, threw one away and shoved the maimed thing into the other, wincing as she worked the fingers, the little one still sticking out stubbornly straight.

Wooden boxes were stacked at the back of the cellar, twenty of them all told. She hobbled to the nearest one and pushed back the lid. Hermon's gold glittered at her. Heaps of coins. A small fortune in that box alone. She touched her fingertips gingerly to the side of her skull, felt the ridges under her skin. Gold. There's so much more you can do with it than just hold your head together.

She dug her hand in and let coins trickle between her fingers. The way you somehow have to if you find yourself alone with a box of money. These would be her weapons. These, and...

She let her gloved hand trail across the blades on the rack, stopped and went back one. A long sword of workmanlike grey steel. It didn't have much in the way of ornamental flourishes, but there was a fearsome beauty about it still, to her eye. The beauty of a thing fitted perfectly to its purpose. It

42

was a Calvez, forged by the best swordsmith in Styria. A gift from her to Benna, not that he'd have known the difference between a good blade and a carrot. He'd worn it for a week then swapped it for an over-priced length of scrap metal with stupid gilt basketwork.

The one he'd been trying to draw when they killed him.

She curled her fingers round the cold grip, strange in her left hand, and slid a few inches of steel from the sheath. It shone bright and eager in the lamplight. Good steel bends, but never breaks. Good steel stays always sharp and ready. Good steel feels no pain, no pity and, above all, no remorse.

She felt herself smile. The first time in months. The first time since Gobba's wire hissed tight around her neck.

Vengeance, then.

Fish out of Water

The cold wind swept in from the sea and gave the docks of Talins a damn good blasting. Or a damn bad one, depending how well dressed you were. Shivers weren't that well dressed at all. He pulled his thin coat tight round his shoulders, though he might as well not have bothered, for all the good it did him. He narrowed his eyes and squinted miserably into the latest gust. He was earning his name today, alright. He had been for weeks.

He remembered sitting warm by the fire, up in the North in a good house in Uffrith, with a belly full of meat and a head full of dreams, talking to Vossula about the wondrous city of Talins. He remembered it with some bitterness, because it was that bloody merchant, with his dewy eyes and his honey tales of home, who'd talked him into this nightmare jaunt to Styria.

Vossula had told him that the sun always shone in Talins. That was why Shivers had sold his good coat before he set off. Didn't want to end up sweating, did he? Seemed now, as he shivered like a curled-up autumn leaf only just still clinging to its branch, that Vossula had been doing some injury to the truth.

Shivers watched the restless waves chew at the quay, throwing icy spray over the few rotting skiffs stirring at their rotting wharves. He listened to the hawsers creaking, to the ill seabirds croaking, to the wind making a loose shutter rattle, to the grunts and grumbles of the men around him. All of 'em huddled on the docks for the sniff of a chance at work, and there'd never been in one place such a crowd of sad stories. Grubby and gaunt, ragged clothes and pinched-in faces. Desperate men. Men just like Shivers, in other words. Except they'd been born here. He'd been stupid enough to choose this.

He slid the last hard heel of bread from his inside pocket as carefully as a miser breaking out his hoard, took a nibble from the end, making sure to taste every crumb of it. Then he caught the man nearest to him staring, licking his pale lips. Shivers felt his shoulders slump, broke some off and handed it over.

"Thanks, friend," as he wolfed it down.

"No bother," said Shivers, though he'd spent hours chopping logs for it. Quite a lot of painful bother, in fact. The rest of 'em were all looking now, big sad eyes like pups needed feeding. He threw up his hands. "If I had bread for everyone, why the fuck would I be stood here?"

They turned away grumbling. He snorted cold snot up and spat it out. Aside from some stale bread it was the only thing to have passed his lips that morning, and going in the wrong direction. He'd come with a pocketful of silver, and a faceful of smiles, and a swelling chestful of happy hope. Ten weeks in Styria, and all three of those were emptied to the bitter dregs.

Vossula had told him the people of Talins were friendly as lambs, welcomed foreigners like guests. He'd found nothing but scorn, and a lot of folk keen to use any rotten trick to relieve him of his dwindling money. They weren't just handing out second chances on the street corners here. No more'n they had been in the North.

A boat had come in now, was tying off at the quay, fishers scurrying over and around it, hauling at ropes and cursing at sailcloth. Shivers felt the rest of the desperate perking up, wondering if there might be a shift of work for one of 'em. He felt a dismal little flare of hope in his own chest, however hard he tried to keep it down, and stood up keen on tiptoes to watch.

Fish slid from the nets onto the dockside, squirming silver in the watery sun. It was a good, honest trade, fishing. A life on the salty brine where no sharp words are spoken, all men set together against the wind, plucking the shining bounty from the sea, and all that. A noble trade, or so Shivers tried to tell himself, in spite of the stink. Any trade that'd have him seemed pretty noble about then.

A man weathered as an old gatepost hopped down from the boat and strutted over, all self-importance, and the beggars jostled each other to catch his eye. The captain, Shivers guessed.

"Need two hands," he said, pushing his battered cap back and looking those hopeful, hopeless faces over. "You, and you."

Hardly needed saying Shivers weren't one of 'em. His head sagged along with the rest as he watched the lucky pair hurrying back to the boat after its captain. One was the bastard he gave his bread to, didn't so much as look round, let alone put in a word for him. Maybe it was what you gave out that made a man, not what you got back, like Shivers' brother used to say, but getting back's a mighty good thing to stop you starving.

"Shit on this." And he started after them, picking his way between the fishers sorting their flapping catch into buckets and barrows. Wearing the friendliest grin he could muster, he walked up to where the captain was busying himself on the deck. "Nice boat you got here," he tried, though it was a slimy tub of shit far as he could see.

"And?"

"Would you think of taking me on?"

"You? What d'you know about fish?"

Shivers was a proven hand with axe, blade, spear and shield. A Named Man who'd led charges and held lines across the North and back. Who'd taken a few bad wounds and given out a lot of worse. But he was set on doing better'n that, and he was clinging to the notion tight as a drowning man to driftwood.

"I used to fish a lot, when I was a boy. Down by the lake, with my father." His bare feet crunching in the shingle. The light glistening on the water. His father's smile, and his brother's.

But the captain didn't come over nostalgic. "Lake? Sea-fishing's what we do, boy."

"Sea-fishing, I've got to say, I've had no practice at."

"Then why you wasting my bloody time? I can get plenty of Styrian fishers for my measure, the best hands, all with a dozen years at sea." He waved at the idle men lining the dock, looked more like they'd spent a dozen years in an ale-cup. "Why should I give work to some Northern beggar?"

"I'll work hard. Had some bad luck is all. I'm just asking for a chance."

"So are we all, but I'm not hearing why I should be the one to give it you."

"Just a chance is—"

"Away from my boat, you big pale bastard!" The captain snatched up a length of rough wood from the deck and had himself a step forwards, as if he was set to beat a dog. "Get off, and take your bad luck with you!"

"I may be no kind of fisher, but I've always had a talent for making men bleed. Best put that stick down before I make you fucking eat it." Shivers gave a look to go with the warning. A killing look, straight out of the North. The captain faltered, stopped, stood there grumbling. Then he tossed his stick away and started shouting at one of his own people.

Shivers hunched his shoulders and didn't look back. He trudged to the mouth of an alley, past the torn bills pasted on the walls, the words daubed over 'em. Into the shadows between the crowded buildings, and the sounds of the docks went muffled at his back. It had been the same story with the smiths, and with the bakers, and with every damn trade in this damn city. There'd even been a cobbler who'd looked like a good enough sort until he told Shivers to fuck himself.

Vossula had said there was work everywhere in Styria, all you had to do was ask. It seemed, for reasons he couldn't fathom, that Vossula had been lying out of his arse the whole way. Shivers had asked him all kinds of questions. But it occurred to him now, as he sank down on a slimy doorstep with his worn-out boots in the gutter and some fish-heads for company, he hadn't asked the one question he should've. The one question staring him in the face ever since he got here.

Tell me, Vossula — if Styria's such a slice of wonder, why the hell are you up here in the North?

"Fucking Styria," he hissed in Northern. He had that pain behind his nose meant he was close to weeping, and he was that far gone he was scarcely even shamed. Caul Shivers. Rattleneck's son. A Named Man who'd faced death in all weathers. Who'd fought beside the biggest names in the North — Rudd Threetrees, Black Dow, the Dogman, Harding Grim. Who'd led the charge against the Union near the Cumnur. Who'd held the line against a thousand Shanka at Dunbrec. Who'd fought seven days of murder up in the High Places. He almost felt a smile tugging at his mouth to think of the wild, brave times he'd come out alive from. He knew he'd been shitting himself the whole way, but what happy days those seemed now. Least he hadn't been alone.

He looked up at the sound of footsteps. Four men were ambling into the alley from the docks, the way he'd come. They had that sorry look men can get when they've got mischief in mind. Shivers hunched into his doorway, hoping whatever mischief they were planning didn't include him.

His heart took a downward turn as they gathered in a half-circle, standing over him. One had a bloated-up red nose, the kind you get from too much drinking. Another was bald as a boot-toe, had a length of wood held by his leg. A third had a scraggy beard and a mouthful of brown teeth. Not a pretty set of men, and Shivers didn't reckon they had anything pretty in mind.

The one at the front grinned down, a nasty-looking bastard with a pointed rat-face. "What you got for us?"

"I wish I'd something worth the taking. But I've not. You might as well just go your way."

Rat Face frowned at his bald mate, annoyed they might get nothing. "Your boots, then."

"In this weather? I'll freeze."

"Freeze. See if I care a shit. Boots, now, before we give you a kicking for the sport of it."

"Fucking Talins," mouthed Shivers under his breath, the ashes of self-pity in his throat suddenly flaring up hot and bloody. It gnawed at him to come this low. Bastards had no use for his boots, just wanted to make themselves feel big. But it'd be a fool's fight four against one, and with no weapon handy. A fool's choice to get killed for some old leather, however cold it was.

He crouched down, muttering as he started to pull his boots off. Then his knee caught Red Nose right in his fruits and doubled him over with a breathy sigh. Surprised himself as much as he did them. Maybe going barefoot was more'n his pride would stretch to. He smashed Rat Face on the chin, grabbed him by the front of his coat and rammed him back into one of his mates, sent them sprawling over together, yelping like cats in a rainstorm.

Shivers dodged the bald bastard's stick as it came down and shrugged it off his shoulder. The man came stumbling past, off balance, mouth wide open. Shivers planted a punch right on the point of his hanging chin and snapped his head up, then hooked his legs away with one boot, sent him squawking onto his back and followed him down. Shivers' fist crunched into his face — two, three, four times, and made a right mess of it, spattering blood up the arm of Shivers' dirty coat.

He scrambled away, leaving Baldy spitting teeth into the gutter. Red Nose was still curled up wailing with his hands between his legs. But the other two had knives out now, sharp metal glinting. Shivers crouched, fists clenched, breathing hard, eyes flicking from one of 'em to the other and his anger wilting fast. Should've just given his boots over. Probably they'd be prising them off his cold, dead feet in a short and painful while. Bloody pride, that rubbish only did a man harm.

Rat Face wiped blood from under his nose. "Oh, you're a dead man now, you Northern fuck! You're good as a—" His leg suddenly went from underneath him and he fell, shrieking, knife bouncing from his hand.

Someone slid out of the shadows behind him. Tall and hooded, sword held loose in a pale left fist, long, thin blade catching such light as there was in the alley and glinting murder. The last of the boot-thieves still standing, the one with the shitty teeth, stared at that length of steel with eyes big as a cow's, his knife looking a piss-poor tool all of a sudden.

"You might want to run for it." Shivers frowned, caught off guard. A woman's voice. Brown Teeth didn't need telling twice. He turned and sprinted off down the alley.

"My leg!" Rat Face was yelling, clutching at the back of his knee with one bloody hand. "My fucking leg!"

"Stop whining or I'll slit the other one."

Baldy was lying there, saying nothing. Red Nose had finally fought his way moaning to his knees.

"Want my boots, do you?" Shivers took a step and kicked him in the fruits again, lifted him up and put him back down mewling on his face. "There's one of 'em, bastard!" He watched the newcomer, blood swoosh-swooshing behind his eyes, not sure how he came through that without getting some steel in his guts. Not sure if he might not still. This woman didn't have the look of good news. "What d'you want?" he growled at her.

"Nothing you'll have trouble with." He could see the corner of a smile inside her hood. "I might have some work for you."

A big plate of meat and vegetables in some kind of gravy, slabs of doughy bread beside. Might've been good, might not have been, Shivers was too busy ramming it into his face to tell. Most likely he looked a right animal, two weeks unshaved, pinched and greasy from dossing in doorways, and not even good ones. But he was far past caring how he looked, even with a woman watching.

She still had her hood up, though they were out of the weather now. She stayed back against the wall, where it was dark. She tipped her head forwards when folk came close, tar-black hair hanging across one cheek. He'd worked out a notion of her face anyway, in the moments when he could drag his eyes away from his food, and he reckoned it was a good one.

Strong, with hard bones in it, a fierce line of jaw and a lean neck, a blue vein showing up the side. Dangerous, he reckoned, though that wasn't such a clever guess since he'd seen her slit the back of a man's knee with small regret. Still, there was something in the way her narrow eyes held him that made him nervous. Calm and cold, as if she'd already got his full measure, and knew just what he'd do next. Knew better'n he did. She had three long marks down one cheek, old cuts still healing. She had a glove on her right hand, and scarcely used it. A limp too he'd noticed on the way here. Caught up in some dark business, maybe, but Shivers didn't have so many friends he could afford to be picky. Right then, anyone who fed him had the full stretch of his loyalty.

She watched him eat. "Hungry?"

"Somewhat."

"Long way from home?"

"Somewhat."

"Had some bad luck?"

"More'n my share. But I made some bad choices, too."

"The two go together."

"That is a fact." He tossed knife and spoon clattering down onto the empty plate. "I should've thought it through." He wiped up the gravy with the last slice of bread. "But I've always been my own worst enemy." They sat facing each other in silence as he chewed it. "You've not told me your name."

"No."

"Like that, is it?"

"I'm paying, aren't I? It's whatever way I say it is."

"Why are you paying? A friend of mine..." He cleared his throat, starting to doubt whether Vossula had been any kind of friend. "A man I know told me to expect nothing for free in Styria."

"Good advice. I need something from you."

Shivers licked at the inside of his mouth and it tasted sour. He had a debt to this woman, now, and he wasn't sure what he'd have to pay. By the look of her, he reckoned it might cost him dear. "What do you need?"

"First of all, have a bath. No one's going to deal with you in that state."

Now the hunger and the cold were gone, they'd left a bit of room for shame. "I'm happier not stinking, believe it or not. I got some fucking pride left."

"Good for you. Bet you can't wait to get fucking clean, then."

He worked his shoulders around, uncomfortable. He had this feeling like he was stepping into a pool with no idea how deep it might be. "Then what?"

"Not much. You go into a smoke-house and ask for a man called Sajaam. You say Nicomo demands his presence at the usual place. You bring him to me."

"Why not do that yourself?"

"Because I'm paying you to do it, fool." She held up a coin in her gloved fist. Silver glinted in the firelight, design of weighing scales stamped into the bright metal. "You bring Sajaam to me, you get a scale. You decide you still want fish, you can buy yourself a barrelful."

Shivers frowned. For some fine-looking woman to come out of nowhere, more'n likely save his life, then make him a golden offer? His luck had never been anywhere near that good. But eating had only reminded him how much he used to enjoy doing it. "I can do that."

"Good. Or you can do something else, and get fifty."

"Fifty?" Shivers' voice was an eager croak. "This a joke?"

"You see me laughing? Fifty, I said, and if you still want fish you can buy your own boat and have change for some decent tailoring, how's that?"

Shivers tugged somewhat shamefacedly at the frayed edge of his coat. With that much he could hop the next boat back to Uffrith and kick Vossula's skinny arse from one end of the town to the other. A dream that had been his one source of pleasure for some time. "What do you want for fifty?"

"Not much. You go into a smoke-house and ask for a man called Sajaam. You say Nicomo demands his presence at the usual place. You bring him to me." She paused for a moment. "Then you help me kill a man."

It was no surprise, if he was honest with himself for once. There was only one kind of work that he was really good at. Certainly only one kind that anyone would pay him fifty scales for. He'd come here to be a better man. But it was just like the Dogman had told him. Once your hands are bloody, it ain't so easy to get 'em clean.

Something poked his thigh under the table and he near jumped out of his chair. The pommel of a long knife lay between his legs. A fighting knife, steel crosspiece gleaming orange, its sheathed blade in the woman's gloved hand.

"Best take it."

"I didn't say I'd kill anyone."

"I know what you said. The blade's just to show Sajaam you mean business."

He had to admit he didn't much care for a woman surprising him with a knife between his thighs. "I didn't say I'd kill anyone."

"I didn't say you did."

"Right then. Just as long as you know." He snatched the blade from her and slid it down inside his coat.

The knife pressed against his chest as he walked up, nuzzling at him like an old lover back for more. Shivers knew it was nothing to be proud of. Any fool can carry a knife. But even so, he wasn't sure he didn't like the weight of it against his ribs. Felt like being someone again.

He'd come to Styria looking for honest work. But when the purse runs empty, dishonest work has to do. Shivers couldn't say he'd ever seen a place with a less honest look about it than this one. A heavy door in a dirty, bare, windowless wall, with a big man standing guard on each side. Shivers could tell it in the way they stood — they had weapons, and were right on the edge of putting 'em to use. One was a dark-skinned Southerner, black hair hanging around his face.

"Need something?" he asked, while the other gave Shivers the eyeball.

"Here to see Sajaam."

"You armed?" Shivers slid out the knife, held it up hilt first, and the man took it off him. "With me, then." The hinges creaked as the door swung open.

The air was thick on the other side, hazy with sweet smoke. It scratched at Shivers' throat and made him want to cough, prickled at his eyes and made them water. It was dim and quiet, too sticky warm for comfort after the nip outside. Lamps of coloured glass threw patterns across the stained walls — green, and red, and yellow flares in the murk. The place was like a bad dream.

Curtains hung about, dirty silk rustling in the gloom. Folk sprawled on cushions, half-dressed and half-asleep. A man lay on his back, mouth wide open, pipe dangling from his hand, trace of smoke still curling from the bowl. A woman was pressed against him, on her side. Both their faces were beaded with sweat, slack as corpses. Looked like an uneasy cross between delight and despair, but tending towards the latter.

"This way." Shivers followed his guide through the haze and down a shadowy corridor. A woman leaning in a doorway watched him pass with dead eyes, saying nothing. Someone was grunting somewhere, "Oh, oh, oh," almost bored.

Through a curtain of clicking beads and into another big room, less smoky but more worrying. Men were scattered about it, an odd mix of types and colours. Judging by their looks, all used to violence. Eight were sitting at a table strewn with glasses, bottles and small money, playing cards. More lounged about in the shadows. Shivers' eye fell right away on a nasty-looking hatchet in easy reach of one, and he didn't reckon it was the only weapon about. A clock was nailed up on the wall, innards dangling, swinging back and forth, tick, tock, tick, loud enough to set his nerves jangling even worse.

A big man sat at the head of the table, the chief's place if this had been the North. An old man, face creased like leather past its best. His skin was oily dark, short hair and beard dusted with iron grey. He had a gold coin he was fiddling with, flipping it across his knuckles from one side of his hand back to the other. The guide leaned down to whisper in his ear, then handed across the knife. His eyes and the eyes of the others were on Shivers, now. A scale was starting to seem a small reward for the task, all of a sudden.

"You Sajaam?" Louder than Shivers had in mind, voice squeaky from the smoke.

The old man's smile was a yellow curve in his dark face. "Sajaam is my name, as all my sweet friends will confirm. You know, you can tell an awful lot about a man from the style of weapon he carries."

"That so?"

Sajaam slid the knife from its sheath and held it up, candlelight glinting on steel. "Not a cheap blade, but not expensive either. Fit for the job, and no frills at the edges. Sharp, and hard, and meaning business. Am I close to the mark?"

"Somewhere round it." It was plain he was one of those who loved to prattle on, so Shivers didn't bother to mention that it weren't even his knife. Less said, sooner he could be on his way.

"What might your name be, friend?" Though the friend bit didn't much convince.

"Caul Shivers."

"Brrrr." Sajaam shook his big shoulders around like he was cold, to much chuckling from his men. Easily tickled, by the look of things. "You are a long, long way from home, my man."

"Don't I fucking know it. I've a message for you. Nicomo demands your presence."

The good humour drained from the room quick as blood from a slit throat. "Where?"

"The usual place."

"Demands, does he?" A couple of Sajaam's people were moving away from the walls, hands creeping in the shadows. "Awfully bold of him. And why would my old friend Nicomo send a big white Northman with a blade to talk to me?" It came to Shivers about then that, for reasons unknown, the woman might've landed him right in the shit. Clearly she weren't this Nicomo character. But he'd swallowed his fill of scorn these last few weeks, and the dead could have him before he tongued up any more.

"Ask him yourself. I didn't come here to swap questions, old man. Nicomo demands your presence in the usual place, and that's all. Now get off your fat black arse before I lose my temper."

There was a long and ugly pause, while everyone had a think about that.

"I like it," grunted Sajaam. "You like that?" he asked one of his thugs.

"It's alright, I guess, if that style o' thing appeals."

"On occasion. Large words and bluster and hairy-chested manliness. Too much gets boring with great speed, but a little can sometimes make me smile. So Nicomo demands my presence, does he?"

"He does," said Shivers, no choice but to let the current drag him where it pleased, and hope to wash up whole.

"Well, then." The old man tossed his cards down on the table and slowly stood. "Let it never be said old Sajaam reneged on a debt. If Nicomo is call-ing…the usual place it is." He pushed the knife Shivers had brought through his belt. "I'll keep hold of this though, hmmm? Just for the moment."

It was late when they got to the place the woman had showed him and the rotten garden was dark as a cellar. Far as Shivers could tell it was empty as one too. Just torn papers twitching on the night air, old news hanging from the slimy bricks.

"Well?" snapped Sajaam. "Where's Cosca?"

"Said she'd be here," Shivers muttered, half to himself.

"She?" His hand was on the hilt of the knife. "What the hell are you—"

"Over here, you old prick." She slid out from behind a tree-trunk and into a scrap of light, hood back. Now Shivers saw her clearly, she was even finer-looking than he'd thought, and harder-looking too. Very fine, and very hard, with a sharp red line down the side of her neck, like the scars you see on hanged men. She had this frown — brows drawn in hard, lips pressed tight, eyes narrowed and fixed in front. Like she'd decided to break a door down with her head, and didn't care a shit for the results.

Sajaam's face had gone slack as a soaked shirt. "You're alive."

"Still sharp as ever, eh?"

"But I heard—"

"No."

Didn't take long for the old man to scrape himself together. "You shouldn't be in Talins, Murcatto. You shouldn't be within a hundred miles of Talins. Most of all, you shouldn't be within a hundred miles of me." He cursed in some language Shivers didn't know, then tipped his face back towards the dark sky. "God, God, why could you not have sent me an honest life to lead?"

The woman snorted. "Because you haven't the guts for it. That and you like money too much."

"All true, regrettably." They might've talked like old friends, but Sajaam's hand hadn't left the knife. "What do you want?"

"Your help killing some men."

"The Butcher of Caprile needs my help killing, eh? As long as none of them are too close to Duke Orso—"

"He'll be the last."

"Oh, you mad bitch." Sajaam slowly shook his head. "How you love to test me, Monzcarro. How you always loved to test us all. You'll never do it. Never, not if you wait until the sun burns out."

"What if I could, though? Don't tell me it hasn't been your fondest wish all these years."

"All these years when you were spreading fire and murder across Styria in his name? Happy to take his orders and his coin, lick his arse like a puppy dog with a new bone? Is it those years you mean? I don't recall you offering your shoulder for me to weep upon."

"He killed Benna."

"Is that so? The bills said Duke Rogont's agents got you both." Sajaam was pointing out some old papers stirring on the wall behind her shoulder. A woman's face on 'em, and a man's. Shivers realised, and with a sharp sinking in his gut, the woman's face was hers. "Killed by the League of Eight. Everyone was so very upset."

"I'm in no mood for jokes, Sajaam."

"When were you ever? But it's no joke. You were a hero round these parts. That's what they call you when you kill so many people the word murderer falls short. Orso gave the big speech, said we all had to fight harder than ever to avenge you, and everyone wept. I am sorry about Benna. I always liked the boy. But I made peace with my devils. You should do the same."

"The dead can forgive. The dead can be forgiven. The rest of us have better things to do. I want your help, and I'm owed. Pay up, bastard."

They frowned at each other for a long moment. Then the old man heaved up a long sigh. "I always said you'd be the death of me. What's your price?"

"A point in the right direction. An introduction here or there. That's what you do, now, isn't it?"

"I know some people."

"Then I need to borrow a man with a cold head and a good arm. A man who won't get flustered at blood spilled."

Sajaam seemed to think about that. Then he turned his head and called over his shoulder. "You know a man like that, Friendly?"

Footsteps scraped out of the darkness from the way Shivers had come. Seemed there'd been someone following them, and doing it well. The woman slid into a fighting crouch, eyes narrowed, left hand on her sword hilt. Shivers would've reached for a weapon too, if he'd had one, but he'd sold all his own in Uffrith and given the knife over to Sajaam. So he settled for a nervous twitching of his fingers, which wasn't a scrap of use to anyone.

The new arrival trudged up, stooped over, eyes down. He was a half-head or more shorter than Shivers but had a fearsome solid look to him, thick neck wider than his skull, heavy hands dangling from the sleeves of a heavy coat.

"Friendly," Sajaam was all smiles at the surprise he'd pulled, "this is an old friend of mine, name of Murcatto. You're going to work for her a while, if you have no objection." The man shrugged his weighty shoulders. "What did you say your name was, again?"

"Shivers."

Friendly's eyes flickered up, then back to the floor, and stayed there. Sad eyes and strange. Silence for a moment.

"Is he a good man?" asked Murcatto.

"This is the best man I know of. Or the worst, if you stand on his wrong side. I met him in Safety."

"What had he done to be locked in there with the likes of you?"

"Everything and more."

More silence. "For a man called Friendly, he's not got much to say."

"My very thoughts when I first met him," said Sajaam. "I suspect the name was meant with some irony."

"Irony? In a prison?"

"All kinds of people end up in prison. Some of us even have a sense of humour."

"If you say so. I'll take some husk as well."

"You? More your brother's style, no? What do you want husk for?"

"When did you start asking your customers why they want your goods, old man?"

"Fair point." He pulled something from his pocket, tossed it to her and she snatched it out of the air.

"I'll let you know when I need something else."

"I shall tick off the hours! I always swore you'd be the death of me, Monzcarro." Sajaam turned away. "The death of me."

Shivers stepped in front of him. "My knife." He didn't understand the fine points of what he'd heard, but he could tell when he was caught up in something dark and bloody. Something where he was likely to need a good blade.

"My pleasure." Sajaam slapped it back into Shivers' palm, and it weighed heavy there. "Though I advise you to find a larger blade if you plan on sticking with her." He glanced round at them, slowly shaking his head. "You three heroes, going to put an end to Duke Orso? When they kill you, do me a favour? Die quickly and keep my name out of it." And with that cheery thought he ambled off into the night.

When Shivers turned back, the woman called Murcatto was looking him right in the eye. "What about you? Fishing's a bastard of a living. Almost as hard as farming, and even worse-smelling." She held out her gloved hand and silver glinted in the palm. "I can still use another man. You want to take your scale? Or you want fifty more?"

Shivers frowned down at that shining metal. He'd killed men for a lot less, when he thought about it. Battles, feuds, fights, in all settings and all weathers. But he'd had reasons, then. Not good ones, always, but something to make it some kind of right. Never just murder, blood bought and paid for.

"This man we're going to kill... what did he do?"

"He got me to pay fifty scales for his corpse. Isn't that enough?"

"Not for me."

She frowned at him for a long moment. That straight-ahead look that was already giving him the worries, somehow. "So you're one of them, eh?"

"One o' what?"

"One of those men that like reasons. That need excuses. You're a dangerous crowd, you lot. Hard to predict." She shrugged. "But if it helps. He killed my brother."

Shivers blinked. Hearing those words, from her mouth, brought that day right back somehow, sharper than he'd remembered it for years. Seeing his father's grey face, and knowing. Hearing his brother was killed, when he'd been promised mercy. Swearing vengeance over the ashes in the long hall, tears in his eyes. An oath he'd chosen to break, so he could walk away from blood and be a better man.

And here she was, out of nowhere, offering him another chance at vengeance. He killed my brother. Felt as if he would've said no to anything else. But maybe he just needed the money.

"Shit on it, then," he said. "Give me the fifty."

Six and One

The dice came up six and one. The highest dice can roll and the lowest. A fitting judgement on Friendly's life. The pit of horror to the heights of triumph. And back.

Six and one made seven. Seven years old, when Friendly committed his first crime. But six years later that he was first caught, and given his first sentence. When they first wrote his name in the big book, and he earned his first days in Safety. Stealing, he knew, but he could hardly remember what he stole. He certainly could not remember why. His parents had worked hard to give him all he needed. And yet he stole. Some men are born to do wrong, perhaps. The judges had told him so.

He scooped the dice up, rattled them in his fist, then let them free across the stones again, watched them as they tumbled. Always that same joy, that anticipation. Dice just thrown can be anything until they stop rolling. He watched them turning, chances, odds, his life and the life of the Northman. All the lives in the great city of Talins turning with them.

Six and one.

Friendly smiled, a little. The odds of throwing six and one a second time were one in eighteen. Long odds, some would say, looking forward into the future. But looking into the past, as he was now, there was no chance of any other numbers. What was coming? Always full of possibilities. What was past? Done, and hardened, like dough turned to bread. There was no going back.

"What do the dice say?"

Friendly glanced up as he gathered the dice with the edge of his hand. He was a big man, this Shivers, but with none of that stringiness tall men sometimes get. Strong. But not like a farmer, or a labourer. Not slow. He understood the work. There were clues, and Friendly knew them all. In Safety, you have to reckon the threat a man poses in a moment. Reckon it, and deal with it, and never blink.

A soldier, maybe, and fought in battles, by his scars, and the set of his face, and the look in his eye as they waited to do violence. Not comfortable, but ready. Not likely to run or get carried away. They are rare, men that keep a sharp head when the trouble starts. There was a scar on his thick left wrist that, if you looked at it a certain way, was like the number seven. Seven was a good number today.

"Dice say nothing. They are dice."

"Why roll 'em, then?"

"They are dice. What else would I do with them?"

Friendly closed his eyes, closed his fist around the dice and pressed them to his cheek, feeling their warm, rounded edges against his palm. What numbers did they hold for him now, waiting to be released? Six and one again? A flicker of excitement. The odds of throwing six and one for a third time were three hundred and twenty-four to one. Three hundred and twenty-four was the number of cells in Safety. A good omen.

"They're here," whispered the Northman.

There were four of them. Three men and a whore. Friendly could hear the vague tinkling of her night-bell on the chill air, one of the men laughing. They were drunk, shapeless outlines lurching down the darkened alley. The dice would have to wait.

He sighed, wrapped them carefully in their soft cloth, once, twice, three times, and he tucked them up tight, safe into the darkness of his inside pocket. He wished that he was tucked up tight, safe in the darkness, but things were what they were. There was no going back. He stood and brushed the street scum from his knees.

"What's the plan?" asked Shivers.

Friendly shrugged. "Six and one."

He pulled his hood up and started walking, hunched over, hands thrust into his pockets. Light from a high window cut across the group as they came closer. Four grotesque carnival masks, leering with drunken laughter. The big man in the centre had a soft face with sharp little eyes and a greedy grin. The painted woman tottered on her high shoes beside him. The man on the left smirked across at her, lean and bearded. The one on the right was wiping a tear of happiness from his grey cheek.

"Then what?" he shrieked through his gurgling, far louder than there was a need for.

"What d'you think? I kicked him 'til he shat himself." More gales of laughter, the woman's falsetto tittering a counterpoint to the big man's bass. "I said, Duke Orso likes men who say yes, you lying—"

"Gobba?" asked Friendly.

His head snapped round, smile fading from his soft face. Friendly stopped. He had taken forty-one steps from the place where he rolled the dice. Six and one made seven. Seven times six was forty-two. Take away the one . . .

"Who're you?" growled Gobba.

"Six and one."

"What?" The man on the right made to shove Friendly away with a drunken arm. "Get out of it, you mad fu—"

The cleaver split his head open to the bridge of his nose. Before his mate on the left's mouth had fallen all the way open, Friendly was across the road and stabbing him in the body. Five times the long knife punched him through the guts, then Friendly stepped back and slashed his throat on the backhand, kicked his legs away and brought him tumbling to the cobbles.

There was a moment's pause as Friendly breathed out, long and slow. The first man had the single great wound yawning in his skull, a black splatter of brains smeared over his crossed eyes. The other had the five stab wounds in his body, and blood pouring from his cut throat.

"Good," said Friendly. "Six and one."

The whore started screaming, spots of dark blood across one powdered cheek.

"You're a dead man!" roared Gobba, taking a stumbling step back, fumbling a bright knife from his belt. "I'll kill you!" But he did not come on.

"When?" asked Friendly, blades hanging loose from his hands. "Tomorrow?"

"I'll—"

Shivers' stick cracked down on the back of Gobba's skull. A good blow, right on the best spot, crumpling his knees easily as paper. He flopped down, slack cheek thumping against the cobbles, knife clattering from his limp fist, out cold.

"Not tomorrow. Not ever." The woman's shriek sputtered out. Friendly turned his eyes on her. "Why aren't you running?" She fled into the darkness, teetering on her high shoes, whimpering breath echoing down the street, her night-bell jangling after.

Shivers frowned down at the two leaking corpses in the road. The two pools of blood worked their way along the cracks between the cobblestones, touched, mingled and became one. "By the dead," he muttered in his Northern tongue.

Friendly shrugged. "Welcome to Styria."

Bloody Instructions

Monza stared down at her gloved hand, lips curled back hard from her teeth, and flexed the three fingers that still worked — in and out, in and out, gauging the pattern of clicks and crunches that came with every closing of her fist. She felt oddly calm considering that her life, if you could call it a life, was balanced on a razor's edge.

Never trust a man beyond his own interests, Verturio wrote, and the murder of Grand Duke Orso and his closest was no one's idea of an easy job. She couldn't trust this silent convict any further than she could trust Sajaam, and that was about as far as she could piss. She had a creeping feeling the Northman was halfway honest, but she'd thought that about Orso, with results that had hardly been happy. It would've been no great surprise to her if they'd brought Gobba in smiling, ready to drag her back to Fontezarmo so they could drop her down the mountain a second time.

She couldn't trust anyone. But she couldn't do it alone.

Hurried footsteps scuffled up outside. The door banged open and three men came through. Shivers was on the right, Friendly on the left. Gobba hung between them, head dangling, an arm over each of their shoulders, his boot-toes scraping through the sawdust scattered across the ground. So it seemed she could trust the pair of them this far, at least.

Friendly dragged Gobba to the anvil — a mass of scarred black iron bolted down in the centre of the floor. Shivers had a length of chain, a manacle on each end, looping it round and round the base. All the while he had this fixed frown. As if he'd got some morals, and they were stinging.

Nice things, morals, but prone to chafe at times like this.

The two men worked well together for a beggar and a convict. No time or movement wasted. No sign of nerves, given they were going about a murder. But then Monza had always had a knack for picking the right men for a job. Friendly snapped the manacles shut on the bodyguard's thick wrists. Shivers reached out and turned the knob on the lamp, the flame fluttering up behind the glass, light spilling out around the grubby forge.

"Wake him up."

Friendly flung a bucket of water in Gobba's face. He coughed, dragged in a breath, shook his head, drops flicking from his hair. He tried to stand and the chain rattled, snatching him back down. He glared around, little eyes hard.

"You stupid bastards! You're dead men, the pair of you! Dead! Don't you know who I am? Don't you know who I work for?"

"I know." Monza did her best to walk smoothly, the way she used to, but couldn't quite manage it. She limped into the light, pushing back her hood.

Gobba's fat face crinkled up. "No. Can't be." His eyes went wide. Then wider still. Shock, then fear, then horror. He lurched back, chains clinking. "No!"

"Yes." And she smiled, in spite of the pain. "How fucked are you? You've put weight on, Gobba. More than I've lost, even. Funny, how things go. Is that my stone you've got there?"

He had the ruby on his little finger, red glimmer on black iron. Friendly reached down, twisted it off and tossed it over to her. She snatched it out of the air with her left hand. Benna's last gift. The one they'd smiled at together as they rode up the mountain to see Duke Orso. The thick band was scratched, bent a little, but the stone still sparkled bloodily as ever, the colour of a slit throat.

"Somewhat damaged when you tried to kill me, eh, Gobba? But weren't we all?" It took her a while to fumble it onto her left middle finger, but in the end she twisted it past the knuckle. "Fits this hand just as well. Piece of luck, that."

"Look! We can make a deal!" There was sweat beading Gobba's face now. "We can work something out!"

"I already did. Don't have a mountain to hand, I'm afraid." She slid the hammer from the shelf — a short-hafted lump hammer with a block of heavy steel for a head — and felt her knuckles shift as she closed her gloved hand tight around it. "So I'm going to break you apart with this, instead.

Hold him, would you?" Friendly folded Gobba's right arm and forced it onto the anvil, clawing fingers spread out pale on the dark metal. "You should've made sure of me."

"Orso'll find out! He'll find out!"

"Of course he will. When I throw him off his own terrace, if not before."

"You'll never do it! He'll kill you!"

"He already did, remember? It didn't stick."

Veins stood out on Gobba's neck as he struggled, but Friendly had him fast, for all his bulk. "You can't beat him!"

"Maybe not. I suppose we'll see. There's only one thing I can tell you for sure." She raised the hammer high. "You won't."

The head came down on his knuckles with a faintly metallic crunch — once, twice, three times. Each blow jarred her hand, sent pain shooting up her arm. But a lot less pain than shot up Gobba's. He gasped, yelped, trembled, Friendly's slack face pressed up against his taut one. Gobba jerked back from the anvil, his hand turning sideways on. Monza felt herself grinning as the hammer hissed down and crushed it flat. The next blow caught his wrist and turned it black.

"Looks worse even than mine did." She shrugged. "Well. When you pay a debt, it's only good manners to add some interest. Get the other hand."

"No!" squealed Gobba, dribbling spit. "No! Think of my children!"

"Think of my brother!"

The hammer smashed his other hand apart. She aimed each blow carefully, taking her time, both eyes on the details. Fingertips. Fingers. Knuckles. Thumb. Palm. Wrist.

"Six and six," grunted Friendly, over Gobba's roars of pain.

The blood was surging in Monza's ears. She wasn't sure she'd heard him right. "Eh?"

"Six times, and six times." He let go of Orso's bodyguard and stood, brushing his palms together. "With the hammer."

"And?" she snapped at him, no clue how that mattered.

Gobba was bent over the anvil, legs braced, dragging on the manacles and spraying spit as he tried vainly to shift the great thing with all his strength, blackened hands flopping.

She leaned towards him. "Did I tell you to get up?" The hammer split his kneecap with a sharp bang. He crumpled onto the floor on his back, was dragging in the air to scream when the hammer crunched into his leg again and snapped it back the wrong way.

"Hard work, this." She winced at a twinge in her shoulder as she dragged her coat off. "But then I'm not as limber as I was." She rolled her black shirtsleeve up past the long scar on her forearm. "You always did tell me you knew how to make a woman sweat, eh, Gobba? And to think I laughed at you." She wiped her face on the back of her arm. "Shows you what I know. Unhook him."

"You sure?" asked Friendly.

"Worried he'll bite your ankles? Let's make a chase of it." The convict shrugged, then leaned down to unlock the cuffs around Gobba's wrists. Shivers was frowning at her from the darkness. "Something wrong?" she snapped at him.

He stayed silent.

Gobba dragged himself to nowhere through the dirty sawdust with his elbows, broken leg slithering along behind. He made a kind of mindless groan while he did it. Something like the ones she'd made when she lay broken at the foot of the mountain beneath Fontezarmo.

"Huuuurrrrhhhh..."

Monza wasn't enjoying this half as much as she'd hoped, and it was making her angrier than ever. Something about those groans was intensely annoying. Her hand was pulsing with pain. She forced a smile onto her face and limped after him, pretended to enjoy it more.

"I've got to say I'm disappointed. Didn't Orso always like to boast about what a hard man he had for a bodyguard? I suppose now we'll find out how hard you really are. Softer than this hammer, I'd—"

Her foot slipped and she yelped as she went over on her ankle, tottered against the brick-lined side of a furnace, put her left hand down to steady herself. It took her a moment to realise the thing was still scalding hot.

"Shit!" Stumbling back the other way like a clown, kicking a bucket and sending dirty water showering up the side of her leg. "Fuck!"

She leaned down over Gobba and lashed petulantly at him with the hammer, suddenly, stupidly angry she'd embarrassed herself. "Bastard! Bastard!" He grunted and gurgled as the steel head thudded into his ribs. He tried to curl up and half-dragged her over on top of him, twisting her leg.

Pain lanced up her hip and made her screech. She dug at the side of his head with the haft of the hammer until she'd torn his ear half-off. Shivers

took a step forwards but she'd already wrenched herself free. Gobba blubbered, somehow dragged himself up to sitting, back against a big water
butt. His hands had swollen up to twice the size they had been. Purple,
flopping mittens.

"Beg!" she hissed. "Beg, you fat fucker!"

But Gobba was too busy staring at the mincemeat on the end of his
arms, and screaming. Hoarse, short, slobbery screams.

"Someone might hear." Friendly looked like he didn't care much either
way.

"Better shut him up, then."

The convict leaned over the barrel from behind with a wire between his
fists, hooked Gobba under the neck and dragged him up hard, cutting his
bellows down to slippery splutters.

Monza squatted in front of him so their faces were level, her knees burning as she watched the wire cut into his fat neck. Just the way it had cut into
hers. The scars it had left on her itched. "How does it feel?" Her eyes flickered over his face, trying to squeeze some sliver of satisfaction from it. "How
does it feel?" Though no one knew better than her. Gobba's eyes bulged,
his jowls trembled, turning from pink, to red, to purple. She pushed herself
up to standing. "I'd say it's a waste of good flesh. But it isn't."

She closed her eyes and let her head drop back, sucked a long breath in
through her nose as she tightened her grip on the hammer, lifted it high.

"Betray me and leave me alive?"

It came down between Gobba's piggy eyes with a sharp bang like a stone
slab splitting. His back arched, his mouth yawned wide but no sound came
out.

"Take my hand and leave me alive?"

The hammer hit him in the nose and caved his face in like a broken egg.
His body crumpled, shattered leg jerking, jerking.

"Kill my brother and leave me alive?"

The last blow broke his skull wide open. Black blood bubbled down
his purple skin. Friendly let go the wire and Gobba slid sideways. Gently,
gracefully almost, he rolled over onto his front, and was still.

Dead. You didn't have to be an expert to see that. Monza winced as she
forced her aching fingers open and the hammer clattered down, its head
gleaming red, a clump of hair stuck to one corner.

One dead. Six left.

"Six and one," she muttered to herself. Friendly stared at her, eyes wide, and she wasn't sure why.

"What's it like?" Shivers, watching her from the shadows.

"What?"

"Revenge. Does it feel good?"

Monza wasn't sure she felt much of anything beyond the pain pulsing through her burned hand and her broken hand, up her legs and through her skull. Benna was still dead, she was still broken. She stood there frowning, and didn't answer.

"You want me to get rid of this?" Friendly waved an arm at the corpse, a heavy cleaver gleaming in his other hand.

"Make sure he won't be found."

Friendly grabbed Gobba's ankle and started dragging him back towards the anvil, leaving a bloody trail through the sawdust. "Chop him up. Into the sewers. Rats can have him."

"Better than he deserves." But Monza felt the slightest bit sick. She needed a smoke. Getting to that time of day. A smoke would settle her nerves. She pulled out a small purse, the one with fifty scales in it, and tossed it to Shivers.

Coins snapped together inside as he caught it. "That's it?"

"That's it."

"Right." He paused, as though he wanted to say something but couldn't think what. "Sorry about your brother."

She looked at his face in the lamplight. Really looking, trying to guess him out. He knew next to nothing about her or Orso. Next to nothing about anything, at a first glance. But he could fight, she'd seen that. He'd walked into Sajaam's place alone, and that took courage. A man with courage, with morals, maybe. A man with pride. That meant he might have some loyalty too, if she could get a grip on it. And loyal men were a rare commodity in Styria.

She'd never spent much time alone. Benna had always been beside her. Or behind her, at any rate. "You're sorry."

"That's right. I had a brother." He started to turn for the door.

"You need more work?" She kept her eyes fixed on his as she came forwards, and while she did it she slid her good hand around behind her back and found the handle of the knife there. He knew her name, and Orso's, and Sajaam's, and that was enough to get them all killed ten times over. One way or another, he had to stay.

"More work like this?" He frowned down at the bloodstained sawdust under her boots.

"Killing. You can say it." She thought about whether to stab him down into the chest or up under the jaw, or wait until he'd turned and take his back. "What did you think it'd be? Milking a goat?"

He shook his head, long hair swaying. "Might sound foolish to you, but I came here to be a better man. You got your reasons, sure, but this feels like a bastard of a stride in the wrong direction."

"Six more men."

"No. No. I'm done." As if he was trying to convince himself. "I don't care how much—"

"Five thousand scales."

His mouth was already open to say no again, but this time the word didn't come. He stared at her. Shocked at first, then thoughtful. Working out how much money that really was. What it might buy him. Monza had always had a knack for reckoning a man's price. Every man has one.

She took a step forwards, looking up into his face. "You're a good man, I see that, and a hard man too. That's the kind of man I need." She let her eyes flick down to his mouth, and then back up. "Help me. I need your help, and you need my money. Five thousand scales. Lot easier to be a better man with that much money behind you. Help me. I daresay you could buy half the North with that. Make a king of yourself."

"Who says I want to be a king?"

"Be a queen, if you please. I can tell you what you won't be doing, though." She leaned in, so close she was almost breathing on his neck. "Begging for work. You ask me, it's not right, a proud man like you in that state. Still." And she looked away. "I can't force you."

He stood there, weighing the purse. But she'd already taken her hand off her knife. She already knew his answer. *Money is a different thing to every man*, Bialoveld wrote, *but always a good thing*.

When he looked up his face had turned hard. "Who do we kill?"

The time was she'd have smirked sideways to see Benna smirking back at her. *We won again*. But Benna was dead, and Monza's thoughts were on the next man to join him. "A banker."

"A what?"

"A man who counts money."

"He makes money counting money?"

"That's right."

"Some strange fashions you folk have down here. What did he do?"

"He killed my brother."

"More vengeance, eh?"

"More vengeance."

Shivers gave a nod. "Reckon I'm hired, then. What do you need?"

"Give Friendly a hand taking out the rubbish, then we're gone tonight. No point loitering in Talins."

Shivers looked towards the anvil, and he took a sharp breath. Then he pulled out the knife she'd given him, walked over to where Friendly was starting work on Gobba's corpse.

Monza looked down at her left hand, rubbed a few specks of blood from the back. Her fingers were trembling some. From killing a man earlier, from not killing one just now, or from needing a smoke, she wasn't sure.

All three, maybe.

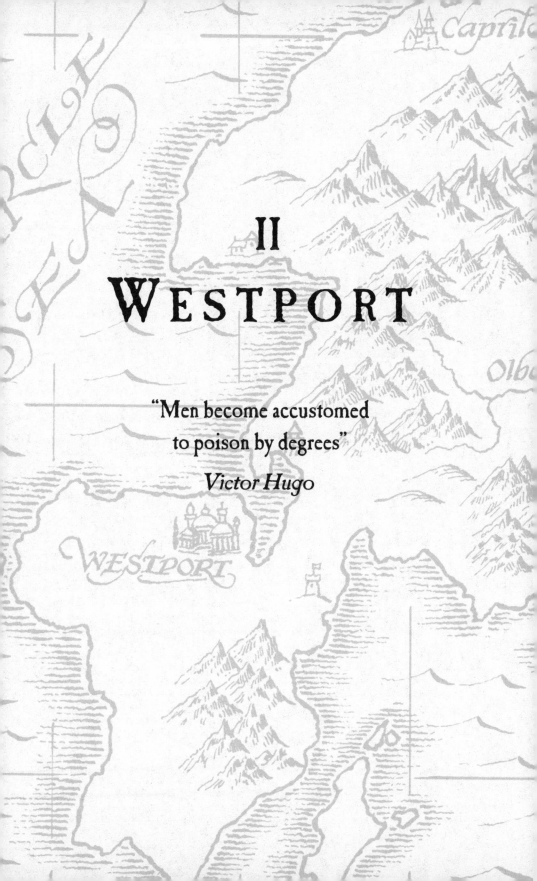

II
WESTPORT

"Men become accustomed
to poison by degrees"

Victor Hugo

The first year they were always hungry, and Benna had to beg in the village while Monza worked the ground and scavenged in the woods.

The second year they took a better harvest, and grew roots in a patch by the barn, and got some bread from old Destort the miller when the snows swept in and turned the valley into a place of white silence.

The third year the weather was fine, and the rain came on time, and Monza raised a good crop in the upper field. As good a crop as her father had ever brought in. Prices were high because of troubles over the border. They would have money, and the roof could be mended, and Benna could have a proper shirt. Monza watched the wind make waves in the wheat, and she felt that pride at having made something with her own hands. That pride her father used to talk about.

A few days before reaping time, she woke in the darkness and heard sounds. She shook Benna from his sleep beside her, one hand over his mouth. She took her father's sword, eased open the shutters, and together they stole through the window and into the woods, hid in the brambles behind a tree-trunk.

There were black figures in front of the house, torches flickering in the darkness.

"Who are they?"

"Shhhh."

She heard them break the door down, heard them crashing through the house and the barn.

"What do they want?"

"Shhhh."

They spread out around the field and set their torches to it, and the fire ate through the wheat until it was a roaring blaze. She heard someone cheering. Another laughing.

Benna stared, face dim-lit with shifting orange, tear-tracks glistening on his thin cheeks. "But why would they . . . why would they . . . ?"

"Shhhh."

Monza watched the smoke rolling up into the clear night. All her work. All her sweat and pain. She stayed there long after the men had gone, and watched it burn.

In the morning more men came. Folk from around the valley, hard-faced and vengeful, old Destort at their head with a sword at his hip and his three sons behind him.

"Came through here too then, did they? You're lucky to be alive. They killed Crevi and his wife, up the valley. Their son too."

"What are you going to do?"

"We're going to track them, then we're going to hang them."

"We'll come."

"You might be better—"

"We'll come."

Destort had not always been a miller, and he knew his business. They caught up with the raiders the next night, working their way back south, camped around fires in the woods without even a proper guard. More thieves than soldiers. Farmers among them too, just from one side of the border rather than the other, chosen to settle some made-up grievance while their lords were busy settling theirs.

"Anyone ain't ready to kill best stay here." Destort drew his sword and the others made their cleavers, and their axes, and their makeshift spears ready.

"Wait!" hissed Benna, clinging at Monza's arm.

"No."

She ran quiet and low, her father's sword in her hand, fires dancing through the black trees. She heard a cry, a clash of metal, the sound of a bowstring.

She came out from the bushes. Two men crouched by a campfire, a pot steaming over it. One had a thick beard, a wood-axe in his fist. Before he lifted it halfway Monza slashed him across the eyes and he fell down, screaming. The other turned to run and she spitted him through the back before he got a stride. The bearded man roared and roared, hands clutching at his face. She stabbed him in the chest, and he groaned out a few wet breaths, then stopped.

She frowned down at the two corpses while the sounds of fighting slowly petered out. Benna crept from the trees, and he took the bearded man's purse from his belt, and he tipped a heavy wedge of silver coins out into his palm.

"He has seventeen scales."

It was twice as much as the whole crop had been worth. He held the other man's purse out to her, eyes wide. "This one has thirty."

"Thirty?" Monza looked at the blood on her father's sword, and thought how strange it was that she was a murderer now. How strange it was that it had been so easy to do. Easier than digging in the stony soil for a living. Far, far easier. Afterwards, she waited for the remorse to come upon her. She waited for a long time.

It never came.

Poison

It was just the kind of afternoon that Morveer most enjoyed. Crisp, even chilly, but perfectly still, immaculately clear. The bright sun flashed through the bare black branches of the fruit trees, found rare gold among dull copper tripod, rods and screws, struck priceless sparks from the tangle of misted glassware. There was nothing finer than working out of doors on a day like this, with the added advantage that any lethal vapours released would harmlessly dissipate. Persons in Morveer's profession were all too frequently despatched by their own agents, after all, and he had no intention of becoming one of their number. Quite apart from anything else, his reputation would never recover.

Morveer smiled upon the rippling lamp flame, nodded in time to the gentle rattling of condenser and retort, the soothing hiss of escaping steam, the industrious pop and bubble of boiling reagents. As the drawing of the blade to the master swordsman, as the jingle of coins to the master merchant, so were these sounds to Morveer. The sounds of his work well done. It was with comfortable satisfaction, therefore, that he watched Day's face, creased with concentration, through the distorting glass of the tapered collection flask.

It was a pretty face, undoubtedly: heart-shaped and fringed with blond curls. But it was an unremarkable and entirely unthreatening variety of prettiness, further softened by a disarming aura of innocence. A face that would attract a positive response, but excite little further comment. A face that would easily slip the mind. It was for her face, above all, that Morveer had selected her. He did nothing by accident.

A jewel of moisture formed at the utmost end of the condenser. It stretched, bloated, then finally tore itself free, tumbled sparkling through space and fell silently to the bottom of the flask.

"Excellent," muttered Morveer.

More droplets swelled and broke away in solemn procession. The last of them clung reluctantly at the edge, and Day reached out and gently flicked the glassware. It fell, and joined the rest, and looked, for all the world, like a little water in the bottom of a flask. Barely enough to wet one's lips.

"And carefully, now, my dear, so very, *very* carefully. Your life hangs by a filament. Your life, and mine too."

She pressed her tongue into her lower lip, ever so carefully twisted the condenser free and set it down on the tray. The rest of the apparatus followed, piece by slow piece. She had fine, soft hands, Morveer's apprentice. Nimble yet steady, as indeed they were required to be. She pressed a cork carefully into the flask and held it up to the light, the sunshine making liquid diamonds of that tiny dribble of fluid, and she smiled. An innocent, a pretty, yet an entirely forgettable smile. "It doesn't look much."

"That is the *entire* point. It is without colour, odour or taste. And yet the most infinitesimal drop consumed, the softest mist inhaled, the gentlest touch upon the skin, even, will kill a man in minutes. There is no antidote, no remedy, no immunity. Truly...this is the King of Poisons."

"The King of Poisons," she breathed, with suitable awe.

"Keep this knowledge close to your heart, my dear, to be used only in the *extreme* of need. Only against the most dangerous, suspicious and cunning of targets. Only against those *intimately* acquainted with the poisoner's art."

"I understand. Caution first, always."

"Very good. That is the most valuable of lessons." Morveer sat back in his chair, making a steeple of his fingers. "Now you know the deepest of my secrets. Your apprenticeship is over, but...I hope you will continue, as my assistant."

"I'd be honoured to stay in your service. I still have much to learn."

"So do we all, my dear." Morveer jerked his head up at the sound of the gate bell tinkling in the distance. "So do we *all*."

Two figures were approaching the house down the long path through the orchard, and Morveer snapped open his eyeglass and trained it upon them. A man and a woman. He was very tall, and powerful-looking with it, wearing a threadbare coat, long hair swaying. A Northman, from his appearance.

"A primitive," he muttered, under his breath. Such men were prone to savagery and superstition, and he held them in healthy contempt.

He trained the eyeglass on the woman, now, though she was dressed much like a man. She looked straight towards the house, unwavering. Straight towards him, it almost seemed. A beautiful face, without doubt, edged with coal-black hair. But it was a hard and unsettling variety of beauty, further sharpened by a brooding appearance of grim purpose. A face that at once issued a challenge and a threat. A face that, having been glimpsed, one would not quickly forget. She did not compare with Morveer's mother in beauty, of course, but who could? His mother had almost transcended the human in her goodly qualities. Her pure smile, kissed by the sunlight, was etched forever into Morveer's memory as if it were a—

"Visitors?" asked Day.

"The Murcatto woman is here." He snapped his fingers towards the table. "Clear all this away. With the *very* greatest care, mark you! Then bring wine and cakes."

"Do you want anything in them?"

"Only plums and apricots. I mean to welcome my guests, not kill them." Not until he had heard what they had to say, at least.

While Day swiftly cleared the table, furnished it with a cloth and drew the chairs back in around it, Morveer took some elementary precautions. Then he arranged himself in his chair, highly polished knee-boots crossed in front of him and hands clasped across his chest, very much the country gentleman enjoying the winter air of his estate. Had he not earned it, after all?

He rose with his most ingratiating smile as his visitors came in close proximity to the house. The Murcatto woman walked with the slightest hint of a limp. She covered it well, but over long years in the trade Morveer had sharpened his perceptions to a razor point, and missed no detail. She wore a sword on her right hip, and it appeared to be a good one, but he paid it little mind. Ugly, unsophisticated tools. Gentlemen might wear them, but only the coarse and wrathful would stoop to actually use one. She wore a glove on her right hand, suggesting she had something she was keen to hide, because her left was bare, and sported a blood-red stone big as his thumbnail. If it was, as it certainly appeared to be, a ruby, it was one of promisingly great value.

"I am—"

"You are Monzcarro Murcatto, once captain general of the Thousand Swords, recently in the service of Duke Orso of Talins." Morveer thought it best to avoid that gloved hand, and so he offered out his left, palm upwards, in a gesture replete with humbleness and submission. "A Kantic gentleman of our mutual acquaintance, one Sajaam, told me to expect your visit." She gave it a brief shake, firm and businesslike. "And your name, my friend?" Morveer leaned unctuously forwards and folded the Northman's big right hand in both of his.

"Caul Shivers."

"Indeed, indeed, I have always found your Northern names *delightfully* picturesque."

"You've found 'em what now?"

"Nice."

"Oh."

Morveer held his hand a moment longer, then let it free. "*Pray* have a seat." He smiled upon Murcatto as she worked her way into her chair, the barest phantom of a grimace on her face. "I must confess I was expecting you to be considerably less beautiful."

She frowned at that. "I was expecting you to be less friendly."

"Oh, I can be *decidedly* unfriendly when it is called for, believe me." Day silently appeared and slid a plate of sweet cakes onto the table, a tray with a bottle of wine and glasses. "But it is hardly called for now, is it? Wine?"

His visitors exchanged a loaded glance. Morveer grinned as he pulled the cork and poured himself a glass. "The two of you are mercenaries, but I can only assume you do not rob, threaten and extort from *everyone* you meet. Likewise, I do not poison my every acquaintance." He slurped wine noisily, as though to advertise the total safety of the operation. "Who would pay me then? You are safe."

"Even so, you'll forgive us if we pass."

Day reached for a cake. "Can I—"

"Gorge yourself." Then to Murcatto. "You did not come here for my wine, then."

"No. I have work for you."

Morveer examined his cuticles. "The deaths of Grand Duke Orso and sundry others, I presume." She sat in silence, but it suited him to speak as though she had demanded an explanation. "It scarcely requires a towering intellect to make the deduction. Orso declares you and your brother killed by agents of the League of Eight. Then I hear from your friend and mine Sajaam that you are less deceased than advertised. Since there has been no tearful reunion with Orso, no happy declaration of your miraculous survival, we can assume the Osprian assassins were in fact... *a fantasy*. The Duke of Talins is a man of notoriously jealous temper, and your many victories made you too popular for your master's taste. Do I come close to the mark?"

"Close enough."

"My heartfelt condolences, then. Your brother, it would appear, could not be with us, and I understood you were inseparable." Her cold blue eyes had turned positively icy now. The Northman loomed grim and silent beside her. Morveer carefully cleared his throat. Blades might be unsophisticated tools, but a sword through the guts killed clever men every bit as thoroughly as stupid ones. "You understand that I am the *very* best at my trade."

"A fact," said Day, detaching herself from her sweetmeat for a moment. "An unchallengeable fact."

"The many persons of quality upon whom I have utilised my skills would so testify, were they able, but, of course, they are not."

Day sadly shook her head. "Not a one."

"Your point?" asked Murcatto.

"The best costs money. More money than you, having lost your employer, can, perhaps, afford."

"You've heard of Somenu Hermon?"

"The name is familiar."

"Not to me," said Day.

Morveer took it upon himself to explain. "Hermon was a destitute Kantic immigrant who rose to become, supposedly, the richest merchant in Musselia. The luxury of his lifestyle was notorious, his largesse legendary."

"And?"

"Alas, he was in the city when the Thousand Swords, in the pay of Grand Duke Orso, captured Musselia by stealth. Loss of life was kept to a minimum, but the city was plundered, and Hermon never heard from again. Nor was his money. The assumption was that this merchant, as merchants often do, greatly exaggerated his wealth, and beyond his gaudy and glorious accoutrements possessed ... precisely ... *nothing*." Morveer took a slow sip of wine, peering at Murcatto over the rim of his glass. "But others would know far better than I. The commanders of that particular campaign were ... what were the names now? A brother and sister ... I believe?"

She stared straight back at him, eyes undeviating. "Hermon was far wealthier than he pretended to be."

"Wealthier?" Morveer wriggled in his chair. "*Wealthier?* Oh my! The advantage to Murcatto! See how I *squirm* at the mention of so infinite a sum of bountiful gold! Enough to pay my meagre fees two dozen times and more, I do not doubt! Why ... my *overpowering* greed has left me quite ..." He lifted his open hand and slapped it down against the table with a bang. "*Paralysed.*"

The Northman toppled slowly sideways, slid from his chair and thumped onto the patchy turf beneath the fruit trees. He rolled gently over onto his back, knees up in the air in precisely the form he had taken while sitting, body rigid as a block of wood, eyes staring helplessly upwards.

"Ah," observed Morveer as he peered over the table. "The advantage to Morveer, it would seem."

Murcatto's eyes flicked sideways, then back. A flurry of twitches ran up one side of her face. Her gloved hand trembled on the tabletop by the slightest margin, and then lay still.

"It worked," murmured Day.

"How could you doubt me?" Morveer, liking nothing better than a captive audience, could not resist explaining how it had been managed. "Yellowseed oil was first applied to my hands." He held them up, fingers outspread. "In order to prevent the agent affecting me, you understand. I would not want to find myself suddenly paralysed, after all. That would be a *decidedly* unpleasant experience!" He chuckled to himself, and Day joined him at a higher pitch while she bent down to check the Northman's pulse, second cake wedged between her teeth. "The active ingredient was a distillation of spider venom. Extremely effective, even on touch. Since I held his hand for longer, your friend has taken a much heavier dose. He'll be lucky to move today ... if I choose to let him move again, of course. You should have retained the power of speech, however."

"Bastard," Murcatto grunted through frozen lips.

"I see that you have." He rose, slipped around the table and perched himself beside her. "I really must apologise, but you understand that I am, as you have been, a person at the precarious *summit* of my profession. We of extraordinary skills and achievements are obliged to take extraordinary precautions. Now, unimpeded by your ability to move, we can speak with absolute candour on the subject of...Grand Duke Orso." He swilled around a mouthful of wine, watched a little bird flit between the branches. Murcatto said nothing, but it hardly mattered. Morveer was happy to speak for them both.

"You have been done a terrible wrong, I see that. Betrayed by a man who owed you so much. Your beloved brother killed and you rendered...less than you were. My own life has been *littered* with painful reverses, believe me, so I entirely empathise. But the world is brimming with the awful and we humble individuals can only alter it by...small degrees." He frowned over at Day, munching noisily.

"What?" she grunted, mouth full.

"Quietly if you must, I am trying to expound." She shrugged, licking her fingers with entirely unnecessary sucking sounds. Morveer gave a disapproving sigh. "The carelessness of youth. She will learn. Time marches in only one direction for us all, eh, Murcatto?"

"Spare me the fucking philosophy," she forced through tight lips.

"Let us confine ourselves to the practical, then. With your notable assistance, Orso has made himself the most powerful man in Styria. I would never pretend to have your grasp of all things military, but it scarcely takes Stolicus himself to perceive that, following your glorious victory at the High Bank last year, the League of Eight are on the verge of collapse. Only a miracle will save Visserine when summer comes. The Osprians will treat for peace or be crushed, depending on Orso's mood, which, as you know far better than most, tends towards crushings. By the close of the year, barring accidents, Styria will have a king at last. An end to the Years of Blood." He drained his glass and waved it expansively. "Peace and prosperity for all and sundry! A better world, surely? Unless one is a mercenary, I suppose."

"Or a poisoner."

"On the contrary, we find more than ample employment in peacetime too. In any case, my point is that killing Grand Duke Orso — quite apart from the apparent impossibility of the task — seems to serve nobody's interests. Not even yours. It will not bring your brother back, or your hand, or your legs." Her face did not flicker, but that might merely have been due to paralysis. "The attempt will more than likely end in your death, and possibly even in mine. My point is that you have to stop this madness, my *dear* Monzcarro. You have to stop it *at once*, and give it no further thought."

Her eyes were pitiless as two pots of poison. "Only death will stop me. Mine, or Orso's."

"No matter the cost? No matter the pain? No matter who's killed along the path?"

"No matter," she growled.

"I find myself *entirely* convinced as to your level of commitment."

"Everything." The word was a snarl.

Morveer positively beamed. "Then we can do business. On that basis, and no other. What do I never deal in, Day?"

"Half-measures," his assistant murmured, eyeing the one cake left on the plate.

"Correct. How many do we kill?"

"Six," said Murcatto, "including Orso."

"Then my rate shall be ten thousand scales per secondary, payable upon proof of their demise, and fifty thousand for the Duke of Talins himself."

Her face twitched slightly. "Poor manners, to negotiate while your client is helpless."

"Manners would be *ludicrous* in a conversation about murder. In any case, I never haggle."

"Then we have a deal."

"I am so glad. Antidote, please."

Day pulled the cork from a glass jar, dipped the very point of a thin knife into the syrupy reduction in its bottom and handed it to him, polished handle first. He paused, looking into Murcatto's cold blue eyes.

Caution first, always. This woman they called the Serpent of Talins was dangerous in the extreme. If Morveer had not known it from her reputation, from their conversation, from the employment she had come to engage him for, he could have seen it at a single glance. He most seriously considered the possibility of giving her a fatal jab instead, throwing her Northern friend in the river and forgetting the whole business.

But to kill Grand Duke Orso, the most powerful man in Styria? To shape the course of history with one deft twist of his craft? For his deed, if not his name, to echo through the ages? What finer way to crown a career of achieving the impossible? The very thought made him smile the wider.

He gave a long sigh. "I hope I will not come to regret this." And he jabbed the back of Murcatto's hand with the point of the knife, a single bead of dark blood slowly forming on her skin.

Within a few moments the antidote was already beginning to take effect. She winced as she turned her head slowly one way, then the other, worked the muscles in her face. "I'm surprised," she said.

"Truly? How so?"

"I was expecting a Master Poisoner." She rubbed at the mark on the back of her hand. "Who'd have thought I'd get such a little prick?"

Morveer felt his grin slip. It only took him a moment to regain his composure, of course. Once he had silenced Day's giggle with a sharp frown. "I hope your temporary helplessness was not too great an inconvenience. I am forgiven, am I not? If the two of us are to cooperate, I would hate to have to labour beneath a shadow."

"Of course." She worked the movement back into her shoulders, the slightest smile at one corner of her mouth. "I need what you have, and you want what I have. Business is business."

"Excellent. Magnificent. Un...*paralleled*." And Morveer gave his most winning smile.

But he did not believe it for a moment. This was a most deadly job, and with a most deadly employer. Monzcarro Murcatto, the notorious Butcher of Caprile, was not a person of the forgiving variety. He was not forgiven. He was not even in the neighbourhood. From now on it would have to be caution first, second and third.

Science and Magic

Shivers pulled his horse up at the top of the rise. The country sloped away, a mess of dark fields with here or there a huddled farm or village, a stand of bare trees. No more'n a dozen miles distant, the line of the black sea, the curve of a wide bay, and along its edge a pale crust of city. Tiny towers clustered on three hills above the chilly brine, under an iron-grey sky.

"Westport," said Friendly, then clicked his tongue and moved his horse on.

The closer they came to the damn place the more worried Shivers got. And the more sore, cold and bored besides. He frowned at Murcatto, riding on her own ahead, hood up, a black figure in a black landscape. The cart's wheels clattered round on the road. The horses clopped and snorted. Some crows caw-cawed from the bare fields. But no one was talking.

They'd been a grim crowd all the way here. But then they'd a grim purpose in mind. Nothing else but murder. Shivers wondered what his father would've made of that. Rattleneck, who'd stuck to the old ways tight as a barnacle to a boat and always looked for the right thing to do. Killing a man you never met for money didn't seem to fit that hole however you twisted it around.

There was a sudden burst of high laughter. Day, perched on the cart next to Morveer, a half-eaten apple in her hand. Shivers hadn't heard much laughter in a while, and it drew him like a moth to flame.

"What's funny?" he asked, starting to grin along at the joke.

She leaned towards him, swaying with the cart. "I was just wondering, when you fell off your chair like a turtle tipped over, if you soiled yourself."

"I was of the opinion you probably did," said Morveer, "but doubted we could have smelled the difference."

Shivers' smile was stillborn. He remembered sitting in that orchard, frowning across the table, trying to look dangerous. Then he'd felt twitchy, then dizzy. He'd tried to lift his hand to his head, found he couldn't. He'd tried to say something about it, found he couldn't. Then the world tipped over. He didn't remember much else.

"What did you do to me?" He lowered his voice. "Sorcery?"

Day sprayed bits of apple as she burst out laughing. "Oh, this just gets better."

"And I said he would be an uninspiring travelling companion." Morveer chuckled. "*Sorcery*. I swear. It's like one of those stories."

"Those big, thick, stupid books! Magi and devils and all the rest!" Day was having herself quite the snigger. "Stupid stories for children!"

"Alright," said Shivers. "I think I get it. I'm slow as a fucking trout in treacle. Not sorcery. What, then?"

Day smirked. "Science."

Shivers didn't much care for the sound of it. "What's that? Some other kind of magic?"

"No, it most *decidedly* is not," sneered Morveer. "Science is a system of rational thought devised to investigate the world and establish the laws by which it operates. The scientist uses those laws to achieve an effect. One which might easily appear magical in the eyes of the primitive." Shivers struggled with all the long Styrian words. For a man who reckoned himself clever, Morveer had a fool's way of talking, seemed meant to make the simple difficult. "Magic, conversely, is a system of lies and nonsense devised to fool idiots."

"Right y'are. I must be the stupidest bastard in the Circle of the World, eh? It's a wonder I can hold my own shit in without paying mind to my arse every minute."

"The thought had occurred."

"There is magic," grumbled Shivers. "I've seen a woman call up a mist."

"Really? And how did it differ from ordinary mist? Magic coloured? Green? Orange?"

Shivers frowned. "The usual colour."

"So a woman called, and there was mist." Morveer raised one eyebrow at his apprentice. "A wonder *indeed*." She grinned, teeth crunching into her apple.

"I've seen a man marked with letters, made one half of him proof against any blade. Stabbed him myself, with a spear. Should've been a killing blow, but didn't leave a mark."

"Ooooooh!" Morveer held both hands up and wiggled his fingers like a child playing ghost. "Magic letters! First, there was no wound, and then... *there was no wound*? I recant! The world is *stuffed* with miracles." More tittering from Day.

"I know what I've seen."

"No, my mystified friend, you *think* you know. There is no such thing as magic. Certainly not here in Styria."

"Just treachery," sang Day, "and war, and plague, and money to be made."

"Why did you favour Styria with your presence, anyway?" asked Morveer. "Why not stay in the North, swaddled in the magic mists?"

Shivers rubbed slowly at the side of his neck. Seemed a strange reason, now, and he felt even more of a fool saying it. "I came here to be a better man."

"Starting from where you are, I hardly think that would prove too difficult."

Shivers had some pride still, and this prick's sniggering was starting to grate on it. He'd have liked to just knock him off his cart with an axe. But he was trying to do better, so he leaned over instead and spoke in Northern, nice and careful. "I think you've got a head full of shit, which is no surprise because your face looks like an arse. You little men are all the same. Always trying to prove how clever y'are so you've something to be proud of. But it don't matter how much you laugh at me, I've won already. You'll never be tall." And he grinned right round his face. "Seeing across a crowded room will always be a dream to you."

Morveer frowned. "And what is that jabber supposed to mean?"

"You're the fucking scientist. You work it out."

Day snorted with high laughter until Morveer caught her with a hard glance. She was still smiling, though, as she stripped the apple core to the pips and tossed it away. Shivers dropped back and watched the empty fields slither by, turned earth half-frozen with a morning frost. Made him think of home. He gave a sigh, and it smoked out against the grey sky. The friends Shivers had made in his life had all been fighters. Carls and Named Men, comrades in the line, most back in the mud, now, one way or another. He reckoned Friendly was the closest thing he'd get to that in the midst of

Styria, so he gave his horse a nudge in the flanks and brought it up next to the convict.

"Hey." Friendly didn't say a word. He didn't even move his head to show he'd heard. Silence stretched out. Looking at that brick wall of a face it was hard to picture the convict a bosom companion, chuckling away at his jokes. But a man's got to clutch at some hope, don't he? "You were a soldier, then?"

Friendly shook his head.

"But you fought in battles?"

And again.

Shivers ploughed on as if he'd said yes. Not much other choice, now. "I fought in a few. Charged in the mist with Bethod's Carls north of the Cumnur. Held the line next to Rudd Threetrees at Dunbrec. Fought seven days in the mountains with the Dogman. Seven desperate days, those were."

"Seven?" asked Friendly, one heavy brow twitching with interest.

"Aye," sighed Shivers. "Seven." The names of those men and those places meant nothing to no one down here. He watched a set of covered carts coming the other way, men with steel caps and flatbows in their hands frowning at him from their seats. "Where did you learn to fight, then?" he asked, the smear of hope at getting some decent conversation drying out quick.

"In Safety."

"Eh?"

"Where they put you when they catch you for a crime."

"Why keep you safe after that?"

"They don't call it Safety because you're safe there. They call it Safety because everyone else is safe from you. They count out the days, months, years they'll keep you. Then they lock you in, deep down, where the light doesn't go, until the days, months, years have all rubbed past, and the numbers are all counted down to nothing. Then you say thank you, and they let you free."

Sounded like a barbaric way of doing things to Shivers. "You do a crime in the North, you pay a gild on it, make it right. That, or if the chieftain decides, they hang you. Maybe put the bloody cross in you, if you've done murders. Lock a man in a hole? That's a crime itself."

Friendly shrugged. "They have rules there that make sense. There's a proper time for each thing. A proper number on the great clock. Not like out here."

"Aye. Right. Numbers, and that." Shivers wished he'd never asked.

Friendly hardly seemed to hear him. "Out here the sky is too high, and every man does what he pleases when he likes, and there are no right numbers for anything." He was frowning off towards Westport, still just a sweep of hazy buildings round the cold bay. "Fucking chaos."

They got to the city walls about midday, and there was already a long line of folk waiting to get in. Soldiers stood about the gate, asking questions, going through a pack or a chest, poking half-hearted at a cart with their spear-butts.

"The Aldermen have been nervous since Borletta fell," said Morveer from his seat. "They are checking everyone who enters. I will do the talking." Shivers was happy enough to let him, since the prick loved the sound of his own voice so much.

"Your name?" asked the guard, eyes infinitely bored.

"Reevrom," said the poisoner, with a massive grin. "A humble merchant from Puranti. And these are my associates—"

"Your business in Westport?"

"Murder." An uncomfortable silence. "I hope to make a veritable *killing* on the sale of Osprian wines! Yes, indeed, I hope to make a *killing* in your city." Morveer chuckled at his own joke and Day tittered away beside him.

"This one doesn't look like the kind we need." Another guard was frowning up at Shivers.

Morveer kept chuckling. "Oh, no need to worry on his account. The man is practically a retard. Intellect of a child. Still, he is good for shifting a barrel or two. I keep him on out of sentiment as much as anything. What am I, Day?"

"Sentimental," said the girl.

"I have too much heart. Always have had. My mother died when I was very young, you see, a wonderful woman—"

"Get on with it!" someone called from behind them.

Morveer took hold of the canvas sheet covering the back of the wagon. "Do you want to check—"

"Do I look like I want to, with half of Styria to get through my bloody gate? On." The guard waved a tired hand. "Move on."

The reins snapped, the cart rolled into the city of Westport, and Murcatto and Friendly rode after. Shivers came last, which seemed about usual lately.

Beyond the walls it was crushed in tight as a battle, and not much less frightening. A paved road struck between high buildings, bare trees planted on either side, crammed with a shuffling tide of folk every shape and colour. Pale men in sober cloth, narrow-eyed women in bright silks, black-skinned men in white robes, soldiers and sell-swords in chain mail and dull plate. Servants, labourers, tradesmen, gentlemen, rich and poor, fine and stinking, nobles and beggars. An awful lot of beggars. Walkers and riders came surging up and away in a blur, horses and carts and covered carriages, women with a weight of piled-up hair and an even greater weight of jewellery, carried past on teetering chairs by pairs of sweating servants.

Shivers had thought Talins was rammed full with strange variety. Westport was way worse. He saw a line of animals with great long necks being led through the press, linked by thin chains, tiny heads swaying sadly about on top. He squeezed his eyes shut and shook his head, but when he opened them the monsters were still there, heads bobbing over the milling crowd, not even remarked upon. The place was like a dream, and not the pleasant kind.

They turned down a narrower way, hemmed in by shops and stalls. Smells jabbed at his nose one after another — fish, bread, polish, fruit, oil, spice and a dozen others he'd no idea of — and they made his breath catch and his stomach lurch. Out of nowhere a boy on a passing cart shoved a wicker cage in Shivers' face and a tiny monkey inside hissed and spat at him, near knocking him from his saddle in surprise. Shouts battered at his ears in a score of different tongues. A kind of a chant came floating up over the top of it, louder and louder, strange but beautiful, made the hairs on his arms bristle.

A building with a great dome loomed over one side of a square, six tall turrets sprouting from its front wall, golden spikes gleaming on their roofs. It was from there the chanting was coming. Hundreds of voices, deep and high together, mingling into one.

"It's a temple." Murcatto had dropped back beside him, her hood still up, not much more of her face showing than her frown.

If Shivers was honest, he was more'n a bit feared of her. It was bad enough that he'd watched her break a man apart with a hammer and give every sign of enjoying it. But he'd had this creeping feeling afterwards, when they were bargaining, that she was on the point of stabbing him. Then there was that hand she always kept a glove on. He couldn't remember ever being scared of a woman before, and it made him shamed and nervous at once. But he could hardly deny that, apart from the glove, and the hammer, and the sick sense of danger, he liked the looks of her. A lot. He wasn't sure he didn't like the danger a bit more than was healthy too. All added up to not knowing what the hell to say from one moment to the next.

"Temple?"

"Where the Southerners pray to God."

"God, eh?" Shivers' neck ached as he squinted up at those spires, higher than the tallest trees in the valley where he was born. He'd heard some folk down South thought there was a man in the sky. A man who'd made the world and saw everything. Had always seemed a mad kind of a notion, but looking at this Shivers weren't far from believing it himself. "Beautiful."

"Maybe a hundred years ago, when the Gurkish conquered Dawah, a lot of Southerners fled before them. Some crossed the water and settled here, and they raised up temples in thanks for their salvation. Westport is almost as much a part of the South as it's a part of Styria. But then it's part of the Union too, since the Aldermen finally had to pick a side, and bought the High King his victory over the Gurkish. They call this place the Crossroads of the World. Those that don't call it a nest of liars, anyway. There are people settled here from across the Thousand Isles, from Suljuk and Sikkur, from Thond and the Old Empire. Northmen even."

"Anything but those stupid bastards."

"Primitives, to a man. I hear some of them grow their hair long like women. But they'll take anyone here." Her gloved finger pointed out a long row of men on little platforms at the far end of the square. A strange bloody crowd, even for this place. Old and young, tall and short, fat and bony, some with strange robes or headgear, some half-naked and painted, one with bones through his face. A few had signs behind 'em in all kinds of letters, beads or baubles hanging. They danced and capered, threw their arms up, stared at the sky, dropped on their knees, wept, laughed, raged, sang, screamed, begged, all blathering away over each other in more languages than Shivers had known about.

"Who the hell are these bastards?" he muttered.

"Holy men. Or madmen, depending who you ask. Down in Gurkhul, you have to pray how the Prophet tells you. Here each man can worship as he pleases."

"They're praying?"

Murcatto shrugged. "More like they're trying to convince everyone else that they know the best way."

People stood watching 'em. Some nodding along with what they were saying. Some shaking their heads, laughing, shouting back even. Some just stood there, bored. One of the holy men, or the madmen, started screaming at Shivers as he rode past in words he couldn't make a smudge of sense from. He knelt, stretching out his arms, beads round his neck rattling, voice raw with pleading. Shivers could see it in his red-rimmed eyes — he thought this was the most important thing he'd ever do.

"Must be a nice feeling," said Shivers.

"What must?"

"Thinking you know all the answers..." He trailed off as a woman walked past with a man on a lead. A big, dark man with a collar of shiny metal, carrying a sack in either hand, his eyes kept on the ground. "You see that?"

"In the South most men either own someone or are owned themselves."

"That's a bastard custom," muttered Shivers. "I thought you said this was part o' the Union, though."

"And they love their freedom over in the Union, don't they? You can't make a man a slave there." She nodded towards some more, being led past meek and humble in a line. "But if they pass through no one's freeing them, I can tell you that."

"Bloody Union. Seems those bastards always want more land. There's more of 'em than ever in the North. Uffrith's full of 'em, since the wars started up again. And what do they need more land for? You should see that city they've got already. Makes this place look a village."

She looked sharply across at him. "Adua?"

"That's the one."

"You've been there?"

"Aye. I fought the Gurkish there. Got me this mark." And he pulled back his sleeve to show the scar on his wrist. When he looked back she had an odd look in her eye. You might almost have called it respect. He liked seeing it. Been a while since anyone looked at him with aught but contempt.

"Did you stand in the shadow of the House of the Maker?" she asked.

"Most of the city's in the shadow of that thing one time o' day or another."

"What was it like?"

"Darker'n outside it. Shadows tend to be, in my experience."

"Huh." The first time Shivers had seen anything close to a smile on her face, and he reckoned it suited her. "I always said I'd go."

"To Adua? What's stopping you?"

"Six men I need to kill."

Shivers puffed out his cheeks. "Ah. That." A surge of worry went through him, and he wondered afresh just why the hell he'd ever said yes. "I've always been my own worst enemy," he muttered.

"Stick with me, then." Her smile had widened some. "You'll soon have worse. We're here."

Not all that heartening, as a destination. A narrow alley, dim as dusk. Crumbling buildings crowded in, shutters rotten and peeling, sheets of plaster cracking away from damp bricks. He led his horse after the cart and through a dim archway while Murcatto swung the creaking doors shut behind them and shot the rusted bolt. Shivers tethered his horse to a rotting post in a yard strewn with weeds and fallen tiles.

"A palace," he muttered, staring up towards the square of grey sky high above, the walls all round coated with dried-up weeds, the shutters hanging miserable from their hinges. "Once."

"I took it for the location," said Murcatto, "not the décor."

They made for a gloomy hall, empty doorways leading into empty chambers. "Lot of rooms," said Shivers.

Friendly nodded. "Twenty-two."

Their boots thump, thumped on the creaking staircase as they made their way up through the rotten guts of the building.

"How are you going to begin?" Murcatto was asking Morveer.

"I already have. Letters of introduction have been sent. We have a *sizeable* deposit to entrust to Valint and Balk tomorrow morning. Sizeable enough to warrant the attention of their most senior officer. I, my assistant and your man Friendly will infiltrate the bank disguised as a merchant and his associates. We will meet with — then seek out an opportunity to kill — Mauthis."

"Simple as that?"

"Seizing an opportunity is more often than not the key in these affairs, but if the moment does not present itself, I will be laying the groundwork for a more...structured approach."

"What about the rest of us?" asked Shivers.

"Our employer, obviously, is possessed of a memorable visage and might be recognised, while *you*," and Morveer sneered back down the stairs at him, "stand out like a cow among the wolves, and would be no more useful than one. You are far too tall and far too scarred and your clothes are far too rural for you to belong in a bank. As for that hair—"

"Pfeeesh," said Day, shaking her head.

"What's that supposed to mean?"

"Exactly how it sounded. You are simply far, far too..." Morveer swirled one hand around. "*North.*"

Murcatto unlocked a flaking door at the top of the last flight of steps and shoved it open. Muddy daylight leaked through and Shivers followed the others out blinking into the sun.

"By the dead." A jumble of mismatched roofs every shape and pitch stretched off all round — red tiles, grey slates, white lead, rotting thatch, bare rafters caked with moss, green copper streaked with dirt, patched with canvas and old leather. A tangle of leaning gables, garrets, beams, paint peeling and sprouting with weeds, dangling gutters and crooked drains, bound up with chains and sagging washing lines, built all over each other at every angle and looking like the lot might slide off into the streets any moment. Smoke belched up from countless chimneys, cast a haze that made the sun a sweaty blur. Here and there a tower poked or a dome bulged above the chaos, the odd tangle of bare wood where some trees had beaten the odds and managed to stick out a twig. The sea was a grey smudge in the distance, the masts of ships in the harbour a far-off forest, shifting uneasily with the waves.

From up here the city seemed to make a great hiss. Noise of work and play, of men and beasts, calls of folk selling and buying, wheels rattling and hammers clanging, splinters of song and scraps of music, joy and despair all mixed up together like stew in a great pot.

Shivers edged to the lichen-crusted parapet beside Murcatto and peered over. People trickled up and down a cobbled lane far below, like water in the bottom of a canyon. A monster of a building loomed up on the other side.

Its wall was a sheer cliff of smooth-cut pale stone, with a pillar every twenty strides that Shivers couldn't have got both arms around, crusted at the top with leaves and faces carved out of stone. There was a row of small windows at maybe twice the height of a man, then another above, then a row of much bigger ones, all blocked by metal grilles. Above that, all along the line of the flat roof, about level with where Shivers was standing, a hedge of black iron spikes stuck out, like the spines on a thistle.

Morveer grinned across at it. "Ladies, gentlemen and savages, I give you the Westport branch...of the Banking House...of Valint and Balk."

Shivers shook his head. "Place looks like a fortress."

"Like a prison," murmured Friendly.

"Like a *bank*," sneered Morveer.

The Safest Place in the World

The banking hall of the Westport office of Valint and Balk was an echoing cavern of red porphyry and black marble. It had all the gloomy splendour of an emperor's mausoleum, the minimum light necessary creeping in through small, high windows, their thick bars casting cross-hatched shadows across the shining floor. A set of huge marble busts stared smugly down from on high: great merchants and financiers of Styrian history, by the look of them. Criminals made heroes by colossal success. Morveer wondered whether Somenu Hermon was among them, and the thought that the famous merchant might indirectly be paying his wages caused his smirk to expand by the slightest margin.

Sixty clerks or more attended identical desks loaded with identical heaps of papers, each with a huge, leather-bound ledger open before him. All manner of men, with all colours of skin, some sporting the skullcaps, turbans or characteristic hairstyles of one Kantic sect or other. The only prejudice here was in favour of those who could turn the fastest coin. Pens rattled in ink bottles, nibs scratched on heavy paper, pages crackled as they were turned. Merchants stood in clumps and haggles, conversing in whispers. Nowhere was a single coin in evidence. The wealth here was made of words, of ideas, of rumours and lies, too valuable to be held captive in gaudy gold or simple silver.

It was a setting intended to awe, to amaze, to intimidate, but Morveer was not a man to be intimidated. He belonged here perfectly, just as he did everywhere and nowhere. He swaggered past a long queue of well-dressed supplicants with the air of studied self-satisfaction that always accompanied new money. Friendly lumbered in his wake, strongbox held close, and Day tiptoed demurely at the rear.

Morveer snapped his fingers at the nearest clerk. "I have an appointment with..." He consulted his letter for effect. "One Mauthis. On the subject of a sizeable deposit."

"Of course. If you would wait for one moment."

"One, but no more. Time and money are the same."

Morveer inconspicuously studied the arrangements for security. It would have been an understatement to call them daunting. He counted twelve armed men stationed around the hall, as comprehensively equipped as the King of the Union's bodyguard. There had been another dozen outside the towering double-doors.

"The place is a fortress," muttered Day under her breath.

"But considerably better defended," replied Morveer.

"How long is this going to take?"

"Why?"

"I'm hungry."

"Already? For pity's *sake*! You will not starve if you — Wait."

A tall man had emerged from a high archway, gaunt-faced with a promi-nent beak of a nose and thinning grey hair, arrayed in sombre robes with a heavy fur collar. "Mauthis," murmured Morveer, from Murcatto's exhaus-tive description. "Our intended."

He was walking behind a younger man, curly haired and with a pleasant smile, not at all richly dressed. So unexceptional, in fact, he would have had a fine appearance for a poisoner. And yet Mauthis, though supposedly in charge of the bank, hurried after with hands clasped, as though he was the junior. Morveer sidled closer, bringing them within earshot.

"...Master Sulfur, I hope you will inform our superiors that everything is under complete control." Mauthis had, perhaps, the very slightest note of panic in his voice. "Absolute and complete—"

"Of course," answered the one called Sulfur, offhand. "Though I rarely find our superiors need informing as to how things stand. They are watch-ing. If everything is under complete control, I am sure they will already be satisfied. If not, well..." He smiled wide at Mauthis, and then at Morveer, and Morveer noticed he had different-coloured eyes, one blue, one green. "Good day." And he strode away and was soon lost in the crowds.

"May I be of assistance?" grated Mauthis. He looked as if he had never laughed in his life. He was running out of time to try it now.

"I certainly hope you may. My name is Reevrom, a merchant of Puranti." Morveer tittered inwardly at his own joke, as he did whenever he utilised the alias, but his face showed nothing but the warmest bonhomie as he offered his hand.

"Reevrom. I have heard of your house. A privilege to make your acquaintance." Mauthis disdained to shake it, and kept a carefully inoffensive distance between them. Evidently a cautious man. Just as well, for his sake. The tiny spike on the underside of Morveer's heavy middle-finger ring was loaded with scorpion venom in a solution of Leopard Flower. The banker would have sat happily through their meeting, then dropped dead within the hour.

"This is my niece," continued Morveer, not in the least downhearted by his failed attempt. "I have been entrusted with the responsibility of escorting her to an introduction with a potential suitor." Day looked up from beneath her lashes with perfectly judged shyness. "And this is my associate." He glanced sideways at Friendly and the man frowned back. "I do him too much credit. My bodyguard, Master Charming. He is not a great conversationalist, but when it comes to bodyguarding, he is ... barely adequate in truth. Still, I promised his old mother that I would take him under my—"

"You have come here on a matter of business?" droned Mauthis.

Morveer bowed. "A *sizeable* deposit."

"I regret that your associates must remain behind, but if you would care to follow me we would, of course, be happy to accept your deposit and prepare a receipt."

"Surely my niece—"

"You must understand that, in the interests of security, we can make no exceptions. Your niece will be perfectly comfortable here."

"Of course, of course you will, my dear. Master Charming! The strongbox!" Friendly handed the metal case over to a bespectacled clerk, left tottering under its weight. "Now wait here, and get up to no mischief!" Morveer gave a heavy sigh as he followed Mauthis into the depths of the building, as though he had insurmountable difficulties securing competent help. "My money will be safe here?"

"The bank's walls are at no point less than twelve feet in thickness. There is only one entrance, guarded by a dozen well-armed men during the day, sealed at night with three locks, made by three different locksmiths, the keys kept by three separate employees. Two parties of men constantly patrol the exterior of the bank until morning. Even then the interior is kept under watch by a most sharp-eyed and competent guard." He gestured towards a bored-looking man in a studded leather jerkin, seated at a desk to the side of the hallway.

"He is locked in?"

"All night."

Morveer worked his mouth with some discomfort. "*Most* comprehensive arrangements."

He pulled out his handkerchief and pretended to cough daintily into it. The silk was soaked in Mustard Root, one of an extensive range of agents to which he had himself long since developed an immunity. He needed only a few moments unobserved, then he could clasp it to Mauthis' face. The slightest inhalation and the man would cough himself to bloody death within moments. But the clerk laboured along between them with the strongbox in his arms, and not the slightest opportunity was forthcoming. Morveer was forced to tuck the lethal cloth away, then narrow his eyes as they turned into a long hallway lined with huge paintings. Light poured in from above, the very roof, far overhead, fashioned from a hundred thousand diamond panes of glass.

"A ceiling of windows!" Morveer turned slowly round and round, head back. "Truly a wonder of architecture!"

"This is an entirely modern building. Your money could not be more secure anywhere, believe me."

"The depths of ruined Aulcus, perhaps?" joked Morveer, as an overblown artist's impression of the ancient city passed by on their left.

"Not even there."

"And making a withdrawal would be *considerably* more testing, I imagine! Ha ha. Ha ha."

"Quite so." The banker did not display even the inkling of a smile. "Our vault door is a foot thickness of solid Union steel. We do not exaggerate when we say this is the safest place in the Circle of the World. This way."

Morveer was ushered into a voluminous chamber panelled with oppressively dark wood, ostentatious yet still uncomfortable, tyrannised by a desk the size of a poor man's house. A sombre oil was set above a looming fireplace: a heavyset bald man glowering down as though he suspected Morveer of being up to no good. Some Union bureaucrat of the dusty past, he suspected. Zoller, maybe, or Bialoveld.

Mauthis took up a high, hard seat and Morveer found one opposite while the clerk lifted the lid of the strongbox and began to count out the money, using a coin-stacker with practised efficiency. Mauthis watched, scarcely blinking. At no stage did he touch either case or coins himself. A cautious man. Damnably, infuriatingly cautious. His slow eyes slid across the desk. "Wine?"

Morveer raised an eyebrow at the distorted glassware behind the windows of a towering cabinet. "Thank you, no. I become quite flustered under its influence, and between the two of us have frequently embarrassed myself. I decided, in the end, to abstain entirely, and stick to selling it to others. The stuff is...*poison*." And he gave a huge smile. "But don't let me stop you." He slid an unobtrusive hand into a hidden pocket within his jacket where the vial of Star Juice was waiting. It would be a small effort to mount a diversion and introduce a couple of drops to Mauthis' glass while he was—

"I too avoid it."

"Ah." Morveer released the vial and instead plucked a folded paper from his inside pocket quite as if that had been his intention from the first. He unfolded it and pretended to read while his eyes darted about the office. "I counted five thousand..." He took in the style of lock upon the door, the fashion of its construction, the frame within which it was set. "Two hundred..." The tiles from which the floor was made, the panels on the walls, the render of the ceiling, the leather of Mauthis' chair, the coals on the unlit fire. "And twelve scales." Nothing seemed promising.

Mauthis showed no emotion at the number. Fortunes and small change, all one. He opened the heavy cover of a huge ledger upon his desk. He licked one finger and flicked steadily through the pages, paper crackling. Morveer felt a warm satisfaction spread out from his stomach to every extremity at the sight, and it was only with an effort that he prevented himself from whooping with triumph. He settled for a prim smile. "Takings from my last trip to Sipani. Wine from Ospria is always a profitable venture, even in these uncertain times. Not everyone has our temperance, Master Mauthis, I am happy to say!"

"Of course." The banker licked his finger once again as he turned the last few pages.

"Five thousand, two hundred and eleven," said the clerk.

Mauthis' eyes flickered up. "Trying to get away with something?"

"Me?" Morveer passed it off with a false chuckle. "Damn that man Charming, he can't count for anything! I swear he has no feel for numbers whatsoever."

The nib of Mauthis' pen scratched across the ledger; the clerk hurried over and blotted the entry as his master neatly, precisely, emotionlessly prepared the receipt. The clerk carried it to Morveer and offered it to him along with the empty strongbox.

"A note for the full amount in the name of the Banking House of Valint and Balk," said Mauthis. "Redeemable at any reputable mercantile institution in Styria."

"Must I sign anything?" asked Morveer hopefully, his fingers closing around the pen in his inside pocket. It doubled as a highly effective blow-gun, the needle concealed within containing a lethal dose of—

"No."

"Very well." Morveer smiled as he folded the paper and slid it away, taking care that it did not catch on the deadly edge of his scalpel. "Better than gold, and a great deal lighter. For now, then, I take my leave. It has been a *decided* pleasure." And he held out his hand again, poisoned ring glinting. No harm in making the effort.

Mauthis did not move from his chair. "Likewise."

Evil Friends

It had been Benna's favourite place in Westport. He'd dragged her there twice a week while they were in the city. A shrine of mirrors and cut glass, polished wood and glittering marble. A temple to the god of male grooming. The high priest — a small, lean barber in a heavily embroidered apron — stood sharply upright in the centre of the floor, chin pointed to the ceiling, as though he'd been expecting them that very moment to enter.

"Madam! A delight to see you again!" He blinked for a moment. "Your husband is not with you?"

"My brother." Monza swallowed. "And no, he…won't be back. I've an altogether tougher challenge for you—"

Shivers stepped through the doorway, gawping about as fearfully as a sheep in a shearing pen. She opened her mouth to speak but the barber cut her off. "I believe I see the problem." He made a sharp circuit of Shivers while the Northman frowned down at him. "Dear, dear. All off?"

"What?"

"All off," said Monza, taking the barber by the elbow and pressing a quarter into his hand. "Go gently, though. I doubt he's used to this and he might startle." She realised she was making him sound like a horse. Maybe that was giving him too much credit.

"Of course." The barber turned, and gave a sharp intake of breath. Shivers had already taken his new shirt off and was looming pale and sinewy in the doorway, unbuckling his belt.

"He means your hair, fool," said Monza, "not your clothes."

"Uh. Thought it was odd, but, well, Southern fashions…" Monza watched him as he sheepishly buttoned his shirt back up. He had a long scar

103

from his shoulder across his chest, pink and twisted. She might've thought it ugly once, but she'd had to change her opinions on scars, along with a few other things.

Shivers lowered himself into the chair. "Had this hair all my life."

"Then it is past time you were released from its suffocating embrace. Head forwards, please." The barber produced his scissors with a flourish and Shivers lurched out of his seat.

"You think I'm letting a man I never met near my face with a blade?"

"I must protest! I trim the heads of Westport's finest gentlemen!"

"You." Monza caught the barber's shoulder as he backed away and marched him forwards. "Shut up and cut hair." She slipped another quarter into his apron pocket and gave Shivers a long look. "You, shut up and sit still."

He sidled back into the chair and clung so tight to its arms that the tendons stood from the backs of his hands. "I'm watching you," he growled.

The barber gave a long sigh and with lips pursed began to work.

Monza wandered around the room while the scissors snip-snipped behind her. She walked along a shelf, absently pulling the stoppers from the coloured bottles, sniffing at the scented oils inside. She caught a glimpse of herself in the mirror. A hard face, still. Thinner, leaner, sharper even than she used to be. Eyes sunken from the nagging pain up her legs, from the nagging need for the husk that made the pain go away.

You look especially beautiful this morning, Monza…

The idea of a smoke stuck in her mind like a bone in her craw. Each day the need crept up on her earlier. More time spent sick, sore and twitchy, counting the minutes until she could creep off and be with her pipe, sink back into soft, warm nothingness. Her fingertips tingled at the thought, tongue working hungrily around her dry mouth.

"Always worn it long. Always." She turned back into the room. Shivers was wincing like a torture victim as tufts of cut hair tumbled down and built up on the polished boards under the chair. Some men clam up when they're nervous. Some men blather. It seemed Shivers was in the latter camp. "Guess my brother had long hair and I went and did the same. Used to try and copy him. Looked up to him. Little brothers, you know… What was your brother like?"

She felt her cheek twitch, remembering Benna's grinning face in the mirror, and hers behind it. "He was a good man. Everyone loved him."

"My brother was a good man. Lot better'n me. My father thought so, anyway. Never missed a chance to tell me...I mean, just saying, nothing strange 'bout long hair where I come from. Folk got other things to cut in a war than their hair, I guess. Black Dow used to laugh at me, 'cause he'd always hacked his right off, so as not to get in the way in a fight. But then he'd give a man shit about anything, Black Dow. Hard mouth. Hard man. Only man harder was the Bloody-Nine his self. I reckon—"

"For someone with a weak grip on the language, you like to talk, don't you? You know what I reckon?"

"What?"

"People talk a lot when they've nothing to say."

Shivers heaved out a sigh. "Just trying to make tomorrow that bit better than today is all. I'm one of those...you've got a word for it, don't you?"

"Idiots?"

He looked sideways at her. "It was a different one I had in mind."

"Optimists."

"That's the one. I'm an optimist."

"How's it working out for you?"

"Not great, but I keep hoping."

"That's optimists. You bastards never learn." She watched Shivers' face emerging from that tangle of greasy hair. Hard-boned, sharp-nosed, with a nick of a scar through one eyebrow. It was a good face, in so far as she cared. She found she cared more than she'd thought she would. "You were a soldier, right? What do they call them up in the North...a Carl?"

"I was a Named Man, as it goes," and she could hear the pride in his voice.

"Good for you. So you led men?"

"I had some looking to me. My father was a famous man, my brother too. A little some of that rubbed off, maybe."

"So why throw it away? Why come down here to be nothing?"

He looked at her in the mirror while the scissors clicked round his face. "Morveer said you were a soldier yourself. A famous one."

"Not that famous." It was only half a lie. Infamous was closer to it.

"That'd be a strange job for a woman, where I come from."

She shrugged. "Easier than farming."

"So you know war, am I right?"

"Yes."

"Daresay you've seen some battles. You've seen men killed."

"Yes."

"Then you've seen what goes with it. The marches, the waiting, the sickness. Folk raped, robbed, crippled, burned out who've done nought to deserve it."

Monza thought of her own field burning, all those years ago. "You've got a point, you can out and say it."

"That blood only makes more blood. That settling one score only starts another. That war gives a bastard of a sour taste to any man that's not half-mad, and it only gets worse with time." She didn't disagree. "So you know why I'd rather be free of it. Make something grow. Something to be proud of, instead of just breaking. Be...a good man, I guess."

Snip, snip. Hair tumbled down and gathered on the floor. "A good man, eh?"

"That's right."

"So you've seen dead men yourself?"

"I've seen my share."

"You've seen a lot together?" she asked. "Stacked up after the plague came through, spread out after a battle?"

"Aye, I've seen that."

"Did you notice some of those corpses had a kind of glow about them? A sweet smell like roses on a spring morning?"

Shivers frowned. "No."

"The good men and the bad, then — all looked about the same, did they? They always did to me, I can tell you that." It was his turn to stay quiet. "If you're a good man, and you try to think about what the right thing is every day of your life, and you build things to be proud of so bastards can come and burn them in a moment, and you make sure and say thank you kindly each time they kick the guts out of you, do you think when you die, and they stick you in the mud, you turn into gold?"

"What?"

"Or do you turn to fucking shit like the rest of us?"

He nodded slowly. "You turn to shit, alright. But maybe you can leave something good behind you."

She barked empty laughter at him. "What do we leave behind but things not done, not said, not finished? Empty clothes, empty rooms, empty spaces in the ones who knew us? Mistakes never made right and hopes rotted down to nothing?"

"Hopes passed on, maybe. Good words said. Happy memories, I reckon."

"And all those dead men's smiles you've kept folded up in your heart, they were keeping you warm when I found you, were they? How did they taste when you were hungry? They raise a smile, even, when you were desperate?"

Shivers puffed out his cheeks. "Hell, but you're a ray of sunshine. Might be they did me some good."

"More than a pocketful of silver would've?"

He blinked at her, then away. "Maybe not. But I reckon I'll try to keep thinking my way, just the same."

"Hah. Good luck, good man." She shook her head as if she'd never heard such stupidity. *Give me only evil men for friends*, Verturio wrote. *Them I understand.*

A last quick clicking of the scissors and the barber stepped away, dabbing at his own sweaty brow with the back of one sleeve. "And we are all finished."

Shivers stared into the mirror. "I look a different man."

"Sir looks like a Styrian aristocrat."

Monza snorted. "Less like a Northern beggar, anyway."

"Maybe." Shivers looked less than happy. "I daresay that's a better-looking man there. A cleverer man." He ran one hand through his short dark hair, frowning at his reflection. "Not sure if I trust that bastard, though."

"And to finish..." The barber leaned forwards, a coloured crystal bottle in his hands, and squirted a fine mist of perfume over Shivers' head.

The Northman was up like a cat off hot coals. "What the *fuck*?" he roared, big fists clenched, shoving the man away and making him totter across the room with a squeal.

Monza burst out laughing. "Looks of a Styrian nobleman, maybe." She pulled out a couple more quarters and tucked them into the gaping barber's apron pocket. "The manners might be a while coming, though."

It was getting dark when they came back to the crumbling mansion, Monza with her hood drawn up and Shivers striding proudly along in his new coat. A cold rain flitted down into the ruined courtyard, a single lamp burned in a window on the first floor. She frowned towards it, and then at Shivers, found the grip of the knife in the back of her belt with her left hand. Best to be ready for every possibility. Up the creaking stairs a peeling door stood ajar, light spilling out across the boards. She stepped up and poked it open with her boot.

A pair of burning logs in the soot-blackened fireplace barely warmed the chamber on the other side. Friendly stood beside the far window, peering through the shutters towards the bank. Morveer had some sheets of paper spread out on a rickety old table, marking his place with an ink-spotted hand. Day sat on the tabletop with her legs crossed, peeling an orange with a dagger. "Definite improvement," she grunted, giving Shivers a glance.

"Oh, I cannot but agree." Morveer grinned. "A dirty, long-haired idiot left the building this morning. A clean, short-haired idiot has returned. It *must* be magic."

Monza let go the grip of her knife while Shivers muttered angrily to himself in Northern. "Since you're not crowing your own praises, I'm guessing the job's not done."

"Mauthis is a *most* cautious and well-protected man. The bank is far too heavily guarded during the day."

"On his way to the bank, then."

"He leaves by an armoured carriage with a dozen guards in attendance. To try and intercept them would be too great a risk."

Shivers tossed another log on the fire and held his palms out towards it. "At his house?"

"Pah," sneered Morveer. "We followed him there. He lives on a walled island in the bay where several of the city's Aldermen have their estates. The public are not admitted. We have no method of gaining advance access to the building even if we can deduce which one is his. How many guards, servants, family members would be in attendance? All unknown. I *flatly* refuse to attempt a job of this difficulty on conjecture. What do I never take, Day?"

"Chances."

"Correct. I deal in *certainties*, Murcatto. That is why you came to me. I am hired for a *certain* man most *certainly* dead, not for a butcher's mess and your target slipped away in the chaos. We are not in Caprile, now—"

"I know where we are, Morveer. What's your plan, then?"

"I have gathered the necessary information and devised a sure means of achieving the desired effect. I need only gain access to the bank during the hours of darkness."

"And how do you plan to do that?"

"How do I plan to do that, Day?"

"Through the rigorous application of observation, logic and method."

Morveer flashed his smug little smile again. "Precisely so."

Monza glanced sideways at Benna. Except Benna was dead, and Shivers was in his place. The Northman raised his eyebrows, blew out a long sigh and looked back to the fire. *Give me only evil men for friends*, Verturio wrote. But there had to be a limit.

Two Twos

The dice came up two twos. Two times two is four. Two plus two is four. Add the dice, or multiply, the same result. It made Friendly feel helpless, that thought. Helpless but calm. All these people struggling to get things done, but whatever they did, it turned out the same. The dice were full of lessons. If you knew how to read them.

The group had formed two twos. Morveer and Day were one pair. Master and apprentice. They had joined together, they stayed together, they laughed together at everyone else. But now Friendly saw that Murcatto and Shivers were forming a pair of their own. They crouched next to each other at the parapet, black outlines against the dim night sky, staring across towards the bank, an immense block of thicker darkness. He had often seen that it was in the nature of people to form pairs. Everyone except him. He was left alone, in the shadows. Maybe there was something wrong with him, the way the judges had said.

Sajaam had chosen him to form a pair with, in Safety, but Friendly had no illusions. Sajaam had chosen him because he was useful. Because he was feared. As feared as anyone in the darkness. But Sajaam had not pretended any differently. He was the only honest man that Friendly knew, and so it had been an honest arrangement. It had worked so well that Sajaam had made enough money in prison to buy his freedom from the judges. But he was an honest man and so, when he was free, he had not forgotten Friendly. He had come back and bought his freedom too.

Outside the walls, where there were no rules, things were different. Sajaam had other business, and Friendly was left alone again. He did not mind, though. He was used to it, and had the dice for company. So he found himself here, in the darkness, on a roof in Westport, in the dead of winter. With these two mismatched pairs of dishonest people.

The guards came in two twos as well, four at a time, and two groups of four, following each other endlessly around the bank all night. It was raining now, a half-frozen sleet spitting down. Still they followed each other, round, and round, and round through the darkness. One party trudged along the lane beneath, well armoured, polearms shouldered.

"Here they come again," said Shivers.

"I see that," sneered Morveer. "Start a count."

Day's whisper came through the night, high and throaty. "One...two... three...four...five..." Friendly stared open-mouthed at her lips moving, the dice forgotten by his limp hand. His own mouth moved silently along with hers. "Twenty-two...twenty-three...twenty-four..."

"How to reach the roof?" Morveer was musing. "How to reach the roof?"

"Rope and grapple?" asked Murcatto.

"Too slow, too noisy, too uncertain. The rope would be left in plain view the entire time, even supposing we could firmly set a grapple. No. We need a method that allows for no accidents."

Friendly wished they would shut their mouths so he could listen to Day's counting. His cock was aching hard from listening to it. "One hundred and twelve...one hundred and thirteen..." He let his eyes close, let his head fall back against the wall, one finger moving back and forth in time. "One hundred and eighty-two...one hundred and eighty-three..."

"No one could climb up there free," came Murcatto's voice. "Not anyone. Too smooth, too sheer. And the spikes to worry on."

"I am in *complete* agreement."

"Up from inside the bank, then."

"Impossible. *Entirely* too many eyes. It must be up the walls, then in via the great windows in the roof. At least the lane is deserted during the hours of darkness. That is something in our favour."

"What about the other sides of the building?"

"The north face is considerably busier and better lit. The east contains the primary entrance, with an additional party of four guards posted all night. The south is identical to this face, but without the advantage of our having access to an adjacent roof. No. This wall is our *only* option."

Friendly saw the faint flicker of light down below in the lane. The next patrol, two times two guards, two plus two guards, four guards working their steady way around the bank.

"All night they keep this up?"

"There are two other parties of four that relieve them. They maintain their vigil uninterrupted until daybreak."

"Two hundred and ninety-one...two hundred and ninety-two...and here comes the next set." Day clicked her tongue. "Three hundred, give or take."

"Three hundred," hissed Morveer, and Friendly could see his head shaking in the darkness. "Not enough time."

"Then how?" snapped Monza.

Friendly swept the dice up again, felt their familiar edges pressing into his palm. It hardly mattered to him how they got into the bank, or even whether they ever did. His hopes mostly involved Day starting to count again.

"There must be a way...there *must* be a—"

"I can do it." They all looked round. Shivers was sitting against the parapet, white hands dangling.

"You?" sneered Morveer. "How?"

Friendly could just make out the curve of the Northman's grin in the darkness. "Magic."

Plans and Accidents

The guards grumbled their way down the lane. Four of 'em — breast-plates, steel caps, halberd blades catching the light from their swing-ing lanterns. Shivers pressed himself deep into the doorway as they clattered past, waited a nervy moment, then padded across the lane and into the shadows beside the pillar he'd chosen. He started counting. Three hundred or so, to make it to the top and onto the roof. He looked up. Seemed a bastard of a long way. Why the hell had he said yes to this? Just so he could slap the smile off that idiot Morveer's face, and show Murcatto he was worth his money?

"Always my own worst enemy," he whispered. Turned out he'd too much pride. That and a terrible weakness for fine-looking women. Who'd have thought it?

He pulled the rope out, two strides long with an eye at one end and a hook at the other. He cast a glance over the windows in the buildings fac-ing him. Most were shuttered against the cold night, but a few were open, a couple still with lights burning inside. He wondered what the chances were of someone looking out and seeing him shinning up the side of a bank. Higher than he'd like, that was sure.

"Worst fucking enemy." He got ready to climb up onto the pillar's base.

"Somewhere here."

"Where, idiot?"

Shivers froze, rope dangling from his hands. Footsteps now, armour jingling. Bastard guards were coming back. They'd never done that in fifty circuits of the place. For all his chat about science, that bloody poisoner had made an arse of it and Shivers was the one left with his fruits dangling in the wind. He squeezed deeper into the shadows, felt the big flatbow on his back scraping stone. How the hell was he going to explain that? Just a midnight stroll, you know, all in black, taking the old bow for a walk.

If he bolted they'd see him, chase him, more'n likely stab him with something. Either way they'd know someone had been trying to creep into the bank and that would be the end of the whole business. If he stayed put... same difference, more or less, except the stabbing got a sight more likely.

The voices came closer. "Can't be far away, all we bloody do is go round and round..."

One of 'em must've lost something. Shivers cursed his shitty luck, and not for the first time. Too late to run. He closed his fist round the grip of his knife. Footsteps thumped, just on the other side of the pillar. Why'd he taken her silver? Turned out he'd a terrible weakness for money too. He gritted his teeth, waited for—

"Please!" Murcatto's voice. She walked out across the lane, hood back, long coat swishing. Might've been the first time Shivers had seen her without a sword. "I'm so, so sorry to bother you. I'm only trying to get home, but I seem to have got myself completely lost."

One of the guards stepped round the pillar, his back to Shivers, and then another. They were no more than arm's length away, between him and her. He could almost have reached out and touched their backplates.

"Where you staying?"

"With some friends, near the fountain on Lord Sabeldi Street, but I'm new in the city, and," she gave a hopeless laugh, "I've quite misplaced it."

One of the guards pushed back his helmet. "I'll say you have. Other side of town, that."

"I swear I've been wandering the city for hours." She began to move away, drawing the men gently after her. Another guard appeared, and another. All four now, with their backs still to Shivers. He held his breath, heart thumping so loud it was a wonder none of them could hear it. "If one of you gentlemen could point me in the right direction I'd be so grateful. Stupid of me, I know."

"No, no. Confusing place, Westport."

"'Specially at night."

"I get lost here myself, time to time." The men laughed, and Monza laughed along, still drawing 'em on. Her eye caught Shivers' just for an instant, and they looked right at each other, and then she was gone round the next pillar, and the guards too, and their eager chatter drifted away. He closed his eyes, and slowly breathed out. Just as well he weren't the only man around with a weakness for women.

He swung himself up onto the square base of the pillar, slid the rope around it and under his rump, hooked it to make a loop. No idea what the count was now, just knew he had to get up there fast. He set off, gripping the stone with his knees and the edges of his boots, sliding the loop of rope up, then dragging it tight while he shifted his legs and set 'em again.

It was a trick his brother taught him, when he was a lad. He'd used it to climb the tallest trees in the valley and steal eggs. He remembered how they'd laughed together when he kept falling off near the bottom. Now he was using it to help kill folk, and if he fell off he'd be dead himself. Safe to say life hadn't turned out quite the way he'd hoped.

Still, he went up quick and smooth. Just like climbing a tree, except no eggs at the end of it and less chance of bark-splinters in your fruits. Hard work, though. He was sweating through by the time he made it up the pillar and still had the hardest part to go. He worked one hand into the mess of stonework at the top, unhooked the rope with the other and dragged it over his shoulder. Then he pulled himself up, fingers and toes digging holds out among the carvings, breath hissing, arms burning. He slipped one leg over a sculpture of a woman's frowning face and sat there, high above the lane, clinging to a pair of stone leaves and hoping they were stronger than the leafy kind.

He'd been in some better spots, but you had to look on the sunny side. It was the first time he'd had a woman's face between his legs in a while. He heard a hiss from across the lane, picked out Day's black shape on the roof. She pointed down. The next patrol were on their way.

"Shit." He pressed himself tight to the stonework, trying to look like rock himself, hands tingling raw from gripping the hemp, hoping no one chose that moment to look up. They clattered by underneath and he let out a long hiss of air, heart pounding in his ears louder than ever. He waited for them to move off round the corner of the building, getting his breath back for the last stretch.

The spikes further along the walls were mounted on poles, could spin round and round. Impossible to get over. At the tops of the pillars, though, they were mortared to the stone. He took his gloves out — heavy smith's gloves — and pulled them on, then he reached up and worked his hands tight around two spikes, took a deep breath. He let go with his legs and swung free, drew himself up, staring a touch cross-eyed at the iron points in front of his face. Just like pulling yourself into the branches, except for the chance of taking your eye out, of course. Be nice to come out of this with both his eyes.

He swung one way, then heaved himself back the other and got one boot up on top. He twisted himself round, felt the spikes scrape against his thick jerkin, digging at his chest as he dragged himself over.

And he was up.

Seventy-eight... seventy-nine... eighty...” Friendly’s lips moved by themselves as he watched Shivers roll over the parapet and onto the roof of the bank.

“He made it,” whispered Day, voice squeaky with disbelief.

“And in good time too.” Morveer chuckled softly. “Who would have thought he would climb... *like an ape*.”

The Northman stood, a darker shape against the dark night sky. He pulled the big flatbow off his back and started to fiddle with it. “Let’s hope he doesn’t shoot like an ape,” whispered Day.

Shivers took aim. Friendly heard the soft click of the bowstring. A moment later he felt the bolt thud into his chest. He snatched hold of the shaft, frowning down. It hardly hurt at all.

“A *happy* circumstance that it has no point.” Morveer unhooked the wire from the flights. “We would do well to avoid any further mishaps, and your untimely death would seem to qualify.”

Friendly tossed the blunt bolt away and tied the rope off to the end of the wire.

“You sure that thing will take his weight?” muttered Day.

“Suljuk silk cord,” said Morveer smugly. “Light as down but strong as steel. It would take all three of us simultaneously, and no one looking up will see a thing.”

“You hope.”

“What do I never take, my dear?”

“Yes, yes.”

The black cord hissed through Friendly’s hands as Shivers started reeling the wire back in. He watched it creep out across the space between the roofs, counting the strides. Fifteen and Shivers had the other end. They pulled it tight between them, then Friendly looped it through the iron ring they'd bolted to the roof timbers and began to knot it, once, twice, three times.

"Are you *entirely* sure of that knot?" asked Morveer. "There is no place in the plan for a lengthy drop."

"Twenty-eight strides," said Friendly.

"What?"

"The drop."

A brief pause. "That is not helpful."

A taut black line linked the two buildings. Friendly knew it was there, and still he could hardly see it in the darkness.

Day gestured towards it, curls stirred by the breeze. "After you."

Morveer fumbled his way over the balustrade, breathing hard. In truth, the trip across the cord had not been a pleasant excursion by any stretch of the imagination. A chilly wind had blown up halfway and set his heart to hammering. There had been a time, during his apprenticeship to the infamous Moumah-yin-Bek, when he had executed such acrobatic exertions with a feline grace, but he suspected it was dwindling rapidly into his past along with a full head of hair. He took a moment to compose himself, wiped chill sweat from his forehead, then realised Shivers was sitting there, grinning at him.

"Is there some manner of a joke?" demanded Morveer.

"Depends what makes you laugh, I reckon. How long will you be in there?"

"Precisely as long as I need to be."

"Best move quicker than you did across that rope, then. You might still be climbing in when they open the place tomorrow." The Northman was still smiling as he slipped over the parapet and back across the cord, swift and sure for all his bulk.

"If there is a God, he has cursed me through my acquaintance." Morveer gave only the briefest consideration to the notion of cutting the knot while the primitive was halfway across, then crept away down a narrow lead channel between low-pitched slopes of slate towards the centre of the building. The great glass roof glowed ahead of him, faint light glittering through thousands of distorting panes. Friendly squatted beside it, already unwinding a second length of cord from around his waist.

"Ah, the modern age." Morveer knelt beside Day, pressing his hands gently to the expanse of glass. "What will they think of next?"

"I feel blessed to live in such exciting times."

"So should we all, my dear." He carefully peered down into the bank's interior. "So should we *all*." The hallway was barely lit, a single lamp burning at each end, bringing a precious gleam to the gilt frames of the huge paintings but leaving the doorways rich with shadow. "Banks," he whispered, a ghost of a smile on his face, "always trying to economise."

He pulled out his glazing tools and began to prise away the lead with pliers, lifting each piece of glass out carefully with blobs of putty. The brilliance of his dexterity was quite undimmed by age, and it took him mere moments to remove nine panes, to snip the lead latticework with pincers and peel it back to leave a diamond-shaped hole ample for his purposes.

"Perfect timing," he murmured. The light from the guard's lantern crept up the panelled walls of the hallway, brought a touch of dawn to the dark canvases. His footsteps echoed as he passed by underneath them, giving vent to a booming yawn, his long shadow stretching out over the marble tiles. Morveer applied the slightest blast of air to his blowpipe.

"Gah!" The guard clapped a hand to the top of his head and Morveer ducked away from the window. There were footsteps below, a scuffling, a gurgle, then the loud thump and clatter of a toppling body. On peering back through the aperture the guard was plainly visible, spreadeagled on his back, lit lamp on its side by one outstretched hand.

"Excellent," breathed Day.

"Naturally."

"However much we talk about science, it always seems like magic."

"We are, one might say, the wizards of the modern age. The rope, if you please, Master Friendly." The convict tossed one end of the silken cord over, the other still knotted around his waist. "You are sure you can take my weight?"

"Yes." There was indeed a sense of terrible strength about the silent man that lent even Morveer a level of confidence. With the rope secured by a knot of his own devising, he lowered first one soft shoe and then the other into the diamond-shaped opening. He worked his hips through, then his shoulders, and he was inside the bank.

"Lower away." And down he drifted, as swiftly and smoothly as if lowered by a machine. His shoes touched the tiles and he slipped the knot with a jerk of his wrist, slid silently into a shadowy doorway, loaded blow-gun ready in one hand. He was expecting but the single guard within the building, but one should never become blinded by expectations.

Caution first, always.

His eyes rolled up and down the darkened hallway, his skin tingling with the excitement of the work under way. There was no movement. Only silence so complete it seemed almost a pressure against his prickling ears.

He looked up, saw Day's face at the gap and beckoned gently to her. She slid through as nimbly as a circus performer and glided down, their equipment folded around her body in a bandolier of black cloth. When her feet touched the ground she slipped free of the rope and crouched there, grinning.

He almost grinned back, then stopped himself. It would not do to let her know the warm admiration for her talents, judgement and character that had developed during their three years together. It would not do to let her even suspect the depth of his regard. It was when he did so that people inevitably betrayed his trust. His time in the orphanage, his apprenticeship, his marriage, his working life — all were scattered with the most poignant betrayals. Truly his heart bore many wounds. He would keep matters entirely professional, and thus protect them both. Him from her, and her from herself.

"Clear?" she hissed.

"As an empty squares board," he murmured, standing over the stricken guard, "and all according to plan. What do we most despise, after all?"

"Mustard?"

"And?"

"Accidents."

"Correct. There are no such things as happy ones. Get his boots."

With considerable effort they manoeuvred him down the hallway to his desk and into his chair. His head flopped back and he began to snore, long moustache fluttering gently around his lips.

"Ahhhhh, he sleeps like a babe. Props, if you please."

Day handed him an empty spirits bottle and Morveer placed it carefully on the tiles beside the guard's boot. She passed him a half-full bottle, and he removed the stopper and sloshed a generous measure down the front of the guard's studded leather jerkin. Then he placed it carefully on its side by his dangling fingers, spirits leaking out across the tiles in an acrid puddle.

Morveer stepped back and framed the scene with his hands. "The tableau...is prepared. What employer does not suspect his nightwatchman of partaking, against his express instructions, of a measure or two after dark? Observe the slack features, the reek of strong spirits, the loud snoring. Ample grounds, upon his discovery at dawn, for his immediate dismissal. He will protest his innocence, but in the total absence of any evidence"— he rummaged through the guard's hair with his gloved fingers and plucked the spent needle from his scalp —"no further suspicions will be aroused. All *perfectly* as normal. Except it will not be normal, will it? Oh no. The silent halls of the Westport office... of the Banking House of Valint and Balk... will conceal *a deadly secret*." He blew out the flame of the guard's lantern, sinking them into deeper darkness. "This way, Day, and do not dither."

They crept together down the hallway, a pair of silent shadows, and stopped beside the heavy door to Mauthis' office. Day's picks gleamed as she bent down to work the lock. It only took a moment for her to turn the tumblers with a meaty clatter, and the door swung silently open.

"Poor locks for a bank," as she slid her picks away.

"They put the good locks where the money is."

"And we're not here to steal."

"Oh no, no, we are rare thieves indeed. We leave *gifts* behind us." He padded around Mauthis' monstrous desk and swung the heavy ledger open, taking care not to move it so much as a hair from its position. "The solution, if you please."

She handed him the jar, full almost to the brim with thin paste, and he carefully twisted the cork out with a gentle thwop. He used a fine paintbrush for the application. The very tool for an artist of his incalculable talents. The pages crackled as he turned them, giving a flick of the brush to the corners of each and every one.

"You see, Day? Swift, smooth and precise, but with every care. With *every* care, most of all. What kills most practitioners of our profession?"

"Their own agents."

"*Precisely* so." With every care, therefore, he swung the ledger closed, its pages already close to dry, slid the paintbrush away and pressed the cork back into the jar.

"Let's go," said Day. "I'm hungry."

"Go?" Morveer's smile widened. "Oh no, my dear, we are *far* from finished. You must still earn your supper. We have a long night's work ahead of us. A *very* long...night's...work."

Here."

Shivers nearly jumped clean over the parapet, he was that shocked, lurched round, heart in his mouth. Murcatto crouched behind, grinning, breath leaving a touch of smoke about her shadowy face.

"By the dead but you gave me a scare!" he hissed.

"Better than what those guards would've given you." She crept to the iron ring and tugged at the knot. "You made it up there, then?" More'n a touch of surprise in her voice.

"You ever doubt I'd do it?"

"I thought you'd break your skull, if you even got high enough to fall."

He tapped his head with a finger. "Least vulnerable part o' me. Shake our friends off?"

"Halfway to bloody Lord Sabeldi Street, I did. If I'd known they'd be that easily led I'd have hooked them in the first place."

Shivers grinned. "Well, I'm glad you hooked 'em in the end, or they'd most likely have hooked me."

"Couldn't have that. We've still got a lot of work to do." Shivers wriggled his shoulders, uncomfortable. It was easy to forget at times that the work they were about was killing a man. "Cold, eh?"

He snorted. "Where I come from, this is a summer day." He dragged the cork from the bottle and held it out to her. "This might help keep you warm."

"Well, that's very thoughtful of you." She took a long swallow, and he watched the thin muscles in her neck shifting.

"I'm a thoughtful man, for one out of a gang of hired killers."

"I'll have you know that some hired killers are very nice people." She took another swig, then handed the bottle back. "None of this crew, of course."

"Hell, no, we're shits to a man. Or woman."

"They're in there? Morveer and his little echo?"

"Aye, a while now, I reckon."

"And Friendly with them?"

"He's with them."

"Morveer say how long he'd be?"

"Him, tell me anything? I thought I was the optimist."

They crouched in cold silence, close together by the parapet, looking across at the dark outline of the bank. For some reason he felt very nervy. Even more than you'd expect going about a murder. He stole a sideways glance at her, then didn't look away quite quick enough when she looked at him.

"Not much for us to do but wait and get colder, then," she said.

"Not much, I reckon. Unless you want to cut my hair any shorter."

"I'd be scared to get the scissors out in case you tried to strip."

That brought a laugh from him. "Very good. Reckon that earns you another pull." He held out the bottle.

"I'm quite the humorist, for a woman who hires killers." She came closer to take it. Close enough to give him a kind of tingle in the side that was near her. Close enough that he could feel the breath in his throat all of a sudden, coming quick. He looked away, not wanting to make a fool of himself any more than he'd been doing the last couple of weeks. Heard her tip the bottle, heard her drink. "Thanks again."

"Not a worry. Anything I can do, Chief, just let me know."

When he turned his head she was looking right at him, lips pressed together in a hard line, eyes fixed on his, that way she had, like she was working out how much he was worth. "There is one other thing."

Morveer pushed the last lips of lead into position with consummate delicacy and stowed his glazing tools.

"Will that do?" asked Day.

"I doubt it will deflect a rainstorm, but it will serve until tomorrow. By then I suspect they will have *considerably* greater worries than a leaking window." He rolled the last smudges of putty away from the glass, then followed his assistant across the rooftop to the parapet. Friendly had already negotiated the cord, a squat shape on the other side of a chasm of empty air. Morveer peered over the edge. Beyond the spikes and the ornamental carvings, the smooth stone pillar dropped vertiginously to the cobbled lane. One of the groups of guards slogged past it, lamps bobbing.

"What about the rope?" Day hissed once they were out of earshot. "When the sun comes up someone will—"

"No detail overlooked." Morveer grinned as he produced the tiny vial from an inside pocket. "A few drops will burn through the knot some time after we have crossed. We need only wait at the far side and reel it in."

As far as could be ascertained by darkness, his assistant appeared unconvinced. "What if it burns more quickly than—"

"It will not."

"Seems like an awful chance, though."

"What do I never take, my dear?"

"Chances, but—"

"You go first, then, by all means."

"You can count on it." Day swung quickly under the rope and swarmed across, hand over hand. It took her no longer than a count of thirty to make it to the other side.

Morveer uncorked the little bottle and allowed a few drops to fall onto the knots. Considering it, he allowed a few more. He had no desire to wait until sunup for the cursed thing to come apart. He allowed the next patrol to pass below, then clambered over the parapet with, it had to be admitted, a good deal less grace than his assistant had displayed. Still, there was no need for undue haste. Caution first, always. He took the rope in his gloved hands, swung beneath it, hooked one shoe over the top, lifted the other—

There was a harsh ripping sound, and the wind blew suddenly cold about his knee.

Morveer peered down. His trouser-leg had caught upon a spike bent upwards well above the others, and torn almost as far as his rump. He thrashed his foot, trying to untangle it, but only succeeded in entrapping it more thoroughly.

"Damn it." Plainly, this had not been part of the plan. Faint smoke was curling now from the balustrade around which the rope was knotted. It appeared the acid was acting more swiftly than anticipated.

"Damn it." He swung himself back to the roof of the bank and perched beside the smoking knot, gripping the rope with one hand. He slid his scalpel from an inside pocket, reached forwards and cut the flapping cloth away from the spike with a few deft strokes. One, two, three and it was almost done, neat as a surgeon. The final stroke and—

"Ah!" He realised with annoyance, then mounting horror, that he had nicked his ankle with the blade. "Damn it!" The edge was tainted with Larync tincture and, since the stuff had always given him a swell of nausea

123

in the mornings, he had allowed his resistance to it to fade. It would not be fatal. Not of itself. But it might cause him to drop off a rope, and he had developed no immunity to a flailing plunge onto hard, hard cobblestones. The irony was bitter indeed. Most practitioners of his profession were killed, after all, by their own agents.

He pulled one glove off with his teeth and fumbled through his many pockets for that particular antidote, gurgling curses around the leather, swaying this way and that as the chill wind gusted up and spread gooseflesh all the way down his bare leg. Tiny tubes of glass rattled against his fingertips, each one etched with a mark that enabled him to identify it by touch.

Under the circumstances, though, the operation was still a testing one. He burped and felt a rush of nausea, a sudden painful shifting in his stomach. His fingers found the right mark. He let the glove fall from his mouth, pulled the phial from his coat with a trembling hand, dragged the cork out with his teeth and sucked up the contents.

He gagged on the bitter extract, spluttered sour spit down onto the faraway cobbles. He clung tight to the rope, fighting dizziness, the black street seeming to tip round and round him. He was a child again, and helpless. He gasped, whimpered, clung on with both hands. As desperately as he had clung to his mother's corpse when they came to take him.

Slowly the antidote had its effect. The dark world steadied, his stomach ceased its mad churning. The lane was beneath him, the sky above, back in their customary positions. His attention was drawn sharply to the knots again, smoking more than ever now and making a slight hissing sound. He could distinctly smell the acrid odour as they burned through.

"Damn it!" He hooked both legs over the rope and set off, pitifully weak from the self-administered dose of Larync. The air hissed in his throat, tightened now by the unmistakable grip of fear. If the cord burned through before he reached the other side, what then? His guts cramped up and he had to pause for a moment, teeth gritted, wobbling up and down in empty air.

On again, but he was lamentably fatigued. His arms trembled, his hands shuffled, bare palm and bare leg burning from friction. Well beyond halfway now, and creeping onwards. He let his head hang back, sucking in air for one more effort. He saw Friendly, an arm out towards him, big hand no more than a few strides distant. He saw Day, staring, and Morveer wondered with some annoyance if he could detect the barest hint of a smile on her shadowy face.

Then there was a faint ripping sound from the far end of the rope.

The bottom dropped out of Morveer's stomach and he was falling, falling, swinging downwards, chill air whooshing in through his gaping mouth. The side of the crumbling building plunged towards him. He started to let go a mad wail, just like the one he made when they tore him from his mother's dead hand. There was a sickening impact that drove his breath out, cut his scream off, tore the cord from his grasping hands.

There was a crashing, a tearing of wood. He was falling, clawing at the air, mind a cauldron of mad despair, eyes bulging sightless. Falling, arms flailing, legs kicking helplessly, the world reeling around him, wind rushing at his face. Falling, falling... no further than a stride or two. His cheek slapped against floorboards, fragments of wood clattering down around him

"Eh?" he muttered.

He was shocked to find himself snatched around the neck, dragged into the air and rammed against a wall with bowel-loosening force, breath driven out in a long wheeze for the second time in a few moments.

"You! What the fuck?" Shivers. The Northman was, for some reason still obscure, entirely naked. The grubby room behind him was dimly lit by some coals banked up in a grate. Morveer's eyes wandered down to the bed. Murcatto was in it, propped up on her elbows, rumpled shirt hanging open, breasts flattened against her ribs. She peered at him with no more than a mild surprise, as if she'd opened her front door to see a visitor she had not been expecting until later.

Morveer's mind clicked into place. Despite the embarrassment of the position, the residual pulsing of mortal terror and the tingling scratches on his face and hands, he began to chuckle. The rope had snapped ahead of time and, by some freak but hugely welcome chance, he had swung down in a perfect arc and straight through the rotten shutters of one of the rooms in the crumbling house. One had to appreciate the irony.

"It seems there *is* such a thing as a happy accident after all!" he cackled.

Murcatto squinted over from the bed, eyes somewhat unfocused. She had a set of curious scars, he noticed, following the lines of her ribs on one side.

"Why you smoking?" she croaked.

Morveer's eyes slid to the husk-pipe on the boards beside the bed, a ready explanation for her lack of surprise at the unorthodox manner of his entrance. "You are confused, but it is easy to see why. I believe it is you that has been smoking. That stuff is absolute *poison*, you realise. Absolute—"

Her arm stretched out, limp finger pointing towards his chest. "Smoking, idiot." He looked down. A few acrid wisps were curling up from his shirt.

"Damn it!" he squeaked as Shivers took a shocked step back and let him fall. He tore his jacket off, fragments of glass from the shattered acid bottle tinkling to the boards. He scrabbled with his shirt, the front of which had begun to bubble, ripped it open and flung it on the floor. It lay there, smoking noticeably and filling the grubby chamber with a foul reek. The three of them stared at it, by a turn of fate that surely no one could have anticipated, all now at least half-naked.

"My apologies." Morveer cleared his throat. "Plainly, this was not part of the plan."

Repaid in Full

Monza frowned at the bed, and she frowned at Shivers in it. He lay flat out, blanket rumpled across his stomach. One big long arm hung off the edge of the mattress, white hand lying limp on its back against the floorboards. One big foot stuck from under the blanket, black crescents of dirt under the nails. His face was turned towards her, peaceful as a child's, eyes shut, mouth slightly open. His chest, and the long scar across it, rose and fell gently with his breathing.

By the light of day, it all seemed like a serious error.

She tossed the coins at Shivers and they jingled onto his chest and scattered across the bed. He jerked awake, blinking around.

"Whassis?" He stared blearily down at the silver stuck to his chest.

"Five scales. More than a fair price for last night."

"Eh?" He pushed sleep out of his eye with two fingers. "You're paying me?" He shoved the coins off his skin and onto the blanket. "I feel something like a whore."

"Aren't you one?"

"No. I've got some pride."

"So you'll kill a man for money, but you won't suck a cunt for it?" She snorted. "There's morals for you. You want my advice? Take the five and stick to killing in future. That you've got a talent for."

Shivers rolled over and dragged the blanket up around his neck. "Shut the door on your way out, eh? It's dreadful cold in here."

* * *

The blade of the Calvez slashed viciously at the air. Cuts left and right, high and low. She spun in the far corner of the courtyard, boots shuffling across the broken paving, lunging with her left arm, bright point darting out chest-high. Her quick breath smoked around her face, shirt stuck to her back in spite of the cold.

Her legs were a little better each day. They still burned when she moved quickly, were stiff as old twigs in the morning and ached like fury by evening time, but at least she could almost walk without grimacing. There was some spring in her knees even, for all their clicking. Her shoulder and her jaw were loosening. The coins under her scalp barely hurt when she pressed them.

Her right hand was as ruined as ever, though. She tucked Benna's sword under her arm and pulled the glove off. Even that was painful. The twisted thing trembled, weak and pale, the scar from Gobba's wire lurid purple round the side. She winced as she forced the crooked fingers closed, little one still stubbornly straight. The thought that she'd be cursed with this hideous liability for the rest of her life brought on a sudden rush of fury.

"Bastard," she hissed through gritted teeth, and dragged the glove back on. She remembered her father giving her a sword to hold for the first time, no more than eight years old. She remembered how heavy it had felt, how strange and unwieldy in her right hand. It hardly felt much better now, in her left. But she had no choice but to learn.

To start from nothing, if that was what it took.

She faced a rotten shutter, blade out straight towards it, wrist turned flat to the ground. She snapped out three jabs and the point tore three slats from the frame, one above the other. She snarled as she twisted her wrist and slashed downwards, splitting it clean in two, splinters flying.

Better. Better each day.

"*Magnificent.*" Morveer stood in a doorway, a few fresh scratches across one cheek. "There is not a shutter in Styria that will dare oppose us." He ambled forwards into the courtyard, hands clasped behind him. "I daresay you were even more impressive when your right hand still functioned."

"I'll worry about that."

"A great deal, I should think. Recovered from your . . . *exertions* of last night with our Northern acquaintance?"

"My bed, my business. And you? Recovered from your little drop through my window?"

"No more than a scratch or two."

"Shame." She slapped the Calvez back into its sheath. "Is it done?"

"It will be."

"He's dead?"

"He will be."

"When?"

Morveer grinned up at the square of pale sky above them. "Patience is the first of virtues, General Murcatto. The bank has only just opened its doors, and the agent I used takes some time to work. Jobs done well are rarely done quickly."

"But it will work?"

"Oh, absolutely so. It will be... *masterful*."

"I want to see it."

"Of course you do. Even in my hands the science of death is never utterly precise, but I would judge about an hour's time to be the best moment. I strongly caution you to touch nothing within the bank, however." He turned away, wagging one finger at her over his shoulder. "And take care you are not recognised. Our work together is only just commencing."

The banking hall was busy. Dozens of clerks worked at heavy desks, bent over great ledgers, their pens scratching, rattling, scratching again. Guards stood bored about the walls, watching half-heartedly or not watching at all. Monza weaved between primped and pretty groups of wealthy men and women, slid between their oiled and bejewelled rows, Shivers shouldering his way through after. Merchants and shopkeepers and rich men's wives, bodyguards and lackeys with strongboxes and money bags. As far as she could tell it was an ordinary day's monumental profits for the Banking House of Valint and Balk.

The place Duke Orso got his money.

Then she caught a glimpse of a lean man with a hook nose, speaking to a group of fur-trimmed merchants and with a clerk flanking him on either side, ledgers tucked under their arms. That vulture face sprang from the crowds like a spark in a cellar, and set a fire in her. Mauthis. The man she'd come to Westport to kill. And it hardly needed saying that he looked very much alive.

Somebody called out over in the corner of the hall but Monza's eyes were fixed ahead, jaw suddenly clenched tight. She started to push through the queues towards Orso's banker.

"What're you doing?" Shivers hissed in her ear, but she shook him off, shoved a man in a tall hat out of her way.

"Give him some air!" somebody shouted. People were looking around, muttering, craning up to see something, the orderly queues starting to dissolve. Monza kept going, closer now, and closer. Closer than was sensible. She had no idea what she'd do when she got to Mauthis. Bite him? Say hello? She was less than ten paces away — as near as she'd been when he peered down at her dying brother.

Then the banker gave a sudden wince. Monza slowed, easing carefully through the crowd. She saw Mauthis double over as if he'd been punched in the stomach. He coughed, and again — hard, retching coughs. He took a lurching step and clutched at the wall. People were moving all around, the place echoing with curious whispers, the odd strange shout.

"Stand back!"

"What is it?"

"Turn him over!"

Mauthis' eyes shimmered with wet, veins bulging from his thin neck. He clawed at one of the clerks beside him, knees buckling. The man staggered, guiding his master slowly to the floor.

"Sir? Sir?"

An atmosphere of breathless fascination seemed to have gripped the whole hall, teetering on the brink of fear. Monza edged closer, peering over a velvet-clad shoulder. Mauthis' starting eyes met hers, and they stared straight at each other. His face was stretched tight, skin turning red, fibres of muscle standing rigid. One quivering arm raised up towards her, one bony finger pointing.

"Muh," he mouthed. "Muh…Muh…"

His eyes rolled back and he started to dance, legs flopping, back arching, jerking madly around on the marble tiles like a landed fish. The men about him stared down, horrified. One of them was doubled up by a sudden coughing fit. People were shouting all over the banking hall.

"Help!"

"Over here!"

"Somebody!"

"Some air, I said!"

A clerk lurched up from his desk, chair clattering over, hands at his throat. He staggered a few steps, face turning purple, then crashed down, a shoe flying off one kicking foot. One of the clerks beside Mauthis was on his knees, fighting for breath. A woman gave a piercing scream.

"By the dead—" came Shivers' voice.

Pink foam frothed from the banker's wide-open mouth. His thrashing settled to a twitching. Then to nothing. His body sagged back, empty eyes goggling up over Monza's shoulder, towards the grinning busts ranged round the walls.

Two dead. Five left.

"Plague!" somebody shrieked, and as if a general had roared for the charge on a battlefield, the place was plunged instantly into jostling chaos. Monza was nearly barged over as one of the merchants who'd been talking to Mauthis turned to run. Shivers stepped up and gave him a shove, sent him sprawling on top of the banker's corpse. A man with skewed eyeglasses clutched at her, bulging eyes horribly magnified in his pink face. She punched on an instinct with her right hand, gasped as her twisted knuckles jarred against his cheek and sent a jolt of pain to her shoulder, chopped at him with the heel of her left and knocked him over backwards.

No plague spreads quicker than panic, Stolicus wrote, *or is more deadly*.

The veneer of civilisation was peeled suddenly away. The rich and self-satisfied were transformed into animals. Those in the way were flung aside. Those that fell were given no mercy. She saw a fat merchant punch a well-dressed lady in the face and she collapsed with a squeal, was kicked to the wall, wig twisted across her bloody face. She saw an old man huddled on the floor, trampled by the mob. A strongbox banged down, silver coins spilling, ignored, kicked across the floor by milling shoes. It was like the madness of a rout. The screaming and the jostling, the swearing and the stink of fear, the scattering of bodies and broken junk.

Someone shoved at her and she lashed out with an elbow, felt something crunch, spots of blood on her cheek. She was caught up by the crush like a twig in a river, jabbed at, twisted, torn and tangled. She was carried snarling through the doorway and into the street, feet scarcely touching the ground, people pressing, thrashing, wriggling up against her. She was swept sideways, slipped from the steps, twisted her leg on the cobbles and lurched against the wall of the bank.

She felt Shivers grab her by the elbow and half-lead, half-carry her off.

A couple of the bank's guards stood, trying ineffectually to stem the flow of panic with the hafts of their halberds. There was a sudden surge in the crowd and Monza was carried back. Between flailing arms she saw a man quivering on the ground, coughing red foam onto the cobbles. A wall of horrified, fascinated faces twitched and bobbed as people fought to get away from him.

Monza felt dizzy, mouth sour. Shivers strode beside her, breathing fast through his nose, glancing back over his shoulder. They rounded the corner of the bank and made for the crumbling house, the maddened clamour fading behind them. She saw Morveer, standing at a high window like a wealthy patron enjoying the theatre from his private box. He grinned down, and waved with one hand.

Shivers growled something in his own tongue as he heaved the heavy door open and Monza came after him. She snatched up the Calvez and made straight for the stairs, taking them two at a time, hardly noticing the burning in her knees.

Morveer still stood by the window when she got there, his assistant cross-legged on the table, munching her way through half a loaf of bread. "There seems to be *quite* the ruckus down in the street!" The poisoner turned into the room, but his smile vanished as he saw Monza's face. "What? He's alive?"

"He's dead. Dozens of them are."

Morveer's eyebrows went up by the slightest fraction. "An establishment of that nature, the books will be in constant movement around the building. I could not take the risk that Mauthis would end up working from another. What do I never take, Day?"

"Chances. Caution first, always." Day tore off another mouthful of bread, and mumbled around it. "That's why we poisoned them all. Every ledger in the place."

"This isn't what we agreed," Monza growled.

"I rather think it is. Whatever it takes, you told me, no matter who gets killed along the way. Those are the only terms under which I work. Anything else allows for *misunderstandings*." Morveer looked somewhat puzzled, somewhat amused. "I am well aware that some individuals are uncomfortable with wholesale murder, but I certainly never anticipated that you, Monzcarro Murcatto, the Serpent of Talins, the Butcher of Caprile, would be one. You need not worry about the money. Mauthis will cost you ten thousand, as we agreed. The rest are free of—"

"It's not a question of money, fool!"

"Then what *is* the question? I undertook a piece of work, as commissioned by you, and was successful, so how can I be at fault? You say you never had in mind any such result, and did not undertake the work yourself, so how can you be at fault? The responsibility seems to drop between us, then, like a *turd* straight from a beggar's *arse* and into an open sewer, to be lost from sight forever and cause nobody any further discomfort. An unfortunate misunderstanding, shall we say? An accident? As if a sudden wind blew up, and a great tree fell, and caught every little insect in that place and squashed...them...*dead*!"

"Squashed 'em," chirped Day.

"If your conscience nags at you—"

Monza felt a stab of anger, gloved hand gripping the sword's scabbard painfully hard, twisted bones clicking as they shifted. "Conscience is an excuse not to do what needs doing. This is about keeping control. We'll stick to one dead man at a time from now on."

"Will we indeed?"

She took a sudden stride into the room and the poisoner edged away, eyes flickering nervously down to her sword, then back. "Don't test me. Not ever. One...at a time...I said."

Morveer carefully cleared his throat. "You are the client, of course. We will proceed as you dictate. There really is no cause to get angry."

"Oh, you'll know if I get angry."

He gave a pained sigh. "What is the tragedy of our profession, Day?"

"No appreciation." His assistant popped the last bit of crust into her mouth.

"*Precisely* so. Come, we will take a turn about the city while our employer decides which name on her little list next merits our attentions. The atmosphere in here feels somewhat tainted by *hypocrisy*." He marched out with an air of injured innocence. Day looked up from under her sandy lashes, shrugged, stood, brushed crumbs from the front of her shirt, then followed her master.

Monza turned back to the window. The crowds had mostly broken up. Groups of nervous city watch had appeared, blocking off the street before the bank, keeping a careful distance from the still shapes sprawled out on the cobbles. She wondered what Benna would've said to this. Told her to calm down, most likely. Told her to think it through.

She grabbed a chest with both hands and snarled as she flung it across the room. It smashed into the wall, sending lumps of plaster flying, clattered down and sagged open, clothes spilling out across the floor.

Shivers stood there in the doorway, watching her. "I'm done."

"No!" She swallowed. "No. I still need your help."

"Standing up and facing a man, that's one thing...but this—"

"The rest will be different. I'll see to it."

"Nice, clean murders? I doubt it. You set your mind to killing, it's hard to pick the number of the dead." Shivers slowly shook his head. "Morveer and his fucking like might be able to step away from it and smile, but I can't."

"So what?" She walked slowly to him, the way you might walk to a skittish horse, trying to stop it bolting with your eyes. "Back to the North with fifty scales for the journey? Grow your hair and go back to bad shirts and blood on the snow? I thought you had pride. I thought you wanted to be better than that."

"That's right. I wanted to be better."

"You can be. Stick. Who knows? Maybe you can save some lives, that way." She laid her left hand gently on his chest. "Steer me down the righteous path. Then you can be good and rich at once."

"I'm starting to doubt a man can be both."

"Help me. I have to do this...for my brother."

"You sure? The dead are past helping. Vengeance is for you."

"For me then!" She forced her voice to drop soft again. "There's nothing I can do to change your mind?"

His mouth twisted. "Going to toss me another five, are you?"

"I shouldn't have done that." She slid her hand up, traced the line of his jaw, trying to judge the right words, pitch the right bargain. "You didn't deserve it. I lost my brother, and he's all I had. I don't want to lose someone else..." She let it hang in the air.

There was a strange look in Shivers' eye, now. Part angry, part hungry, part ashamed. He stood there silent for a long moment, and she felt the muscles clenching and unclenching on the side of his face.

"Ten thousand," he said.

"Six."

"Eight."

"Done." She let her hand fall, and they stared at each other. "Get packed, we leave within the hour."

"Right." He slunk guiltily out of the door without meeting her eye and left her there, alone.

And that was the trouble with good men. Just so damned expensive.

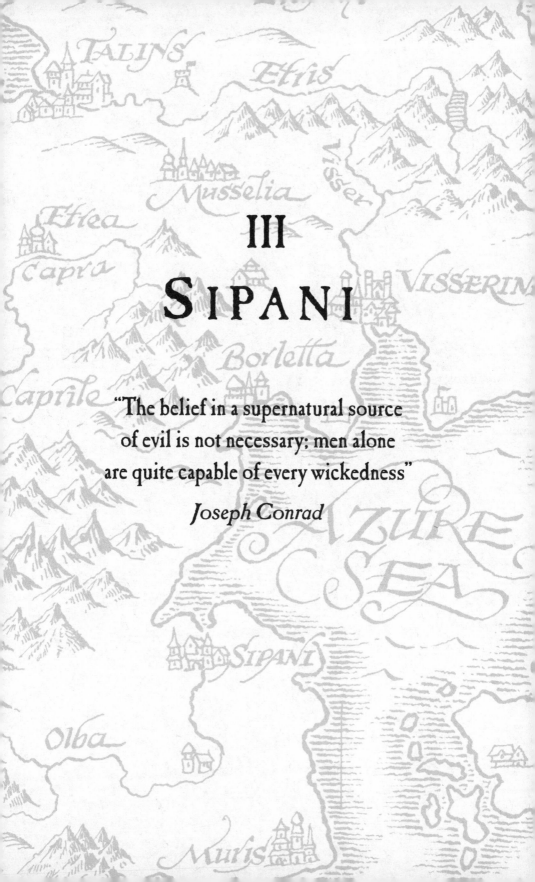

III
SIPANI

"The belief in a supernatural source
of evil is not necessary; men alone
are quite capable of every wickedness"

Joseph Conrad

Not two weeks later, men came over the border looking to even the tally, and they hanged old Destort and his wife, and burned the mill. A week after that his sons set out for vengeance, and Monza took down her father's sword and went with them, Benna snivelling along behind. She was glad to go. She had lost the taste for farming.

They left the valley to settle a score, and for two years they did not stop. Others joined them, men who had lost their work, their farms, their families. Before too long it was them burning crops, breaking into farmhouses, taking what they could find. Before too long it was them doing the hangings. Benna grew up quickly, and sharpened to a merciless edge. What other choice? They avenged killings, then thefts, then slights, then the rumours of slights. There was war, so there was never any shortage of wrongs to avenge.

Then, at the end of summer, Talins and Musselia made peace with nothing gained on either side but corpses. A man with a gold-edged cloak rode into the valley with soldiers behind him and forbade reprisals. Destort's sons and the rest split up, took their spoils with them, went back to what they had been doing before the madness started or found new madness to take a hand in. By then, Monza's taste for farming had grown back.

They made it as far as the village.

A vision of martial splendour stood at the edge of the broken fountain in a breastplate of shining steel, a sword hilt set with glinting gemstones at his hip. Half the valley had gathered to listen to him speak.

"My name is Nicomo Cosca, captain of the Company of the Sun — a noble brotherhood fighting with the Thousand Swords, greatest mercenary brigade in Styria! We have a Paper of Engagement from the young Duke Rogont of Ospria and are looking for men! Men with experience of war, men with courage, men with a love of adventure and a taste for money! Are any of you sick of grubbing in the mud for a living? Do any of you hope for something better? For honour? For glory? For riches? Join us!"

"We could do that," Benna hissed.

"No," said Monza, "I'm done with fighting."

"There will be little fighting!" shouted Cosca, as if he could guess her thoughts. "That I promise you! And what there is you will be well paid for thrice over! A scale a week, plus shares of booty! And there will be plenty of booty, lads, believe me! Our cause is just . . . or just enough, and victory is a certainty."

"We could do that!" hissed Benna. "You want to go back to tossing mud? Broken down tired every night and dirt under your fingernails? I won't!"

Monza thought of the work she would have just to clear the upper field, and how much she might make from doing it. A line had formed of men keen to join the Company of the Sun, beggars and farmers mostly. A black-skinned notary took their names down in a ledger.

Monza shoved past them.

"I am Monzcarro Murcatto, daughter of Jappo Murcatto, and this is my brother Benna, and we are fighters. Can you find work for us in your company?"

Cosca frowned at her, and the black-skinned man shook his head. "We need men with experience of war. Not women and boys." He tried to move her away with his arm.

She would not be moved. "We've experience. More than these scrapings."

"I've work for you," said one of the farmers, made bold by signing his mark on the paper. "How about you suck my cock?" He laughed at that. Until Monza knocked him down in the mud and made him swallow half his teeth with the heel of her boot.

Nicomo Cosca watched this methodical display with one eyebrow slightly raised. "Sajaam, the Paper of Engagement. Does it specify men, exactly? What is the wording?"

The notary squinted at a document. "Two hundred cavalry and two hundred infantry, those to be persons well equipped and of quality. Persons is all it says."

"And quality is such a vague term. You, girl! Murcatto! You are hired, and your brother too. Make your marks."

She did so, and so did Benna, and as simply as that they were soldiers of the Thousand Swords. Mercenaries. The farmer clutched at Monza's leg.

"My teeth."

"Pick through your shit for them," she said.

Nicomo Cosca, famed soldier of fortune, led his new hirings from the vil-

lage to the sound of a merry pipe, and they camped under the stars that night, gathered round fires in the darkness, talking of making it rich in the coming campaign.

Monza and Benna huddled together with their blanket around their shoulders. Cosca came out of the murk, firelight glinting on his breastplate. "Ah! My war-children! My lucky mascots! Cold, eh?" He swept his crimson cloak off and tossed it down to them. "Take this. Might keep the frost from your bones."

"What d'you want for it?"

"Take it with my compliments, I have another."

"Why?" she grunted, suspicious.

"'A captain looks first to the comfort of his men, then to his own,' Stolicus said."

"Who's he?" asked Benna.

"Stolicus? Why, the greatest general of history!" Monza stared blankly at him. "An emperor of old. The most famous of emperors."

"What's an emperor?" asked Benna.

Cosca raised his brows. "Like a king, but more so. You should read this." He slid something from a pocket and pressed it into Monza's hand. A small book, with a red cover scuffed and scarred.

"I will." She opened it and frowned at the first page, waiting for him to go.

"Neither of us can read," said Benna, before Monza could shut him up.

Cosca frowned, twisting one corner of his waxed moustache between finger and thumb. Monza was waiting for him to tell them to go back to the farm, but instead he lowered himself slowly and sat cross-legged beside them. "Children, children." He pointed at the page. "This here is the letter 'A.'"

Fogs and Whispers

Sipani smelled of rot and old salt water, of coal smoke, shit and piss, of fast living and slow decay. Made Shivers feel like puking, though the smell mightn't have mattered so much if he could've seen his hand before his face. The night was dark, the fog so thick that Monza, walking close enough to touch, weren't much more than a ghostly outline. His lamp scarcely lit ten cobbles in front of his boots, all shining with cold dew. More than once he'd nearly stepped straight off into water. It was easily done. In Sipani, water was hiding round every corner.

Angry giants loomed up, twisted, changed to greasy buildings and crept past. Figures charged from the mist like the Shanka did at the Battle of Dunbrec, then turned out to be bridges, railings, statues, carts. Lamps swung on poles at corners, torches burned by doorways, lit windows glowed, hanging in the murk, treacherous as marsh-lights. Shivers would set his course by one set, squinting through the mist, only to see a house start drifting. He'd blink, and shake his head, the ground shifting dizzily under his boots. Then he'd realise it was a barge, sliding past in the water beside the cobbled way, bearing its lights off into the night. He'd never liked cities, fog or salt water. The three together were like a bad dream.

"Bloody fog," Shivers muttered, holding his lamp higher, as though that helped. "Can't see a thing."

"This is Sipani," Monza tossed over her shoulder. "City of Fogs. City of Whispers."

The chill air was full of strange sounds, alright. Everywhere the slap, slop of water, the creaking of ropes as rowing boats squirmed on the shifting canals. Bells tolling in the darkness, folk calling out, all kinds of voices.

Prices. Offers. Warnings. Jokes and threats spilling over each other. Dogs barked, cats hissed, rats skittered, birds croaked. Snatches of music, lost in the mist. Ghostly laughter fluttered past on the other side of the seething water, lamps bobbing through the gloom as some revel wended into the night from tavern, to brothel, to gambling den, to smoke-house. Made Shivers' head spin, and left him sicker than ever. Felt like he'd been sick for weeks. Ever since Westport.

Footsteps echoed from the darkness and Shivers pressed himself against the wall, right hand on the haft of the hatchet tucked in his coat. Men loomed up and away, brushing past him. Women too, one holding a hat to her piled-up hair as she ran. Devil faces, smeared with drunken smiles, reeling past in a flurry and gone into the night, mist curling behind their flapping cloaks.

"Bastards," hissed Shivers after them, letting go his axe and peeling himself away from the sticky wall. "Lucky I didn't split one of 'em."

"Get used to it. This is Sipani. City of Revels. City of Rogues."

Rogues were in long supply, alright. Men slouched around steps, on corners, beside bridges, dishing out hard looks. Women too, black outlines in doorways, lamps glowing behind, some of 'em hardly dressed in spite of the cold. "A scale!" one called at him from a window, letting one thin leg dangle in the murk. "For a scale you get the night of your life! Ten bits then! Eight!"

"Selling themselves," Shivers grunted.

"Everyone's selling themselves," came Monza's muffled voice. "This is—"

"Yes, yes. This is fucking Sipani."

Monza stopped and he nearly walked into her. She pushed her hood back and squinted at a narrow doorway in a wall of crumbling brickwork. "This is it."

"You take a man to all the finest places, eh?"

"Maybe later you'll get the tour. For now we've got business. Look dangerous."

"Right y'are, Chief." Shivers stood up tall and fixed his hardest frown. "Right y'are."

She knocked, and not long after the door wobbled open. A woman stared out from a dim-lit hallway, long and lean as a spider. She had a way of standing, hips loose and tilted to one side, arm up on the doorframe, one thin finger tapping at the wood. Like the fog was hers, and the night, and them too. Shivers brought his lamp up a touch closer. A hard, sharp face with a knowing smile, spattered with freckles, short red hair sprouting all ways from her head.

"Shylo Vitari?" asked Monza.

"You'll be Murcatto, then."

"That's right."

"Death suits you." She narrowed her eyes at Shivers. Cold eyes, with a hint of a cruel joke in 'em. "Who's your man?"

He spoke for himself. "Name's Caul Shivers, and I'm not hers."

"No?" She grinned at Monza. "Whose is he, then?"

"I'm my own."

She gave a sharp laugh at that. Seemed everything about her had an edge on it. "This is Sipani, friend. Everyone belongs to someone. Northman, eh?"

"That a problem?"

"Got tossed down a flight of stairs by one once. Haven't been entirely comfortable around them since. Why Shivers?"

She caught him off balance with that one. "What?"

"Up in the North, the way I heard it, a man earns his name. Great deeds done, and all that. Why Shivers?"

"Er..." The last thing he needed was to look the fool in front of Monza. He was still hoping to make it back into her bed at some point. "Because my enemies shiver with fear when they face me," he lied.

"That so?" Vitari stood back from the door, giving him a mocking grin as he ducked under the low lintel. "You must have some cowardly bloody enemies."

"Sajaam says you know people here," said Monza as the woman led them into a narrow sitting room, barely lit by some smoky coals on a grate.

"I know everyone." She took a steaming pot off the fire. "Soup?"

"Not me," said Shivers, leaning against the wall and folding his arms over his chest. He'd been a lot more careful about hospitality since he met Morveer.

"Nor me," said Monza.

"Suit yourselves." Vitari poured a mug out for herself and sat, folding one long leg over the other, pointed toe of her black boot rocking backwards and forwards.

Monza took the only other chair, wincing a touch as she lowered herself into it. "Sajaam says you can get things done."

"And just what is it that the two of you need doing?"

Monza glanced across at Shivers, and he shrugged back at her. "I hear the King of the Union is coming to Sipani."

"So he is. Seems he's got it in mind that he's the great statesman of the age." Vitari smiled wide, showing two rows of clean, sharp teeth. "He's going to bring peace to Styria."

"Is he now?"

"That's the rumour. He's brought together a conference to negotiate terms, between Grand Duke Orso and the League of Eight. He's got all their leaders coming — those who are still alive, at least, Rogont and Salier at the front. He's got old Sotorius to play host — neutral ground here in Sipani, is the thinking. And he's got his brothers-in-law on their way, to speak for their father."

Monza craned forwards, eager as a buzzard at a carcass. "Ario and Foscar both?"

"Ario and Foscar both."

"They're going to make peace?" asked Shivers, and soon regretted saying anything. The two women each gave him their own special kind of sneer.

"This is Sipani," said Vitari. "All we make here is fog."

"And that's all anyone will be making at this conference, you can depend on that." Monza eased herself back into her chair, scowling. "Fogs and whispers."

"The League of Eight is splitting at the seams. Borletta fallen. Cantain dead. Visserine will be under siege when the weather breaks. No talk's going to change that."

"Ario will sit, and smirk, and listen, and nod. Scatter a little trail of hopes that his father will make peace. Right up until Orso's troops appear outside the walls of Visserine."

Vitari lifted her cup again, narrow eyes on Monza. "And the Thousand Swords alongside them."

"Salier and Rogont and all the rest will know that well enough. They're no fools. Misers and cowards, maybe, but no fools. They're only playing for time to manoeuvre."

"Manoeuvre?" asked Shivers, chewing on the strange word.

"Wriggle," said Vitari, showing him her teeth again. "Orso won't make peace, and the League of Eight aren't looking for it. The only man who's come here hoping for anything but fog is his August Majesty, but they say he's got a talent for self-deception."

"Comes with the crown," said Monza, "but he's nothing to me. Ario and Foscar are my business. What will they be about, other than feeding lies to their brother-in-law?"

"There's going to be a masked ball in honour of the king and queen at Sotorius' palace on the first night of the conference. Ario and Foscar will be there."

"That'll be well guarded," said Shivers, doing his best to keep up. Didn't help that he thought he could hear a child crying somewhere.

Vitari snorted. "A dozen of the best-guarded people in the world, all sharing a room with their bitterest enemies? There'll be more soldiers than at the Battle of Adua, I'll be bound. Hard to think of a spot where the brothers would be less vulnerable."

"What else, then?" snapped Monza.

"We'll see. I'm no friend of Ario's, but I know someone who is. A close, close friend."

Monza's black brows drew in. "Then we should be talking to—"

The door creaked suddenly open and Shivers spun round, hatchet already halfway out.

A child stood in the doorway. A girl maybe eight years old, dressed in a too-long shift with bony ankles and bare feet sticking out the bottom, red hair poking from her head in a tangled mess. She stared at Shivers, then Monza, then Vitari with wide blue eyes. "Mama. Cas is crying."

Vitari knelt down and smoothed the little girl's hair. "Never you mind, baby, I hear. Try and soothe him. I'll be up soon as I can, and sing to you all."

"Alright." The girl gave Shivers another look, and he pushed his axe away, somewhat shamefaced, and tried to make a grin. She backed off and pulled the door shut.

"My boy's got a cough," said Vitari, her voice with its hard edge again. "One gets ill, then they all get ill, then I get ill. Who'd be a mother, eh?"

Shivers lifted his brows. "Can't say I've got the equipment."

"Never had much luck with family," said Monza. "Can you help us?"

Vitari's eyes flickered over to Shivers, and back. "Who else you got along with you?"

"A man called Friendly, as muscle."

"Good, is he?"

"Very," said Shivers, thinking of the two men hacked bloody on the streets of Talins. "Bit strange, though."

"You need to be in this line of work. Who else?"

"A poisoner and his assistant."

"A good one?"

"According to him. Name of Morveer."

"Gah!" Vitari looked as if she'd the taste of piss in her mouth. "Castor Morveer? That bastard's about as trustworthy as a scorpion."

Monza looked back, hard and level. "Scorpions have their uses. Can you help us, I asked?"

Vitari's eyes were two slits, shining in the firelight. "I can help you, but it'll cost. If we can get the job done, something tells me I won't be welcome in Sipani anymore."

"Money isn't a problem. Just as long as you can get us close. You know someone who can help with that?"

Vitari drained her mug, then tossed the dregs hissing onto the coals. "Oh, I know all kinds of people."

The Arts of Persuasion

It was early, and the twisting streets of Sipani were quiet. Monza hunched in a doorway, coat wrapped tight around her, hands wedged under her armpits. She'd been hunched there for an hour at least, steadily getting colder, breathing fog into the foggy air. The edges of her ears and her nostrils tingled unpleasantly. It was a wonder the snot hadn't frozen in her nose. But she could be patient. She had to be.

Nine-tenths of war is waiting, Stolicus wrote, and she felt he'd called it low.

A man wheeled past a barrow heaped with straw, tuneless whistling deadened by the thinning mist, and Monza's eyes slid after him until he became a murky outline and was gone. She wished Benna was with her.

And she wished he'd brought his husk pipe with him.

She shifted her tongue in her dry mouth, trying to push the thought out of her mind, but it was like a splinter under her thumbnail. The painful, wonderful bite at her lungs, the taste of the smoke as she let it curl from her mouth, her limbs growing heavy, the world softening. The doubt, the anger, the fear all leaking away...

Footsteps clapped on wet flagstones and a pair of figures rose out of the gloom. Monza stiffened, fists clenching, pain flashing through her twisted knuckles. A woman in a bright red coat edged with gold embroidery. "Hurry up!" Snapped in a faint Union accent to a man lumbering along behind with a heavy trunk on one shoulder. "I do not mean to be late again —"

Vitari's shrill whistle cut across the empty street. Shivers slid from a doorway, loomed up behind the servant and pinned his arms. Friendly came out of nowhere and sank four heavy punches into his gut before he could even shout, sent him to the cobbles blowing vomit.

Monza heard the woman gasp, caught a glimpse of her wide-eyed face as she turned to run. Before she'd gone a step Vitari's voice echoed out of the gloom ahead. "Carlot dan Eider, unless I'm much mistaken!"

The woman in the red coat backed towards the doorway where Monza was standing, one hand held up. "I have money! I can pay you!"

Vitari sauntered out of the murk, loose and easy as a mean cat in her own garden. "Oh, you'll pay alright. I must say I was surprised when I learned Prince Ario's favourite mistress was in Sipani. I heard you could hardly be dragged from his bedchamber." Vitari herded her towards the doorway and Monza backed off, into the dim corridor, wincing at the sharp pains through her legs as she started to move.

"Whatever the League of Eight are paying, I'll—"

"I don't work for them, and I'm hurt by the assumption. Don't you remember me? From Dagoska? Don't you remember trying to sell the city to the Gurkish? Don't you remember getting caught?" And Monza saw her let something drop and clatter against the cobbles — a cross-shaped blade, dancing and rattling on the end of a chain.

"Dagoska?" Eider's voice had a note of strange terror in it now. "No! I've done everything he asked! Everything! Why would he—"

"Oh, I don't work for the Cripple anymore." Vitari leaned in close. "I've gone freelance."

The woman in the red coat stumbled back over the threshold and into the corridor. She turned and saw Monza waiting, gloved hand slack on the pommel of her sword. She stopped dead, ragged breath echoing from the damp walls. Vitari shut the door behind them, latch dropping with a final-sounding click.

"This way." She gave Eider a shove and she nearly fell over her own coat-tails. "If it please you." Another shove as she found her feet and she sprawled through the doorway on her face. Vitari dragged her up by one arm and Monza followed them slowly into the room beyond, jaw clenched tight.

Like her jaw, the room had seen better days. The crumbling plaster was stained with black mould, bubbling up with damp, the stale air smelled of rot and onions. Day leaned back in one corner, a carefree smile on her face as she buffed a plum the colour of a fresh bruise against her sleeve. She offered it to Eider.

"Plum?"

"What? No!"

"Suit yourself. They're good though."

"Sit." Vitari shoved Eider into the rickety chair that was the only furniture. Usually a good thing, getting the only seat. But not now. "They say history moves in circles but who'd ever have thought we'd meet like this again? It's enough to bring tears to our eyes, isn't it? Yours, anyway."

Carlot dan Eider didn't look like crying any time soon, though. She sat upright, hands crossed in her lap. Surprising composure, under the circumstances. Dignity, almost. She was past the first flush of youth, but a most striking woman still, and everything carefully plucked, painted and powdered to make the best show of it. A necklace of red stones flashed around her throat, gold glittered on her long fingers. She looked more like a countess than a mistress, as out of place in the rotting room as a diamond ring in a rubbish heap.

Vitari prowled slowly around the chair, leaning down to hiss in her ear. "You're looking well. Always did know how to land on your feet. Quite the tumble, though, isn't it? From head of the Guild of Spicers to Prince Ario's whore?"

Eider didn't even flinch. "It's a living. What do you want?"

"Just to talk." Vitari's voice purred low and husky as a lover's. "Unless we don't get the answers we want. Then I'll have to hurt you."

"No doubt you'll enjoy that."

"It's a living." She punched Ario's mistress suddenly in the ribs, hard enough to twist her in the chair. She doubled up, gasping, and Vitari leaned over her, bringing her fist up again. "Another?"

"No!" Eider held her hand up, teeth bared, eyes flickering round the room then back to Vitari. "No...ah...I'll be helpful. Just...just tell me what you need to know."

"Why are you down here, ahead of your lover?"

"To make arrangements for the ball. Costumes, masks, all kinds of—"

Vitari's fist thumped into her side in just the same spot, harder than the first time, the sharp thud echoing off the damp walls. Eider whimpered, arms wrapped around herself, took a shuddering breath then coughed it out, face twisted with pain. Vitari leaned down over her like a black spider over a bound-up fly. "I'm losing patience. Why are you here?"

"Ario's putting on…another kind of celebration…afterwards. For his brother. For his brother's birthday."

"What kind of celebration?"

"The kind for which Sipani is famous." Eider coughed again, turned her head and spat, a few wet specks settling across the shoulder of her beautiful coat.

"Where?"

"At Cardotti's House of Leisure. He's hired the whole place for the night. For him, and for Foscar, and for their gentlemen. He sent me here to make the arrangements."

"He sent his mistress to hire whores?"

Monza snorted. "Sounds like Ario. What arrangements?"

"To find entertainers. To make the place ready. To make sure it's safe. He…trusts me."

"More fool him." Vitari chuckled. "I wonder what he'd do if he knew who you really worked for, eh? Who you really spy for? Our mutual friend at the House of Questions? Our crippled friend from his Majesty's Inquisition? Keeping an eye on Styrian business for the Union, eh? You must have trouble remembering who you're supposed to betray from week to week."

Eider glowered back at her, arms still folded around her battered ribs. "It's a living."

"A dying, if Ario learns the truth. One little note is all it would take."

"What do you want?"

Monza stepped from the shadows. "I want you to help us get close to Ario, and to Foscar. I want you to let us into Cardotti's House of Leisure on the night of this celebration of yours. When it comes to arranging the entertainments, I want you to hire who we say, when we say, how we say. Do you understand?"

Eider's face was very pale. "You mean to kill them?" No one spoke, but the silence said plenty. "Orso will guess I betrayed him! The Cripple will know I betrayed him! There aren't two worse enemies in the Circle of the World! You might as well kill me now!"

"Alright." The blade of the Calvez rang gently as she drew it. Eider's eyes went wide.

"Wait—"

Monza reached out, resting the glinting point of the sword in the hollow between Eider's collarbones, and gently pushed. Ario's mistress arched back over the chair, hands opening and closing helplessly.

"Ah! Ah!" Monza twisted her wrist, steel flashing as the slender blade tilted one way and the other, the point grinding, digging, screwing ever so slowly into Eider's neck. A line of dark blood trickled from the wound it made and crept down her breastbone. Her squealing grew more shrill, more urgent, more terrified. "No! Ah! Please! No!"

"No?" Monza held her there, pinned over the back of the chair. "Not quite ready to die after all? Not many of us are, when it comes to the moment." She slid the Calvez free and Eider rocked forwards, touching one trembling fingertip to her bloody neck, breath coming in ragged gasps.

"You don't understand. It isn't just Orso! It isn't just the Union! They're both backed by the bank. By Valint and Balk. Owned by the bank. The Years of Blood are no more than a sideshow to them. A skirmish. You've no idea whose garden you're pissing in—"

"Wrong." Monza leaned down and made Eider shrink back. "I don't care. There's a difference."

"Now?" asked Day.

"Now."

The girl's hand darted out and pricked Eider's ear with a glinting needle. "Ah!"

Day yawned as she slipped the splinter of metal into an inside pocket. "Don't worry, it's slow-working. You've got at least a week."

"Until what?"

"Until you get sick." Day took a bite out of her plum and juice ran down her chin. "Bloody hell," she muttered, catching it with a fingertip.

"Sick?" breathed Eider.

"Really, really sick. A day after that you'll be deader than Juvens."

"Help us, you get the antidote, and at least the chance to run." Monza rubbed the blood from the point of Benna's sword with gloved thumb and forefinger. "Try and tell anyone what we're planning, here or in the Union, Orso, or Ario, or your friend the Cripple, and..." She slid the blade back into its sheath and slapped the hilt home with a sharp snap. "One way or another, Ario will be short one mistress."

Eider stared round at them, one hand still pressed to her neck. "You evil bitches."

Day gave the plum pit a final suck then tossed it away. "It's a living."

"We're done." Vitari dragged Ario's mistress to her feet by one elbow and started marching her towards the door.

Monza stepped in front of them. "What will you be telling your battered manservant, when he comes round?"

"That…we were robbed?"

Monza held out her gloved hand. Eider's face fell even further. She unclasped her necklace and dropped it into Monza's palm, then followed it with her rings. "Convincing enough?"

"I don't know. You seem like the kind of woman to put up a struggle." Monza punched her in the face. She squawked, stumbled, would've fallen if Vitari hadn't caught her. She looked up, blood leaking from her nose and her split lip, and for an instant she had this strange expression. Hurt, yes. Afraid, of course. But more angry than either one. Like the look Monza had herself, maybe, when they threw her from the balcony.

"Now we're done," she said.

Vitari yanked at Eider's elbow and dragged her out into the hallway, towards the front door, their footsteps scraping against the grubby boards. Day gave a sigh, then pushed herself away from the wall and brushed plaster-dust from her backside. "Nice and neat."

"No thanks to your master. Where is he?"

"I prefer employer, and he said there were some errands he had to run."

"Errands?"

"That a problem?"

"I paid for the master, not the dog."

Day grinned. "Woof, woof. There's nothing Morveer can do that I can't."

"That so?"

"He's getting old. Arrogant. That rope burning through was nearly the death of him, in Westport. I wouldn't want any carelessness like that to interfere with your business. Not for what you're paying. No one worse to have next to you than a careless poisoner."

"You'll get no argument from me on that score."

Day shrugged. "Accidents happen all the time in our line of work. Especially to the old. It's a young person's trade, really." She sauntered out into the corridor, passed Vitari stalking back the other way. The look of glee was long gone from her sharp face, and the swagger with it. She lifted one black boot and shoved the chair angrily away into one corner.

"There's our way in, then," she said.

"Seems so."

"Just what I promised you."

"Just what you promised."

"Ario and Foscar, both together, and a way to get to them."

"A good day's work."

They looked at each other, and Vitari ran her tongue around the inside of her mouth as if it tasted bitter. "Well." She shrugged her bony shoulders. "It's a living."

The Life of the Drinker

A drink, a drink, a drink. Where can a man find a drink?"

Nicomo Cosca, famed soldier of fortune, tottered against the wall of the alley, rooting through his purse yet again with quivering fingers. There was still nothing in it but a tuft of grey fluff. He dug it out, blew it from his fingertips and watched it flutter gently down. All his fortune.

"Bastard purse!" He flung it in the gutter in a feeble rage. Then he thought better of it and had to stoop to pick it up, groaning like an old man. He was an old man. A lost man. A dead man, give or take a final rattle of breath. He sank slowly to his knees, gazing at his broken reflection in the black water gathered between the cobblestones.

He would have given all he owned for the slightest taste of liquor. He owned nothing, it had to be said. But his body was his, still. His hands, which had raised up princes to the heights of power and flung them down again. His eyes, which had surveyed the turning points of history. His lips, which had softly kissed the most celebrated beauties of the age. His itching cock, his aching guts, his rotting neck, he would happily have sold it all for a single measure of grape spirit. But it was hard to see where he would find a buyer.

"I have become myself…an empty purse." He raised his leaden arms imploringly and roared into the murky night. "Someone give me a fucking drink!"

"Stop your mouth, arsehole!" a rough voice called back, and then, with the clatter of shutters closing, the alley plunged into deeper gloom.

He had dined at the tables of dukes. He had sported in the beds of countesses. Cities had trembled at the name of Cosca.

"How did it ever come...to this?" He clambered up, swallowing the urge to vomit. He smoothed his hair back from his throbbing temples, fumbled with the limp ends of his moustaches. He made for the lane with something approaching his famous swagger of old. Out between the ghostly buildings and into a patch of lamplight in the mist, moist night breeze tickling at his sore face. Footsteps approached and Cosca lurched round, blinking.

"Good sir! I find myself temporarily without funds, and wonder whether you would be willing to advance me a small loan until—"

"Away and piss, beggar." The man shoved past, barging him against the wall.

Cosca's skin flushed with greasy outrage. "You address none other than Nicomo Cosca, famed soldier of fortune!" The effect was somewhat spoiled by the brittle cracking of his ravaged voice. "Captain general of the Thousand Swords! Ex-captain general, that is." The man made an obscene gesture as he disappeared into the fog. "I dined...at the beds...of dukes!" Cosca collapsed into a fit of hacking coughs and was obliged to bend over, shaking hands on his shaking knees, aching ribcage going like a creaky bellows.

Such was the life of the drinker. A quarter on your arse, a quarter on your face, a quarter on your knees and the rest of your time bent over. He finally hawked up a great lump of phlegm, and with one last cough blew it spinning from his sore tongue. Would this be his legacy? Spit in a hundred thousand gutters? His name a byword for petty betrayal, avarice and waste? He straightened with a groan of the purest despair, staring up into nothingness, even the stars denied him by Sipani's all-cloaking fog.

"One last chance. That's all I'm asking." He had lost count of the number of last chances he had wasted. "Just one more. God!" He had never believed in God for an instant. "Fates!" He had never believed in Fates either. "Anyone!" He had never believed in anything much beyond the next drink. "Just one...more...chance."

"Alright. One more."

Cosca blinked. "God? Is that...you?"

Someone chuckled. A woman's voice, and a sharp, mocking, most ungodlike sort of a chuckle. "You can kneel if you like, Cosca."

He squinted into the sliding mist, pickled brains spurred into something approaching activity. Someone knowing his name was unlikely to be a good thing. His enemies far outnumbered his friends, and his creditors far outnumbered both. He fished drunkenly for the hilt of his gilded sword, then realised he had pawned it months ago in Osperia and bought a cheap one. He fished drunkenly for the hilt of that instead, then realised he had pawned that one when he first reached Sipani. He let his shaky hand drop. Not much lost. He doubted he could have swung a blade even if he'd had one.

"Who the bloody hell's out there? If I owe you money, make ready"— his stomach lurched and he gave vent to a long, acrid burp —"to die?"

A dark shape rose suddenly from the murk at his side and he spun, tripped over his own feet and went sprawling, head cracking against the wall and sending a blinding flash across his vision.

"So you're alive, still. You are alive, aren't you?" A long, lean woman, a sharp face mostly in shadow, spiky hair tinted orange. His mind fumbled sluggishly to recognition.

"Shylo Vitari, well I never." Not an enemy, perhaps, but certainly not a friend. He propped himself up on one elbow, but from the way the street was spinning, decided that was far enough. "Don't suppose you might consent... to buy a man a drink, might you?"

"Goat's milk?"

"What?"

"I hear it's good for the digestion."

"They always said you had a flint for a heart, but I never thought even you would be so cold as to suggest I drink *milk*, damn you! Just one more shot of that old grape spirit." A drink, a drink, a drink. "Just one more and I'm done."

"Oh, you're done alright. How long you been drunk this time?"

"I've a notion it was summer when I started. What is it now?"

"Not the same year, that's sure. How much money have you wasted?"

"All there is and more. I'd be surprised if there's a coin in the world that hasn't been through my purse at some point. But I seem to be out of funds right now, so if you could just spare some change—"

"You need to make a change, not spend some."

He drew himself up, as far as his knees at least, and jabbed at his chest with a crabbing finger. "Do you suppose the shrivelled, piss-soaked, horrified better part of me, the part that screams to be released from this torture, doesn't know that?" He gave a helpless shrug, aching body collapsing on itself. "But for a man to change he needs the help of good friends, or, better yet, good enemies. My friends are all long dead, and my enemies, I am forced to admit...have better things to do."

"Not all of us." Another woman's voice, but one that sent a creeping shiver of familiarity down Cosca's back. A figure formed out of the gloom, mist sucked into smoky swirls after her flicking coat-tails.

"No..." he croaked.

He remembered the moment he first laid eyes on her: a wild-haired girl of nineteen with a sword at her hip and a bright stare rich with anger, defiance and the slightest fascinating hint of contempt. There was a hollowness to her face now, a twist of pain about her mouth. The sword hung on the other side, gloved right hand resting slack on the pommel. Her eyes still had that unwavering sharpness, but there was more anger, more defiance and a long stretch more contempt. Who could blame her for that? Cosca was beyond contemptible, and knew it.

He had sworn a thousand times to kill her, of course, if he ever saw her again. Her, or her brother, or Andiche, Victus, Sesaria, Faithful Carpi or any of the other treacherous bastards from the Thousand Swords who had once betrayed him. Stolen his place from him. Sent him fleeing from the battlefield at Afieri with his reputation and his clothes both equally tattered.

He had sworn a thousand times to kill her, but Cosca had broken all manner of oaths in his life, and the sight of her brought no rage. Instead what welled up in him was a mixture of worn-out self-pity, sappy joy and, most of all, piercing shame at seeing in her face how far he had fallen. He felt the ache in his nose, behind his cheeks, tears welling in his stinging eyes. For once he was grateful that they were red as wounds at the best of times. If he wept, no one could tell the difference.

"Monza." He tried to tug his filthy collar straight, but his hands were shaking too badly to manage it. "I must confess I heard you were dead. I was meaning to take revenge, of course—"

"On me or for me?"

He shrugged. "Difficult to remember...I stopped on the way for a drink."

"Smells like it was more than one." There was a hint of disappointment in her face that pricked at his insides almost worse than steel. "I heard you finally got yourself killed in Dagoska."

He managed to lift one arm high enough to wave her words away. "There have always been false reports of my death. Wishful thinking, on the part of my many enemies. Where is your brother?"

"Dead." Her face did not change.

"Well. I'm sorry for that. I always liked the boy." The lying, gutless, scheming louse.

"He always liked you." They had detested each other, but what did it matter now?

"If only his sister had felt as warmly about me, things might be so much different."

"'Might be' takes us nowhere. We've all got . . . regrets."

They looked at each other for a long moment, her standing, him on his knees. Not quite how he had pictured their reunion in his dreams. "Regrets. The cost of the business, Sazine used to tell me."

"Perhaps we should put the past behind us."

"I can hardly remember yesterday," he lied. The past weighed on him like a giant's suit of armour.

"The future, then. I've a job for you, if you'll take it. Reckon you're up to a job?"

"What manner of job?"

"Fighting."

Cosca winced. "You always were far too attached to fighting. How often did I tell you? A mercenary has no business getting involved with that nonsense."

"A sword is for rattling, not for drawing."

"There's my girl. I've missed you." He said it without thinking, had to cough down his shame and nearly coughed up a lung.

"Help him up, Friendly."

A big man had silently appeared while they were talking, not tall but heavyset, with an air of calm strength about him. He hooked Cosca under his elbow and pulled him effortlessly to his feet.

"That's a strong arm and a good deed," he gurgled over a rush of nausea. "Friendly is your name? Are you a philanthropist?"

"A convict."

"I see no reason why a man cannot be both. My thanks in any case. Now if you could just point us in the direction of a tavern—"

"The taverns will have to wait for you," said Vitari. "No doubt causing a slump in the wine industry. The conference begins in a week and we need you sober."

"I don't do sober anymore. Sober hurts. Did someone say conference?"

Monza was still watching him with those disappointed eyes. "I need a good man. A man with courage and experience. A man who won't mind crossing Grand Duke Orso." The corner of her mouth curled up. "You're as close as we could find at short notice."

Cosca clung to the big man's arm while the misty street tipped around. "From that list, I have... experience?"

"I'll take one of four, if he needs money too. You need money, don't you, old man?"

"Shit, yes. But not as much as I need a drink."

"Do the job right and we'll see."

"I accept." He found he was standing tall, looking down at Monza now, chin held high. "We should have a Paper of Engagement, just like the old days. Written in swirly script, with all the accoutrements, the way Sajaam used to write them. Signed with red ink and... where can a man find a notary this time of night?"

"Don't worry. I'll take your word."

"You must be the only person in Styria who would ever say that to me. But as you please." He pointed decisively down the street. "This way, my man, and try to keep up." He boldly stepped forwards, his leg buckled and he squawked as Friendly caught him.

"Not that way," came the convict's slow, deep voice. He slid one hand under Cosca's arm and half-led him, half-carried him in the opposite direction.

"You are a gentleman, sir," muttered Cosca.

"I am a murderer."

"I see no reason why a man cannot be both..." Cosca strained to focus on Vitari, loping along up ahead, then at the side of Friendly's heavy face. Strange companions. Outsiders. Those no one else would find a use for. He watched Monza walking, the purposeful stride he remembered from long ago turned slightly crooked. Those who were willing to cross Grand Duke Orso. And that meant madmen, or those with no choices. Which was he?

The answer was in easy reach. There was no reason a man could not be both.

Left Out

Friendly's knife flashed and flickered, twenty strokes one way and twenty the other, grazing the whetstone with a sharpening kiss. There was little worse than a blunt knife and little better than a sharp one, so he smiled as he tested the edge and felt that cold roughness against his fingertip. The blade was keen.

"Cardotti's House of Leisure is an old merchant's palace," Vitari was saying, voice chilly calm. "Wood-built, like most of Sipani, round three sides of a courtyard with the Eighth Canal right at its rear."

They had set up a long table in the kitchen at the back of the warehouse, and the six of them sat about it now. Murcatto and Shivers, Day and Morveer, Cosca and Vitari. On the table stood a model of a large wooden building on three sides of a courtyard. Friendly judged that it was one thirty-sixth the size of the real Cardotti's House of Leisure, though it was hard to be precise, and he liked very much to be precise.

Vitari's fingertip trailed along the windows on one side of the tiny building. "There are kitchens and offices on the ground floor, a hall for husk and another for cards and dice." Friendly pressed his hand to his shirt pocket and was comforted to feel his own dice nuzzling against his ribs. "Two staircases in the rear corners. On the first floor thirteen rooms where guests are entertained—"

"Fucked," said Cosca. "We're all adults here, let's call it what it is." His bloodshot eyes flickered up to the two bottles of wine on the shelf, then back. Friendly had noticed they did that a lot.

Vitari's finger drifted up towards the model's roof. "Then, on the top floor, three large suites for the . . . *fucking* of the most valued guests. They say the Royal Suite in the centre is fit for an emperor."

"Then Ario might just consider it fit for himself," growled Murcatto.

The group had grown from five to seven, so Friendly cut each of the two loaves into fourteen slices, the blade hissing through the crust and sending up puffs of flour dust. There would be twenty-eight slices in all, four slices each. Murcatto would eat less, but Day would make up for it. Friendly hated to leave a slice of bread uneaten.

"According to Eider, Ario and Foscar will have three or four dozen guests, some of them armed but not keen to fight, as well as six bodyguards."

"She telling the truth?" Shivers' heavy accent.

"Chance may play a part, but she won't lie to us."

"Keeping charge o' that many . . . we'll need more fighters."

"Killers," interrupted Cosca. "Again, let's call them what they are."

"Twenty, maybe," came Murcatto's hard voice, "as well as you three."

Twenty-three. An interesting number. Heat kissed the side of Friendly's face as he unhooked the door of the old stove and pulled it creaking open. Twenty-three could be divided by no other number, except one. No parts, no fractions. No half-measures. Not unlike Murcatto herself. He hauled the big pot out with a cloth around his hands. Numbers told no lies. Unlike people.

"How do we get twenty men inside without being noticed?"

"It's a revel," said Vitari. "There'll be entertainers. And we'll provide them."

"Entertainers?"

"This is Sipani. Every other person in the city is an entertainer or a killer. Shouldn't be too difficult to find a few who are both."

Friendly was left out of the planning, but he did not mind. Sajaam had asked him to do what Murcatto said, and that was the end of it. He had learned long ago that life became much easier if you ignored what was not right before you. For now the stew was his only concern.

He dipped in his wooden spoon and took a taste, and it was good. He rated it forty-one out of fifty. The smell of cooking, the sight of the steam rising, the sound of the fizzing logs in the stove, it all put him in comforting mind of the kitchens in Safety. Of the stews, and soups, and porridge they used to make in the great vats. Long ago, back when there was an infinite weight of comforting stone always above his head, and the numbers added, and things made sense.

"Ario will want to drink for a while," Murcatto was saying, "and gamble, and show off to his idiots. Then he'll be brought up to the Royal Suite."

Cosca split a crack-lipped grin. "Where women will be waiting for him, I take it?"

"One with black hair and one with red." Murcatto exchanged a hard look with Vitari.

"A surprise fit for an emperor," chuckled Cosca, wetly.

"When Ario's dead, which will be quickly, we'll move next door and pay Foscar the same kind of visit." Murcatto shifted her scowl to Morveer. "They'll have brought guards upstairs to watch things while they're busy. You and Day can handle them."

"Can we indeed?" The poisoner took a brief break from sneering at his fingernails. "A *fit* purpose for our talents, I am sure."

"Try not to poison half the city this time. We should be able to kill the brothers without raising any unwanted attention, but if something goes wrong, that's where the entertainers come in."

The old mercenary jabbed at the model with a quivery finger. "Take the courtyard first, the gaming and smoking halls, and from there secure the staircases. Disarm the guests and round them up. Politely, of course, and in the best taste. Keep control."

"Control." Murcatto's gloved forefinger stabbed the tabletop. "That's the word I want at the front of your tiny minds. We kill Ario, we kill Foscar. If any of the rest make trouble, you do what you have to, but keep the murder to a minimum. There'll be trouble enough for us afterwards without a bloodbath. You all got that?"

Cosca cleared his throat. "Perhaps a drink would help me to commit it all to—"

"I've got it." Shivers spoke over him. "Control, and as little blood as possible."

"Two murders." Friendly set the pot down in the middle of the table. "One and one, and no more. Food." And he began to ladle portions out into the bowls.

He would have liked very much to ensure that everyone had the exact same number of pieces of meat. The same number of pieces of carrot and onion too, the same number of beans. But by the time he had counted them out the food would have been cold, and he had learned that most people found that level of precision upsetting. It had led to a fight in the mess in Safety once, and Friendly had killed two men and cut a hand from another. He had no wish to kill anyone now. He was hungry. So he satisfied himself by giving each one of them the same number of ladles of stew, and coped with the deep sense of unease it left him.

"This is good," gurgled Day, around a mouthful. "This is excellent. Is there more?"

"Where did you learn to cook, my friend?" Cosca asked.

"I spent three years in the kitchens in Safety. The man who taught me used to be head cook to the Duke of Borletta."

"What was he doing in prison?"

"He killed his wife, and chopped her up, and cooked her in a stew, and ate it."

There was quiet around the table. Cosca noisily cleared his throat. "No one's wife in this stew, I trust?"

"The butcher said it was lamb, and I've no reason to doubt him." Friendly picked up his fork. "No one sells human meat that cheap."

There was one of those uncomfortable silences that Friendly always seemed to produce when he said more than three words at once. Then Cosca gave a gurgling laugh. "Depends on the circumstances. Reminds me of when we found those children, do you remember, Monza, after the siege at Muris?" Her scowl grew even harder than usual, but there was no stopping him. "We found those children, and we wanted to sell them on to some slavers, but you thought we could—"

"Of course!" Morveer almost shrieked. "*Hilarious!* What could possibly be more amusing than orphan children sold into slavery?"

There was another awkward silence while the poisoner and the mercenary gave each other a deadly glare. Friendly had seen men exchange that very look in Safety. When new blood came in, and prisoners were forced into a cell together. Sometimes two men would just catch each other wrong. Hate each other from the moment they met. Too different. Or too much the same. Things were harder to predict out here, of course. But in Safety, when you saw two men look at each other that way you knew, sooner or later, there would be blood.

* * *

A drink, a drink, a drink. Cosca's eyes lurched from that preening louse Morveer and down to the poisoner's full wine glass, around the glasses of the others, reluctantly back to his own sickening mug of water and finally to the wine bottle on the table, where his gaze was gripped as if by burning pincers. A quick lunge and he could have it. How much could he swallow before they wrestled it from his hands? Few men could drink faster when circumstances demanded—

Then he noticed Friendly watching him, and there was something in the convict's sad, flat eyes that made him think again. He was Nicomo Cosca, damn it! Or he had been once, at least. Cities had trembled, and so on. He had spent too many years never thinking beyond his next drink. It was time to look further. To the drink after next, at any rate. But change was not easy.

He could almost feel the sweat springing out of his skin. His head was pulsing, booming with pain. He clawed at his itchy neck but that only made it itch the more. He was smiling like a skull, he knew, and talking far too much. But it was smile, and talk, or scream his exploding head off.

"...saved my life at the siege of Muris, eh, Monza? At Muris, was it?" He hardly even knew how his cracking voice had wandered onto the subject. "Bastard came at me out of nowhere. A quick thrust!" He nearly knocked his water cup over with a wayward jab of his finger. "And she ran him through! Right through the heart, I swear. Saved my life. At Muris. Saved my...life..."

And he almost wished she had let him die. The kitchen seemed to be spinning, tossing, tipping wildly like the cabin of a ship in a fatal tempest. He kept expecting to see the wine slosh from the glasses, the stew spray from the bowls, the plates slide from the see-sawing table. He knew the only storm was in his head, yet still found himself clinging to the furniture whenever the room appeared to heel with particular violence.

"...wouldn't have been so bad if she hadn't done it again the next day. I took an arrow in the shoulder and fell in the damn moat. Everyone saw, on both sides. Making me look a fool in front of my friends is one thing, but in front of my enemies—"

"You've got it wrong."

Cosca squinted up the table at Monza. "I have?" Though he had to admit he could hardly remember his last sentence, let alone the events of a siege a dozen drunken years ago.

"It was me in the moat, you that jumped in to pull me out. Risked your life, and took an arrow doing it."

"Seems astoundingly unlikely I'd have done a thing like that." It was hard to think about anything beyond his violent need for a drink. "But I'm finding it somewhat difficult to recall the details, I must confess. Perhaps if one of you could just see your way to passing me the wine I could—"

"Enough." She had that same look she always used to have when she dragged him from one tavern or another, except even angrier, even sharper and even more disappointed. "I've five men to kill, and I've no time to be saving anyone anymore. Especially from their own stupidity. I've no use for a drunk." The table was silent as they all watched him sweat.

"I'm no drunk," croaked Cosca. "I simply like the taste of wine. So much so that I have to drink some every few hours or become violently ill." He clung to his fork while the room swayed around him, fixed his aching smile while they chuckled away. He hoped they enjoyed their laughter while they could, because Nicomo Cosca always laughed last. Provided he wasn't being sick, of course.

Morveer was feeling left out. He was a scintillating conversationalist face to face, it hardly needed to be said, but had never been at his ease in large groups. This scenario reminded him unpleasantly of the dining room in the orphanage, where the larger children had amused themselves by throwing food at him, a terrifying prelude to the whisperings, beatings, dunkings and other torments in the nocturnal blackness of the dormitories.

Murcatto's two new assistants, on the hiring of whom he had not been given even the most superficial consultation, were far from putting his mind at ease. Shylo Vitari was a torturer and broker in information, highly competent but possessed of an abrasive personality. He had collaborated with her once before, and the experience had not been a happy one. Morveer found the whole notion of inflicting pain with one's own hands thoroughly repugnant. But she knew Sipani, so he supposed he could suffer her. For now.

Nicomo Cosca was infinitely worse. A notoriously destructive, treacherous and capricious mercenary with no code or scruple but his own profit. A drunkard, dissipater and womaniser with all the self-control of a rabid dog. A self-aggrandising backslider with an epically inflated opinion of his own abilities, he was everything Morveer was not. But now, as well as taking this dangerously unpredictable element into their confidence and involving him intimately in their plans, the group seemed to be paying court to the trembling shell. Even Day, his own assistant, was chortling at his jokes whenever she did not have her mouth full, which, admittedly, was but rarely.

"...a group of miscreants hunched around a table in an abandoned warehouse?" Cosca was musing, bloodshot eyes rolling round the table. "Talking of masks, and disguises, and weaponry? I cannot imagine how a man of my high calibre ended up in such company. One would think there was some underhand business taking place!"

"My own thoughts exactly!" Morveer shrilly interjected. "I could never countenance such a stain upon my conscience. That is why I applied an extract of Widow's Blossom to your bowls. I hope you all enjoy your last few agonising moments!"

Six faces frowned back at him, entirely silent.

"A jest, of course," he croaked, realising instantly that his conversational foray had suffered a spectacular misfire. Shivers exhaled long and slow. Murcatto curled her tongue sourly around one canine tooth. Day was frowning down at her bowl.

"I've taken more amusing punches in the face," said Vitari.

"Poisoners' humour." Cosca glowered across the table, though the effect was somewhat spoiled by the rattling of his fork against his bowl as his right hand vibrated. "A lover of mine was murdered by poison. I have had nothing but disgust for your profession ever since. And all its members, naturally."

"You can hardly expect me to take responsibility for the actions of every person in my line of work." Morveer thought it best not to mention that he had, in fact, been personally responsible, having been hired by Grand Duchess Sefeline of Ospria to murder Nicomo Cosca some fourteen years before. It was becoming a matter of considerable annoyance that he had missed the mark and killed his mistress instead.

"I crush wasps whenever I find them, whether they have stung me or not. To my mind you people — if I can call you people — are all equally worthy of contempt. A poisoner is the filthiest kind of coward."

"Second only to a drunkard!" returned Morveer with a suitable curling of his upper lip. "Such human refuse might almost evoke pity were they not so utterly repellent. No animal is more predictable. Like a befouled homing pigeon, the drunk returns ever to the bottle, unable to change. It is their one route of escape from the misery they leave in their wake. For them the sober world is so crowded with old failures and new fears that they suffocate in it. There is a *true* coward." He raised his glass and took a long, self-satisfied gulp of wine. He was unused to drinking rapidly and felt, in fact, a powerful urge to vomit, but forced a queasy smile onto his face nonetheless.

Cosca's thin hand clutched the table with a white-knuckled intensity as he watched Morveer swallow. "How little you understand me. I could stop drinking whenever I wish. In fact, I have already resolved to do so. I would prove it to you." The mercenary held up one wildly flapping hand. "If I could just get half a glass to settle these damn palsies!"

The others laughed, the tension diffused, but Morveer caught the lethal glare on Cosca's face. The old soak might have seemed harmless as a village dunce, but he had once been counted among the most dangerous men in Styria. It would have been folly to take such a man lightly, and Morveer was nobody's fool. He was no longer the orphan child who had blubbered for his mother while they kicked him.

Caution first, each and every time.

Monza sat still, said no more than she had to and ate less, gloved hand painfully clumsy with the knife. She left herself out, up here at the head of the table. The distance a general needs to keep from the soldiers, an employer from the hirelings, a wanted woman from everyone, if she's got any sense. It wasn't hard to do. She'd been keeping her distance for years and leaving Benna to do the talking, and the laughing, and be liked. A leader can't afford to be liked. Especially not a woman. Shivers kept glancing up the table towards her, and she kept not meeting his eye. She'd let things slip in Westport, made herself look weak. She couldn't let that happen again.

"The pair o' you seem pretty familiar," Shivers was saying now, eyes moving between her and Cosca. "Old friends, are you?"

"Family, rather!" The old mercenary waved his fork wildly enough to have someone's eye out. "We fought side by side as noble members of the

Thousand Swords, most famous mercenary brigade in the Circle of the World!" Monza frowned sideways at him. His old bloody stories were bringing back things done and choices made she'd sooner have left in the past. "We fought across Styria and back, while Sazine was captain general. Those were the days to be a mercenary! Before things started to get... complicated."

Vitari snorted. "You mean bloody."

"Different words for the same thing. People were richer back then, and scared more easily, and the walls were all lower. Then Sazine took an arrow in the arm, then lost the arm, then died, and I was voted to the captain general's chair." Cosca poked his stew around. "Burying that old wolf, I realised that fighting was too much hard work, and I, like most persons of quality, wished to do as little of it as possible." He gave Monza a twitchy grin. "So we split the brigade in two."

"You split the brigade in two."

"I took one half, and Monzcarro and her brother Benna took the other, and we spread a rumour we'd had a falling out. We hired ourselves out to both sides of every argument we could find — and we found plenty — and... pretended to fight."

"Pretended?" muttered Shivers.

Cosca's trembling knife and fork jabbed at each other in the air. "We'd march around for weeks at a time, picking the country clean all the while, mount the odd harmless skirmish for the show of it, then leave off at the end of each season a good deal richer but with no one dead. Well, a few of the rot, maybe. Every bit as profitable as having at the business in earnest, though. We even mounted a couple of fake battles, didn't we?"

"We did."

"Until Monza took an engagement with Grand Duke Orso of Talins, and decided she was done with fake battles. Until she decided to mount a proper charge, with swords well sharpened and swung in earnest. Until you decided to make a difference, eh, Monza? Shame you never told me we weren't faking anymore. I could've warned my boys and saved some lives that day."

"Your boys." She snorted. "Let's not pretend you ever cared for anyone's life but your own."

"There have been a few others I valued higher. I never profited by it, though, and neither did they." Cosca hadn't taken his bloodshot eyes from

Monza's. "Which of your own people turned on you? Faithful Carpi, was it? Not so faithful in the end, eh?"

"He was as faithful as you could wish for. Right up until he stabbed me."

"And now he's taken the captain general's chair, no doubt?"

"I hear he's managed to wedge his fat arse into it."

"Just as you slipped your skinny one into it after mine. But he couldn't have taken anything without the consent of some other captains, could he? Fine lads, those. That bastard Andiche. That big leech Sesaria. That sneering maggot Victus. Were those three greedy hogs still with you?"

"They still had their faces in the trough. All of them turned on me, I'm sure, just the way they turned on you. You're telling me nothing I don't know."

"No one thanks you, in the end. Not for the victories you bring them. Not for the money you make them. They get bored. And the first sniff of something better—"

Monza was out of patience. A leader can't afford to look soft. Especially not a woman. "For such an expert on people, it's a wonder you ended up a friendless, penniless drunk, eh, Cosca? Don't pretend I didn't give you a thousand chances. You wasted them all, like you wasted everything else. The only question that interests me is — are you set on wasting this one too? Can you do as I fucking tell you? Or are you set on being my enemy?"

Cosca only gave a sad smile. "In our line of work, enemies are things to be proud of. If experience has taught the two of us anything, it's that your friends are the ones you need to watch. My congratulations to the cook." He tossed his fork down in his bowl, got up and strutted from the kitchen in almost a straight line. Monza frowned at the sullen faces he left around the table.

Never fear your enemies, Verturio wrote, *but your friends, always.*

A Few Bad Men

The warehouse was a draughty cavern, cold light finding chinks in the shutters and leaving bright lines across the dusty boards, across the empty crates piled up in one corner, across the old table in the middle of the floor. Shivers dropped into a rickety chair next to it, felt the grip of the knife Monza had given him pressing at his calf. A sharp reminder of what he'd been hired for. Life was getting way more dark and dangerous than back home in the North. As far as being a better man went, he was going backwards, and quicker every day.

So why the hell was he still here? Because he wanted Monza? He had to admit it, and the fact she'd been cold with him since Westport only made him want her more. Because he wanted her money? That too. Money was a damn good thing for buying stuff. Because he needed the work? He did. Because he was good at the work? He was.

Because he enjoyed the work?

Shivers frowned. Some men aren't stamped out for doing good, and he was starting to reckon he might be one of 'em. He was less and less sure with every day that being a better man was worth all the effort.

The sound of a door banging tugged him from his thoughts, and Cosca came down the creaking wooden steps from the rooms where they were sleeping, scratching slowly at the splatter of red rash up the side of his neck.

"Morning."

The old mercenary yawned. "So it seems. I can barely remember the last one of these I saw. Nice shirt."

Shivers twitched at his sleeve. Dark silk, with polished bone buttons and clever stitching round the cuff. A good stretch fancier than he'd have picked out, but Monza had liked it. "Hadn't noticed."

"I used to be one for fine clothes myself." Cosca dropped into a rickety chair next to Shivers. "So did Monza's brother, for that matter. He had a shirt just like that one, as I recall."

Shivers weren't sure what the old bastard was getting at, but he was sure he didn't like it. "And?"

"Spoken much about her brother, has she?" Cosca had a strange little smile, like he knew something Shivers didn't.

"She told me he's dead."

"So I hear."

"She told me she's not happy about it."

"Most decidedly not."

"Something else I should know?"

"I suppose we could all be wiser than we are. I'll leave that up to her, though."

"Where is she?" snapped Shivers, patience drying up.

"Monza?"

"Who else?"

"She doesn't want anyone to see her face that doesn't have to. But not to worry. I have hired fighting men all across the Circle of the World. And my fair share of entertainers too, as it goes. Do you have any issue with my taking charge of the proceedings?"

Shivers had a pile of issues with it. It was plain the only thing Cosca had taken charge of for a good long while was a bottle. After the Bloody-Nine killed his brother, and cut his head off, and had it nailed up on a standard, Shivers' father had taken to drinking. He'd taken to drinking, and rages, and having the shakes. He'd stopped making good choices, and he'd lost the respect of his people, and he'd wasted all he'd built, and died leaving Shivers nought but sour memories.

"I don't trust a man who drinks," he growled, not bothered about dressing it up. "A man takes to drinking, then he gets weak, then his mind goes."

Cosca sadly shook his head. "You have it back to front. A man's mind goes, then he gets weak, then he takes to drink. The bottle is the symptom, not the cause. But though I am touched to my core by your concern, you need not worry on my account. I feel a great deal steadier today!" He spread his hands out above the tabletop. It was true they weren't shaking as bad as they had been. A gentle quiver rather than a mad jerk. "I'll be back to my best before you know it."

"I can hardly wait to see that." Vitari strutted out from the kitchen, arms folded.

"None of us can, Shylo!" And Cosca slapped Shivers on the arm. "But enough about me! What criminals, footpads, thugs and other such human filth have you dug from the slimy backstreets of old Sipani? What fighting entertainers have you for our consideration? Musicians who murder? Deadly dancers? Singers with swords? Jugglers who...who..."

"Kill?" offered Shivers.

Cosca's grin widened. "Brusque and to the point, as always."

"Brusque?"

"Thick." Vitari slid into the last chair and unfolded a sheet of paper on the scarred tabletop. "First up, there's a band I found playing for bits near the docks. I reckon they make a fair stretch more from robbing passers-by than serenading them, though."

"Rough-and-tumble fellows, eh? The very type we need." Cosca stretched out his scrawny neck like a cock about to crow. "Enter!"

The door squealed open and five men wandered in. Even where Shivers came from they would've been reckoned a rough-looking set. Greasy-haired. Pock-faced. Rag-dressed. Their eyes darted about, narrow and suspicious, dirty hands clutching a set of stained instruments. They shuffled up in front of the table, one of them scratching his groin, another prodding at a nostril with his drumstick.

"And you are?" asked Cosca.

"We're a band," the nearest said.

"And has your band a name?"

They looked at each other. "No. Why would it?"

"Your own names, then, if you please, and your specialities both as entertainer and fighter."

"My name's Solter. I play the drum, and the mace." Flicking his greasy coat back to show the dull glint of iron. "I'm better with the mace, if I'm honest."

"I'm Morc," said the next in line. "Pipe, and cutlass."

"Olopin. Horn, and hammer."

"Olopin, as well." Jerking a thumb sideways. "Brother to this article.

174

Fiddle, and blades." Whipping a pair of long knives from his sleeves and spinning 'em round his fingers.

The last had the most broken nose Shivers had ever seen, and he'd seen some bad ones. "Gurpi. Lute, and lute."

"You fight with your lute?" asked Cosca.

"I hits 'em with it just so." The man showed off a sideways swipe, then flashed two rows of shit-coloured teeth. "There's a great-axe hidden in the body."

"Ouch. A tune, then, if you please, my fellows, and make it something lively!"

Shivers weren't much for music, but even he could tell it was no fine playing. The drum was out of time. The pipe was tuneless tooting. The lute was flat, probably on account of all the ironware inside. But Cosca nodded along, eyes shut, like he'd never heard sweeter music.

"My days, what multi-talented fellows you are!" he shouted after a couple of bars, bringing the din to a stuttering halt. "You're hired, each one of you, at forty scales per man for the night."

"Forty...scales...a man?" gawped the drummer.

"Paid on completion. But it will be tough work. You will undoubtedly be called upon to fight, and possibly even to play. It may have to be a fatal performance, for our enemies. You are ready for such a commitment?"

"For forty scales a man?" They were all grinning now. "Yes, sir, we are! For that much we're fearless."

"Good men. We know where to find you."

Vitari leaned across as the band made their way out. "Ugly set of bastards."

"One of the many advantages of a *masked* revel," whispered Cosca. "Stick 'em in motley and no one will be any the wiser."

Shivers didn't much care for the idea of trusting his life to those lot. "They'll notice the playing, no?"

Cosca snorted. "People don't visit Cardotti's for the music."

"Shouldn't we have checked how they fight?"

"If they fight like they play we should have no worries."

"They play about as well as runny shit."

"They play like lunatics. With luck they fight the same way."

"That's no kind of—"

"I hardly thought of you as the fussy type." Cosca peered at Shivers down his long nose. "You need to learn to live a little, my friend. All victories worth the winning are snatched with vim and brio!"

"With who?"

"Carelessness," said Vitari.

"Dash," said Cosca. "And seizing the moment."

"And what do you make of all this?" Shivers asked Vitari. "Vim and whatever."

"If the plan goes smoothly we'll get Ario and Foscar away from the others and—" She snapped her fingers with a sharp crack. "Won't matter much who strums the lute. Time's running out. Four days until the great and good of Styria descend on Sipani for their conference. I'd find better men, in an ideal world. But this isn't one."

Cosca heaved a throaty sigh. "It most certainly is not. But let's not be downhearted — a few moments in and we're five men to the good! Now, if I could just get a glass of wine we'd be well on our way to—"

"No wine," growled Vitari.

"It's coming to something when a man can't even wet his throat." The old mercenary leaned close enough that Shivers could pick out the broken veins across his cheeks. "Life is a sea of sorrows, my friend. Enter!"

The next man barely fit through the warehouse door, he was that big. A few fingers taller than Shivers but a whole lot weightier. He had thick stubble across his great chunk of jaw and a mop of grey curls though he didn't seem old. His heavy hands fussed with each other as he came towards the table, a bit stooped like he was shamed of his own size, boards giving a complaining creak every time one of his great boots came down.

Cosca whistled. "My, my, that is a big one."

"Found him in a tavern down by the First Canal," said Vitari, "drunk as shit but everyone too scared to move him. Hardly speaks a word of Styrian."

Cosca leaned towards Shivers. "Perhaps you might take the lead with this one? The brotherhood of the North?"

Shivers didn't remember there being that much brotherhood up there in the cold, but it was worth a try. The words felt strange in his mouth, it was that long since he'd used them. "What's your name, friend?"

The big man looked surprised to hear Northern. "Greylock." He pointed at his hair. "S'always been this colour."

"What brought you all the way down here?"

"Come looking for work."

"What sort o' work?"

"Whatever'll have me, I reckon."

"Even if it's bloody?"

"Likely it will be. You're a Northman?"

"Aye."

"You look like a Southerner."

Shivers frowned, drew his fancy cuffs back and out of sight under the table. "Well, I'm not one. Name's Caul Shivers."

Greylock blinked. "Shivers?"

"Aye." He felt a flush of pleasure that the man knew his name. He still had his pride, after all. "You heard o' me?"

"You was at Uffrith, with the Dogman?"

"That's right."

"And Black Dow too, eh? Neat piece o' work, the way I heard it."

"That it was. Took the city with no more'n a couple dead."

"No more'n a couple." The big man nodded slowly, eyes never leaving Shivers' face. "That must've been real smooth."

"It was. He was a good chief for keeping folk alive, the Dogman. Best I took orders from, I reckon."

"Well, then. Since the Dogman ain't here his self, it'd be my honour to stand shoulder to shoulder with a man like you."

"Right you are. Likewise. Pleased to have you along. He's in," said Shivers in Styrian.

"Are you sure?" asked Cosca. "He has a certain…sourness to his eye that worries me."

"You need to learn to live a little," grunted Shivers. "Get some fucking brio in."

Vitari snorted laughter and Cosca clutched his chest. "Gah! Run through with my own rapier! Well, I suppose you can have your little friend. What could we do with a pair of Northmen, now?" He threw up one finger. "We could mount a re-enactment! A rendering of that famous Northern duel — you know the one, Fenris the Feared, or whatever, and…you know, what's-his-name now…"

Shivers' back went cold as he said the name. "The Bloody-Nine."

"You've heard of it?"

"I was there. Right in the thick. I held a shield at the edge of the circle."

"Excellent! You should be able to bring a frisson of historical accuracy to the proceedings, then."

"Frisson?"

"Bit," grunted Vitari.

"Why not just bloody say bit, then?"

But Cosca was too busy grinning at his own notion. "A whiff of violence! Ario's gentlemen will lap it up! And what better excuse for weapons in plain sight?" Shivers was a sight less keen. Dressing up as the man who killed his brother, a man he'd nearly killed himself, and pretending to fight. The one thing in its favour was he wouldn't have to strum a lute, at least.

"What's he saying?" rumbled Greylock in Northern.

"The two of us are going to pretend to have a duel."

"Pretend?"

"I know, but they pretend all kinds o' shit down here. We'll put a show on. Act it out, you know. Entertainment."

"The circle's no laughing matter," and the big man didn't look like laughing either.

"Down here it is. First we pretend, then we might have some others to fight for real. Forty scales if you can make it work."

"Right you are, then. First we pretend. Then we fight for real. Got it." Greylock gave Shivers a long, slow look, then lumbered away.

"Next!" bellowed Cosca. A skinny man pranced through the doorway in orange tights and a bright red jacket, big bag in one hand. "Your name?"

"I am none other than"— he gave a fancy bow —"the Incredible Ronco!"

The old mercenary's brows shot up as fast as Shivers' heart sank. "And your specialities, both as entertainer and fighter?"

"They are one and the same, sirs!" Nodding to Cosca and Shivers. "My lady!" Then to Vitari. He turned slowly round, reaching stealthily into his bag, then spun about, one hand to his face, cheeks puffed out—

There was a rustle and a blaze of brilliant fire shot from Ronco's lips, close enough for Shivers to feel the heat sting his cheek. He would've dived from his chair if he'd had the time, but instead he was left rooted — blinking, staring, gasping, as his eyes got used to the darkness of the warehouse again. A couple of patches of fire clung to the table, one just beyond the ends of Cosca's trembling fingers. The flames sputtered, in silence, and died, leaving behind a smell that made Shivers want to puke.

The Incredible Ronco cleared his throat. "Ah. A slightly more...vigorous demonstration than I intended."

"But damned impressive!" Cosca wafted the smoke away from his face. "Undeniably entertaining, and undeniably deadly. You are hired, sir, at the price of forty scales for the night."

The man beamed. "Delighted to be of service!" He bowed even lower this time round. "Sirs! My lady! I take...my leave!"

"You sure about that?" asked Shivers as Ronco strutted to the door. "Bit of a worry, ain't it? Fire in a wooden building?"

Cosca looked down his nose again. "I thought you Northmen were all wrath and bad teeth. If things turn sour, fire in a wooden building could be just the equaliser we need."

"The what we need, now?"

"Leveller," said Vitari.

That seemed a bad word to pick. They called death the Great Leveller, up in the hills of the North. "Fire indoors could end up levelling the lot of us, and in case you didn't notice, that bastard weren't too precise. Fire is dangerous."

"Fire is pretty. He's in."

"But won't he—"

"Ah." Cosca held up a silencing hand.

"We should—"

"Ah."

"Don't tell me—"

"Ah, I said! Do you not have the word 'ah' in your country? Murcatto put me in charge of the entertainers and, with the greatest of respect, that means I say who is in. We are not taking votes. You concentrate on mounting a show to make Ario's gentlemen cheer. I'll handle the planning. How does that sound?"

"Like a short cut to disaster," said Shivers.

"Ah, disaster!" Cosca grinned. "I can't wait. Who have we to consider in the meantime?"

Vitari cocked one orange brow at her list. "Barti and Kummel — tumblers, acrobats, knife-artists and walkers on the high wire."

Cosca nudged Shivers in the ribs with his elbow. "Walkers on the high wire, there you go. How could *that* end badly?"

The Peacemakers

It was a rare clear day in the City of Fogs. The air was crisp and cold, the sky was perfectly blue and the King of the Union's conference of peace was due to begin its noble work. The ragged rooflines, the dirty windows, the peeling doorways were all thick with onlookers, waiting eagerly for the great men of Styria to appear. They trickled down both gutters of the wide avenue below, a multicoloured confusion, pressing up against the grim grey lines of soldiers deployed to hold them back. The hubbub of the crowd was a weight on the air. Thousands of murmuring voices, stabbed through here and there by the shouts of hawkers, bellowed warnings, squeals of excitement. Like the sound of an army before a battle.

Nervously waiting for the blood to start spilling.

Five more dots, perched on the roof of a crumbling warehouse, were nothing to remark upon. Shivers stared down, big hands dangling over the parapet. Cosca had his boot propped carelessly on the cracked stonework, scratching at his scabby neck. Vitari leaned back against the wall, long arms folded. Friendly stood bolt upright to the side, seeming lost in a world of his own. The fact that Morveer and his apprentice were away on their own business gave Monza scant confidence. When she first met the poisoner, she hadn't trusted him at all. Since Westport, she trusted him an awful lot less. And these were her troops. She sucked in a long, bitter breath, licked her teeth and spat down into the crowd below.

When God means to punish a man, the Kantic scriptures say, *he sends him stupid friends, and clever enemies.*

"That's a lot o' people," said Shivers, eyes narrowed against the chilly glare. Just the kind of stunning revelation Monza had come to expect from the man. "An awful lot."

"Yes." Friendly's eyes flickered over the crowds, lips moving silently, giving Monza the worrying impression that he was trying to count them.

"This is nothing." Cosca dismissed half of Sipani with an airy wave. "You should have seen the throng that packed the streets of Ospria after my victory at the Battle of the Isles! They filled the air with falling flowers! Twice as many, at the least. You should have been there!"

"I was there," said Vitari, "and there were half as many at the most."

"Does pissing on my dreams give you some sick satisfaction?"

"A little." Vitari smirked at Monza, but she didn't laugh. She was thinking of the triumph they'd put on for her in Talins, after the fall of Caprile. Or the massacre at Caprile, depending on who you asked. She remembered Benna grinning while she frowned, standing in his stirrups and blowing kisses to the balconies. The people chanting her name, even though Orso was riding in thoughtful silence just behind with Ario at his shoulder. She should've seen it coming then . . .

"Here they are!" Cosca shielded his eyes with one hand, leaning out dangerously far over the railing. "All hail our great leaders!"

The noise of the crowd swelled as the procession came into view. Seven mounted standard-bearers brought up the front, flags on lances all at the exact same angle — the illusion of equality deemed necessary for peace talks. The cockleshell of Sipani. The white tower of Ospria. The three bees of Visserine. The black cross of Talins. The symbols of Puranti, Affoia and Nicante stirred lazily in the breeze alongside them. A man in gilded armour rode behind, the golden sun of the Union drooping from his black lance.

Sotorius, Chancellor of Sipani, was the first of the great and good to appear. Or the mean and evil, depending on who you asked. He was truly ancient, with thin white hair and beard, hunched under the weight of the heavy chain of office he'd worn since long before Monza was born. He hobbled along doggedly with the aid of a cane and with the eldest of his many sons, probably in his sixties himself, at his elbow. Several columns of Sipani's leading citizens followed, sun twinkling on jewels and polished leather, bright silk and cloth of gold.

"Chancellor Sotorius," Cosca was noisily explaining to Shivers. "According to tradition, the host goes on foot. Still alive, the old bastard."

"Looks like he needs a rest though," muttered Monza. "Someone get the man a coffin."

"Not quite yet, I think. Half-blind he may be, but he still has clearer sight than most. The long-established master of the middle ground. One way or another he's kept Sipani neutral for two decades. Right through the Years of Blood. Ever since I gave him a bloody nose at the Battle of the Isles!"

Vitari snorted. "Didn't stop you taking his coin when it all turned sour with Sefeline of Ospria, as I recall."

"Why should it have? Paid soldiers can't be too picky over their employers. You have to blow with the wind in this business. Loyalty on a mercenary is like armour on a swimmer." Monza frowned sideways, wondering whether that was meant for her, but Cosca was blathering on as though it meant nothing to anyone. "Still, he never suited me much, old Sotorius. It was a wedding of necessity, an unhappy marriage and, once victory was won, a divorce we were both happy to agree to. Peaceful men find little work for mercenaries, and the old Chancellor of Sipani has made a rich and glorious career from peace."

Vitari sneered down at the wealthy citizens tramping by below. "Looks like he's hoping to make an export of it."

Monza shook her head. "One thing Orso will never be buying."

The leaders of the League of Eight came next. Orso's bitter enemies, which had meant Monza's too, until her tumble down a mountain. They were attended by a regiment of hangers-on, all decked out in a hundred clashing liveries. Duke Rogont rode at the front on a great black charger, reins in one sure hand, giving the occasional nod to the crowds as someone shouted for him. He was a popular man, and was called on to nod often, almost to the point that his head bobbed like a turkey's. Salier had somehow been wedged into the saddle of a stocky roan beside Rogont, pink jowls bulging out over the gilded collar of his uniform, on one side, then the other, in time to the movement of his labouring mount.

"Who's the fat man?" asked Shivers.

"Salier, Grand Duke of Visserine."

Vitari sniggered. "For another month or two, maybe. He squandered his city's soldiers in the summer." Monza had charged them down on the High Bank, with Faithful Carpi beside her. "His city's food in the autumn."

Monza had merrily burned the fields about the walls and driven off the farmers. "And he's fast running out of allies." Monza had left Duke Cantain's head rotting on the walls of Borletta. "You can almost see him sweating from here, the old bastard."

"Shame," said Cosca. "I always liked the man. You should see the galleries in his palace. The greatest collection of art in the world, or so he says. Quite the connoisseur. Kept the best table in Styria too, in his day."

"It shows," said Monza.

"One does wonder how they get him in his saddle."

"Block and tackle," snapped Vitari.

Monza snorted. "Or dig a trench and ride the horse up underneath him."

"What about the other one?" asked Shivers.

"Rogont, Grand Duke of Ospria."

"He looks the part." True enough. Tall and broad-shouldered with a handsome face and a mass of dark curls.

"Looks it." Monza spat again. "But not much more."

"The nephew of my one-time employer, now thankfully deceased, the Duchess Sefeline." Cosca had made his neck bleed with his scratching. "They call him the Prince of Prudence. The Count of Caution. The Duke of Delay. A fine general, by all accounts, but doesn't like to gamble."

"I'd be less charitable," said Monza.

"Few people are less charitable than you."

"He doesn't like to fight."

"No good general likes to fight."

"But every good general has to, from time to time. Rogont's been pitted against Orso throughout the Years of Blood and never fought more than a skirmish. The man's the best withdrawer in Styria."

"Toughest thing to manage, a retreat. Maybe he just hasn't found his moment yet."

Shivers gave a faraway sigh. "We're all of us waiting for our moment."

"He's wasted all his chances now," said Monza. "Once Visserine falls, the way to Puranti is open, and beyond that nothing but Ospria itself, and Orso's crown. No more delays. The sand's run through on caution."

Rogont and Salier passed underneath them. The two men who, along with honest, honourable, dead Duke Cantain, had formed the League of

Eight to defend Styria against Orso's insatiable ambition. Or to frustrate his rightful claims so they could fight among themselves for whatever was left, depending on who you asked. Cosca had a faraway smile on his face as he watched them go. "You live long enough, you see everything ruined. Caprile, a shell of her former glory."

Vitari grinned at Monza. "That was one of yours, no?"

"Musselia most shamefully capitulated to Orso in spite of her impenetrable walls."

Vitari grinned wider. "Wasn't that one of yours too?"

"Borletta fallen," Cosca lamented, "bold Duke Cantain dead."

"Yes," growled Monza, before Vitari could open her mouth.

"The invincible League of Eight has withered to a company of five and will soon dwindle to a party of four, with three of those far from keen on the whole notion."

Monza could just hear Friendly's whisper, "Eight...five...four...three..."

Those three followed now, glittering households trailing them like the wake behind three ducks. Junior partners in the League. Lirozio, the Duke of Puranti, defiant in elaborate armour and even more elaborate moustaches. The young Countess Cotarda of Affoia — a pasty girl whose pale yellow silks weren't helping her complexion, her uncle and first advisor, some said her first lover, hovering close at her shoulder. Patine came last, First Citizen of Nicante — his hair left wild, dressed in sackcloth with a knotted rope for a belt, to show he was no better than the lowest peasant in his care. The rumour was he wore silken undergarments and slept on a golden bed, and with no shortage of company. So much for the humility of the powerful.

Cosca was already looking to the next chapter in the procession of greatness. "By the Fates. Who are these young gods?"

They were a magnificent pair, there was no denying that. They rode identical greys with effortless confidence, arrayed in matching white and gold. Her snowy gown clung to her impossibly tall and slender form and spread out behind her, fretted with glittering thread. His gilded breastplate was polished to a mirror-glare, simple crown set with a single stone so big Monza could almost see its facets glittering a hundred strides distant.

"How incredibly fucking regal," she sneered.

"One can almost smell the majesty," threw in Cosca. "I would kneel if I thought my knees could bear it."

"His August Majesty, the High King of the Union." Vitari's voice was greasy with irony. "And his queen, of course."

"Terez, the Jewel of Talins. She sparkles brightly, no?"

"Orso's daughter," Monza forced out through clenched teeth. "Ario and Foscar's sister. Queen of the Union, and a royal cunt into the bargain."

Even though he was a foreigner on Styrian soil, even though Union ambitions were treated with the greatest suspicion here, even though his wife was Orso's daughter, the crowd found themselves cheering louder for a foreign king than they had for their own geriatric chancellor.

The people far prefer a leader who appears great, Bialoveld wrote, *to one who is.*

"Hardly the most neutral of mediators, you'd think." Cosca puffed his cheeks out thoughtfully. "Bound so tight to Orso and his brood you can hardly see the light between them. Husband, and brother, and son-in-law to Talins?"

"No doubt he considers himself above such earthly considerations." Monza's lip curled as she watched the royal pair approach. It looked as if they'd ridden from the pages of a lurid storybook and out into the drab and slimy city by accident. Wings on their horses were all they needed to complete the fantasy. It was a wonder someone hadn't glued some on. Terez wore a great necklace of huge stones, flashing so brilliantly in the sun they were painful to look at.

Vitari was shaking her head. "How many jewels can you pile on one woman?"

"Not many more without burying the bitch," growled Monza. The ruby that Benna had given her seemed a child's trinket by comparison.

"Jealousy is a terrible thing, ladies." Cosca nudged Friendly in the ribs. "She seems well enough in my eyes, eh, my friend?" The convict said nothing. Cosca tried Shivers instead. "Eh?"

The Northman glanced sideways at Monza, then away. "Don't get the fuss, myself."

"Well, a pretty pair, the two of you! I never met such cold-blooded fighting men. I may be past my prime but I'm nothing like so withered inside as you set of long faces. My heart can still be moved by a young couple in love."

Monza doubted there could be that much fire between them, however they might grin at one another. "Few years ago now, well before she was a queen in anything but her own mind, Benna had a bet with me that he could bed her."

Cosca raised one brow. "Your brother always liked to sow his seed widely, as I recall. The results?"

"Turned out he wasn't her type." It had turned out Monza interested her a great deal more than Benna ever could.

A household even grander than the whole League of Eight had fielded followed respectfully behind the royal couple. A score at least of ladies-in-waiting, each one dripping jewels of her own. A smattering of Lords of Midderland, Angland and Starikland, weighty furs and golden chains about their shoulders. Men-at-arms plodded behind, armour stained with dust from the hooves in front. Each man choking on the dirt of his betters. The ugly truth of power.

"King of the Union, eh?" mused Shivers, watching the royal couple move off. "That there is the most powerful man in the whole Circle of the World?"

Vitari snorted. "That there is the man he stands behind. Everyone kneels to someone. You don't know too much about politics, do you?"

"About what?"

"Lies. The Cripple rules the Union. That boy with all the gold is the mask he wears."

Cosca sighed. "If you looked like the Cripple, I daresay you'd get a mask too…"

Such cheering as there was moved off slowly after the king and queen, and left a sullen silence behind it. Quiet enough that Monza could hear the clattering of the wheels as a gilded carriage rattled down the avenue. Several score of grim guardsmen tramped in practised columns to either side, weapons less well polished than the Union's had been, but better used. A crowd of well-dressed and entirely useless gentlemen followed.

Monza closed her right fist tight, crooked bones shifting. The pain crept across her knuckles, through her hand, up her arm, and she felt her mouth twist into a grim smile.

"There they are," said Cosca.

Ario sat on the right, draped over his cushions, swaying gently with the movement of the carriage, his customary look of lazy contempt smeared across his face. Foscar sat pale and upright beside him, head starting this way and that at every smallest sound. Preening tomcat and eager puppy dog, placed neatly together.

Gobba had been nothing. Mauthis had been just a banker. Orso would scarcely have remarked on the new faces around him when they were replaced. But Ario and Foscar were his sons. His precious flesh. His future. If she could kill them, it would be the next best thing to sticking the blade in Orso's own belly. Her smile grew, imagining his face as they brought him the news.

Your Excellency! Your sons... are dead...

A sudden shriek split the silence. "Murderers! Scum! Orso's bastards!" Some limbs flailed down in the crowd below, someone trying to break through the cordon of soldiers. "You're a curse on Styria!" There was a swell of angry mutterings, a nervous ripple spread out through the onlookers. Sotorius might have called himself neutral, but the people of Sipani had no love for Orso or his brood. They knew when he broke the League of Eight, they'd be next. Some men always want more.

A couple of the mounted gentlemen drew steel. Metal gleamed at the edge of the crowd, there was a thin scream. Foscar was almost standing in the carriage, staring off into the heaving mass of people. Ario pulled him down and slouched back in his seat, careless eyes fixed on his fingernails.

The disturbance was finished. The carriage rattled off, gentlemen finding their formation again, soldiers in the livery of Talins tramping behind. The last of them passed under the roof of the warehouse, and off down the avenue.

"And the show is over," sighed Cosca, pushing himself from the railing and making for the door that led to the stairs.

"I wish it could've gone on forever," sneered Vitari as she turned away.

"One thousand eight hundred and twelve," said Friendly.

Monza stared at him. "What?"

"People. In the parade."

"And?"

"One hundred and five stones in the queen's necklace."

"Did I fucking ask?"

"No." Friendly followed the others back to the stairs.

She stood there alone, frowning into the stiffening wind for a moment longer, glaring off up the avenue as the crowd began to disperse, her fist and her jaw still clenched aching tight.

"Monza." Not alone. When she turned her head, Shivers was looking her in the eye, and from closer than she'd have liked. He spoke as if finding the words was hard work. "Seems like we haven't...I don't know. Since West-port...I just wanted to ask—"

"Best if you don't." She brushed past him and away.

Cooking up Trouble

Nicomo Cosca closed his eyes, licked his smiling lips, breathed in deep through his nose in anticipation and raised the bottle. A drink, a drink, a drink. The familiar promise of the tap of glass against his teeth, the cooling wetness on his tongue, the soothing movement of his throat as he swallowed... if only it hadn't been water.

He had crept from his sweat-soaked bed and down to the kitchen in his clammy nightshirt to hunt for wine. Or any old piss that could make a man drunk. Something to make his dusty bedroom stop shaking like a carriage gone off the road, banish the ants he felt were crawling all over his skin, sponge away his pounding headache, whatever the costs. Shit on change, and Murcatto's vengeance too.

He had hoped that everyone would be in bed, and squirmed with trembling frustration when he had seen Friendly at the stove, making porridge for breakfast. Now, though, he had to admit, he was strangely glad to have found the convict here. There was something almost magical about Friendly's aura of calmness. He had the utter confidence to stay silent and simply not care what anyone thought. Enough to take Cosca a rare step towards calmness himself. Not silence, though. Indeed he had been talking, virtually uninterrupted, since the first light began to creep through the chinks in the shutters and turn to dawn.

"...why the hell am I doing this, Friendly? Fighting, at my age? Fighting! I've never enjoyed that part of the business. And on the same side as that self-congratulating vermin Morveer! A poisoner? Stinking way to kill a man, that. And I am acutely aware, of course, that I am breaking the soldier's first rule."

Friendly cocked one eyebrow a fraction as he slowly stirred the porridge. Cosca strongly suspected the convict knew exactly why he had come here, but if he did, he had better manners than to bring it up. Convicts, in the main, are wonderfully polite. Bad manners can be fatal in prison. "First?" he asked.

"Never fight for the weaker side. Much though I have always despised Duke Orso with a flaming passion, there is a huge and potentially fatal gulf between hating the man and actually doing anything about it." He thumped his fist gently against the tabletop and made the model of Cardotti's rattle gently. "Particularly on behalf of a woman who already betrayed me once..."

Like a homing pigeon drawn endlessly back to its loved and hated cage, his mind was dragged back through nine wasted years to Afieri. He pictured the horses thundering down the long slope, sun flashing behind them, as he had so many times since in a hundred different stinking rooms, and bone-cheap boarding houses, and broken-down slum taverns across the Circle of the World. A fine pretence, he had thought as the cavalry drew closer, smiling through the haze of drink to see it done so well. He remembered the cold dismay as the horsemen did not slow. The sick lurch of horror as they crashed into his own slovenly lines. The mixture of fury, hopelessness, disgust and dizzy drunkenness as he scrambled onto his horse to flee, his ragtag brigade ripped apart around him and his reputation with it. That mixture of fury, hopelessness, disgust and dizzy drunkenness that had followed him as tightly as his shadow ever since. He frowned at the distorted reflection of his wasted face in the bubbly glass of the water bottle.

"The memories of our glories fade," he whispered, "and rot away into half-arsed anecdotes, thin and unconvincing as some other bastard's lies. The failures, the disappointments, the regrets, they stay raw as the moments they happened. A pretty girl's smile, never acted on. A petty wrong we let another take the blame for. A nameless shoulder that knocked us in a crowd and left us stewing for days, for months. Forever." He curled his lip. "This is the stuff the past is made of. The wretched moments that make us what we are."

Friendly stayed silent, and it drew Cosca out better than any coaxing.

"And none more bitter than the moment Monzcarro Murcatto turned on me, eh? I should be taking my revenge on her, instead of helping her take hers. I should kill her, and Andiche, and Sesaria, and Victus, and all my other one-time bastard friends from the Thousand Swords. So what the *shit* am I doing here, Friendly?"

"Talking."

Cosca snorted. "As ever. I always had poor judgement where women were concerned." He barked with sudden laughter. "In truth, I always had dire judgement on every issue. That is what has made my life such a series of thrills." He slapped the bottle down on the table. "Enough penny philosophy! The fact is I need the chance, I need to change and, much more importantly, I desperately need the money." He stood up. "Fuck the past. I am Nicomo Cosca, damn it! I laugh in the face of fear!" He paused for a moment. "And I am going back to bed. My earnest thanks, Master Friendly, you make as fine a conversation as any man I've known."

The convict looked away from his porridge for just a moment. "I've hardly said a word."

"Exactly."

Morveer's morning repast was arranged upon the small table in his small bedchamber, once perhaps an upstairs storeroom in an abandoned warehouse in an insalubrious district of Sipani, a city he had always despised. Refreshment consisted of a misshapen bowl of cold oatmeal, a battered cup of steaming tea, a chipped glass of sour and lukewarm water. Beside them, in a neat row, stood seventeen various vials, bottles, jars and tins, each filled with its own pastes, liquids or powders in a range of colours from clear, to white, through dull buff to the verdant blue of the scorpion oil.

Morveer reluctantly spooned in a mouthful of mush. While he worked it around his mouth with scant relish, he removed the stoppers from the first four containers, slid a glinting needle from its packet, dipped it in the first and pricked the back of his hand. The second, and the same. The third, and the fourth, and he tossed the needle distastefully away. He winced as he watched a tiny bead of blood well from one of the prick-marks, then dug another spoonful from the bowl and sat back, head hanging, while the wave of dizziness swept over him.

"Damn Larync!" Still, it was far preferable that he should endure a tiny dose and a little unpleasantness every morning, than that a large dose, administered by malice or misadventure, should one day burst every blood vessel in his brain.

He forced down another mouthful of salty slop, opened the tin next in line, scooped out a tiny pinch of Mustard Root, held one nostril closed and snorted it up the other. He shivered as the powder burned at his nasal passages, licked at his teeth as his mouth turned unpleasantly numb. He took a mouthful of tea, found it unexpectedly scalding as he swallowed and nearly coughed it back up.

"Damn Mustard Root!" That he had employed it against targets with admirable efficacy on several occasions gave him no extra love for consuming the blasted stuff himself. Quite the opposite. He gargled a mouthful of water in a vain attempt to sluice away the acrid taste, knowing full well that it would be creeping from the back of his nose for hours to come.

He lined up the next six receptacles, unscrewed, uncorked, uncapped them. He could have swallowed their contents one at a time, but long years of such breakfasts had taught him it was better to dispose of them all at once. So he squirted, flicked and dripped the appropriate amounts into his glass of water, mixed them carefully with his spoon, gathered himself and forced it back in three ugly swallows.

Morveer set the glass down, wiped the tears from under his eyes and gave vent to a watery burp. He felt a momentary nudge of nausea, but it swiftly calmed. He had been doing this every morning for twenty years, after all. If he was not accustomed to it by—

He dived for the window, flung the shutters open and thrust his head through just in time to spray his meagre breakfast into the rotten alley beside the warehouse. He gave a bitter groan as he slumped back, dashed the burning snot from his nose and picked his way unsteadily to the washstand. He scooped water from the basin and rubbed it over his face, stared at his reflection in the mirror as moisture dripped from his brows. The worst of it was that he would now have to force more oatmeal into his rebellious guts. One of the many unappreciated sacrifices he was forced to make, simply in order to excel.

The other children at the orphanage had never appreciated his special talents. Nor had his master, the infamous Moumah-yin-Bek. His wife had not appreciated him. His many apprentices had not. And now it seemed his latest employer, also, had no appreciation for his selfless, for his discomforting, for his — no, no, it was no exaggeration — *heroic* efforts on her behalf. That dissolute old wineskin Nicomo Cosca was afforded greater respect than he.

"I am doomed," he murmured disconsolately. "Doomed to give, and give, and get *nothing* in return."

A knock at the door, and Day's voice. "You ready?"

"Soon."

"They're getting everyone together downstairs. We need to be off to Cardotti's. Lay the groundwork. The importance of preparation and all that." It sounded as if she was talking with her mouth full. It would, in fact, have been a surprise had she not been.

"I will catch up with you!" He heard her footsteps moving off. There, at least, was one person with the requisite admiration for his magisterial skills, who rendered him the fitting respect, exceeded his lofty expectations. He was coming to rely on her a great deal, he realised, both practically and emotionally. More than was cautious, perhaps.

But even a man of Morveer's extraordinary talents could not manage everything himself. He gave a long sigh, and turned from the mirror.

The entertainers, or the killers, for they were both, were scattered around the warehouse floor. Twenty-five of them, if Friendly counted himself. The three Gurkish dancers sat crossed-legged — two with their ornate cat-face masks pushed up on their oiled black hair. The last had her mask down, eyes glistening darkly behind the slanted eyeholes, rubbing carefully at a curved dagger. The band were already dressed in smart black jackets and tights striped grey and yellow, their silvered masks in the shape of musical notes, practising a jig they had finally managed to play half-decently.

Shivers stood nearby in a stained leather tunic with balding fur on the shoulders, a big round wooden shield on his arm and a heavy sword in the other hand. Greylock loomed opposite, an iron mask covering his whole face, a great club set with iron studs in his fists. Shivers was talking fast in Northern, showing how he was going to swing his sword, how he wanted Greylock to react, practising the show they would put on.

Barti and Kummel, the acrobats, wore tight-fitting chequered motley, arguing with each other in the tongue of the Union, one of them passionately waving a short stabbing sword. The Incredible Ronco watched from behind a mask painted vivid red, orange and yellow, like dancing flames. Beyond him the three jugglers were filling the air with a cascade of shining knives, flashing and flickering in the half-darkness. Others lounged against crates, sat cross-legged on the floor, capered about, sharpened blades, tinkered with costumes.

Friendly hardly recognised Cosca himself, dressed in a velvet coat heavy with silver embroidery, a tall hat on his head and a long black cane in his hand with a heavy golden knob on the end. The rash on his neck was disguised with powder. His greying moustaches were waxed to twinkling curves, his boots were polished to a glistening shine, his mask was crusted with splinters of sparkling mirror, but his eyes sparkled more.

He swaggered towards Friendly with the smirk of a ringmaster at a circus. "My friend, I hope you are well. My thanks again for your ear this morning."

Friendly nodded, trying not to grin. There was something almost magical about Cosca's aura of good humour. He had the utter confidence to talk, and talk, and know he would be listened to, laughed with, understood. It almost made Friendly want to talk himself.

Cosca held something out. A mask in the shape of a pair of dice, showing double one with eyeholes where the spots should have been. "I hoped you might do me the favour of minding the dice table tonight."

Friendly took the mask from him with a trembling hand. "I would like that very much."

Their mad crew wound through the twisting streets as the morning mists were clearing — down grey alleys, over narrow bridges, through hazy, rotting gardens and along damp tunnels, footfalls hollow in the gloom. The treacherous water was never far off, Shivers wrinkling his nose at the salt stink of the canals.

Half the city was masked and in costume, and it seemed they all had something to celebrate. Folk who weren't invited to the great ball in honour of Sipani's royal visitors had their own revels planned, and a lot of 'em were getting started good and early. Some hadn't gone too wild with their costumes — holiday coats and dresses with a plain mask around their eyes. Some had gone wild, then further still — huge trousers, high shoes, gold and silver faces locked up in animal snarls and madman grins. Put Shivers in mind of the Bloody-Nine's face when he fought in the circle, devil smile spattered with blood. That did nothing for his nerves. Didn't help he was wearing fur and leather like he used to in the North, carrying a heavy sword and shield not much different from ones he'd used in earnest.

A crowd poured past all covered in yellow feathers, masks with great beaks, squawking like a flock of crazy seagulls. That did nothing for his nerves either.

Off in the mist, half-glimpsed round corners and across hazy squares, there were stranger shapes still, their hoots and warbles echoing down the wooden alleyways. Monsters and giants. Made Shivers' palms itch, thinking of the way the Feared rose out of the mist up at Dunbrec, bringing death with him. These were just silly bastards on stilts, of course, but still. You put a mask on a person, something weird happens. Changes the way they act along with the way they look. Sometimes they don't seem like people at all no more, but something else.

Shivers wouldn't have liked the flavour of it even if they hadn't been planning murder. Felt like the city was built on the borders of hell and devils were spilling out into the streets, mixing with the everyday and no one acting like there was much special about it. He had to keep reminding himself that, of all the strange and dangerous-seeming crowds, his was much the strangest and most dangerous they were likely to happen across. If there were devils in the city, he was one of the worst. Wasn't actually that comforting a thought, once it'd taken root.

"This way, my friends!" Cosca led them across a square planted with four clammy, leafless trees and a building loomed up from the gloom — a large wooden building on three sides of a courtyard. The same building that had been sitting on the kitchen table at the warehouse the last few days. Four well-armed guards were frowning around a gate of iron bars, and Cosca sprang smartly up the steps towards them, heels clicking. "A fine morning to you, gentlemen!"

"Cardotti's is closed today," the nearest growled back, "and tonight too."

"Not to us." Cosca took in the mismatched troupe with a sweep of his cane. "We are the entertainers for this evening's private function, selected and hired especially for the purpose by Prince Ario's consort, Carlot dan Eider. Now open that gate quick sharp, we have a great deal of preparation to attend to. In we come, my children, and don't dally! People must be entertained!"

The yard was bigger'n Shivers had been expecting, and a lot more of a disappointment too, since this was supposed to be the best brothel in the world. A stretch of mossy cobbles with a couple of rickety tables and chairs, painted in flaking gilt. Lines were strung from upstairs windows, sheets flapping sluggishly as they dried. A set of wine-barrels were badly stacked in one corner. A bent old man was sweeping with a worn-out broom, a fat woman was giving what might've been some underwear a right thrashing on a washboard. Three skinny women sat about a table, bored. One had an open book in her hand. Another frowned at her nails as she worked 'em with a file. The last slouched in her chair, watching the entertainers file in while she blew smoke from a little clay chagga pipe.

Cosca sighed. "There's nothing more mundane, or less arousing, than a whorehouse in the daytime, eh?"

"Seems not." Shivers watched the jugglers find a space over in one corner and start to unpack their tools, gleaming knives among 'em.

"I've always thought it must be a fine enough life, being a whore. A successful one, at any rate. You get the days off, and when finally you are called upon to work you can get most of it done lying down."

"Not much honour in it," said Shivers.

"Shit at least makes flowers grow. Honour isn't even that useful."

"What happens when you get old, though, and no one wants you no more? Seems to me all you're doing is putting off the despair and leaving a pack of regrets behind you."

Below Cosca's mask, his smile had a sad twist. "That's all any of us are doing, my friend. Every business is the same, and ours is no different. Soldiering, killing, whatever you want to call it. No one wants you when you get old." He strutted past Shivers and into the courtyard, cane flicking backwards and forwards with each stride. "One way or another, we're all of us whores!" He snatched a fancy cloth from a pocket, waved it at the three women as he passed and gave a bow. "Ladies. A most profound honour."

"Silly old cock," Shivers heard one of them mutter in Northern, before she went back to her pipe. The band were already tuning up, making almost as sour a whine as when they were actually playing.

Two tall doorways led from the yard — left to the gaming hall, right to the smoking hall, from those to the two staircases. His eyes crept up the ivy-covered wall, herringbone planks of weather-darkened wood, to the row of narrow windows on the first floor. Rooms for the entertainment of guests. Higher still, to bigger windows of coloured glass, just under the roofline. The Royal Suite, where the most valued visitors were welcomed. Where they planned to welcome Prince Ario and his brother Foscar in a few hours.

"Oy." A touch on his shoulder, and he turned, and stood blinking.

A tall woman stood behind him, a shining black fur draped around her shoulders, long black gloves on her long arms, black hair scraped over to one side and hanging soft and smooth across her white face. Her mask was scattered with chips of crystal, eyes gleaming through the narrow slots and set on him.

"Er..." Shivers had to make himself look away from her chest, the shadow between her tits drawing his eyes like a bear's to a beehive. "Something I can...you know..."

"I don't know, is there?" Her painted lips twisted up at one corner, part sneer and part smile. Seemed as if there was something familiar about that voice. Through the slit in her skirts he could just see the end of a long pink scar on her thigh.

"Monza?" he whispered.

"Who else as fine as this would have anything to say to the likes of you?" She eyed him up and down. "This brings back memories. You look almost as much of a savage as when I first met you."

"That's the idea, I reckon. You look, er..." He struggled for the word.

"Like a whore?"

"A damn pricey one, maybe."

"I'd hate to look a cheap one. I'm headed upstairs, to wait for our guests. All goes well, I'll see you at the warehouse."

"Aye. If all goes well." Shivers' life had a habit of not going well. He frowned up at those stained-glass windows. "You going to be alright?"

"Oh, I can handle Ario. I've been looking forward to it."

"I know, but, I'm just saying...if you need me closer—"

"Stick your tiny mind to keeping things under control down here. Let me worry about me."

"I'm worried enough that I can spare some."

"Thought you were an optimist," she tossed over her shoulder as she walked away.

"Maybe you talked me out of it," he muttered at her back. He didn't like it much when she spoke to him that way, but he liked it a lot better'n when she wouldn't speak to him at all. He saw Greylock glowering at him as he turned, and stabbed an angry finger at the big bastard. "Don't just stand there! Let's get this damn fake circle marked out, 'fore we get old!"

* * *

Monza was a long way from comfortable as she teetered through the gambling hall, Cosca beside her. She wasn't used to the high shoes. She wasn't used to the draught around her legs. Corsets were torture at the best of times, and it hardly helped that this one had two of the bones removed and replaced with long, thin knives, the points up between her shoulder blades and the grips hidden in the small of her back. Her ankles, and her knees, and her hips were already throbbing. The notion of a smoke tickled at the back of her mind, just like always, but she forced it away. She'd endured enough pain, these past few months. A little more was a light price to pay if it got her close to Ario. Close enough to stick a blade in his sneering face. The thought alone put some swagger back into her step.

Carlot dan Eider waited for them at the end of the room, standing with regal superiority between two card tables covered with grey sheets, wearing a red dress fit for an empress of legend.

"Will you look at the two of us?" sneered Monza as she came close. "A general dressed like a whore and a whore dressed like a queen. Everyone's pretending to be someone else tonight."

"That's politics." Ario's mistress frowned over at Cosca. "Who's this?"

"Magister Eider, what a delightful and unexpected honour." The old mercenary bowed as he swept his hat off, exposing his scabrous, sweat-beaded bald patch. "I never dreamed the two of us would meet again."

"You!" Eider stared coldly back at him. "I might have known you'd be caught up in this. I thought you died in Dagoska!"

"So did I, but it turned out I was only very, *very* drunk."

"Not so drunk you couldn't fumble your way to betraying me."

The old mercenary shrugged. "It's always a crying shame when honest people are betrayed. When it happens to the treacherous, though, one cannot avoid a certain sense of... cosmic justice." Cosca grinned from Eider, to Monza, and back. "Three people as loyal as us all on one side? I can hardly wait to see how this turns out."

Monza's guess was that it would turn out bloody. "When will Ario and Foscar get here?"

"When Sotorius' grand ball begins to break up. Midnight, or just before."

"We'll be waiting."

"The antidote," snapped Eider. "I've done my part."

"You'll get it when I get Ario's head on a plate. Not before."

"What if something goes wrong?"

"You'll die along with the rest of us. Better hope things run smoothly."

"What's to stop you from letting me die anyway?"

"My dazzling reputation for fair play and good behaviour."

Unsurprisingly, Eider didn't laugh. "I tried to do the right thing in Dagoska." She jabbed at her chest with a finger. "I tried to do the right thing! I tried to save people! Look what it's cost me!"

"There might be a lesson in there about doing the right thing." Monza shrugged. "I've never had that problem."

"You can joke! Do you know what it's like, to live in fear every moment?"

Monza took a quick step towards her and she shrank back against the wall. "Living in fear?" she snarled, their masks almost scraping together. "Welcome to *my* fucking life! Now quit whining and smile for Ario and the other bastards at the ball tonight!" She dropped her voice to a whisper. "Then bring him to us. Him and his brother. Do as I tell you, and you might still get a happy ending."

She knew that neither one of them thought that very likely. There'd be precious few happy endings to tonight's festivities.

Day turned the drill one last time, bit squealing through wood, then eased it gently free. A chink of light peeped up into the darkness of the attic and brightly illuminated a circular patch of her cheek. She grinned across at Morveer, and he was touched by a sudden bitter-sweet memory of his mother's smiling face by candlelight. "We're through."

Now was hardly the time for nostalgia. He swallowed the upwelling of emotion and crept over, taking the greatest care to set his feet only upon the rafters. A black-clad leg bursting through the ceiling and kicking wildly would no doubt give Orso's sons and their guards some cause for concern. Peering down through the hole, doubtless invisible among the thick mouldings, Morveer could see an opulent stretch of panelled corridor with a rich Gurkish carpet and two high doorways. A crown was carved into the wood above the nearer one.

"*Perfect* positioning, my dear. The Royal Suite." From here they had an unobstructed view of guards stationed by either door. He reached into his jacket, and frowned. He patted at his other pockets, panic stabbing at him.

"Damn it! I forgot my spare blowpipe! What if—"

"I brought two extra, just in case."

Morveer pressed one hand to his chest. "Thank the Fates. No! Damn the Fates. Thank your prudent planning. Where would I be without you?"

Day grinned her innocent little grin. "About where you are now, but with less charming company. Caution first, always."

"*So* true." He dropped his voice back to a whisper. "And here they come." Murcatto and Vitari appeared, both masked, powdered and dressed, or rather undressed, like the many female employees of the establishment. Vitari opened the door beneath the crown and entered. Murcatto glanced briefly up at the ceiling, nodded, then followed her. "They are within. So far all proceeds according to plan." But there was ample time yet for disasters. "The yard?"

Day wriggled on her stomach to the far edge of the attic where roof met rafters, and peered through the holes they had drilled overlooking the building's central courtyard. "Looks as if they're ready to welcome our guests. What now?"

Morveer crept to the minuscule, grubby window and brushed some cobwebs away with the side of one hand. The sun was sinking behind the ragged rooftops, casting a muddy flare over the City of Whispers. "The masked ball should soon be under way at Sotorius' palace." On the far side of the canal, behind Cardotti's House of Leisure, the torches were being lit, lamplight spilling from the windows in the black residences and into the blue evening. Morveer flicked the cobwebs from his fingers with some distaste. "Now we sit here in this mouldering attic, and wait for his Highness Prince Ario to arrive."

Sex and Death

By darkness, Cardotti's House of Leisure was a different world. A fantasy land, as far removed from drab reality as the moon. The gaming hall was lit by three hundred and seventeen flickering candles. Friendly had counted them as they were hoisted up on tinkling chandeliers, bracketed to gleaming sconces, twisted into glittering candlesticks.

The sheets had been flung back from the gaming tables. One of the dealers was shuffling his cards, another was sitting, staring into space, a third carefully stacking up his counters. Friendly counted silently along with him. At the far end of the room an old man was oiling the lucky wheel. Not too lucky for those that played it, by Friendly's assessment of the odds. That was the strange thing about games of chance. The chances were always against the player. You might beat the numbers for a day, but you could never beat them in the end.

Everything shone like hidden treasure, and the women most of all. They were dressed now, and masked, transformed by warm candlelight into things barely human. Long, thin limbs oiled and powdered and dusted with glitter, eyes shining darkly through the eyeholes of gilded masks, lips and nails painted black-red like blood from a fatal wound.

The air was full of strange, frightening smells. There had been no women in Safety, and Friendly felt greatly on edge. He calmed himself by rolling the dice over and over, and adding the scores one upon another. He had reached already four thousand two hundred and...

One of the women swept past, her ruffled dress swishing against the Gurkish carpet, one long, bare leg sliding out from the blackness with each step. Two hundred and...His eyes seemed glued to that leg, his heart beating

201

very fast. Two hundred and ... twenty-six. He jerked his eyes away and back to the dice.

Three and two. Utterly normal, and nothing to worry about. He straightened, and stood waiting. Outside the window, in the courtyard, the guests were beginning to arrive.

Welcome, my friends, welcome to Cardotti's! We have everything a growing boy needs! Dice and cards, games of skill and chance are this way! For those who relish the embrace of mother husk, that door! Wine and spirits on demand. Drink deep, my friends! There will be various entertainments mounted here in the yard throughout the evening! Dancing, juggling, music ... even perhaps a little violence, for those with a taste for blood! As for female companionship, well ... that you will find throughout the building ..."

Men were pouring into the courtyard in a masked and powdered flow. The place was already heaving with expensively tailored bodies, the air thick with their braying chatter. The band were sawing out a merry tune in one corner of the yard, the jugglers flinging a stream of sparkling glasses high into the air in another. Occasionally one of the women would strut through, whisper to someone, lead him away into the building. And upstairs, no doubt. Cosca could not help wondering ... could he be spared for a few moments?

"Quite utterly charmed," he murmured, tipping his hat at a willowy blonde as she swayed past.

"Stick to the guests!" she snarled viciously in his face.

"Only trying to lift the mood, my dear. Only trying to help."

"You want to help, you can suck a prick or two! I've enough to get through!" Someone touched her on the shoulder and she turned, smiling radiantly, took him by the arm and swept away.

"Who are all these bastards?" Shivers, muttering in his ear. "Three or four dozen, weren't we told, a few armed but not keen to fight? There must be twice that many in already!"

Cosca grinned as he clapped the Northman on the shoulder. "I know! Isn't it a thrill when you throw a party and you get more guests than you expected? Somebody's popular!"

Shivers did not look amused. "I don't reckon it's us! How do we keep control of all this?"

"What makes you think I have the answers? In my experience, life rarely turns out the way you expect. We must bend with the circumstances, and simply do our best."

"Maybe six guards, weren't we told? So who are they?" The Northman jerked his head towards a grim-looking knot of men gathered in one corner, all with polished breastplates over their padded black jackets, with serious masks of plain steel, serious swords and long knives at their hips, serious frowns on their chiselled jaws. Their eyes darted carefully about the yard as though looking for threats.

"Hmmm," mused Cosca. "I was wondering the same thing."

"Wondering?" The Northman's big fist was uncomfortably tight round Cosca's arm. "When does wondering turn into shitting yourself?"

"I've often wondered." Cosca peeled the hand away. "But it's a funny thing. I simply don't get scared." He made off through the crowd, clapping backs, calling for drinks, pointing out attractions, spreading good humour wherever he went. He was in his element, now. Vice, and high living, but danger too.

He feared old age, failure, betrayal and looking a fool. Yet he never feared before a fight. Cosca's happiest moments had been spent waiting for battles to begin. Watching the countless Gurkish march upon the walls of Dagoska. Watching the forces of Sipani deploy before the Battle of the Isles. Scrambling onto his horse by moonlight when the enemy sallied from the walls of Muris. Danger was the thing he most enjoyed. Worries for the future, purged. Failures of the past, erased. Only the glorious now remained. He closed his eyes and sucked in air, felt it tingling pleasantly in his chest, heard the excited babbling of the guests. He scarcely even felt the need for a drink anymore.

He snapped his eyes open to see two men stepping through the gate, others scraping away to make grovelling room for them. His Highness Prince Ario was dressed in a scarlet coat, silken cuffs drooping from his embroidered sleeves in a manner that implied he would never have to grip anything for himself. A spray of multicoloured feathers sprouted from the top of his golden mask, thrashing like a peacock's tail as he looked about him, unimpressed.

"Your Highness!" Cosca swept off his hat and bowed low. "We are truly, *truly* honoured by your presence."

"Indeed you are," said Ario. "And by the presence of my brother." He wafted a languid hand at the man beside him, dressed all in spotless white with a mask in the form of half a golden sun, somewhat twitchy and reluctant-seeming, Cosca rather thought. Foscar, no doubt, though he had grown a beard which very much suited him. "Not to mention that of our mutual friend, Master Sulfur."

"Alas, I cannot stay." A nondescript fellow had slipped in behind the two brothers. He had a curly head of hair, a simple suit and a faint smile. "So much to do. Never the slightest peace, eh?" And he grinned at Cosca. Inside the holes of his plain mask, his eyes were different colours: one blue, one green. "I must to Talins tonight, and speak to your father. We cannot allow the Gurkish a free hand."

"Of course not. Damn those Gurkish bastards. Good journey to you, Sulfur." Ario gave the slightest bow of his head.

"Good journey," growled Foscar, as Sulfur turned for the gate.

Cosca jammed his hat back on his head. "Well, your two honours are certainly most welcome! Please, enjoy the entertainments! Everything is at your disposal!" He sidled closer, flashing his most mischievous grin. "The top floor of the building has been reserved for you and your brother. Your Highness will find, I rather think, a particularly surprising diversion in the Royal Suite."

"There, brother. Let us see if, in due course, we can divert you from your cares." Ario frowned towards the band. "By the heavens, could that woman not have found some better music?"

The thickening throng parted to let the brothers pass. Several sneering gentlemen followed in their wake, as well as four more of the grim men with their swords and armour. Cosca frowned after their shining backplates as they stepped through the door into the gaming hall.

Nicomo Cosca felt no fear, that was a fact. But a measure of sober concern at all these well-armed men seemed only prudent. Monza had asked for control, after all. He hopped over to the entrance and touched one of the guards outside upon his arm. "No more in tonight. We are full." He shut the gate in the man's surprised face, turned the key in the lock and slipped it into his waistcoat pocket. Prince Ario's friend Master Sulfur would have the honour of being the last man to pass through the front gate tonight.

He flung one arm up at the band. "Something livelier lads, strike up a tune! We are here to entertain!"

Morveer knelt, hunched in the darkness of the attic, peering from the eaves of the roof into the courtyard far below. Men in ostentatious attire formed knots that swelled, dissolved, shifted and flowed in and out through the two doors that led into the building. They glittered and gleamed in pools of lamplight. Ribald exclamations and hushed chatter, poor music and good-natured laughter floated up through the night, but Morveer was not inclined to celebrate.

"Why so many?" he whispered. "We were anticipating less than half this number. Something... is *awry*."

A gout of incandescent flame went up into the frigid night and there was an eruption of clapping. That imbecile Ronco, endangering his own existence and that of every other person in the yard. Morveer slowly shook his head. If that was a good idea then he was the Emperor of—

Day hissed at him, and he fumbled his way back across the rafters, old wood creaking gently, and applied his eye to one of the holes. "Someone's coming."

A group of eight persons emerged from the stairway, all of them masked. Four were evidently guards, armoured in highly polished breastplates. Two were even more evidently women employed by Cardotti's. It was the final two men that were of interest to Morveer.

"Ario and Foscar," whispered Day.

"So it would *undoubtedly* appear." Orso's sons exchanged a brief word while their guards took up positions flanking the two doors. Then Ario bowed low, his snigger echoing faintly around the attic. He swaggered down the corridor to the second door, one of the women on each arm, leaving his brother to approach the Royal Suite.

Morveer frowned. "Something is most seriously *awry*."

It was an idiot's idea of what a king's bedchamber might look like. Everything was overpatterned, gaudy with gold and silver thread. The bed was a monstrous four-poster suffocated with swags of crimson silk. An obese cabinet burst with coloured liquor bottles. The ceiling was crusted with shadowy mouldings and an enormous, tinkling chandelier that hung too

205

low. The fireplace was carved like a pair of naked women holding up a plate of fruit, all in green marble.

There was a huge canvas in a gleaming frame on one wall — a woman with an improbable bosom bathing in a stream, and seeming to enjoy it a lot more than was likely. Monza never had understood why getting out a tit or two made for a better painting. But painters seemed to think it did, so tits is what you got.

"That bloody music's giving me a headache," Vitari grumbled, hooking a finger under her corset and scratching at her side.

Monza jerked her head sideways. "That fucking bed's giving me a headache. Especially against that wallpaper." A particularly vile shade of azure blue and turquoise stripes with gilt stars splashed across them.

"Enough to drive a woman to smoking." Vitari prodded at the ivory pipe lying on the marbled table beside the bed, a lump of husk in a cut-glass jar beside it. Monza hardly needed it drawn to her attention. For the last hour her eyes had rarely been off it.

"Mind on the job," she snapped, jerking her eyes away and back towards the door.

"Always." Vitari hitched up her skirt. "Not easy with these bloody clothes. How does anyone—"

"Shhh." Footsteps, coming down the corridor outside.

"Our guests. You ready?"

The grips of the two knives jabbed at the small of Monza's back as she shifted her hips. "Bit late for second thoughts, no?"

"Unless you've decided you'd rather fuck them instead."

"I think we'll stick to murder." Monza slid her right hand up the window frame in what she hoped was an alluring pose. Her heart was thumping, the blood surging painfully loud in her ears.

The door creaked ever so slowly open, and a man stepped through into the room. He was tall and dressed all in white, his golden mask in the shape of half a rising sun. He had an impeccably trimmed beard, which failed to disguise a ragged scar down his chin. Monza blinked at him. He wasn't Ario. He wasn't even Foscar.

"Shit," she heard Vitari breathe.

Recognition hit Monza like spit in the face. It wasn't Orso's son, but his son-in-law. None other than the great peacemaker himself, his August Majesty, the High King of the Union.

* * *

Ready?" asked Cosca.

Shivers cleared his throat one more time. It had felt like there was something stuck in it ever since he'd walked into this damn place. "Bit late for second thoughts, no?"

The old mercenary's mad grin spread even wider. "Unless you've decided you'd rather fuck them instead. Gentlemen! Ladies! Your attention, please!" The band stopped playing and the violin began to hack out a single, sawing note. It didn't make Shivers feel much better.

Cosca jabbed with his cane, clearing the guests out of the circle they'd marked in the middle of the yard. "Step back, my friends, for you are in the gravest danger! One of the great moments of history is about to be acted out before your disbelieving eyes!"

"When do I get a fuck?" someone called, to ragged laughter.

Cosca leaped forwards, nearly took the man's eye out on the end of his cane. "Once someone dies!" The drum had joined in now, whack, whack, whack. Folk pressed round the circle by flickering torchlight. A ring of masks — birds and beasts, soldiers and clowns, leering skulls and grinning devils. Men's faces underneath — drunk, bored, angry, curious. At the back, Barti and Kummel teetered on each other's shoulders, whichever was on top clapping along with the drumbeats.

"For your education, edification and enjoyment..." Shivers hadn't a clue what that meant. "Cardotti's House of Leisure presents to you..." He took a rough breath, hefting sword and shield, and pushed through into the circle. "The infamous duel between Fenris the Feared..." Cosca flicked his cane out towards Greylock as he lumbered into the circle from the other side. "And Logen Ninefingers!"

"He's got ten fingers!" someone called, making a ripple of drunken laughter.

Shivers didn't join 'em. Greylock might've been a long way less frightening than the real Feared had been, but he was a long way clear of a comforting sight still, big as a house with that mask of black iron over his face, left side of his shaved head and his great left arm painted blue. His club looked awful heavy and very dangerous, right then, clutched in those big fists. Shivers had to keep telling himself they were on the same side. Just pretending was all. Just pretending.

"You gentlemen would be well advised to make room!" shouted Cosca, and the three Gurkish dancers pranced round the edge of the circle, black-cat masks over their black faces, herding the guests towards the walls. "There may be blood!"

"There'd better be!" Another wave of laughter. "I didn't come here to watch a pair of idiots dance with each other!"

The onlookers whooped, whistled, booed. Mostly booed. Shivers somehow doubted his plan — hop around the circle for a few minutes flailing at the air, then stab Greylock between his arm and his side while the big man burst a bladder of pig blood — was going to get these fuckers clapping. He remembered the real duel, outside the walls of Carleon with the fate of all the North hanging on the outcome. The cold morning, the breath smoking on the air, the blood in the circle. The Carls gathered round the edge, shaking their shields, screaming and roaring. He wondered what those men would've made of this nonsense. Life took you down some strange paths, alright.

"Begin!" shouted Cosca, springing back into the crowd.

Greylock gave a mighty roar and came charging forwards, swinging the club and swinging it hard. Gave Shivers the bastard of a shock. He got his shield up in time, but the weight of the blow knocked him clean over, sliding across the ground on his arse, left arm struck numb. He sprawled out, all tangled up with his sword, nicked his eyebrow on the edge. Lucky not to get the point in his eye. He rolled, the club crashing down where he'd lain a moment before and sending stone chips flying. Even as he was clambering up, Greylock was at him again, looking like he meant deadly business, and Shivers had to scramble away with all the dignity of a cat in a wolf-pen. He didn't remember this being what they discussed. Seemed the big man meant to give these bastards a show to remember after all.

"Kill him!" Someone laughed.

"Give us some blood, you idiots!"

Shivers tightened his hand round the grip of the sword. He suddenly had a bad feeling. Even worse'n before.

Rolling dice normally made Friendly feel calm, but not tonight. He had a bad feeling. Even worse than before. He watched them tumble, clatter, spin, their clicking seeming to dig at his clammy skin, and come to rest.

"Two and four," he said.

"We see the numbers!" snapped the man with the mask like a crescent moon. "Damn dice hate me!" He tossed them angrily over, bouncing against the polished wood.

Friendly frowned as he scooped them up and rolled them gently back. "Five and three. House wins."

"It seems to be making a habit of it," growled the one with the mask like a ship, and some of their friends muttered angrily. They were all of them drunk. Drunk and stupid. The house always makes a habit of winning, which is why it hosts games of chance in the first place. But it was hardly Friendly's job to educate them on that point. Someone at the far end of the room cried out with shrill delight as the lucky wheel brought up their number. A few of the card players clapped with mild disdain.

"Bloody dice." Crescent Moon slurped from his glass of wine as Friendly carefully gathered up the counters and added them to his own swelling stacks. He was having trouble breathing, the air was so thick with strange smells — perfume, and sweat, and wine, and smoke. He realised his mouth was hanging open, and snapped it shut.

The King of the Union looked from Monza, to Vitari, and back — handsome, regal and most extremely unwelcome. Monza realised her mouth was hanging open, and snapped it shut.

"I mean no disrespect, but one of you will be more than adequate and I have...always had a weakness for dark hair." He gestured to the door. "I hope I will not offend by asking you to leave us. I will make sure you are paid."

"How generous." Vitari glanced sideways and Monza gave her the tiniest shrug, her mind flipping around like a frog in hot water as it sought desperately for a way clear of this self-made trap. Vitari pushed herself away from the wall and strutted to the door. She brushed the front of the king's coat with the back of her hand on the way past. "Curse my red-haired mother," she sneered. The door clicked shut.

"A most..." The king cleared his throat. "Pleasing room."

"You're easily pleased."

He snorted with laughter. "My wife would not say so."

"Few wives say good things about their husbands. That's why they come to us."

"You misunderstand. I have her blessing. My wife is expecting our third child and therefore…well, that hardly interests you."

"I'll seem interested whatever you say. That's what I'm paid for."

"Of course." The king rubbed his hands somewhat nervously together. "Perhaps a drink."

She nodded towards the cabinet. "There they are."

"Do you need one?"

"No."

"No, of course, why would you?" Wine gurgled from the bottle. "I suppose this is nothing new for you."

"No." Though in fact it was hard to remember the last time she'd been disguised as a whore in a room with a king. She had two choices. Bed him, or murder him. Neither one held much appeal. Killing Ario would make trouble enough. To kill a king — even Orso's son-in-law — would be asking for a great deal more.

When faced with two dark paths, Stolicus wrote, *a general should always choose the lighter.* She doubted these were quite the circumstances he'd had in mind, but that changed nothing. She slid one hand around the nearest bedpost, lowered herself until she was sitting awkwardly on the garish covers. Then her eye fell on the husk pipe.

When faced with two dark paths, Farans wrote, *a general should always find a third.*

"You seem nervous," she murmured.

The king had made it as far as the foot of the bed. "I must confess it's been a long time since I visited…a place like this one."

"Something to calm you, then." She turned her back on him before he had the chance to say no, and began to fill the pipe. It didn't take her long to make it ready. She did it every night, after all.

"Husk? I'm not sure that I —"

"You need your wife's blessing for this too?" She held it out to him.

"Of course not."

She stood, lifting the lamp, holding his eye, and set the flame to the bowl. His first breath in he coughed out straight away. The second not much later. The third he managed to hold, then blow out in a plume of white smoke.

"Your turn," he croaked, pressing the pipe back into her hand as he sank down on the bed, smoke still curling up from the bowl and tickling her nose.

"I..." Oh, how she wanted it. She was trembling with her need for it. "I..." Right there, right in her hand. But this was no time to indulge herself. She needed to stay in control.

His mouth curled up in a gormless grin. "Whose blessing do you need?" he croaked. "I promise I won't tell a...oh."

She was already setting the flame to the grey-brown flakes, sucking the smoke in deep, feeling it burn at her lungs.

"Damn boots," the king was saying as he tried to drag his highly polished footwear off. "Don't bloody fit me. You pay...a hundred marks...for some boots...you expect them to—" One flew off and clattered into the wall, leaving a bright trace behind it. Monza was finding it hard to stand up.

"Again." She held the pipe out.

"Well...where's the harm?" Monza stared at the lamp flame as it flared up. Shimmering, shining, all the colours of a hoard of priceless jewels, the crumbs of husk glowing orange, turning from sweet brown to blazing red to used-up grey ash. The king breathed a long plume of sweet-smelling smoke in her face and she closed her eyes and sucked it in. Her head was full of it, swelling with it, ready to burst open.

"Oh."

"Eh?"

He stared around. "That is...rather..."

"Yes. Yes it is." The room was glowing. The pains in her legs had become pleasurable tickles. Her bare skin fizzed and tingled. She sank down, mattress creaking under her rump. Just her and the King of the Union, perched on an ugly bed in a whorehouse. What could've been more comfortable?

The king licked lazily at his lips. "My wife. The queen. You know. Did I mention that? Queen. She does not always—"

"Your wife likes women," Monza found she'd said. Then she snorted with laughter, and had to wipe some snot off her lip. "She likes them a lot."

The king's eyes were pink inside the eyeholes of his mask. They crawled lazily over her face. "Women? What were we talking of?" He leaned forwards. "I don't feel...nervous...anymore." He slid one clumsy hand up the side of her leg. "I think..." he muttered, working his tongue around his mouth. "I...think..." His eyes rolled up and he flopped back on the bed, arms outspread. His head tipped slowly sideways, mask skewing across his face, and he was still, faint snoring echoing in Monza's ears.

He looked so peaceful there. She wanted to lie down. She was always thinking, thinking, worrying, thinking. She needed to rest. She deserved to. But there was something nagging at her — something she needed to do first. What was it? She drifted to her feet, swaying uncertainly.

Ario.

"Uh. That's it." She left his Majesty sprawled across the bed and made for the door, the room tipping one way and then the other, trying to catch her out. Tricky bastard. She bent down and tore one of the high shoes off, tottered sideways and nearly fell. She flung the other away and it floated gently through the air, like an anchor sinking through water. She had to force her eyes open wide as she looked at the door, because there was a mosaic of blue glass between her and the world, candle flames beyond it leaving long, blinding smears across her sight.

Morveer nodded to Day, and she nodded back, a deeper black shape crouched in the fizzing darkness of the attic, the slightest strip of blue light across her grin. Behind her, the joists, the laths, the rafters were all black outlines touched down the edges with the faintest glow. "I will deal with the pair beside the Royal Suite," he whispered. "You...take the others."

"Done, but when?"

When was the question of paramount importance. He put his eye to the hole, blowpipe in one hand, fingertips of the other rubbing nervously against his thumb. The door to the Royal Suite opened and Vitari emerged from between the guards. She frowned up, then walked away down the corridor. There was no sign of Murcatto, no sign of Foscar, no further sign of anything. This was not part of the plan, of that Morveer was sure. He had still to kill the guards, of course, he had been paid to do so and always followed through on a contracted task. That was one thing among many that separated him from the obscene likes of Nicomo Cosca. But when, when, when...

Morveer frowned. He was sure he could hear the vague sound of someone chewing. "Are you eating?"

"Just a bun."

"Well stop it! We are at work, for pity's sake, and I am trying to think! Is an *iota* of professionalism too much to ask?"

Time stretched out to the vague accompaniment of the incompetent musicians down in the courtyard, but with the exception of the guards rocking gently from side to side, there was no further sign of movement. Morveer slowly shook his head. In this case, it seemed, as in so many, one moment was much like another. He breathed in deep, lifted the pipe to his lips, taking aim on the furthest of his allotted pair—

The door to Ario's chamber banged open. The two women emerged, one still adjusting her skirts. Morveer held his breath, cheeks puffed out. They pulled the door shut then made off down the corridor. One of the guards said something to the other, and he laughed. There was the most discreet of hisses as Morveer discharged his pipe, and the laughter was cut short.

"Ah!" The nearest guard pressed one hand to his scalp.

"What?"

"Something... I don't know, stung me."

"Stung you? What would've—" It was the other guard's turn to rub at his head. "Bloody hell!"

The first had found the needle in his hair, and now held it up to the light. "A needle." He fumbled for his sword with a clumsy hand, lurched back against the wall and slid down onto his backside. "I feel all..."

The second guard took an unsteady stride into the corridor, reached up at nothing, then pitched over on his face, arm outstretched. Morveer allowed himself the slightest nod of satisfaction, then crept over to Day, crouching over two of the holes with her blowpipe in her hand.

"Success?" he asked.

"Of course." She held the bun in the other, and now took a bite from it. Through the hole Morveer saw the two guards beside Ario's suite slumped motionless.

"Fine work, my dear. But that, *alas*, is all the work with which we were trusted." He began to gather up their equipment.

"Should we stay, see how it goes?"

"I see no reason so to do. The best we can hope for is that men will die, and that I have witnessed before. Frequently. Take it from me. One death is *much* like another. You have the rope?"

"Of course."

"Never too soon to secure the means of escape."

"Caution first, always."

"*Precisely* so."

Day uncoiled the cord from her pack and made one end of it fast around a heavy joist. She lifted one foot and kicked the little window from its frame. Morveer heard the sound of it splashing down into the canal behind the building.

"Most neatly done. *What* would I do without you?"

D ie!" And Greylock came charging across the circle with that great lump of wood high over his head. Shivers gasped along with the crowd, only just scrambled clear in time, felt the wind of it ripping at his face. He caught the big man in a clumsy hug and they tottered together round the outside of the circle.

"What the fuck are you after?" Shivers hissed in his ear.

"Vengeance!" Greylock dealt him a knee in the side then flung him off.

Shivers stumbled away, finding his balance, picking his brains for some slight he'd given the man. "Vengeance? For what, you mad bastard?"

"For Uffrith!" He slapped his great foot down, feinting, and Shivers hopped back, peering over the top of his shield.

"Eh? No one got killed there!"

"You sure?"

"A couple o' men down on the docks, but—"

"My brother! No more'n fourteen years old!"

"I had no part o' that, you great turd! Black Dow did them killings!"

"Black Dow ain't before me now, and I swore to my mother I'd make someone pay. You'd a big enough part for me to knock it out o' you, fucker!" Shivers gave a girlish kind of squeak as he ducked back from another great sweep, heard men cheering around him, as keen for blood as the watchers might be at a real duel.

Vengeance, then. A double-edged blade if ever there was one. You never could tell when that bastard was going to cut you. Shivers stood, blood creeping down the side of his face from a knock he took just before, and all he could think was how fucking unfair it was. He'd tried to do the right thing, just the way his brother had always told him he should. He'd tried to be a better man. Hadn't he? This was where good intentions put you. Right in the shit.

"But I just...I done my best!" he bellowed in Northern.

Greylock sent spit spinning through the mouth-hole of his mask. "So did my brother!" He came on, club coming down in a blur. Shivers ducked round it, jerked his shield up hard and smashed the rim under the big man's jaw, sent him staggering back, spluttering blood.

Shivers still had his pride. That much he'd kept for himself. He was damned if he was going to be put in the mud by some great thick bastard who couldn't tell a good man from a bad. He felt the fury boiling up his throat, the way it used to back home in the North, when the battle was joined and he was in the thick of it.

"Vengeance, is it?" he screamed. "I'll show you fucking vengeance!"

Cosca winced as Shivers caught a blow on his shield and staggered sideways. He snarled something extremely angry-sounding in Northern, lashed at the air with his sword and missed Greylock by no more than the thickness of a finger, almost chopping deep into the onlookers on the backswing and making them shuffle nervously away.

"Amazing stuff!" someone frothed. "It looks almost real! I must hire them for my daughter's wedding..."

It was true, the Northmen were mounting a good show. Rather too good. They circled warily, eyes fixed on each other, one of them occasionally jabbing forwards with foot or weapon. The furious, concentrated caution of men who knew the slightest slip could mean death. Shivers had his hair matted to the side of his face with blood. Greylock had a long scratch through the leather on his chest and a cut under his chin where the shield-rim had cracked him.

The onlookers had stopped yelling obscenities, cooing and gasping instead, eyes locked hungrily on the fighters, caught between wanting to press forwards to see, and press back when the weapons were swung. They felt something on the air in the courtyard. Like the weight of the sky before a great storm. Genuine, murderous rage.

The band had more than got the trick of the battle music, the fiddle stabbing as Shivers slashed with the sword, drum booming whenever Greylock heaved his great club, adding significantly to the near-unbearable tension.

Quite clearly they were trying to kill each other, and Cosca had not the ghost of a notion how to stop them. He winced as the club crashed into Shivers' shield again and nearly knocked him off his feet. He glanced worriedly up towards the stained-glass windows high above the yard.

Something told him they were going to leave more than two corpses behind tonight.

The corpses of the two guards lay beside the door. One was sitting up, staring at the ceiling. The other lay on his face. They hardly looked dead. Just sleeping. Monza slapped her own face, tried to shake the husk out of her head. The door wobbled towards her and a hand in a black glove reached out and grabbed the knob. Damn it. She needed to do that. She stood there, swaying, waiting for the hand to let go.

"Oh." It was her hand. She turned it and the door came suddenly open. She fell through, almost pitched on her face. The room swam around her, walls flowing, melting, streaming waterfalls. Flames crackled, sparkling crystal in a fireplace. One window was open and music floated in, men shouting from down below. She could see the sounds, happy smears curling in around the glass, reaching across the changing space between, tickling at her ears.

Prince Ario lay on the bed, stark naked, body white on the rumpled cover, legs and arms spread out wide. His head turned towards her, the spray of feathers on his mask making long shadows creep across the glowing wall behind.

"More?" he murmured, taking a lazy swallow from a wine bottle.

"I hope we haven't...tired you out...already." Monza's own voice seemed to boom out of a faraway bucket as she padded towards the bed, a ship tossing on a choppy red sea of soft carpet.

"I daresay I can rise to the occasion," said Ario, fumbling with his cock. "You seem to have the advantage of me, though." He waved a finger at her. "Too many clothes."

"Uh." She shrugged the fur from her shoulders and it slithered to the floor.

"Gloves off." He swatted with his hand. "Don't care for them."

"Nor me." She pulled them off, tickling at her forearms. Ario was staring at her right hand. She held it up in front of her eyes, blinked at it. There was a long, pink scar down her forearm, the hand a blotchy claw, palm squashed, fingers twisted, little one sticking out stubbornly straight.

"Ah." She'd forgotten about that.

"A crippled hand." Ario wriggled eagerly down the bed towards her, his cock and the feathers sprouting from his head waggling from side to side with the movements of his hips. "How terribly...exotic."

"Isn't it?" The memory of Gobba's boot crunching down across it flashed through her mind and snatched her into the cold moment. She felt herself smile. "No need for this." She took hold of the feathers and plucked the mask from his head, tossed it away into the corner.

Ario grinned at her, pink marks around his eyes where the mask had sat. She felt the glow of the husk leaking from her mind as she stared into his face. She saw him stabbing her brother in the neck, heaving him off the terrace, complaining at being cut. And here he was, before her now. Orso's heir.

"How rude." He clambered up from the bed. "I must teach you a lesson."

"Or maybe I'll teach you one."

He came closer, so close that she could smell his sweat. "Bold, to bandy words with me. Very bold." He reached out and ran one finger up her arm. "Few women are as bold as that." Closer, and he slipped his other hand into the slit in her skirts, up her thigh, squeezing at her arse. "I almost feel as if I know you."

Monza took hold of the corner of her mask with her ruined right hand as Ario drew her closer still. "Know me?" She slid her other fist gently behind her back, found the grip of one of the knives. "Of course you know me."

She pulled her mask away. Ario's smile lingered for a moment longer as his eyes flickered over her face. Then they went staring wide.

"Somebody—!"

A hundred scales on this next throw!" Crescent Moon bellowed, holding the dice up high. The room grew quiet as people turned to watch.

"A hundred scales." It meant nothing to Friendly. None of it was his money, and money only interested him as far as counting it went. Losses and gains were exactly the same.

Crescent Moon rattled the dice in his hand. "Come on, you shits!" The man flung them recklessly across the table, bouncing and tumbling.

"Five and six."

"Hah!" Moon's friends whooped, chuckled, slapped him on the back as though he had achieved something fine by throwing one number instead of another.

The one with the mask like a ship threw his arms in the air. "Have that!"

The one with the fox mask made an obscene gesture.

The candles seemed to have grown uncomfortably bright. Too bright to count. The room was very hot, close, crowded. Friendly's shirt was sticking to him as he scooped up the dice and tossed them gently back. A few gasps round the table. "Five and six. House wins." People often forgot that any one score is just as likely as any other, even the same score. So it was not entirely a shock that Crescent Moon lost his sense of perspective.

"You cheating bastard!"

Friendly frowned. In Safety he would have cut a man who spoke to him like that. He would have had to, so that others would have known not to try. He would have started cutting him and not stopped. But they were not in Safety now, they were outside. Control, he had been told. He made himself forget the warm handle of his cleaver, pressing into his side. Control. He only shrugged. "Five and six. The dice don't lie."

Crescent Moon grabbed hold of Friendly's wrist as he began to sweep up the counters. He leaned forwards and poked him in the chest with a drunken finger. "I think your dice are loaded."

Friendly felt his face go slack, the breath hardly moving in his throat, it had constricted so painfully tight. He could feel every drop of sweat tickling at his forehead, at his back, at his scalp. A calm, cold, utterly unbearable rage seared through every part of him. "You think my dice are what?" he could barely whisper.

Poke, poke, poke. "Your dice are liars."

"My dice . . . are *what*?" Friendly's cleaver split the crescent mask in half and the skull underneath it wide open. His knife stabbed the man with the ship over his face through his gaping mouth and the point emerged from the back of his head. Friendly stabbed him again, and again, squelch, squelch, the grip of the blade turning slippery. A woman gave a long, shrill scream.

Friendly was vaguely aware that everyone in the hall was gaping at him, four times three times four of them, or more, or less. He flung the dice table over, sending glasses, counters, coins flying. The man with the fox mask was staring, eyes wide inside the eyeholes, spatters of dark brains across his pale cheek.

Friendly leaned forwards into his face. "Apologise!" he roared at the very top of his lungs. "Apologise to my fucking dice!"

* * *

Somebody—!"

Ario's cry turned to a breathy wheeze of an in-breath. He stared down, and she did too. Her knife had gone in the hollow where his thigh met his body, just beside his wilting cock, and was buried in him to the grip, blood running out all over her fist. For the shortest moment he gave a hideous, high-pitched shriek, then the point of Monza's other knife punched in under his ear and slid out of the far side of his neck.

Ario stayed there, eyes bulging, one hand plucking weakly at her bare shoulder. The other crept trembling up and fumbled at the handle of the blade. Blood leaked out of him thick and black, oozing between his fingers, bubbling down his legs, running down his chest in dark, treacly streaks, leaving his pale skin all smeared and speckled with red. His mouth yawned, but his scream was nothing but a soft farting sound, breath squelching around the wet steel in his throat. He tottered back, his other arm fishing at the air, and Monza watched him, fascinated, his white face leaving a bright trace across her vision.

"Three dead," she whispered. "Four left."

His bloody thighs slapped against the windowsill and he fell, head smashing against the stained glass and knocking the window wide. He tumbled through and out into the night.

The club came over, a blow that could've smashed in Shivers' skull like an egg. But it was tired, sloppy, left Greylock's side open. Shivers ducked it, already spinning, snarling as he whipped the heavy sword round. It cut into the big man's blue-painted forearm with a meaty thump, hacked it off clean, carried on through and chopped deep into the side of his stomach. Blood showered from the stump and into the faces of the onlookers. The club clattered to the cobbles, hand and wrist along with it. Someone gave a thin shriek. Someone else laughed.

"How'd they do that?"

Then Greylock started squealing like he'd caught his foot in a door. "Fuck! It hurts! Ah! Ah! What's my...by the—"

He reached around with the one hand he had left, fumbling at the gash in his side, dark mush bulging out. He lurched forwards onto one knee, head tipping back, and started to scream. Until Shivers' sword hit his mask right in the forehead and made a clang that cut his roar off dead, left a huge dent between the eyeholes. The big man crashed over on his back, his boots flew up in the air, then thumped down.

And that was the end of the evening's entertainment.

The band spluttered out a last few wobbly notes, then the music died. Apart from some vague yelling leaking from the gaming hall, the yard was silent. Shivers stared down at Greylock's corpse, blood bubbling out from beneath the stoved-in mask. His fury had suddenly melted, leaving him only with a painful arm, a scalp prickling with cold sweat and a healthy sense of creeping horror.

"Why do things like this always happen to me?"

"Because you're a bad, bad man," said Cosca, peering over his shoulder.

Shivers felt a shadow fall across his face. He was just looking up when a naked body crashed down headfirst into the circle from above, showering the already gaping crowd with blood.

That's Entertainment

All at once, things got confused.

"The king!" someone squealed, for no reason that made any sense. The blood-spattered space that had been the circle was suddenly full of stumbling bodies, running to nowhere. Everyone was bawling, wailing, shouting. Men's voices and women's, a noise fit to deafen the dead. Someone shoved at Shivers' shield and he shoved back on an instinct, sent them sprawling over Greylock's corpse.

"It's Ario!"

"Murder!" A guest started to draw his sword, and one of the band stepped calmly forwards and smashed his skull apart with a sharp blow of a mace.

More screams. Steel rang and grated. Shivers saw one of the Gurkish dancers slit a man's belly open with a curved knife, saw him fumble his sword as he vomited blood, stab the man behind him in the leg. There was a crash of tinkling glass and a flailing body came flying through one of the windows of the gambling hall. Panic and madness spread like fire in a dry field.

One of the jugglers was flinging knives, flying metal clattering about the yard, thudding into flesh and wood, just as deadly to friends as enemies. Someone grabbed hold of Shivers' sword arm and he elbowed them in the face, lifted his sword to hack at them and realised it was Morc, the pipe player, blood running from his nose. There was a loud whomp and a glare of orange through the heaving bodies. The screaming went up a notch, a mindless chorus.

"Fire!"

"Water!"

"Out of my way!"

"The juggler! Get the—"

"Help! Help!"

"Knights of the Body, to me! To me!"

"Where's the prince? Where's Ario?"

"Somebody help!"

"Back!" shouted Cosca.

"Eh?" Shivers called at him, not sure who was howling at who. A knife flickered past in the darkness, rattled away between the thrashing bodies.

"Back!" Cosca sidestepped a sword-thrust, whipped his cane around, a long, thin blade sliding free of it, ran a man through the neck with a swift jab. He slashed at someone else, missed and almost stabbed Shivers as he lurched past. One of Ario's gentlemen, mask like a squares board, nearly caught Cosca with a sword. Gurpi loomed up behind and smashed his lute over the man's head. The wooden body shattered, the axe blade inside split his shoulder right down to his chest and crushed his butchered wreckage into the cobbles.

Another surge of flame went up, people stumbled away, shoving madly, a ripple through the straining crowd. They suddenly parted and the Incredible Ronco came thrashing straight at Shivers, white fire wreathing him like some devil burst out of hell. Shivers tottered back, smashed him away with his shield. Ronco reeled into the wall, bounced off it and into another, showering globs of liquid fire, folk scrambling away, steel stabbing about at random. The flames spread up the dry ivy, first a crackle, then a roar, leaped to the wooden wall, bathing the heaving courtyard in wild, flickering light. A window shattered. The locked gates clattered as men clutched at 'em, screaming to be let out. Shivers beat the flames on his shield against the wall. Ronco was rolling on the ground, still burning, making a thin screech like a boiling kettle, the flames casting a crazy glare across the bobbing masks of guests and entertainers — twisted monsters' faces, everywhere Shivers looked.

There was no time to make sense of any of it. All that mattered was who lived and who died, and he'd no mind to join the second lot. He backed off, keeping close to the wall, shoving men away with his scorched shield as they grabbed at him.

A couple of the guards in breastplates were forcing their way through the press. One of 'em chopped Barti or Kummel down with his sword, hard to say which, caught one of Ario's gentlemen on the backswing and took part of his skull off. He staggered round, squealing, one hand clapped to his head, blood running out between his fingers, over his golden mask and down his face in black streaks. Barti or Kummel, whichever was left, stabbed a knife into the top of the swordsman's head, right up to the hilt, then hooted as the point of a blade slid out of the front of his chest.

Another armoured guard shouldered his way towards Shivers, sword held high, shouting something, sounded like the Union tongue. Didn't much matter where he was from, he had a mind for killing, that was clear, and Shivers didn't plan on giving him the first blow. He snarled as he swung, full-blooded, but the guard lurched back out of the way and Shivers' sword chopped into something else with a meaty thwack. A woman's chest, just happened to be stumbling past. She fell against the wall, scream turning to a gurgle as she slid down through the ivy, mask half-torn off, one eye staring at him, blood bubbling from her nose, from her mouth, pouring down her white neck.

The courtyard was a place of madness, lit by spreading flames. A fragment of a night-time battlefield, but a battle with no sides, no purpose, no winners. Bodies were kicked around under the panicking crowd — living, dead, split and bloodied. Gurpi was flailing, all tangled up with the wreckage of his lute, not even able to swing his axe for the broken strings and bits of wood. While Shivers watched, one of the guards hacked him down, sent blood showering black in the firelight.

"The smoking hall!" hissed Cosca, chopping someone out of their way with his sword. Shivers thought it might've been one of the jugglers, there was no way of telling. He dived through the open doorway after the old mercenary, together they started to heave the door shut. A hand came through and got caught against the frame, clutching wildly. Shivers bashed at it with the pommel of his sword until it slithered back trembling through the gap. Cosca wrestled the door closed and the latch dropped, then he tore the key around and flung it jingling away across the boards.

"What now?"

The old mercenary stared at him, eyes wild. "What makes you think I've got the fucking answers?"

The hall was long and low, scattered with cushions, split up by billowing curtains, lit by guttering lamps, smelling of sweet husk-smoke. The sounds of violence out in the yard were muffled. Someone snored. Someone else giggled. A man sat against the wall opposite, a beaked mask and a broad smile on his face, pipe dangling from his hand.

"What about the others?" hissed Shivers, squinting into the half-light.

"I think we've reached the point of every man for himself, don't you?" Cosca was busy trying to drag an old chest in front of the door, already shuddering from blows outside. "Where's Monza?"

"They'll get in by the gaming hall, no? Won't they—" Something crashed against a window and it burst inwards, spraying twinkling glass into the room. Shivers shuffled further into the murk, heart thumping hard as a hammer at the inside of his skull. "Cosca?" Nought but smoke and darkness, flickering light through the windows, flickering lamps on tables. He got tangled with a curtain, tore it down, fabric ripping from the rail above. Smoke was scratching at his throat. Smoke from the husk in here, smoke from the fire out there, more and more. The air was hazy with it.

He could hear voices. Crashing and screaming on his left like a bull going mad in the burning building. "My dice! My dice! Bastards!"

"Help!"

"Somebody send for...somebody!"

"Upstairs! The king! Upstairs!"

Someone was beating at a door with something heavy, he could hear the wood shuddering under the blows. A figure loomed at him. "Excuse me, could you—" Shivers smashed him in the face with his shield and knocked him flying, stumbled past, a vague idea he was after the stairs. Monza was upstairs. Top floor. He heard the door burst open behind him, shifting light, brown smoke, writhing figures began to pour through into the smoking hall, blades shining in the gloom. One of 'em pointed at him. "There! There he is!"

Shivers snatched a lamp up in his shield hand and flung it, missed the man at the front and hit the wall. It burst apart, showering burning oil across a curtain. People scattered, one of them screaming, arm on fire. Shivers ran the other way, deeper into the building, half-falling as cushions and tables tripped him in the darkness. He felt a hand grab his ankle and hacked at it with his sword. He staggered through the choking shadows to a doorway, a faint chink of light down the edge, shouldered it open, sure he'd get stabbed between the shoulder blades any moment.

He started up a set of spiral steps two at a time, panting with effort, legs burning as he climbed up towards the rooms where guests were entertained. Or fucked, depending how you looked at it. A panelled corridor met the stairway and a man came barrelling out of it just as Shivers got there, almost ran straight into him. They ended up staring into each other's masks. One of the bastards with the polished breastplates. He clutched at Shivers' shoulder with his free hand, showing his teeth, tried to pull his sword back for a thrust but got his elbow caught on the wall behind.

Shivers butted him in the face on an instinct, felt the man's nose crunch under his forehead. No room for the sword. Shivers chopped him in the hip with the edge of his shield, gave him a knee in the fruits that made him whoop, then swung him round and bundled him down the stairs, watched him flop over and over around the corner, sword clattering away. He kept going, upwards, not stopping for breath, starting to cough.

He could hear more shouting behind him, crashing, screaming. "The king! Protect the king!" He staggered on, one step at a time now, sword aching heavy in his hand, shield dangling from his limp arm. He wondered who was still alive. He wondered about the woman he'd killed in the courtyard, the hand he'd smashed in the doorway. He tottered into the hallway at the top of the stairs, wafting his shield in front of his face to try and clear the haze.

There were bodies here, black shapes sprawled under the wide windows. Maybe she was dead. Anyone could've been dead. Everyone. He heard coughing. Smoke rolled around near the ceiling, pouring into the corridor over the tops of the doors. He squinted into it. A woman, bent over, bare arms stretched out in front of her, black hair hanging.

Monza.

He ran towards her, trying to hold his breath, keep down low under the smoke. He caught her round the waist, she grabbed his neck, snarling. She had blood spotted across her face, soot around her nose and her mouth.

"Fire," she croaked at him.

"Over here." He turned back the way he came, and stopped still.

Down at the end of the corridor, two men with breastplates were getting to the top of the steps. One of them pointed at him.

"Shit." He remembered the model. Cardotti's backed onto the Eighth Canal. He lifted one boot and kicked the window wide. A long way down below, beyond the blowing smoke, water shifted, busy with the reflections of fire.

"My own worst fucking enemy," he forced through his gritted teeth.

"Ario's dead," Monza drawled in his ear. Shivers dropped his sword, grabbed hold of her. "What're you—" He threw her out of the window,

225

heard her choking shriek as she started falling. He tore his shield from his arm and flung it at the two men as they ran down the corridor towards him, climbed up on the window ledge and jumped.

Smoke washed and billowed around him. The rushing air tore at his hair, his stinging eyes, his open mouth. He hit the water feet first and it dragged him down. Bubbles rushed in the blackness. The cold gripped him, almost forced him to suck in a breath of water. He hardly knew which way was up, flailing about, struck his head on something.

A hand grabbed him under the jaw, pulled at it, his face burst into the night and he gasped in cold air and cold water. He was dragged along through the canal, choking on the smoke he'd breathed, on the water he'd breathed, on the stink of the rotten water he was breathing now. He thrashed and jerked, wheezing, gasping.

"Still, you bastard!"

A shadow fell across his face, his shoulder scraped on stone. He fished around and his hand closed on an old iron ring, enough to hold his head above the water while he coughed up a lungful of canal. Monza was pressed to him, treading water, arm around his back, holding him tight. Her quick, scared, desperate breathing and his own hissed out together, merged with the slapping of the water and echoed under the arch of a bridge.

Beyond its black curve he could see the back of Cardotti's House of Leisure, the fire shooting high into the sky above the buildings around it, flames crackling and roaring, showers of sparks fizzing and popping, ash and splinters flying, smoke pouring up in a black-brown cloud. Light flickered and danced on the water and across one half of Monza's pale face — red, orange, yellow, the colours of fire.

"Shit," he hissed, shivering at the cold, at the aching lag-end of battle, at what he'd done back there in the madness. He felt tears burning at his eyes. Couldn't stop himself crying. He started to shake, to sob, only just managing to keep his grip on the ring. "Shit...shit...shit..."

"Shhh." Monza's hand clapped over his mouth. Footsteps snapped against the road above, shouted voices echoing back and forth. They shrank back together, pressing against the slimy stonework. "Shhh." Few hours ago he'd have given a lot to be pressed up against her like this. Somehow, right then, he didn't feel much in the way of romance, though.

"What happened?" she whispered.

Shivers couldn't even look at her. "I've no fucking idea."

What Happened

Nicomo Cosca, infamous soldier of fortune, skulked in the shadows and watched the warehouse. All seemed quiet, shutters dark in their rotting frames. No vengeful mob, no clamour of guards. His instincts told him simply to walk off into the night, and pay no further mind to Monzcarro Murcatto and her mad quest for vengeance. But he needed her money, and his instincts had never been worth a runny shit. He shrank back into the doorway as a woman in a mask ran down the lane, skirts held up, giggling. A man chased after her. "Come back! Kiss me, you bitch!" Their footsteps clattered away.

Cosca strutted across the street as if he owned it, into the alley behind the warehouse, then plastered himself to the wall. He sidled up to the back door. He slid the sword from his cane with a faint ring of steel, blade coldly glittering in the night. The knob turned, the door crept open. He eased his way through into the darkness—

"Far enough." Metal kissed his neck. Cosca opened his hand and let the sword clatter to the boards.

"I am undone."

"Cosca, that you?" The blade came away. Vitari, pressed into the shadows behind the door.

"Shylo, you changed? I much preferred the clothes you had at Cardotti's. More...ladylike."

"Huh." She pushed past him and down the dark passageway. "That underwear, such as it was, was torture."

"I shall have to content myself with seeing it in my dreams."

"What happened at Cardotti's?"

"What happened?" Cosca bent over stiffly and fished his sword up between two fingers. "I believe the word 'bloodbath' would fit the circumstances. Then it caught fire. I must confess...I made a quick exit." He was, in truth, disgusted with himself for having fled and saved his own worthless skin. But the decided habits of a whole life, especially a wasted life, were hard to change. "Why don't you tell me what happened?"

"The King of the Union happened."

"The what?" Cosca remembered the man in white, with the mask like the rising sun. The man who had not looked very much like Foscar. "Aaaaaah. That would explain all the guards."

"What about your entertainers?"

"Hugely expendable. None of them have shown their faces here?"

Vitari shook her head. "Not so far."

"Then, I would guess, they are largely, if not entirely, expended. So it always is with mercenaries. Easily hired, even more easily discharged and never missed once they are gone."

Friendly sat in the darkened kitchen, hunched over the table, rolling his dice gently in the light from a single lamp. A heavy and extremely threatening cleaver gleamed on the wood beside it.

Cosca came close, pointing to the dice. "Three and four, eh?"

"Three and four."

"Seven. A most ordinary score."

"Average."

"May I?"

Friendly looked sharply up at him. "Yes."

Cosca gathered the dice and gently rolled them back. "Six. You win."

"That's my problem."

"Really? Losing is mine. What happened? No trouble in the gaming hall?"

"Some."

There was a long streak of half-dried blood across the convict's neck, dark in the lamplight. "You've got something...just here," said Cosca.

Friendly wiped it off, looked down at his red-brown fingertips with all the emotion of an empty sink. "Blood."

"Yes. A lot of blood, tonight." Now Cosca was back to something approaching safety, the giddy rush of danger was starting to recede, and all the old regrets crowded in behind it. His hands were shaking again.

A drink, a drink, a drink. He wandered through the doorway into the warehouse.

"Ah! The ringmaster for tonight's circus of murder!" Morveer leaned against the rail of the stairs, sneering down, Day not far behind, her dangling hands slowly peeling an orange.

"Our poisoners! I'm sorry to see you made it out alive. What happened?"

Morveer's lip curled still further. "Our allotted role was to remove the guards on the top floor of the building. That we accomplished with *absolute* speed and secrecy. We were not asked to remain in the building thereafter. Indeed we were ordered not to. Our employer does not entirely trust us. She was concerned that there be no *indiscriminate slaughter.*"

Cosca shrugged. "Slaughter, by its very definition, would not appear to discriminate."

"Either way, your responsibility is over. I doubt anyone will object if you take this, now."

Morveer flicked his wrist and something sparkled in the darkness. Cosca snatched it from the air on an instinct. A metal flask, liquid sloshing inside. Just like the one he used to carry. The one he sold...where was it now? That sweet union of cold metal and strong liquor lapped at his memory, brought the spit flooding into his dry mouth. A drink, a drink, a drink—

He was halfway through unscrewing the cap before he stopped himself. "It would seem a sensible life lesson never to swallow gifts from poisoners."

"The only poison in there is the same kind you have been swallowing for years. The same kind you will never stop swallowing."

Cosca lifted the flask. "Cheers." He upended it and let the spirit inside spatter over the warehouse floor, then tossed it clattering away into a corner. He made sure he noted where it ended up, though, in case there was a trickle left inside. "No sign of our employer?" he called to Morveer. "Or her Northern puppy?"

"None. We should give some consideration to the possibility that there may never be any."

"He's right." Vitari was a black shape in the lamplit doorway to the kitchen. "Chances are good they're dead. What do we do then?"

Day looked at her fingernails. "I, for one, will weep a river."

Morveer had other plans. "We should have a scheme for dividing such money as Murcatto has here—"

"No," said Cosca, for some reason intensely irritated at the thought. "I say we wait."

"This place is not safe. One of the entertainers could have been captured by the authorities, could even now be divulging its location."

"Exciting, isn't it? I say we wait."

"Wait if you please, but I—"

Cosca whipped his knife out in one smooth motion. The blade whirred shining through the darkness and thumped, vibrating gently, into the wood no more than a foot or two from Morveer's face. "A little gift of my own."

The poisoner raised one eyebrow at it. "I do not appreciate drunks throwing knives at me. What if your aim had been off?"

Cosca grinned. "It was. We wait."

"For a man of *notoriously* fickle loyalties, I find your attachment to a woman who once betrayed you...perplexing."

"So do I. But I've always been an unpredictable bastard. Perhaps I'm changing my ways. Perhaps I've made a solemn vow to be sober, loyal and diligent in all my dealings from now on."

Vitari snorted. "That'll be the day."

"And how long do we wait?" demanded Morveer.

"I suppose you'll know when I say you can leave."

"And suppose...I choose...to leave before?"

"You're nothing like as clever as you think you are." Cosca held his eye. "But you're cleverer than that."

"Everyone be calm," snarled Vitari, in the most uncalming voice imaginable.

"I don't take orders from you, you pickled *remnant*!"

"Maybe I need to teach you how—"

The warehouse door banged open and two figures burst through. Cosca whipped his sword from his stick, Vitari's chain rattled, Day had produced a small flatbow from somewhere and levelled it at the doorway. But the new arrivals were not representatives of the authorities. They were none other than Shivers and Monza, both wet through, stained with dirt and soot and panting for breath as though they had been pursued through half the streets of Sipani. Perhaps they had.

Cosca grinned. "You need only mention her name and up she springs! Master Morveer was just now discussing how we should divide your money if it turned out you were burned to a cinder in the shell of Cardotti's."

"Sorry to disappoint you," she croaked.

Morveer gave Cosca a deadly glare. "I am by *no* means disappointed, I assure you. I have a vested interested in your survival to the tune of many thousands of scales. I was simply considering…a contingency."

"Best to be prepared," said Day, lowering the bow and sucking the juice from her orange.

"Caution first, *always*."

Monza lurched across the warehouse floor, one bare foot dragging, jaw muscles clenched tight against evident pain. Her clothes, which had not left too much to the imagination in the first instance, were badly ripped. Cosca could see a long red scar up one thin thigh, more across her shoulder, down her forearm, pale and prickly with gooseflesh. Her right hand was a mottled, bony claw, pressed against her hip as though to keep it out of sight.

He felt an unexpected stab of dismay at the sight of those marks of violence. Like seeing a painting one had always admired wilfully defaced. A painting one had secretly hoped to own, perhaps? Was that it? He shrugged his coat off and held it out to her as she came past him. She ignored it.

"Do we gather you are less than satisfied with tonight's endeavours?" asked Morveer.

"We got Ario. It could've been worse. I need some dry clothes. We leave Sipani right away." She limped up the steps, torn skirts dragging in the dust behind her, and shouldered past Morveer. Shivers swung the warehouse door shut and leaned against it, head back.

"That is one stone-hearted bitch," muttered Vitari as she watched her go.

Cosca pursed his lips. "I always said she had a devil in her. But of the two, her brother was the truly ruthless one."

"Huh." Vitari turned back into the kitchen. "It was a compliment."

Monza managed to shut the door and make it a few steps into her room before her insides clenched up as if she'd been punched in the guts. She retched so hard she could hardly breathe, a long string of bitter drool dangling from her lip and spattering against the boards.

She shivered with revulsion, started trying to twist her way out of the whore's clothes. Her flesh crept at the touch of them, her guts cramped at the rotten canal stink of them. Numb fingers wrestled with hooks and eyes, clawed at buttons and buckles. Gasping and grunting, she tore the damp rags off and flung them away.

She caught sight of herself in the mirror, in the light of the one lamp. Hunched like a beggar, shivering like a drunk, red scars standing out from white skin, black hair hanging lank and loose. A drowned corpse, standing. Just about.

You're a dream. A vision. The very Goddess of War!

She was doubled over by another stab of sickness, stumbled to her chest and started dragging fresh clothes on with trembling hands. The shirt had been one of Benna's. For a moment it was almost like having his arms around her. As close as she could ever get, now.

She sat on the bed, her own arms clamped around herself, bare feet pressed together, rocking back and forth, willing the warmth to spread. Another rush of nausea dragged her up and had her spitting bile. Once it passed she shoved Benna's shirt down behind her belt, bent to drag her boots on, grimacing at the cold aches through her legs.

She delved her hands into the washbasin and threw cold water on her face, started to scrape away the traces of paint and powder, the smears of blood and soot, digging at her ears, at her hair, at her nose.

"Monza!" Cosca's voice outside the door. "We have a distinguished visitor."

She pulled the leather glove back over her twisted joke of a hand, winced as she worked her bent fingers into it. She took a long, shuddering breath, then slid the Calvez out from under her mattress and into the clasp on her belt. It made her feel better just having it there. She pulled the door open.

Carlot dan Eider stood in the middle of the warehouse floor, gold thread gleaming in her red coat, watching Monza as she came down the steps, trying not to limp, Cosca following after.

"What in hell happened? Cardotti's is still burning! The city's in uproar!"

"What happened?" barked Monza. "Why don't you tell me what happened? His August fucking Majesty was where Foscar was supposed to be!"

The black scab on Eider's neck shifted as she swallowed. "Foscar wouldn't go. He said he had a headache. So Ario took his brother-in-law along in his place."

"And he happened to bring a dozen Knights of the Body with him," said Cosca. "The king's own bodyguards. As well as a far greater volume of guests than anyone anticipated. The results were not happy. For anyone."

"Ario?" muttered Eider, face pale.

Monza stared into her eyes. "Deader than *fuck*."

"The king?" she almost whispered.

"Alive. When I left him. But the building did tend to burn down after that. Maybe they got him out."

Eider looked at the floor, rubbing at one temple with her gloved hand. "I'd hoped you might fail."

"No such luck."

"There will be consequences now. You do a thing like this, there are consequences. Some you see coming, and some you don't." She held out one hand. "My antidote."

"There isn't one."

"I kept my side of the bargain!"

"There was no poison. Just a jab with a dry needle. You're free."

Eider barked despairing laughter at her. "Free? Orso won't rest until he's fed me to his dogs! Perhaps I can keep ahead of him, but I'll never keep ahead of the Cripple. I let him down, and put his precious king in harm's way. He won't let that pass. He never lets anything pass. Are you happy now?"

"You talk as if there was a choice. Orso and the rest die, or I do, and that's all. Happy isn't part of the sum." Monza shrugged as she turned away. "You'd better start running."

"I sent a letter."

She stopped, then turned back. "Letter?"

"Earlier today. To Grand Duke Orso. It was written in some passion, so I forget exactly what was said. The name Shylo Vitari was mentioned, though. And the name Nicomo Cosca."

Cosca waved it away with one hand. "I've always had a lot of powerful enemies. I consider it a point of pride. Listing them makes excellent dinner conversation."

Eider turned her sneer from the old mercenary back to Monza. "Those two names, and the name of Murcatto as well."

Monza frowned. "Murcatto."

"How much of a fool do you take me for? I know who you are, and now Orso will know too. That you're alive, and that you killed his son, and that you had help. A petty revenge, perhaps, but the best I could manage."

"Revenge?" Monza nodded slowly. "Well. Everyone's at it. It would've been better if you hadn't done that." The Calvez rattled gently as she rested her hand on its hilt.

"Why, will you kill me for it? Hah! I'm good as dead already!"

"Then why should I bother? You're not on my list. You can go." Eider stared at her for a moment, mouth slightly open as though she was about to speak, then she snapped it shut and turned for the door. "Aren't you going to wish me luck?"

"What?"

"The way I see it, your best hope now is that I kill Orso."

Ario's one-time mistress paused in the doorway. "Some fucking chance of that!" And she was gone.

IV

VISSERINE

"War without fire is
as worthless as sausages
without mustard"

Henry V

The Thousand Swords fought for Ospria against Muris. They fought for Muris against Sipani. They fought for Sipani against Muris, then for Ospria again. Between contracts, they sacked Oprile on a whim. A month later, judging they had perhaps not been thorough enough, they sacked it again, and left it in smouldering ruins. They fought for everyone against no one, and no one against everyone, and all the while they hardly did any fighting at all.

But robbery and plunder, arson and pillage, rape and extortion, yes.

Nicomo Cosca liked to surround himself with the curious that he might seem strange and romantic. A nineteen-year-old swordswoman inseparable from her younger brother seemed to qualify, so he kept them close. At first he found them interesting. Then he found them useful. Then he found them indispensable.

He and Monza would spar together in the cold mornings — the flicker and scrape of steel, the hiss and smoke of snatched breath. He was stronger, and she quicker, and so they were well matched. They would taunt each other, and spit at each other, and laugh. Men from the company would gather to watch them, laugh to see their captain bested by a girl half his age, often as not. Everyone laughed, except Benna. He was no swordsman.

He had a trick for numbers, though, and he took charge of the company's books, and then the buying of the stocks, and then the management and resale of the booty and the distribution of the proceeds. He made money for everyone, and had an easy manner, and soon was well loved.

Monza was a quick study. She learned what Stolicus wrote, and Verturio, and Bialoveld, and Farans. She learned all that Nicomo Cosca had to teach. She learned tactics and strategy, manoeuvre and logistics, how to read the ground and how to read an enemy. She learned by watching, then she learned by doing. She learned all the arts and all the sciences that were of use to the soldier.

"You have a devil in you," Cosca told her, when he was drunk, which was not rarely. She saved his life at Muris, then he saved hers. Everyone laughed, except Benna, again. He was no lifesaver.

Old Sazine died of an arrow, and the captains of the companies that made up the Thousand Swords voted Nicomo Cosca to the captain general's chair. Monza and Benna went with him. She carried Cosca's orders. Then she told him what his orders should be. Then she gave orders while he was passed out drunk and pretended they were his. Then she stopped pretending they were his, and no one minded because her orders were better than his would have been, even had he been sober.

As the months passed and turned to years, he was sober less and less. The only orders he gave were in the tavern. The only sparring he did was with a bottle. When the Thousand Swords had picked one part of the country clean and it came time to move on, Monza would search for him through the taverns, and the smoke-houses, and the brothels, and drag him back.

She hated to do it, and Benna hated to watch her do it, but Cosca had given them a home and they owed him, so she did it still. As they wended their way to camp in the dusk, him stumbling under the weight of drink, and her stumbling under the weight of him, he would whisper in her ear.

"Monza, Monza. What would I do without you?"

Vengeance, Then

General Ganmark's highly polished cavalry boots click-clicked against the highly polished floor. The chamberlain's shoes squeak-squeaked along behind. The echoes of both snap-snapped from the glittering walls and around the great, hollow space, their hurry setting lazy dust motes swirling through bars of light. Shenkt's own soft work boots, scuffed and supple from long use, made no sound whatsoever.

"Upon entering the presence of his Excellency," the chamberlain's words frothed busily out, "you advance towards him, without undue speed, looking neither right nor left, your eyes tilted down towards the ground and at no point meeting those of his Excellency. You stop at the white line upon the carpet. Not before the line and under no circumstances beyond it but *precisely* at the line. You then kneel—"

"I do not kneel," said Shenkt.

The chamberlain's head rotated towards him like an affronted owl's. "Only the heads of state of foreign powers are excepted! Everyone must—"

"I do not kneel."

The chamberlain gasped with outrage, but Ganmark snapped over him. "For pity's sake! Duke Orso's son and heir has been murdered! His Excellency does not give a damn whether a man kneels if he can bring him vengeance. Kneel or not, as it suits you." Two white-liveried guardsmen lifted their crossed halberds to let them pass, and Ganmark shoved the double doors wide open.

The hall beyond was dauntingly cavernous, opulent, grand. Fit for the throne room of the most powerful man in Styria. But Shenkt had stood in greater rooms, before greater men, and had no awe left in him. A thin red carpet stretched away down the mosaic floor, a white line at its lonely end. A high dais rose beyond it, a dozen men in full armour standing guard in front. Upon the dais was a golden chair. Within the chair was Grand Duke Orso of Talins. He was dressed all in black, but his frown was blacker yet.

A strange and sinister selection of people, three score or more, of all races, sizes and shapes, knelt before Orso and his retinue in a wide arc. They carried no weapons now, but Shenkt guessed they usually carried many. He knew some few of them by sight. Killers. Assassins. Hunters of men. Persons in his profession, if the whitewasher could be said to be in the same profession as the master painter.

He advanced towards the dais, without undue speed, looking neither right nor left. He passed through the half-circle of assorted murderers and stopped precisely at the line. He watched General Ganmark stride past the guards and up the steps to the throne, lean to whisper in Orso's ear while the chamberlain took up a disapproving pose at his other elbow.

The grand duke stared at Shenkt for a long moment and Shenkt stared back, the hall cloaked all the while in that oppressive silence that only great spaces can produce. "So this is he. Why is he not kneeling?"

"He does not kneel, apparently," said Ganmark.

"Everyone else kneels. What makes you special?"

"Nothing," said Shenkt.

"But you do not kneel."

"I used to. Long ago. No more."

Orso's eyes narrowed. "And what if a man tried to make you?"

"Some have tried."

"And?"

"And I do not kneel."

"Stand, then. My son is dead."

"You have my sorrow."

"You do not sound sorrowful."

"He was not my son."

The chamberlain nearly choked on his tongue, but Orso's sunken eyes did not deviate. "You like to speak the truth, I see. Blunt counsel is a valuable thing to powerful men. You come to me with the highest recommendations."

Shenkt said nothing.

"That business in Keln. I understand that was your work. All of that, your work alone. It is said that the things that were left could hardly be called corpses."

Shenkt said nothing.

"You do not confirm it."

Shenkt stared into Duke Orso's face, and said nothing.

"You do not deny it, though."

More nothing.

"I like a tight-lipped man. A man who says little to his friends will say less than nothing to his enemies."

Silence.

"My son is murdered. Thrown from the window of a brothel like rubbish. Many of his friends and associates, my citizens, were also killed. My son-in-law, his Majesty the King of the Union, no less, only just escaped the burning building with his life. Sotorius, the half-corpse Chancellor of Sipani who was their host, wrings his hands and tells me he can do nothing. I am betrayed. I am bereaved. I am…*embarrassed*. Me!" he screamed suddenly, making the chamber ring, and every person in it flinch.

Every person except Shenkt. "Vengeance, then."

"Vengeance!" Orso smashed the arm of his chair with his fist. "Swift and terrible."

"Swift I cannot promise. Terrible — yes."

"Then let it be slow, and grinding, and merciless."

"It may be necessary to cause some harm to your subjects and their property."

"Whatever it takes. Bring me their heads. Every man, woman or child involved in this, to the slightest degree. Whatever is necessary. Bring me their heads."

"Their heads, then."

"What will be your advance?"

"Nothing."

"Not even—"

"If I complete the job, you will pay me one hundred thousand scales for the head of the ringleader, and twenty thousand for each assistant to a maximum of one quarter of a million. That is my price."

"A very high one!" squeaked the chamberlain. "What will you do with so much money?"

"I will count it and laugh, while considering how a rich man need not answer the questions of idiots. You will find no employer, anywhere, unsatisfied with my work." Shenkt moved his eyes slowly to the half-circle of scum at his back. "You can pay less to lesser men, if you please."

"I will," said Orso. "If one of them should find the killers first."

"I would accept no other arrangement, your Excellency."

"Good," growled the duke. "Go, then. All of you, go! Bring…me… revenge!"

"You are dismissed!" screeched the chamberlain. There was a rustling, rattling, clattering as the assassins rose to leave the great chamber. Shenkt turned and walked back down the carpet towards the great doors, without undue speed, looking neither right nor left.

One of the killers blocked his path, a dark-skinned man of average height but wide as a door, lean slabs of muscle showing through the gap in his brightly coloured shirt. His thick lip curled. "You are Shenkt? I expected more."

"Pray to whatever god you believe in that you never see more."

"I do not pray."

Shenkt leaned close, and whispered in his ear. "I advise you to start."

Although a large room by most standards, General Ganmark's study felt cluttered. An oversized bust of Juvens frowned balefully from above the fireplace, his stony bald spot reflected in a magnificent mirror of coloured Visserine glass. Two monumental vases loomed either side of the desk almost to shoulder height. The walls were crowded with canvases in gilded frames, two of them positively vast. Fine paintings. Far too fine to be squeezed.

"A most impressive collection," said Shenkt.

"That one is by Coliere. It would have burned in the mansion in which I found it. And these two are Nasurins, that by Orhus." Ganmark pointed them out with precise jabs of his forefinger. "His early period, but still. Those vases were made as tribute to the first Emperor of Gurkhul, many hundreds of years ago, and somehow found their way to a rich man's house outside Caprile."

"And from there to here."

"I try to rescue what I can," said Ganmark. "Perhaps when the Years of Blood end, Styria will still have some few treasures worth keeping."

"Or you will."

"Better I have them than the flames. The campaign season begins, and I will be away to Visserine in the morning, to take the city under siege. Skirmishes, sacks and burnings. March and counter-march. Famine and pestilence, naturally. Maim and murder, of course. All with the awful randomness of a stroke from the heavens. Collective punishment. Of everyone, for nothing. War, Shenkt, war. And to think I once dreamed of being an honourable man. Of doing good."

"We all dream of that."

The general raised one eyebrow. "Even you?"

"Even me." Shenkt slid out his knife. A Gurkish butcher's sickle, small but sharp as fury.

"I wish you joy of it, then. The best I can do is strive to keep the waste to the merely... epic."

"These are wasteful times." Shenkt took the little lump of wood from his pocket, dog's head already roughly carved into the front.

"Aren't they all? Wine? It is from Cantain's own cellar."

"No."

Shenkt worked carefully with his knife while the general filled his own glass, woodchips scattering across the floor between his boots, the hindquarters of the dog slowly taking shape. Hardly a work of art like those around him, but it would serve. There was something calming in the regular movements of the curved blade, in the gentle fluttering down of the shavings.

Ganmark leaned against the mantel, drew out the poker and gave the fire a few unnecessary jabs. "You have heard of Monzcarro Murcatto?"

"The captain general of the Thousand Swords. A most successful soldier. I heard she was dead."

"Can you keep a secret, Shenkt?"

"I keep many hundreds."

"Of course you do. Of course." He took a long breath. "Duke Orso ordered her death. Hers and her brother's. Her victories had made her popular in Talins. Too popular. His Excellency feared she might usurp his throne, as mercenaries can do. You are not surprised?"

"I have seen every kind of death, and every kind of motive."

"Of course you have." Ganmark frowned at the fire. "This was not a good death."

"None of them are."

"Still. This was not a good one. Two months ago Duke Orso's bodyguard vanished. No great surprise, he was a foolish man, took little care over his safety, was prone to vice and bad company and had made many enemies. I thought nothing of it."

"And?"

"A month later, the duke's banker was poisoned in Westport, along with half his staff. This was a different matter. He took a very great deal of care over his safety. To poison him was a task of the greatest difficulty, carried out with a formidable professionalism and an exceptional lack of mercy. But he dabbled widely in the politics of Styria, and the politics of Styria is a fatal game with few merciful players."

"True."

"Valint and Balk themselves suspected a long enmity with Gurkish rivals might be the motive."

"Valint and Balk."

"You are familiar with the institution?"

Shenkt paused. "I believe they employed me once. Go on."

"But now Prince Ario, murdered." The general pushed one fingertip under his ear. "Stabbed in the very spot in which he stabbed Benna Murcatto, then thrown down from a high window?"

"You think Monzcarro Murcatto is still alive?"

"A week after his son's death, Duke Orso received a letter. From one Carlot dan Eider, Prince Ario's mistress. We had long suspected she was here to spy for the Union, but Orso tolerated the affair."

"Surprising."

Ganmark shrugged. "The Union is our confirmed ally. We helped them win the latest round of their endless wars against the Gurkish. We both enjoy the backing of the Banking House of Valint and Balk. Not to mention the fact that the King of the Union is Orso's son-in-law. Naturally we send each other spies, by way of neighbourly good manners. If one must entertain a spy, she might as well be a charming one, and Eider was, undeniably, charming. She was with Prince Ario in Sipani. After his death she disappeared. Then the letter."

"And it said?"

"That she was compelled through poison to assist Prince Ario's murderers. That they included among their number a mercenary named Nicomo

Cosca and a torturer named Shylo Vitari, and were led by none other than Murcatto herself. Very much alive."

"You believe it?"

"Eider had no reason to lie to us. No letter will save her from his Excellency's wrath if she is found, and she must know it. Murcatto was alive when she went over the balcony, that much I am sure of. I have not seen her dead."

"She is seeking revenge."

Ganmark gave a joyless chuckle. "These are the Years of Blood. Everyone is seeking revenge. The Serpent of Talins, though? The Butcher of Caprile? Who loved nothing in the world but her brother? If she lives, she is on fire with it. There are few more single-minded enemies a man could find."

"Then I should find this woman Vitari, this man Cosca and this serpent Murcatto."

"No one must learn she might still live. If it was known in Talins that Orso was the one who planned her death...there could be unrest. Revolt, even. She was much loved among the people. A talisman. A mascot. One of their own, risen through merit. As the wars drag on and the taxes mount, his Excellency is...less well liked than he could be. I can trust you to keep silent?"

Shenkt kept silent.

"Good. There are associates of Murcatto's still in Talins. Perhaps one of them knows where she is." The general looked up, the orange glow of the fire splashed across one side of his tired face. "But what am I saying? It is your business to find people. To find people, and to..." He stabbed again at the glowing coals and sent up a shower of dancing sparks. "I need not tell you your business, need I?"

Shenkt put away his half-finished carving, and his knife, and turned for the door. "No."

Downwards

They came upon Visserine as the sun was dropping down behind the trees and the land was turning black. You could see the towers even from miles distant. Dozens of 'em. Scores. Sticking up tall and slim as lady's fingers into the cloudy blue-grey sky, pricks of light scattered where lamps burned in high windows.

"Lot o' towers," Shivers muttered to himself.

"There always was a fashion for them in Visserine." Cosca grinned sideways at him. "Some date all the way back to the New Empire, centuries old. The greatest families compete to build the tallest ones. It is a point of pride. I remember when I was a boy, one fell before it was finished, not three streets from where I lived. A dozen poor dwellings were destroyed in the collapse. It's always the poor who are crushed under rich men's ambitions. And yet they rarely complain, because... well..."

"They dream of having towers o' their own?"

Cosca chuckled. "Why, yes, I suppose they do. They don't see that the higher you climb, the further you have to fall."

"Men rarely see that 'til the ground's rushing at 'em."

"All too true. And I fear many of the rich men of Visserine will be tumbling soon..."

Friendly lit a torch, Vitari too, and Day a third, set at the front of the cart to light the way. Torches were lit all round them, 'til the road was a trickle of tiny lights in the darkness, winding through the dark country towards the sea. Would've made a pretty picture, at another time, but not now. War was coming, and no one was in a pretty mood.

The closer they came to the city, the more choked the road got with people, and the more rubbish was scattered either side of it. Half of 'em seemed desperate to get into Visserine and find some walls to hide behind, the other half to get out and find some open country to run through. It was a bastard of a choice for farmers, when war was on the way. Stick to your land and get a dose of fire and robbery for certain, with rape or murder more'n likely. Make for a town on the chance they'll find room for you, risk being robbed by your protectors, or caught up in the sack if the place falls. Or run for the hills to hide, maybe get caught, maybe starve, maybe just die of an icy night.

War killed some soldiers, sure, but it left the rest with money, and songs to sing, and a fire to sit around. It killed a lot more farmers, and left the rest with nought but ashes.

Just to lift the mood rain started flitting down through the darkness, spitting and hissing as it fell on the flickering torches, white streaks through the circles of light around 'em. The road turned to sticky mud. Shivers felt the wet tickle his scalp, but his thoughts were far off. Same place they'd tended to stray to these last few weeks. Back to Cardotti's, and the dark work he'd done there.

His brother had always told him it was about the lowest thing a man could do, kill a woman. Respect for womenfolk, and children, sticking to the old ways and your word, that was what set men apart from animals, and Carls from killers. He hadn't meant to do it, but when you swing steel in a crowd you can't duck the blame for the results. The good man he'd come here to be should've been gnawing his nails to the bloody quick over what he'd done. But all he could get in his head when he thought of his blade chopping a bloody chunk out of her ribs, the hollow sound it made, her staring face as she slid dying down the wall, was relief he'd got away with it.

Killing a woman by mistake in a brothel was murder, evil as it got, but killing a man on purpose in a battle was all kinds of noble? A thing to take pride in, sing songs of? Time was, gathered round a fire up in the cold North, that had seemed simple and obvious. But Shivers couldn't see the difference so sharp as he'd used to. And it wasn't like he'd got himself confused. He'd suddenly got it clear. You set to killing folk, there's no right place to stop that means a thing.

"You look as if you've dark thoughts in mind, my friend," said Cosca.

"Don't seem the time for jokes."

The mercenary chuckled. "My old mentor Sazine once told me you should laugh every moment you live, for you'll find it decidedly difficult afterwards."

"That so? And what became of him?"

"Died of a rotten shoulder."

"Poor punchline."

"Well, if life's a joke," said Cosca, "it's a black one."

"Best not to laugh, then, in case the joke's on you."

"Or trim your sense of humour to match."

"You'd need a twisted sense of humour to make laughs o' this."

Cosca scratched at his neck as he looked towards the walls of Visserine, rising up black out of the thickening rain. "I must confess, for now I'm failing to see the funny side."

You could tell from the lights there was an ugly press at the gate, and it got no prettier the closer they came. Folk were coming out from time to time — old men, young men, women carrying children, gear packed up on mules or on their backs, cartwheels creaking round through the sticky mud. Folk were coming out, easing nervous through the angry crowd, but there weren't many being let the other way. You could feel the fear, heavy on the air, and the thicker they all crowded the worse it got.

Shivers swung down from his horse, stretched his legs and made sure he loosened his sword in its sheath.

"Alright." Under her hood, Monza's hair was stuck black to the side of her scowling face. "I'll get us in."

"You are *absolutely* convinced that we should enter?" demanded Morveer.

She gave him a long look. "Orso's army can't be more than two days behind us. That means Ganmark. Faithful Carpi too, maybe, with the Thousand Swords. Wherever they are is where we need to be, and that's all."

"You are my employer, of course. But I feel duty-bound to point out that there is such a thing as being *too* determined. Surely we can devise a less perilous alternative to trapping ourselves in a city that will soon be surrounded by hostile forces."

"We'll do no good waiting out here."

"No good will be done if we are all *killed*. A plan too brittle to bend with circumstance is worse than no—" She turned before he'd finished and made off towards the archway, shoving her way between the bodies. "Women," Morveer hissed through gritted teeth.

"What about them?" growled Vitari.

"Present company entirely excepted, they are prone to think with heart rather than head."

"For what she's paying she can think with her arse for all I care."

"Dying rich is still dying."

"Better'n dying poor," said Shivers.

Not long after, a half-dozen guards came shoving through the crowd, herding folk away with their spears, clearing a muddy path to the gate. An officer came frowning with 'em, Monza just behind his shoulder. No doubt she'd sown a few coins, and this was the harvest.

"You six, with the cart there." The officer pointed a gloved finger at Shivers and the rest. "You're coming in. You six and no one else."

There were some angry mutters from the rest stood about the gate. Somebody gave the cart a kick as it started moving. "Shit on this! It ain't right! I paid my taxes to Salier all my life, and I get left out?" Someone snatched at Shivers' arm as he tried to lead his horse after. A farmer, from what he could tell in the torchlight and the spitting rain, even more desperate than most. "Why should these bastards be let through? I've got my family to—"

Shivers smashed his fist into the farmer's face. He caught him by his coat as he fell and dragged him up, followed the first punch with another, knocked him sprawling on his back in the ditch by the road. Blood bubbled down his face, black in the dusk as he tried to push himself up. You start some trouble, it's best to start it and finish it all at once. A bit of sharp violence can save you a lot worse down the line. That's the way Black Dow would've handled it. So Shivers stepped forwards quick, planted his boot on the man's chest and shoved him back into the mud.

"Best stay where y'are." A few others stood behind, dark outlines of men, a woman with two children around her legs. One lad looking straight at him, bent over like he was thinking of doing something about it all. The farmer's son, maybe. "I do this shit for a living, boy. You feel a pressing need to lie down?"

The lad shook his head. Shivers took hold of his horse's bridle again, clicked his tongue and made for the archway. Not too fast. Good and ready in case anyone was fool enough to test him. But they were already back to shouting before he'd got a stride or two, calling out how they were special, why they should be let in while the rest were left to the wolves. A man getting his front teeth knocked out was nothing to cry about in all this. Those that hadn't seen far worse guessed they'd be seeing it soon enough, and all their care was to make sure they weren't on the sharp end of it. He followed the others, blowing on his skinned knuckles, under the archway and into the darkness of the long tunnel.

Shivers tried to remember what the Dogman had told him, a hundred years ago it seemed now, back in Adua. Something about blood making more blood, and it not being too late to be better'n that. Not too late to be a good man. Rudd Threetrees had been a good man, none better. He'd stuck to the old ways all his life, never took the easy path, if he thought it was the wrong one. Shivers was proud to say he'd fought beside the man, called him chief, but in the end, what had Threetrees' honour got him? A few misty-eyed mentions around the fire. That, and a hard life, and a place in the mud at the end of it. Black Dow had been as cold a bastard as Shivers ever knew. A man who never faced an enemy if he could take him in the back, burned villages without a second thought, broke his own oaths and spat on the results. A man as merciful as the plague, and with a conscience the size of a louse's cock. Now he sat in Skarling's chair with half the North at his feet and the other half feared to say his name.

They came out from the tunnel and into the city. Water spattered from broken gutters and onto worn cobbles. A wet procession of men, women, mules, carts, waiting to get out, watching them as they tramped the other way. Shivers tipped his head back, eyes narrowed against the rain flitting down into his face as they went under a great tower, soaring up into the black night. Must've been three times the height of the tallest thing in Carleon, and it weren't even the biggest one around.

He glanced sideways at Monza, the way he'd got so good at doing. She had her usual frown, eyes fixed right ahead, light from passing torches shifting across the hard bones in her face. She set her mind to a thing, and did whatever it took. Shit on conscience and consequences both. Vengeance first, questions later.

He moved his tongue around in his mouth and spat. The more he saw, the more he saw she was right. Mercy and cowardice were the same. No one was giving prizes for good behaviour. Not here, not in the North, not anywhere. You want a thing, you have to take it, and the greatest man is the one that snatches most. Maybe it would've been nice if life was another way.

But it was how it was.

Monza was stiff and aching, just like always. She was angry and tired, just like always. She needed a smoke, worse than ever. And just to sprinkle some spice on the evening, she was getting wet, cold and saddle-sore besides.

She remembered Visserine as a beautiful place, full of twinkling glass and graceful buildings, fine food, laughter and freedom. She'd been in a rare good mood when she last visited, true, in a warm summer rather than a chill spring, with no one but Benna looking to her for leadership and no four men she had to kill.

But even so, the place was a long way from the bright pleasure garden of her memory.

Where there was a lamp burning the shutters were closed tight, light just leaking out around the edges, catching the little glass figures in their niches above the doors and making them twinkle. Household spirits, a tradition from long ago, before the time of the New Empire even, put there to bring prosperity and drive off evil. Monza wondered what good those chunks of glass would be when Orso's army broke through into the city. Not much. The streets were thick with fear, the sense of threat so heavy it seemed to stick to Monza's clammy skin and make the hairs on her neck prickle.

Not that Visserine wasn't crawling with people. Some were running, making for docks or gates. Men and women with packs, everything they could save on their backs, children in tow, elders shuffling behind. Wagons rattled along stacked with sacks and boxes, with mattresses and chests of drawers, with all manner of useless junk that would no doubt end up abandoned, lining one road or another out of Visserine. A waste of time and effort, trying to save anything but your lives at a time like this.

You chose to run, you'd best run fast.

But there were plenty who'd chosen to run into the city for refuge, and found to their great dismay it was a dead end. They lined the streets in places. They filled the doorways, huddled under blankets against the rain. They crammed the shadowy arcades of an empty market in their dozens, cowering as a column of soldiers tramped past, armour beaded up with moisture, gleaming by torchlight. Sounds came echoing through the murk. Crashes of breaking glass or tearing wood. Angry shouts, or fearful. Once or twice an outright scream.

Monza guessed a few of the city's own people were making an early start on the sacking. Settling a score or two, or snatching a few things they'd always envied while the eyes of the powerful were fixed on their own survival. This was one of those rare moments when a man could get something for free, and there'd be more and more taking advantage of it as Orso's army gathered outside the city. The stuff of civilisation, already starting to dissolve.

Monza felt eyes following her and the rest of the merry band as they rode slowly through the streets. Fearful eyes, suspicious eyes, and the other kind — trying to judge if they were soft enough or rich enough to be worth robbing. She kept the reins in her right hand, for all it hurt her to tug at them, so her left could rest on her thigh, close to the hilt of her sword. The only law in Visserine now was at the edge of a blade. And the enemy hadn't even arrived yet.

I have seen hell, Stolicus wrote, *and it is a great city under siege.*

Up ahead the road passed under a marble arch, a long rivulet of water spattering from its high keystone. A mural was painted on the wall above. Grand Duke Salier sat enthroned at the top, optimistically depicted as pleasantly plump rather than massively obese. He held one hand up in blessing, a heavenly light radiating from his fatherly smile. Beneath him an assortment of Visserine's citizens, from the lowest to the highest, humbly enjoyed the benefits of his good governance. Bread, wine, wealth. Under them, around the top of the archway, the words *charity, justice, courage* were printed in gold letters high as a man. Someone with an appetite for truth had managed to climb up there and daub over them in streaky red, *greed, torture, cowardice.*

"The arrogance of that fat fucker Salier." Vitari grinned sideways at her, orange hair black-brown with rain. "Still, I reckon he's made his last boast, don't you?"

Monza only grunted. All she could think about as she looked into Vitari's sharp-boned face was how far she could trust her. They might be in the middle of a war, but the greatest threats were still more than likely from within her own little company of outcasts. Vitari? Here for the money — ever a risky motivation since there's always some bastard with deeper pockets. Cosca? How can you trust a notoriously treacherous drunk you once betrayed yourself? Friendly? Who knew how the hell that man's mind worked?

But they were all tight as family beside Morveer. She stole a glance over her shoulder, caught him frowning at her from the seat of his cart. The man was poison, and the moment he could profit by it he'd murder her easily as crushing a tick. He was already suspicious of the choice to come into Visserine, but the last thing she wanted was to share her reasoning. That Orso would have Eider's letter by now. Would have offered a king's ransom of Valint and Balk's money for her death and got half the killers in the Circle of the World scouring Styria hoping to put her head in a bag. Along with the heads of anyone who'd helped her, of course.

The chances were high they'd be safer in the middle of a battle than outside it.

Shivers was the only one she could even halfway trust. He rode hunched over, big and silent beside her. His babble had been quite the irritation in Westport, but now it had dried up, strange to say, it had left a gap. He'd saved her life, in foggy Sipani. Monza's life wasn't all it had been, but a man saving it still raised him a damn sight higher in her estimation.

"You're quiet, all of a sudden."

She could hardly see his face in the darkness, just the hard set of it, shadows in his eye sockets, in the hollows under his cheeks. "Don't reckon I've much to say."

"Never stopped you before."

"Well. I'm starting to see all kinds o' things different."

"That so?"

"You might think it comes easy to me, but it's an effort, trying to stay hopeful. An effort that don't ever seem to pay off."

"I thought being a better man was its own reward."

"I guess it ain't reward enough for all the work. In case you hadn't noticed, we're in the middle of a war."

"Believe me, I know what a war looks like. I've been living in one most of my life."

"Well, what are the odds o' that? Me too. From what I've seen, and I've seen plenty, a war ain't really the place for bettering yourself. I'm thinking I might try it your way, from now on."

"Pick out a god and praise him! Welcome to the real world!" She wasn't sure she didn't feel a twinge of disappointment though, for all her grinning. Monza might have given up on being a decent person long ago, but somehow she liked the idea that she could have pointed one out. She pulled on her reins and eased her horse up, the cart clattering to a halt behind her. "We're here."

The place she and Benna had bought in Visserine was an old one, built before the city had good walls, and rich men each took their own care to guard what was theirs. A stone tower-house on five storeys, hall and stables to one side, with slit windows on the ground floor and battlements on the high roof. It stood big and black against the dark sky, a very different beast from the low brick-and-timber houses that crowded in close around it. She lifted the key to the studded door, then frowned. It was open a crack, light gathering on the rough stone down its edge. She put her finger to her lips and pointed towards it.

Shivers raised one big boot and kicked it shuddering open, wood clattering on the other side as something was barged out of the way. Monza darted in, left hand on the hilt of her sword. The kitchen was empty of furniture and full of people. Grubby and tired-looking, every one of them staring at her, shocked and fearful, in the light of one flickering candle. The nearest, a stocky man with one arm in a sling, stumbled up from an empty barrel and caught hold of a length of wood.

"Get back!" he screamed at her. A man in a dirty farmer's smock took a stride towards her, waving a hatchet.

Shivers stepped around Monza's shoulder, ducking under the lintel and straightening up, big shadow shifting across the wall behind him, his heavy sword drawn and gleaming down by his leg. "You get back."

The farmer did as he was told, scared eyes fixed on that length of bright metal. "Who the hell are you?"

"Me?" snapped Monza. "This is my house, bastard."

"Eleven of them," said Friendly, slipping through the doorway on the other side.

As well as the two men there were two old women and a man even older, bent right over, gnarled hands dangling. There was a woman about Monza's age, a baby in her arms and two little girls sat near her, staring with big eyes, like enough to be twins. A girl of maybe sixteen stood by the empty fireplace. She had a rough-forged knife out that she'd been gutting a fish with, her other arm across a boy, might've been ten or so, pushing him behind her shoulder.

Just a girl, looking out for her little brother.

"Put your sword away," Monza said.

"Eh?"

"No one's getting killed tonight."

Shivers raised one heavy brow at her. "Now who's the optimist?"

"Lucky for you I bought a big house." The one with his arm in a sling looked like the head of the family, so she fixed her eye on him. "There's room for all of us."

He let his club drop. "We're farmers from up the valley, just looking for somewhere safe. Place was like this when we found it, we didn't steal nothing. We'll be no trouble—"

"You'd better not be. This all of you?"

"My name's Furli. That's my wife—"

"I don't need your names. You'll stay down here, and you'll stay out of our way. We'll be upstairs, in the tower. You don't come up there, you understand? That way no one gets hurt."

He nodded, fear starting to mix with relief. "I understand."

"Friendly, get the horses stabled, and that cart off the street." Those farmers' hungry faces — helpless, weak, needy — made Monza feel sick. She kicked a broken chair out of the way then started up the stairs, winding into the darkness, her legs stiff from a day in the saddle. Morveer caught up with her on the fourth landing, Cosca and Vitari just behind him, Day at the back, a trunk in her arms. Morveer had brought a lamp with him, light pooling on the underside of his unhappy face.

"Those peasants are a decided threat to us," he murmured. "A problem easily solved, however. It will hardly be necessary to utilise the King of Poisons. A charitable contribution of a loaf of bread, dusted with Leopard Flower of course, and they would cease to—"

"No."

He blinked. "If your intention is to leave them at liberty down there, I must most strongly protest at—"

"Protest away. Let's see if I care a shit. You and Day can take that room." As he turned to peer into the darkness, Monza snatched the lamp out of his hand. "Cosca, you're on the second floor with Friendly. Vitari, seems like you get to sleep alone next door."

"Sleeping alone." She kicked some fallen plaster away across the boards. "Story of my life."

"I will to my cart, then, and bring my equipment into the Butcher of Caprile's hostel for *displaced peasantry*." Morveer was shaking his head with disgust as he turned for the stairs.

"Do that," snapped Monza at his back. She loitered for a moment, until she'd heard his boots scrape down a few flights and out of earshot. Until, apart from Cosca's voice burbling away endlessly to Friendly downstairs, it was quiet on the landing. Then she followed Day into her room and gently pushed the door closed. "We need to talk."

The girl had opened her trunk and was just getting a chunk of bread out of it. "What about?"

"The same thing we talked about in Westport. Your employer."

"Picking at your nerves, is he?"

"Don't tell me he isn't picking at yours."

"Every day for three years."

"Not an easy man to work for, I reckon." Monza took a step into the room, holding the girl's eye. "Sooner or later a pupil has to step out from her master's shadow, if she's ever going to become the master herself."

"That why you betrayed Cosca?"

That gave Monza a moment's pause. "More or less. Sometimes you have to take a risk. Grasp the nettle. But then you've got much better reasons even than I had." Said offhand, as though it was obvious.

Day's turn to pause. "What reasons?"

Monza pretended to be surprised. "Well... because sooner or later Morveer will betray me, and go over to Orso." She wasn't sure of it, of course, but it was high time she guarded herself against the possibility.

"That so?" Day wasn't smiling any longer.

"He doesn't like the way I do things."

"Who says I like the way you do things?"

"You don't see it?" Day only narrowed her eyes, food, for once, forgotten in her hand. "If he goes to Orso, he'll need someone to blame. For Ario. A scapegoat."

Now she got the idea. "No," she snapped. "He needs me."

"How long have you been with him? Three years, did you say? Managed before, didn't he? How many assistants do you think he's had? See a lot of them around, do you?"

Day opened her mouth, blinked, then thoughtfully shut it.

"Maybe he'll stick, and we'll stay a happy family and part friends. Most poisoners are good sorts, when you get to know them." Monza leaned down close to whisper. "But when he tells you he's going over to Orso, don't say I didn't warn you."

She left Day frowning at her chunk of bread, slipped quietly through the door and brushed it shut with her fingertips. She peered down the stairwell, but there was no sign of Morveer, only the handrail spiralling down into the shadows. She nodded to herself. The seed was planted now, she'd have to see what sprouted from it. She pushed her tired legs up the narrow steps to the top of the tower, through the creaking door and into the high chamber under the roof, faint sound of rain drumming above.

The room where she and Benna had spent a happy month together, in the midst of some dark years. Away from the wars. Laughing, talking, watching the world from the wide windows. Pretending at how life might have been if they'd never taken up warfare, and somehow made it rich some other way. She found she was smiling, despite herself. The little glass figure still gleamed in its niche above the door. Their household spirit. She remembered Benna grinning over his shoulder as he pushed it up there with his fingertips.

So it can watch over you while you sleep, the way you've always watched over me.

Her smile leaked away, and she walked to the window and dragged open one of the flaking shutters. Rain had thrown a grey veil across the dark city, pelting down now, spattering against the sill. A stroke of distant lightning picked out the tangle of wet roofs below for an instant, the grey outlines of other towers looming from the murk. A few moments later the thunder crackled sullen and muffled across the city.

"Where do I sleep?" Shivers stood in the doorway, arm up on the frame and some blankets over one shoulder.

"You?" She glanced up to the little glass statue above his head, then back to Shivers' face. Maybe she'd had high standards, long ago, but back then she'd had Benna, and both her hands, and an army behind her. She had nothing behind her now but six well-paid misfits, a good sword and a lot of money. A general should keep her distance from her troops, maybe, and a wanted woman from everyone, but Monza wasn't a general anymore. Benna was dead, and she needed something. You can weep over your misfortunes, or you can pick yourself up and make the best of things, shit though they may be. She elbowed the shutter closed, sank down wincing on the bed and set the lamp on the floor.

"You're in here, with me."

His brows went up. "I am?"

"That's right, optimist. Your lucky night." She leaned back on her elbows, old bed-frame creaking, and stuck one foot up at him. "Now shut the door and help me get my fucking boots off."

Rats in a Sack

Cosca squinted as he stepped out onto the roof of the tower. Even the sunlight seemed set on tormenting him, but he supposed he richly deserved it. Visserine was spread out around him: jumbles of brick-and-timber houses, villas of cream-coloured stone, the green tops of leafing trees where the parks and broad avenues were laid out. Everywhere windows glinted, statues of coloured glass on the rooflines of the grandest buildings catching the morning sun and shining like jewels. Other towers were widely scattered, dozens of them, some far taller than the one he stood on, each casting its own long shadow across the sprawl.

Southwards the grey-blue sea, the smoke of industry still rising from the city's famous glass-working district on its island just offshore, the gliding specks of seabirds circling above it. To the east the Visser was a dark snake glimpsed through the buildings, four bridges linking the two halves of the city. Grand Duke Salier's palace squatted jealously on an island in its midst. A place where Cosca had spent many enjoyable evenings, an honoured guest of the great connoisseur himself. When he had still been loved, feared and admired. So long ago it seemed another man's life.

Monza stood motionless at the parapet, framed by the blue sky. The blade of her sword and her sinewy left arm made a line, perfectly straight, from shoulder to point. The steel shone bright, the ruby on her middle finger glittered bloody, her skin gleamed with sweat. Her vest stuck to her with it. She let the sword drop as he came closer, as he lifted the wine jug and took a long, cool swallow.

"I wondered how long it would take you."

"Only water in it, more's the pity. Did you not witness my solemn oath never to touch wine again?"

She snorted. "That I've heard before, with small results."

"I am in the slow and agonising process of mending my ways."

"I've heard that too, with even smaller ones."

Cosca sighed. "Whatever must a man do to be taken seriously?"

"Keep his word once in his life?"

"My fragile heart, so often broken in the past! Can it take such a buffeting?" He wedged one boot up on the battlements beside her. "I was born in Visserine, you know, no more than a few streets away. A happy childhood but a wild youth, full of ugly incidents. Including the one that obliged me to flee the city to seek my fortune as a paid soldier."

"Your whole life has been full of ugly incidents."

"True enough." He had few pleasant memories, in fact. And most of those, Cosca realised as he peered sideways at Monza, had involved her. Most of the best moments of his life, and the very worst of all. He took a sharp breath and shielded his eyes with a hand, looking westwards, past the grey line of the city walls and out into the patchwork of fields beyond. "No sign of our friends from Talins yet?"

"Soon. General Ganmark isn't a man to turn up late to an engagement." She paused for a moment, frowning, as always. "When are you going to say you told me?"

"Told you what?"

"About Orso."

"You know what I told you."

"Never trust your own employer." A lesson he had learned at great cost from Duchess Sefeline of Ospria. "And now I'm the one paying your wages."

Cosca made an effort at a grin, though it hurt his sore lips to do it. "But we are fittingly suspicious in all our dealings with each other."

"Of course. I wouldn't trust you to carry my shit to the stream."

"A shame. Your shit smells sweet as roses, I am sure." He leaned back against the parapet and blinked into the sun. "Do you remember how we used to spar, in the mornings? Before you got too good."

"Before you got too drunk."

"Well, I could hardly spar afterwards, could I? There is a limit to how much a man should be willing to embarrass himself before breakfast. Is that a Calvez you have there?"

She lifted the sword, sun's gleam gliding along its edge. "I had it made for Benna."

"For Benna? What the hell would he do with a Calvez? Use it as a spit and cook apples on it?"

"He didn't even do that much, as it goes."

"I used to have one, you know. Damn good sword. Lost it in a card game. Drink?" He held out the jug.

She reached for it. "I could—"

"Hah!" He flung the water in her face and she yelped, stumbling back, drops flying. He ripped his sword from its sheath and as the jug shattered against the roof he was already swinging. She managed to parry the first cut, ducked desperately under the second, slipped, sprawled, rolled away as Cosca's blade squealed down the roofing lead where she had been a moment before. She came up in a crouch, sword at the ready.

"You're getting soft, Murcatto." He chuckled as he paced out into the centre of the roof. "You'd never have fallen for the old water in the face ten years ago."

"I didn't fall for it just now, idiot." She wiped her brow slowly with her gloved hand, water dripping from the ends of her wet hair, never taking her eyes from his. "You got anything more than water in the face, or is that as far as your swordsmanship reaches these days?"

Not much further, if he was honest. "Why don't we find out?"

She sprang forwards and their blades feathered together, metal ringing and scraping. She had a long scar on her bare right shoulder, another curving round her forearm and into her black glove.

He waved his sword at it. "Fighting left-handed, eh? Hope you're not taking pity on an old man."

"Pity? You know me better than that." He flicked away a jab, but another came so quickly behind it he only just got out of the way, the blade punching a ragged hole in his shirt before it whipped back out.

He raised his brows. "Good thing I lost some weight during my last binge."

"You could lose more, if you're asking me." She circled him, the point of her tongue showing between her teeth.

"Trying to get the sun behind you?"

"You never should've taught me all those dirty tricks. Care to use your left, even things up a little?"

"Give up an advantage? You know me better than that!" He feinted right then went the other way and left her lunging at nothing. She was quick, but not near as quick as she had been with her right hand. He trod on her boot as she passed, made her stumble, the point of his sword left a neat scratch across the scar on her shoulder, and made a cross of it.

She peered down at the little wound, a bead of blood forming at its corner. "You old bastard."

"A little something to remember me by." And he twirled his sword around and slashed ostentatiously at the air. She lunged at him again and their swords rang together, cut, cut, jab and parry. All a touch clumsy, like sewing with gloves on. The time was they had given exhibitions, but it seemed time had done nothing for either of them. "One question..." he murmured, keeping his eyes on hers. "Why did you betray me?"

"I got tired of your fucking jokes."

"I deserved to be betrayed, of course. Every mercenary ends up stabbed in the front or the back. But by you?" He jabbed at her, followed it with a cut that made her shuffle back, wincing. "After all I taught you? All I gave you? Safety, and money, and a place to belong? I treated you like my own daughter!"

"Like your mother, maybe. You've left out getting so drunk you'd shit in your clothes. I owed you, but there's a limit." She circled him, looking for an opening, no more than the thickness of a finger between the points of their swords. "I might've followed you to hell, but I wasn't taking my brother there with me."

"Why not? He'd have been right at home."

"Fuck yourself!" She tricked him with a feint, switched angle and forced him to hop away with all the grace of a dying frog. He had forgotten how much work swordplay required. His lungs were burning already, shoulder, forearm, wrist, hand, all aching with a vengeance. "If it hadn't been me it would've been one of the other captains. Sesaria! Victus! Andiche!" She pushed home each hated name with a sharp cut, jarring the sword in his hand. "They were all falling over themselves to be rid of you at Afieri!"

"Can we not mention that *damn place*!" He parried her next effort and switched smartly to the attack with something close to his old vigour, driving her back towards the corner of the roof. He needed to bring this to a close before he died of exhaustion. He lunged again and caught her sword on his. He drove her off balance against the parapet, bent her back over the battlements, guards scraping together until their faces were no more than a few inches apart, the long drop to the street looming into view behind her head. He could feel her quick breath on his cheek. For the briefest moment he almost kissed her, and he almost pushed her off the roof. Perhaps it was only because he could not decide which to do that he did neither one.

"You were better with your right hand," he hissed.

"You were better ten years ago." She slid from under his sword and her gloved little finger came from nowhere and poked him in the eye.

"Eeeee!" he squealed, free hand clapped to his face. Her knee thudded almost silently into his fruits and sent a lance of pain through his belly as far as his neck. "Ooooof…" He tottered, blade clattering from his clutching fingers, bent over, unable to breathe. "A little something to remember me by." And the glittering point of Monza's sword left him a burning scratch across his cheek.

"Gah!" He sank down slowly to the roofing lead. Back on his knees. There really is no place like home…

Through the savage pain he heard slow clapping coming from the stairway. "Vitari," he croaked, squinting over at her as she ambled out into the sunlight. "Why is it…you always find me…at my lowest moments?"

"Because I enjoy them so."

"You bitches don't know your luck…that you'll never feel the pain…of a blow to the fruits."

"Try childbirth."

"A charming invitation…if I were a little less bruised in the relevant areas, I would definitely take you up on it."

But, as so often, his wit was wasted. Vitari's attention was already fixed far beyond the battlements, and Monza's too. Cosca dragged himself up, bow-legged. A long column of horsemen had crested a rise to the west of the city, framed between two nearby towers, a cloud of dust rising from the hooves of their horses and leaving a brown smear across the sky.

"They're here," said Vitari. From somewhere behind them a bell began to ring, soon joined by others.

"And there," said Monza. A second column had appeared. And a pillar of smoke, drifting up beyond a hill to the north.

Cosca stood as the sun slowly rose into the blue sky, no doubt administering a healthy dose of sunburn to his spreading bald patch, and watched Duke Orso's army steadily deploy in the fields outside the city. Regiment after regiment smoothly found their positions, well out of bowshot from the walls. A large detachment forded the river to the north and completed the encirclement. The horse screened the foot as they formed neat lines, then fell back behind them, no doubt to set about the business of ravaging anything carelessly left unravaged last season.

Tents began to appear, and carts too as the supplies came up, stippling the muddy land behind the lines. The tiny defenders at the walls could do nothing but watch as the Talinese dug in around them, as orderly as the workings of a gigantic clock. Not Cosca's style, of course, even when sober. More engineering than artistry, but one had to admire the discipline.

He spread his arms wide. "Welcome, one and all, to the siege of Visserine!"

The others had all gathered on the roof to watch Ganmark's grip on the city tighten. Monza stood with her left hand on her hip, gloved right slack on the pommel of her sword, black hair stirring around her scowl. Shivers was on Cosca's other side, staring balefully out from under his brows. Friendly sat near the door to the stairs, rolling his dice between his crossed legs. Day and Vitari muttered to each other further along the parapet. Morveer looked even more sour than usual, if that was possible.

"Can no one's sense of humour withstand so small a thing as a siege? Cheer up, my comrades!" Cosca gave Shivers a hearty clap on his broad back. "It isn't every day you get to see so large an army handled so well! We should all congratulate Monza's friend General Ganmark on his exceptional patience and discipline. Perhaps we should pen him a letter."

"My dear General Ganmark." Monza worked her mouth, curled her tongue and blew spit over the battlements. "Yours ever, Monzcarro Murcatto."

"A simple missive," observed Morveer, "but no doubt he will treasure it."

"Lot o' soldiers down there," Shivers grunted.

Friendly's voice drifted gently over. "Thirteen thousand four hundred, or thereabouts."

"Mostly Talinese troops." Cosca waved at them with the eyeglass. "Some regiments from Orso's older allies — flags of Etrisani on the right wing, there, near the water, and some others of Cesale in the centre. All regulars, though. No sign of our old comrades-in-arms, the Thousand Swords. Shame. It would be fine to renew some old friendships, wouldn't it, Monza? Sesaria, Victus, Andiche. Faithful Carpi too, of course." Renew old friendships... and be revenged on old friends.

"The mercenaries will be away to the east." Monza jerked her head across the river. "Holding off Duke Rogont and his Osprians."

"Great fun for all involved, no doubt. But we, at least, are here." Cosca gestured towards the crawling soldiers outside the city. "General Ganmark, one presumes, is there. The plan, to bring us all together in a happy reunion? We presume you have a plan?"

"Ganmark is a cultured man. He has a taste for art."

"And?" demanded Morveer.

"No one has more art than Grand Duke Salier."

"His collection is impressive." Cosca had admired it on several occasions, or at any rate pretended to, while admiring his wine.

"The finest in Styria, they say." Monza strode to the opposite parapet, looking towards Salier's palace on its island in the river. "When the city falls, Ganmark will make straight for the palace, eager to rescue all those priceless works from the chaos."

"To steal them for himself," threw in Vitari.

Monza's jaw was set even harder than usual. "Orso will want to be done with this siege quickly. Leave as much time as possible to put an end to Rogont. Finish the League of Eight for good and claim his crown before winter comes. That means breaches, and assaults, and bodies in the streets."

"Marvellous!" Cosca clapped his hands. "Streets may boast noble trees, and stately buildings, but they never feel complete without a dusting of corpses, do they?"

"We take armour, uniforms, weapons from the dead. When the city falls, which will be soon, we disguise ourselves as Talinese. We find our way into the palace, and while Ganmark is going about the rescue of Salier's collection and his guard is down…"

"Kill the bastard?" offered Shivers.

There was a pause. "I believe I perceive the most *minute* of flaws in the scheme." Morveer's whining words were like nails driven into the back of Cosca's skull. "Grand Duke Salier's palace will be among the best-guarded locations in Styria at the present moment, and *we* are not in it. Nor likely to receive an invitation."

"On the contrary, I have one already." Cosca was gratified to find them all staring at him. "Salier and I were quite close some years ago, when he employed me to settle his boundary issues with Puranti. We used to dine together once a week and he assured me I was welcome whenever I found myself in the city."

The poisoner's face was a caricature of contempt. "Would this, by any chance, have been *before* you became a wine-ravaged sot?"

Cosca waved one careless hand while filing that slight carefully away with the rest. "During my long and most enjoyable transformation into one. Like a caterpillar turning into a beautiful butterfly. In any case, the invitation still stands."

Vitari narrowed her eyes at him. "How the hell do you plan to make use of it?"

"I imagine I will address the guards at the palace gate, and say something along the lines of — 'I am Nicomo Cosca, famed soldier of fortune, and I am here for dinner.'"

There was an uncomfortable silence, quite as if he had contributed a giant turd rather than a winning idea.

"Forgive me," murmured Monza, "but I doubt your name opens doors the way it used to."

"*Latrine* doors, maybe." Morveer gave a sneering shake of his head. Day chuckled softly into the wind. Even Shivers had a dubious curl to his lip.

"Vitari and Morveer, then," snapped Monza. "That's your job. Watch the palace. Find us a way in." The two of them gave each other an unenthusiastic frown. "Cosca, you know something about uniforms."

He sighed. "Few men more. Every employer wants to give you one of their own. I had one from the Aldermen of Westport cut from cloth of gold, about as comfortable as a lead pipe up the—"

"Something less eye-catching might be better suited to our purpose."

Cosca drew himself up and snapped out a vibrating salute. "General Murcatto, I will do my straining utmost to obey your orders!"

"Don't strain. Man of your age, you might rupture something. Take Friendly with you, once the assaults begin." The convict shrugged, and went back to his dice.

"We will most nobly strip the dead to their naked arses!" Cosca turned towards the stairs, but was brought up short by the sight in the bay. "Ah! Duke Orso's fleet has joined the fun." He could just see ships moving on the horizon, white sails marked with the black cross of Talins.

"More guests for Duke Salier," said Vitari.

"He always was a conscientious host, but I'm not sure even he can be prepared for so many visitors at once. The city is entirely cut off." And Cosca grinned into the wind.

"A prison," said Friendly, and almost with a smile of his own.

"We are helpless as rats in a sack!" snapped Morveer. "You speak quite as if that were a *good thing*."

"Five times I have been under siege, and always quite relished the experience. It has a wonderful way of limiting the options. Of freeing the mind." Cosca took a long breath in through his nose and blew it happily out. "When life is a cell, there is nothing more liberating than captivity."

The Forlorn Hope

F ire.

Visserine by night had become a place of flame and shadow. An endless maze of broken walls, fallen roofs, jutting rafters. A nightmare of disembodied cries, ghostly shapes flitting through the darkness. Buildings loomed, gutted shells, the eyeless gaps of window and doorway screaming open, fire spurting out, licking through, tickling at the darkness. Charred beams stabbed at the flames and they stabbed back. Showers of white sparks climbed into the black skies, and a black snow of ash fell softly the other way. The city had new towers now, crooked towers of smoke, glowing with the light of the fires that gave them birth, smudging out the stars.

"How many did we get the last time?" Cosca's eyes gleamed yellow from the flames across the square. "Three was it?"

"Three," croaked Friendly. They were safe in the chest in his room: the armour of two Talinese soldiers, one with the square hole left by a flatbow bolt, and the uniform of a slight young lieutenant he had found crushed under a fallen chimney. Bad luck for him, but then Friendly supposed it was his side throwing the fire everywhere.

They had catapults beyond the walls, five on the west side of the river, and three on the east. They had catapults on the twenty-two white-sailed ships in the harbour. The first night, Friendly had stayed up until dawn watching them. They had thrown one hundred and eighteen burning missiles over the walls, scattering fires about the city. Fires shifted, and burned out, and split, and merged one with another, and so they could not be counted. The numbers had deserted Friendly, and left him alone and afraid. It had taken but six short days, three nights times two, for peaceful Visserine to turn to this.

The only part of the city untouched was the island on which Duke Salier's palace stood. There were paintings there, Murcatto said, and other pretty things that Ganmark, the leader of Orso's army, the man they were here to kill, wished to save. He would burn countless houses, and countless people in them, and order murder night and day, but these dead things of paint had to be protected. Friendly thought this was a man who should be put in Safety, so that the world outside could be a safer place. But instead he was obeyed, and admired, and the world burned. It seemed all turned around, all wrong. But then Friendly could not tell right from wrong, the judges had told him so.

"You ready?"

"Yes," lied Friendly.

Cosca flashed a crazy grin. "Then to the breach, dear friend, once more!" And he trotted off down the street, one hand on the hilt of his sword, the other clasping his hat to his head. Friendly swallowed, then followed, lips moving silently as he counted the steps he took. He had to count something other than the ways he could die.

It only grew worse the closer they got to the city's western edge. The fires rose up in terrible magnificence, creaking and roaring, towering devils, gnawing at the night. They burned Friendly's eyes and made them weep. Or perhaps he wept anyway, to see the waste of it. If you wanted a thing, why burn it? And if you did not want it, why fight to take it from someone else? Men died in Safety. They died there all the time. But there was no waste like this. There was not enough there to risk destroying what there was. Each thing was valued.

"Bloody Gurkish fire!" Cosca cursed as they gave another roaring blaze a wide berth. "Ten years ago no one had dreamed of using that stuff as a weapon. Then they made Dagoska an ash-heap with it, knocked holes in the walls of the Agriont with it. Now no sooner does a siege begin than everyone's clamouring to blow things up. We liked to torch a building or two in my day, just to get things moving, but nothing like this. War used to be about making money. Some degree of modest misery was a regrettable side effect. Now it's just about destroying things, and the more thoroughly the better. Science, my friend, science. Supposed to make life easier, I thought."

Lines of sooty soldiers tramped by, armour gleaming orange with reflected flames. Lines of sooty civilians passed buckets of water from hand

269

to hand, desperate faces half-lit by the glow of unquenchable fires. Angry ghosts, black shapes in the sweltering night. Behind them, a great mural on a shattered wall. Duke Salier in full armour, sternly pointing the way to victory. He had been holding a flag, Friendly thought, but the top part of the building had collapsed, and his raised arm along with it. Dancing flames made it look as if his painted face was twitching, as if his painted mouth was moving, as if the painted soldiers around him were charging onwards to the breach.

When Friendly was young, there had been an old man in the twelfth cell on his corridor who had told tales of long ago. Tales of the time before the Old Time, when this world and the world below were one, and devils roamed the earth. The inmates had laughed at that old man, and Friendly had laughed at him too, since it was wise in Safety to do just as others did and never to stand out. But he had gone back when no one else was near, to ask how many years, exactly, it had been since the gates were sealed and Euz shut the devils out of the world. The old man had not known the number. Now it seemed the world below had broken through the gates between again, flooding out into Visserine, chaos spreading with it.

They hurried past a tower in flames, fire flickering in its windows, pluming up from its broken roof like a giant's torch. Friendly sweated, coughed, sweated more. His mouth was endlessly dry, his throat endlessly rough, his fingertips chalky with soot. He saw the toothed outline of the city's walls at the end of a street strangled with rubble.

"We're getting close! Stay with me!"

"I . . . I . . ." Friendly's voice croaked to nothing on the smoky air. He could hear a noise, now, as they sidled down a narrow alley, red light flickering at its end. A clattering and clashing, a surging tide of furious voices. A noise like the great riot had made in Safety, before the six most feared convicts, Friendly among them, had agreed to put a stop to the madness. Who would stop the madness here? There was a boom that made the earth shudder, and a ruddy glare lit the night sky.

Cosca slipped up to the trunk of a scorched tree, keeping low, and crouched against it. The noise grew louder as Friendly crept after, terribly loud, but his heart pounding in his ears almost drowned it out.

The breach was no more than a hundred strides off, a ragged black patch of night torn from the city wall and clogged with heaving Talinese troops. They crawled like ants over the nightmare of fallen masonry and broken timbers that formed a ragged ramp down into a burned-out square at the city's edge. There might have been an orderly battle when the first assault came, but now it had dissolved into a shapeless, furious mêlée, defenders crowding in from barricades thrown up before the gutted buildings, attackers fumbling their way on, on through the breach, adding their mindless weight to the fight, their breathless corpses to the carnage.

Axe and sword blades flashed and glinted, pikes and spears waved and tangled, a torn flag or two hung limp over the press. Arrows and bolts flitted up and down, from the Talinese crowding outside the walls, from defenders at their barricades, from a crumbling tower beside the breach. While Friendly watched, a great chunk of masonry was sent spinning down from the top of the wall and into the boiling mass below, tearing a yawning hole through them. Hundreds of men, struggling and dying by the hellish glare of burning torches, of burning missiles, of burning houses. Friendly could hardly believe it was real. It all looked false, fake, a model staged for a lurid painting.

"The breach at Visserine," he whispered to himself, framing the scene with his hands and imagining it hanging on some rich man's wall.

When two men set out to kill each other, there is a pattern to it. A few men, for that matter. A dozen, even. With a situation like that, Friendly had always been entirely comfortable. There is a form to be followed, and by being faster, stronger, sharper, you can come out alive. But this was otherwise. The mindless press. Who could know when you would be pushed, by the simple pressure of those behind, onto a pike? The awful randomness. How could you predict an arrow, or a bolt, or a falling rock from above? How could you see death coming, and how could you avoid it? It was one colossal game of chance with your life as the stake. And like the games of chance at Cardotti's House of Leisure, in the long run, the players could only lose.

"Looks like a hot one!" Cosca screamed in his ear.

"Hot?"

"I've been in hotter! The breach at Muris looked like a slaughter yard when we were done!"

Friendly could hardly bring himself to speak, his head was spinning so much. "You've been...in that?"

Cosca waved a dismissive hand. "A few times. But unless you're mad you soon tire of it. Looks like fun, maybe, but it's no place for a gentleman."

271

"How do they know who's on whose side?" hissed Friendly.

Cosca's grin gleamed in his soot-smeared face. "Guesswork, mostly. You just try to stay pointed in the right direction and hope for the...ah."

A fragment had broken from the general mêlée and was flowing forwards, bristling with weapons. Friendly could not even tell whether they were the besiegers or the besieged, they hardly seemed like men at all. He turned to see a wall of spears advancing down the street from the opposite direction, shifting light gleaming on dull metal, across stony faces. Not individual men, but a machine for killing.

"This way!" Friendly felt a hand grab his arm, shove him through a broken doorway in a tottering piece of wall. He stumbled and slipped, pitched over on his side. He half-ran, half-slid down a great heap of rubble, through a cloud of choking ash, and lay on his belly beside Cosca, staring up towards the combat in the street above. Men crashed together, killed and died, a formless soup of rage. Over their screams, their bellows of anger, the clash and squeal of metal, Friendly could hear something else. He stared sideways. Cosca was bent over on his knees, shaking with ill-suppressed mirth.

"Are you laughing?"

The old mercenary wiped his eyes with a sooty finger. "What's the alternative?"

They were in a kind of darkened valley, choked with rubble. A street? A drained canal? A sewer? Ragged people picked through the rubbish. Not far away a dead man lay face down. A woman crouched over the corpse with a knife out, in the midst of cutting the fingers from one limp hand for his rings.

"Away from that body!" Cosca lurched up, drawing his sword.

"This is ours!" A scrawny man with tangled hair and a club in his hand.

"No." Cosca brandished the blade. "This is ours." He took a step forwards and the scavenger stumbled back, falling through a scorched bush. The woman finally got through the bone with her knife, pulled the ring off and stuffed it in her pocket, flung the finger at Cosca along with a volley of abuse, then scuttled off into the darkness.

The old mercenary peered after them, weighing his sword in his hand. "He's Talinese. His gear, then!"

Friendly crept numbly over and began to unbuckle the dead man's armour. He pulled the backplate away and slid it into his sack.

"Swiftly, my friend, before those sewer rats return."

Friendly had no mind to delay, but his hands were shaking. He was not sure why. They did not normally shake. He pulled the soldier's greaves off, and his breastplate, rattling into the sack with the rest. Four sets, this would be. Three plus one. Three more and they would have one each. Then perhaps they could kill Ganmark, and be done, and he could go back to Talins, and sit in Sajaam's place, counting the coins in the card game. What happy times those seemed now. He reached out and snapped off the flatbow bolt in the man's neck.

"Help me." Hardly more than a whisper. Friendly wondered if he had imagined it. Then he saw the soldier's eyes were wide open. His lips moved again. "Help me."

"How?" whispered Friendly. He undid the hooks and eyes on the man's padded jacket and, as gently as he could, stripped it from him, dragging the sleeve carefully over the oozing stumps of his severed fingers. He stuffed his clothes into the sack, then gently rolled him back over onto his face, just as he had found him.

"Good!" Cosca pointed towards a burned-out tower leaning precariously over a collapsed roof. "That way, maybe?"

"Why that way?"

"Why not that way?"

Friendly could not move. His knees were trembling. "I don't want to go."

"Understandable, but we should stay together." The old mercenary turned and Friendly caught his arm, words starting to burble out of his mouth.

"I'm losing count! I can't...I can't think. What number are we up to, now? What...what...have I gone mad?"

"You? No, my friend." Cosca was smiling as he clapped his hand down on Friendly's shoulder. "You are entirely sane. This. All this!" He swept his hat off and waved it wildly around. "This is insanity!"

Mercy and Cowardice

Shivers stood at the window, one half open and the other closed, the frame around him like the frame around a painting, watching Visserine burn. There was an orange edge to his black outline from the fires out towards the city walls — down the side of his stubbly face, one heavy shoulder, one long arm, the twist of muscle at his waist and the hollow in the side of his bare arse.

If Benna had been there he'd have warned her she was taking some long chances, lately. Well, first he'd have asked who the big naked Northman was, then he'd have warned her. Putting herself in the middle of a siege, death so close she could feel it tickling at her neck. Letting her guard down even this much with a man she was meant to be paying, walking the soft line with those farmers downstairs. She was taking risks, and she felt that tingling mix of fear and excitement that a gambler can't do without. Benna wouldn't have liked it. But then she'd never listened to his warnings when he was alive. If the odds stand long against you, you have to take long chances, and Monza had always had a knack for picking the right ones.

Up until they killed Benna and threw her down the mountain, at least.

Shivers' voice came out of the darkness. "How'd you come by this place, anyway?"

"My brother bought it. Long time ago." She remembered him standing at the window, squinting into the sun, turning to her and smiling. She felt a grin tug at the corner of her own mouth, just for a moment.

Shivers didn't turn, now, and he didn't smile either. "You were close, eh? You and your brother."

"We were close."

"Me and my brother were close. Everyone that knew him felt close to him. He had that trick. He got killed, by a man called the Bloody-Nine. He got killed when he'd been promised mercy, and his head nailed to a standard."

Monza didn't much care for this story. On the one hand it was boring her, on the other it was making her think of Benna's slack face as they tipped him over the parapet. "Who'd have thought we had so much in common? Did you take revenge?"

"I dreamed of it. My fondest wish, for years. I had the chance, more'n once. Vengeance on the Bloody-Nine. Something a lot of men would kill for."

"And?"

She saw the muscles working on the side of Shivers' head. "The first time I saved his life. The second I let him go, and chose to be a better man."

"And you've been wandering round like a tinker with his cart ever since, peddling mercy to anyone who'll take? Thanks for the offer, but I'm not buying."

"Not sure I'm selling anymore. I been acting the good man all this time, talking up the righteous path, hoping to convince myself I done the right thing walking away. Breaking the circle. But I didn't, and that's a fact. Mercy and cowardice are the same, just like you told me, and the circle keeps turning, whatever you try. Taking vengeance…it might not answer no questions. It sure won't make the world a fairer place or the sun shine warmer. But it's better'n not taking it. It's a damn stretch better."

"I thought you were all set on being Styria's last good man."

"I've tried to do the right thing when I could, but you don't get a name in the North without doing some dark work, and I done my share. I fought beside Black Dow, and Crummock-i-Phail, and the Bloody-Nine his self, for that matter." He gave a snort. "You think you got cold hearts down here? You should taste the winters where I come from." There was something in the set of his face she hadn't seen before, and hadn't expected to. "I'd like to be a good man, that's true. But you need it the other way, then I know how."

There was silence for a moment, while they looked at each other. Him leaning against the window frame, her sprawled on the bed with one hand behind her head.

"If you really are such a snow-hearted bastard, why did you come back for me? In Cardotti's?"

"You still owe me money."

She wasn't sure if he was joking. "I feel warm all over."

"That and you're about the best friend I've got in this mad fucking country."

"And I don't even like you."

"I'm still hoping you'll warm to me."

"You know what? I might just be getting there."

She could see his grin in the light from beyond the window. "Letting me in your bed. Letting Furli and the rest stay in your house. If I didn't know better I'd be thinking I'd peddled you some mercy after all."

She stretched out. "Maybe beneath this harsh yet beautiful shell I'm really still a soft-hearted farmer's daughter, only wanting to do good. You think of that?"

"Can't say I did."

"Anyway, what's my choice? Put them out on the street, they might start talking. Safer here, where they owe us something."

"They're safest of all in the mud."

"Why don't you go downstairs and put all our minds at rest, then, killer? Shouldn't be a problem for the hero that used to carry Black Now's luggage."

"Dow."

"Whoever. Best put some trousers on first, though, eh?"

"I'm not saying we should've killed 'em or nothing, I'm just pointing out the fact. Mercy and cowardice are the same, I heard."

"I'll do what needs doing, don't worry. I always have. But I'm not Morveer. I'm not murdering eleven farmers just for my convenience."

"Nice to hear, I guess. All those little people dying in the bank didn't seem to bother you none, long as one of 'em was Mauthis."

She frowned. "That wasn't the plan."

"Nor the folk at Cardotti's."

"Cardotti's didn't go quite the way I had in mind either, in case you didn't notice."

"I noticed pretty good. The Butcher of Caprile, they call you, no? What happened there?"

"What needed doing." She remembered riding up in the dusk, the stab of worry as she saw the smoke over the city. "Doing it and liking it are different things."

"Same results, no?"

"What the hell would you know about it? I don't remember you being there." She shook the memory off and slid from the bed. The careless warmth of the last smoke was wearing through and she felt strangely awkward in her own scarred skin, crossing the room with his eyes on her, stark naked but for the glove still on her right hand. The city, and its towers, and its fires spread out beyond the window, blurred through the bubbly glass panes in the closed half. "I didn't bring you up here to remind me of my mistakes. I've made enough of the bastards."

"Who hasn't? Why did you bring me up here?"

"Because I've an awful weakness for big men with tiny minds, what do you think?"

"Oh, I try not to think much, makes my tiny mind hurt. But I'm starting to get the feeling you might not be quite so hard as you make out."

"Who is?" She reached out and touched the scar on his chest. Fingertip trailing through hair, over rough, puckered skin.

"We've all got our wounds, I guess." He slid his hand down the long scar on her hip bone, and her stomach clenched up tight. That gambler's mix of fear and excitement still, with a trace of disgust mixed in.

"Some worse than others." The words sour in her mouth.

"Just marks." His thumb slid across the scars on her ribs, one by one. "They don't bother me any."

She pulled the glove off her crooked right hand and stuck it in his face. "No?"

"No." His big hands closed gently around her ruined one, warm and tight. She stiffened up at first, almost dragged it away, breath catching with ugly shock, as if she'd caught him caressing a corpse. Then his thumbs started to rub at her twisted palm, at the aching ball of her thumb, at her crooked fingers, all the way to the tips. Surprisingly tender. Surprisingly pleasant. She let her eyes close and her mouth open, stretched her fingers out as wide as they'd go, and breathed.

She felt him closer, the warmth of him, his breath on her face. Not much chance to wash lately and he had a smell — sweat and leather and a hint of bad meat. Sharp, but not entirely unpleasant. She knew she had a smell herself. His face brushed hers, rough cheek, hard jaw, nudging against her nose, nuzzling at her neck. She was half-smiling, skin tingling in the draught from the window, carrying that familiar tickle of burning buildings to her nose.

One of his hands still held hers, out to the side now, the other slid up her flank, over the knobble of her hip bone, slid under her breast, thumb rubbing back and forth over her nipple, slightly pleasant, slightly clumsy. Her free hand brushed against his cock, already good and hard, up, and down, damp skin sticky on her palm. She lifted one foot, heel scraping loose plaster from the wall, wedged it on the windowsill so her legs were spread wide. His fingers slid back and forth between them with a soft squelch, squelch.

Her right hand was round under his jaw, twisted fingers pulling at his ear, turning his head sideways, thumb dragging his mouth open so she could push her tongue into it. It tasted of the cheap wine they'd been drinking, but hers probably did too, and who cared a shit anyway?

She drew him close, pressing up against him, skin sliding against skin. Not thinking about her dead brother, not thinking about her crippled hand, not thinking about the war outside, or needing a smoke, or the men she had to kill. Just his fingers and her fingers, his cock and her cunt. Not much, maybe, but something, and she needed something.

"Get on and fuck me," she hissed in his ear.

"Right," he croaked at her, hooked her under one knee, lifted her to the bed and dumped her on her back, frame creaking. She wriggled away, making room, and he knelt down between her open knees, working his way forwards, fierce grin on his face as he looked down at her. Same grin she had, keen to get on with it. She felt the end of his cock sliding around between her thighs, one side, then the other. "Where the fuck..."

"Bloody Northmen, couldn't find your arse with a chair."

"My arse ain't the hole I'm looking for."

"Here." She dragged some spit off her tongue with her fingers, propped herself up on one elbow, reached down and took hold of him, working his cock around until she found the spot.

"Ah."

"Ah," she grunted back. "That's it."

"Aye." He moved his hips in circles, easing deeper with each one. "That... is... it." He ran his hands up her thighs, fingers into the short hair, started rubbing at her with his thumb.

"Gently!" She slapped his hand away and slid her own down in its place, middle finger working slowly round and round. "You're not trying to crack a nut, fool."

"Your nut, your business, I reckon." His cock slid out as he worked his way forwards, onto his arms above her, but she slid it back in easy enough. They started finding a rhythm, patient but building, bit by bit.

She kept her eyes open, looking in his face, and she could see the gleam of his in the darkness looking back. Both of them with teeth bared, breathing hard. He opened his mouth to meet hers, then moved his head away as she craned up to kiss him, always just out of reach until she had to slump back flat with a gasp that sent a warm shiver through her.

She slid her right hand onto his backside, squeezing at one buttock as it tensed and relaxed, tensed and relaxed. Faster now, damp skin slap-slapping, and she pushed her twisted hand round further, down into the crack of his arse. She strained her head up off the bed again, biting at his lips, at his teeth, and he nipped at her, grunting in his throat and her grunting back. He came down onto one elbow, his other hand sliding up over her ribs, squeezing hard at one breast then the other, almost painful.

Creak, creak, creak, and her feet were off the bed and in the air, his hand tangled in her hair, fingers rubbing at the coins under her skin, dragging her head back, her face up against his, and she sucked his tongue out of his mouth and into hers, bit at it, licked at it. Deep, slobbery, hungry, snarling kisses. Hardly kisses at all. She pushed her finger into his arsehole, up to the first knuckle.

"What the fuck?" He broke clear of her as if she'd slapped him in the face, stopped moving, still and tense above her. She jerked her right hand back, left still busy between her legs.

"Alright," she hissed. "Doesn't make you less of a man, you know. Your arse, your business. I'll keep clear of it in—"

"Not that. D'you hear something?"

Monza couldn't hear anything but her own fast breath and the faint sound of her fingers still sliding wetly up and down. She pushed her hips back up against him. "Come on. There's nothing but—"

The door crashed open, wood flying from the splintered lock. Shivers scrambled from the bed, tangled with the blanket. Monza was dazzled by lamplight, caught a glimpse of bright metal, armour, a shout and a sword swung.

There was a metallic thud, Shivers gave a squawk and went down hard on the boards. Monza felt spots of blood patter on her cheek. She had the hilt of the Calvez in her hand. Right hand, stupidly, by force of habit, blade a few inches drawn.

"No you don't." A woman coming through the ruins of the door, loaded flatbow levelled, hair scraped back from a soft-looking round face. A man turned from standing over Shivers and towards Monza, sword in hand. She could scarcely see more of him than the outline of his armour, his helmet. Another soldier stomped through the door, lantern in one fist and an axe in the other, curved blade gleaming. Monza let her twisted fingers open and the Calvez clattered down beside the bed half-drawn.

"That's better," said the woman.

Shivers gave a groan, tried to push himself up, eyes narrowed against the light, blood trickling down his face from a cut in his hair. Must have been clubbed with the flat. The one with the axe stepped forwards and swung a boot into his ribs, thud, thud, made him grunt, curled up naked against the wall. A fourth soldier walked in, some dark cloth over one arm.

"Captain Langrier."

"What did you find?" asked the woman, handing him the flatbow.

"This, and some others."

"Looks like a Talinese uniform." She held the jacket up so Monza could see it. "Got anything to say about this?"

The jolt of cold shock was fading, and an even frostier fear was pressing in fast behind it. These were Salier's soldiers. She'd been so fixed on killing Ganmark, so fixed on Orso's army, she hadn't spared a thought for the other side. They'd got her attention now, alright. She felt a sudden need for another smoke, so bad she was nearly sick. "It's not what you think," she managed to croak out, acutely aware she was stark naked and smelled sharply of fucking.

"How do you know what I think?"

Another soldier with a big drooping moustache appeared in the doorway. "A load of bottles and suchlike in one of the rooms. Didn't fancy touching 'em. Looked like poison to me."

"Poison, you say, Sergeant Pello?" Langrier stretched her head to one side and rubbed at her neck. "Well, that is damn suspicious."

"I can explain it." Monza's mouth was dry. She knew she couldn't. Not in any way these bastards would believe.

"You'll get your chance. Back at the palace, though. Bind 'em up."

Shivers grimaced as the axeman dragged his wrists behind his back and snapped manacles shut on them, hauled him to his feet. One of the others grabbed Monza's arm, twisted it roughly behind her as he jammed the cuffs on.

"Ah! Mind my hand!" One of them dragged her off the bed, shoved her stumbling towards the door and she nearly slipped, getting her balance back without much dignity. There wasn't much dignity to be had in all of this. Benna's little glass statue watched from its niche. So much for house-hold spirits. "Can we get some clothes at least?"

"I don't see why." They hauled her out onto the landing, into the light of another lantern. "Wait there." Langrier squatted down, frowning at the zig-zag scars on Monza's hip and along her thigh, neat pink dots of the pulled stitches almost faded. She prodded at them with one thumb as though she was checking a joint of meat in a butcher's for rot. "You ever seen marks like that before, Pello?"

"No."

She looked up at Monza. "How did you get these?"

"I was shaving my cunt and the razor slipped."

The woman spluttered with laughter. "I like that. That's funny."

Pello was laughing too. "That is funny."

"Good thing you've got a sense of humour." Langrier stood up, brushing dust from her knees. "You'll need that later." She thumped Monza on the side of the head with an open hand and sent her tumbling down the stairs. She fell on her shoulder with a jarring impact, the steps battered her back, skinned her knees, her legs went flying over. She squealed and grunted as the wood drove the air out of her, then the wall cracked her in the nose and knocked her sprawling, one leg buckled against the plaster. She lifted her head, groggy as a drunkard, the stairway still reeling. Her mouth tasted of blood. She spat it out. It filled up again.

"Fuh," she grunted.

"No more jokes? We've got a few more flights if you're still feeling witty."

She wasn't. She let herself be dragged up, grunting as pain ground at her battered shoulder-joint.

"What's this?" She felt the ring pulled roughly off her middle finger, saw Langrier smiling as she held her hand up to the light, ruby glinting.

"Looks good on you," said Pello. Monza kept her silence. If the worst she lost out of this was Benna's ring, she'd count herself lucky indeed.

There were more soldiers on the floors below, rooting through the tower, dragging gear from the chests and boxes. Glass crunched and tinkled as they upended one of Morveer's cases onto the floor. Day was sitting on a bed nearby, yellow hair hanging over her face, hands bound behind her. Monza met her eye for a moment, and they stared at each other, but there wasn't much pity to spare. At least she'd been lucky enough to have her shift on when they came.

They shoved Monza down into the kitchen and she leaned against the wall, breathing fast, stark naked but past caring. Furli was down there, and his brother too. Langrier walked over to them and pulled a purse from her back pocket.

"Looks like you were right. Spies." She counted coins out into the farmer's waiting palm. "Five scales for each of them. Duke Salier thanks you for your diligence, citizen. You say there were more?"

"Four others."

"We'll keep a watch on the tower and pick them up later. You'd better find somewhere else for your family."

Monza watched Furli take the money, licking at the blood running out of her nose and thinking this was where charity got you. Sold for five scales. Benna would probably have been upset by the size of the bounty, but she had far bigger worries. The farmer gave her a last look as they dragged her stumbling out through the door. There was no guilt in his eyes. Maybe he felt he'd done the best thing for his family, in the midst of a war. Maybe he was proud that he'd had the courage to do it. Maybe he was right to be.

Seemed it was as true now as it had been when Verturio wrote the words. *Mercy and cowardice are the same.*

The Odd Couple

It was Morveer's considered opinion that he was spending entirely too much of his time in lofts, of late. It did not help in the slightest that this one was exposed to the elements. Large sections of the roof of the ruined house were missing, and the wind blew chill into his face. It reminded him most unpleasantly of that crisp spring night, long ago, when two of the prettiest and most popular girls had lured him onto the roof of the orphanage then locked him up there in his nightshirt. He was found in the morning, grey-lipped and shivering, close to having frozen to death. How they had all laughed.

The company was far from warming him. Shylo Vitari crouched in the darkness, her head a spiky outline with the night sky behind, one eye shut, her eyeglass to the other. Behind them in the city, fires burned. War might be good for a poisoner's business, but Morveer had always preferred to keep it at arm's length. Considerably beyond, in fact. A city under siege was no place for a civilised man. He missed his orchard. He missed his good goose-down mattress. He attempted to shift the collars of his coat even higher around his ears, and transferred his attention once again to the palace of Grand Duke Salier, brooding on its long island in the midst of the fast-flowing Visser.

"Why ever a man of my talents should be called upon to survey a scene of this nature is entirely beyond me. I am no general."

"Oh no. You're a murderer on a much smaller scale."

Morveer frowned sideways. "As are you."

"Surely, but I'm not the one complaining."

"I resent being dropped into the centre of a war."

"It's Styria. It's spring. Of course there's a war. Let's just come up with a plan and get back out of the night."

"Huh. Back to Murcatto's charitable institution for the housing of displaced agricultural workers, do you mean? The stench of self-righteous hypocrisy in that place causes my bile to rise."

Vitari blew into her cupped hands. "Better than out here."

"Is it? Downstairs, the farmer's brats wail into the night. Upstairs, our employer's profoundly unsubtle erotic adventures with our barbarian companion keep the floorboards groaning at all hours. I ask you, is there anything more unsettling than the sound of other...people...*fucking*?"

Vitari grinned. "You've got a point there. They'll have that floor in before they're done."

"They'll have my skull in before that. I ask you, is an iota of professionalism too much to ask for?"

"Long as she's paying, who cares?"

"I care if her carelessness leads to my untimely demise, but I suppose we must make do."

"Less whining and more work, then, maybe? A way in."

"A way in, because the noble leaders of Styrian cities are trusting folk, always willing to welcome uninvited guests into their places of residence..."

Morveer moved his eyeglass carefully across the front of the sprawling building, rising up sheer from the frothing waters of the river. For the home of a renowned aesthete, it was an edifice of minimal architectural merit. A confusion of ill-matched styles awkwardly mashed together into a jumble of roofs, turrets, cupolas, domes and dormers, its single tower thrusting up into the heavens. The gatehouse was comprehensively fortified, complete with arrow loops, bartizans, machicolations and gilded portcullis facing the bridge into the city. A detachment of fifteen soldiers were gathered there in full armour.

"The gate is far too well guarded, the front elevation far too visible to climb, either to roof or window."

"Agreed. The only spot we'd have a chance of getting in without being seen is the north wall."

Morveer swung his eyeglass towards the narrow northern face of the building, a sheer expanse of mossy grey stone pierced by darkened stained-glass windows and with a begargoyled parapet above. Had the palace been a ship sailing upriver, that would have been its prow, and fast-flowing water foamed with particular energy around its sloping base. "Unobserved, perhaps, but also the most difficult to reach."

"Scared?" Morveer lowered his eyeglass with some irritation to see Vitari grinning at him.

"Let us say rather that I am dubious as to our chances of success. Though I confess I feel some warmth at the prospect of your *plunging* from a rope into the frothing river, I am far from attracted by the prospect of following you."

"Why not just say you're scared?"

Morveer refused to rise to such ham-fisted taunting. It had not worked in the orphanage; it would most certainly not work now. "We would require a boat, of course."

"Shouldn't be too hard to find something upriver."

He pursed his lips as he weighed the benefits. "The plan would have the added advantage of providing a means of egress, an aspect of the venture by which Murcatto seems decidedly untroubled. Once Ganmark has been put paid to, we might hope to reach the roof, still disguised, and back down the rope to the boat. Then we could simply float out to sea and—"

"Look at that." Vitari pointed at a group moving briskly along the street below, and Morveer trained his eyeglass upon them. Perhaps a dozen armoured soldiers marched on either side of two stumbling figures, entirely naked, hands bound behind them. A woman and a large man.

"Looks like they've caught some spies," said Vitari. "Bad luck for them."

One of the soldiers jabbed the man with the butt of his spear and knocked him over in the road, bare rump sticking into the air. Morveer chuckled. "Oh yes, indeed, even among Styrian prisons, the dungeons beneath Salier's palace enjoy a black reputation." He frowned through the eyeglass. "Wait, though. The woman looks like—"

"Murcatto. It's fucking them!"

"Can nothing run smoothly?" Morveer felt a mounting sense of horror he had in no way expected. Stumbling along at the back in her nightshirt, hands bound behind her, was Day. "Curse it all! They have my assistant!"

"Piss on your assistant. They have our employer! That means they have my pay!"

Morveer could do nothing but grind his teeth as the prisoners were herded across the bridge and into the palace, the heavy gates tightly sealed behind them. "Damn it! The tower-house is no longer safe! We cannot return there!"

"An hour ago you couldn't stand the thought of going back to that den of hypocrisy and erotic adventure."

"But my equipment is there!"

"I doubt it." Vitari nodded her spiky head towards the palace. "It'll be with all the boxes they carried in there."

Morveer slapped petulantly at the bare rafter by his head, winced as he took a splinter in his forefinger and was forced to suck it. "Damn and shitting *blast*!"

"Calm, Morveer, calm."

"I am calm!" The sensible thing to do was undeniably to find a boat, to float silently up to Duke Salier's palace, then past it and out to sea, writing off his losses, return to the orchard and train another assistant, leaving Murcatto and her imbecile Northman to reap the consequences of their stupidity. Caution first, always, but...

"I cannot leave my assistant behind in there," he barked. "I simply *cannot*!"

"Why?"

"Well, because..." He was not sure why. "I *flatly* refuse to go through the trouble of instructing another!"

Vitari's irritating grin had grown wider. "Fine. You need your girl and I need my money. You want to cry about it or work on a way in? I still say boat down the river to the north wall, then rope and grapple to the roof."

Morveer squinted unhopefully towards the sheer stonework. "You can truthfully secure a grapple up there?"

"I could get a grapple through a fly's arse. It's you getting the boat into position that worries me."

He was not about to be outdone. "I challenge you to find a more accomplished oarsman! I could hold a boat steady in a deluge twice as fierce, but it will not be needful. I can drive a hook into that stonework and anchor the boat against those rocks all night."

"Good for you."

"Good. Excellent." His heart was beating with considerable urgency at the argument. He might not have liked the woman, but her competence was in no doubt. Given the circumstances he could not have selected a more suitable companion. A most handsome woman, too, in her own way, and no doubt every bit as firm a disciplinarian as the sternest nurse at the orphanage had been...

Her eyes narrowed. "I hope you're not going to make the same suggestion you made last time we worked together."

Morveer bristled. "There will be no repetition of that *whatsoever,* I can assure you!"

"Good. Because I'd still rather fuck a hedgehog."

"You made your preferences *quite* clear on that occasion!" he answered shrilly, then moved with all despatch to shift the topic. "There is no purpose in delay. Let us find a vessel appropriate to our needs." He took one last look down as he slithered back into the attic, and paused. "Who's this now?" A single figure was striding boldly towards the palace gates. Morveer felt his heart sink even lower. There was no mistaking the flamboyant gait. "*Cosca.* Whatever is that horrible old drunkard about?"

"Who knows what goes through that scabby head?"

The mercenary strode towards the guards quite as if it was his palace rather than Duke Salier's, waving one arm. Morveer could just hear his voice in between the sighing of the wind, but had not the slightest notion of the words. "What are they saying?"

"You can't read lips?" Vitari muttered.

"No."

"Nice to find there's one subject you're not the world's greatest expert on. The guards are challenging him."

"Of course!" That much was clear from the halberds lowered at Cosca's chest. The old mercenary swept off his hat and bowed low.

"He is replying...my name is Nicomo Cosca...famed soldier of fortune...and I am here..." She lowered the eyeglass, frowning.

"Yes?"

Vitari's eyes slid towards him. "And I am here for dinner."

Darkness

Utter dark. Monza opened her eyes wide, squinted and stared, and saw nothing but fizzing, tingling blackness. She wouldn't have been able to see her hand before her face. But she couldn't move her hand there anyway, or anywhere else.

They'd chained her to the ceiling by her wrists, to the floor by her ankles. If she hung limp, her feet just brushed the clammy stones. If she stretched up on tiptoe, she could ease the throbbing ache through her arms, through her ribs, through her sides, a merciful fraction. Soon her calves would start to burn, though, worse and worse until she had to ease back down, teeth gritted, and swing by her skinned wrists. It was agonising, humiliating, terrifying, but the worst of it was, she knew — this was as good as things were going to get.

She wasn't sure where Day was. Probably she'd blinked those big eyes, shed a single fat tear and said she knew nothing, and they'd believed her. She had the sort of face that people believed. Monza never had that sort of face. But then she probably didn't deserve one. Shivers was struggling somewhere in the inky black, metal clinking as he twisted at his chains, cursing in Northern, then Styrian. "Fucking Styria. Fucking Vossula. Shit. Shit."

"Stop!" she hissed at him. "Might as well . . . I don't know . . . keep your strength."

"Strength going to help us, you reckon?"

She swallowed. "Couldn't hurt." Couldn't help. Nothing could.

"By the dead, but I need to piss."

"Piss, then," she snapped into the darkness. "What's the difference?"

A grunt. The sound of liquid spattering against stone. She might've joined him if her bladder hadn't been knotted up tight with fear. She pushed up on her toes again, legs aching, wrists, arms, sides burning with every breath.

"You got a plan?" Shivers' words sank away and died on the buried air.

"What fucking plan do you think I'd have? They think we're spies in their city, working for the enemy. They're sure of it! They're going to try and get us to talk, and when we don't have anything to say they want to hear, they're going to fucking kill us!" An animal growl, more rattles. "You think they didn't plan for you struggling?"

"What d'you want me to do?" His voice was strangled, shrill, as if he was on the verge of sobbing. "Hang here and wait for them to start cutting us?"

"I..." She felt the unfamiliar thickness of tears at the back of her own throat. She didn't have the shadow of an idea of a way clear of this. Helpless. How could you get more helpless than chained up naked, deep underground, in the pitch darkness? "I don't know," she whispered. "I don't know."

There was the clatter of a lock turning and Monza jerked her head up, skin suddenly prickling. A door creaked open and light stabbed at her eyes. A figure came down stone steps, boots scraping, a torch flickering in his hand. Another came behind him.

"Let's see what we're doing, shall we?" A woman's voice. Langrier, the one who'd caught them in the first place. The one who'd knocked Monza down the stairs and taken her ring. The other one was Pello, with the moustache. They were both dressed like butchers, stained leather aprons and heavy gloves. Pello went around the room, lighting torches. They didn't need torches, they could've had lamps. But torches are that bit more sinister. As if, at that moment, Monza needed scaring. Light crept out across rough stone walls, slick with moisture, splattered with green moss. There were a couple of tables about, heavy cast-iron implements on them. Unsubtle-looking implements.

She'd felt better when it was dark.

Langrier bent over a brazier and got it lit, blowing patiently on the coals, orange glow flaring across her soft face with each breath.

Pello wrinkled his nose. "Which one of you pissed?"

"Him," said Langrier. "But what's the difference?" Monza watched her slide a few lengths of iron into the furnace, and felt her throat close up tight. She looked sideways at Shivers, and he looked back at her, and said nothing. There was nothing to say. "More than likely they'll both be pissing soon enough."

"Alright for you, you don't have to mop it up."

"I've mopped up worse." She looked at Monza, and her eyes were bored. No hate in them. Not much of anything. "Give them some water, Pello."

The man offered a jug. She would've liked to spit in his face, scream obscenities, but she was thirsty, and it was no time for pride. So she opened her mouth and he stuck the spout in it, and she drank, and coughed, and drank, and water trickled down her neck and dripped to the cold flags between her bare feet.

Langrier watched her get her breath back. "You see, we're just people, but I have to be honest, that's probably the last kindness you'll be getting out of us if you're not helpful."

"It's a war, boy." Pello offered the jug to Shivers. "A war, and you're on the other side. We don't have the time to be gentle."

"Just give us something," said Langrier. "Just a little something I can give to my colonel, then we can leave you be, for now, and we'll all be a lot happier."

Monza looked her right in the eye, unwavering, and did her best to make her believe. "We're not with Orso. The opposite. We're here—"

"You had his uniforms, didn't you?"

"Only so we could drop in with them if they broke into the city. We're here to kill Ganmark."

"Orso's Union general?" Pello raised his brows at Langrier and she shrugged back.

"It's either what she said, or they're spies, working with the Talinese. Here to assassinate the duke, maybe. Now which of those seems the more likely?"

Pello sighed. "We've been in this game a long time, and the obvious answer, nine times out of ten, is the right one."

"Nine times out of ten." Langrier spread her hands in apology. "So you might have to do better than that."

"I can't do any fucking better," Monza hissed through gritted teeth, "that's all I—"

Langrier's gloved fist thudded suddenly into her ribs. "The truth!" Her other fist into Monza's other side. "The truth!" A punch in the stomach.

"The truth! The truth! The truth!" She sprayed spit in Monza's face as she screamed it, knocking her back and forth, the sharp thumps and Monza's wheezing grunts echoing dully from the damp walls of the place.

She couldn't do any of the things her body desperately needed to do — bring her arms down, or fold up, or fall over, or breathe even. She was helpless as a carcass on a hook. When Langrier got tired of pounding the guts out of her she shuddered silently for a moment, eyes bulging, every muscle cramped up bursting tight, creaking back and forth by her wrists. Then she coughed watery puke into her armpit, heaved half a desperate, moaning breath in and drooled out some more. She drooped limp as a wet sheet on a drying line, hair tangled across her face, heard that she was whimpering like a beaten dog with every shallow breath but couldn't stop it and didn't care.

She heard Langrier's boots scraping over to Shivers. "So she's a fucking idiot, that's proven. Let's give you a chance, big man. I'll start with something simple. What's your name?"

"Caul Shivers," voice high and tight with fear.

"Shivers." Pello chuckled.

"Northerners. Who dreams up all these funny names? What about her?"

"Murcatto, she calls herself. Monzcarro Murcatto." Monza slowly shook her head. Not because she blamed him for saying her name. Just because she knew the truth couldn't help.

"What do you know? The Butcher of Caprile herself in my little cell! Murcatto's dead, idiot, months ago, and I'm getting bored. You'd think none of us would ever die, the way you're wasting our time."

"You reckon they're very stupid," asked Pello, "or very brave?"

"What's the difference?"

"You want to hold him?"

"You mind doing it?" Langrier winced as she worked one elbow around. "Damn shoulder's aching today. Wet weather always gets it going."

"You and your bloody shoulder." Metal rattled as Pello let a stride of chain out through the pulley above and Shivers' hands dropped down around his head. Any relief he felt was short lived, though. Pello came up behind and kicked him in the back of his legs, sent him lurching onto his knees, arms stretched out again, kept him there by planting one boot on the back of his calves.

"Look!" It was cold but Shivers' face was all beaded up with sweat. "We're not with Orso! I don't know nothing about his army. I just…I just don't know!"

"It's the truth," Monza croaked, but so quiet no one could hear her. Even that started her coughing, each heave stabbing through her battered ribs.

Pello slid one arm around Shivers' head, elbow under his jaw, his other hand firm behind, tilting his face back.

"No!" squawked Shivers, the one bulging eye Monza could see rolling towards her. "It was her! Murcatto! She hired me! To kill seven men! Vengeance, for her brother! And…and—"

"You've got him?" asked Langrier.

"I've got him."

Shivers' voice rose higher. "It was her! She wants to kill Duke Orso!" He was trembling now, teeth chattering together. "We did Gobba, and a banker! A banker…called Mauthis! Poisoned him, and then…and then… Prince Ario, in Sipani! At Cardotti's! And now—"

Langrier stuck a battered wooden dowel between his jaws, putting a quick end to his wasted confession. "Wouldn't want you to chew your tongue off. Still need you to tell me something worth hearing."

"I've got money!" croaked Monza, her voice starting to come back.

"What?"

"I've got money! Gold! Boxes full of it! Not with me, but…Hermon's gold! Just—"

Langrier chuckled. "You'd be amazed how everyone remembers buried treasure at a time like this. Doesn't often work out."

Pello grinned. "If I had just a tenth of what I've been promised in this room I'd be a rich man. I'm not, in case you're wondering."

"But if you did have boxes full of gold, where the hell would I spend it now? You came a few weeks too late to bribe us. The Talinese are all around the city. Money's no use here." Langrier rubbed at her shoulder, winced, worked her arm in a circle, then dragged an iron from the brazier. It squealed out with the sound of metal on metal, sent up a drifting shower of orange sparks and a sick twist of fear through Monza's churning guts.

"It's true," she whispered. "It's true." But all the strength had gone out of her.

"'Course it is." And Langrier stepped forwards and pressed the yellow-hot metal into Shivers' face. It made a sound like a slice of bacon dropped into a pan, but louder, and with his mindless, blubbering screech on top of it, of course. His back arched, his body thrashed and trembled like a fish on a line, but Pello kept his grip on him, grim-faced.

Greasy steam shot up, a little gout of flame that Langrier blew out with a practised puff of air through pursed lips, grinding the iron one way then the other, into his eye. While she did it, she had the same look she might have had wiping a table. A tedious, distasteful chore that had fallen to her and unfortunately had to be done.

The sizzling grew quieter. Shivers' scream had become a moaning hiss, the last air in his lungs being dragged out of him, spit spraying from his stretched-back lips, frothing from the wood between his bared teeth. Langrier stepped away. The iron had cooled to dark orange, smeared down one side with smoking black ash. She tossed it clattering back into the coals with some distaste.

Pello let go and Shivers' head dropped forwards, breath bubbling in his throat. Monza didn't know if he was awake or not, aware or not. She prayed not. The room smelled of charred meat. She couldn't look at his face. Couldn't look. Had to look. A glimpse of a great blackened stripe across his cheek and through his eye, raw-meat-red around it, bubbled and blistered, shining oily with fat cooked from his face. She jerked her eyes back to the floor, wide open, the air crawling in her throat, all her skin as clammy-cold as a corpse dragged from a river.

"There we go. Aren't we all better off for that, now? All so you could keep your secrets for a few minutes longer? What you won't tell us, we'll just get out of that little yellow-haired bitch later." She waved a hand in front of her face. "Damn, that stinks. Drop her down, Pello."

The chains rattled and she went down. Couldn't stand, even. Too scared, too hurting. Her knees grazed the stone. Shivers' breath crackled. Langrier rubbed at her shoulder. Pello clicked his tongue softly as he made the chains fast. Monza felt the sole of his boot dig into the backs of her calves.

"Please," she whispered, whole body shivering, teeth rattling. Monzcarro Murcatto, the dreaded Butcher of Caprile, the fearsome Serpent of Talins, that monster who'd washed herself in the Years of Blood, all that was a distant memory. "Please."

"You think we enjoy doing this? You think we wouldn't rather get on with people? I'm well liked mostly, aren't I, Pello?"

"Mostly."

"For pity's sake, give me something I can use. Just tell me…" Langrier closed her eyes and rubbed at them with the back of her wrist. "Just tell me who you get your orders from, at least. Let's just start with that."

"Alright, alright!" Monza's eyes were stinging. "I'll talk!" She could feel tears running down her face. "I'm talking!" She wasn't sure what she was saying. "Ganmark! Orso! Talins!" Gibberish. Nothing. Anything. "I…I work for Ganmark!" Anything to keep the irons in the brazier for a few more moments. "I take my orders from him!"

"From him directly?" Langrier frowned over at Pello, and he took a break from picking at the dry skin on one palm to frown back. "Of course you do, and his Excellency Grand Duke Salier is constantly down here checking how we're getting along. Do you think I'm a fucking idiot?" She cuffed Monza across the face, one way and back the other, turned her mouth bloody and set her skin burning, made the room jerk and sway. "You're making this up as you go along!"

Monza tried to shake the mud out of her head. "Wha' d'you wan' me to tell you?" Words all mangled in her swollen mouth.

"Something that fucking helps me!"

Monza's bloody lip moved up and down, but nothing came out except a string of red drool. Lies were useless. The truth was useless. Pello's arm snaked around her head from behind, tight as a noose, dragged her face back towards the ceiling.

"No!" she squawked. "No! N—" The piece of wood was wedged into her mouth, wet with Shivers' spit.

Langrier loomed into Monza's blurry vision, shaking one arm out. "My damn shoulder! I swear I'm in more pain than anyone, but no one has mercy on me, do they?" She dragged a fresh iron clear of the coals, held it up, yellow-white, casting a faint glow across her face, making the beads of sweat on her forehead glisten. "Is there anything more boring than other people's pain?"

She raised the iron, Monza's weeping eye jammed wide open and fixed on its white tip as it loomed towards her, fizzing ever so softly. The breath wheezed and shuddered in her throat. She could almost feel the heat from it on her cheek, almost feel the pain already. Langrier leaned forwards.

"Stop." Out of the corner of her eye, she saw a blurry figure in the doorway. She blinked, eyelids fluttering. A great fat man, standing at the top of the steps in a white dressing gown.

"Your Excellency!" Langrier shoved the iron back into the brazier as though it was her it was burning. The grip round Monza's neck was suddenly released, Pello's boot came off the back of her calves.

Grand Duke Salier's eyes shifted slowly in his great expanse of pale face, from Monza, to Shivers, and back to Monza. "Are these they?"

"Indeed they are." Nicomo Cosca peered over the duke's shoulder and down into the room. Monza couldn't remember ever in her life being so glad to see someone. The old mercenary winced. "Too late for the Northman's eye."

"Early enough for his life, at least. But whatever have you done to her skin, Captain Langrier?"

"The scars she had already, your Excellency."

"Truly? Quite the collection." Salier slowly shook his head. "A most regrettable case of mistaken identity. For the time being, these two people are my honoured guests. Some clothes for them, and do what you can for his wound."

"Of course." She snatched the dowel out of Monza's mouth and bowed her head. "I deeply regret my mistake, your Excellency."

"Quite understandable. This is war. People get burned." The duke gave a long sigh. "General Murcatto, I hope you will accept a bed in my palace, and join us for breakfast in the morning?"

The chains rattled free and her limp hands fell down into her lap. She thought she managed to gasp out a "yes" before she started sobbing so hard she couldn't speak, tears running free down her face.

Terror, and pain, and immeasurable relief.

The Connoisseur

Anyone would have supposed it was an ordinary morning of peace and plenty in Duke Salier's expansive dining chamber, a room in which his Excellency no doubt spent much of his time. Four musicians struck up sweet music in a far-distant corner, all smiling radiantly, as though serenading the doomed in a palace surrounded by enemies was all they had ever wished for. The long table was stacked high with delicacies: fish and shellfish, breads and pastries, fruits and cheeses, sweets, meats and sweetmeats, all arranged as neatly on their gilded plates as medals on a general's chest. Too much food for twenty, and there were but three to dine, and two of those not hungry.

Monza did not look well. Both of her lips were split, her face was ashen in the centre, swollen and bruised shiny pink on both sides, the white of one eye red with bloodshot patches, fingers trembling. Cosca felt raw to look at her, but he supposed it might have been worse. Small help to their Northern friend. He could have sworn he could hear the groans through the walls all night long.

He reached out with his fork, ready to spear a sausage, well-cooked meat striped black from the grill. An image of Shivers' well-cooked, black-striped face drifted through his mind, and he cleared his throat and caught himself instead a hard-boiled egg. It was only when it was halfway to his plate that he noticed its similarity to an eyeball. He shook it hastily off his fork and into its dish with a rumbling of nausea, and contented himself with tea, silently pretending it was heavily laced with brandy.

Duke Salier was busy reminiscing on past glories, as men are prone to do when their glories are far behind them. One of Cosca's own favourite pastimes, and, if it was even a fraction as boring when he did it, he resolved to give it up. "...Ah, but the banquets I have held in this very room! The great men and women who have enjoyed my hospitality at this table! Rogont, Cantain, Sotorius, Orso himself, for that matter. I never trusted that weasel-faced liar, even back then."

"The courtly dance of Styrian power," said Cosca. "Partners never stay together long."

"Such is politics." The roll of fat around Salier's jaw shifted softly as he shrugged. "Ebb and flow. Yesterday's hero, tomorrow's villain. Yesterday's victory..." He frowned at his empty plate. "I fear the two of you will be my last guests of note and, if you will forgive me, you both have seen more notable days. Still! One takes the guests one has, and makes the merry best of it!" Cosca gave a weary grin. Monza did not stretch herself even that far. "No mood for levity? Anyone would think my city was on fire by your long faces! We will do no more good at the breakfast table, anyway. I swear I've eaten twice what the two of you have combined." Cosca reflected that the duke undoubtedly weighed more than twice what the two of them did combined. Salier reached for a glass of white liquid and raised it to his lips.

"Whatever are you drinking?"

"Goat's milk. Somewhat sour, but wondrous for the digestion. Come, friends — and enemies, of course, for there is nothing more valuable to a powerful man than a good enemy — take a turn with me." He struggled from his chair with much grunting, tossed his glass away and led them briskly across the tiled floor, one plump hand waving in time to the music. "How is your companion, the Northman?"

"Still in very great pain," murmured Monza, looking in some herself.

"Yes...well...a terrible business. Such is war, such is war. Captain Langrier tells me there were seven of you. The blond woman with the child's face is with us, and your man, the quiet one who brought the Talinese uniforms and has apparently been counting every item in my larder since the crack of dawn this morning. One does not need his uncanny facility with numbers to note that two of your band are still...at large."

"Our poisoner and our torturer," said Cosca. "A shame, it's so hard to find good ones."

"Fine company you keep."

"Hard jobs mean hard company. They'll be out of Visserine by now,

297

I daresay." They would be halfway to being out of Styria by now, if they had any sense, and Cosca was far from blaming them.

"Abandoned, eh?" Salier gave a grunt. "I know the feeling. My allies have abandoned me, my soldiers, my people. I am distraught. My sole remaining comfort is my paintings." One fat finger pointed to a deep archway, heavy doors standing open and bright sunlight spilling through.

Cosca's trained eye noted a deep groove in the stonework, metal points gleaming in a wide slot in the ceiling. A portcullis, unless he was much mistaken. "Your collection is well protected."

"Naturally. It is the most valuable in Styria, long years in the making. My great-grandfather began it." Salier ushered them into a long hallway, a strip of gold-embroidered carpet beckoning them down the centre, many-coloured marble gleaming in the light from huge windows. Vast and brooding oils crowded the opposite wall in long procession, gilt frames glittering.

"This hall is given over to the Midderland masters, of course," Salier observed. There was a snarling portrait of bald Zoller, a series of Kings of the Union — Harod, Arnault, Casimir, and more. One might have thought they all shat molten gold, they looked so smug. Salier paused a moment before a monumental canvas of the death of Juvens. A tiny, bleeding figure lost in an immensity of forest, lightning flaring across a lowering sky. "Such brushwork. Such colouring, eh, Cosca?"

"Astounding." Though one daub looked much like another to his eye.

"The happy days I have spent in profound contemplation of these works. Seeking the hidden meanings in the minds of the masters." Cosca raised his brows at Monza. More time in profound contemplation of the campaign map and less on dead painters and perhaps Styria would not have found itself in the current fix.

"Sculptures from the Old Empire," murmured the duke as they passed through a wide doorway and into a second airy gallery, lined on both sides with ancient statues. "You would not believe the cost of shipping them from Calcis." Heroes, emperors, gods. Their missing noses, missing arms, scarred and pitted bodies gave them a look of wounded surprise. The forgotten winners of ten centuries ago, reduced to confused amputees. *Where am I? And for pity's sake, where are my arms?*

"I have been wondering what to do," said Salier suddenly, "and would value your opinion, General Murcatto. You are renowned across Styria and beyond for your ruthlessness, single-mindedness and commitment. Decisiveness has never been my greatest talent. I am too prone to think on what is lost by a certain course of action. To look with longing at all those doors that will be closed, rather than the possibilities presented by the one that I must open."

"A weakness in a soldier," said Monza.

"I know it. I am a weak man, perhaps, and a poor soldier. I have relied on good intentions, fair words and righteous causes, and it seems I and my people now will pay for it." Or for that and his avarice, betrayals and endless warmongering, at least. Salier examined a sculpture of a muscular boatman. Death poling souls to hell, perhaps. "I could flee the city, by small boat in the hours of darkness. Down the river and away, to throw myself upon the mercy of my ally Grand Duke Rogont."

"A brief sanctuary," grunted Monza. "Rogont will be next."

"True. And a man of my considerable dimensions, fleeing? Terribly undignified. Perhaps I could surrender myself to your good friend General Ganmark?"

"You know what would follow."

Salier's soft face turned suddenly hard. "Perhaps Ganmark is not so utterly bereft of mercy as some of Orso's other dogs have been?" Then he seemed to sink back down, face settling into the roll of fat under his chin. "But I daresay you are right." He peered significantly sideways at a statue that had lost its head some time during the last few centuries. "My fat head on a spike would be the best that I could hope for. Just like good Duke Cantain and his sons, eh, General Murcatto?"

She looked evenly back at him. "Just like Cantain and his sons." Heads on spikes, Cosca reflected, were still as fashionable as ever.

Around a corner and into another hall, still longer than the first, walls crowded with canvases. Salier clapped his hands. "Here hang the Styrians! Greatest of our countrymen! Long after we are dead and forgotten, their legacy will endure." He paused before a scene of a bustling marketplace. "Perhaps I could bargain with Orso? Curry favour by delivering to him a mortal enemy? The woman who murdered his eldest son and heir, perhaps?"

Monza did not flinch. She never had been the flinching kind. "The best of luck."

"Bah. Luck has deserted Visserine. Orso would never negotiate, even if I could give him back his son alive, and you have put well and truly paid to that possibility. We are left with suicide." He gestured at a huge, dark-framed effort, a half-naked soldier offering his sword to his defeated general. Presumably so they could make the last sacrifice that honour demanded. That was where honour got a man. "To plunge the mighty blade into my bared breast, as did the fallen heroes of yesteryear!"

The next canvas featured a smirking wine merchant leaning on a barrel and holding a glass up to the light. Oh, a drink, a drink, a drink. "Or poison? Deadly powders in the wine? Scorpion in the bedsheets? Asp down one's undergarments?" Salier grinned round at them. "No? Hang myself? I understand men often spend, when they are hanged." And he flapped his hands away from his groin in demonstration, as though they had been in any doubt as to his meaning. "Sounds like more fun than poison, anyway." The duke sighed and stared glumly at a painting of a woman surprised while bathing. "Let us not pretend I have the courage for such exploits. Suicide, that is, not spending. That I still manage once a day, in spite of my size. Do you still manage it, Cosca?"

"Like a fucking fountain," he drawled, not to be outdone in vulgarity.

"But what to do?" mused Salier. "What to—"

Monza stepped in front of him. "Help me kill Ganmark." Cosca felt his brows go up. Even beaten, bruised and with the enemy at the gates, she could not wait to draw the knives again. Ruthlessness, single-mindedness and commitment indeed.

"And why ever would I wish to do that?"

"Because he'll be coming for your collection." She had always had a knack for tickling people where they were most ticklish. Cosca had seen her do it often. To him, among others. "Coming to box up all your paintings, and your sculptures, and your jars, and ship them back to Fontezarmo to adorn Orso's latrines." A nice touch, his latrines. "Ganmark is a connoisseur, like yourself."

"That Union cocksucker is nothing like me!" Anger suddenly flared red across the back of Salier's neck. "A common thief and braggart, a degenerate man-fucker, tramping blood across the sweet soil of Styria as though its mud were not fit for his boots! He can have my life, but he'll never have my paintings! I will see to it!"

"I can see to it," hissed Monza, stepping closer to the duke. "He'll come here, when the city falls. He'll rush here, keen to secure your collection. We can be waiting, dressed as his soldiers. When he enters," she snapped her fingers, "we drop your portcullis, and we have him! You have him! Help me."

But the moment had passed. Salier's veneer of heavy-lidded carelessness had descended again. "These are my two favourites, I do believe," gesturing, all nonchalance, towards two matching canvases. "Parteo Gavra's studies of the woman. They were intended always as a pair. His mother, and his favourite whore."

"Mothers and whores," sneered Monza. "A curse on fucking artists. We were talking of Ganmark. Help me!"

Salier blew out a tired sigh. "Ah, Monzcarro, Monzcarro. If only you had sought my help five seasons ago, before Sweet Pines. Before Caprile. Even last spring, before you spiked Cantain's head above his gate. Even then, the good we could have done, the blows we could have struck together for freedom. Even—"

"Forgive me if I'm blunt, your Excellency, but I spent the night being beaten like a sack of *meat*." Monza's voice cracked slightly on the last word. "You ask for my opinion. You've lost because you're too weak, too soft and too slow, not because you're too good. You fought alongside Orso happily enough when you shared the same goals, and smiled happily enough at his methods, as long as they brought you more land. Your men spread fire, rape and murder when it suited you. No love of freedom then. The only open hand the farmers of Puranti had from you back in those days was the one that crushed them flat. Play the martyr if you must, Salier, but not with me. I feel sick enough already."

Cosca felt himself wincing. There was such a thing as too much truth, especially in the ears of powerful men.

The duke's eyes narrowed. "Blunt, you say? If you spoke to Orso in such a manner it is small wonder he threw you down a mountain. I almost wish I had a long drop handy. Tell me, since candour seems the fashion, what did you do to anger Orso so? I thought he loved you like a daughter? Far more than his own children, not that any of those three ever were so very lovable — fox, shrew and mouse."

Her bruised cheek twitched. "I became too popular with his people."

"Yes. And?"

"He was afraid I might steal his throne."

"Indeed? And I suppose your eyes were never turned upon it?"

"Only to keep him in it."

"Truly?" Salier grinned sideways at Cosca. "It would hardly have been the first chair your loyal claws tore from under its owner, would it?"

"I did nothing!" she barked. "Except win his battles, make him the greatest man in Styria. Nothing!"

The Duke of Visserine sighed. "I have a fat body, Monzcarro, not a fat head, but have it your way. You are all innocence. Doubtless you handed out cakes at Caprile as well, rather than slaughter. Keep your secrets if you please. Much good may they do you now."

Cosca narrowed his eyes against the sudden glare as they stepped out of an open doorway, through an echoing arcade and into the pristine garden at the centre of Salier's gallery. Water trickled in pools at its corners. A pleasant breeze made the new flowers nod, stirred the leaves of the topiary, plucked specks of blossom from Suljuk cherry trees, no doubt torn from their native soil and brought across the sea for the amusement of the Duke of Visserine.

A magnificent sculpture towered over them in the midst of a cobbled space, twice life-size or more, carved from perfectly white, almost translucent marble. A naked man, lean as a dancer and muscular as a wrestler, one arm extended and with a bronze sword, turned dark and streaked with green, thrust forwards in the fist. As if directing a mighty army to storm the dining room. He had a helmet pushed back on the top of his head, a frown of stern command on his perfect features.

"The Warrior," murmured Cosca, as the shadow of the great blade fell across his eyes, the glare of sunlight blazing along its edge.

"Yes, by Bonatine, greatest of all Styrian sculptors, and this perhaps his greatest work, carved at the height of the New Empire. It originally stood on the steps of the Senate House in Borletta. My father took it as an indemnity after the Summer War."

"He fought a war?" Monza's split lip curled. "For this?"

"Only a small one. But it was worth it. Beautiful, is it not?"

"Beautiful," Cosca lied. To the starving man, bread is beautiful. To the homeless man, a roof is beautiful. To the drunkard, wine is beautiful. Only those who want for nothing else need find beauty in a lump of rock.

"Stolicus was the inspiration, I understand, ordering the famous charge at the Battle of Darmium."

Monza raised an eyebrow. "Leading a charge, eh? You'd have thought he'd have put some trousers on for work like that."

"It's called artistic licence," snapped Salier. "It's a fantasy, one can do as one pleases."

Cosca frowned. "Really? I always felt a man makes more points worth making if he steers always close to the truth..."

Hurried boot heels cut him off and a nervous-looking officer rushed across the garden, face touched with sweat, a long smear of black mud down the left side of his jacket. He came to one knee on the cobbles, head bowed.

"Your Excellency."

Salier did not even look at him. "Speak, if you must."

"There has been another assault."

"So close to breakfast time?" The duke winced as he placed a hand on his belly. "A typical Union man, this Ganmark, he has no more regard for mealtimes than you did, Murcatto. With what result?"

"The Talinese have forced a second breach, towards the harbour. We drove them back, but with heavy losses. We are greatly outnumbered—"

"Of course you are. Order your men to hold their positions as long as possible."

The colonel licked his lips. "And then...?"

"That will be all." Salier did not take his eyes from the great statue.

"Your Excellency." The man retreated towards the door. And no doubt to a heroic, pointless death at one breach or another. The most heroic deaths of all were the pointless ones, Cosca had always found.

"Visserine will soon fall." Salier clicked his tongue as he stared up at the great image of Stolicus. "How profoundly...depressing. Had I only been more like this."

"Thinner waisted?" murmured Cosca.

"I meant warlike, but while we are wishing, why not a thin waist too? I thank you for your...almost uncomfortably honest counsel, General Murcatto. I may have a few days yet to make my decision." To delay the inevitable at the cost of hundreds of lives. "In the meantime, I hope the two of you will remain with us. The two of you, and your three friends."

"Your guests," asked Monza, "or your prisoners?"

"You have seen how my prisoners are treated. Which would be your choice?"

Cosca took a deep breath, and scratched slowly at his neck. A choice that more or less made itself.

Vile Jelly

Shivers' face was near healed. Faint pink stripe left across his forehead, through his brow, across his cheek. More'n likely it would fade altogether in a few days more. His eye still ached a bit, but he'd kept his looks alright. Monza lay in the bed, sheet round her waist, skinny back turned towards him. He stood a moment, grinning, watching her ribs shift gently as she breathed, patches of shadow between them shrinking and growing. Then he padded from the mirror across to the open window, looking out. Beyond it the city was burning, fires lighting up the night. Strange thing though, he wasn't sure which city, or why he was there. Mind was moving slowly. He winced, rubbing at his cheek.

"Hurts," he grunted. "By the dead it hurts."

"Oh, *that* hurts?" He whipped round, stumbling back against the wall. Fenris the Feared loomed over him, bald head brushing the ceiling, half his body tattooed with tiny letters, the rest all cased in black metal, face writhing like boiling porridge.

"You're . . . you're fucking dead!"

The giant laughed. "I'll say I'm fucking dead." He had a sword stuck right through his body, the hilt above one hip, point of the blade sticking out under his other arm. He jerked one massive thumb at the blood dripping from the pommel and scattering across the carpet. "I mean, this *really* hurts. Did you cut your hair? I liked you better before."

Bethod pointed to his smashed-in head, a twisted mess of blood, brains, hair, bone. "Shuth uth, the pair o' youth." He couldn't speak right because his mouth was all squashed in on itself. "Thith ith whath hurts lookth like!" He gave the Feared a pointless shove. "Why couldn't you win, you thtupid half-devil bathtard?"

"I'm dreaming," Shivers said to himself, trying to think his way through it, but his face was throbbing, throbbing. "I must be dreaming."

Someone was singing. "I...am made...of death!" Hammer banging on a nail. "I am the Great Leveller!" Bang, bang, bang, each time sending a jolt of pain through Shivers' face. "I am the storm in the High Places!" The Bloody-Nine hummed to himself as he cut the corpse of Shivers' brother into bits, stripped to the waist, body a mass of scars and twisted muscle all daubed-up with blood. "So you're the good man, eh?" He waved his knife at Shivers, grinning. "You need to fucking toughen up, boy. You should've killed me. Now help me get his arms off, optimist."

"The dead know I don't like this bastard any, but he's got a point." Shivers' brother's head peered down at him from its place nailed to Bethod's standard. "You need to toughen up. Mercy and cowardice are the same. You reckon you could get this nail out?"

"You're a fucking embarrassment!" His father, slack face streaked with tears, waving his jug around. "Why couldn't you be the one dead, and your brother lived? You useless little fuck! You useless, gutless, disappointing speck o' shit!"

"This is rubbish," snarled Shivers through gritted teeth, sitting down on his crossed legs by the fire. His whole head was pulsing. "This is just...just rubbish!"

"What's rubbish?" gurgled Tul Duru, blood leaking from his cut throat as he spoke.

"All this. Faces from the past, saying meaningful stuff. Bit fucking obvious, ain't it? Couldn't you do better'n this shit?"

"Uh," said Grim.

Black Dow looked a bit put out. "Don't blame us, boy. Your dream, no? You cut your hair?"

Dogman shrugged. "If you was cleverer, maybe you'd have cleverer dreams."

He felt himself grabbed from behind, face twisted round. The Bloody-Nine was there beside him, hair plastered to his head with blood, scarred face all dashed with black. "If you was cleverer, maybe you wouldn't have got your eye burned out." And he ground his thumb into Shivers' eye, harder and harder. Shivers thrashed, and twisted, and screamed, but there was no way free. It was already done.

He woke up screaming, 'course. He always did now. You could hardly call it a scream anymore, his voice was worn down to a grinding stub, gravel in his raw throat.

It was dark. Pain tore at his face like a wolf at a carcass. He thrashed free of the blankets, reeled to nowhere. Like the iron was still pressed against him, burning. He crashed into a wall, fell on his knees. Bent over, hands squeezing the sides of his skull like they might stop his head from cracking open. Rocking, every muscle flexed to bursting. He groaned and moaned, whimpered and snarled, spat and blubbered, drooled and gibbered, mad from it, mindless with it. Touch it, press it. He held his quivering fingers to the bandages.

"Shhhh." He felt a hand. Monza, pawing at his face, pushing back his hair.

Pain split his head where his eye used to be like an axe splitting a log, split his mind too, broke it open, thoughts all spilling out in a mad splatter. "By the dead...make it stop...shit, shit." He grabbed her hand and she winced, gasped. He didn't care. "Kill me! Kill me. Just make it stop." He wasn't even sure what tongue he was talking. "Kill me. By the..." He was sobbing, tears stinging the eye he still had. She tore her hand away and he was rocking again, rocking, pain ripping through his face like a saw through a tree-stump. He'd tried to be a good man, hadn't he?

"I tried, I fucking tried. Make it stop...please, please, please, please—"

"Here." He snatched hold of the pipe and sucked at it, greedy as a drunkard at the bottle. He hardly even marked the smoke biting, just heaved in air until his lungs were full, and all the while she held him, arms tight around him, rocking him back and forwards. The darkness was full of colours, now. Covered with glittering smears. The pain was a step away, 'stead of pressed burning against him. His breathing had softened to a whimper, aching body all washed out.

She helped him up, dragging him to his feet, pipe clattering from his limp hand. The open window swayed, a painting of another world. Hell maybe, red and yellow spots of fire leaving long brushstrokes through the dark. The bed came up and swallowed him, sucked him down. His face throbbed still, pulsed a dull ache. He remembered, remembered why.

"The dead…" he whispered, tears running down his other cheek. "My eye. They burned my eye out."

"Shhhh," she whispered, gently stroking the good side of his face. "Quiet now, Caul. Quiet."

The darkness was reaching for him, wrapping him up. Before it took him he twisted his fingers clumsily in her hair and dragged her face towards his, close enough almost to kiss his bandages.

"Should've been you," he whispered at her. "Should've been you."

Other People's Scores

T hat's his place," said the one with the sore on his cheek. "Sajaam's place."

A stained door in a stained wall, pasted with fluttering old bills decrying the League of Eight as villains, usurpers and common criminals. A pair of caricature faces stared from each one, a bloated Duke Salier and a sneering Duke Rogont. A pair of common criminals stood at the doorway, scarcely less caricatures themselves. One dark-skinned, the other with a heavy tattoo down one arm, both sweeping the street with identical scowls.

"Thank you, children. Eat, now." Shenkt pressed a scale into each grubby hand, twelve pairs of eyes wide in smudged faces to have so much money. Once a few days had passed, let alone a few years, he knew it would have done them little good. They were the beggars, thieves, whores, early dead of tomorrow. But Shenkt had done much harm in his life, and so he tried, wherever possible, to be kind. It put nothing right, he knew that. But perhaps a coin could tip the scales of life by that vital degree, and one among them would be spared. It would be a good thing, to spare even one.

He hummed quietly to himself as he crossed the street, the two men at the door frowning at him all the way. "I am here to speak to Sajaam."

"You armed?"

"Always." He and the dark-skinned guard stared at each other for a moment. "My ready wit could strike at any moment."

Neither one of them smiled, but Shenkt had not expected them to, and did not care into the bargain. "What've you got to say to Sajaam?"

"'Are you Sajaam?' That shall be my opening gambit."

"You mocking us, little man?" The guard put one hand on the mace hanging at his belt, no doubt thinking himself fearsome.

"I would not dare. I am here to enjoy myself, and have money to spend, nothing more."

"Maybe you came to the right place after all. With me."

He led Shenkt through a hot, dim room, heavy with oily smoke and shadows. Lit blue, green, orange, red by lamps of coloured glass. Husk-smokers sprawled around it, pale faces twisted with smiles, or hanging slack and empty. Shenkt found that he was humming again, and stopped himself.

A greasy curtain pushed aside into a large back room that smelled of unwashed bodies, smoke and vomit, rotten food and rotten living. A man covered in tattoos sat cross-legged upon a sweat-stained cushion, an axe leaning against the wall beside him. Another man sat on the other side of the room, digging at an ugly piece of meat with a knife, a loaded flatbow beside his plate. Above his head an old clock hung, workings dangling from its underside like the intestines from a gutted corpse, pendulum swinging, tick, tick, tick.

Upon a long table in the centre of the room were the chattels of a card game. Coins and counters, bottles and glasses, pipes and candles. Men sat about it, six of them in all. A fat man at Shenkt's right hand, a scrawny one at the left, stuttering out a joke to his neighbour.

"...he fuh, fuh, fucked her!"

Harsh laughter, harsh faces, cheap lives of cheap smoke, cheap drink, cheap violence. Shenkt's guide walked around to the head of the table, leaned down to speak to a broad-shouldered man, black-skinned, white-haired, with the smile of comfortable ownership on his lined face. He toyed with a golden coin, flipping it glinting across the tops of his knuckles.

"You are Sajaam?" asked Shenkt.

He nodded, entirely at his ease. "Do I know you?"

"No."

"A stranger, then? We do not entertain many strangers here, do we, my friends?" A couple of them grinned half-heartedly. "Most of my customers are well known to us. What can Sajaam do for you, stranger?"

"Where is Monzcarro Murcatto?"

Like a man plunging through thin ice, the room was sucked into sudden, awful silence. That heavy quiet before the heavens split. That pregnant stillness, bulging with the inevitable.

"The Snake of Talins is dead," murmured Sajaam, eyes narrowing.

Shenkt felt the slow movement of the men around him. Their smiles creeping off, their feet creeping to the balance for killing, their hands creeping to their weapons. "She is alive and you know where. I want only to talk to her."

"Who the shuh, shit does this bastard thuh, think he is?" asked the scrawny card player, and some of the others laughed. Tight, fake laughs, to hide their tension.

"Only tell me where she is. Please. Then no one's conscience need grow any heavier today." Shenkt did not mind pleading. He had given up his vanity long ago. He looked each man in the eyes, gave each a chance to give him what he needed. He gave everyone a chance, where he could. He wished more of them took it.

But they only smiled at him, and at each other, and Sajaam smiled widest of all. "I carry my conscience lightly enough."

Shenkt's old master might have said the same. "Some of us do. It is a gift."

"I tell you what, we'll toss for it." Sajaam held his coin up to the light, gold flashing. "Heads, we kill you. Tails, I tell you where Murcatto is…" His smile was all bright teeth in his dark face. "Then we kill you." There was the slightest ring of metal as he flicked his coin up.

Shenkt sucked in breath through his nose, slow, slow.

The gold crawled into the air, turning, turning.

The clock beat deep and slow as the oars of a great ship.

Boom…boom…boom…

Shenkt's fist sank into the great gut of the fat man on his right, almost to the elbow. Nothing left to scream with, he gave the gentlest fragment of a sigh, eyes popping. An instant later the edge of Shenkt's open hand caved his astonished face in and ripped his head half-off, bone crumpling like paper. Blood sprayed across the table, black spots frozen, the expressions of the men around it only now starting to shift from rage to shock.

Shenkt snatched the nearest of them from his chair and flung him into the ceiling. His cry was barely begun as he crashed into a pair of beams, wood bursting, splinters spinning, mangled body falling back down in a languid shower of dust and broken plaster. Long before that one hit the floor, Shenkt had seized the next player's head and rammed his face through the table, through the floor beneath it. Cards, and broken glasses, chunks

310

of planking, fragments of wood and flesh made a swelling cloud. Shenkt ripped the half-drawn hatchet from his fist as he went down, sent it whirling across the room and into the chest of the tattooed man, halfway up from his cushion and the first note of a war cry throbbing from his lips. It hit him haft first, so hard it scarcely mattered, spun him round and round like a child's top, ripped wide open, blood gouting from his body in all directions.

The flatbow twanged, deep and distorted, string twisting as it pushed the bolt towards him, swimming slowly through the dust-filled air as if through treacle, shaft flexing lightly back and forth. Shenkt snatched it from its path and drove it clean through a man's skull, his face folding into itself, meat bursting from torn skin. Shenkt caught him under the jaw and sent his corpse hurtling across the room with a flick of his wrist. He crashed into the archer, the two bodies mashed together, flailing bonelessly into the wall, through the wall, out into the alley on the other side, leaving a ragged hole in the shattered planks behind them.

The guard from the door had his mace raised, mouth open, air rushing in as he made ready to roar. Shenkt leaped the ruins of the table and slapped him backhanded across the chest, burst his ribcage and sent him reeling, twisting up like a corkscrew, mace flying from his lifeless hand. Shenkt stepped forwards and snatched Sajaam's coin from the air as it spun back down, metal slapping into his palm.

He breathed out, and time flowed again.

The last couple of corpses tumbled across the floor. Plaster dropped, settled. The tattooed man's left boot rattled against the boards, leg quivering as he died. One of the others was groaning, but not for much longer. The last spots of blood rained softly from the air around them, misting across the broken glass, the broken wood, the broken bodies. One of the cushions had burst, the feathers still fluttering down in a white cloud.

Shenkt's fist trembled before Sajaam's slack face. Steam hissed from it, then molten gold, trickling from between his fingers, running down his forearm in shining streaks. He opened his hand and showed it, palm forwards, daubed with black blood, smeared with glowing metal.

"Neither heads nor tails."

"Fuh...fuh...fuh..." The stuttering man still sat at his place, where the table had been, cards clutched in his rigid hand, every part of him spattered, spotted, sprayed with blood.

"You," said Shenkt. "Stuttering man. You may live."

"Fuh ... fuh ..."

"You alone are spared. Out, before I reconsider."

The mumbling beggar dropped his cards, fled whimpering for the door and tumbled through it. Shenkt watched him go. A good thing, even to spare one.

As he turned back, Sajaam was swinging his chair over his head. It burst apart across Shenkt's shoulder, broken pieces bouncing from the floor and clattering away. A futile gesture, Shenkt scarcely even felt it. The edge of his hand chopped into the man's big arm, snapped it like a dead twig, spun him around and sent him rolling over and over across the floor.

Shenkt walked after him, his scuffed work boots making not the slightest sound as they found the gaps between the debris. Sajaam coughed, shook his head, started to worm away on his back, gurgling through gritted teeth, hand dragging behind him the wrong way up. The heels of his embroidered Gurkish slippers kicked at the floor, leaving stuttering trails through the detritus of blood, dust, feathers and splinters that had settled across the whole room like leaves across a forest floor in autumn.

"A man sleeps through most of his life, even when awake. You get so little time, yet still you spend it utterly oblivious. Angry, frustrated, fixated on meaningless nothings. That drawer does not close flush with the front of my desk. What cards does my opponent hold, and how much money can I win from him? I wish I were taller. What will I have for dinner, for I am not fond of parsnips?" Shenkt rolled a mangled corpse out of his way with the toe of one boot. "It takes a moment like this to jerk us to our senses, to draw our eyes from the mud to the heavens, to root our attention in the present. Now you realise how precious is each moment. That is my gift to you."

Sajaam reached the back wall and propped himself up against it, worked himself slowly to standing, broken arm hanging limp.

"I despise violence. It is the last tool of feeble minds." Shenkt stopped a stride away. "So let us have no more foolishness. Where is Monzcarro Murcatto?"

To give the man his due for courage, he made for the knife at his belt.

Shenkt's pointed finger sank into the hollow where chest met shoulder, just beneath his collarbone. It punched through shirt, skin, flesh, and as the rest of his fist smacked hard against Sajaam's chest and drove him back against the wall, his fingernail was already scraping against the inside surface of his shoulder blade, buried in his flesh right to the knuckles. Sajaam screamed, knife clattering from his dangling fingers.

"No more foolishness, I said. Where is Murcatto?"

"In Visserine the last I heard!" His voice was hoarse with pain. "In Visserine!"

"At the siege?" Sajaam nodded, bloody teeth clenched tight together. If Visserine had not fallen already, it would have by the time Shenkt got there. But he never left a job half-done. He would assume she was still alive, and carry on the chase. "Who does she have with her?"

"Some Northman beggar, called himself Shivers! A man of mine named Friendly! A convict! A convict from Safety!"

"Yes?" Shenkt twisted his finger in the man's flesh, blood trickling from the wound and down his hand, around the streaks of gold dried to his forearm, dripping from his elbow, tap, tap, tap.

"Ah! Ah! I put her in touch with a poisoner called Morveer! In Westport, and in Sipani with a woman called Vitari!" Shenkt frowned. "A woman who can get things done!"

"Murcatto, Shivers, Friendly, Morveer . . . Vitari."

A desperate nod, spit flying from Sajaam's gritted teeth with every heaving, agonised breath.

"And where are these brave companions bound next?"

"I'm not sure! Gah! She said seven men! The seven men who killed her brother! Ah! Puranti, maybe! Keep ahead of Orso's army! If she gets Ganmark, maybe she'll try for Faithful next, for Faithful Carpi!"

"Maybe she will." Shenkt jerked his finger free with a faint sucking sound and Sajaam collapsed, sliding down until his rump hit the floor, his shivering, sweat-beaded face twisted with pain.

"Please," he grunted. "I can help you. I can help you find her."

Shenkt squatted down in front of him, blood-smeared hands dangling on the knees of his blood-smeared trousers. "But you have helped. You can leave the rest to me."

"I have money! I have money."

Shenkt said nothing.

"I was planning on turning her in to Orso, sooner or later, once the price was high enough."

More nothing.

"That doesn't make any difference, does it?"

Silence.

"I told that bitch she'd be the death of me."

"You were right. I hope that is a comfort."

"Not much of one. I should have killed her then."

"But you saw money to be made. Have you anything to say?"

Sajaam stared at him. "What would I say?"

"Some people want to say things, at the end. Do you?"

"What are you?" he whispered.

"I have been many things. A student. A messenger. A thief. A soldier in old wars. A servant of great powers. An actor in great events. Now?" Shenkt puffed out an unhappy breath as he gazed around at the mangled corpses hunched, sprawled, huddled across the room. "Now, it seems, I am a man who settles other people's scores."

The Fencing Master

Monza's hands were shaking again, but that was no surprise. The danger, the fear, not knowing if she was going to live out the next moment. Her brother murdered, herself broken, everything she'd worked for gone. The pain, the withering need for husk, trusting no one, day after day, week after week. Then there was all the death she'd been the cause of, in Westport, in Sipani, gathering on her shoulders like a great weight of lead.

The last few months had been enough to make anyone's hands shake. But maybe it was just watching Shivers have his eye burned out and thinking she'd be next.

She looked nervously towards the door between her room and his. He'd be awake soon. Screaming again, which was bad enough, or silent, which was worse. Kneeling there, looking at her with his one eye. That accusing look. She knew she should have been grateful, should have cared for him the way she used to for her brother. But a growing part of her just wanted to kick him and not stop. Maybe when Benna died everything warm, or decent, or human in her had been left rotting on the mountainside with his corpse.

She pulled her glove off and stared at the thing inside. At the thin pink scars where the shattered bones had been put back together. The deep red line where Gobba's wire had cut into her. She curled the fingers into a fist, or something close, except the little one, still pointing off like a signpost to nowhere. It didn't hurt as badly as it used to, but more than enough to bring a grimace to her face, and the pain cut through the fear, crushed the doubts.

"Revenge," she whispered. Kill Ganmark, that was all that mattered now. His soft, sad face, his weak, watery eyes. Calmly stabbing Benna through the stomach. Rolling his corpse off the terrace. *That's that.* She squeezed her fist tighter, bared her teeth at it.

"Revenge." For Benna and for herself. She was the Butcher of Caprile, merciless, fearless. She was the Snake of Talins, deadly as the viper and no more regretful. Kill Ganmark, and then...

"Whoever's next." And her hand was steady.

Running footsteps slapped hard along the hallway outside and away. She heard someone shout in the distance, couldn't make out the words, but couldn't miss the edge of fear in the voice. She crossed to the window and pulled it open. Her room, or her cell, was high up on the north face of the palace. A stone bridge spanned the Visser upstream, tiny dots moving fast across it. Even from this distance she could tell people running for their lives.

A good general gets to know the smell of panic, and suddenly it was reeking. Orso's men must have finally carried the walls. The sack of Visserine had begun. Ganmark would be on his way to the palace, even now, to take possession of Duke Salier's renowned collection.

The door creaked open and Monza spun about. Captain Langrier stood in the doorway in a Talinese uniform, a bulging sack in one hand. She had a sword at one hip and a long dagger at the other. Monza had nothing of the kind, and she found herself acutely aware of the fact. She stood, hands by her sides, trying to look as if every muscle wasn't ready to fight. And die, more than likely.

Langrier moved slowly into the room. "So you really are Murcatto, eh?"

"I'm Murcatto."

"Sweet Pines? Musselia? The High Bank? You won all those battles?"

"That's right."

"You ordered all those folk killed at Caprile?"

"What the fuck do you want?"

"Duke Salier says he's decided to do it your way." Langrier dumped the sack on the floor and it sagged open. Metal gleamed inside. The Talinese armour Friendly had stolen out near the breach. "Best put this on. Don't know how long we'll have before your friend Ganmark gets here."

Alive, then. For now. Monza dragged a lieutenant's jacket from the sack and pulled it on over her shirt, started to button it up. Langrier watched her for a minute, then started talking.

"I just wanted to say...while there's a chance. Well. That I always admired you, I guess."

Monza stared at her. "What?"

"A woman. A soldier. Getting where you've been. Doing what you've done. You might've stood on the other side from us, but you always were something of a hero to—"

"You think I care a shit?" Monza didn't know which sickened her more — being called a hero or who was saying it.

"Can't blame me for not believing you. Woman with your reputation, thought you'd be harder in a fix like that—"

"You ever watched someone have their eye burned out of their head and thought you'd be next?"

Langrier worked her mouth. "Can't say I've sat on that side of the issue."

"You should try it, see how fucking hard you end up." Monza pulled some stolen boots on, not so bad a fit.

"Here." Langrier was holding Benna's ring out to her, big stone gleaming the colour of blood. "Doesn't suit me anyway."

Monza snatched it from her hand, twisted it onto her finger. "What? Give me back what you stole in the first place and think that makes us even?"

"Look, I'm sorry about your man's eye and the rest, but it isn't about you, understand? Someone's a threat to my city, I have to find out how. I don't like it, it's just what has to be done. Don't pretend you haven't done worse. I don't expect we'll ever share any jokes. But for now, while we've got this task to be about, we'll need to put it behind us."

Monza kept her silence as she dressed. It was true enough. She'd done worse, alright. Watched it done, anyway. Let it be done, which was no better. She buckled on the breastplate, must've come from some lean young officer and fitted her well enough, pulled the last strap through. "I need something to kill Ganmark with."

"Once we get to the garden you can have a blade, not—"

Monza saw a hand close around the grip of Langrier's dagger. She started to turn, surprised. "Wha—" The point slid out of the front of her neck. Shivers' face loomed up beside hers, white and wasted, bandages bound tight over one whole side of it, a pale stain through the cloth where his eye used to be. His left arm slid around Langrier's chest from behind and drew her tight against him. Tight as a lover.

"It ain't about you, understand?" He was almost kissing at her ear as blood began to run from the point of the knife and down her neck in a thick black line. "You take my eye, I've got to take your life." She opened her mouth, and her tongue flopped out, and blood started to trickle from the tip of it and down her chin. "I don't like it." Her face turned purple, eyes rolling up. "Just what has to be done." Her legs kicked, her boot heels clattering against the boards as he lifted her up in the air. "Sorry about your neck." The blade ripped sideways and opened her throat up wide, black blood showering out across the bedclothes, spraying up the wall in an arc of red spots.

Shivers let her drop and she crumpled, sprawling face down as if her bones had turned to mud, another gout of blood spurting sideways. Her boots moved, toes scraping. One set of nails scratched at the floor. Shivers took a long breath in through his nose, then he blew it out, and he looked up at Monza, and he smiled. A friendly little grin, as if they'd shared some private joke that Langrier just hadn't got.

"By the dead but I feel better for that. Ganmark's in the city, did she say?"

"Uh." Monza couldn't speak. Her skin was flushed and burning.

"Then I reckon we got work ahead of us." Shivers didn't seem to notice the rapidly spreading slick of blood creep between his toes, around the sides of his big bare feet. He dragged the sack up and peered inside. "Armour in here, then? Guess I'd better get dressed, eh, Chief? Hate to arrive at a party in the wrong clothes."

The garden at the centre of Salier's gallery showed no signs of imminent doom. Water trickled, leaves rustled, a bee or two floated lazily from one flower to another. White blossom occasionally filtered down from the cherry trees and dusted the well-shaved lawns.

Cosca sat cross-legged and worked the edge of his sword with a whet-stone, metal softly ringing. Morveer's flask pressed into his thigh, but he felt no need for it. Death was at the doorstep, and so he was at peace. His blissful moment before the storm. He tipped his head back, eyes closed, sun warm on his face, and wondered why he could never feel this way unless the world was burning down around him.

Calming breezes washed through the shadowy colonnades, through doorways into hallways lined with paintings. Through one open window Friendly could be seen, in the armour of a Talinese guardsman, counting every soldier in Nasurin's colossal painting of the Second Battle of Oprile. Cosca grinned. He tried always to be forgiving of other men's foibles. He had enough of his own, after all.

Perhaps a half-dozen of Salier's guards had remained, disguised as soldiers from Duke Orso's army. Men loyal enough to die beside their master at the last. He snorted as he ran the whetstone once more down the edge of his sword. Loyalty had always sat with honour, discipline and self-restraint on his list of incomprehensible virtues.

"Why so happy?" Day sat beside him on the grass, a flatbow across her knees, chewing at her lip. The uniform she wore must have come from some dead drummer-boy, it fit her well. Very well. Cosca wondered if it was wrong of him to find something peculiarly alluring about a pretty girl in a man's clothes. He wondered furthermore if she might be persuaded to give a comrade-in-arms…a little help sharpening his weapon before the fighting started? He cleared his throat. Of course not. But a man could dream.

"Perhaps something is wrong in my head." He rubbed a blemish from the steel with his thumb. "Getting out of bed." Metal rang. "A day of honest work." Whetstone scraped. "Peace. Normality. Sobriety." He held the sword up to the light and watched the metal gleam. "These are the things that terrify me. Danger, by contrast, has long been my only relief. Eat something. You'll need your strength."

"I've no appetite," she said glumly. "I've never faced certain death before."

"Oh, come, come, don't say such a thing." He stood, brushed the blossom from the captain's insignia on the sleeves of his stolen uniform. "If there is one thing I have learned in all my many last stands, it is that death is never certain, only…extremely likely."

"Truly inspirational words."

"I try. Indeed I do." Cosca slapped his sword into its sheath, picked up Monza's Calvez and ambled away towards the statue of The Warrior. His Excellency Duke Salier stood in its muscular shadow, arrayed for a noble death in a spotless white uniform festooned with gold braid.

"How did it end like this?" he was musing. The very same question Cosca had so often asked himself, while sucking the last drop from one cheap bottle or another. Waking baffled in one unfamiliar doorway, or another. Carrying out one hateful, poorly paid act of violence. Or another. "How did it end...like this?"

"You underestimated Orso's venomous ambition and Murcatto's ruthless competence. Don't feel too badly, though, we've all done it."

Salier's eyes rolled sideways. "The question was intended to be rhetorical. But you are right, of course. It seems I have been guilty of arrogance, and the penalty will be harsh. No less than everything. But who could have expected a young woman would win one unlikely victory over us after another? How I laughed when you made her your second, Cosca. How we all laughed when Orso gave her command. We were already planning our triumphs, dividing his lands between us. Our chuckles are become sobs now, eh?"

"I find chuckles have a habit of doing so."

"I suppose that makes her a very great soldier and me a very poor one. But then I never aspired to be a soldier, and would have been perfectly happy as merely a grand duke."

"Now you are nothing, instead, and so am I. Such is life."

"Time for one last performance, though."

"For both of us."

The duke grinned back. "A pair of dying swans, eh, Cosca?"

"A brace of old turkeys, maybe. Why aren't you running, your Excellency?"

"I must confess I am wondering myself. Pride, I think. I have spent my life as the Grand Duke of Visserine, and insist on dying the same way. I refuse to be simply fat Master Salier, once of importance."

"Pride, eh? Can't say I ever had much of the stuff."

"Then why aren't you running, Cosca?"

"I suppose..." Why was he not running? Old Master Cosca, once of importance, who always kept his last thought for his own skin? Foolish love? Mad bravery? Old debts to pay? Or simply so that merciful death could spare him from further shame? "But look!" He pointed to the gate. "Only think of her and she appears."

She wore a Talinese uniform, hair gathered up under a helmet, jaw set hard. Just like a serious young officer, clean-shaven this morning and keen to get stuck into the manly business of war. If Cosca had not known, he swore he would never have guessed. A tiny something in the way she walked, perhaps? In the set of her hips, the length of her neck? Again, the women in men's clothes. Did they have to torture him so?

"Monza!" he called. "I was worried you might not make it!"

"And leave you to die gloriously alone?" Shivers came behind her wearing breastplate, greaves and helmet stolen from a big corpse out near the breach. Bandages stared accusingly from one blind eyehole. "From what I can hear, they're at the palace gate already."

"So soon?" Salier's tongue darted over his plump lips. "Where is Captain Langrier?"

"She ran. Seems glory didn't appeal."

"Is there no loyalty left in Styria?"

"I never noticed any before." Cosca tossed the Calvez over in its scabbard and Monza snatched it smartly from the air. "Unless you count each man for himself. Is there any plan, besides wait for Ganmark to come calling?"

"Day!" She pointed up to the narrower windows on the floor above. "I want you up there. Drop the portcullis once we've had a try at Ganmark. Or once he's had a try at us."

The girl looked greatly relieved to be put at least temporarily out of harm's way, though Cosca feared it would be no more than temporary. "Once the trap's sprung. Alright." She hurried off towards one of the doorways.

"We wait here. When Ganmark arrives we tell him we've captured Grand Duke Salier. We bring your Excellency close, and then . . . you realise we may well all die today?"

The duke smiled weakly, jowls trembling. "I am not a fighter, General Murcatto, but nor am I a coward. If I am to die, I might as well spit from my grave."

"I couldn't agree more," said Monza.

"Oh, nor me," Cosca threw in. "Though a grave's a grave, spit or no. You are quite sure he'll come?"

"He'll come."

"And when he does?"

"Kill," grunted Shivers. Someone had given him a shield and a heavy studded axe with a long pick on the reverse. Now he took a brutal-looking practice swipe with it.

Monza's neck shifted as she swallowed. "I guess we just wait and see."

"Ah, wait and see." Cosca beamed. "My kind of plan."

* * *

A crash came from somewhere in the palace, distant shouting, maybe even the faint clash and clatter of steel. Monza worked her left hand nervously around the hilt of the Calvez, hanging drawn beside her leg.

"Did you hear that?" Salier's soft face was pale as butter beside her. His guards, scattered about the garden fingering their borrowed weapons, looked hardly more enthusiastic. But that was the thing about facing death, as Benna had often pointed out. The closer it gets, the worse an idea it seems. Shivers didn't look like he had any doubts. Hot iron had burned them out of him, maybe. Cosca neither, his happy grin widening with each moment. Friendly sat cross-legged, rolling his dice across the cobbles.

He looked up at her, face blank as ever. "Five and four."

"That a good thing?"

He shrugged. "It's nine." Monza raised her brows. A strange group she'd gathered, surely, but when you have a half-mad plan you need men at least half-mad to see it through.

Sane ones might be tempted to look for a better idea.

Another crash, and a thin scream, closer this time. Ganmark's soldiers, working their way through the palace towards the garden at its centre. Friendly threw his dice once more, then gathered them up and stood, sword in hand. Monza tried to stay still, eyes fixed on the open doorway ahead, the hall lined with paintings beyond it, beyond that the archway that led into the rest of the palace. The only way in.

A helmeted head peered round the side of the arch. An armoured body followed. A Talinese sergeant, sword and shield raised and ready. Monza watched him creep carefully under the portcullis, across the marble tiles. He stepped cautiously out into the sunlight, frowning about at them.

"Sergeant," said Cosca brightly.

"Captain." The man straightened up, letting his sword point drop. More men followed him. Well-armed Talinese soldiers, watchful and bearded veterans tramping into the gallery with weapons at the ready. They looked surprised, at first, to see their own side already in the garden, but not unhappy. "That him?" asked the sergeant, pointing to Salier.

"This is him," said Cosca, grinning back.

"Well, well. Fat fucker, ain't he?"

"That he is."

More soldiers were coming through the entrance now, and behind them a knot of staff officers in pristine uniforms, with fine swords but no armour. Striding at their head with an air of unchallengeable authority came a man with a soft face and sad, watery eyes.

Ganmark.

Monza might have felt some grim satisfaction that she'd predicted his actions so easily, but the swell of hatred at the sight of him crowded it away. He had a long sword at his left hip, a shorter one at his right. Long and short steels, in the Union style.

"Secure the gallery!" he called in his clipped accent as he marched out into the garden. "Above all, ensure no harm comes to the paintings!"

"Yes, sir!" Boots clattered as men moved to follow his orders. Lots of men. Monza watched them, jaw set aching hard. Too many, maybe, but there was no use weeping about it now. Killing Ganmark was all that mattered.

"General!" Cosca snapped out a vibrating salute. "We have Duke Salier."

"So I see. Well done, Captain, you were quick off the mark, and shall be rewarded. Very quick." He gave a mocking bow. "Your Excellency, an honour. Grand Duke Orso sends his brotherly greetings."

"Shit on his greetings," barked Salier.

"And his regrets that he could not be here in person to witness your utter defeat."

"If he was here, I'd shit on him too."

"Doubtless. He was alone?"

Cosca nodded. "Just waiting here, sir, looking at this." And he jerked his head towards the great statue in the centre of the garden.

"Bonatine's Warrior." Ganmark paced slowly towards it, smiling up at the looming marble image of Stolicus. "Even more beautiful in person than by report. It shall look very well in the gardens of Fontezarmo." He was no more than five paces away. Monza tried to keep her breath slow, but her heart was hammering. "I must congratulate you on your wonderful collection, your Excellency."

"I shit on your congratulations," sneered Salier.

"You shit on a great many things, it seems. But then a person of your size no doubt produces a vast quantity of the stuff. Bring the fat man closer."

Now was the moment. Monza gripped the Calvez tight, stepped forwards, gloved right hand on Salier's elbow, Cosca moving up on his other side. Ganmark's officers and guards were spreading out, staring at the statue, at the garden, at Salier, peering through the windows into the hallways. A couple still stuck close to their general, one with his sword drawn, but they didn't look worried. Didn't look ready. All comrades together.

Friendly stood, still as a statue, sword in hand. Shivers' shield hung loose, but she saw his knuckles white on the haft of his axe, saw his good eye flickering from one enemy to another, judging the threat. Ganmark's grin spread as they led Salier forwards.

"Well, well, your Excellency. I still remember the text of that rousing speech, the one you made when you formed the League of Eight. What was it you said? That you'd rather die than kneel to a dog like Orso? I'd very much like to see you kneel, now." He grinned at Monza as she came closer, no more than a couple of strides between them. "Lieutenant, could you—" His pale eyes narrowed for an instant, and he knew her. She sprang at him, barging his nearest guard out of the way, lunging for his heart.

She felt the familiar scrape of steel on steel. In that flash Ganmark had somehow managed to get his sword half-drawn, enough to send her thrust wide by a hair. He jerked his head to one side and the point of the Calvez left him a long cut across his cheek before he flicked it away, his sword ringing clear from its sheath.

Then it was chaos in the garden.

Monza's blade left a long scratch down Ganmark's face. The nearest officer gave Friendly a puzzled look. "But—"

Friendly's sword hacked deep into his head. The blade stuck in his skull as he fell, and Friendly let it go. A clumsy weapon, he preferred to work closer. He slid out the cleaver, the knife from his belt, felt the comfort of the familiar grips in his fists, the overwhelming relief that things were now simple. Kill as many as possible while they were surprised. Even the odds. Eleven against twenty-six were not good ones.

He stabbed a red-haired officer in the stomach before he could draw his sword, shoved him back into a third and sent his arm wide, crowded in close and hacked the cleaver into his shoulder, heavy blade splitting cloth and flesh. He dodged a spear-thrust and the soldier who held it stumbled past. Friendly sank the knife into his armpit, and out, blade scraping against the edge of his breastplate.

There was a screeching, rattling sound as the portcullis dropped. Two soldiers were standing in the archway. The gate came down just behind one, sealing him into the gallery with everyone else. The other must have leaned back, trying to get out of the way. The plummeting spikes caught him in the stomach and crushed him helpless into the floor, stoving in his breastplate, one leg folded underneath him, the other kicking wildly. He began to scream, but it hardly mattered. By then everyone was screaming.

The fight spread out across the garden, spilled into the four beautiful hallways surrounding it. Cosca dropped a guard with a slash across the backs of his thighs. Shivers had cut one man near in half when the fight began, and now was hemmed in by three more, backing towards the hall full of statues, swinging wildly, making a strange noise between a laugh and a roar.

The red-haired officer Friendly had stabbed limped away, groaning, through the doorway into the first hall, leaving a scattering of bloody spots across the polished floor. Friendly sprang after, rolled under a panicky sweep of his sword, came up and took the back of his head off with the cleaver. The soldier pinned under the portcullis gibbered, gurgled, tore pointlessly at the bars. The other one, only just now working out what was happening, pointed his halberd at Friendly. A confused-looking officer with a birthmark across one cheek turned from contemplation of one of the seventy-eight paintings in the hall and drew his sword.

Two of them. One and one. Friendly almost smiled. This he understood.

Monza slashed at Ganmark again but one of his soldiers got in her way, bundled into her with his shield. She slipped, rolled sideways and scrambled up, the fight thrashing around her.

She saw Salier give a bellow, whip out a narrow small-sword from behind his back and cut one astonished officer down with a slash across the face. He thrust at Ganmark, surprisingly agile for a man of his size, but nowhere near agile enough. The general sidestepped and calmly ran the Grand Duke of Visserine right through his big belly. Monza saw a bloody foot of metal slide out from the back of his white uniform. Just as it had slid out through the back of Benna's white shirt.

"Oof," said Salier. Ganmark raised a boot and shoved him off, sent him stumbling back across the cobbles and into The Warrior's marble pedestal.

The duke slid down it, plump hands clutched to the wound, blood soaking through the soft white cloth.

"Kill them all!" bellowed Ganmark. "But mind the pictures!"

Two soldiers came at Monza. She hopped sideways so they got in each other's way, slid round a careless overhead chop from one, lunged and ran him through the groin, just under his breastplate. He made a great shriek, falling to his knees, but before she could find her balance again the other was swinging at her. She only just parried, the force almost jarring the Calvez from her hand. He slammed her in the chest with his shield and the rim of her breastplate dug into her stomach and drove her breath out, left her helpless. He raised his sword again, squawked, lurched sideways. One knee buckled and he pitched on his face, sliding forwards. The flights of a flatbow bolt stuck from the nape of his neck. Monza saw Day leaning from a window above, bow in her hands.

Ganmark pointed up towards her. "Kill the blond woman!" She vanished inside, and the last of the Talinese soldiers hurried obediently after her.

Salier stared down at the blood leaking out over his plump hands, eyes slightly unfocused. "Whoever would've thought...I'd die fighting?" And his head dropped back against the statue's pedestal.

"Is there no end to the surprises the world throws up?" Ganmark undid the top button of his jacket and pulled a handkerchief from inside it, dabbed at the bleeding cut on his face, then carefully wiped Salier's blood from the blade of his sword. "It's true, then. You are still alive."

Monza had her breath back now, and her brother's sword up. "It's true, cocksucker."

"I always did admire the subtlety of your rhetoric." The one Monza had stabbed through the groin was groaning as he tried to drag himself towards the entrance. Ganmark stepped carefully over him on his way towards her, tucking the bloody handkerchief into a pocket and doing his top button up again with his free hand. The crash, scrape, cry of fighting leaked from the halls beyond the colonnades, but for now they were alone in the garden. Unless you counted all the corpses scattered around the entrance. "Just the two of us, then? It's been a while since I drew steel in earnest, but I'll endeavour not to disappoint you."

"Don't worry about that. Your death will be entirely satisfying."

He gave his weak smile, and his damp eyes drifted down to her sword. "Fighting left-handed?"

"Thought I'd give you some kind of chance."

"The least I can do is extend to you the same courtesy." He flicked his sword smartly from one palm into the other, switched his guard and pointed the blade towards her. "Shall we—"

Monza had never been one to wait for an invitation. She lunged at him but he was ready, sidestepped it, came back at her with a sharp pair of cuts, high and low. Their blades rang together, slid and scraped, darting back and forth, glittering in the strips of sunlight between the trees. Ganmark's immaculately polished cavalry boots glided across the cobbles as nimbly as a dancer's. He jabbed at her, lightning fast. She parried once, twice, then nearly got caught and only just twisted away. She had to stumble back a few quick steps, take a breath and set herself afresh.

It is a deplorable thing to run from the enemy, Farans wrote, *but often better than the alternative.*

She watched Ganmark as he paced forwards, gleaming point of his sword moving in gentle little circles. "You keep your guard too low, I am afraid. You are full of passion, but passion without discipline is no more than a child's tantrum."

"Why don't you shut your fucking mouth and fight?"

"Oh, I can talk and cut pieces from you both at once." He came at her in earnest, pushing her from one side of the garden to the other, parrying desperately, jabbing weakly back when she could, but not often, and to no effect.

She'd heard it said he was one of the greatest swordsmen in the world, and it wasn't hard to believe, even with his left hand. A good deal better than she'd been at her best, and her best was squashed under Gobba's boot and scattered down the mountainside beneath Fontezarmo. Ganmark was quicker, stronger, sharper. Which meant her only chance was to be cleverer, trickier, dirtier. Angrier.

She screeched as she came at him, feinted left, jabbed right. He sprang back, and she pulled her helmet off and flung it in his face. He saw it just in time to duck, it bounced from the top of his head and made him grunt. She came in after it but he twisted sideways and she only nicked the gold braid on the shoulder of his uniform. She jabbed and he parried, well set again.

"Tricky."

"Get your arse fucked."

"I think I might be in the mood, once I've killed you." He slashed at her, but instead of backing off she came in close, caught his sword, their hilts scraping. She tried to trip him but he stepped around her boot, just kept his balance. She kicked at him, caught his knee, his leg buckled for the briefest moment. She cut viciously, but Ganmark had already slid away and she only hacked a chunk from some topiary, little green leaves fluttering.

"There are easier ways to trim hedges, if that's your aim." Almost before she knew it he was on her with a series of cuts, driving her across the cobbles. She hopped over the bloody corpse of one of his guards, ducked behind the great legs of the statue, keeping it between them, trying to think out some way to come at him. She undid the buckles on one side of her breastplate, pulled it open and let it clatter down. It was no protection against a swordsman of his skill, and the weight of it was only tiring her.

"No more tricks, Murcatto?"

"I'll think of something, bastard!"

"Think fast, then." Ganmark's sword darted between the statue's legs and missed by a hair as she jerked out of its way. "You don't get to win, you know, simply because you think yourself aggrieved. Because you believe yourself justified. It is the best swordsman who wins, not the angriest."

He seemed about to slide around The Warrior's huge right leg, but came instead the other way, jumping over Salier's corpse slumped against the pedestal. She saw it coming, knocked his sword wide then hacked at his head with small elegance but large force. He ducked just in time. The blade of the Calvez clanged against Stolicus' well-muscled calf and sent chips of marble flying. She only just kept a hold on the buzzing grip, left hand aching as she reeled away.

Ganmark frowned, gently touched the crack in the statue's leg with his free hand. "Pure vandalism." He leaped at her, caught her sword and drove her back, once, then twice, her boots sliding from the cobbles and up onto the turf beside, fighting all the while to tease, or trick, or bludgeon out some opening she could use. But Ganmark saw everything well before it came, handled it with the simple efficiency of masterful skill. He was scarcely even breathing hard. The longer they fought the more he had her measure, and the slimmer dwindled her chances.

"You should mind that backswing," he said. "Too high. It limits your options and leaves you open." She cut at him, and again, but he flicked them dismissively away. "And you are prone to tilt your steel to the right when extended." She jabbed and he caught the blade on his, metal sliding on metal, his sword whipping around hers. With an effortless twist of his wrist he tore the Calvez from her hand and sent it skittering across the cobbles. "See what I mean?"

She took a shocked step back, saw the gleam of light as Ganmark's sword darted out. The blade slid neatly through the palm of her left hand, point passing between the bones and pricking her in the shoulder, bending her arm back and holding it pinned like meat and onions on a Gurkish skewer. The pain came an instant later, making her groan as Ganmark twisted the sword and drove her helplessly down onto her knees, bent backwards.

"If that feels undeserved from me, you can tell yourself it's a gift from the townsfolk of Caprile." He twisted his sword the other way and she felt the point grind into her shoulder, the steel scrape against the bones in her hand, blood running down her forearm and into her jacket.

"Fuck you!" she spat at him, since it was that or scream.

His mouth twitched into that sad smile. "A gracious offer, but your brother was more my type." His sword whipped out of her and she lurched onto all fours, chest heaving. She closed her eyes, waiting for the blade to slide between her shoulder blades and through her heart, just the way it had through Benna's.

She wondered how much it would hurt, how long it would hurt for. A lot, most likely, but not for long.

She heard boot heels clicking away from her on cobbles, and slowly raised her head. Ganmark hooked his foot under the Calvez and flicked it up into his waiting hand. "One touch to me, I rather think." He tossed the sword arrow-like and it thumped into the turf beside her, wobbling gently back and forth. "What do you say? Shall we make it the best of three?"

The long hall that housed Duke Salier's Styrian masterpieces was now further adorned by five corpses. The ultimate decoration for any palace, though the discerning dictator needs to replace them regularly if he is to avoid an odour. Especially in warm weather. Two of Salier's disguised soldiers and one of Ganmark's officers all sprawled bloodily in attitudes of scant dignity, though one of the general's guards had managed to die in a position approaching comfort, curled around an occasional table with an ornamental vase on top.

Another guard was dragging himself towards the far door, leaving a greasy red trail across the polished floor as he went. The wound Cosca had given him was in his stomach, just under his breastplate, and it was tough to crawl and hold your guts in all at once.

That left two young staff officers, bright swords drawn and bright eyes full of righteous hate, and Cosca. Probably they would both have been nice enough people under happier circumstances. Probably their mothers loved them and probably they loved their mothers back. Certainly they did not deserve to die here in this gaudy temple to greed simply for choosing one self-serving side over another. But what choice for Cosca other than to do his very best to kill them? The lowest slug, weed, slime struggle always to stay alive. Why should Styria's most infamous mercenary hold himself to another standard?

The two officers moved apart, one heading for the tall windows, the other for the paintings, herding Cosca towards the end of the room and, more than likely, the end of his life. He was prickly with sweat under the Talinese uniform, the breath burning his lungs. Fighting to the death was undeniably a young man's game.

"Now, now, lads," he muttered, weighing his sword. "How about you face me one at a time? Have you no honour?"

"No honour?" sneered one. "Us?"

"You disguised yourself in order to launch a cowardly attack upon our general by stealth!" hissed the other, face pinking with outrage.

"True. True." Cosca let the point of his sword drop. "And the shame of it stabs at me. I surrender."

The one on the left was not taken in for a moment. The one on the right looked somewhat puzzled, though, lowered his sword for an instant. It was him that Cosca flung his knife at.

It twittered through the air and thudded into the young man's side, doubling him over. Cosca charged in behind it, aiming for the chest. Perhaps the boy leaned forwards, or perhaps Cosca's aim was wayward, but the blade caught the officer's neck and, in a spectacular justification of all the sharpening, took his head clean off. It spun away, spraying spots of blood, bounced from one of the paintings with a hollow clonk and a flapping of canvas. The body keeled forwards, blood welling from the severed neck in long spurts and creeping out across the floor.

Even as Cosca yelped with surprised triumph, the other officer was on him, slashing away like a man beating a carpet. Cosca ducked, weaved, parried, jerked helplessly back from a savage cut, tripped over the headless corpse and went sprawling in the slick of blood around it.

The officer gave a shriek as he sprang to finish the work. Cosca's flailing hand clutched for the nearest thing, gripped it, flung it. The severed head. It caught the young man in the face and sent him stumbling. Cosca floundered to his blade and snatched it up, spun about, hand, sword, face, clothes all daubed with red. Strangely fitting, for a man who had lived the life he had.

The officer was already at him again with a flurry of furious cuts. Cosca gave ground as fast as he could without falling over, sword drooping, pretending at complete exhaustion and not having to pretend all that much. He collided with the table, nearly fell, his free hand fished behind him, found the rim of the ornamental jar. The officer came forwards, lifting his sword with a yelp of triumph. It turned to a gurgle of shock as the jar came flying at him. He managed to smash it away with the hilt of his sword, fragments of pottery bursting across one side of him, but that left his blade wide for a moment. Cosca made one last desperate lunge, felt a gentle resistance as his blade punched through the officer's cheek and out through the back of his head with textbook execution.

"Oh." The officer wobbled slightly as Cosca whipped his sword back and capered sharply away. "Is that…" His look was one of bleary-eyed surprise, like a man who had woken up drunk to find himself robbed and tied naked to a post. Cosca could not quite remember whether it was in Etrisani or Westport that had happened to him, those years all rather blended into one.

"Whasappenah?" The officer slashed with exaggerated slowness and Cosca stepped out of the way, let him spin round in a wide circle and sprawl over onto his side. He laboriously rolled, clambered up, blood running gently from the neat little slit beside his nose. The eye above it was flickering now, face on that side gone slack as old leather.

"Sluviduviduther," he drooled.

"Your pardon?" asked Cosca.

"Slurghhh!" And he raised his quivering sword and charged. Directly sideways into the wall. He crashed into the painting of the girl surprised while bathing, tore a great gash through it with his flailing sword arm, brought the great canvas keeling down on top of him as he fell, one boot sticking out from underneath the gilded frame. He did not move again.

"The lucky bastard," Cosca whispered. To die beneath a naked woman. It was the way he had always wanted to go.

The wound in Monza's shoulder burned. The one through her left hand burned far worse. Her palm, her fingers, sticky with blood. She could barely make a fist, let alone grip a blade. No choice, then. She dragged the glove from her right hand with her teeth, reached out and took hold of the Calvez' hilt with it, feeling the crooked bones shift as her twisted fingers closed around the grip, little one still painfully straight.

"Ah. Right-handed?" Ganmark flicked his sword spinning into the air, snatched it back with his own right hand as nimbly as a circus trickster. "I always did admire your determination, if not the goals on which you trained it. Revenge, now, eh?"

"Revenge," she snarled.

"Revenge. If you could even get it, what good would it do you? All this expenditure of effort, pain, treasure, blood, for what? Who is ever left better off for it?" His sad eyes watched her slowly stand. "Not the avenged dead, certainly. They rot on, regardless. Not those who are avenged upon, of course. Corpses all. And what of the ones who take vengeance, what of them? Do they sleep easier, do you suppose, once they have heaped murder on murder? Sown the bloody seeds of a hundred other retributions?" She circled around, trying to think of some trick to kill him with. "All those dead men at that bank in Westport, that was your righteous work, I suppose? And the carnage at Cardotti's, a fair and proportionate reply?"

"What had to be done!"

"Ah, what had to be done. The favourite excuse of unexamined evil echoes down the ages and slobbers from your twisted mouth." He danced at her, their swords rang together, once, twice. He jabbed, she parried and jabbed back. Each contact sent a jolt of pain up her arm. She ground her teeth together, forced the scowl to stay on her face, but there was no disguising how much it hurt her, or how clumsy she was with it. If she'd had small chances with her left, she had none at all with her right, and he knew it already.

"Why the Fates chose you for saving I will never guess, but you should have thanked them kindly and slunk away into obscurity. Let us not pretend you and your brother did not deserve precisely what you received."

"Fuck yourself! I didn't deserve that!" But even as she said it, she had to wonder. "My brother didn't!"

Ganmark snorted. "No one is quicker to forgive a handsome man than I, but your brother was a vindictive coward. A charming, greedy, ruthless, spineless parasite. A man of the very lowest character imaginable. The only thing that lifted him from utter worthlessness, and utter inconsequence, was you." He sprang at her with lethal speed and she reeled away, fell against a cherry tree with a grunt and stumbled back through the shower of white blossom. He could surely have spitted her but he stayed still as a statue, sword at the ready, smiling faintly as he watched her thrash her way clear.

"And let us face the facts, General Murcatto. You, for all your undeniable talents, have hardly been a paragon of virtue. Why, there must be a hundred thousand people with just reasons to fling your hated carcass from that terrace!"

"Not Orso. Not him!" She came low, jabbing sloppily at his hips, wincing as he flicked her sword aside and jarred the grip in her twisted palm.

"If that's a joke, it's not a funny one. Quibble with the judge, when the sentence is self-evidently more than righteous?" He placed his feet with all the watchful care of an artist applying paint to a canvas, steering her back onto the cobbles. "How many deaths have you had a hand in? How much destruction? You are a bandit! A glorified profiteer! You are a maggot grown fat on the rotting corpse of Styria!" Three more blows, rapid as a sculptor's hammer on his chisel, snapping her sword this way and that in her aching grip. "Did not deserve, you say to me, *did not deserve*? That excuse for a right hand is embarrassing enough. Pray do not shame yourself further."

She made a tired, pained, clumsy lunge. He deflected it disdainfully, already stepping around her and letting her stumble past. She expected his sword in her back; instead she felt his boot thud into her arse and send her sprawling across the cobbles, Benna's sword bouncing from her numb fingers one more time. She lay there a moment, panting for breath, then slowly rolled over, came up to her knees. There hardly seemed much point standing. She'd be back here soon enough, once he ran her through. Her right hand throbbed, trembled. The shoulder of her stolen uniform was dark with blood, the fingers of her left hand were dripping with it.

Ganmark flicked his wrist, whipped the head from a flower and into his waiting palm. He lifted it to his face and breathed in deep. "A beautiful day, and a good place to die. We should have finished you up at Fontezarmo, along with your brother. But now will do."

She couldn't think of much in the way of sharp last words, so she just tipped her head back and spat at him. It spattered against his neck, his collar, the pristine front of his uniform. Not much vengeance, maybe, but something. Ganmark peered down at it. "A perfect lady to the end."

His eyes flickered sideways and he jerked away as something flashed past him, twittered into a flower bed behind. A thrown knife. There was a snarl and Cosca was on him, barking like a mad dog as he harried the general back across the cobbles.

"Cosca!" Fumbling her sword up. "Late, as ever."

"I was somewhat occupied next door," growled the old mercenary, pausing to catch his breath.

"Nicomo Cosca?" Ganmark frowned at him. "I thought you were dead."

"There have always been false reports of my death. Wishful thinking—"

"On the part of his many enemies." Monza stood, shaking the weakness out of her limbs. "You've got a mind to kill me, you should get it done instead of talking about it."

Ganmark backed slowly away, sliding his short steel from its sheath with his left hand, pointing it towards her, the long towards Cosca, his eyes flitting back and forth between them. "Oh, there's still time."

Shivers weren't himself. Or maybe he finally was. The pain had turned him mad. Or the eye they'd left him wasn't working right. Or he was still all broken up from the husk he'd been sucking at the past few days. Whatever the reasons, he was in hell.

And he liked it.

The long hall pulsed, glowed, swam like a rippling pool. Sunlight burned through the windows, stabbing and flashing at him through a hundred hundred glittering squares of glass. The statues shone, smiled, sweated, cheered him on. He might've had one eye less than before, but he saw things clearer. The pain had swept away all his doubts, his fears, his questions, his choices. All that shit had been dead weight on him. All that shit was weakness, and lies, and a waste of effort. He'd made himself think things were complicated when they were beautifully, awfully simple. His axe had all the answers he needed.

Its blade caught the sunlight and left a great white, fizzing smear, hacked into a man's arm sending black streaks flying. Cloth flapping. Flesh torn. Bone splintered. Metal bent and twisted. A spear squealed across Shivers' shield and he could taste the roar in his mouth, sweet as he swung the axe again. It crashed into a breastplate and left a huge dent, sent a body flailing into a pitted urn, burst it apart, writhing on the floor in a mass of shattered pottery.

The world was turned inside out, like the glistening innards of the officer he'd gutted a few moments before. He used to get tired when he fought. Now he got stronger. The rage boiled up in him, leaked out of him, set his skin on fire. With every blow he struck it got worse, better, muscles burning until he had to scream it out, laugh it out, weep, sing, thrash, dance, shriek.

He smashed a sword away with his shield, tore it from a hand, was on the soldier behind it, arms around him, kissing his face, licking at him. He roared as he ran, ran, legs pounding, rammed him into one of the statues, sent it over, crashing into another, and another beyond that, tipping, smashing on the floor, breaking apart into chunks in a cloud of dust.

The guard groaned, sprawling in the ruins, tried to roll over. Shivers' axe stoved the top of his helmet in deep with a hollow clonk, drove the metal rim right down over his eyes and squashed his nose flat, blood running out from underneath.

"Fucking die!" Shivers bashed in the side of the helmet and sent his head one way. "Die!" Swung back and crumpled the other side, neck crunching like a sock full of gravel. "Die! Die!" Bonk, bonk, like pots and pans clattering in the river after mealtime. A statue looked on, disapproving.

"Look at me?" Shivers smashed its head off with his axe. Then he was on top of someone, not knowing how he got there, ramming the edge of his shield into a face until it was nothing but a shapeless mess of red. He could hear someone whispering, whispering in his ear. Mad, hissing, croaking voice.

"I am made of death. I am the Great Leveller. I am the storm in the High Places." The Bloody-Nine's voice, but it came from his own throat. The hall was strewn with fallen men and fallen statues, scattered with bits of both. "You." Shivers pointed his bloody axe at the last of them, cringing at the far end of the dusty hallway. "I see you there, fucker. No one gets away." He realised he was talking in Northern. The man couldn't understand a word he said. Hardly mattered, though.

He reckoned he got the gist.

Monza forced herself on down the arcade, wringing the last strength from her aching legs, snarling as she lunged, jabbed, cut clumsily, not letting up for a moment. Ganmark was on the retreat, dropping back through sunlight, then shadow, then sunlight again, frowning with furious concentration. His eyes flickered from side to side, parrying her blade and Cosca's as it jabbed at him from between the pillars on her right, their hard breathing, their shuffling footsteps, the quick scraping of steel echoing from the vaulted ceiling.

She cut at him, then back the other way, ignoring the burning pain in her fist as she tore the short steel from his hand and sent it clattering into the shadows. Ganmark lurched away, only just turned one of Cosca's thrusts wide with his long steel, left his unguarded side facing her. She grinned, was pulling her arm back to lunge when something crashed into the window on her left, sent splinters of glass flying into her face. She thought she heard Shivers' voice, roaring in Northern from the other side. Ganmark slipped between two pillars as Cosca slashed at him and away across the lawn, backing off into the centre of the garden.

"Could you get on and kill this bastard?" wheezed Cosca.

"Doing my best. You go left."

"Left it is." They moved apart, herding Ganmark towards the statue. He looked spent now, blowing hard, soft cheeks turned blotchy pink and shining with sweat. She smiled as she feinted at him, sensing victory, felt her smile slip as he suddenly sprang to meet her. She dodged his first thrust, slashed at his neck, but he caught it and pushed her away. He was a lot less spent than she'd thought, and she was a lot more. Her foot came down badly and she tottered sideways. Ganmark darted past and his sword left a burning cut across her thigh. She tried to turn, screeched as her leg crumpled, fell and rolled, the Calvez tumbling from her limp fingers and bouncing away.

Cosca sprang past with a hoarse cry, swinging wildly. Ganmark dropped under his cut, lunged from the ground and ran him neatly through the stomach. Cosca's sword clanged hard into The Warrior's shin and flew from his hand, stone chips spinning. The general whipped his blade free and Cosca dropped to his knees, sagged sideways with a long groan.

"And that's that." Ganmark turned towards her, Bonatine's greatest work looming up behind him. A few flakes of marble trickled from the statue's ankle, already cracked where Monza's sword had chopped into it. "You've given me some exercise, I'll grant you that. You are a woman — or have been a woman — of remarkable determination." Cosca dragged himself across the cobbles, leaving spotty smears of blood behind him. "But in keeping your eyes always ahead, you blinded yourself to everything around you. To the nature of the great war you fight in. To the natures of the people closest to you." Ganmark flicked out his handkerchief again, dabbed sweat from his forehead, carefully wiped blood from his steel. "If Duke Orso and his state of Talins are no more than a sword in the hand of Valint and Balk, then you were never more than that sword's ruthless point." He flicked the shining point of his own sword with his forefinger. "Always stabbing, always killing, but never considering why." There was a gentle creaking, and over his shoulder The Warrior's own great sword wobbled ever so slightly. "Still. It hardly matters now. For you the fight is over." Ganmark still wore his sad smile as he came to a stop a stride from her. "Any pithy last words?"

"Behind you," growled Monza through gritted teeth, as The Warrior rocked ever so gently forwards.

"You must take me for—" There was a loud bang. The statue's leg split in half and the whole vast weight of stone toppled inexorably forwards.

Ganmark was just beginning to turn as the point of Stolicus' giant sword pinned him between the shoulder blades, drove him onto his knees, burst out through his stomach and crashed into the cobbles, spraying blood and rock chips in Monza's stinging face. The statue's legs broke apart as they hit the ground, noble feet left on the pedestal, the rest cracking into muscular chunks and rolling around in a cloud of white marble dust. From the hips up, the proud image of the greatest soldier of history stayed in one magnificent piece, staring sternly down at Orso's general, impaled on his monstrous sword beneath him.

Ganmark made a sucking sound like water draining from a broken bath, and coughed blood down the front of his uniform. His head fell forwards, steel clattering from his dangling hand.

There was a moment of stillness.

"Now that," croaked Cosca, "is what I call a happy accident."

Four dead, three left. Monza saw someone creep out from one of the colonnades, grimaced as she shuffled to her sword and dragged it up for the third time, hardly sure which ruined hand to hold it in. It was Day, loaded flatbow levelled. Friendly trudged along behind her, knife and cleaver hanging from his fists.

"You got him?" asked the girl.

Monza looked at Ganmark's corpse, kneeling spitted on the great length of bronze. "Stolicus did."

Cosca had kicked his way as far as one of the cherry trees and sat with his back against the trunk. He looked just like a man relaxing on a summer's day. Apart from the bloody hand pressed to his stomach. She limped up to him, stuck the Calvez point-first into the turf and knelt down.

"Let me have a look." She fumbled with the buttons on Cosca's jacket, but before she got the second one undone he reached up, gently took her bloody hand and her twisted one in his.

"I've been waiting years for you to tear my clothes off, but I think I'll have politely to decline. I'm finished."

"You? Never."

He squeezed her hands tighter. "Right through the guts, Monza. It's over." His eyes rolled towards the gate, and she could hear the faint clattering as soldiers on the other side struggled to lever the portcullis open. "And you'll have other problems soon enough. Four of seven, though, girl." He grinned. "Never thought you'd make four of seven."

"Four of seven," muttered Friendly, behind her.

"I wish I could've made Orso one of them."

"Well." Cosca raised his brows. "It's a noble calling, but I guess you can't kill everyone."

Shivers was walking slowly over from one of the doorways. He barely even glanced at Ganmark's impaled corpse as he passed. "None left?"

"Not in here." Friendly nodded towards the gate. "Some out there, though."

"Reckon so." The Northman stopped not far away. His hanging axe, his dented shield, his pale face and the bandages across one half of it were all dashed and speckled dark red.

"You alright?" asked Monza.

"Don't rightly know what I am."

"Are you hurt, I'm asking?"

He touched one hand to the bandages. "No worse'n before we started . . . reckon I must be beloved o' the moon today, as the hillmen say." His eye rolled down to her bloody shoulder, her bloody hand. "You're bleeding."

"My fencing lesson turned ugly."

"You need a bandage?"

She nodded towards the gateway, the noise of the Talinese soldiers on the other side getting louder with every moment. "We'll be lucky if we get the time to bleed to death."

"What now, then?"

She opened her mouth, but nothing came out. There was no use fighting, even if she'd had the strength. The palace would be swarming with Orso's soldiers. There was no use surrendering, even if she'd been the type. They'd be lucky if they made it back to Fontezarmo to be killed. Benna had always warned her she didn't think far enough ahead, and it seemed he'd had a point—

"I've an idea." Day's face had broken out in an unexpected smile. Monza followed her pointing finger, up to the roofline above the garden, and squinted into the sun. A black figure crouched there against the bright sky.

"A *fine* afternoon to you!" She never thought she'd be glad to hear Castor Morveer's scraping whine. "I was hoping to view the Duke of Visserine's famous collection and I appear to have become entirely lost! I don't suppose any of you kind gentlefolk know where I might find it? I hear he has Bonatine's greatest work!"

Monza jerked her bloody thumb at the ruined statue. "Not all it's cracked up to be!"

Vitari had appeared beside the poisoner now, was smoothly lowering a rope. "We're rescued," grunted Friendly, in just the same tone as he might have said, "We're dead."

Monza hardly had the energy even to feel pleased. She hardly knew if she was pleased. "Day, Shivers, get up there."

"No doubt." Day tossed her bow away and ran for it. The Northman frowned at Monza for a moment, then followed.

Friendly was looking down at Cosca. "What about him?" The old mercenary seemed to have dozed off for a moment, eyelids flickering.

"We'll have to pull him up. Get a hold."

The convict slid one arm around his back and started to lift him. Cosca woke with a jolt, grimaced. "Dah! No, no, no, no, no." Friendly let him carefully back down and Cosca shook his scabby head, breathing ragged. "I'm not screaming my way up a rope just so I can die on a roof. Here's as good a place as any, and this as good a time. I've been promising to do it for years. Might as well keep my word this once."

She squatted down beside him. "I'd rather call you a liar one more time, and keep you watching my back."

"I only stayed there...because I like looking at your arse." He bared his teeth, winced, gave a long growl. The clanging at the gate was getting louder.

Friendly offered Cosca's sword to him. "They'll be coming. You want this?"

"Why would I? It was messing with those things got me into this fix in the first place." He tried to shift, winced and sagged back, his skin already carrying that waxy sheen that corpses have.

Vitari and Morveer had bundled Shivers over the gutter and onto the roof. Monza jerked her head at Friendly. "Your turn."

He crouched there for a moment, not moving, then looked to Cosca. "Do you want me to stay?"

The old mercenary took Friendly's big hand and smiled as he gave it a squeeze. "I am touched beyond words to hear you make the offer. But no, my friend. This I had better handle alone. Give your dice a roll for me."

"I will." Friendly stood and strode off towards the rope without a backward glance. Monza watched him go. Her hands, her shoulder, her leg burned, her battered body ached. Her eyes slunk over the bodies scattered across the garden. Sweet victory. Sweet vengeance. Men turned into meat.

"Do me one favour." Cosca had a sad smile, almost as if he guessed her thoughts.

"You came back for me, didn't you? I can stretch to one."

"Forgive me."

She made a sound — half-snort, half-retch. "I thought I was the one betrayed you?"

"What does it matter now? Treachery is commonplace. Forgiveness is rare. I'd rather go without any debts. Except all the money I owe in Ospria. And Adua. And Dagoska." He weakly waved one bloody hand. "Let's say no debts to you, anyway, and leave it at that."

"That I can do. We're even."

"Good. I lived like shit. Glad to see at least I got the dying right. Get on."

Part of her wanted to stay with him, to be with him when Orso's men broke through the gate, make sure there really were no debts. But not that big a part. She'd never been prone to sentiment. Orso had to die, and if she was killed here, who'd get it done? She pulled the Calvez from the ground, slid it back into its sheath and turned without another word. Words are poor tools at a time like that. She limped to the rope, tied it off under her hips the best she could, twisted it around her wrist.

"Let's go!"

From the roof Monza could see right across the city. The wide curve of the Visser and its graceful bridges. The many towers poking at the sky, dwarfed by pillars of smoke still rising from the scattered fires. Day had already got a pear from somebody and was biting happily into it, yellow curls blowing on the breeze, juice gleaming on her chin.

Morveer raised one eyebrow at the carnage down in the garden. "I am relieved to observe that, in my absence, you succeeded in keeping the slaughter under tight control."

"Some things never change," she snapped at him.

"Cosca?" asked Vitari.

"Not coming."

Morveer gave a sickening little grin. "He failed to save his own skin this time? So a drunkard can change after all."

Rescue or not, Monza would have stabbed him at that moment if she'd had a good hand to do it with. From the way Vitari scowled at the poisoner, she was feeling much the same. She jerked her spiky head towards the river instead. "We should have the tearful reunion down in the boat. The city's full of Orso's troops. High time we were floating out to sea."

Monza took one last look back. All was still down in the garden. Salier had slid from the fallen statue's pedestal and rolled onto his back, arms outstretched as if welcoming a dear old friend. Ganmark knelt in a wide slick of blood, impaled on The Warrior's great bronze blade, head dangling. Cosca's eyes were closed, hands resting in his lap, a slight smile still on his tipped-back face. Cherry blossom wafted down and settled across his stolen uniform.

"Cosca, Cosca," she murmured. "What will I do without you?"

V
PURANTI

"For mercenaries are disunited, thirsty for power, undisciplined, and disloyal; they are brave among their friends and cowards before the enemy; they have no fear of God, they do not keep faith with their fellow men; they avoid defeat just as long as they avoid battle; in peacetime you are despoiled by them and in wartime by the enemy"

Niccolò Machiavelli

F or two years, half the Thousand Swords pretended to fight the other half. Cosca, when he was sober enough to speak, boasted that never before in history had men made so much for doing so little. They sucked the coffers of Nicante and Affoia bone dry, then turned north when their hopes were dashed by the sudden outbreak of peace, seeking new wars to profit from, or ambitious employers to begin them.

No employer was more ambitious than Orso, the new Grand Duke of Talins, kicked to power after his elder brother was kicked by his favourite horse. He was all too eager to sign a Paper of Engagement with the well-known mercenary Monzcarro Murcatto. Especially since his enemies in Etrea had but lately hired the infamous Nicomo Cosca to lead their troops.

It proved difficult to bring the two to battle, however. Like two cowards circling before a brawl, they spent a whole season in ruinously expensive manoeuvrings, doing much harm to the farmers of the region but little to each other. They were finally urged together in ripe wheat-fields near the village of Afieri, where a battle seemed sure to follow. Or something that looked very like one.

But that evening Monza had an unexpected visitor to her tent. None other than Duke Orso himself.

"Your Excellency, I had not expected—"

"No need for pleasantries. I know what Nicomo Cosca has planned for tomorrow."

Monza frowned. "I imagine he plans to fight, and so do I."

"He plans no such thing, and neither do you. The pair of you have been making fools of your employers for the past two years. I do not care to be made a fool of. I can see fake battles in the theatre at a fraction of the cost. That is why I will pay you twice to fight him in earnest."

Monza had not been expecting this. "I . . ."

"You have loyalty to him, I know. I respect that. Everyone must stick at *something in their lives. But Cosca is the past, and I have decided that you are the future. Your brother agrees with me."*

Monza had certainly not been expecting that. She stared at Benna, and he grinned back. "It's better like this. You deserve to lead."

"I can't... the other captains will never—"

"I spoke to them already," said Benna. "All except Faithful, and that old dog will follow along when he sees how the wind's blowing. They're sick of Cosca, and his drinking, and his foolishness. They want a long contract and a leader they can be proud of. They want you."

The Duke of Talins was watching. She could not afford to seem reluctant. "Then I accept, of course. You had me at paid twice," she lied.

Orso smiled. "I have a feeling you and I will do well for one another, General Murcatto. I will look forward to news of your victory tomorrow." And he left.

When the tent flap dropped Monza cuffed her brother across the face and knocked him to the ground. "What have you done, Benna? What have you done?"

He looked sullenly up at her, one hand to his bloody mouth. "I thought you'd be pleased."

"No you fucking didn't! You thought you'd be. I hope you are."

But there was nothing she could do but forgive him, and make the best of it. He was her brother. The only one who really knew her. And Sesaria, Victus, Andiche and most of the other captains had agreed. They were tired of Nicomo Cosca. So there could be no turning back. The next day, as dawn slunk out of the east and they prepared for the coming battle, Monza ordered her men to charge in earnest. What else could she do?

By evening she was sitting in Cosca's chair, with Benna grinning beside her and her newly enriched captains drinking to her first victory. Everyone laughed but her. She was thinking of Cosca, and all he had given her, what she had owed him and how she had paid him back. She was in no mood to celebrate.

Besides, she was captain general of the Thousand Swords. She could not afford to laugh.

Sixes

The dice came up a pair of sixes.

In the Union they call that score suns, like the sun on their flag. In Baol they call it twice won, because the house pays double on it. In Gurkhul they call it the Prophet or the Emperor, depending where a man's loyalty lies. In Thond it is the golden dozen. In the Thousand Isles, twelve winds. In Safety they call two sixes the jailer, because the jailer always wins. All across the Circle of the World men cheer for that score, but to Friendly it was no better than any other. It won him nothing. He turned his attention back to the great bridge of Puranti, and the men crossing it.

The faces of the statues on their tall columns might have worn to pitted blobs, the roadway might have cracked with age and the parapet crumbled, but the six arches still soared tall and graceful, scornful of the dizzy drop below. The great piers of rock from which they sprang, six times six strides high, still defied the battering waters. Six hundred years old and more, but the Imperial bridge was still the only way across the Pura's deep gorge at this time of year. The only way to Ospria by land.

The army of Grand Duke Rogont marched across it in good order, six men abreast. The regular tramp, tramp of their boots was like a mighty heartbeat, accompanied by the jingle and clatter of arms and harness, the occasional calls of officers, the steady murmur of the watching crowd, the rushing throb of the river far below. They had been marching across it all morning, now, by company, by battalion, by regiment. Moving forests of spear tips, gleaming metal and studded leather. Dusty, dirty, determined faces. Proud flags hanging limp on the still air. Their six-hundredth rank

347

had passed not long before. Some four thousand men across already and at least as many more to follow. Six, by six, by six, they came.

"Good order. For a retreat." Shivers' voice had withered to a throaty whisper in Visserine.

Vitari snorted. "If there's one thing Rogont knows how to manage it's a retreat. He's had enough practice."

"One must appreciate the irony," observed Morveer, watching the soldiers pass with a look of faint scorn. "Today's proud legions march over the last vestiges of yesterday's fallen empire. So it always is with military splendour. Hubris made flesh."

"How incredibly profound." Murcatto curled her lip. "Why, travelling with the great Morveer is both pleasure and education."

"I am philosopher and poisoner all in one. I *pray* you not to worry, though, my fee covers both. Remunerate me for my bottomless insights, the poison comes free of charge."

"Does our luck have no end?" she grated back.

"Does it even have a beginning?" murmured Vitari.

The group was down to six, and those more irritable than ever. Murcatto, hood drawn up, black hair hanging lank from inside, only her pointed nose and chin and hard mouth visible. Shivers, half his head still bandaged and the other half milk-pale, his one eye sunk in a dark ring. Vitari, sitting on the parapet with her legs stretched out and her shoulders propped against a broken column, freckled face tipped back towards the bright sun. Morveer, frowning down at the churning water, his apprentice leaning nearby. And Friendly, of course. Six. Cosca was dead. In spite of his name, Friendly rarely kept friends long.

"Talking of remuneration," Morveer droned on, "we should visit the nearest bank and have a note drawn up. I hate to have debts outstanding between myself and an employer. It leaves a sour taste on our otherwise honey-sweet relationship."

"Sweet," grunted Day, around a mouthful, though whether she was talking about her cake or the relationship, it was impossible to say.

"You owe me for my part in General Ganmark's demise, a peripheral yet vital one, since it prevented you from partaking in a demise of your own. I have also to replace the equipment so carelessly lost in Visserine. Need I once again point out that, had you allowed me to remove our problematic farmers as I desired, there would have been no—"

"Enough," hissed Murcatto. "I don't pay you to be reminded of my mistakes."

"I imagine that service too is free of charge." Vitari slid down from the parapet. Day swallowed the last of her cake and licked her fingers. They all made ready to move, except for Friendly. He stayed, looking down at the water.

"Time to move," said Murcatto.

"Yes. I am going back to Talins."

"You're what?"

"Sajaam was sending word to me here, but there is no letter."

"It's a long way to Talins. There's a war—"

"This is Styria. There's always a war."

There was a pause while she looked at him, her eyes almost hidden in her hood. The others watched, none showing much feeling at his going. People rarely did, when he went, and nor did he. "You're sure?" she asked.

"Yes." He had seen half of Styria — Westport, Sipani, Visserine and much of the country in between — and hated it all. He had felt shiftless and scared sitting in Sajaam's smoke-house, dreaming of Safety. Now those long days, the smell of husk, the endless cards and posturing, the routine rounds of the slums collecting money, the occasional moments of predictable and well-structured violence, all seemed like some happy dream. There was nothing for him out here, where every day was under a different sky. Murcatto was chaos, and he wanted no more of her.

"Take this then." She pulled a purse out from her coat.

"I am not here for your money."

"Take it anyway. It's a lot less than you deserve. Might make the journey easier." He let her press it into his hand.

"Luck be at your back," said Shivers.

Friendly nodded. "The world is made of six, today."

"Six be at your back, then."

"It will be, whether I want it or not." Friendly swept up the dice with the side of his hand, wrapped them carefully in their cloth and tucked them down inside his jacket. Without a backward glance he slipped off through the crowds lining the bridge, against the endless current of soldiers, over the endless current of water. He left both behind, struck on into the smaller, meaner part of the city on the river's western side. He would pass the time by counting the number of strides it took him to reach Talins. Since he said his goodbyes he had made already three hundred and sixty-six—

"Master Friendly!" He jerked round, frowning, hands itching ready to move to knife and cleaver. A figure leaned lazily in a doorway off the street, arms and boots crossed, face all in shadow. "Whatever are the odds of meeting you here?" The voice sounded terribly familiar. "Well, you would know the odds better than me, I'm sure, but a happy chance indeed, on that we can agree."

"We can," said Friendly, beginning to smile as he realised who it was.

"Why, I feel almost as if I threw a pair of sixes..."

The Eye-Maker

A bell tinkled as Shivers shoved the door open and stepped through into the shop, Monza at his shoulder. It was dim inside, light filtering through the window in a dusty shaft and falling across a marble counter, shadowy shelves down one wall. At the back, under a hanging lamp, was a big chair with a leather pad to rest your head on. Might've looked inviting, except for the straps to hold the sitter down. On a table beside it a neat row of instruments were laid out. Blades, needles, clamps, pliers. Surgeon's tools.

That room might've given him a cold tremble fit to match his name once, but no more. He'd had his eye burned out of his face, and lived to learn the lessons. The world hardly seemed to have any horrors left. Made him smile, to think how scared he'd always been before. Scared of everything and nothing. Smiling tugged at the great wound under his bandages and made his face burn, so he stopped.

The bell brought a man creeping through a side door, hands rubbing nervously together. Small and dark-skinned with a sorry face. Worried they were here to rob him, more'n likely, what with Orso's army not far distant. Everyone in Puranti seemed worried, scared they'd lose what they had. Apart from Shivers himself. He hadn't much to lose.

"Sir, madam, can I be of assistance?"

"You're Scopal?" asked Monza. "The eye-maker?"

"I am Scopal," he bent a nervous bow, "scientist, surgeon, physician, specialising in all things relating to the vision."

Shivers undid the knot at the back of his head. "Good enough." And he started unwinding the bandages. "Fact is I've lost an eye."

351

That perked the surgeon up. "Oh, don't say lost, my friend!" He came forwards into the light from the window. "Don't say lost until I have had a chance to view the damage. You would be amazed at what can be achieved! Science is leaping forwards every day!"

"Springy bastard, ain't it."

Scopal gave an uncertain chuckle. "Ah...most elastic. Why, I have returned a measure of sight to men who thought themselves blind for life. They called me a magician! Imagine that! They called me...a..."

Shivers peeled away the last bandages, the air cold against his tingling skin, and he stepped up closer, turning the left side of his face forwards. "Well? What do you reckon? Can science make that big a jump?"

The man gave a polite nod. "My apologies. But even in the area of replacement I have made great discoveries, never fear!"

Shivers took a half-step further, looming over the man. "Do I look feared to you?"

"Not in the least, of course, I merely meant...well..." Scopal cleared his throat and sidled to the shelves. "My current process for an ocular prosthesis is—"

"The fuck?"

"Fake eye," said Monza.

"Oh, much, much more than that." Scopal slid out a wooden rack. Six metal balls sat on it, gleaming silver-bright. "A perfect sphere of the finest Midderland steel is inserted into the orbit where it will, one hopes, remain permanently." He brought down a round board, flipped it towards them with a showy twist. It was covered with eyes. Blue ones, green ones, brown ones. Each had the colour of a real eye, the gleam of a real eye, some of the whites even had a red vein or two in 'em. And still they looked about as much like a real eye as a boiled egg might've.

Scopal waved at his wares with high smugness. "A curved enamel such as these, painted with care to match perfectly your other eye, is then inserted between metal ball and eyelid. These are prone to wear, and must therefore be regularly changed, but, believe me, the results can be uncanny."

The fake eyes stared, unblinking, at Shivers. "They look like dead men's eyes."

An uncomfortable pause. "When glued upon a board, of course, but properly fitted within a living face—"

"Reckon it's a good thing. Dead men tell no lies, eh? We'll have no more lies." Shivers strode to the back of the shop, dropped down into the chair, stretched out and crossed his legs. "Get to it, then."

"At once?"

"Why not?"

"The steel will take an hour or two to fit. Preparing a set of enamels usually requires at least a fortnight—" Monza tossed a stack of silver coins onto the counter and they jingled as they spilled across the stone. Scopal humbly bowed his head. "I will fit the closest I have, and have the rest ready by tomorrow evening." He turned the lamp up so bright Shivers had to shield his good eye with one hand. "It will be necessary to make some incisions."

"Some whats, now?"

"Cuts," said Monza.

"'Course it will. Nothing in life worth doing that doesn't need a blade, eh?"

Scopal shuffled the instruments around on the little table. "Followed by some stitches, the removal of the useless flesh—"

"Dig out the dead wood? I'm all for it. Let's have a fresh start."

"Might I suggest a pipe?"

"Fuck, yes," he heard Monza whisper.

"Suggest away," said Shivers. "I'm getting bored o' pain the last few weeks."

The eye-maker bowed his head, eased off to charge the pipe. "I remember you getting your hair cut," said Monza. "Nervous as a lamb at its first shearing."

"Heh. True."

"Now look at you, keen to be fitted for an eye."

"A wise man once told me you have to be realistic. Strange how fast we change, ain't it, when we have to?"

She frowned back at him. "Don't change too far. I've got to go."

"No stomach for the eye-making business?"

"I've got to renew an acquaintance."

"Old friend?"

"Old enemy."

Shivers grinned. "Dearer yet. Watch you don't get killed, eh?" And he settled back in the chair, pulled the strap tight round his forehead. "We've still got work to do." He closed his good eye, the lamplight glowing pink through the lid.

Prince of Prudence

Grand Duke Rogont had made his headquarters in the Imperial Bath-Hall. The building was still one of the greatest in Puranti, casting half the square at the east end of the old bridge into shadow. But like the rest of the city, it had seen better centuries. Half its great pediment and two of the six mighty pillars that once held it up had collapsed lifetimes before, the stone pilfered for the mismatched walls of newer, meaner buildings. The stained masonry sprouted with grass, with dead ivy, with a couple of stubborn little trees, even. Probably baths had been a higher priority when it was built, before everyone in Styria started trying to kill each other. Happy times, when keeping the water hot enough had been anyone's biggest worry. The crumbling building might have whispered of the glories of a lost age, but made a sad comment on Styria's long decline.

If Monza had cared a shit.

But she had other things on her mind. She waited for a gap to appear between one tramping company of Rogont's retreating army and the next, then she forced her shoulders back and strode across the square. Up the cracked steps of the Bath-Hall, trying to walk with all her old swagger while her crooked hip bone clicked back and forth in its socket and sent stings right through her arse. She pushed her hood back, keeping her eyes fixed on the foremost of the guards, a grizzled-looking veteran wide as a door with a scar down one colourless cheek.

"I need to speak to Duke Rogont," she said.

"Of course."

"I'm Mon...what?" She'd been expecting to explain herself. Probably to be laughed at. Possibly to be strung up from one of the pillars. Certainly not to be invited in.

"You're General Murcatto." The man had a twist to his grey mouth that came somewhere near a smile. "And you're expected. I'll need the sword, though." She frowned as she handed it over, liking the feel of this less than if they'd kicked her down the street.

There was a great pool in the marble hall beyond, surrounded by tall columns, murky water smelling strongly of rot. Her old enemy Grand Duke Rogont was poring over a map on a folding table, in a sober grey uniform, lips thoughtfully pursed. A dozen officers clustered about him, enough gold braid between them to rig a carrack. A couple looked up as she made her way around the fetid pond towards them.

"It's her," she heard one say, his lip well curled.

"Mur...cat...to," another, as if the very name was poison. No doubt it was to them. She'd been making fools of these very men for the past few years and the more of a fool a man is, the less he cares to look like one. Still, *the general with the smallest numbers should remain always on the offensive*, Stolicus wrote. So she walked up unhurried, the thumb of her bandaged left hand hooked carelessly in her belt, as if this was her bath and she was the one with all the swords.

"If it isn't the Prince of Prudence, Duke Rogont. Well met, your Cautiousness. A proud-looking set of comrades you've got here, for men who've spent seven years retreating. Still, at least you're not retreating today." She let it sink in for a moment. "Oh, wait. You are."

That forced a few chins to haughtily rise, a nostril or two to flare. But the dark eyes of Rogont himself shifted up from the map without any rush, a little tired, perhaps, but still irritatingly handsome and at ease. "General Murcatto, what a pleasure! I wish we could have met after a great battle, preferably with you as a crestfallen prisoner, but my victories have been rather thin on the ground."

"Rare as summer snows."

"And you, so cloaked in glories. I feel quite naked under your victorious glare." He peered towards the back of the hall. "But wherever are your all-conquering Thousand Swords now?"

Monza sucked her teeth. "Faithful Carpi's borrowed them from me."

"Without asking? How...rude. I fear you are too much soldier and not enough politician. I fear I am the opposite. Words may hold more power than swords, as Juvens said, but I have discovered to my cost that there are times when there is no substitute for pointy metal."

"These are the Years of Blood."

"Indeed they are. We are all the prisoners of circumstance, and circumstances have left me once again with no other choice but bitter retreat. The noble Lirozio, Duke of Puranti and owner of this wonderful bath, was as staunch and warlike an ally as could be imagined when Duke Orso's power was long leagues away on the other side of the great walls of Musselia. You should have heard him gnash his teeth, his sword never so eager to spring forth and spill hot blood."

"Men love to talk about fighting." Monza let her eyes wander over the sullen faces of Rogont's advisors. "Some like to dress for it, too. Getting blood on the uniforms is a different matter."

A couple of angry head-tosses from the peacocks, but Rogont only smiled. "My own sad realisation. Now Musselia's great walls are breached, thanks to you, Borletta fallen, thanks to you, and Visserine burned too. The army of Talins, ably assisted by your erstwhile comrades, the Thousand Swords, are picking the country clean on Lirozio's very doorstep. The brave duke finds his enthusiasm for drum and bugle much curtailed. Powerful men are as inconstant as the shifting water. I should have picked weaker allies."

"Bit late for that."

The duke puffed out his cheeks. "Too late, too late, shall be my epitaph. At Sweet Pines I arrived but two days tardy, and rash Salier had fought and lost without me. So Caprile was left helpless before your well-documented wrath." That was a fool's version of the story, but Monza kept it to herself, for now. "At Musselia I arrived with all my power, prepared to hold the great walls and block the Gap of Etris against you, and found you had stolen the city the day before, picked it clean already and now held the walls against me." More injury to the truth, but Monza kept her peace. "Then at the High Bank I found myself unavoidably detained by the late General Ganmark, while the also late Duke Salier, quite determined not to be fooled by you a second time, was fooled by you a second time and his army scattered like chaff on a stiff wind. So Borletta..." He stuck his tongue between his lips, jerked his thumb towards the floor and blew a loud farting sound. "So brave Duke Cantain..." He drew one finger across his throat and blew another. "Too late, too late. Tell me, General Murcatto, how come you are always first to the field?"

"I rise early, shit before daybreak, check I'm pointed in the right direction and let nothing stop me. That and I actually try to get there."

"Your meaning?" demanded a young man at Rogont's elbow, his face even sourer than the rest.

"My meaning?" she parroted, goggling like an idiot, and then to the duke himself, "Is that you could have reached Sweet Pines on time but chose to dither, knowing proud, fat Salier would piss before his trousers were down and more than likely waste all his strength whether he won or not. He lost, and looked the fool, and you the wiser partner, just as you hoped." It was Rogont's turn to stay carefully silent. "Two seasons later you could have reached the Gap in time and held it against the world, but it suited you to delay, and let me teach the proud Musselians the lesson you wanted them to learn. Namely to be humble before your prudent Excellency."

The whole chamber was very still as her voice grated on. "When did you realise time was running out? That you'd delayed so much you'd let your allies wane too weak, let Orso wax too strong? No doubt you would have liked to make it to the High Bank for once on time, but Ganmark got in your way. As far as playing the good ally, by that time it was..." She leaned forwards and whispered it. "*Too late.* All your policy was making sure you were the strongest partner when the League of Eight won, so you could be the first among them. A grand notion, and carefully managed. Except, of course, Orso has won, and the League of Eight..." She stuck her tongue between her lips and blew a long fart at the assembled flower of manhood. "So much for too late, fuckers."

The shrillest of the brood stepped towards her, fists clenched. "I will not listen to one word more of this, you...you devil! My father died at Sweet Pines!"

It seemed everyone had their own wrongs to avenge, but Monza had too many wounds of her own to be much stung by other people's. "Thank you," she said.

"What?"

"Since your father was presumably among my enemies, and the aim of a battle is to kill them, I take his death as a compliment. I shouldn't have to explain that to a soldier."

His face had turned a blotchy mixture of pink and white. "If you were a man I'd kill you where you stand."

"If you were a man, you mean. Still, since I took your father, it's only fair I give you something in trade." She curled her tongue and blew spit in his face.

He came at her clumsily, and with his hands, just as she'd guessed he would. Any man who needs to be worked up to it that hard isn't likely to be too fearful when he finally gets there. She was ready, dodged around him, grabbed the top and bottom rims of his gilded breastplate, used his own weight to swing him, caught his toe with one well-placed boot. She grabbed the hilt of his sword as he stumbled helplessly past, bent almost double, part running and part falling, and whipped it from his belt. He squawked as he splashed into the pool, sending up a fountain of shining spray, and she spun round, blade at the ready.

Rogont rolled his eyes. "Oh, for pity's—" His men bundled past, all fumbling their swords out, cursing, nearly knocking the table over in their haste to get at her. "Less steel, gentlemen, if you please, less steel!" The officer had surfaced now, or at least was fighting to, splashing and floundering, hauled down by the weight of his ornamental armour. Two of Rogont's other attendants hurried to drag him from the pool while the rest shuffled towards Monza, jostling at each other in their efforts to stab her first.

"Shouldn't you be the ones retreating?" she hissed as she backed away past the pillars.

The nearest jabbed at her. "Die, you damned—"

"Enough!" roared Rogont. "Enough! Enough!" His men scowled like naughty children called to account. "No swordplay in the bath, for pity's sake! Will my shame never end?" He gave a long sigh, then waved an arm. "Leave us, all of you!"

His foremost attendant's moustache bristled with horror. "But, your Excellency, with this . . . foul creature?"

"Never fear, I will survive." He arched one eyebrow at them. "I can swim. Now out, before someone hurts themselves. Shoo! Go!"

Reluctantly they sheathed their swords and grumbled their way from the hall, the soaked man leaving a squelching trail of wet fury behind him. Monza grinned as she tossed his gilded sword into the pool, where it vanished with a splash. A small victory, maybe, but she had to enjoy the ones she got these days.

Rogont waited in silence until they were alone, then gave a heavy sigh. "You told me she would come, Ishri."

"It is well that I never tire of being right." Monza started. A dark-skinned woman lay on her back on a high windowsill, a good stride or two above Rogont's head. Her legs were crossed, up against the wall, one arm and her head hanging off the back of the narrow ledge so that her face was almost upside down. "For it happens often." She slid off backwards, flipped over at the last moment and dropped silently to all fours, nimble as a lizard.

Monza wasn't sure how she'd missed her in the first place, but she didn't like that she had. "What are you? An acrobat?"

"Oh, nothing so romantic as an acrobat. I am the East Wind. You can think of me as but one of the many fingers on God's right hand."

"You talk enough rubbish to be a priest."

"Oh, nothing so dry and dusty as a priest." Her eyes rolled to the ceiling. "I am a passionate believer, in my way, but only men may take the robe, thanks be to God."

Monza frowned. "An agent of the Gurkish Emperor."

"Agent sounds so very…underhanded. Emperor, Prophet, Church, State. I would call myself a humble representative of Southern Powers."

"What's Styria to them?"

"A battlefield." And she smiled wide. "Gurkhul and the Union may be at peace, but…"

"The fighting goes on."

"Always. Orso's allies are our enemies, so his enemies are our allies. We find ourselves with common cause."

"The downfall of Grand Duke Orso of Talins," muttered Rogont. "Please God."

Monza curled her lip at him. "Huh. Praying to God now, Rogont?"

"To whoever will listen, and most fervently."

The Gurkish woman stood, stretching up on tiptoe to the ends of her long fingers. "And you, Murcatto? Are you the answer to this poor man's desperate prayers?"

"Maybe."

"And he to yours, perhaps?"

"I've been often disappointed by the powerful, but I can hope."

"You'd hardly be the first friend I've disappointed." Rogont nodded towards the map. "They call me the Count of Caution. The Duke of Delay. The Prince of Prudence. Yet you would make an ally of me?"

"Look at me, Rogont, I'm almost as desperate as you are. 'Great tempests,' Farans said, 'wash up strange companions.'"

"A wise man. How can I help my strange companion, then? And, more importantly, how can she help me?"

"I need to kill Faithful Carpi."

"Why would we care for treacherous Carpi's death?" Ishri sauntered forwards, head falling lazily onto one side, then further still. Too far to look at comfortably, let alone to do. "Are there not other captains among the Thousand Swords? Sesaria, Victus, Andiche?" Her eyes were pitch black, as empty and dead as the eye-maker's replacements. "Will not one of those infamous vultures fill your old chair, keen to pick at the corpse of Styria?"

Rogont pouted. "And so my weary dance continues, but with a fresh partner. I win only the most fleeting reprieve."

"Those three have no loyalty to Orso beyond their pockets. They were persuaded easily enough to betray Cosca for me, and me for Faithful, when the price was right. If the price is right, with Faithful gone I can bring them back to me, and from Orso's service to yours."

A slow silence. Ishri raised her fine black brows. Rogont tipped his head thoughtfully back. The two of them exchanged a lingering glance. "That would go a long way towards evening the odds."

"You are sure you can buy them?" asked the Gurkish woman.

"Yes," Monza lied smoothly. "I never gamble." An even bigger lie, so she delivered it with even greater confidence. There was no certainty where the Thousand Swords were concerned, and even less with the faithless bastards who commanded them. But there might be a chance, if she could kill Faithful. Get Rogont's help with that, then they'd see.

"How high would be the price?"

"To turn against the winning side? Higher than I can afford, that's sure." Even if she'd had the rest of Hermon's gold to hand, and most of it was still buried thirty strides from her dead father's ruined barn. "But you, the Duke of Ospria—"

Rogont gave a sorry chuckle. "Oh, the bottomless purse of Ospria. I am in hock up to my neck and beyond. I'd sell my arse if I thought I could get more than a few coppers for it. No, you will coax no gold from me, I fear."

"What about your Southern Powers?" asked Monza. "I hear the mountains of Gurkhul are made of gold."

Ishri wriggled back against one of the pillars. "Of mud, like everyone else's. But there may be much gold in them, if one knows where to dig. How do you plan to put an end to Faithful?"

"Lirozio will surrender to Orso's army as soon as it arrives."

"Doubtless," said Rogont. "He is every bit as proficient at surrender as I am at retreat."

"The Thousand Swords will push on southwards towards Ospria, picking the country clean, and the Talinese will follow."

"I need no military genius to tell me this."

"I'll find a place, somewhere between, and bring Carpi out. With two-score men I can get him killed. Small risk for either one of you."

Rogont cleared his throat. "If you can bring that loyal old hound out of his kennel, then I can surely spare some men to put him down."

Ishri watched Monza, just as Monza might have watched an ant. "And once he is at peace, if you can buy the Thousand Swords then I can furnish the money."

If, if, if. But that was more than Monza had any right to hope for here. She could just as easily have left the meeting feet first. "Then it's as good as done. To strange companions, eh?"

"Indeed. God has truly blessed you." Ishri gave an extravagant yawn. "You came looking for one friend, and you leave with two."

"Lucky me," said Monza, far from sure she was leaving with any. She turned towards the gate, boot heels scraping against the worn marble, hoping she didn't start shaking before she got there.

"One more thing, Murcatto!" She looked back to Rogont, standing alone now by his maps. Ishri had vanished as suddenly as she'd appeared. "Your position is weak, and so you are obliged to play at strength. I see that. You are what you are, bold beyond recklessness. I would not have it any other way. But I am what I am, also. Some more respect, in future, will make our marriage of mutual desperation run ever so much more smoothly."

Monza gave an exaggerated curtsey. "Your Resplendence, I am not only weak, but abject with regret."

Rogont slowly shook his head. "That officer of mine really should have drawn and run you through."

"Is that what you'd have done?"

"Oh, pity, no." He looked back to his charts. "I'd have asked for more spit."

Neither Rich nor Poor

Shenkt hummed to himself as he walked down the shabby corridor, his footfalls making not the slightest sound. The exact tune always somehow eluded him. A nagging fragment of something his sister sang when he was a child. He could see the sunlight still, through her hair, the window at her back, face in shadow. All long ago, now. All faded, like cheap paints in the sun. He had never been much of a singer himself. But he hummed, at least, and imagined his sister's voice singing along with him, and that was some comfort.

He put his knife away, and the carved bird too, almost finished now, though the beak was giving him some trouble and he did not wish to break it by rushing. Patience. As vital to the wood-carver as it is to the assassin. He stopped before the door. Soft, pale pine, full of knots, badly jointed, light shining through a split. He wished, sometimes, that his work took him to better places. He raised one boot, and burst the lock apart with a single kick.

Eight sets of hands leaped to weapons as the door splintered from its hinges. Eight hard faces snapped towards him, seven men and a woman. Shenkt recognised most of them. They had been among the kneeling half-circle in Orso's throne room. Killers, sent after Prince Ario's murderers. Comrades, of a kind, in the hunt. If the flies on a carcass can be said to be comrades to the lion that made the kill. He had not expected such as these to beat him to his quarry, but he was long past being surprised by the turns life took. His twisted like a snake in its death throes.

"Have I come at a bad time?" he asked.

"It's him."

"The one who wouldn't kneel."

"Shenkt." This last from the man who had blocked his path in Orso's throne room. The one he had advised to pray. Shenkt hoped he had taken the advice, but did not think it likely. A couple of them relaxed when they recognised his face, pushed back their half-drawn blades, thinking him one of their number.

"Well, well." A man with a pockmarked face and long, black hair seemed to be in charge. He reached out and gently pushed the woman's bow towards the floor with one finger. "My name's Malt. You're just in time to help us bring them in."

"Them?"

"The ones his Excellency Duke Orso's paying us to find, who do you think? Over there, in the smoke-house yonder."

"All of them?"

"The leader, anyway."

"How do you know you have the right man?"

"Woman. Pello knows, don't you, Pello?"

Pello was possessed of a ragged moustache and a look of sweaty desperation. "It's Murcatto. The same one who led Orso's army at Sweet Pines. She was in Visserine, not but a month ago. Took her prisoner. Questioned her myself. That's where the Northman lost his eye." The Northman called Shivers, that Sajaam had spoken of. "In Salier's palace. She killed Ganmark there, that general of Orso's, few days afterward."

"The Snake of Talins herself," said Malt proudly, "and still alive. What do you think of that?"

"I am all amazed." Shenkt walked slowly to the window and peered out across the street. A shabby-looking place for a famous general, but such was life. "She has men with her?"

"Just this Northman. Nothing we can't deal with. Lucky Nim and two of her boys are waiting in the alley at the back. When the big clock next chimes, we go in the front. They won't be getting away."

Shenkt looked slowly round at each suspicious face, and gave each man a chance. "You all are determined to do this? All of you?"

"Of fucking course we are. You'll find no faint hearts here, my friend." Malt looked at him through narrowed eyes. "You want to come in with us?"

"With you?" Shenkt took a long breath, then sighed. "Great tempests wash up strange companions."

"I'll take that as a yes."

"We don't need this fucker." The one Shenkt had told to pray, again, making a great show of a curved knife. A man of small patience, evidently. "I say we cut his throat, and one less share to pay."

Malt gently pushed his knife down. "Come now, no need to be greedy. I've been on jobs like that before, everyone stuck on the money not the work, watching their backs every minute. Bad for your health and your business. We'll do this civilised, or not at all. What do you say?"

"I say civilised," said Shenkt. "For pity's sake, let's kill like honest men."

"Exactly so. With what Orso's paying, there'll be enough for everyone. Equal shares all round, and we can all be rich."

"Rich?" Shenkt smiled sadly as he shook his head. "The dead are neither rich nor poor." The look of mild surprise was just forming on Malt's face when Shenkt's pointing finger split it neatly in half.

Shivers sat on the greasy bed, back pressed to the dirty wall, with Monza sprawled on top of him. Her head lay in his lap, breath hissing shallow, in and out. The pipe was still in her bandaged left hand, smoke twisting from the embers in a brown streak. He frowned at it creeping through the shafts of light, rippling, spreading, filling the room with sweet haze.

Husk was good stuff for pain. Too good, to Shivers' mind. So good you always needed more. So good that after a while stubbing your toe seemed like excuse enough. Took your edge off, all that smoking, left you soft. Maybe Monza had more edge than she wanted, but he didn't trust it. The smoke was tickling at his nose, making him feel sick and needy both together. His eye was itching under the bandages. Would've been easy to do it. Where was the harm...?

He had a sudden panic, wriggling out from under her like he was buried alive. Monza gave an irritated burble then fell back, eyelids flickering, hair stuck across her clammy face. Shivers ripped back the bolt on the window and pulled the wonky shutters open, getting a nice view of the rotting alley behind the building and a face full of cold, piss-smelling air. At least that smell was honest.

There were two men down there by a back door, and a woman holding one hand up. A bell rang out, from a high clock tower in the next street.

The woman nodded, the men pulled out a bright sword and a heavy mace. She opened the door and they hurried in.

"Shit," hissed Shivers, hardly able to believe it. Three of 'em and, from the way they'd been waiting, most likely more coming in the front. Too late to run. But then Shivers was sick of running anyway. He had his pride, still, didn't he? Running from the North and down here to fucking Styria was what landed him in this one-eyed mess in the first place.

He reached towards Monza, but stopped short. State she was in she'd be no use. So he let her be, slid out the heavy knife she'd given him the first day they met. The grip was firm in his hand and he squeezed it tight. They were better armed, maybe, but big weapons and small rooms don't mix. Surprise was on his side, and that's the best weapon a man can have. He pressed himself into the shadows behind the door, feeling his heart thumping, the breath burning in his throat. No fear, no doubt, just furious readiness.

He heard their soft steps on the stairs and had to stop himself laughing. A bit of a giggle crept out all the same, and he didn't know why, 'cause there was nothing funny. A creak and a muttered curse. Not the sharpest assassins in the whole Circle of the World. He bit on his lip, trying to stop his ribs shaking. Monza stirred, stretched out smiling on the greasy blanket.

"Benna..." she murmured. The door was yanked open and the swordsman sprang in. Monza's eyes came blearily open. "Whathe—"

The second man barged in like a fool, knocking his mate off balance, lifting his mace over his head, tip scraping a little shower of plaster from the low ceiling. It was almost like he was offering it up. Would've seemed rude to turn it down, so Shivers snatched it from his hand while he stabbed the first one in the back.

The blade slid in and out of him. Quick, quiet scrapes, up to the hilt. Shivers growled through his teeth, half-sniggering with the leftover shreds of laughter, arm pumping in and out. The stabbed man made a shocked little hoot each time, not sure what was happening yet, twisted round, jerking the knife out of Shivers' hand.

The other one turned, eyes wide, too close to swing at. "Wha—"

Shivers thumped him in the nose with the butt of the mace and felt it pop, sent him reeling towards the empty fireplace. The stabbed man's knees went, he caught his sword point on the wall above Monza and pitched on top of her. No need to worry about him. Shivers took a short stride, dropping onto his knees so the mace wouldn't hit the ceiling, roaring as he swung the big lump of metal. It hit its previous owner in the forehead with a meaty crunch, stove his skull in, spattered the ceiling with spots of blood.

He heard a scream behind, twisted round. The woman sprang through the door, a short blade in each hand. Monza's kicking leg tripped her as she struggled out from under the dying swordsman. Happy chance, the woman's scream switching from fury to shock as she blundered into Shivers' arms, fumbling one of her knives. He grabbed her other wrist as he went down under her, on top of the maceman's corpse, his head smacking against the side of the fireplace and leaving him blinded for a moment.

He kept his grip on her wrist, felt her nails tearing at his bandages. They growled stupidly at each other, her hair hanging down and tickling at him, tongue stuck between her teeth with the effort as she tried to push the blade into his neck with all her weight. Her breath smelled of lemons. He wrenched himself round and punched her under the jaw, snapped her head up, teeth sinking deep into her tongue.

Same moment the sword hacked clumsily into her arm, the point almost catching Shivers' shoulder, making him jerk back. Monza's white face behind her, eyes hardly focused. The woman howled, tried to drag herself free. Another fumbling sword blow caught the top of her head with the flat and knocked her sideways. Monza floundered into the wall, tripped over the bed, almost stabbing herself as the sword clattered from her hand. Shivers twisted the blade from the woman's limp grip and stabbed her under the jaw right to the hilt, blood spraying out across Monza's shirt and up the wall.

He kicked himself free of the tangle of limbs, scrabbling up the mace, pulling his knife from the dead swordsman's back and pushing it into his belt, stumbling for the door. The corridor outside was empty. He grabbed Monza's wrist and dragged her up. She was staring down at herself, soaked with the woman's blood.

"Wha...wha..."

He pulled her limp arm over his shoulder and hauled her through the door, bundled her down the stairs, her boots clattering against the treads. Out through the open back door into sunlight. She tottered a step and blew thin vomit down the wall. Groaned and heaved again. He pushed the haft of the mace up his sleeve, the bloody head in his fist, ready to let it drop if he needed to. He realised he was sniggering again as he did it. Couldn't see why. Still nothing funny. Quite the opposite, far as he could tell. Still laughing, though.

Monza took a drunken step or two, bent almost double. "I got stop smoking," she muttered, spitting bile.

"'Course. Just as soon as my eye grows back." He grabbed her elbow, pulled her after him towards the end of the alley, folk moving in the sunlit street. He paused at the corner, took a quick look both ways, then dragged her arm around his shoulder again, and away.

Aside from the three corpses, the room was empty. Shenkt padded to the window, stepping carefully around the slick of blood across the boards, and peered out. Of Murcatto and the one-eyed Northman there was no sign. But it was better they should escape than someone else should find them before he did. That he would not allow. When Shenkt took on a job, he always saw it through.

He squatted down, forearms resting on his knees, hands dangling. He had hardly made a worse mess of Malt and his seven friends than Murcatto and her Northman had of these three. The walls, the floor, the ceiling, the bed, all spattered and smeared with red. One man lay by the fireplace, his skull roundly pulped. The other was face down, the back of his shirt ripped with stab-wounds, soaked through with blood. The woman had a yawning gash in her neck.

Lucky Nim, he presumed. It seemed her luck had deserted her.

"Just Nim, then."

Something gleamed in the corner, by the wall. He stooped and picked it up, held it to the light. A golden ring with a large, blood-red ruby. Far too fine a ring for any of these scum to wear. Murcatto's ring, even? Still warm from her finger? He slid it onto his own, then took hold of Nim's ankle and dragged her corpse up onto the bed, humming to himself as he stripped it bare.

Her right leg had a patch of scaly rash across the thigh, so he took the left instead, cut it free, buttock and all, with three practised movements of his butcher's sickle. He popped the bone from the hip joint with a sharp twist of his wrists, took the foot off with two jerks of the curved blade, wrapped her belt around the neatly butchered leg to hold it folded and slid it into his bag.

A rump steak, then, thick-cut and pan-fried. He always carried a special mix of Suljuk four-spice with him, crushed to his taste, and the oil native to the region around Puranti had a wonderful nutty flavour. Then salt, and crushed pepper. Good meat was all in the seasoning. Pink in the centre, but not bloody. Shenkt had never been able to understand people who liked their meat bloody, the notion disgusted him. Onions sizzling alongside. Perhaps then dice the shank and make stew, with roots and mushrooms, a broth from the bones, a dash of that old Muris vinegar to give it ...

"Zing."

He nodded to himself, carefully wiped the sickle clean, shouldered the bag, turned for the door and ... stopped.

He had passed a baker's earlier, and thought what fine, crusty, new-baked loaves they had in the window. The smell of fresh bread. That glorious scent of honesty and simple goodness. He would very much have liked to be a baker, had he not been ... what he was. Had he never been brought before his old master. Had he never followed the path laid out for him, and had he never rebelled against it. How well that bread would be, he now thought, sliced and thickly smeared with a coarse pâté. Perhaps with a quince jelly, or some such, and a good glass of wine. He drew his knife again and went in through Lucky Nim's back for her liver.

After all, it was no use to her now.

Heroic Efforts, New Beginnings

The rain stopped, and the sun came out over the farmland, a faint rainbow stretching down from the grey heavens. Monza wondered if there was an elf-glade where it touched the ground, the way her father used to tell her. Or if there was just shit, like everywhere else. She leaned from her saddle and spat into the wheat.

Elf shit, maybe.

She pushed her wet hood back and scowled to the west, watching the showers roll off towards Puranti. If there was any justice they'd dump a deluge on Faithful Carpi and the Thousand Swords, their outriders probably no more than a day's ride behind. But there was no justice, and Monza knew it. The clouds pissed where they pleased.

The damp winter wheat was spattered with patches of red flowers, like smears of blood across the tawny country. It would be ready to harvest soon, except there'd be no one here to do the reaping. Rogont was doing what he was best at — pulling back, and the farmers were taking everything they could carry and pulling back with him towards Ospria. They knew the Thousand Swords were coming, and knew better than to be there when they did. There were no more infamous foragers in the world than the men Monza used to lead.

Forage, Farans wrote, *is robbery so vast that it transcends mere crime, and enters the arena of politics.*

She'd lost Benna's ring. She kept fussing at her middle finger with her thumb, endlessly disappointed to find it wasn't there. A pretty piece of rock hadn't changed the fact Benna was dead. But still it felt as if she'd lost some last little part of him she'd managed to cling on to. One of the last little parts of herself worth keeping.

She was lucky a ring was all she'd lost back in Puranti, though. She'd been careless, and it had nearly been the end of her. She had to stop smoking. Make a new beginning. Had to, and yet she was smoking more than ever. Each time she woke from sweet oblivion she told herself it would have to be the last, but a few hours later and she'd be sweating desperation from every pore. Waves of sick need, like an incoming tide, each one higher than the last. Each one resisted took a heroic effort, and Monza was no hero, however the people of Talins might once have cheered for her. She'd thrown her pipe away, then in a sticky panic bought another. She wasn't sure how many times she'd hidden the dwindling lump of husk down at the bottom of one bag or another. But she'd found there's a problem with hiding a thing yourself.

You always know where it is.

"I do not care for this country." Morveer stood from his swaying seat and peered out across the flat land. "This is good country for an ambush."

"That's why we're here," Monza growled back. Hedgerows, the odd stand of trees, brown houses and barns alone or in groups away across the fields — plenty of hiding places. Scarcely a thing moved. Scarcely a sound but for the crows, the wind flapping the canvas on the cart, the wheels rattling, splattering through an occasional puddle.

"Are you sure it is prudent to put your faith in Rogont?"

"You don't win battles with prudence."

"No, one plans murders with it. Rogont is *notoriously* untrustworthy even for a grand duke, and an old enemy of yours besides."

"I can trust him as far as what's in his own interest." The question was all the more irritating as it was one she'd been asking herself ever since they left Puranti. "Small risk for him killing Faithful Carpi, but a hell of a pay-off if I can bring him the Thousand Swords."

"But it would hardly be your first miscalculation. What if we are *marooned* out here in the path of an army? You are paying me to kill one man at a time, not fight a war single—"

"I paid you to kill one man in Westport, and you murdered fifty at a throw. I need no lessons from you in taking care."

"Scarcely more than forty, and that was due to too much care to get your man, not too little! Was your butcher's bill any shorter at Cardotti's House of Leisure? Or in Duke Salier's palace? Or at Caprile, for that matter? Forgive me if I have *scant* faith in your ability to keep violence contained!"

"Enough!" she snarled at him. "You're like a goat that won't stop bleating! Do the job I pay you for, and that's the end of it!"

Morveer pulled up the cart suddenly with a haul on the reins and Day squawked as she nearly fumbled her apple. "Is this the thanks I get for your timely rescue in Visserine? After you so *pointedly* ignored my sage advice?"

Vitari, sprawling among the supplies on the back of the cart, stuck up one long arm. "That rescue was as much my doing as his. No one's thanked me."

Morveer ignored her. "Perhaps I should find a more grateful employer!"

"Perhaps I should find a more obedient fucking poisoner!"

"Perhaps...! But wait." Morveer held up a finger, squeezing his eyes shut. "But wait." He puckered his lips and sucked in a deep breath, held it for a moment, then slowly blew it out. And again. Shivers rode up, raised his one eyebrow at Monza. One more breath, and Morveer's eyes came open, and he gave a chuckle of sickening falseness. "Perhaps...I should most *sincerely* apologise."

"What?"

"I realise I am...not always the easiest company." A sharp burst of laughter from Vitari and Morveer winced, but carried on. "If I seem always contrary it is because I want only the best for you and your venture. It has ever been a failing of mine to be too *intransigent* in my pursuit of excellence. There is no more important characteristic than *pliability* in a man who must, perforce, be your *humble* servant. Can I entreat you to make with me...a heroic effort? To put this unpleasantness behind us?" He snapped the reins and moved the cart on, still smiling thinly over his shoulder. "I feel it! A new beginning!"

Monza caught Day's eye as she passed, rocking gently on her seat. The blond girl lifted her brows, stripped her apple to the last fragment of stalk and flicked it away into the field. Vitari was on the back of the cart, just pulling off her coat and sprawling out on the canvas in the sunlight. "Sun's coming out. New beginning." She pointed across the country, one hand pressed to her chest. "And aaaaaaaw, a rainbow! You know, they say there's an elf-glade where it touches the ground!"

Monza scowled after them. Seemed more likely they'd stumble on an elf-glade than that Morveer would make a new beginning. She trusted this sudden obedience even less than his endless carping.

"Maybe he just wants to be loved," came Shivers' whispery voice as they set off again.

"If men can change like that." And Monza snapped her fingers in his face.

"That's the only way they do change, ain't it?" His one eye stayed on her. "If things change enough around 'em? Men are brittle, I reckon. They don't bend into new shapes. They get broken into them. Crushed into them."

Burned into them, maybe. "How's your face?" she muttered.

"Itchy."

"Did it hurt, at the eye-maker's?"

"On a scale between stubbing your toe and having your eye burned out, it was down near the bottom."

"Most everything is."

"Falling down a mountain?"

"Not that bad, as long as you lie still. It's when you try to get up it starts to sting some." That got a grin from him, though he was grinning a lot less than he used to. Small surprise after what he'd been through, maybe. What she'd put him through. "I suppose...I should be thanking you for saving my life, again. It's getting to be a habit."

"What you're paying me for, ain't it, Chief? Work well done is its own reward, my father always used to tell me. Fact is I'm good at it. As a fighter I'm a man you need to respect. As anything else I'm just a big shiftless fuck wasted a dozen years in the wars, with nothing to show for it but bloody dreams and one less eye than most. I've got my pride, still. Man's got to be what he is, I reckon. Otherwise what is he? Just pretending, no? And who wants to spend all the time they're given pretending to be what they ain't?"

Good question. Luckily they crested a rise, and she was spared having to think of an answer. The remains of the Imperial road stretched away, an arrow-straight stripe of brown through the fields. Eight centuries old, and still the best road in Styria. A sad comment on the leadership since. There was a farm not far from it. A stone house of two storeys, windows shuttered, roof of red tiles turned mossy brown with age, a small stable-block beside. A waist-high wall of lichen-splattered drystone round a muddy yard, a couple of scrawny birds pecking at the dirt. Opposite the house a wooden barn, roof slumping in the middle. A weather vane in the shape of a winged snake flapped limply on its leaning turret.

"That's the place!" she called out, and Vitari stuck her arm up to show she'd heard.

A stream wound past the buildings and off towards a mill-house a mile or two distant. The wind came up, shook the leaves on a hedgerow, made soft waves in the wheat, drove the ragged clouds across the sky, their shadows flowing over the land beneath.

It reminded Monza of the farm where she was born. She thought of Benna, a boy running through the crop, just the top of his head showing above the ripening grain, hearing his high laughter. Long ago, before their father died. Monza shook herself and scowled. Maudlin, self-indulgent, nostalgic shit. She'd hated that farm. The digging, the ploughing, the dirt under her nails. And all for what? There weren't many things you worked so hard at to make so little.

The only other one she could think of right off was revenge.

Since his earliest remembrances, Morveer seemed always to have had an uncanny aptitude for saying the wrong thing. When he meant to contribute, he would find he was complaining. When he intended to be solicitous, he would discover he was insulting. When he sought earnestly to provide support, he would be construed as undermining. He wanted only to be valued, respected, included, and yet somehow every attempt at good fellowship only made matters worse.

He was almost starting to believe, after thirty years of failed relationships — a mother who had left him, a wife who had left him, apprentices who had left, robbed or attempted to kill him, usually by poison but on one memorable occasion with an axe — that he simply was not very good with people. He should have been glad, at least, that the loathsome drunk Nicomo Cosca was dead, and indeed he had at first felt some relief. But the dark clouds had soon rolled back to re-establish the eternal baseline of mild depression. He found himself once more squabbling with his troublesome employer over every detail of their business.

Probably it would have been better if he had simply retired to the mountains and lived as a hermit, where he could injure nobody's feelings. But the thin air had never suited his delicate constitution. So he had resolved, once more, to make a heroic effort at camaraderie. To be more compliant, more graceful, more indulgent of the shortcomings of others. He had taken the first step, therefore, while the rest of the party were out surveying the land for signs of the Thousand Swords, by pretending at a headache and preparing a pleasant surprise, in the form of his mother's recipe for mushroom soup. Perhaps the only tangible thing which she had left her only son.

He nicked his finger while slicing, singed his elbow upon the hot stove, both of which events almost caused him to forsake his new beginning in a torrent of unproductive rage. But by the time he heard the horses returning to the farm, just as the sun was sinking and the shadows in the yard outside were stretching out, he had the table set, two stubs of candle casting a welcoming glow, two loaves of bread sliced and the pot of soup at the ready, exuding a wholesome fragrance.

"Excellent." His rehabilitation was assured.

His new vein of optimism did not survive the arrival of the diners, however. When they entered, incidentally without removing their boots and therefore treading mud across his gleaming floor, they looked towards his lovingly cleaned kitchen, his carefully laid table, his laboriously prepared potage with all the enthusiasm of convicts being shown the executioner's block.

"What's this?" Murcatto's lips were pushed out and her brows drawn down in even deeper suspicion than usual.

Morveer did his best to float over it. "This is an apology. Since our number-obsessed cook has returned to Talins, I thought I might occupy the vacuum and prepare dinner. My mother's recipe. Sit, sit, pray sit!" He hurried round dragging out chairs and, notwithstanding some uncomfortable sideways glances, they all found seats.

"Soup?" Morveer advanced on Shivers with pan and ladle at the ready.

"Not for me. You did, what do you call it…"

"Paralyse," said Murcatto.

"Aye. You paralysed me that time."

"You mistrust me?" he snapped.

"Almost by definition," said Vitari, watching him from under her ginger brows. "You're a poisoner."

"After all we have been through together? You mistrust me, over a little *paralysis*?" He was making heroic efforts to repair the foundering ship of their professional relationship, and nobody appreciated it one whit. "If my intention was to poison you, I would simply sprinkle Black Lavender on your pillow and lull you to a sleep that would *never end*. Or put Amerind thorns in your boots, Larync on the grip of your axe, Mustard Root in your water flask." He leaned down towards the Northman, knuckles white around the ladle. "There are a thousand thousand ways that I could kill you and you would never suspect the merest *shadow* of a thing. I would not go to all the trouble of *cooking* you *dinner*!"

Shivers' one eye stared levelly back into his for what seemed a very long time. Then the Northman reached out, and for the briefest moment Morveer wondered if he was about to receive his first punch in the face for many years. But instead Shivers only folded his big hand round Morveer's with exaggerated care, tipping the pan so soup spilled out into his bowl. He picked up his spoon, dipped it in his soup, blew delicately on it and slurped up the contents. "It's good. Mushroom, is it?"

"Er . . . yes, it is."

"Nice." Shivers held Morveer's eye a moment longer before letting go his hand.

"Thank you." Morveer hefted the ladle. "Now, does anyone *not* want soup?"

"Me!" The voice barked out of nowhere like boiling water squirted in Morveer's ear. He jerked away, the pan tumbling, hot soup flooding out across the table and straight into Vitari's lap. She leaped up with a screech, wet cutlery flying. Murcatto's chair went clattering over as she lurched out of it, fumbling for her sword. Day dropped a half-eaten slice of bread as she took a shocked step back towards the door. Morveer whipped around, dripping ladle clutched pointlessly in one fist—

A Gurkish woman stood smiling beside him, arms folded. Her skin was smooth as a child's, flawless as dark glass, eyes midnight black.

"Wait!" barked Murcatto, one hand up. "Wait. She's a friend."

"She's no friend of mine!" Morveer was still desperately trying to understand how she could have appeared from nothing in such a manner. There was no door near her, the window was tightly shuttered and barred, the floor and ceiling intact.

"You have no friends, poisoner," she purred at him. Her long, brown coat hung open. Underneath, her body seemed to be swaddled entirely in white bandages.

"Who are you?" demanded Day. "And where the hell did you come from?"

"They used to call me the East Wind." The woman displayed two rows of utterly perfect white teeth as she turned one finger gracefully round and round. "But now they call me Ishri. I come from the sun-bleached South."

"She meant—" began Morveer.

"Magic," murmured Shivers, the only member of the party who had remained in his seat. He calmly raised his spoon and slurped up another mouthful. "Pass the bread, eh?"

"Damn your bread!" he snarled back. "And your magic too! How did you get in here?"

"One of them." Vitari had a table-knife in her fist, eyes narrowed to deadly slits as the remains of the soup dripped from the table and tapped steadily on the floor. "An Eater."

The Gurkish woman pushed one fingertip through the spilled soup and curled her tongue around it. "We must all eat something, no?"

"I don't care to be on the menu."

"You need not worry. I am very picky about my food."

"I tangled with your kind before, in Dagoska." Morveer did not fully understand what was being said, a sensation which was among his least favourite, but Vitari seemed worried, and that made him worried. She was by no means a woman prone to high-blown fancies. "What deals have you been making, Murcatto?"

"The ones that needed making. She works for Rogont."

Ishri let her head fall to one side, so far that it was almost horizontal. "Or perhaps he works for me."

"I don't care who's the rider and who's the donkey," snapped Murcatto, "as long as one or the other of you is sending men."

"He is sending them. Two score of his best."

"In time?"

"Unless the Thousand Swords come early, and they will not. Their main body are camped six miles distant still. They were held up picking a village clean. Then they just had to burn the place. A destructive little crowd." Her gaze fell on Morveer. Those black eyes made him unnecessarily nervous. He did not like the fact that she was wrapped up in bandages. He found himself curious as to why—

"They keep me cool," she said. He blinked, wondering whether he might have spoken the question out loud. "You did not." He felt himself turn cold to the roots of his hair. Just as he had when the nurses uncovered his secret materials at the orphanage, and guessed their purpose. He could not escape the irrational conclusion that this Gurkish devil somehow knew his private thoughts. Knew the things he had done, that he had thought no one would ever know...

"I will be in the barn!" he screeched, voice far more shrill than he had intended. He dragged it down with difficulty. "I must prepare, if we are to have visitors tomorrow. Come, Day!"

"I'll just finish this." She had quickly grown accustomed to their visitor, and was busy buttering three slices of bread at once.

"Ah...yes...I see." He stood twitching for a moment, but there was nothing he could achieve by staying but further embarrassment. He stalked towards the door.

"You need your coat?" asked Day.

"I will be more than warm enough!"

It was only when he was through the door of the farmhouse and into the darkness, the wind sighing chill across the wheat and straight through his shirt, that he realised he would not be warm enough by any stretch of the imagination. It was too late to return without looking entirely the fool, and that he steadfastly refused to do.

"Not *me*." He cursed most bitterly as he picked his way across the darkened farmyard, wrapping his arms around himself and already beginning to shiver. He had allowed some Gurkish charlatan to unnerve him with simple parlour tricks. "Bandaged *bitch*." Well, they would all see. "Oh *yes*." He had got the better of the nurses at the orphanage, in the end, for all the whippings. "We'll see who whips who *now*." He peered over his shoulder to make sure he was unobserved. "Magic!" he sneered. "I'll show you a trick or—"

"Eeee!" His boot squelched, slid, and he went over on his back in a patch of mud. "Bah! Damn it to your bastard *arse*!" So much for heroic efforts, and new beginnings too.

The Traitor

Shivers reckoned it was an hour or two short of dawn. The rain had slacked right off but water still drip-dripped from the new leaves, pattering in the dirt. The air was weighty with chill damp. A swollen stream gurgled near the track, smothering the muddy falls of his horse's hooves. He knew he was close, could see the faintest ruddy campfire glow at the edges of the slick tree-trunks.

Dark times are the best for dark business, Black Dow always used to say, and he should've known.

Shivers nudged his horse through the wet night, hoping some drunk sentry didn't get nervous and serve him up an arrow through the guts. One of those might hurt less than having your eye burned out, but it was nought to look forward to. Luckily, he saw the first guard before the guard saw him, pressed up against a tree, spear resting on his shoulder. He had an oilskin draped right over his head, couldn't have seen a thing, even if he'd been awake.

"Oy!" The man jerked round, dropped his spear in the muck. Shivers grinned as he watched him fumbling for it in the dark, arms crossed loose on his saddle-bow. "You want to give me a challenge, or shall I just head on and leave you to it?"

"Who goes there?" he growled, tearing his spear up along with a clump of wet grass.

"My name's Caul Shivers, and Faithful Carpi's going to want to talk to me."

The Thousand Swords' camp looked pretty much like camps always do. Men, canvas, metal and mud. Mud in particular. Tents scattered every which way. Horses tethered to trees, breath smoking in the darkness. Spears stacked up one against the other. Campfires, some burning, some down to fizzling embers, the air sharp with their smoke. A few men still awake, wrapped in blankets mostly, on guard or still drinking, frowning as they watched Shivers pass.

Reminded him of all the cold, wet nights he'd spent in camps across the North and back. Huddled around fires, hoping to the dead the rain didn't get heavier. Roasting meat, spitted on dead men's spears. Curled up shivering in the snow under every blanket he could find. Sharpening blades for dark work on the morrow. He saw faces of men dead and gone back to the mud, that he'd shared drink and laughter with. His brother. His father. Tul Duru, that they'd called the Thunderhead. Rudd Threetrees, the Rock of Uffrith. Harding Grim, quieter than the night. Brought up a swell of unexpected pride, those memories. Then a swell of unexpected shame at the work he was about now. More feeling than he'd had since he lost his eye, or he'd expected to have again.

He sniffed, and his face stung underneath the bandages, and the soft moment slipped away and left him cold again. They stopped at a tent big as a house, lamplight leaking out into the night round the edges of its flap.

"Now you'd best behave yourself in here, you Northern bastard." The guard jabbed at Shivers with his own axe. "Or I'll—"

"Fuck yourself, idiot." Shivers brushed him out of the way with one arm and pushed on through. Inside it smelled of stale wine, mouldy cloth, unwashed men. Ill-lit by flickering lamps, hung round the edges with slashed and tattered flags, trophies from old battlefields.

A chair of dark wood set with ivory, stained, scarred and polished with hard use, stood on a pair of crates up at the far end. The captain general's chair, he guessed. The one that had been Cosca's, then Monza's, and now was Faithful Carpi's. Didn't look much more than some battered rich man's dining chair. Surely didn't look like much to kill folk over, but then small reasons often serve for that.

There was a long table set up in the midst, men sat down each side. Captains of the Thousand Swords. Rough-looking men, scarred, stained and battered as the chair, and with quite a collection of weapons too, between 'em. But Shivers had smiled in harder company, and he smiled now. Strange thing was, he felt more at home with these lot than he had in months. He knew the rules here, he reckoned, better'n he did with Monza. Seemed as if they'd started out doing some planning, by the maps that were spread across the wood, but some time in the middle of the night the strategy had turned to dice. Now the maps were weighted down with scattered coins, with half-full bottles, with old cups, chipped glasses. One great chart was soaked red with spilled wine.

A big man stood at the head of the table — a faceful of scars, short hair grey and balding. He had a bushy moustache, the rest of his thick jaw covered in white stubble. Faithful Carpi himself, from what Monza had said. He was shaking the dice in one chunk of fist. "Come on, you shits, come on and give me nine!" They came up one and three, to a few sighs and some laughter. "Damn it!" He tossed some coins down the table to a tall, pock-faced bastard with a hook-nose and the ugly mix of long black hair and a big bald patch. "One of these days I'll work your trick out, Andiche."

"No trick. I was born under a lucky star." Andiche scowled at Shivers, about as friendly a look as a fox spares for a chicken. "Who the hell's this bandaged arsehole?"

The guard pushed in past Shivers, giving him a dirty look sideways. "General Carpi, sir, this Northman says he needs to speak to you."

"That a fact?" Faithful spared Shivers a quick glance, then went back to stacking up his coins. "And why would I want to speak to the likes of him? Toss me the dice there, Victus, I ain't done."

"That's the problem with generals." Victus was bald as an egg and gaunt as famine, bunches of rings on his fingers and chains round his neck doing nothing to make him look prettier. "They never do know when they're done." And he tossed the dice back down the table, couple of his fellows chuckling.

The guard swallowed. "He says he knows who killed Prince Ario!"

"Oh, you do, do you? And who was that?"

"Monzcarro Murcatto." Every hard face in the tent turned sharp towards Shivers. Faithful carefully set the dice down, eyes narrowed. "Looks like you know the name."

"Should we hire him for a jester or hang him for a liar?" Victus grated out.

"Murcatto's dead," another.

"That so? I wonder who it is I been fucking for the past month, then?"

"If you've been fucking Murcatto I'd advise you to get back to it." Andiche grinned around him. "From what her brother told me, no one here can suck a cock as well as she could."

A good few chuckles at that. Shivers wasn't sure what he meant about her brother, but it didn't matter none. He'd already undone the bandages, and now he dragged the lot off in one go, turned his face towards the lamplight. Such laughter as there was mostly sputtered out. He had the kind of face now put a sharp end to mirth. "Here's what she's cost me so far. For a handful of silver? Shit on that, I ain't half the fool she takes me for, and I've got my pride, still. I'm done with the bitch."

Faithful Carpi was frowning at him. "Describe her."

"Tall, lean, black hair, blue eyes, frowns a lot. Sharp tongue on her."

Victus waved one jewel-crusted hand at him. "Common knowledge!"

"She's got a broken right hand, and marks all over. From falling down a mountain, she says." Shivers pushed his finger into his stomach, keeping his eyes on Faithful. "Got a scar just here, and one matching in her back. Says a friend of hers gave it to her. Stabbed her through with her own dagger."

Carpi's face had turned grim as a gravedigger's. "You know where she is?"

"Hold up just a trice, there." Victus looked even less happy than his chief. "You saying Murcatto's alive?"

"I'd heard a rumour," said Faithful.

A huge black-skinned man with long ropes of iron-grey hair stood up sharp from the table. "I'd heard all kinds of rumours," voice slow and deep as the sea. "Rumours and facts are two different things. When were you planning to fucking tell us?"

"When you fucking needed to know, Sesaria. Where is she?"

"At a farm," said Shivers. "Maybe an hour's hard ride distant."

"How many does she have with her?"

"Just four. A whining poisoner and his apprentice, hardly more'n a girl. A red-haired woman name of Vitari and some brown bitch."

"Where exactly?"

Shivers grinned. "Well, that's why I'm here, ain't it? To sell you the where exactly."

"I don't like the smell of this shit," snarled Victus. "If you're asking me—"

"I'm not," growled Faithful, without looking round. "What's your price for it?"

"A tenth part of what Duke Orso's offering on the head o' Prince Ario's killer."

"Just a tenth?"

"I reckon a tenth is plenty more'n I'll get from her, but not enough to get me killed by you. I want no more'n I can carry away alive."

"Wise man," said Faithful. "Nothing we hate more than greed, is there, boys?" A couple of chuckles, but most were still looking far from happy at their old general's sudden return from the land of the dead. "Alright, then, a tenth part is fair. You've a deal." And Faithful stepped forwards and slapped his hand into Shivers', looking him right in the face. "If we get Murcatto."

"You need her dead or alive?"

"Sorry to say, I'd prefer dead myself."

"Good, so would I. Last thing I want is a running score with that crazy bitch. She don't forget."

Faithful nodded. "So it seems. I reckon we can do business, you and me. Swolle?"

"General?" A man with a heavy beard stepped up.

"Get three-score horsemen ready to ride, and quick, those with the fastest—"

"Might be best to keep it to fewer," said Shivers.

"That so? And how would fewer men be better?"

"The way she tells it, she's got friends here still." Shivers let his eye wander round the hard faces in the tent. "The way she tells it, there's plenty o' men in this camp wouldn't say no to having her back in charge. The way she tells it, they won victories to be proud of with her, and with you they skulk around and scout, while Orso's men get all the prizes." Faithful's eyes darted sideways, then back. Enough to let Shivers know he'd touched a wound. There's no chief in the world so sure of himself he don't worry some. No chief of men like these, leastways. "Best keep it to a few, and them ones you're sure of. I've no problem stabbing Murcatto in the back, I reckon she's got it coming. Getting stabbed by one o' these is another matter."

"Five all told, and four of 'em women?" Swolle grinned. "A dozen should do it."

Faithful kept his eyes on Shivers. "Still. Make it three score, like I said, just in case there's more at the party than we're expecting. I'd be all embarrassed to arrive at a job short-handed."

"Sir." And Swolle shouldered his way out through the tent flap.

Shivers shrugged. "Have it your way."

"Why, that I will. You can depend on it." Faithful turned to his frowning captains. "Any of you old bastards want to come out on the hunt?"

Sesaria shook his big head, long hair swaying. "This is your mess, Faithful. You can swing the broom."

"I've foraged enough for one night." Andiche was already pushing out through the flap, a few others following in a muttering crowd, some looking suspicious, some looking careless, some looking drunk.

"I too must take my leave, General Carpi." The speaker stood out among all these rough, scarred, dirty men, if only 'cause nothing much about him stood out. He had a curly head of hair, no weapon Shivers could see, no scar, no sneer, no fighter's air of menace in the least. But Faithful still chuckled up to him like he was a man needed respect.

"Master Sulfur!" Folding his hand in both of his big paws and giving it a squeeze. "My thanks for stopping by. You're always welcome here."

"Oh, I am loved wherever I go. Easy to remain on good terms with the man who brings the money."

"Tell Duke Orso, and your people at the bank, they've nothing to worry on here. It'll all be taken care of, like we discussed. Just as soon as I've dealt with this little problem."

"Life does love to throw up problems, doesn't it?" Sulfur gave Shivers a splinter of a smile. He had odd-coloured eyes, one blue, one green. "Happy hunting, then." And he ambled out into the dawn.

Faithful was back in Shivers' face right away. "An hour's ride, you said?"

"If you move quick for your age."

"Huh. How do you know she won't have missed you by then, slipped away?"

"She's asleep. Husk sleep. She smokes more o' that shit every day. Half her time drooling with it, the rest drooling for it. She won't be waking any time soon."

"Best to waste no time, though. That woman can cause unpleasant surprises."

"That's a fact. And she's expecting help. Two-score men from Rogont, coming by tomorrow afternoon. They're planning to shadow you, lay an ambush as you turn south."

"No better feeling than flipping a surprise around, eh?" Faithful grinned. "And you'll be riding at the front."

"For a tenth part o' the take I'll ride at the front side-saddle."

"Just in front will do. Right next to me and you can point out the ground. We honest men need to stick together."

"That we do," said Shivers. "No doubt."

"Alright." Faithful clapped his big hands and rubbed them together. "A piss, then I'm getting my armour on."

King of Poisons

oss?" came Day's high voice. "You awake?"

Morveer exhaled a racking sigh. "Merciful slumber has indeed released me from her soft bosom...and back into the *frigid* embrace of an uncaring world."

"What?"

He waved it bitterly away. "Never mind. My words fall like seeds...on stony ground."

"You said to wake you at dawn."

"Dawn? Oh, harsh mistress!" He threw back his one thin blanket and struggled up from the prickling straw, truly a humble repose for a man of his matchless talents, stretched his aching back and clambered stiffly down the ladder to the floor of the barn. He was forced to concede that he had long been too advanced in years, not to mention too refined in tastes, for haylofts.

Day had assembled the apparatus during the hours of darkness and now, as the first anaemic flicker of dawn niggled at the narrow windows, the burners were alight. Reagents happily simmered, steam carelessly condensed, distillations merrily dripped into the collecting flasks. Morveer processed around the makeshift table, rapping his knuckles against the wood as he passed, making the glassware clink and tinkle. Everything appeared to be entirely in order. Day had learned her business from a master, after all, perhaps the greatest poisoner in all the wide Circle of the World, who would say nay? But even the sight of the good work well done could not coax Morveer from his maudlin mood.

He puffed out his cheeks and gave vent to a weary sigh. "No one understands me. I am *doomed* to be misunderstood."

"You're a complex person," said Day.

"Exactly! *Exactly* so! *You* see it!" Perhaps she alone appreciated that beneath his stern and masterful exterior there were reservoirs of feeling deep as mountain lakes.

"I've made tea." She held a battered metal mug out to him, steam curling from within. His stomach grumbled unpleasantly.

"No. I am grateful for your kind attentions, of course, but no. My digestion is unsettled this morning, *terribly* unsettled."

"Our Gurkish visitor making you nervous?"

"Absolutely and entirely *not*," he lied, suppressing a shiver at the very remembrance of those midnight eyes. "My dyspepsia is the result of my ongoing difference of opinion with our employer, the notorious Butcher of Caprile, the ever-contrary Murcatto! I simply cannot seem to find the correct approach with that woman! However cordially I behave, however spotless my intentions, she bears it *ill*!"

"She's somewhat prickly, true."

"In my opinion she passes beyond prickly and enters the arena of... sharp," he finished, lamely.

"Well, the betrayal, the being thrown down the mountain, the dead brother and all—"

"Explanations, not excuses! We all have suffered painful reverses! I declare, I am half-tempted to abandon her to her inevitable fate and seek out fresh employment." He snorted with laughter at a sudden thought. "With *Duke Orso*, perhaps!"

Day looked up sharply. "You're joking."

It had, in fact, been intended as a witticism, for Castor Morveer was not the man to abandon an employer once he had accepted a contract. Certain standards of behaviour had to be observed, in his business more than any other. But it amused him to explore the notion further, counting off the points one by one upon his outstretched digits. "A man who can undoubtedly afford my services. A man who undoubtedly *requires* my services. A man who has proved himself unencumbered by the slightest troublesome moral qualm."

"A man with a record of pushing his employees down mountains."

Morveer dismissed it. "One should never be foolish enough to trust the sort of person who would hire a poisoner. In that he is no worse an employer than any other. Why, it is a profound wonder the thought did not occur sooner!"

"But...we killed his son."

"Bah! Such difficulties are easily explained away when two men find they need each other." He airily waved one hand. "Some invention will suffice. Some wretched scapegoat can always be found to shoulder the blame."

She nodded slowly, mouth set hard. "A scapegoat. Of course."

"A *wretched* one." One less mutilated Northman in the world would be no loss to posterity. Nor one less insane convict or abrasive torturer, for that matter. He was almost warming to the notion. "But I daresay for the time being we are stuck with Murcatto and her futile quest for revenge. *Revenge.* I swear, is there a more pointless, destructive, unsatisfying motive in all the world?"

"I thought motives weren't our business," observed Day, "only jobs and the pay."

"Correct, my dear, very correct, every motive is a pure one that necessitates our services. You see straight to the heart of the matter as always, as though the matter were entirely *transparent*. Whatever would I do without you?" He came smiling around the apparatus. "How are our preparations proceeding?"

"Oh, I know what to do."

"Good. Very good. Of course you do. You learned from a master."

She bowed her head. "And I marked your lessons well."

"Most *excellent* well." He leaned down to flick at a condenser, watched the Larync essence dripping slowly down into the retort. "It is vital to be exhaustively prepared for any and every eventuality. Caution first, always, of—Ah!" He frowned down at his forearm. A tiny speck of red swelled, became a dot of blood. "What..." Day backed slowly away from him, an expression of the most peculiar intensity on her face. She held a mounted needle in her hand.

"Someone to take the blame?" she snarled at him. "Scapegoat, am I? Fuck yourself, bastard!"

Come on, come on, come on." Faithful was pissing again, stood by his horse, back to Shivers, shaking his knees around. "Come on, come on. Bloody years catching up on me, that's what this is."

"That or your dark deeds," said Swolle.

"I've done nothing black enough to deserve this shit, surely. You feel like you never had to go so bad in your life, then when you finally get your prick out, you end up stood here in the wind for an age of…ah…ah… there's the fucker!" He leaned backwards, showing off his big bald spot. A brief spatter, then another. One more, he worked his shoulders around as he shook the drips off, and started lacing up again.

"That's it?" asked Swolle.

"What's your interest?" snapped the general. "To bottle it? Years catching up on me is all it is." He picked his way up the slope bent over, heavy red cloak held out of the mud in one hand, and squatted down next to Shivers. "Right then. Right then. That's the place?"

"That's the place." The farm sat at the end of an open paddock, in the midst of a sea of grey wheat, under the grey sky, clouds smudged with watery dawn. Faint light flickered at the narrow windows of the barn, but no more signs of life. Shivers rubbed his fingers slowly against his palms. He'd never done much treachery. Nothing so sharply cut as this, leastways, and it was making him nervy.

"Looks peaceful enough." Faithful ran a slow hand over his white stubble. "Swolle, you get a dozen men and take 'em round the side, out of sight, into that stand of trees down there, get on the flank. Then if they see us and make a run for it you can finish up."

"Right y'are, General. Nice and simple, eh?"

"Nothing worse than too much plan. More there is to remember, more there is to make a shit of. Don't need to tell you not to make a shit of it, do I, Swolle?"

"Me? No, sir. Into the trees, then if I see anyone running, charge. Just like at the High Bank."

"Except Murcatto's on the other side now, right?"

"Right. Fucking evil bitch."

"Now, now," said Faithful. "Some respect. You were happy enough to clap for her when she brought you victories, you can clap for her now. Shame things have come to this, is all. Nothing else for it. Don't mean there can't be some respect."

"Right. Sorry." Swolle paused for a moment. "Sure it wouldn't be better to try and creep down there on foot? I mean, we can't ride into that farmhouse, can we?"

Faithful gave him a long look. "Did they pick a new captain general while I was away, and are you it?"

"Well, no, 'course not, just—"

"Creeping up ain't my style, Swolle. Knowing how often you wash, more than likely Murcatto'd fucking smell you before we got within a hundred strides, and be ready. No, we'll ride down there and spare my knees the wear. We can always get down once we've given the place the check over. And if she's got any surprises for us, well, I'd rather be in my saddle." He frowned sideways at Shivers. "You see a problem with that, boy?"

"Not me." From what Shivers had seen he reckoned Faithful was one o' those men make a good second and a poor chief. Lots of bones but no imagination. Looked like he'd got stuck to one way of doing things over the years and had to do it now whether it fit the job or not. But he weren't about to say so. Strong leaders might like it when someone brings 'em a better idea, but weak ones never do. "You reckon I could get my axe back, though?"

Faithful grinned. "'Course you can. Just as soon as I see Murcatto's dead body. Let's go." He nearly tripped on his cloak as he turned for the horses, angrily dragged it up and tossed it over his shoulder. "Bloody thing. Knew I should've got a shorter one."

Shivers took one last look at the farm before he followed, shaking his head. There's nothing worse'n too much plan, that's true. But too little comes in close behind.

Morveer blinked. "But…" He took a slow step towards Day. His ankle wobbled and he slumped sideways against the table, knocking over a flask and making the fizzing contents spill across the wood. He clutched one hand to his throat, his skin flushing, burning. He knew already what she must have done, the realisation spreading out frigid through his veins. He knew already what the consequences would have to be. "The King…" he rasped, "of Poisons?"

"What else? Caution first, always."

He grimaced, at the meagre pain of the tiny prick in his arm, and at the far deeper wound of bitter betrayal besides. He coughed, fell forwards onto his knees, one hand stretching, trembling upwards. "But—"

Day kicked his hand away with the toe of one shoe. "Doomed to be misunderstood?" Her face was twisted with contempt. With hatred, even. The pleasing mask of obedience, of admiration, of innocence too, finally dropped. "What do you think there is to understand about you, you swollen-headed parasite? You're thin as tissue paper!" There was the deepest cut of all — ingratitude, after all he had given her! His knowledge, his money, his...fatherly affection! "The personality of a baby in the body of a murderer! Bully and coward in one. Castor Morveer, greatest poisoner in the world? Greatest bore in the world, maybe, you—"

He sprang forwards with consummate nimbleness, nicked her ankle with his scalpel as he passed, rolled under the table and came up on the other side, grinning at her through the complexity of apparatus, the flickering flames of the burners, the distorting shapes of twisted tubes, the glinting surfaces of glass and metal.

"Ha *ha*!" He shouted, entirely alert and not dying in the least. "*You*, poison *me*? The *great* Castor Morveer, undone by his *assistant*? I think *not*!" She stared down at her bleeding ankle, and then up at him, eyes wide. "There is no King of Poisons, fool!" he cackled. "The method I showed you, that produces a liquid that smells, tastes and looks like water? It makes water! Entirely *harmless*! Unlike the concoction with which I just now pricked you, which was enough to kill a dozen horses!"

He slipped his hand inside his shirt, deft fingertips unerringly selecting the correct vial and sliding it out into the light. Clear fluid gleamed inside. "The antidote." She winced as she saw it, made to dive one way around the table then came the other, but her feet were clumsy and he evaded her with negligible effort. "*Most* undignified, my dear! Chasing each other around our apparatus, in a barn, in the middle of rural Styria! Most *terribly* undignified!"

"Please," she hissed at him. "Please, I'll...I'll—"

"Don't embarrass us both! You have displayed your true nature now, you...you ingrate *harpy*! You are unmasked, you treacherous *cuckoo*!"

"I didn't want to take the blame is all! Murcatto said sooner or later you'd go over to Orso! That you'd want to use me as the scapegoat! Murcatto said—"

"*Murcatto?* You listen to *Murcatto* over *me*? That degenerate, husk-addled and notorious *butcher* of the *bloody battlefield*? Oh, *commendable* guiding *light*! Curse me for an imbecile to trust either one of you! It seems you were correct, at least, that I am like to a baby. All *unspoiled innocence*! All *unde-served mercy*!" He flicked the vial through the air at Day. "Let it never again be said," as he watched her fumbling through the straw for it, "that I am not," as she clawed it up and ripped out the cork, "as generous, merciful and forgiving as any poisoner," as she sucked down the contents, "within the *entire* Circle of the World."

Day wiped her mouth and took a shuddering breath. "We need…to talk."

"We certainly do. But not for long." She blinked, then a strange spasm passed over her face. Just as he had known it would. He wrinkled his nose as he tossed his scalpel clattering across the table. "The blade carried no poison, but you have just consumed a vial of undiluted Leopard Flower."

She flopped over, eyes rolling back, skin turning pink, began to jerk around in the straw, froth gurgling from her mouth.

Morveer stepped forwards, leaned down over her, baring his teeth, stab-bing at his chest with a clawing finger. "Kill *me*, would you? *Poison* me? Castor *Morveer*?" The heels of her shoes drummed out a rapid beat on the hard-packed earth, sending up puffs of straw-dust. "*I* am the only King of Poisons, you…you child-faced *fool*!" Her thrashing became a locked-up trembling, back arched impossibly far. "The simple *insolence* of you! The *arrogance*! The *insult*! The, the, the…" He fumbled breathlessly for the right word, then realised she was dead. There was a long, slow silence as her corpse gradually relaxed.

"Shit!" he barked. "Entirely *shit*!" The scant satisfaction of victory was already fast melting, like an unseasonable flurry of snow on a warm day, before the crushing disappointment, wounding betrayal and simple incon-venience of his new, assistant-less, employer-less situation. For Day's final words had left him in no doubt that Murcatto was to blame. That after all his thankless, selfless toil on her behalf she had plotted his death. Why had he not anticipated this development? How could he not have expected it, after all the painful reverses he had suffered in his life? He was simply too soft a personage for this harsh land, this unforgiving epoch. Too trusting and too comradely for his own good. He was prone to see the world in the rosy tones of his own benevolence, cursed always to expect the best from people.

"Thin as paper, am I? Shit! You…*shit*!" He kicked Day's corpse petu-lantly, his shoe thudding into her body over and over and making it shudder

again. "*Swollen-headed?*" He near shrieked it. "*Me?* Why, I am *humility*...
its...fucking...*self*!" He realised suddenly that it ill befit a man of his
boundless sensitivity to kick a person already dead, especially one he had
cared for almost as a daughter. He felt a sudden bubbling-up of melodra-
matic regret.

"I'm sorry! So sorry." He knelt beside her, gently pushed her hair back,
touched her face with trembling fingers. That vision of innocence, never
more to smile, never more to speak. "I'm so sorry, but...but why? I will
always remember you, but—Oh...urgh!" There was a sharp smell of
urine. The corpse voiding itself, an inevitable side effect of a colossal dose
of Leopard Flower that a man of his experience really should have seen
coming. The pool had already spread out through the straw and soaked the
knees of his trousers. He tottered up, wincing with disgust.

"Shit! Shit!" He snatched up a flask and flung it against the wall in a fury,
fragments of glass scattering. "Bully and coward in one?" He gave Day's
body another petulant kick, bruised his toes and set off limping around the
barn at a great pace.

"Murcatto!" That evil witch had incited his apprentice to treachery.
The best and most loved apprentice he had trained since he was obliged to
pre-emptively poison Aloveo Cray back in Ostenhorm. He knew he should
have killed Murcatto in his orchard, but the scale, the importance and the
apparent impossibility of the work she offered had appealed to his vanity.
"Curse my vanity! The *one* flaw in my character!"

But there could be no vengeance. "*No.*" Nothing so base and uncivilised, for that was not Morveer's way. He was no savage, no animal like the
Serpent of Talins and her ilk, but a refined and cultured gentleman of the
highest ethical standards. He was considerably out of pocket, now, after
all his hard and loyal work, so he would have to find a proper contract. A
proper employer and an entirely orderly and clean-motived set of murders,
resulting in "a proper, honest *profit*."

And who would pay him to murder the Butcher of Caprile and her barbaric cronies? The answer was not so very difficult to fathom.

He faced a window and practised his most sycophantic bow, the one
with the full finger twirl at the end. "Grand Duke Orso, an incom...par-
able *honour*." He straightened, frowning. At the top of the long rise, silhou-
etted against the grey dawn, were several dozen riders.

* * *

For honour, glory and, above all, a decent pay-off!" A scattering of laughter as Faithful drew his sword and held it up high. "Let's go!" And the long line of horsemen started moving, keeping loosely together as they thrashed through the wheat and out into the paddock, upping the pace to a trot.

Shivers went along with 'em. There wasn't much choice since Faithful was right at his side. Hanging back would've seemed poor manners. He would've liked his axe to hand, but hoping for a thing often brought on the opposite. Besides, as they picked up speed to a healthy canter, keeping both hands on the reins seemed like an idea with some weight to it.

Maybe a hundred strides out now, and all still looking peaceful. Shivers frowned at the farmhouse, at the low wall, at the barn, gathering himself, making ready. It all seemed like a bad plan, now. It had seemed a bad plan at the time, but having to do it made it seem a whole lot worse. The ground rushed past hard under his horse's hooves, the saddle jolted at his sore arse, the wind nipped at his narrowed eye, tickled at the raw scars on the other side of his face, bitter cold without the bandages. Faithful rode on his right, sitting up tall, cloak flapping behind him, sword still raised, shouting, "Steady! Steady!" On his left the line shifted and buckled, eager faces of men and horses in a twisting row, spears jolting up and down at all angles. Shivers worked his boots free of the stirrups.

Then the shutters of the farmhouse flew open all together with an echoing bang. Shivers saw the Osprians at the windows, first light glinting on their steel caps as a long row of 'em came up from behind the wall together, flatbows levelled. Comes a time you just have to do a thing, shit on the consequences. The air whooped in his throat as he sucked in a great breath and held it, then threw himself sideways and tumbled from the saddle. Over the batter of hooves, the clatter of metal, the rushing of wind he heard Monza's sharp cry.

Then the dirt struck him, jarred his teeth together. He rolled, grunting, over and over, took a mouthful of mud. The world spun, all dark sky and flicking soil, flying horses, falling men. Hooves thudded around him, mud spattered in his eyes. He heard screams, fought his way up as far as his knees. A corpse dropped, flailing, crashed into Shivers and knocked him on his back again.

* * *

Morveer made it to the double doors of the barn and wrestled one wide enough to stick his head through, just in time to see the Osprian soldiers rise from behind the farmyard wall and deliver a disciplined and deadly volley of flatbow fire.

Out in the grassy paddock men jerked and tumbled from their saddles, horses fell and threw their riders. Flesh plunged down, ploughed into the wet dirt, limbs flailing. Beasts and men roared and wailed in shock and fury, pain and fear. Perhaps a dozen riders dropped, but the rest broke into a full charge without the slightest hint of reluctance, weapons raised and gleaming, releasing war cries to match the death screams of their fallen comrades.

Morveer whimpered, shoved the door shut and pressed his back against it. Red-edged battle. Rage and randomness. Pointed metal moving at great speed. Blood spilled, brains dashed, soft bodies ripped open and their innards laid sickeningly bare. A most uncivilised way to carry on, and decidedly not his area of expertise. His own guts, thankfully still within his abdomen, shifted with a first stab of bestial terror and revulsion, then constricted with a more reasoned wash of fear. If Murcatto won, her lethal intentions towards him had already been clearly displayed. She had not balked for a moment at engineering the death of his innocent apprentice, after all. If the Thousand Swords won, well, he was an accomplice of Prince Ario's killer. In either case his life would undoubtedly be painfully forfeit.

"Damn it!"

Beyond the one doorway the farmyard was rapidly becoming a slaughteryard, but the windows were too narrow to squeeze through. Hide in the hayloft? No, no, what was he, five years old? Lie down beside poor Day and play dead? What? Lie down in urine? Never! He dashed to the back of the barn with all despatch, poked desperately at the planking for a way through. He found a loose board and began kicking at it.

"Break, you wooden *bastard*! Break! Break! *Break!*" The sounds of mortal combat were growing ever more intense in the yard behind him. Something crashed against the side of the barn and made him startle, dust filtering down from the rafters with the force of it. He turned back to the carpentry, whimpering now with fear and frustration, face prickling with sweat. One last kick and the wood tore free. Wan daylight slunk in through a narrow gap between two ragged-edged planks. He knelt, turning sideways on, forced his head through the crack, splinters digging at his scalp, gained a view of flat country, brown wheat, a stand of trees perhaps two hundred strides distant. Safety. He worked one arm through into the free air, clutching vainly at the weathered outside of the barn. One shoulder, half his chest, and then he stuck fast.

It had been optimistic of him, to say the least, to imagine that he might have effortlessly slipped through that gap. Ten years ago he had been slender as a willow-swatch, could have glided through a space half the width with the grace of a dancer. Too many pastries in the interim had rendered such an operation impossible, however, and there appeared to be a growing prospect that they might have cost him his life. He wriggled, squirmed, sharp wood digging at his belly. Is this how they would find him? Is this the tale that they would snigger over in after years? Would that be his legacy? The great Castor Morveer, death without a face, most feared of all poisoners, finally brought to book, wedged in a crack in the back of a barn while fleeing?

"Damn *pastries*!" he screamed, and with one last effort tore himself through, teeth gritted as a rogue nail ripped his shirt half-off and left him a long and painful cut down his ribs. "Damn it! Shit!" He dragged his aching legs through after him. Finally liberated from the clawing embrace of poor-quality joinery and riddled with splinters, he began to dash towards the proffered safety of the trees, waist-high wheat stalks tripping him, thrashing him, snatching at his legs.

He had progressed no further than five wobbly strides when he fell headlong, sprawling in the damp crop with a squeal. He struggled up, cursing. One of his shoes had been snatched off by the jealous wheat as he went down. "Damn *wheat*!" He was just beginning to cast about for it when he became aware of a loud drumming sound. To his disbelieving horror, a dozen horsemen had burst from the trees towards which he had been fleeing, and were even now bearing down on him at full gallop, spears lowered.

He gave vent to a breathless squeak, spun, slipped on his bare foot, began to limp back to the crack that had so mauled him on their first acquaintance. He wedged one leg through, whimpered at a stab of agony as he accidentally squashed his fruits against a plank. His back prickled as the hammering of hooves grew louder. The riders were no more than fifty strides from him, eyes of men and beasts starting, teeth of men and beasts bared, brightening morning sun catching warlike metal, chaff flying from threshing hooves. He would never tear his bleeding body back through the narrow gap in time. Would he be thrashed, now? Poor, humble Castor Morveer, who only ever wanted to be—

The corner of the barn exploded in a gout of bright flame. It made no sound beyond the crack and twang of shattering wood. The air suddenly swarmed with spinning debris: a tumbling chunk of flaming beam, ripped planks, bent nails, a scouring cloud of splinters and sparks. A cone of wheat was flattened in one great rustling wave, sucking up a rippling swell of dust, stalk, grain, embers. Two not insignificant barrels were suddenly exposed, standing proud in the midst of the levelled crop, directly in the path of the charging horsemen. Flames leaped up from them, black char spreading spontaneously across their sides.

The right-hand barrel exploded with a blinding flash, the left almost immediately after. Two great fountains of soil were hurled into the sky. The lead horse, trapped between them, seemed to stop, frozen, twist, then burst apart along with its rider. Most of the rest were enveloped in the spreading clouds of dust and, presumably, reduced to flying mincemeat.

A wave of wind flattened Morveer against the side of the barn, tearing at his ripped shirt, his hair, his eyes. A moment later the thunderous double detonation reached his ears and made his teeth rattle. A couple of horses at either end of the line remained largely in one piece, flapping bonelessly as they were tossed through the air like an angry toddler's toys, one mount turned mostly inside out, crashing down to leave bloody scars through the crop near the trees from which they had first emerged.

Clods of earth rattled against the plank wall. Dust began to settle. Patches of damp wheat burned reluctantly around the edges of the blast, sending up smudges of acrid smoke. Charred splinters of wood, blackened chaff, smouldering fragments of men and beasts still rained from the sky. Ash wafted softly down on the breeze.

Morveer stood, still wedged in the side of the barn, struck to the heart with cold amazement. Gurkish fire, it seemed, or something darker, more... magical? A figure appeared around the smouldering corner of the barn just as he wrenched himself free and dived into the wheat, peering up between the stalks.

The Gurkish woman, Ishri. One arm and the hem of her brown coat were thoroughly on fire. She seemed suddenly to notice as the flames licked up around her face, shrugged the burning garment off without rush and tossed it aside, standing bandaged from neck to toe, unburned and pristine as the body of some ancient desert queen embalmed and ready for burial. She took one long look towards the trees, then smiled and slowly shook her head.

She said something happily in Kantic. Morveer's mastery of the tongue was not supreme, but it sounded like, "You still have it, Ishri." She swept the wheat where Morveer was hiding with her black eyes, at which he ducked down with the greatest alacrity, then she turned and disappeared behind the shattered corner of the barn from whence she came. He heard her faintly chuckling to herself.

"You still have it."

Morveer was left only with an overpowering — but in his opinion entirely justifiable — desire to flee, and never look back. So he wormed his way through the gore-spattered crops on his belly. Towards the trees, inch by painful inch, breath wheezing in his burning chest, terror pricking at his arse all the long way.

397

No Worse

Monza jerked the Calvez back and the man gave a wheezing grunt, face all squeezed up with shock, clutching at the little wound in his chest. He took a tottering step forwards, hauling up his short-sword as if it weighed as much as an anvil. She stepped out to the left and ran him through the side, just under his ribs, a foot of well-used blade sliding through his studded leather jerkin. He turned his head in her direction, face pink and trembling, veins bulging in his stretched-out neck. When she pulled the sword out, he dropped as if it had been the only thing holding him up. His eyes rolled towards her.

"Tell my…" he whispered.

"What?"

"Tell…her—" He strained up from the boards, dust caked across one side of his face, then coughed black vomit and stopped moving.

Monza placed him, all of a sudden. Baro, his name had been, or Paro, something with an "o" on the end. Some cousin of old Swolle's. He'd been there at Musselia, after the siege, after they sacked the town. He'd laughed at one of Benna's jokes. She remembered because it hadn't seemed the time for jokes, after they'd murdered Hermon and stolen his gold. She hadn't felt much like laughing, she knew that.

"Varo?" she muttered, trying to think what that joke had been. She heard a board creak, saw movement just in time to drop down. Her head jolted, the floor hit her in the face. She got up, the room tipped over and she ploughed into the wall, put one elbow out of the window, almost fell right through it. Roaring outside, clatter and clash of combat.

Through a head full of lights she saw something come at her and she

398

tumbled out of the way, heard it smash into plaster. Splinters in her face. She screamed, reeling off balance, slashed at a black shape with the Calvez, saw her hand was empty. Dropped it already. There was a face at the window.

"Benna?" And some blood trickled from her mouth.

No time for jokes. Something clattered into her back and drove her breath out. She saw a mace, dull metal gleaming. Saw a man's face, snarling. A chain whipped around his neck and jerked him up. The room was settling, blood whooshing in her head, she tried to stand and only rolled onto her back.

Vitari had him round the throat and they lurched together about the dim room. He elbowed at her, other hand fiddling at the chain, but she dragged it tight, eyes ground to two furious little slits. Monza struggled up, made it to her feet, wobbled towards them. He fished at his belt for a knife but Monza got there first, pinned his free arm with her left hand, drew the blade with her right and started stabbing him with it.

"Uh, uh, uh." Squelch, scrape, thud, honking and spitting in each other's faces, her stuttering moan, and his squealing grunts, and Vitari's low growl all mingling together into an echoing, animal mess. Pretty much the same sounds they would have made if they were fucking rather than killing each other. Scrape, thud, squelch. "Uh, ah, uh."

"Enough!" hissed Vitari. "He's done!"

"Uh." She let the knife clatter to the boards. Her arm was sticky wet inside her coat all the way to her elbow, gloved hand locked up into a burning claw. She turned to the door, narrowing her stinging eyes against the brightness, stepped clumsily over the corpse of an Osprian soldier and through the broken wood in the doorway.

A man with blood down his cheek clawed at her, near dragged her over as he fell, smearing gore across her coat. A mercenary was stabbed from behind as he tried to stagger up from the yard, went down thrashing on his face. Then the Osprian soldier who'd speared him got kicked in the head by a horse, his steel cap flying right off and him toppling sideways like a felled tree. Men and mounts strained all around — a deadly storm of thumping boots, hooves, clattering metal, swinging weapons and flying dirt.

And not ten strides from her, through the mass of writhing bodies, Faithful Carpi sat on his big warhorse, roaring like a madman. He hadn't much changed — the same broad, honest, scarred face. The bald pate, the thick white moustache and the white stubble round it. He'd got himself a shiny breastplate and a long red cloak better suited to a duke than a mercenary. He had a flatbow bolt sticking from his shoulder, right arm hanging useless, the other raised to point a heavy sword towards the house.

The strange thing was that she felt a rush of warmth when she first laid eyes on him. That happy pang you get when you see a friend's face in a crowd. Faithful Carpi, who'd led five charges for her. Who'd fought for her in all weathers and never let her down. Faithful Carpi, who she would've trusted with her life. Who she had trusted with her life, so he could sell it cheap for Cosca's old chair. Sell her life, and sell her brother's too.

The warmth didn't last long. The dizziness faded with it, left her a dose of anger scalding her guts and a stinging pain down the side of her head where the coins held her skull together.

The mercenaries could be bitter fighters when they had no other choice, but they much preferred foraging to fighting and they'd been withered by that first volley, rattled by the shock of men where they hadn't expected them. They had spears ahead, enemies in the buildings, archers at the windows and on the flat stable roof, shooting down at their leisure. A rider shrieked as he was dragged from his saddle, spear tumbling from his hand and clattering at Monza's feet.

A couple of his comrades turned their horses to run. One made it back into the paddock. The other was poked wailing from his saddle with a sword, foot caught in one stirrup, dancing upside down while his horse thrashed about. Faithful Carpi was no coward, but you don't last thirty years as a mercenary without knowing when to make a dash for it. He wheeled his horse around, chopping an Osprian soldier down and laying his skull wide open in the mud. Then he was gone round the side of the farmhouse.

Monza clawed up the fallen spear in her gloved hand, snatched hold of the bridle of the riderless horse with the other and dragged herself into the saddle, her sudden bitter need to kill Carpi putting some trace of the old spring back into her lead-filled legs. She pulled the horse around to face the farmyard wall, gave it her heels and jumped it, an Osprian soldier flinging his flatbow down and diving out of her way with a cry. She thumped down on the other side, jolting in the saddle and near stabbing herself in the face, crashed out into the wheat, stalks thrashing at the legs of her stolen horse as it struggled up the long slope. She fumbled the spear across into her left hand, took the reins in her right, crouched down and drummed up a jagged

canter with her heels. She saw Carpi stop at the top of the rise, a black outline against the bright eastern sky, then turn his horse and tear away.

She burst out from the wheat and across a field spotted with thorny
bushes, downhill now, clods of mud flying from the soft ground as she dug
her mount to a full gallop. Not far ahead of her Carpi jumped a hedgerow,
greenery thrashing at his horse's hooves. He landed badly, flailing in the
saddle to keep his balance. Monza picked her spot better, cleared the hedge
easily, gaining on him all the time. She kept her eyes ahead, always ahead.
Not thinking of the speed, or the danger, or the pain in her hand. All that
was in her mind was Faithful Carpi, and his horse, and the overpowering
need to stick her spear into one or the other.

They thundered across an unplanted field, hooves hammering at the
thick mud, towards a crease in the ground that looked like a stream. A
whitewashed building gleamed beside it in the brightening morning sun, a
mill-house from what Monza could tell with the world shaking, wobbling,
rushing around her. She strained forwards over her horse's neck, gripping
hard at the spear couched under her arm, wind rushing at her narrowed
eyes. Willing herself closer to Faithful Carpi. Willing herself closer to vengeance. It looked as though his horse might have picked up a niggle when
he spoiled that jump, she was making ground on him now, making ground
fast.

There were just three lengths between them, then two, specks of mud
from the hooves of Carpi's warhorse flicking in her face. She drew herself
up in the saddle, pulling back the spear, sun twinkling on the tip for a
moment. She caught a glimpse of Faithful's familiar face as he jerked his
head round to look over his shoulder, one grey eyebrow thick with blood,
streaks down his stubbly cheek from a cut on his forehead. She heard him
growl, digging hard with his spurs, but his horse was a heavy beast, better suited to charging than fleeing. The bobbing head of her mount crept
slowly closer and closer to the streaming tail of Carpi's, the ground a brown
blur rushing by between the two.

She screamed as she rammed the spear point into the horse's rump. It
jerked, twisted, head flailing, one eye rolling wild, foam on its bared teeth.
Faithful jolted in the saddle, one boot torn from the stirrup. The warhorse
carried on for a dizzy moment, then its wounded leg twisted underneath
it and all at once it went down, pitching forwards, head folding under its
hurtling weight, hooves flailing, mud flying. She heard Carpi squeal as she

flashed past, heard the thumping behind her as his horse tumbled over and over across the muddy field.

She hauled on the reins with her right hand, pulled her horse up, snorting and tossing, legs shaky from the hard ride. She saw Carpi pushing himself drunkenly from the ground, tangled with his long red cloak, all spattered and streaked with dirt. She was surprised to see him still alive, but not unhappy. Gobba, Mauthis, Ario, Ganmark, they'd had their part in what Orso had done to her, done to her brother, and they'd paid their price for it. But none of them had been her friends. Faithful had ridden beside her. Eaten with her. Drunk from her canteen. Smiled, and smiled, then stabbed her when it suited him, and stolen her place.

She had a mind to stretch this out.

He took a dizzy step, mouth hanging open, eyes wide in his bloody face. He saw her and she grinned, held the spear up high and gave a whoop. Like a hunter might do, seeing the fox in the open. He started limping desperately away towards the edge of the field, wounded arm cradled against his chest, the shaft of the flatbow bolt jutting broken from his shoulder.

The smile tugged hard at her face as she trotted up closer, close enough to hear his wheezing breath as he struggled pointlessly towards the stream. The sight of that treacherous bastard crawling for his life made her happier than she'd been in a long while. He hauled his sword from its scabbard with his left hand, floundering desperately forwards, using it as a crutch.

"Takes time," she called to him, "to learn to use the wrong hand! I should know! You don't have that much fucking time, Carpi!" He was close to the stream, but she'd be on him before he got there, and he knew it.

He turned, clumsily raising the blade. She jerked the reins and sent her mount sideways so he hacked nothing but air. She stood in the stirrups, stabbed down with the spear, caught him in the shoulder and tore the armour from it, ripped a gash in his cloak and knocked him to his knees, sword left stuck in the earth. He moaned through gritted teeth, blood trickling down his breastplate, struggling to get up again. She pulled one boot from the stirrup, brought her horse closer and kicked him in the face, snapped his head back and sent him rolling down the bank and into the stream.

She tossed the spear point-first into the soil, swung her leg over the saddle and slid down. She stood a moment, watching Carpi floundering, shaking the life back into her stiff legs. Then she snatched the spear up, took a long, slow breath and started picking her way down the bank to the water's edge.

Not far downstream the mill-house stood, waterwheel clattering as it slowly turned. The far bank had been walled up with rough stone, all bearded with moss. Carpi was fumbling at it, cursing, trying to drag himself up onto the far side. But weighed down with armour, his cloak heavy with water, a flatbow bolt in one shoulder and a spear wound in the other, he had less than no chance. So he waded doggedly along, up to his waist in the stream, while she shadowed him on the other bank, grinning, spear levelled.

"You keep on going, Carpi, I'll give you that. No one could call you a coward. Just an idiot. Stupid Carpi." She forced out a laugh. "I can't believe you fell for this shit. All those years taking my orders, you should've known me better. Thought I'd be sitting waiting, did you, weeping over my misfortunes?"

He edged back through the water, eyes fixed on the point of her spear, breathing hard. "That fucking Northman lied to me."

"Almost as if you can't trust anyone these days, eh? You should've stabbed me in the heart, Faithful, instead of the guts."

"Heart?" he sneered. "You don't have one!" He floundered through the water at her, sending up a shower of glittering spray, dagger in his fist. She thrust at him, felt the spear's shaft jolt in her aching right hand as the point took him in the hip, twisted him round and sent him over backwards. He struggled up again, snarling through his gritted teeth. "I'm better'n you at least, you murdering scum!"

"If you're so much better than me, how come you're the one in the stream and I'm the one with the spear, fucker?" She moved the point in slow circles, shining with wet. "You keep on coming, Carpi, I'll give you that. No one could call you a coward. Just a fucking liar. Traitor Carpi."

"Me a traitor?" He dragged himself down the wall towards the slowly clattering waterwheel. "Me? After all those years I stuck with you? I wanted to be loyal to Cosca! I *was* loyal to him. I'm Faithful!" He thumped his wet breastplate with his bloody hand. "That's what I am. What I was. You stole that from me! You and your fucking brother!"

"I didn't throw Cosca down a mountain, bastard!"

"You think I wanted to do it? You think I wanted any of this?" There were tears in the old mercenary's eyes as he struggled away from her. "I'm not made to lead! Ario comes to me, says Orso's decided you can't be trusted! That you have to go! That you're the past and I'm the future, and

403

the rest of the captains already agreed. So I took the easy way. What was my choice?"

Monza wasn't enjoying herself anymore. She remembered Orso standing smiling in her tent. *Cosca is the past, and I have decided that you are the future.* Benna smiling beside him. *It's better like this. You deserve to lead.* She remembered taking the easy way. What had been her choice? "You could've warned me, given me a chance to—"

"Like you warned Cosca? Like you warned me? Fuck yourself, Murcatto! You pointed out the path and I followed, that's all! You sow bloody seeds, you'll reap a bloody harvest, and you sowed seeds across Styria and back! You did this to yourself! You did this to—Gah!" He twisted backwards, fumbling weakly at his neck. That fine cloak of his had floated back and got all caught up in the gears of the waterwheel. Now the red cloth was winding tighter and tighter, dragging him hard against the slowly turning wood.

"Fucking..." He fumbled with his one half-good arm at the mossy slats, at the rusted bolts of the great wheel, but there was no stopping it. Monza watched, mouth half-open but no words to say, spear hanging slack from her hands as he was dragged down, down under the wheel. Down, down, into the black water. It surged and bubbled around his chest, then around his shoulders, then around his neck.

His bulging eyes rolled up towards her. "I'm no worse'n you, Murcatto! Just did what I had to!" He was fighting to keep his mouth above the frothing water. "I'm...no worse...than—"

His face disappeared.

Faithful Carpi, who'd led five charges for her. Who'd fought for her in all weathers and never let her down. Faithful Carpi, who she'd trusted with her life.

Monza floundered down into the stream, cold water closing around her legs. She caught hold of Faithful's clutching hand, felt his fingers grip hers. She pulled, teeth gritted, growling with the effort. She lifted the spear, rammed it into the gears hard as she could, felt the shaft jam there. She hooked her gloved hand under his armpit, up to her neck in surging water, fighting to drag him out, straining with every burning muscle. She felt him starting to come up, arm sliding out of the froth, elbow, then shoulder, she started fumbling at the buckle on his cloak with her gloved hand but she couldn't make the fingers work. Too cold, too numb, too broken. There was a crack as the spear shaft splintered. The waterwheel started turning, slowly, slowly, metal squealing, cogs grating, and dragged Faithful back under.

The stream kept on flowing. His hand went limp, and that was that.

Five dead, two left.

She let it go, breathing hard. She watched as his pale fingers slipped under the water, then she waded out of the stream and limped up onto the bank, soaked to the skin. There was no strength left in her, legs aching deep in the bones, right hand throbbing all the way up her forearm and into her shoulder, the wound on the side of her head stinging, blood pounding hard as a club behind her eyes. It was all she could manage to get one foot in the stirrup and drag herself into the saddle.

She took a look back, felt her guts clench and double her over, spat a mouthful of scalding sick into the mud, then another. The wheel had pulled Faithful right under and now it was dragging him up on the other side, limbs dangling, head lolling, eyes wide open and his tongue hanging out, some waterweed tangled around his neck. Slowly, slowly, it hoisted him up into the air, like an executed traitor displayed as an example to the public.

She wiped her mouth on the back of her arm, scraped her tongue over her teeth and tried to spit the bitterness away while her sore head spun. Probably she should have cut him down from there, given him some last shred of dignity. He'd been her friend, hadn't he? No hero, maybe, but who was? A man who'd wanted to be loyal in a treacherous business, in a treacherous world. A man who'd wanted to be loyal and found it had gone out of fashion. Probably she should have dragged him up onto the bank at least, left him somewhere he could lie still. But instead she turned her horse back towards the farm.

Dignity wasn't much help to the living, it was none to the dead. She'd come here to kill Faithful, and he was killed.

No point weeping about it now.

Harvest Time

Shivers sat on the steps of the farmhouse, trimming some loose skin from the big mass of grazes on his forearm and watching some man weep over a corpse. Friend. Brother, even. He weren't trying to hide it, just sat slumped over, tears dripping off his chin. A moving sight, most likely, if you were that way inclined.

And Shivers always had been. His brother had called him pig-fat when he was a boy on account of his being that soft. He'd cried at his brother's grave and at his father's. When his friend Dobban got stabbed through with a spear and took two days going back to the mud. The night after the fight at Dunbrec, when they buried half his crew along with Threetrees. After the battle in the High Places, even, he'd gone off and found a spot on his own, let fall a full puddle of salt water. Though that might've been relief the fighting was done, rather than sorrow some lives were.

He knew he'd wept all those times, and he knew why, but he couldn't remember for the life of him how it had felt to do it. He wondered if there was anyone left in the world he'd cry for now, and he wasn't sure he liked the answer.

He took a swig of sour water from his flask, and watched a couple of Osprian soldiers picking over the bodies. One rolled a dead man over, some bloody guts slithering out of his split side, wrestled his boot off, saw it had a hole in the sole, tossed it away. He watched another pair, shirt-sleeves rolled up, one with a shovel over his shoulder, arguing the toss over where'd be easiest to start digging. He watched the flies, floating about in the soupy air, already gathering round the open mouths, the open eyes, the open wounds. He looked at ragged gashes and broken bone, cut-off limbs and spilled innards, blood in sticky streaks, drying spots and spatters, red-black pools across the stony yard, and felt no pleasure at a job well done, but no disgust either, no guilt and no sorrow. Just the stinging of his grazes, the uncomfortable stickiness of the heat, the tiredness in his bruised limbs and a niggling trace of hunger, since he'd missed breakfast.

There was a man screaming inside the farmhouse, where they were dealing with the wounded. Screaming, screaming, hoarse and blubbery. But there was a bird tweeting happily from the eaves of the stable too, and Shivers found without too much effort he could concentrate on one and forget the other. He smiled and nodded along with the bird, leaned back against the door frame and stretched his leg out. Seemed a man could get used to anything, in time. And he was damned if he was going to let some screaming shift him off a good spot on the doorstep.

He heard hoofbeats, looked round. Monza, trotting slowly down the slope, a black figure with the bright-blue sky behind her. He watched her pull her lathered horse up in the farmyard, frowning at the bodies. Her clothes were sodden wet, as if she'd been dunked in a stream. Her hair was matted with blood on one side, her pale cheek streaked with it.

"Aye aye, Chief. Good to see you." Should've been true but it felt like some kind of a lie, still. He felt not much of anything either way. "Faithful dead, is he?"

"He's dead." She slid stiffly down. "Have any trouble getting him here?"

"Not much. He wanted to bring more friends than we'd planned for, but I couldn't bring myself to turn 'em down. You know how it is when folk hear about a party. They looked so eager, poor bastards. Have any trouble killing him?"

She shook her head. "He drowned."

"Oh aye? Thought you'd have stabbed him." He picked her sword up and offered it to her.

"I stabbed him a bit." She looked at the blade for a moment, then took it from his hand and sheathed it. "Then I let him drown."

Shivers shrugged. "Up to you. Drowning'll do it, I reckon."

"Drowning did it."

"Five of seven, then."

"Five of seven." Though she didn't look like celebrating. Hardly any more than the man crying over his dead friend. It weren't much of a joyous occasion for anyone, even on the winning side. There's vengeance for you.

"Who's that screaming?"

"Someone. No one." Shivers shrugged. "Listen to the bird instead."

"What?"

"Murcatto!" Vitari stood, arms folded, in the open doorway of the barn. "You'll want to see this."

It was cool and dim inside, sunlight coming in through a ragged hole in the corner, through the narrow windows, throwing bright stripes across the darkened straw. One fell over Day's corpse, yellow hair tangled across her face, body twisted awkwardly. No blood. No marks of violence at all.

"Poison," muttered Monza.

Vitari nodded. "Oh, the irony."

A hellish-looking mess of copper rods, glass tubes and odd-shaped bottles was stood on the table beside the body, a couple of lamps with yellow-blue flames flickering underneath, stuff bubbling away inside, trickling, dripping. Shivers liked the look of the poisoner's equipment even less than the look of the poisoner's corpse. Bodies he was good and familiar with, science was all unknown.

"Fucking science," he muttered. "Even worse'n magic."

"Where's Morveer?" asked Monza.

"No sign." The three of them looked hard at each other for a moment.

"Not among the dead?"

Shivers slowly shook his head. "It's a shame, but I didn't see him."

Monza took a worried step back. "Best not touch anything."

"You think?" growled Vitari. "What happened?"

"Difference of opinion between master and apprentice, by the look of things."

"Serious difference," muttered Shivers.

Vitari slowly shook her spiky head. "That's it. I'm finished."

"You're what?" asked Monza.

"I'm out. In this business you have to know when to quit. It's war now, and I try not to get involved with that. Too hard to pick the outcome." She nodded towards the yard where, out in the sunshine, they were piling up the corpses. "Visserine was a step too far for me, and this is a step further. That and I've no taste for being on the wrong side of Morveer. I could do without looking over my shoulder every day of my life."

"You'll still be looking over your shoulder for Orso," said Monza.

"Knew it when I took the job. Needed the money." Vitari held out her open palm. "Talking of which..."

Monza frowned at her hand, then her face. "You've only come halfway. Halfway, half what we agreed."

"Seems fair. All the money and dead is no kind of payment. I'll settle for half and live."

"I'd sooner keep you on. I can use you. And you won't be safe as long as Orso's alive—"

"Then you'd best get on and kill the bastard, hadn't you? But without me."

"Your choice." Monza reached inside her coat and pulled out a flat leather pouch, a little stained with water. She unfolded it twice and slid a paper from inside, damp at one corner, covered with fancy-looking script. "More than half what we agreed. Five thousand two hundred and twelve scales, in fact." Shivers frowned at it. He still couldn't see how you could turn such a weight of silver into a scrap of paper.

"Fucking banking," he murmured. "Even worse'n science."

Vitari took the bill from Monza's gloved hand, gave it a quick look over. "Valint and Balk?" Her eyes went even narrower than usual, which was some achievement. "This paper better pay. If not, there's no place in the Circle of the World you'll be safe from—"

"It'll pay. If there's one thing I don't need it's more enemies."

"Then let's part friends." Vitari folded the paper and pushed it down into her shirt. "Maybe we'll work together again some time."

Monza stared right into her face, that way she had. "I'll count the minutes."

Vitari backed off for a few steps, then turned towards the sunlit square of the doorway.

"I fell in a river!" Shivers called after her.

"What?"

"When I was young. First time I went raiding. I got drunk, and I went for a piss, and I fell in the river. Current sucked my trousers off, dumped me half a mile downstream. Time I got back to camp I'd more or less turned blue with cold, shivering so bad I near shook my fingers off."

"And?"

"That's why they called me Shivers. You asked. Back in Sipani." And he grinned. Seemed like he could see the funny side of it, these days. Vitari stood there for a moment, a lean black outline, then slid out through the door. "Well, Chief, looks like it's just you and me—"

"And me!" He snapped round, reaching for his axe. Beside him Monza crouched, sword already half-drawn, both straining into the darkness. Ishri's grinning face hung on one side, over the edge of the hayloft. "And a fine afternoon to my two heroes." She slid down the ladder face first, as smooth as if her bandaged body had no bones in it. Up onto her feet, looking impossibly thin without her coat, and she sauntered across the straw towards Day's corpse. "One of your killers killed the other. There's killers for you." She looked at Shivers, eyes black as coal, and he gripped his axe tight.

"Fucking magic," he mumbled. "Even worse'n banking."

She crept up, all white-toothed, hungry grin, touched one finger to the pick on the back of his axe and pushed it gently down towards the floor. "Do I take it you murdered your old friend Faithful Carpi to your satisfaction?"

Monza slapped her sword back into its sheath. "Faithful's dead, if that's the point of your fucking performance."

"You have a strange manner of celebration." She lifted her long arms to the ceiling. "Vengeance is yours! Praise be to God!"

"Orso still lives."

"Ah, yes." Ishri opened her eyes very wide, so wide Shivers wondered if they might drop out. "When Orso dies you will smile."

"What do you care whether I smile?"

"I, care? Not a particle. You Styrians have a habit of boasting, and boasting, and never following through. I am pleased to find one who can get the job done. Do the job, scowl by all means." She ran her fingers across the table-top then casually snuffed the flames of the burners out with the palm of her hand. "Speaking of which, you told our mutual friend Duke Rogont you could bring the Thousand Swords over to his side, as I recall?"

"If the Emperor's gold is forthcoming—"

"In your shirt pocket."

Monza frowned as she pulled something from her pocket and held it up to the light. A big red-gold coin, shining with that special warmth gold has that somehow makes you want to hold it. "Very nice, but it'll take more than one."

"Oh, there'll be more. The mountains of Gurkhul are made of gold, I hear." She peered at the charred edges of the hole in the corner of the barn, then happily clicked her tongue. "I still have it." And she twisted her body through the gap like a fox through a fence and was gone.

Shivers left it a moment, then leaned close to Monza. "Can't put my finger on it, but there's something odd about her."

"You've got this amazing sense for people, haven't you?" She turned without smiling and left the barn.

Shivers stood there a moment longer, frowning down at Day's body, working his face around, feeling the scars on the left side stretching, shifting, itching. Cosca dead, Day dead, Vitari gone, Friendly gone, Morveer fled and, by the look of things, turned against them. So much for the merry company. He should've been all nostalgic for the happy friends of long ago, the bands of brothers he'd been a part of. United in a common cause, even if it was no more'n staying alive. Dogman, and Harding Grim, and Tul Duru. Black Dow, even, all men with a code. All faded into the past, and left him alone. Down here in Styria, where no one had any code that meant a thing.

Even then, his right eye was about as close to crying as his left.

He scratched at the scar on his cheek. Ever so gently, just with his fingertips. He winced, scratched harder. And harder still. He stopped himself, hissing through his teeth. Now it itched worse than ever, and hurt into the bargain. He'd yet to work out a way to scratch that itch that didn't make matters worse.

There's vengeance for you.

The Old New Captain General

Monza had seen wounds past counting, in all their wondrous variety. The making of them had been her profession. She'd witnessed bodies ruined in every conceivable manner. Men crushed, slashed, stabbed, burned, hanged, skinned, gutted, gored. But Caul Shivers' scar might well have been the worst she'd ever seen on the face of a living man.

It started as a pink mark near the corner of his mouth, became a ragged groove thick as a finger below his cheekbone, then widened, a stream of mottled, melted flesh flowing towards his eye. Streaks and spots of angry red spread out from it across his cheek, down the side of his nose. There was a thin mark to match slanting across his forehead and taking off half his eyebrow. Then there was the eye itself. It was bigger than the other. Lashes gone, lids shrivelled, the lower one drooping. When he blinked with his right eye, the left only twitched, and stayed open. He'd sneezed a while back, and it had puckered up like a swallowing throat, the dead enamelled pupil still staring at her through the pink hole. She'd had to will herself not to spew, and yet she was gripped with a horrified fascination, constantly looking to see if it would happen again, and it hardly helped that she knew he couldn't see her looking.

She should have felt guilt. She'd been the cause of it, hadn't she? She should have felt sympathy. She'd scars of her own, after all, and ugly enough. But disgust was as close as she could get. She wished she'd started off riding on the other side of him, but it was too late now. She wished he'd never taken the bandages off, but she could hardly tell him to put them back on. She told herself it might heal, might get better, and maybe it would.

But not much, and she knew it.

He turned suddenly, and she realised why he'd been staring at his saddle. His right eye was on her. His left, in the midst of all that scar, still looked straight downwards. The enamel must have slipped, and now his mismatched eyes gave him a look of skewed confusion.

"What?"

"Your, er…" She pointed at her face. "It's slipped…a bit."

"Again? Fucking thing." He put his thumb in his eye and slid it back up. "Better?" Now the false one was fixed straight ahead while the real one glared at her. It was almost worse than it had been.

"Much," she said, doing her best to smile.

Shivers spat something in Northern. "Uncanny results, did he say? If I happen back through Puranti I'll give that eye-making bastard a visit…"

The mercenaries' first picket came into view around a curve in the track — a scattering of shady-looking men in mismatched armour. She knew the one in charge by sight. She'd made it her business to know every veteran in the Thousand Swords, and what he was good for. Secco was this one's name, a tough old wolf who'd served as a corporal for six years or more.

He pointed his spear at her as they brought their horses to a walk, his fellows around him, flatbows, swords, axes at the ready. "Who goes—"

She pushed her hood back. "Who do you think, Secco?"

The words froze on his lips and he stood, spear limp, as she rode past. On into the camp, men going about their morning rituals, eating their breakfasts, getting ready to march. A few looked up as she and Shivers passed on the track, or at any rate the widest stretch of mud between the tents. A few of them started staring. Then a few more, watching, following at a distance, gathering along the way.

"It's her."

"Murcatto."

"She's alive?"

She rode through them the way she used to, shoulders back, chin up, sneer locked on her mouth, not even bothering to look. As if they were nothing to her. As if she was a better kind of animal than they were. And all the while she prayed silently they didn't work out what they'd never worked out yet, but what she was always afraid to the pit of her stomach they would.

That she didn't know what the hell she was doing, and a knife would kill her just as dead as anyone else.

But none of them spoke to her, let alone tried to stop her. Mercenaries are cowards, on the whole, even more so than most people. Men who'll kill because it's the easiest way they've found to make a living. Mercenaries have no loyalty in them, on the whole, by definition. Not much to their leaders, even less to their employers.

That was what she was counting on.

The captain general's tent was pitched on a rise in a big clearing, red pennant hanging limp from its tallest pole, well above the jumble of badly pitched canvas around it. Monza kicked her horse up, making a couple of men scurry out of her way, trying not to let the nerves that were boiling up her throat show. It was a long enough gamble as it was. Show one grain of fear and she'd be done.

She swung down from her horse, tossed the reins carelessly round a sapling trunk. She had to sidestep a goat someone had tethered there, then strode up towards the flap. Nocau, the Gurkish outcast who'd guarded the tent during the daylight since way back in Sazine's time, stood staring, his big scimitar not even drawn.

"You can shut your mouth now, Nocau." She leaned in close and pushed his slack jaw shut with her gloved finger so his teeth snapped together. "Wouldn't want a bird nesting in there, eh?" And she pushed through the flap.

The same table, even if the charts on it were of a different stretch of ground. The same flags hanging about the canvas, some of them that she'd added, won at Sweet Pines and the High Bank, at Musselia and Caprile. And the same chair, of course, that Sazine had supposedly stolen from the Duke of Cesale's dining table the day he formed the Thousand Swords. It stood empty on a pair of crates, waiting for the arse of the new captain general. For her arse, if the Fates were kind.

Though she had to admit they weren't usually.

The three most senior captains left in the great brigade stood close to the improvised dais, muttering to each other. Sesaria, Victus, Andiche. The three Benna had persuaded to make her captain general. The three who'd persuaded Faithful Carpi to take her place. The three she needed to persuade to give it back to her. They looked up, and they saw her, and they straightened.

"Well, well," rumbled Sesaria.

"Well, well, well," muttered Andiche. "If it isn't the Serpent of Talins."

"The Butcher of Caprile herself," whined Victus. "Where's Faithful?"

She looked him right in the eye. "Not coming. You boys need a new captain general."

The three of them swapped glances, and Andiche sucked noisily at his yellowed teeth. A habit Monza had always found faintly disgusting. One of many disgusting things about the lank-haired rat of a man. "As it happens, we'd reached the same conclusion on our own."

"Faithful was a good fellow," rumbled Sesaria.

"Too good for the job," said Victus.

"A decent captain general needs to be an evil shit at best."

Monza showed her teeth. "Any one of you three is more than evil enough, I reckon. There aren't three bigger shits in Styria." It was no kind of joke. She should've murdered these three rather than Faithful. "Too big a set of shits to work for each other, though."

"True enough," said Victus sourly.

Sesaria tipped his head back and stared at her down his flat nose. "We need someone new."

"Or someone old," said Monza.

Andiche grinned at his two fellows. "As it happens, we'd reached the same conclusion on our own," he said again.

"Good for you." This was going more smoothly even than she'd hoped. Eight years she'd led the Thousand Swords, and she knew how to handle the likes of these three. Greed, nice and simple. "I'm not the type to let a little bad blood get in the way of a lot of good money, and I damn well know that none of you are." She held Ishri's coin up to the light, a Gurkish double-headed coin, Emperor on one side, Prophet on the other. She flicked it to Andiche. "There'll be plenty more like that, to go over to Rogont."

Sesaria stared at her from under his thick grey brows. "Fight for Rogont, against Orso?"

"Fight all the way back across Styria?" The chains round Victus' neck rattled as he tossed his head. "The same ground we've fought over the past eight years?"

Andiche looked up from the coin to her, and puffed out his acne-scarred cheeks. "Sounds like an awful lot of fighting."

"You've won against longer odds, with me in charge."

"Oh, that's a fact." Sesaria gestured at the tattered flags. "We've won all kinds of glory with you in the chair, all kinds of pride."

"But try paying a whore with that." Victus was grinning, and that weasel never grinned. Something was wrong about their smiles, something mocking in them.

"Look." Andiche rested one lazy hand on the arm of the captain general's chair and dusted the seat off with the other. "We don't doubt for a moment that when it comes to a fight, you're the best damn general a man could ask for."

"Then what's the problem?"

Victus' face twisted into a snarl. "We don't want to fight! We want to make... fucking... money!"

"Who ever brought you more money than me?"

"Ahem," came a voice right in her ear. Monza jerked round, and froze, hand halfway to the hilt of her sword. Standing just behind her, with a faintly embarrassed smile, was Nicomo Cosca.

He'd shaved off his moustache, and all his hair besides, left only a black and grey stubble over his knobbly skull, his sharp jaw. The rash had faded to a faint pink splash up the side of his neck. His eyes were less sunken, his face no longer trembling or beaded with sweat. But the smile was the same. The faint little smile and the playful gleam in his dark eyes. The same he used to have, when she first met him.

"A delight to see you both well."

"Uh," grunted Shivers. Monza found she'd made a kind of strangled cough, but no words came with it.

"I am in resplendent health, your concern for my welfare is most touching." Cosca strolled past, slapping a puzzled-looking Shivers on the back, more captains of the Thousand Swords pushing their way through the flap after him and spreading out around the edges of the tent. Men whose names, faces, qualities, or lack of them, she knew well. A thick-set man with a stoop, a worn coat and almost no neck came at the rear. He raised his heavy brows at her as he passed.

"Friendly?" she hissed. "I thought you were going back to Talins!"

He shrugged, as if it was nothing. "Didn't make it all the way."

"So I fucking see!"

Cosca stepped up onto the packing cases and turned to the assembly with a self-satisfied flourish. He'd acquired a grand black breastplate with golden scrollwork from somewhere, a sword with a gilded hilt, fine black boots with shining buckles. He settled himself into the captain general's chair with as much pomp as an Emperor into his throne, Friendly standing watchful beside the cases, arms crossed. As Cosca's arse touched the wood the tent broke into polite applause, every captain tapping their fingers against their palms as daintily as fine ladies attending the theatre. Just as they had for Monza, when she stole the chair. If she hadn't felt suddenly so sick she might almost have laughed.

Cosca waved away the applause while obviously encouraging it. "No, no, really, entirely undeserved. But it's good to be back."

"How the hell—"

"Did I survive? The wound, it appears, was not quite so fatal as we all supposed. The Talinese took me, on account of my uniform, for one of their own, and bore me directly to an excellent surgeon, who was able to staunch the bleeding. I was two weeks abed, then slipped out of a window. I made contact in Puranti with my old friend Andiche, who I had gathered might be desirous of a change in command. He was, and so were all his noble fellows." He gestured to the captains scattered about the tent, then to himself. "And here I am."

Monza snapped her mouth shut. There was no planning for this. Nicomo Cosca, the very definition of an unpredictable development. Still, a plan too brittle to bend with circumstances is worse than no plan at all. "My congratulations, then, General Cosca," she managed to grate. "But my offer still stands. Gurkish gold in return for your services to Duke Rogont—"

"Ah." Cosca winced, sucking air through his teeth. "Tiny little problem there, unfortunately. I already signed a new engagement with Grand Duke Orso. Or with his heir, to be precise, Prince Foscar. A promising young man. We'll be moving against Ospria just as Faithful Carpi planned, prior to his untimely demise." He poked at the air with his forefinger. "Putting paid to the League of Eight! Taking the fight to the Duke of Delay! There's plenty to sack in Ospria. It was a good plan." Agreeing mutters from the captains. "Why work out another?"

"But you hate Orso!"

"Oh, I despise him utterly, that's well known, but I've nothing against his money. It's the exact same colour as everybody else's. You should know. He paid you enough of it."

"You old cunt," she said.

"You really shouldn't talk to me that way." Cosca stuck his lips out at her. "I am a mature forty-eight. Besides, I gave my life for you!"

"You didn't fucking die!" she snarled.

"Well. Rumours of my death are often exaggerated. Wishful thinking, on the part of my many enemies."

"I'm beginning to know how they feel."

"Oh, come, come, whatever were you thinking? A noble death? Me? Very much not my style. I mean to go with my boots off, a bottle in my hand and a woman on my cock." His eyebrows went up. "It's not that job you've come for, is it?"

Monza ground her teeth. "If it's a question of money—"

"Orso has the full support of the Banking House of Valint and Balk, and you'll find no deeper pockets anywhere. He's paying well, and better than well. But it's not about the money, actually. I signed a contract. I gave my solemn word."

She stared at him. "When have you ever cared a shit about your word?"

"I'm a changed man." Cosca pulled a flask from a back pocket, unscrewed it and took a long swig, never taking his amused eyes from her face. "And I must admit I owe it all to you. I've put the past behind me. Found my principles." He grinned at his captains, and they grinned back. "Bit mossy, but they should polish up alright. You forged a good relationship with Orso. Loyalty. Honesty. Stability. Hate to toss all your hard work down the latrine. Besides, there's the soldier's first rule to consider, isn't there, boys?"

Victus and Andiche spoke in unison, just the way they'd used to, before she took the chair. "Never fight for the losing side!"

Cosca's grin grew wider. "Orso holds the cards. Find a good hand of your own, my ears are always open. But we'll stick with Orso for now."

"Whatever you say, General," said Andiche.

"Whatever you say," echoed Victus. "Good to have you back."

Sesaria leaned down, muttering something in Cosca's ear. The new captain general recoiled as though stung. "Give them over to Duke Orso? Absolutely not! Today is a happy day! A joyous occasion for one and all! There'll be no killing here, not today." He wafted a hand at her as though he was shooing a cat out of the kitchen. "You can go. Better not come back tomorrow, though. We might not be so joyous, then."

Monza took a step towards him, a curse half-out of her mouth. There was a rattling of metal as the assorted captains began to draw their weapons. Friendly blocked her path, arms coming uncrossed, hands dropping to his sides, expressionless face turned towards her. She stopped still. "I need to kill Orso!"

"And if you manage it, your brother will live again, yes?" Cosca cocked his head to one side. "You'll get your hand back? No?"

She was cold all over, skin prickling. "He deserves what's coming!"

"Ah, but most of us do. All of us will get it regardless. How many others will you suck into your little vortex of slaughter in the meantime?"

"For Benna—"

"No. For you. I know you, don't forget. I've stood where you stand now, beaten, betrayed, disgraced, and come out the other side. As long as you have men to kill you are still Monzcarro Murcatto, the great and fearsome! Without that, what are you?" Cosca's lip curled. "A lonely cripple with a bloody past."

The words were strangled in her throat. "Please, Cosca, you have to—"

"I don't have to do a thing. We're even, remember? More than even, say I. Out of my sight, snake, before I pack you off back to Duke Orso in a jar. You need a job, Northman?"

Shivers' good eye crept across to Monza, and for a moment she was sure he'd say yes. Then he slowly shook his head. "I'll stick with the chief I've got."

"Loyalty, eh?" Cosca snorted. "Be careful with that nonsense, it can get you killed!" A scattering of laughter. "The Thousand Swords is no place for loyalty, eh, boys? We'll have none of that childishness here!" More laughter, a score or more hard grins all aimed at Monza.

She felt dizzy. The tent seemed too bright and too dark at once. Her nose caught a waft of something — sweaty bodies, or strong drink, or stinking cooking, or a latrine pit too close to the headquarters, and her stomach turned over, set her mouth to watering. A smoke, oh please, a smoke. She turned on her heel, somewhat unsteadily, shoved her way between a couple of chuckling men and through the flap, out of the tent and into the bright morning.

Outside it was far worse. Sunlight stabbed at her. Faces, dozens of them, blurred together into a mass of eyes, all fixed on her. A jury of scum. She tried to look ahead, always ahead, but she couldn't stop her lids from flickering. She tried to walk in the old way, head back, but her knees were trembling so hard she was sure they must be able to hear them slapping against the insides of her trousers. It was as if she'd been putting off the fear, the weakness, the pain. Putting it off, storing it up, and now it was breaking on her in one great wave, sweeping her under, helpless. Her skin was icy with cold sweat. Her hand was aching all the way to her neck. They saw what she really was. Saw she'd lost. A lonely cripple with a bloody past, just like Cosca said. Her guts shifted and she gagged, an acid tickle at the back of her throat. The world lurched.

Hate only keeps you standing so long.

"Can't," she whispered. "Can't." She didn't care what happened, as long as she could stop. Her leg buckled and she started to fall, felt Shivers grab hold of her arm and drag her up.

"Walk," he hissed in her ear.

"Can't—"

His fist dug hard into her armpit, and the pain stopped the world spinning for a moment. "Fucking walk, or we're finished."

Enough strength, with Shivers' help, to make it to the horses. Enough to put a boot in a stirrup. Enough, with an aching groan, to get herself into the saddle, pull her horse around and get it facing the right way. As they rode from the camp she could hardly see. The great captain general, Duke Orso's would-be nemesis, sagging in her saddle like dead meat.

You make yourself too hard, you make yourself brittle too. Crack once, crack all to pieces.

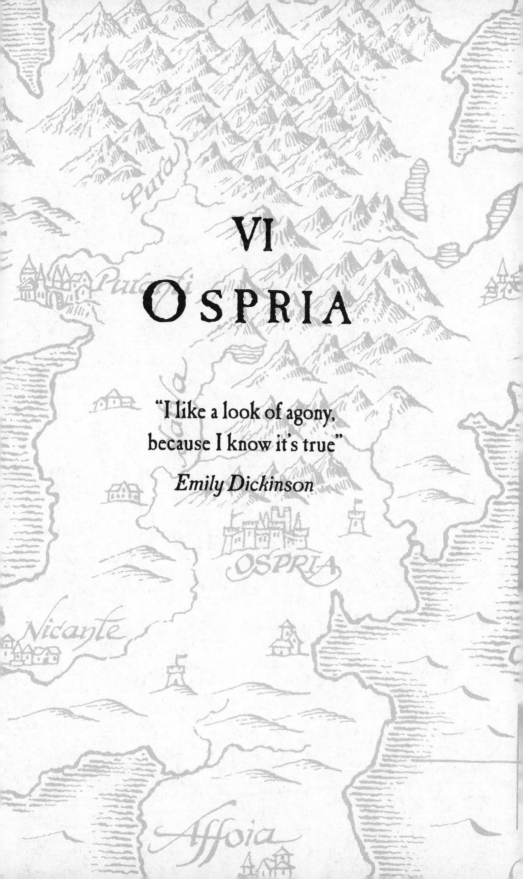

VI
OSPRIA

"I like a look of agony,
because I know it's true"

Emily Dickinson

It seemed a little gold could spare a lot of blood.

Musselia could not be captured without an indefinite siege, this was well known. It had once been a great fortress of the New Empire, and its inhabitants placed great pride in their ancient walls. Too much pride in walls, perhaps, and not enough gold in the pockets of their defenders. It was for a sum almost disappointing that Benna arranged for a small side gate to be left unlocked.

Even before Faithful and his men had taken possession of the defences, and long before the rest of the Thousand Swords spilled out into the city to begin the sack, Benna was leading Monza through the darkened streets. Him leading her was unusual enough in itself.

"Why did you want to be at the front?"

"You'll see."

"Where are we going?"

"To get our money back. Plus interest."

Monza frowned as she hurried after him. Her brother's surprises tended always to have a sting in them. Through a narrow archway in a narrow street. A cobbled courtyard inside, lit by two flickering torches. A Kantic man in simple travelling clothes stood beside a canvas-covered cart, horse hitched and ready. Monza did not know him, but he knew Benna, coming forwards, hands out, his smile gleaming in the darkness.

"Benna, Benna. It is good to see you!" They embraced like old comrades.

"And you, my friend. This is my sister, Monzcarro."

The man bowed to her. "The famous and fearsome. An honour."

"Somenu Hermon," said Benna, smiling wide. "Greatest merchant of Musselia."

"No more than a humble trader, like any other. There are only a few last... things... to move. My wife and children have already left."

"Good. That makes this much easier."

Monza frowned at her brother. "What's going —"

Benna snatched her dagger from her belt and stabbed Hermon overhand in his face. It happened so fast that the merchant was still smiling as he fell.

Monza drew her sword on an instinct, staring into the shadows around the courtyard, out into the street, but all was quiet.

"What the hell have you done?" she snarled at him. He was up on the cart, ripping back the canvas, a mad, eager look on his face. He fumbled open the lid of a box underneath, delved inside and let coins slowly drop with the jingling rattle of falling money.

Gold.

She hopped up beside him. More gold than she had ever seen at once. With a sickly widening of her eyes she realised there were more boxes. She pushed the canvas back with trembling hands. Many more.

"We're rich!" squeaked Benna. "We're rich!"

"We were already rich." She was looking down at her knife stuck through Hermon's eye, blood black in the lamplight. "Did you have to kill him?"

He stared at her as if she had gone mad. "Rob him and leave him alive? He would have told people we had the money. This way we're safe."

"Safe? This much gold is the opposite of safe, Benna!"

He frowned, as though he was hurt by her. "I thought you'd be pleased. You of all people, who slaved in the dirt for nothing." As though he was disappointed in her. "This is for us. For us, do you understand?" As though he was disgusted with her. "Mercy and cowardice are the same, Monza! I thought you knew that."

What could she do? Unstab Hermon's face?

It seemed a little gold could cost a lot of blood.

His Plan of Attack

The southernmost range of the Urval Mountains, the spine of Styria, all shadowy swales and dramatic peaks bathed in golden evening light, marched boldly southwards, ending at the great rock into which Ospria itself was carved. Between the city and the hill on which the headquarters of the Thousand Swords had been pitched, the deep and verdant valley was patched with wild flowers in a hundred colours. The Sulva wound through its bottom and away towards the distant sea, touched by the setting sun and turned the orange of molten iron.

Birds twittered in the olive trees of an ancient grove, grasshoppers chirped in the waving long grass, the wind kissed at Cosca's face and made the feather on his hat, held gently in one hand, heroically thrash and flutter. Vineyards were planted on the slopes to the north of the city, green rows of vines on the dusty hillsides that drew Cosca's eye and made his mouth water with an almost painful longing. The best vintages in the Circle of the World were trampled out on that very ground...

"Sweet mercy, a drink," he mouthed.

"Beautiful," breathed Prince Foscar.

"You never before looked upon fair Ospria, your Highness?"

"I had heard stories, but..."

"Breathtaking, isn't she?" The city was built upon four huge shelves cut into the cream-coloured rock of the steep hillside, each one surrounded by its own smooth wall, crammed with lofty buildings, stuffed with a tangle of roofs, domes, turrets. The ancient Imperial aqueduct curved gracefully down from the mountains to meet its outermost rampart, fifty arches or more, the tallest of them twenty times the height of a man. The citadel clung impossibly to the highest crag, four great towers picked out against the darkening azure sky. The lamps were being lit in the windows as the sun sank, the outline of the city dusted with pinprick points of light. "There can be no other place quite like this one."

A pause. "It seems almost a shame to spoil it with fire and sword," observed Foscar.

"Almost, your Highness. But this is war, and those are the tools available."

Cosca had heard that Count Foscar, now Prince Foscar following his brother's mishap in a famous Sipanese brothel, was a boyish, callow, weak-nerved youth, and was therefore pleasantly impressed by what he had seen thus far. The lad was fresh-faced, true, but every man begins young, and he seemed thoughtful rather than weak, sober rather than bloodless, polite rather than limp. A young man very much like Cosca himself had been at that age. Only the absolute reverse in every particular, of course.

"They appear to be most powerful fortifications…" murmured the prince, scanning the towering walls of the city with his eyeglass.

"Oh, indeed. Ospria was the furthest outpost of the New Empire, built as a bastion to hold back the restless Baolish hordes. Parts of the walls have been standing firm against the savage for more than five hundred years."

"Then will Duke Rogont not simply retreat behind them? He does seem prone to avoid battle whenever possible…"

"He'll give battle, your Highness," said Andiche.

"He must," rumbled Sesaria, "or we'll just camp in his pretty valley and starve him out."

"We outnumber him three to one or more," whined Victus.

Cosca could not but agree. "Walls are only useful if one expects help, and no help is coming to the League of Eight now. He must fight. He will fight. He is desperate." If there was one thing he understood, it was desperation.

"I must confess I have some…concerns." Foscar nervously cleared his throat. "I understood that you always hated my father with a passion."

"Passion. Hah." Cosca dismissed it with a wave. "As a young man I let my passion lead me by the nose, but I have learned numerous harsh lessons in favour of a cool head. I and your father have had our disagreements but I am, above all else, a mercenary. To let my personal feelings reduce the weight of my purse would be an act of criminal unprofessionalism."

"Hear, hear." Victus wore an unsightly leer. Even more so than usual.

"Why, my own three closest captains," and Cosca took them in with a the-
atrical sweep of his hat, "betrayed me utterly and put Murcatto in my chair.
They fucked me to their balls, as they say in Sipani. To their balls, your Highness. If I had a taste for vengeance, it would be on these three heaps of human
shit." Then Cosca chuckled, and they chuckled, and the vaguely uncomfortable atmosphere was swiftly dispelled. "But we can all be useful to each other,
and so I have forgiven them everything, and your father too. Vengeance brings
no man a brighter tomorrow, and when placed on the scales of life, does not
outweigh a single...scale. You need not worry on that score, Prince Foscar, I
am all business. Bought and paid for, and entirely your man."

"You are generosity itself, General Cosca."

"I am avarice itself, which is not quite the same, but will do in a pinch.
Now, perhaps, for dinner. Would any of you gentlemen care for a drink?
We came by a crate of a very fine vintage in a manor house upstream only
yesterday, and—"

"It might be best if we were to discuss our strategy before the levity begins." Colonel Rigrat's shrill voice was as a file applied directly to
Cosca's sensitive back teeth. He was a sharp-faced, sharp-voiced, sharply
self-satisfied man in his late thirties and a well-pressed uniform, previously
General Ganmark's second in command and now Foscar's. Presumably the
military brains behind the Talinese operation, such as they were. "Now,
while everyone still has their wits close to hand."

"Believe me, young man," though he was neither young, nor yet a man
as far as Cosca was concerned, "my wits and I are not easily parted. You
have a plan in mind?"

"I do!" Rigrat produced his baton with a flourish. Friendly loomed out
from under the nearest olive tree, hands moving to his weapons. Cosca sent
him melting back into the shadows with the faintest smile and shake of his
head. No one else even noticed.

Cosca had been a soldier all his life, of a kind, and had yet to understand
what the purpose of a baton truly was. You could not kill a man with one,
or even look like you might. You could not hammer in a tent peg, cook a
good side of meat or even pawn it for anything worthwhile. Perhaps they
were intended for scratching those hard-to-reach places in the small of the
back? Or stimulating the anus? Or perhaps simply for marking a man out
as a fool? For that purpose, he reflected as Rigrat pointed self-importantly
towards the river with his baton, they served admirably.

"There are two fords across the Sulva! Upper...and lower! The lower is much the wider and more reliable crossing." The colonel indicated the point where the dirty stripe of the Imperial road met the river, glimmering water flaring out in the gently sloping bottom of the valley. "But the upper, perhaps a mile upstream, should also be usable at this time of year."

"Two fords, you say?" It was a fact well known there were two damn fords. Cosca himself had crossed in glory by one when he came into Ospria to be toasted by Grand Duchess Sefeline and her subjects, and fled by another just after the bitch had tried to poison him. Cosca slid his battered flask from his jacket pocket. The one that Morveer had flung at him back in Sipani. He unscrewed the cap.

Rigrat gave him a sharp glance. "I thought we agreed that we would drink once we had discussed strategy."

"You agreed. I just stood here." Cosca closed his eyes, took a deep breath, tilted up the flask and took a long swallow, then another, felt the coolness fill his mouth, wash at his dry throat. A drink, a drink, a drink. He gave a happy sigh. "Nothing like a drink of an evening."

"May I continue?" hissed Rigrat, riddled with impatience.

"Of course, my boy, take your time."

"The day after tomorrow, at dawn, you will lead the Thousand Swords across the lower ford—"

"Lead? From the front, do you mean?"

"Where else would a commander lead from?"

Cosca exchanged a baffled glance with Andiche. "Anywhere else. Have you ever been at the front of a battle? The chances of being killed there really are very high."

"Extremely high," said Victus.

Rigrat ground his teeth. "Lead from what position pleases you, but the Thousand Swords will cross the lower ford, supported by our allies from Etrisani and Cesale. Duke Rogont will have no choice but to engage you with all his power, hoping to crush your forces while you are still crossing the river. Once he is committed, our Talinese regulars will break from hiding and cross the upper ford. We will take the enemy in the flank, and—" He snapped his baton into his waiting palm with a smart crack.

"You'll hit them with a stick?"

Rigrat was not amused. Cosca had to wonder whether he ever had been.

"With steel, sir, with steel! We will rout them utterly and put them to flight, and thus put an end to the troublesome League of Eight!"

There was a long pause. Cosca frowned at Andiche, and Andiche frowned back. Sesaria and Victus shook their heads at one another. Rigrat tapped his baton impatiently against his leg. Prince Foscar cleared his throat once more, nervously pushed his chin forwards. "Your opinion, General Cosca?"

"Hmm." Cosca gloomily shook his head, eyeing the sparkling river with the weightiest of frowns. "Hmm. Hmm. Hmmmm."

"Hmmm." Victus tapped his pursed lips with one finger.

"Humph." Andiche puffed out his cheeks.

"Hrrrrrm." Sesaria's unconvinced voice throbbed at a deeper pitch.

Cosca removed his hat, scratched his head and placed it back with a flick at the feather. "Hmmmmmmmmmmmmmm—"

"Are we to take it that you disapprove?" asked Foscar.

"I somehow let slip my misgivings? Then I cannot in good conscience suppress them. I am not convinced that the Thousand Swords are well suited to the task you have assigned."

"Not convinced," said Andiche.

"Not well suited," said Victus.

Sesaria was a silent mountain of reluctance.

"Have you not been well paid for your services?" demanded Rigrat.

Cosca chuckled. "Of course, and the Thousand Swords will fight, you may depend on that!"

"They will fight, every man!" asserted Andiche.

"Like devils!" added Victus.

"But it is how they are to be made to fight best that concerns me as their captain general. They have lost two leaders in a brief space." He hung his head as if he regretted the fact, and had in no way benefited hugely himself.

"Murcatto, then Faithful." Sesaria sighed as if he had not been one of the prime agents in the changes of command.

"They have been relegated to support duties."

"Scouting," lamented Andiche.

"Clearing the flanks," growled Victus.

"Their morale is at a terribly low ebb. They have been paid, but money is never the best motivation for a man to risk his life." Especially a mercenary, it needed hardly to be said. "To throw them into a pitched mêlée against a stubborn and desperate enemy, toe to toe...I'm not saying they might break, but...well..." Cosca winced, scratching slowly at his neck. "They might break."

"I hope this is not an example of your notorious reluctance to fight," sneered Rigrat.

"Reluctance...to fight? Ask anyone, I am a tiger!" Victus snorted snot down his chin but Cosca ignored him. "This is a question of picking the right tool for the task. One does not employ a rapier to cut down a stubborn tree. One employs an axe. Unless one is a complete arse." The young colonel opened his mouth to retort but Cosca spoke smoothly over him. "The plan is sound, in outline. As one military man to another I congratulate you upon it unreservedly." Rigrat paused, unbalanced, not sure if he was being taken for a fool or not, though he most obviously was.

"But it would be wiser counsel for your regular Talinese troops — tried and tested recently in Visserine, then Puranti, committed to their cause, used to victory and with the very firmest of morale — to cross the lower ford and engage the Osprians, supported by your allies of Etrisani and Cesale, and so forth." He waved his flask towards the river, a far more useful implement to his mind than a baton, since a baton makes no man drunk. "The Thousand Swords would be far better deployed concealed upon the high ground. Waiting to seize the moment! To drive across the upper ford, with dash and vigour, and take the enemy in the rear!"

"Best place to take an enemy," muttered Andiche. Victus sniggered.

Cosca finished with a flourish of his flask. "Thus, your earthy courage and our fiery passion are used where they are best suited. Songs will be sung, glory will be seized, history will be made, Orso will be king..." He gave Foscar a gentle bow. "And yourself, your Highness, in due course."

Foscar frowned towards the fords. "Yes. Yes, I see. The thing is, though—"

"Then we are agreed!" Cosca flung an arm around his shoulders and guided him back towards the tent. "Was it Stolicus who said great men march often in the same direction? I believe it was! Let us march now towards dinner, my friends!" He pointed one finger back towards the darkening mountains, where Ospria glimmered in the sunset. "I swear, I am so hungry I could eat a city!" Warm laughter accompanied him back into the tent.

Politics

Shivers sat there frowning, and drank.

Duke Rogont's great dining hall was the grandest room he'd ever got drunk in by quite a stretch. When Vossula told him Styria was packed with wonders it was this type of thing, rather than the rotting docks of Talins, that Shivers had in mind. It must've had four times the floor of Bethod's great hall in Carleon and a ceiling three times as high or more. The walls were pale marble with stripes of blue-black stone through it, all fretted with veins of glitter, all carved with leaves and vines, all grown up and crept over with ivy so the real plants and the sculpted tangled together in the dancing shadows. Warm evening breezes washed in through open windows wide as castle gates, made the orange flames of a thousand hanging lamps flicker and sway, striking a precious gleam from everything.

A place of majesty and magic, built by gods for the use of giants.

Shame the folk gathered there fell a long way short of either. Women in gaudy finery, brushed, jewelled and painted to look younger, or thinner, or richer than they were. Men in bright-coloured jackets who wore lace at their collars and little gilded daggers at their belts. They looked at him first with mild disdain on their powdered faces, like he was made of rotting meat. Then, once he'd turned the left side of his face forwards, with a sick horror that gave him three parts grim satisfaction and one part sick horror of his own.

Always at every feast there's some stupid, ugly, mean bastard got a big score to settle with no one in particular, drinks way too much and makes the night a worry for everyone. Seemed tonight it was him, and he was taking to the part with a will. He hawked up phlegm and spat it noisily across the gleaming floor.

A man at the next table in a yellow coat with long tails to it looked round, the smallest sneer on his puffed-up lips. Shivers leaned towards him, grinding the point of his knife into the polished table-top. "Something to say to me, piss-coat?" The man paled and turned back to his friends without a word. "Bunch o' bastard cowards," Shivers growled into his quickly emptying wine-cup, good and loud enough to be heard three tables away. "Not a single bone in the whole fucking crowd!"

He thought about what the Dogman might've made of this crew of tittering dandies. Or Rudd Threetrees. Or Black Dow. He gave a grim snort to think of it, but his laughter choked off short. If there was a joke, it was on him. Here he was, in the midst of 'em, after all, leaning on their charity without a friend to his name. Or so it seemed.

He scowled towards the high table, up on a raised dais at the head of the room. Rogont sat in the midst of his most favoured guests, grinning around as though he was a star shining from the night sky. Monza sat beside him. Hard to tell from where Shivers was, specially with everything smeared up with anger and too much wine, but he thought he saw her laughing. Enjoying herself, no doubt, without her one-eyed errand boy to drag her down.

He was a fine-looking bastard, the Prince of Prudence. Had both his eyes, anyway. Shivers would've liked to break his smooth, smug face open. With a hammer, like Monza had broken Gobba's head. Or just with his fists. Crush it in his hands. Pound it to red splinters. He gripped his knife trembling tight, spinning out a whole mad story of how he'd go about it. Picking over all the bloody details, shifting them about until they made him look as big a man as possible, Rogont wailing for mercy and pissing himself, twisting it into crazy shapes where Monza wanted him more'n ever at the end of it. And all the while he watched the two of 'em through one twitching, narrowed eye.

He goaded himself with the notion they were laughing at him, but he knew that was foolishness. He didn't matter enough to laugh at, and that made him stew hotter than ever. He was still clinging to his pride, after all, like a drowning man to a twig way too small to keep him afloat. He was a maimed embarrassment, after he'd saved her life how many times? Risked his life how many times? And after all the bloody steps he'd climbed to get to the top of this bastard mountain too. Might've hoped for something better'n scorn at the end of it.

He jerked his knife from the split wood. The knife Monza had given him the first day they met. Back when he had both his eyes and a lot less blood on his hands. Back when he had it in mind to leave killing behind him, and be a good man. He could hardly remember what that had felt like.

Monza sat there frowning, and drank.

She hadn't much taste for food lately, had less for ceremony, and none at all for tonguing arses, so Rogont's banquet of the doomed came close to a nightmare. Benna had been the one for feasting, form and flattery. He would have loved this — pointing, laughing, slapping backs with the worst of them. If he'd found a moment clear of soaking up the flattery of people who despised him, he would have leaned over, and touched her arm with a soothing hand, and whispered in her ear to grin and take it. Baring her teeth in a rictus snarl was about as close as she could come.

She had a bastard of a headache, pulsing away down the side where the coins were screwed, and the genteel rattle of cutlery might as well have been nails hammered into her face. Her guts seemed to have been cramping up ever since she left Faithful drowned on the millwheel. It was the best she could do not to turn to Rogont and spew, and spew, and spew all over his gold-embroidered white coat.

He leaned towards her with polite concern. "Why so glum, General Murcatto?"

"Glum?" She swallowed the rising acid enough to speak. "Orso's army are on their way."

Rogont turned his wine glass slowly round and round by the stem. "So I hear. Ably assisted by your old mentor Nicomo Cosca. The scouts of the Thousand Swords have already reached Menzes Hill, overlooking the fords."

"No more delays, then."

"It would appear not. My designs on glory will soon be ground into the dust. As such designs often are."

"You sure the night before your own destruction is the best time to celebrate?"

"The day after might be too late."

"Huh." True enough. "Perhaps you'll get a miracle."

"I've never been a great believer in divine intervention."

"No? What are they here for, then?" Monza jerked her head towards a knot of Gurkish just below the high table, dressed in the white robes and skullcaps of the priesthood.

The duke peered down at them. "Oh, their help goes well beyond the spiritual. They are emissaries of the Prophet Khalul. Duke Orso has his allies in the Union, the backing of their banks. I must find friends of my own. And even the Emperor of Gurkhul kneels before the Prophet."

"Everyone kneels to someone, eh? I guess Emperor and Prophet can console each other after their priests bring news of your head on a spike."

"They'll soon get over it. Styria is a sideshow to them. I daresay they're already preparing the next battlefield."

"I hear the war never ends." She drained her glass and slung it rattling back across the wood. Maybe they pressed the best wine in the world in Ospria, but it tasted of vomit to her. Everything did. Her life was made of sick. Sick and frequent, painful, watery shits. Raw-gummed, saw-tongued, rough-toothed, sore-arsed. A horse-faced servant in a powdered wig flowed around her shoulder and let fall a long stream of wine into the empty glass, as though flourishing the bottle as far above her as possible would make it taste better. He retreated with consummate ease. Retreat was the speciality down in Ospria, after all. She reached for the glass again. The most recent smoke had stopped her hand shaking, but nothing more.

So she prayed for mindless, shameful, stupefying drunkenness to swarm over and blot out the misery.

She let her eyes crawl over Ospria's richest and most useless citizens. If you really looked for it, the banquet had an edge of shrill hysteria. Drinking too much. Talking too fast. Laughing too loud. Nothing like a dash of imminent annihilation to lower the inhibitions. The one consolation of Rogont's coming rout was that a good number of these fools would lose everything along with him.

"You sure I should be up here?" she grunted.

"Someone has to be." Rogont glanced sideways at the girlish Countess Cotarda of Affoia without great enthusiasm. "The noble League of Eight, it seems, has become a League of Two." He leaned close. "And to be entirely honest I'm wondering if it's not too late for me to get out of it. The sad fact is I'm running short of notable guests."

"So I'm an exhibit to stiffen your wilting prestige, am I?"

"Exactly so. A perfectly charming one, though. And those stories about my wilting are all scurrilous rumours, I assure you." Monza couldn't find the strength even to be irritated, let alone amused, and settled for a weary snort. "You should eat something." He gestured at her untouched plate with his fork. "You look thin."

"I'm sick." That and her right hand hurt so badly she could scarcely hold the knife. "I'm always sick."

"Really? Something you ate?" Rogont forked meat into his mouth with all the relish of a man likely to live out the week. "Or something you did?"

"Maybe it's just the company."

"I wouldn't be at all surprised. My Aunt Sefeline was always revolted by me. She was a woman much prone to nausea. You remind me of her in a way. Sharp mind, great talents, will of iron, but a weaker stomach than might have been expected."

"Sorry to disappoint you." The dead knew she disappointed herself enough.

"Me? Oh, quite the reverse, I assure you. We are none of us made from flint, eh?"

If only. Monza gagged down more wine and scowled at the glass. A year ago, she'd had nothing but contempt for Rogont. She remembered laughing with Benna and Faithful over what a coward he was, what a treacherous ally. Now Benna was dead, she'd murdered Faithful and she'd run to Rogont for shelter like a wayward child to her rich uncle. An uncle who couldn't even protect himself, in this case. But he was far better company than the alternative. Her eyes were dragged reluctantly towards the bottom of the long table on the right, where Shivers sat alone.

The hard fact was he sickened her. It was an effort just to stand beside him, let alone touch him. It was far more than the simple ugliness of his maimed face. She'd seen enough that was ugly, and done enough too, to have no trouble at least pretending to be comfortable around it. It was the silences, when before she couldn't shut him up. They were full of debts she couldn't pay. She'd see that skewed, dead ruin of an eye and remember him whispering at her, *It should've been you.* And she'd know it should have been. When he did talk he said nothing about doing the right thing anymore, nothing about being a better man. Maybe it should have pleased her to have won that argument. She'd tried hard enough. But all she could think was that she'd taken a halfway decent man and somehow made a halfway evil one. She wasn't only rotten herself, she rotted everything she touched.

Shivers sickened her, and the fact she was disgusted when she knew she should have been grateful only sickened her even more.

"I'm wasting time," she hissed, more at her glass than anyone else.

Rogont sighed. "We all are. Just passing the ugly moments until our ignominious deaths in the least horrible manner we can find."

"I should be gone." She tried to make a fist of her gloved hand, but the pain only made her weaker now. "Find a way...find a way to kill Orso." But she was so tired she could hardly find the strength to say it.

"Revenge? Truly?"

"Revenge."

"I would be crushed if you were to leave."

She could hardly be bothered to take care what she said. "Why the hell would you want me?"

"I, want you?" Rogont's smile slipped for a moment. "I can delay no longer, Monzcarro. Soon, perhaps tomorrow, there will be a great battle. One that will decide the fate of Styria. What could be more valuable than the advice of one of Styria's greatest soldiers?"

"I'll see if I can find you one," she muttered.

"And you have many friends."

"Me?" She couldn't think of a single one alive.

"The people of Talins love you still." He raised his eyebrows at the gathering, some of them still glowering at her with scant friendliness. "Less popular here, of course, but that only serves to prove the point. One man's villain is another's hero, after all."

"They think I'm dead in Talins, and don't care into the bargain." She hardly cared herself.

"On the contrary, agents of mine are in the process of making the citizens well aware of your triumphant survival. Bills posted at every crossroads dispute Duke Orso's story, charge him with your attempted murder and proclaim your imminent return. The people care deeply, believe me, with that bottomless passion common folk sometimes have for great figures they have never met, and never will. If nothing else, it turns them further against Orso, and gives him difficulties at home."

"Politics, eh?" She drained her glass. "Small gestures, when war is knocking at your gates."

"We all make the gestures we can. But in war and politics both you are still an asset to be courted." His smile was back now, and broader than ever. "Besides, what extra reason should a man require to keep cunning and beautiful women close at hand?"

She scowled sideways. "Fuck yourself."

"When I must." He looked straight back at her. "But I'd much rather have help."

You look almost as bitter as I feel."

"Eh?" Shivers prised his scowl from the happy couple. "Ah." There was a woman talking to him. "Oh." She was very good to look at, so much that she seemed to have a glow about her. Then he saw everything had a glow. He was drunk as shit.

She seemed different from the rest, though. Necklace of red stones round her long neck, white dress that hung loose, like the ones he'd seen black women wearing in Westport, but she was very pale. There was something easy in the way she stood, no stiff manners to her. Something open in her smile. For a moment, it almost had him smiling with her. First time in a while.

"Is there space here?" She spoke Styrian with a Union accent. An outsider, like him.

"You want to sit...with me?"

"Why not, do you carry the plague?"

"With my luck I wouldn't be surprised." He turned the left side of his face towards her. "This seems to keep most folk well clear o' me by itself, though."

Her eyes moved over it, then back, and her smile didn't flicker. "We all have our scars. Some of us on the outside, some of us—"

"The ones on the inside don't take quite such a toll on the looks, though, eh?"

"I've found that looks are overrated."

Shivers looked her slowly up and down, and enjoyed it. "Easy for you to say, you've plenty to spare."

"Manners." She puffed out her cheeks as she looked round the hall. "I'd despaired of finding any among this crowd. I swear, you must be the only honest man here."

"Don't count on it." Though he was grinning wide enough. There was never a bad time for flattery from a fine-looking woman, after all. He had his pride. She held out one hand to him and he blinked at it. "I kiss it, do I?"

"If you like. It won't dissolve."

It was soft and smooth. Nothing like Monza's hand — scarred, tanned, callused as any Named Man's. Even less like her other one, twisted as a nettle root under that glove. Shivers pressed his lips to the woman's knuckles, caught a giddy whiff of scent. Like flowers, and something else that made the breath sharpen in his throat.

"I'm, er . . . Caul Shivers."

"I know."

"You do?"

"We've met before, though briefly. Carlot dan Eider is my name."

"Eider?" Took him a moment to place it. A half-glimpsed face in the mist. The woman in the red coat, in Sipani. Prince Ario's lover. "You're the one that Monza—"

"Beat, blackmailed, destroyed and left for dead? That would be me." She frowned up towards the high table. "Monza, is it? Not only first-name terms, but an affectionate shortening. The two of you must be very close."

"Close enough." Nowhere near as close as they had been, though, in Visserine. Before they took his eye.

"And yet she sits up there, with the great Duke Rogont, and you sit down here, with the beggars and the embarrassments."

Like she knew his own thoughts. His fury flickered up again and he tried to steer the talk away from it. "What brings you here?"

"After the carnage in Sipani I had no other choices. Duke Orso is doubtless offering a pretty price for my head. I've spent the last three months expecting every person I passed to stab me, poison me, throttle me, or worse."

"Huh. I know that feeling."

"Then you have my sympathy."

"The dead know I could do with some."

"You can have all mine, for what that's worth. You're just as much a piece in this sordid little game as I am, no? And you've lost even more than I. Your eye. Your face."

She didn't seem to move, but she seemed to keep getting closer. Shivers hunched his shoulders. "I reckon."

"Duke Rogont is an old acquaintance. A somewhat unreliable man, though undoubtedly a handsome one."

"I reckon," he managed to grate out.

"I was forced to throw myself upon his mercy. A hard landing, but some succour, for a while. Though it seems he has found a new diversion now."

"Monza?" The fact he'd been thinking it himself all night didn't help any. "She ain't like that."

Carlot dan Eider gave a disbelieving snort. "Really? Not a treacherous, murdering liar who'll use anyone and anything to get her way? She betrayed Nicomo Cosca, no, and stole his chair? Why do you think Duke Orso tried to kill her? Because it was his chair she was planning to steal next." The drink had made him half-stupid, he couldn't think of a thing to say to it. "Why not use Rogont to get her way? Or is she in love with someone else?"

"No," he growled. "Well... how would I know — fucking no! You've got it twisted!"

She touched one hand to her pale chest. "*I* have it twisted? There's a reason why they call her the Snake of Talins! A snake loves nothing but itself!"

"You'd say anything. She used you in Sipani. You hate her!"

"I'd shed no tears over her corpse, that's true. The man who put a blade in her could have my gratitude and more besides. But that doesn't make me a liar." She was halfway to whispering in his ear. "Monzcarro Murcatto, the Butcher of Caprile? They murdered children there." He could almost feel her breath on him, his skin tingling with having her so near, anger and lust all mangled hot together. "Murdered! In the streets! She wasn't even faithful to her brother, from what I hear —"

"Eh?" Shivers wished he'd drunk less, the hall was getting some spin to it.

"You didn't know?"

"Know what?" An odd mix of curiosity, and fear, and disgust creeping up on him.

Eider laid one hand on his arm, close enough that he caught another waft of scent — sweet, dizzying, sickening. "She and her brother were *lovers*." She purred the last word, dragging it out long.

"What?" His scarred cheek was burning like he'd been slapped.

"Lovers. They used to sleep together, like husband and wife. They used to *fuck* each other. It's no kind of secret. Ask anyone. Ask her."

Shivers found he could hardly breathe. He should've known it. Few things made sense now had tripped him at the time. He had known it, maybe. But still he felt tricked. Betrayed. Laughed at. Like a fish tickled

439

from a stream and left choking. After all he'd done for her, after all he'd lost. The rage boiled up in him so hot he could hardly keep hold of himself.

"Shut your fucking mouth!" He flung Eider's hand off. "You think I don't see you goading me?" He was up from his bench somehow, standing over her, hall tipping around him, blurred lights and faces swaying. "You take me for a fool, woman? D'you set me at nothing?"

Instead of cringing back she came forwards, pressing against him almost, eyes seeming big as dinner plates. "Me? You've made no sacrifices for me! Am *I* the one who's cut you off? Am *I* the one who sets you at nothing?"

Shivers' face was on fire. The blood was battering at his skull, so hard it felt like it might pop his eye right out. Except it was burned out already. He gave a strangled sort of a yelp, throat closed up with fury. He staggered back, since it was that or throttle her, lurched straight into a servant, knocking his silver tray from his hands, glasses falling, bottle shattering, wine spraying.

"Sir, I most humbly—"

Shivers' left fist thudded into his ribs and twisted him sideways, right crunched into the man's face before he could fall. He bounced off the wall and sprawled in the wreckage of his bottles. There was blood on Shivers' fist. Blood, and a white splinter between his fingers. A piece of tooth. What he wanted, more'n anything, was to kneel over this bastard, take his head in his hands and smash it against the beautiful carvings on the wall until his brains came out. He almost did it.

But instead he made himself turn. Made himself turn and stumble away.

Time crawled.

Monza lay on her side, back to Shivers, at the very edge of the bed. Keeping as much space between them as she possibly could without rolling onto the floor. The first traces of dawn were creeping from between the curtains now, turning the room dirty grey. The wine was wearing through and leaving her more nauseous, weary, hopeless than ever. Like a wave washing up on a dirty beach that you hope will wash it clean, but only sucks back out and leaves a mass of dead fish behind it.

She tried to think what Benna would have said. What he'd have done, to make her feel better. But she couldn't remember what his voice had sounded like anymore. He was leaking away, and taking the best of her with him. She thought of him a boy, long ago, small and sickly and helpless. Needing her to take care of him. She thought of him a man, laughing, riding up the mountain to Fontezarmo. Still needing her to take care of him. She knew what colour his eyes had been. She knew there had been creases at their corners, from smiling often. But she couldn't see his smile.

Instead the faces that came to her in all their bloodied detail were the five men she'd killed. Gobba, fumbling at Friendly's garrotte with his great bloated, ruined hands. Mauthis, flapping around on his back like a puppet, gurgling pink foam. Ario, hand to his neck as black blood spurted from him. Ganmark, grinning up at her, stuck through the back with Stolicus' outsize sword. Faithful, drowned and dripping, dangling from his waterwheel, no worse than her.

The faces of the five men she'd killed, and of the two she hadn't. Eager little Foscar, barely even a man himself. And Orso, of course. Grand Duke Orso, who'd loved her like a daughter.

Monza, Monza, what would I do without you…

She tore the blankets back and swung her sweaty legs from the bed, dragged her trousers on, shivering though it was too hot, head pounding with worn-out wine.

"What you doing?" came Shivers' croaky voice.

"Need a smoke." Her fingers were trembling so badly she could hardly turn the lamp up.

"Maybe you should be smoking less, think of that?"

"Thought of it." She fumbled with the lump of husk, wincing as she moved her ruined fingers. "Decided against."

"It's the middle of the night."

"Go to sleep, then."

"Shitty fucking habit." He was sitting up on the side of the bed, broad back to her, head turned so he was frowning out of the corner of his one good eye.

"You're right. Maybe I should take up knocking servants' teeth out instead." She picked up her knife and started hacking husk into the bowl of the pipe, scattering dust. "Rogont wasn't much impressed, I can tell you that."

"Wasn't long ago you weren't much impressed with him, as I recall. Seems your feelings about folk change with the wind, though, don't it?"

Her head was splitting. She'd no wish to talk to him, let alone argue. But it's at times like those people bite each other hardest. "What's eating at you?" she snapped, knowing full well already and not wanting to hear about it either.

"What d'you think?"

"You know what, I've my own problems."

"You leaving me, is what!"

She'd have jumped at the chance. "Leaving you?"

"Tonight! Down with the shit while you sat up there lording it with the Duke of Delay!"

"You think I was in charge of the fucking *seating*?" she sneered at him. "He put me there to make him look good, is all."

There was a pause. He turned his head away from her, shoulders hunching. "Well. I guess looking good ain't something I can help with these days."

She twitched — awkward, annoyed. "Rogont can help me. That's all. Foscar's out there, with Orso's army. Foscar's out there..." And he had to die, whatever the costs.

"Vengeance, eh?"

"They killed my brother. I shouldn't have to explain it to you. You know how I feel."

"No. I don't."

She frowned. "What about your brother? Thought you said the Bloody-Nine killed him? I thought—"

"I hated my fucking brother. Folk called him Skarling reborn, but the man was a bastard. He'd show me how to climb trees, and fish, nick me under the chin and laugh when our father was there. When he was gone, he used to kick me 'til I couldn't breathe. He said I'd killed our mother. All I did was be born." His voice was hollow, no anger left in it. "When I heard he was dead, I wanted to laugh, but I cried instead because everyone else was. I swore vengeance on his killer and all the rest 'cause, well, there's a form to be followed, ain't there? Wouldn't want to fall short. But when I heard the Bloody-Nine nailed my bastard of a brother's head up, I didn't know whether I hated the man for doing it, or hated that he'd robbed me o' the chance, or wanted to kiss him for the favour like you'd kiss...a brother, I guess..."

For a moment she was about to get up, go to him, put her hand on his shoulder. Then his one eye moved towards her, cold and narrow. "But you'd know all about that, I reckon. Kissing your brother."

The blood pounded suddenly behind her eyes, worse than ever. "What my brother was to me is my fucking business!" She realised she was stabbing at him with the knife, tossed it away across the table. "I'm not in the habit of explaining myself. I don't plan to start with the men I hire!"

"That's what I am to you, is it?"

"What else would you be?"

"After what I've done for you? After what I've lost?"

She flinched, hands trembling worse than ever. "Well paid, aren't you?"

"Paid?" He leaned towards her, pointing at his face. "How much is my eye worth, you evil cunt?"

She gave a strangled growl, jerked up from the chair, snatched up the lamp, turned her back on him and made for the door to the balcony.

"Where you going?" His voice had turned suddenly wheedling, as if he knew he'd stepped too far.

"Clear of your self-pity, bastard, before I'm sick!" She ripped the door open and stepped out into the cold air.

"Monza—" He was sitting slumped on the bed, the saddest sort of look on his face. On the half of it that still worked, anyway. Broken. Hopeless. Desperate. Fake eye pointing off sideways. He looked as if he was about to weep, to fall down, to beg to be forgiven.

She slammed the door shut. It suited her to have an excuse. She preferred the passing guilt of turning her back on him to the endless guilt of facing him. Much, much preferred it.

The view from the balcony might well have been among the most breathtaking in the world. Ospria dropped away below, a madman's maze of streaky copper roofs, each one of the four tiers of the city surrounded by its own battlemented walls and towers. Tall buildings of old, pale stone crowded tight behind them, narrow-windowed and striped with black marble, pressed in alongside steeply climbing streets, crooked alleys of a thousand steps, deep and dark as the canyons of mountain streams. A few early lights shone from scattered windows, flickering dots of sentries' torches moved on the walls. Beyond them the valley of the Sulva was sunk in the shadows of the mountains, only the faintest glimmer of the river in its bottom. At the summit of the highest hill on the other side, against the dark velvet of the sky, perhaps the pinpricks of the campfires of the Thousand Swords.

Not a place for anyone with a fear of heights.

But Monza had other things on her mind. All that mattered was to make nothing matter, and as fast as she could. She crabbed down into the deepest corner, hunched jealously over her lamp and her pipe like a freezing man over a last tongue of fire. She gripped the mouthpiece in her teeth, lifted the rattling hood with trembling hands, leaned forwards—

A sudden gust came up, swirled into the corner, whipped her greasy hair in her eyes. The flame fluttered and went out. She stayed there, frozen, staring at the dead lamp in achy confusion, then sweaty disbelief. Her face went slack with horror as the implications fumbled their way into her thumping head.

No flame. No smoke. No way back.

She sprang up, took a step towards the parapet and flung the lamp out across the city with all her strength. She tilted her head back, taking a great breath, grabbed the parapet, rocked forwards and screamed her lungs out. Screamed her hatred at the lamp as it tumbled down, at the wind that had blown it out, at the city spread out below her, at the valley beyond it, at the world and everyone in it.

In the distance, the angry sun was beginning to creep up behind the mountains, staining the sky around their darkened slopes with blood.

No More Delays

Cosca stood before the mirror, making the final adjustments to his fine lace collar, turning his five rings so the jewels faced precisely outwards, adjusting each bristle of his beard to his satisfaction. It had taken him an hour and a half, by Friendly's calculation, to make ready. Twelve passes of the razor against the sharpening strap. Thirty-one movements to trim away the stubble. One tiny nick left under his jaw. Thirteen tugs of the tweezers to purge the nose hairs. Forty-five buttons done up. Four pairs of hooks and eyes. Eighteen straps to tighten and buckles to fasten.

"And all is ready. Master Friendly, I wish you to take the post of first sergeant of the brigade."

"I know nothing about war." Nothing except that it was madness, and threw him out of all compass.

"You need know nothing. The role would be to keep close to me, to keep silent but sinister, to support and follow my lead where necessary and most of all to watch my back and yours. The world is full of treachery, my friend! The odd bloody task too, and on occasion to count out sums of money paid and received, to take inventory of the numbers of men, weapons and sundries at our disposal…"

That was, to the letter, what Friendly had done for Sajaam, in Safety then outside it. "I can do that."

"Better than any man alive, I never doubt! Could you begin by fastening this buckle for me? Bloody armourers. I swear they only put it there to vex me." He jerked his thumb at the side strap on his gilded breastplate, stood tall and held his breath, sucking in his gut as Friendly tugged it closed.

"Thank you, my friend, you are a rock! An anchor! An axle of calm about which I madly spin. Whatever would I do without you?"

Friendly did not understand the question. "The same things."

"No, no. Not the same. Though we are not long acquainted, I feel there is...an understanding between us. A bond. We are much alike, you and I."

Friendly sometimes felt he feared every word he had to speak, every new person and every new place. Only by counting everything and anything could he claw by his fingernails from morning to night. Cosca, by sharp contrast, drifted effortlessly through life like blossom on the wind. The way that he could talk, smile, laugh, make others do the same seemed like magic as surely as when Friendly had seen the Gurkish woman Ishri form from nowhere. "We are nothing alike."

"You see my point exactly! We are entire opposites, like earth and air, yet we are both...missing something...that others take for granted. Some part of that machinery that makes a man fit into society. But we each miss different cogs on the wheel. Enough that we may make, perhaps, between the two of us, one half-decent human."

"One whole from two halves."

"An extraordinary whole, even! I have never been a reliable man — no, no, don't try to deny it." Friendly had not. "But you, my friend, are constant, clear-sighted, single-minded. You are...*honest* enough...to make me more honest."

"I've spent most of my life in prison."

"Where you did more to spread honesty among Styria's most dangerous convicts than all the magistrates in the land, I do not doubt!" Cosca slapped Friendly on his shoulder. "Honest men are so very rare, they are often mistaken for criminals, for rebels, for madmen. What were your crimes, anyway, but to be different?"

"Robbery the first time, and I served seven years. When they caught me again there were eighty-four counts, with fourteen murders."

Cosca cocked an eyebrow. "But were you truly guilty?"

"Yes."

He frowned for a moment, then waved it away. "Nobody's perfect. Let's leave the past behind us." He gave his feather a final flick, jammed his hat onto his head at its accustomed rakish angle. "How do I look?"

Black pointed knee-boots set with huge golden spurs in the likeness of bull's heads. Breastplate of black steel with golden adornments. Black velvet sleeves slashed with yellow silk, cuffs of Sipanese lace hanging at the wrists. A sword with flamboyant gilded basketwork and matching dagger, slung ridiculously low. An enormous hat, its yellow feather threatening to brush the ceiling. "Like a pimp who lost his mind in a military tailor's."

Cosca broke out in a radiant grin. "Precisely the look I was aiming at! So to business, Sergeant Friendly!" He strode forwards, flung the tent flap wide and stepped through into the bright sunlight.

Friendly stuck close behind. It was his job, now.

The applause began the moment he stepped up onto the big barrel. He had ordered every officer of the Thousand Swords to attend his address, and here they were indeed; clapping, whooping, cheering and whistling to the best of their ability. Captains to the fore, lieutenants crowding further back, ensigns clustering at the rear. In most bodies of fighting men these would have been the best and brightest, the youngest and highest born, the bravest and most idealistic. This being a brigade of mercenaries, they were the polar opposite. The longest serving, the most steeped in vice, the slyest back-stabbers, most practised grave-robbers and fastest runners, the men with fewest illusions and most betrayals under their belts. Cosca's very own constituency, in other words.

Sesaria, Victus and Andiche lined up beside the barrel, all three clapping gently, the biggest, blackest crooks of the lot. Unless you counted Cosca himself, of course. Friendly stood not far behind, arms tightly folded, eyes darting over the crowd. Cosca wondered if he was counting them, and decided it was a virtual certainty.

"No, no! No, no! You do me too much honour, boys! You shame me with your fond attentions!" And he waved the adulation down, fading into an expectant silence. A mass of scarred, pocked, sunburned and diseased faces turned towards him, waiting. As hungry as a gang of bandits. They were one.

"Brave heroes of the Thousand Swords!" His voice rang out into the balmy morning. "Well, let us say brave men of the Thousand Swords, at least. Let us say men, anyway!" Scattered laughter, a whoop of approval. "My boys, you all know my stamp! Some of you have fought beside me... or at any rate in front." More laughter. "The rest of you know my...spotless reputation." And more yet. "You all know that I, above all, am one of you. A soldier, yes! A fighter, of course! But one who would much prefer to sheathe his weapon." And he gave a gentle cough as he adjusted his groin. "Than draw his blade!" And he slapped the hilt of his sword to widespread merriment.

"Let it never be said that we are not masters and journeymen of the glorious profession of arms! As much so as any lapdog at some noble's boots! Men strong of sinew!" And he slapped Sesaria's great arm. "Men sharp of wits!" And he pointed at Andiche's greasy head. "Men hungry for glory!" He jerked his thumb towards Victus. "Let it never be said we will not brave risks for our rewards! But let the risks be kept as lean as possible, and the rewards most hearty!" Another swell of approval.

"Your employer, the young Prince Foscar, was keen that you carry the lower ford and meet the enemy head on in pitched battle..." Nervous silence. "But I declined! Though you are paid to fight, I told him, you are far keener on the pay than the fighting!" A rousing cheer. "We'll wet our boots higher up, therefore, and with considerably lighter opposition! And whatever occurs today, however things may seem, you may always depend upon it that I have your...best interests closest to my own heart!" And he rubbed his fingers against his thumb to an even louder cheer.

"I will not insult you by calling for courage, for steadfastness, for loyalty and honour! All these things I already know you possess in the highest degree!" Widespread laughter. "So to your units, officers of the Thousand Swords, and await my order! May Mistress Luck be always at your side and mine! She is drawn, after all, to those who least deserve her! May darkness find us victorious! Uninjured! And above all — rich!"

There was a rousing cheer. Shields and weapons, mailed and plated arms, gauntleted fists shaken in the air.

"Cosca!"

"Nicomo Cosca!"

"The captain general!"

He hopped smiling down from his barrel as the officers began to disperse, Sesaria and Victus going with them to make their regiments — or their gangs of opportunists, criminals and thugs — ready for action. Cosca strolled away towards the brow of the hill, the beautiful valley opening out before him, shreds of misty cloud clinging to the hollows in its sides. Ospria looked proudly down on all from her mountain, fairer than ever by daylight, all cream-coloured stone banded with blue-black stripes of masonry,

roofs of copper turned pale green by the years or, on a few buildings recently
repaired, shining brilliantly in the morning glare.

"Nice speech," said Andiche. "If your taste runs to speeches."

"Most kind. Mine does."

"You've still got the trick of it."

"Ah, my friend, you have seen captain generals come and go. You well
know there is a happy time, after a man is elevated to command, in which
he can say and do no wrong in the eyes of his men. Like a husband in
the eyes of his new wife, just following the marriage. Alas, it cannot last.
Sazine, myself, Murcatto, ill-fated Faithful Carpi, our tides all flowed out
with varying speed and left each one of us betrayed or dead. And so shall
mine again. I will have to work harder for my applause in future."

Andiche split a toothy grin. "You could always appeal to the cause."

"Hah!" Cosca lowered himself into the captain general's chair, set out in
the dappled shade of a spreading olive tree with a fine view of the glittering fords. "My curse on fucking causes! Nothing but big excuses. I never
saw men act with such ignorance, violence and self-serving malice as when
energised by a just cause." He squinted at the rising sun, brilliant in the
bright blue sky. "As we will no doubt witness, in the coming hours…"

Rogont drew his sword with a faint ring of steel.

"Free men of Ospria! Free men of the League of Eight! Great hearts!"

Monza turned her head and spat. Speeches. Better to move fast and hit
hard than waste time talking about it. If she'd found herself with time for a
speech before a battle she would have reckoned she'd missed her moment,
pulled back and looked for another. It took a man with a bloated sense of
himself to think his words might make all the difference.

So it was no surprise that Rogont had his all well worked out.

"Long have you followed me! Long have you waited for the day you
would prove your mettle! My thanks for your patience! My thanks for your
courage! My thanks for your faith!" He stood in his stirrups and raised his
sword high above his head. "Today we fight!"

He cut a pretty picture, there was no denying that. Tall, strong and handsome, dark curls stirred by the breeze. His armour was studded with glittering gems, steel polished so bright it was almost painful to look at. But his
men had made an effort too. Heavy infantry in the centre, well armoured

under a forest of polearms or clutching broadswords in their gauntleted fists, shields and blue surcoats all stitched with the white tower of Ospria. Light infantry on the wings, all standing to stiff attention in studded leather, pikes kept carefully vertical. Archers too, steel-capped flatbowmen, hooded longbowmen. A detachment of Affoians on the far right slightly spoiled the pristine organisation, weapons mismatched and their ranks a little skewed, but still a good stretch neater than any men Monza had ever led.

And that was before she turned to the cavalry lined up behind her, a gleaming row in the shadow of the outermost wall of Ospria. Every man noble of birth and spirit, horses in burnished bardings, helmets with sculpted crests, lances striped, polished and ready to be steeped in glory. Like something out of a badly written storybook.

She snorted some snot from the back of her nose, and spat again. In her experience, and she had plenty, clean men were the keenest to get into battle and the keenest to get clear of it.

Rogont was busy cranking up his rhetoric to new heights. "We stand now upon a battlefield! Here, in after years, men will say heroes fought! Here, men will say the fate of Styria was decided! Here, my friends, here, on our own soil! In sight of our own homes! Before the ancient walls of proud Ospria!" Enthusiastic cheering from the companies drawn up closest to him. She doubted the rest could hear a word of it. She doubted most could even see him. For those that could, she doubted the sight of a shiny speck in the distance would do much for their morale.

"Your fate is in your own hands!" Their fate had been in Rogont's hands, and he'd frittered it away. Now it was in Cosca's and Foscar's, and it was likely to be a bloody one.

"Now for freedom!" Or at best a better-looking brand of tyranny.

"Now for glory!" A glorious place in the mud at the bottom of the river.

Rogont jerked on the reins with his free hand and made his chestnut charger rear, lashing at the air with its front hooves. The effect was only slightly spoiled by a few heavy clods of shit that happened to fall from its rear end at the same moment. It sped off past the massed ranks of infantry, each company cheering Rogont as he passed, lifting their spears in unison and giving a roar. It might have been an impressive sight. But Monza had seen it all before, with grim results. A good speech wasn't much compensation for being outnumbered three to one.

The Duke of Delay trotted up towards her and the rest of his staff, the same gathering of heavily decorated and lightly experienced men she'd made fools of in the baths at Puranti, arrayed for battle now rather than the parade ground. Safe to say they hadn't warmed to her. Safe to say she didn't care.

"Nice speech," she said. "If your taste runs to speeches."

"Most kind." Rogont turned his horse and drew it up beside her. "Mine does."

"I'd never have guessed. Nice armour too."

"A gift from the young Countess Cotarda." A knot of ladies had gathered to observe at the top of the slope in the shade of the city walls. They sat side-saddle in bright dresses and twinkling jewels, as if they were expecting to attend a wedding rather than a slaughter. Cotarda herself, milk-pale in flowing yellow silks, gave a shy wave and Rogont returned it without much vigour. "I think her uncle has it in mind that we might marry. If I live out the day, of course."

"Young love. My heart is all aglow."

"Damp down your sentimental soul, she's not at all my type. I like a woman with a little... bite. Still, it is a fine armour. An impartial observer might mistake me for some kind of hero."

"Huh. 'Desperation bakes heroes from the most rotten flour,' Farans wrote."

Rogont blew out a heavy sigh. "We are running short of time for this particular loaf to rise."

"I thought that talk about you having trouble rising was all scurrilous rumours..." There was something familiar about one of the ladies in Countess Cotarda's party, more simply dressed than the others, long-necked and elegant. She turned her head and then her horse, began to ride down the grassy slope towards them. Monza felt a cold twinge of recognition. "What the hell is she doing here?"

"Carlot dan Eider? You know her?"

"I know her." If punching someone in the face in Sipani counted.

"An old... friend." He said the word in a way that implied more than that. "She came to me in peril of her life, begging for protection. Under what circumstances could I possibly refuse?"

"If she'd been ugly?"

Rogont shrugged with a faint rattling of steel. "I freely admit it, I'm every bit as shallow as the next man."

"Far shallower, your Excellency." Eider nudged her horse up close to them, and gracefully inclined her head. "And who is this? The Butcher of Caprile! I thought you were but a thief, blackmailer, murderer of innocents and keen practiser of incest! Now it seems you are a soldier too."

"Carlot dan Eider, such a surprise! I thought this was a battle but now it smells more like a brothel. Which is it?"

Eider raised one eyebrow at the massed regiments. "Judging by all the swords I'd guess... the former? But I suppose you'd be the expert. I saw you at Cardotti's and I see you here, equally comfortable dressed as warrior or whore."

"Strange how it goes, eh? I wear the whore's clothes and you do the whore's business."

"Perhaps I should turn my hand to murdering children instead?"

"For pity's sake, enough!" snapped Rogont. "Am I doomed to be always surrounded by women, showing off? Have the two of you not noticed I have a battle to lose? All I need now is for that vanishing devil Ishri to spring out of my horse's arse and give me my death of shock to complete the trio! My Aunt Sefeline was the same, always trying to prove she had the biggest cock in the chamber! If all your purpose is to posture, the two of you can get that done behind the city walls and leave me out here to ponder my downfall alone."

Eider bowed her head. "Your Excellency, I would hate to intrude. I am here merely to wish you the best of fortune."

"Sure you wouldn't care to fight?" snapped Monza at her.

"Oh, there are other ways of fighting than bloody in the mud, Murcatto." She leaned from her saddle and hissed it. "You'll see!"

"Your Excellency!" A shrill call, soon joined by others, a ripple of excitement spreading through the horsemen. One of Rogont's officers was pointing over the river, towards the ridge on the far side of the valley. There was movement there against the pale sky. Monza nudged her horse towards it, sliding out a borrowed eyeglass and scanning across the ridge.

A scattering of horsemen came first. Outriders, officers and standard-bearers, banners held high, white flags carrying the black cross of Talins, the names of battles stitched along their edges in red and silver thread. It hardly helped that a good number of the victories she'd had a hand in herself. A wide column of men tramped into view behind them, marching steadily down the brown stripe of the Imperial road towards the lower ford, spears shouldered.

The foremost regiment stopped and began to spread out about a half-mile from the water. Other columns began to spill from the road, forming battle lines across the valley. There was nothing clever about the plan, as far as she could see.

But they had the numbers. They didn't need to be clever.

"The Talinese have arrived," murmured Rogont, pointlessly.

Orso's army. Men she'd fought alongside this time last year, led to victory at Sweet Pines. Men Ganmark had led until Stolicus fell on him. Men Foscar was leading now. That eager young lad with the fluff moustache who'd laughed with Benna in the gardens of Fontezarmo. That eager young lad she'd sworn to kill. She chewed her lip as she moved the eyeglass across the dusty front ranks, more men and more flooding over the hill behind them.

"Regiments from Etrisani and Cesale on their right wing, some Baolish on their left." Ragged-marching men in fur and heavy chain mail, savage fighters from the hills and the mountains in the far east of Styria.

"The great majority of Duke Orso's regular troops. But where, oh where, are your comrades of the Thousand Swords?"

Monza nodded up towards Menzes Hill, a green lump speckled with olive groves above the upper ford. "I'd bet my life they're there, behind the brow. Foscar will cross the lower ford in strength and give you no choice but to meet him head on. Once you're committed, the Thousand Swords will cross the upper ford unopposed and take you in the flank."

"Very likely. What would be your advice?"

"You should've turned up to Sweet Pines on time. Or Musselia. Or the High Bank."

"Alas, I was late for those battles then. I am extremely late for them now."

"You should have attacked long before this. Taken a gamble as they marched down the Imperial road from Puranti." Monza frowned at the valley, the great number of soldiers on both sides of the river. "You have the smaller force."

"But the better position."

"To get it you gave up the initiative. Lost your chance at surprise. Trapped yourself. The general with the smallest numbers is well advised to stay always on the offensive."

"Stolicus, is it? I never had you down for book learning."

"I know my business, Rogont, books and all."

"My epic thanks to you and your friend Stolicus for explaining my failures. Perhaps one of you might furnish an opinion on how I might now achieve success?"

Monza let her eyes move over the landscape, judging the angles of the slopes, the distances from Menzes Hill to the upper ford, from the upper to the lower, from the striped walls of the city to the river. The position seemed better than it was. Rogont had too much ground to cover and not enough men for the job.

"All you can do now is the obvious. Hit the Talinese with all your archers as they cross, then all your foot as soon as their front ranks touch dry land. Keep the cavalry here to at least hold up the Thousand Swords when they show. Hope to break Foscar quickly, while his feet are in the river, then turn to the mercenaries. They won't stick if they see the game's against them. But breaking Foscar..." She watched the great body of men forming up into lines as wide as the wide ford, more columns belching from the Imperial road to join them. "If Orso thought you had a chance at it he'd have picked a commander more experienced and less valuable. Foscar's got more than twice your numbers on his own, and all he has to do is hold you." She peered up the slope. The Gurkish priests sat observing the battle not far from the Styrian ladies, their white robes bright in the sunlight, their dark faces grim. "If the Prophet sent you a miracle, now might be the time."

"Alas, he sent only money. And kind words."

Monza snorted. "You'll need more than kind words to win today."

"*We'll* need," he corrected, "since you fight beside me. Why do you fight beside me, by the way?"

Because she was too tired and too sick to fight alone anymore. "Seems I can't resist pretty men in lots of trouble. When you held all the cards I fought for Orso. Now look at me."

"Now look at us both." He took in a long breath, and gave a happy sigh.

"What the hell are you so pleased about?"

"Would you rather I despaired?" Rogont grinned at her, handsome and doomed. Maybe the two went together. "If the truth be known, I'm relieved the waiting is over, whatever odds we face. Those of us who carry great responsibilities must learn patience, but I have never had much taste for it."

"That's not your reputation."

"People are more complicated than their reputations, General Murcatto. You should know that. We will settle our business here, today. No more delays." He twitched his horse away to confer with one of his aides, and left Monza slumped in her saddle, arms limp across the bow, frowning up towards Menzes Hill.

She wondered if Nicomo Cosca was up there, squinting towards them through his eyeglass.

Cosca squinted through his eyeglass towards the mass of soldiery on the far side of the river. The enemy, though he held no personal rancour towards them. The battlefield was no place for rancour. Blue flags carrying the white tower of Ospria fluttered above them, but one larger than the others, edged with gold. The standard of the Duke of Delay himself. Horsemen were scattered about it, a group of ladies too, by the look of things, ridden out to watch the battle, all in their best. Cosca fancied he could even see some Gurkish priests, though he could not imagine what their interest might be. He wondered idly whether Monzcarro Murcatto was there. The notion of her sitting side-saddle in floating silks fit for a coronation gave him a brief moment of amusement. The battlefield was most definitely a place for amusement. He lowered his eyeglass, took a swig from his flask and happily closed his eyes, feeling the sun flicker through the branches of the old olive trees.

"Well?" came Andiche's rough voice.

"What? Oh, you know. Still forming up."

"Rigrat sends word the Talinese are beginning their attack."

"Ah! So they are." Cosca sat forwards, training his eyeglass on the ridge to his right. The front ranks of Foscar's foot were close to the river now, spread out across the flower-dotted sward in orderly lines, the hard dirt of the Imperial road invisible beneath that mass of men. He could faintly hear the tramping of their feet, the disembodied calls of their officers, the regular thump, thump of their drums floating on the warm air, and he waved one hand gently back and forth in time. "Quite the spectacle of military splendour!"

He moved his round window on the world down the road to the glittering, slow-flowing water, across it to the far bank and up the slope. The Osprian regiments were deploying to meet them, perhaps a hundred strides above the river. Archers had formed a long line behind them on higher ground, kneeling, making ready their bows. "Do you know, Andiche…

I have a feeling we will shortly witness some bloodshed. Order the men forwards, up behind us here. Fifty strides, perhaps, beyond the brow of the hill."

"But... they'll be seen. We'll lose the surprise—"

"Shit on the surprise. Let them see the battle, and let the battle see them. Give them a taste for it."

"But General—"

"Give the orders, man. Don't fuss."

Andiche turned away, frowning, and beckoned over one of his sergeants. Cosca settled back with a satisfied sigh, stretched his legs out and crossed one highly polished boot over the other. Good boots. How long had it been since he'd last worn good boots? The front rank of Foscar's men were in the river. Wading forwards with grim determination, no doubt, up to their knees in cold water, looking without relish at the considerable body of soldiers drawn up in good order on the high ground to their front. Waiting for the arrows to start falling. Waiting for the charge to come. An unenviable task, forcing that ford. He had to admit to being damn pleased he had talked his way clear of it.

He raised Morveer's flask and wet his lips, just a little.

Shivers heard the faint cries of the orders, the rattling rush of a few hundred shafts loosed together. The first volley went up from Rogont's archers, black splinters drifting, and rained down on the Talinese as they waded on through the shallows.

Shivers shifted in his saddle, rubbed gently at his itching scar as he watched the lines twist and buckle, holes opening up, flags drooping. Some men slowing, wanting to get back, others moving faster, wanting to press on. Fear and anger, two sides to the same coin. No one's favourite job, trying to march tight over bad terrain while men shoot arrows at you. Stepping over corpses. Friends, maybe. The horrible chance of it, knowing a little gust might be the difference between an arrow in the earth by your boot or an arrow through your face.

Shivers had seen battles enough, of course. A lifetime of 'em. He'd watched them play out or listened to the sounds in the distance, waiting to hear the call and take his own part, fretting on his chances, trying to hide his fear from those he led and those he followed. He remembered Black

Well, running through the mist, heart pounding, startling at shadows. The Cumnur, where he'd screamed the war cry with five thousand others as they thundered down the long slope. Dunbrec, where he'd followed Rudd Threetrees in a charge against the Feared, damn near given his life to hold the line. The battle in the High Places, Shanka boiling up out of the valley, mad Easterners trying to climb the wall, fighting back to back with the Bloody-Nine, stand or die. Memories sharp enough to cut himself on — the smells, the sounds, the feel of the air on his skin, the desperate hope and mad anger.

He watched another volley go up, watched the great mass of Talinese coming on through the water, and felt nothing much but curious. No kinship with either side. No sorrow for the dead. No fear for himself. He watched men dropping under the hail of fire, and he burped, and the mild burning up his throat gave him a sight more worry than if the river had suddenly flooded and washed every one of those bastards down there out to the ocean. Drowned the fucking world. He didn't care a shit about the outcome. It wasn't his war.

Which made him wonder why he was ready to fight in it, and more'n likely on the losing side.

His eye twitched from the brewing battle to Monza. She clapped Rogont on the shoulder and Shivers felt his face burn like he'd been slapped. Each time they spoke it stung at him. Her black hair blew back for a moment, showed him the side of her face, jaw set hard. He didn't know if he loved her, or wanted her, or just hated that she didn't want him. She was the scab he couldn't stop picking, the split lip he couldn't stop biting at, the loose thread he couldn't stop tugging 'til his shirt came all to pieces.

Down in the valley the front rank of the Talinese had worse troubles, floundering from the river and up onto the bank, lost their shape from slogging across the ford under fire. Monza shouted something at Rogont, and he called to one of his men. Shivers heard the cries creep up from the slopes below. The order to charge. The Osprian foot lowered their spears, blades a glittering wave as they swung down together, then began to move. Slow at first, then quicker, then breaking into a jog, pouring away from the archers, still loading and firing fast as they could, down the long slope towards the sparkling water, and the Talinese trying to form some kind of line on the bank.

Shivers watched the two sides come together, merge. A moment later he heard the contact, faint on the wind. That rattling, clattering, jangling din of metal, like a hailstorm on a lead roof. Roars, wails, screams from nowhere floating with it. Another volley fell among the ranks still struggling through the water. Shivers watched it all, and burped again.

Rogont's headquarters was quiet as the dead, everyone staring down towards the ford, mouths and eyes wide, faces pale and reins clenched tight with worry. The Talinese had flatbowmen of their own ready now, sent a wave of bolts up from the water, flying flat and hissing among the archers. More'n one fell. Someone started squealing. A rogue bolt thudded into the turf not far from one of Rogont's officers, made his horse startle and near dumped him from the saddle. Monza urged her own mount a pace or two forwards, standing in the stirrups to get a better view, borrowed armour gleaming dully in the morning sun. Shivers frowned.

One way or another, he was here for her. To fight for her. Protect her. Try to make things right between them. Or maybe just hurt her like she'd hurt him. He closed his fist, nails digging into his palm, knuckles sore from knocking that servant's teeth out. They weren't done yet, that much he knew.

All Business

The upper ford was a patch of slow-moving water, sparkling in the morning sun as it broke up in the shallows. A faint track led from the far bank between a few scattered buildings, then through an orchard and up the long slope to a gate in the black-banded outermost wall of Ospria. All seemingly deserted. Rogont's foot were mostly committed to the savage fight at the lower ford. Only a few small units hung back to guard the archers, loading and firing into the mass of men in the midst of the river as fast as they possibly could.

The Osprian cavalry were waiting in the shadow of the walls as a last reserve, but too few, and too far away. The Thousand Swords' path to victory appeared unguarded. Cosca stroked gently at his neck. In his judgement, now was the perfect moment to attack.

Andiche evidently agreed. "Getting hot down there. Should I tell the men to mount up?"

"Let's not trouble them quite yet. It's still early."

"You sure?"

Cosca turned to look evenly back at him. "Do I look unsure?" Andiche puffed out his pitted cheeks, then stomped off to confer with some of his own officers. Cosca stretched out, hands clasped behind his head, and watched the battle slowly develop. "What was I saying?"

"A chance to leave all this behind," said Friendly.

"Ah yes! I had the chance to leave all this behind. Yet I chose to come back. Change is not a simple thing, eh, Sergeant? I entirely see and understand the pointlessness and waste of it all, yet I do it anyway. Does that make me worse or better than the man who does it thinking himself ennobled by a righteous cause? Or the man who does it for his own profit, without the slightest grain of thought for right or wrong? Or are we all the same?"

Friendly only shrugged.

"Men dying. Men maimed. Lives destroyed." He might as well have been reciting a list of vegetables for all the emotion he felt. "I have spent half my life in the business of destruction. The other half in the dogged pursuit of self-destruction. I have created nothing. Nothing but widows, orphans, ruins and misery, a bastard or two, perhaps, and a great deal of vomit. Glory? Honour? My piss is worth more, that at least makes nettles grow." But if his aim was to prick his own conscience into wakefulness it still slumbered on regardless. "I have fought in many battles, Sergeant Friendly."

"How many?"

"A dozen? A score? More? The line between battle and skirmish is a fuzzy one. Some of the sieges dragged on, with many engagements. Do those count as one, or several?"

"You're the soldier."

"And even I don't have the answers. In war, there are no straight lines. What was I saying?"

"Many battles."

"Ah, yes! Many! And though I have tried always to avoid becoming closely involved in the fighting, I have often failed. I am fully aware of what it's like in the midst of that mêlée. The flashing blades. Shields cloven and spears shattered. The crush, the heat, the sweat, the stink of death. The tiny heroics and the petty villainies. Proud flags and honourable men crushed underfoot. Limbs lopped off, showers of blood, split skulls, spilled guts, and all the rest." He raised his eyebrows. "Reasonable to suppose some drownings too, under the circumstances."

"How many, would you say?"

"Difficult to be specific." Cosca thought of the Gurkish drowning in the channel at Dagoska, brave men swept out to sea, their corpses washed up on every tide, and gave a long sigh. "Still, I find I can watch without much sentiment. Is it ruthlessness? Is it the fitting detachment of command? Is it the configuration of the stars at my birth? I find myself always sanguine in the face of death and danger. More so than at any other time. Happy when I should be horrified, fearful when I should be calm. I am a riddle, to be sure, even to myself. I am a back-to-front man, Sergeant Friendly!" He laughed, then chuckled, then sighed, then was silent. "A man upside down and inside out."

"General." Andiche was leaning over him again, lank hair hanging.

"What, for pity's sake? I am trying to philosophise!"

"The Osprians are fully engaged. All their foot are tackling Foscar's troops. They've no reserves but a few horse."

Cosca squinted down towards the valley. "I see that, Captain Andiche. We all quite clearly see that. There is no need to state the obvious."

"Well...we'll sweep those bastards away, no trouble. Give me the order and I'll see to it. We'll get no easier chance."

"Thank you, but it looks dreadfully hot out there now. I am quite comfortable where I am. Perhaps later."

"But why not—"

"It amazes me, that after so long on campaign, the whole business of the chain of command still confounds you! You will find it far less worrisome if, rather than trying to anticipate my orders, you simply wait for me to give them. It really is the simplest of military principles."

Andiche scratched his greasy head. "I understand the concept."

"Then act according to it. Find a shady spot, man, take the weight from your feet. Stop running to nowhere. Take a lesson from my goat. Do you see her fussing?"

The goat lifted her head from the grass between the olive trees for a moment, and bleated.

Andiche put his hands on his hips, winced, stared down at the valley, up at Cosca, frowned at the goat, then turned away and walked off, shaking his head.

"Everyone rushing, rushing, Sergeant Friendly, do we get no peace? Is a quiet moment out of the sun really too much to ask? What was I saying?"

Why isn't he attacking?"

When Monza had seen the Thousand Swords easing onto the brow of the hill, the tiny shapes of men, horses, spears black against the blue morning sky, she'd known they were about to charge. To splash happily across the upper ford and take Rogont's men in the flank, just the way she'd said they would. Just the way she'd have done. To put a bloody end to the battle, to the League of Eight, to her hopes, such as they were. No man was quicker to pluck the easy fruit than Nicomo Cosca, and none quicker to wolf it down than the men she used to lead.

But the Thousand Swords only sat there, in plain view, on top of Menzes Hill, and waited. Waited for nothing. Meanwhile Foscar's Talinese struggled on the banks of the lower ford, at push of pike with Rogont's Osprians, water, ground and slope all set against them, arrows raining down on the men behind the front line with punishing regularity. Bodies were carried by the current, limp shapes washing up on the bank of the river, bobbing in the shallows below the ford.

Still the Thousand Swords didn't move.

"Why show himself in the first place, if he doesn't mean to come down?" Monza chewed at her lip, not trusting it. "Cosca's no fool. Why give away the surprise?"

Duke Rogont only shrugged. "Why complain about it? The longer he waits, the better for us, no? We have enough to worry on with Foscar."

"What's he up to?" Monza stared up at the mass of horsemen ranged across the crest of the hill, beside the olive grove. "What's that old bastard about?"

Colonel Rigrat whipped his well-lathered horse between the tents, sending idle mercenaries scattering, and reined the beast in savagely not far away. He slid from the saddle, nearly fell, tore his boot from the stirrup and stormed up, ripping off his gloves, face flushed with sweaty fury. "Cosca! Nicomo Cosca, damn you!"

"Colonel Rigrat! A fine morning, my young friend! I hope all is well?"

"Well? Why are you not attacking?" He stabbed one finger down towards the river, evidently having misplaced his baton. "We are engaged in the valley! Most hotly engaged!"

"Why, so you are." Cosca rocked forwards and rose smoothly from the captain general's chair. "Perhaps it would be better if we were to discuss this away from the men. Not good form, to bicker. Besides, you're scaring my goat."

"What?"

Cosca patted the animal gently on the back as he passed. "She's the only one who truly understands me. Come to my tent. I have fruit there! Andiche! Come join us!"

He strode off, Rigrat blustering after, Andiche falling into puzzled step behind. Past Nocau, on guard before the flap with his great scimitar drawn, and into the cool, dim interior of the tent, draped all around with the victories of the past. Cosca ran the back of his hand affectionately down one swathe of threadbare cloth, edges blackened by fire. "The flag that hung upon the walls of Muris, during the siege...was it truly a dozen years ago?" He turned to see Friendly sidle through the flap after the others and lurk near the entrance. "I brought it down from the highest parapet with my own hand, you know."

"After you tore it from the hand of the dead hero who was up there first," said Andiche.

"Whatever is the purpose of dead heroes, if not to pass on stolen flags to more prudent fellows in the rank behind?" He snatched the bowl of fruit from the table and shoved it under Rigrat's nose. "You look ill, Colonel. Have a grape."

The man's trembling face was rapidly approaching grape colour. "Grape? Grape?" He lashed at the flap with his gloves. "I demand that you attack at once! I flatly demand it!"

"Attack." Cosca winced. "Across the upper ford?"

"Yes!"

"According to the excellent plan you laid out to me last night?"

"Yes, damn it! Yes!"

"In all honesty, nothing would please me more. I love a good attack, ask anyone, but the problem is...you see..." Pregnant silence stretched out as he spread his hands wide. "I took such an enormous sum of money from Duke Rogont's Gurkish friend not to."

Ishri came from nowhere. Solidified from the shadows at the edges of the tent, slid from the folds in the ancient flags and strutted into being. "Greetings," she said. Rigrat and Andiche both stared at her, equally stunned.

Cosca peered up at the gently flapping roof of the tent, tapping at his pursed lips with one finger. "A dilemma. A moral quandary. I want so badly to attack, but I cannot attack Rogont. And I can scarcely attack Foscar, when his father has also paid me so handsomely. In my youth I jerked this way and that just as the wind blew me, but I am trying earnestly to change, Colonel, as I explained to you the other evening. Really, in all good conscience, the only thing I can do is sit here." He popped a grape into his mouth. "And do nothing."

Rigrat gave a splutter and made a belated grab for his sword, but Friend-ly's big fist was already around the hilt, knife gleaming in his other hand. "No, no, no." The colonel froze as Friendly slid his sword carefully from its sheath and tossed it across the tent.

Cosca snatched it from the air and took a couple of practice swipes. "Fine steel, Colonel, I congratulate you on your choice of blades, if not of strategy."

"You were paid by both? To fight neither?" Andiche was smiling ear to ear as he draped one arm around Cosca's shoulders. "My old friend! Why didn't you tell me? Damn, but it's good to have you back!"

"Are you sure?" Cosca ran him smoothly through the chest with Rigrat's sword, right to the polished hilt. Andiche's eyes bulged, his mouth dropped open and he dragged in a great long wheeze, his pockmarked face twisted, trying to scream. But all that came out was a gentle cough.

Cosca leaned close. "You think a man can turn on me? Betray me? Give my chair to another for a few pieces of silver, then smile and be my friend? You mistake me, Andiche. Fatally. I may make men laugh, but I'm no clown."

The mercenary's coat glistened with dark blood, his trembling face had turned bright red, veins bulging in his neck. He clawed weakly at Cosca's breastplate, bloody bubbles forming on his lips. Cosca let go the hilt, wiped his hand on Andiche's sleeve and shoved him over. He fell on his side, spit-ted, gave a gentle groan and stopped moving.

"Interesting." Ishri squatted over him. "I am rarely surprised. Surely Murcatto is the one who stole your chair. You let her go free, no?"

"On reflection, I doubt the facts of my betrayal quite match the story. But in any case, a man can forgive all manner of faults in beautiful women that in ugly men he finds entirely beyond sufferance. And if there's one thing I absolutely cannot abide, it's disloyalty. You have to stick at something in your life."

"Disloyalty?" screeched Rigrat, finally finding his voice. "You'll pay for this, Cosca, you treacherous—"

Friendly's knife thumped into his neck and out, blood showered across the floor of the tent and spattered the Musselian flag that Sazine had taken the day the Thousand Swords were formed.

Rigrat fell to his knees, one hand clutched to his throat, blood pouring down the sleeve of his jacket. He flopped forwards onto his face, trembled for a moment, then was still. A dark circle bloomed out through the material of the groundsheet and merged with the one already creeping from Andiche's corpse.

"Ah," said Cosca. He had been planning to ransom Rigrat back to his family. It did not seem likely now. "That was...ungracious of you, Friendly."

"Oh." The convict frowned at his bloody knife. "I thought...you know. Follow your lead. I was being first sergeant."

"Of course you were. I take all the blame myself. I should have been more specific. I have ever suffered from...unspecificity? Is that a word?"

Friendly shrugged. So did Ishri.

"Well." Cosca scratched gently at his neck as he looked down at Rigrat's body. "An annoying, pompous, swollen-headed man, from what I saw. But if those were capital crimes I daresay half the world would hang, and myself first to the gallows. Perhaps he had many fine qualities of which I was unaware. I'm sure his mother would say so. But this is a battle. Corpses are a sad inevitability." He crossed to the tent flap, took a moment to compose himself, then clawed it desperately aside. "Some help here! For pity's sake, some help!"

He hurried back to Andiche's body and squatted beside it, knelt one way and then another, found what he judged to be the most dramatic pose just as Sesaria burst into the tent.

"God's breath!" as he saw the two corpses, Victus bundling in behind, eyes wide.

"Andiche!" Cosca gestured at Rigrat's sword, still where he had left it. "Run through!" He had observed that people often state the obvious when distressed.

"Someone get a surgeon!" roared Victus.

"Or better yet a priest." Ishri swaggered across the tent towards them. "He's dead."

"What happened?"

"Colonel Rigrat stabbed him."

"Who the hell are you?"

"Ishri."

"He was a great heart!" Cosca gently touched Andiche's staring-eyed, gape-mouthed, blood-spattered face. "A true friend. He stepped before the thrust."

"Andiche did?" Sesaria did not look convinced.

"He gave his life...to save mine." Cosca's voice almost croaked away to nothing at the end, and he dashed a tear from the corner of his eye. "Thank the Fates Sergeant Friendly moved as quickly as he did or I'd have been done for too." He beat at Andiche's chest, fist squelching on his warm, blood-soaked coat. "My fault! My fault! I blame myself!"

"Why?" snarled Victus, glaring down at Rigrat's corpse. "I mean, why did this bastard do it?"

"My fault!" wailed Cosca. "I took money from Rogont to stay out of the battle!"

Sesaria and Victus exchanged a glance. "You took money...to stay out?"

"A huge amount of money! There will be shares by seniority, of course." Cosca waved his hand as though it was a trifle now. "Danger pay for every man, in Gurkish gold."

"Gold?" rumbled Sesaria, eyebrows going up as though Cosca had pronounced a magic word.

"But I would sink it all in the ocean for one minute longer in my old friend's company! To hear him speak again! To see him smile. But never more. Forever..." Cosca swept off his hat, laid it gently over Andiche's face and hung his head. "Silent."

Victus cleared his throat. "How much gold are we talking about, exactly?"

"A...huge...quantity." Cosca gave a shuddering sniff. "As much again as Orso paid us to fight on his behalf."

"Andiche dead. A heavy price to pay." But Sesaria looked as if he perceived the upside.

"Too heavy a price. Far too heavy." Cosca slowly stood. "My friends... could you bring yourselves to make arrangements for the burial? I must observe the battle. We must stumble on. For him. There is one consolation, I suppose."

"The money?" asked Victus.

Cosca slapped down a hand on each captain's shoulder. "Thanks to my bargain we will not need to fight. Andiche will be the only casualty the Thousand Swords suffer today. You could say he died for all of us. Sergeant Friendly!" And Cosca turned and pushed past into the bright sunlight. Ishri glided silently at his elbow.

"Quite the performance," she murmured. "You really should have been an actor rather than a general."

"There's not so much air between the two as you might imagine." Cosca walked to the captain general's chair and leaned on the back, feeling suddenly tired and irritable. Considering the long years he had dreamed of taking revenge for Afieri, it was a disappointing pay-off. He was in terrible need of a drink, fumbled for Morveer's flask, but it was empty. He frowned down into the valley. The Talinese were engaged in a desperate battle perhaps half a mile wide at the bank of the lower ford, waiting for help from the Thousand Swords. Help that would never come. They had the numbers, but the Osprians were still holding their ground, keeping the battle narrow, choking them up in the shallows. The great mêlée heaved and glittered, the ford crawling with men, bobbing with bodies.

Cosca gave a long sigh. "You Gurkish think there's a point to it all, don't you? That God has a plan, and so forth?"

"I've heard it said." Ishri's black eyes flicked from the valley to him. "And what do you think God's plan is, General Cosca?"

"I have long suspected that it might be to annoy me."

She smiled. Or at least her mouth curled up to show sharp white teeth. "Fury, paranoia and epic self-centredness in the space of a single sentence."

"All the fine qualities a great military leader requires..." He shaded his eyes, squinting off to the west, towards the ridge behind the Talinese lines. "And here they are. Perfectly on schedule." The first flags were showing there. The first glittering spears. The first of what appeared to be a considerable body of men.

The Fate of Styria

Up there." Monza's gloved forefinger, and her little finger too, of course, pointed towards the ridge.

More soldiers were coming over the crest, a mile or two to the south of where the Talinese had first appeared. A lot more. It seemed Orso had kept a few surprises back. Reinforcements from his Union allies, maybe. Monza worked her sore tongue around her sour mouth and spat. From faint hopes to no hopes. A small step, but one nobody ever enjoys taking. The leading flags caught a gust of wind and unfurled for a moment. She peered at them through her eyeglass, frowned, rubbed her eye and peered again. There was no mistaking the cockleshell of Sipani.

"Sipanese," she muttered. Until a few moments ago, the world's most neutral men. "Why the hell are they fighting for Orso?"

"Who says they are?" When she turned to Rogont, he was smiling like a thief who'd whipped the fattest purse of his career. He spread his arms out wide. "Rejoice, Murcatto! The miracle you asked for!"

She blinked. "They're on our side?"

"Most certainly, and right in Foscar's rear! And the irony is that it's all your doing."

"Mine?"

"Entirely yours! You remember the conference in Sipani, arranged by that preening mope the King of the Union?"

The great procession through the crowded streets, the cheering as Rogont and Salier led the way, the jeering as Ario and Foscar followed. "What of it?"

"I had no more intention of making peace with Ario and Foscar than they

468

had with me. My only care was to talk old Chancellor Sotorius over to my side. I tried to convince him that if the League of Eight lost then Duke Orso's greed would not end at Sipani's borders, however neutral they might be. That once my young head was off, his ancient one would be next on the block."

More than likely true. Neutrality was no better defence against Orso than it was against the pox. His ambitions had never stopped at one river or the next. One reason why, until the moment he'd tried to kill her, he'd made Monza such a fine employer.

"But the old man clung to his cherished neutrality, tight as a captain to the wheel of his sinking ship, and I despaired of dislodging him. I am ashamed to admit I began to despair entirely, and was seriously considering fleeing Styria for happier climes." Rogont closed his eyes and tilted his face towards the sun. "And then, oh, happy day, oh, serendipity..." He opened them and looked straight at her. "You murdered Prince Ario."

Black blood pumping from his pale throat, body tumbling through the open window, fire and smoke as the building burned. Rogont grinned with all the smugness of a magician explaining the workings of his latest trick.

"Sotorius was the host. Ario was under his protection. The old man knew Orso would never forgive him for the death of his son. He knew the doom of Sipani was sounded. Unless Orso could be stopped. We came to an agreement that very night, while Cardotti's House of Leisure was still burning. In secret, Chancellor Sotorius brought Sipani into the League of Nine."

"Nine," muttered Monza, watching the Sipanese host march steadily down the gentle hillside towards the fords, and Foscar's almost undefended rear.

"My long retreat from Puranti, which you thought so ill-advised, was intended to give him time to prepare. I backed willingly into this little trap so I could play the bait in a greater one."

"You're cleverer than you look."

"Not difficult. My aunt always told me I looked a dunce."

She frowned across the valley at the motionless host on top of Menzes Hill. "What about Cosca?"

"Some men never change. He took a very great deal of money from my Gurkish backers to keep out of the battle."

It suddenly seemed she didn't understand the world nearly as well as she'd thought. "I offered him money. He wouldn't take it."

"Imagine that, and negotiation so very much your strong point. He wouldn't take the money from *you*. Ishri, it seems, talks more sweetly. 'War is but the pricking point of politics. Blades can kill men, but only words can move them, and good neighbours are the surest shelter in a storm.' I quote from Juvens' *Principles of Art*. Flim-flam and superstition mostly, but the volume on the exercise of power is quite fascinating. You should read more widely, General Murcatto. Your book-learning is narrow in scope."

"I came to reading late," she grunted.

"You may enjoy the full use of my library, once I've butchered the Talinese and conquered Styria." He smiled happily down towards the bottom of the valley, where Foscar's army were in grave danger of being surrounded. "Of course, if Orso's troops had a more seasoned leader today than the young Prince Foscar, things might have been very different. I doubt a man of General Ganmark's abilities would have fallen so completely into my trap. Or even one of Faithful Carpi's long experience." He leaned from his saddle and brought his self-satisfied smirk a little closer. "But Orso has suffered some unfortunate losses in the area of command, lately."

She snorted, turned her head and spat. "So glad to be of help."

"Oh, I couldn't have done it without you. All we need do is hold the lower ford until our brave allies of Sipani reach the river, crush Foscar's men between us, and Duke Orso's ambitions will be drowned in the shallows."

"That all?" Monza frowned towards the water. The Affoians, an untidy red-brown mass on the neglected far right of the battle, had been forced back from the bank. No more than twenty paces of churned-up mud, but enough to give the Talinese a foothold. Now it looked as if some Baolish had waded through the deeper water upstream and got around their flank.

"It is, and it appears that we are already well on our way to...ah." Rogont had seen it too. "Oh." Men were beginning to break from the fighting, struggling up the hillside towards the city.

"Looks as if your brave allies of Affoia have tired of your hospitality."

The mood of smug jubilation that had swept through Rogont's headquarters when the Sipanese appeared was fading rapidly as more and more dots crumbled from the back of the bulging Affoian lines and began to scatter in every direction. Above them the companies of archers grew ragged as bowmen looked nervously up towards the city. No doubt they weren't keen to get closer acquainted with the men they'd been shooting arrows down at for the last hour.

"If those Baolish bastards break through they'll take your people in the flank, roll your whole line up. It'll be a rout."

Rogont chewed at his lip. "The Sipanese are less than half an hour away."

"Excellent. They'll turn up just in time to count our corpses. Then theirs."

He glanced nervously back towards the city. "Perhaps we should retire to our walls—"

"You haven't the time to disengage from that mess. Even as skilled a withdrawer as you are."

The duke's face had lost its colour. "What do we do?"

It suddenly seemed she understood the world perfectly. Monza drew her sword with a faint ringing of steel. A cavalry sword she'd borrowed from Rogont's armoury — simple, heavy and murderously well-sharpened. His eyes rolled down to it. "Ah. That."

"Yes. That."

"I suppose there comes a time when a man must truly cast prudence to one side." Rogont set his jaw, muscles working on the side of his head. "Cavalry. With me…" His voice died to a throaty croak.

A loud voice to a general, Farans wrote, *is worth a regiment*.

Monza stood in her stirrups and screamed at the top of her lungs. "Form the horse!"

The duke's staff began to screech, point, wave their swords. Mounted men drew in all around, forming up in long ranks. Harnesses rattled, armour clanked, lances clattered against each other, horses snorted and pawed at the ground. Men found their places, tugged their restless mounts around, cursed and bellowed, strapped on helmets and slapped down visors.

The Baolish were breaking through in earnest, boiling out of the widening gaps in Rogont's shattered right wing like the rising tide through a wall of sand. Monza could hear their shrill war cries as they streamed up the slope, see their tattered banners waving, the glitter of metal on the move. The lines of archers above them dissolved all at once, men tossing away their bows and running for the city, mixed up with fleeing Affoians and a few Osprians who were starting to think better of the whole business. It had always amazed her how quickly an army could come apart once the panic started to spread. Like pulling out the keystone of a bridge, the whole thing, so firm and ordered one minute, could be nothing but ruins the next. They were on the brink of that moment of collapse now, she could feel it.

Monza felt a horse pull up beside her and Shivers met her eye, axe in one hand, reins and a heavy shield in the other. He hadn't bothered with armour. Just wore the shirt with the gold thread on the cuffs. The one she'd picked out for him. The one that Benna might have worn. It didn't seem to suit him much now. Looked like a crystal collar on a killing dog.

"Thought maybe you'd headed back North."

"Without all that money you owe me?" His one eye shifted down into the valley. "Never yet turned my back on a fight."

"Good. Glad to have you." It was true enough, at that moment. Whatever else, he had a handy habit of saving her life. She'd already looked away by the time she felt him look at her. And by that time, it was time to go.

Rogont raised his sword, and the noon sun caught the mirror-bright blade and struck flashing fire from it. Just like in the stories.

"Forward!"

Tongues clicked, heels kicked, reins snapped. Together, as if they were one animal, the great line of horsemen started to move. First at a walk, horses stirring, snorting, jerking sideways. The ranks twisted and flexed as eager men and mounts broke ahead. Officers bellowed, bringing them back into formation. Faster they moved, and faster, armour and harness clattering, and Monza's heart beat faster with them. That tingling mix of fear and joy that comes when the thinking's done and there's nothing left but to do. The Baolish had seen them, were struggling to form some kind of line. Monza could see their snarling faces in the moments when the world held still, wild-haired men in tarnished chain mail and ragged fur.

The lances of the horsemen around her began to swing down, points gleaming, and they broke into a trot. The breath hissed cold in Monza's nose, sharp in her dry throat, burned hot in her chest. Not thinking about the pain or the husk she needed for it. Not thinking about what she'd done or what she'd failed to do. Not thinking about her dead brother or the men who'd killed him. Just gripping with all her strength to her horse and to her sword. Just staying fixed on the scattering of Baolish on the slope in front of her, already wavering. They were tired out and ragged from fighting in the valley, running up the hill. And a few hundred tons of horseflesh bearing down on a man could tax his nerve at the best of times.

Their half-formed line began to crumble.

"Charge!" roared Rogont. Monza screamed with him, heard Shivers bellowing beside her, shouts and wails from every man in the line. She dug her heels in hard and her horse swerved, righted itself, sprang down the hill at a bone-cracking gallop. Hooves thudded at the ground, mud and grass flicked and flew, Monza's teeth rattled in her head. The valley bounced and shuddered around her, the sparkling river rushed up towards her. Her eyes were full of wind, she blinked back wet, the world turned to a blurry, sparkling smear then suddenly, mercilessly sharp again. She saw the Baolish scattering, flinging down weapons as they ran. Then the cavalry were among them.

A horse ahead of the pack was impaled on a spear, shaft bending, shattering. It took spearman and rider with it, tumbling over and over down the slope, straps and harness flailing in the air.

She saw a lance take a running man in the back, rip him open from his arse to his shoulders and send the corpse reeling. The fleeing Baolish were spitted, hacked, trampled, broken.

One was flung spinning from the chest of a horse in front, chopped across the back with a sword, clattered shrieking against Monza's leg and was broken apart under the hooves of Rogont's charger.

Another dropped his spear, turning away, his face a pale blur of fear. She swung her sword down, felt the jarring impact up her arm as the heavy blade stoved his helmet deep in with a hollow clonk.

Wind rushed in her ears, hooves pounded. She was screaming still, laughing, screaming. Cut another man down as he tried to run, near taking his arm off at the shoulder and sending blood up in a black gout. Missed another with a full-blooded sweep and only just kept her saddle as she was twisted round after her sword. Righted herself just in time, clinging to the reins with her aching hand.

They were through the Baolish now, had left their torn and bloody corpses in their wake. Shattered lances were flung aside, swords were drawn. The slope levelled off as they plunged on, closer to the river, the ground spotted with Affoian bodies. The battle was a tight-packed slaughter ahead, brought out in greater detail now, more and more Talinese crossing the ford, adding their weight to the mindless press on the banks. Polearms waved and glittered, blades flashed, men struggled and strained. Over the wind and her own breath Monza could hear it, like a distant storm, metal and voices mangled together. Officers rode behind the lines, screaming vainly, trying to bring some trace of order to the madness.

A fresh Talinese regiment had started to push through the gap the Baolish had made on the far right — heavy infantry, well armoured. They'd wheeled and were pressing at the end of the Osprian line, the men in blue straining to hold them off but sorely outnumbered now, more men coming up from the river every moment and forcing the gap wider.

Rogont, shining armour streaked with blood, turned in his saddle and pointed his sword towards them, screamed something no one could hear. It hardly mattered. There was no stopping now.

The Talinese were forming a wedge around a white battle flag, black cross twisting in the wind, an officer at the front stabbing madly at the air as he tried to get them ready to meet the charge. Monza wondered briefly whether she'd ever met him. Men knelt, a mass of glittering armour at the point of the wedge, bristling with polearms, waving and rattling further back, half still caught up with the Osprians, tangled together every which way, a thicket of blades.

Monza saw a cloud of bolts rise from the press in the ford. She winced as they flickered towards her, held her breath for no reason that made any sense. Held breath won't stop an arrow. Rattle and whisper as they showered down, clicking into turf, pinging from heavy armour, thudding into horseflesh.

A horse took a bolt in the neck, twisted, went over on its flank. Another careered into it and its rider came free of the saddle, thrashing at the air, his lance tumbling down the hillside, digging up clods of black soil. Monza wrenched her horse around the wreckage. Something rattled off her breastplate and spun up into her face. She gasped, rolling in her saddle, pain down her cheek. Arrow. The flights had scratched her. She opened her eyes to see an armoured man clutching at a bolt in his shoulder, jolting, jolting, then tumbling sideways, dragged clanking after his madly galloping horse, foot still caught in one stirrup. The rest of them plunged on, horses flowing round the fallen or over them, leaving them trampled.

She'd bitten her tongue somewhere. She spat blood, digging her spurs in again and forcing her mount on, lips curled right back, wind rushing cold at her mouth.

"We should've stuck to farming," she whispered. The Talinese came pounding up to meet her.

* * *

Shivers never had understood where the eager fools came from in every battle, but there were always enough of the bastards to make a show. These ones drove their horses straight for the white flag, at the point of the wedge where the spears were well set. The front horse checked before it got there, skidded and reared, rider just clinging on. The horse behind crashed into it and sent beast and man both onto the gleaming points, blood and splinters flying. Another bucked behind, pitching its rider forwards over its head and tumbling into the muck where the front rank gratefully stabbed at him.

Calmer-headed horsemen broke to the sides, flowing round the wedge like a stream round a rock and into its softer flanks where the spears weren't set. Squealing soldiers clambered over each other as the riders bore down, fighting to be anywhere but the front, spears wobbling at all angles.

Monza went left and Shivers followed, his eye fixed on her. Up ahead a couple of horses jumped the milling front rank and into the midst, riders lashing about with swords and maces. Others crashed into the scrambling men, crushing them, trampling them, sending them spinning, screaming, begging, driving through 'em towards the river. Monza chopped some stumbling fool down as she passed and was into the press, hacking away with her sword. A spearman jabbed at her and caught her in the backplate, near tore her from the saddle.

Black Dow's words came to mind — there's no better time to kill a man than in a battle, and that goes double when he's on your own side. Shivers gave his horse the spurs and urged it up beside Monza, standing tall in his stirrups, bringing his axe up high above her head. His lips curled back. He swung it down with a roar and right into the spearman's face, burst it wide open and sent his corpse tumbling. He heaved the axe all the way over to the other side and it crashed into a shield and left a great dent in it, knocked the man who held it under the threshing hooves of the horse beside. Might've been one of Rogont's people, but it was no time to be thinking on who was who.

Kill everyone not on a horse. Kill anyone on a horse who got in his way.

Kill everyone.

He screamed his war cry, the one he'd used outside the walls of Adua, when they scared the Gurkish off with screams alone. The high wail, out of the icy North, though his voice was cracked and creaking now. He laid about him, hardly looking what he was chopping at, axe blade clanking, banging, thudding, voices crying, blubbering, screeching.

A broken voice roared in Northern. "Die! Die! Back to the mud, fuckers!" His ears were full of mindless roar and rattle. A shifting sea of jabbing weapons, squealing shields, shining metal, bone shattered, blood spattered, furious, terrified faces washing all round him, squirming and wriggling, and he hacked and chopped and split them like a mad butcher going at a carcass.

His muscles were throbbing hot, his skin was on fire to the tips of his fingers, damp with sweat in the burning sun. Forwards, always forwards, part of the pack, towards the water, leaving a bloody path of broken bodies, dead men and dead horses behind them. The battle opened up and he was through, men scattering in front of him. He spurred his horse between two of them, jolting down the bank and into the shallow river. He hacked one between the shoulders as they fled then chopped deep into the other's neck on the backswing, sent him spinning into the water.

There were riders all round him now, splashing into the ford, hooves sending up showers of bright spray. He caught a glimpse of Monza, still ahead, horse struggling through deeper water, sword blade twinkling as it went up and cut down. The charge was spent. Lathered horses floundered in the shallows. Riders leaned down, chopping, barking, soldiers stabbed back at them with spears, cut at their legs and their mounts with swords. A horseman floundered desperately in the water, crest of his helmet skewed while men battered at him with maces, knocking him this way and that, leaving great dents in his heavy armour.

Shivers grunted as something grabbed him round the stomach, was bent back, shirt ripping. He flailed with his elbow but couldn't get a good swing. A hand clutched at his head, fingers dug at the scarred side of his face, nails scraping at his dead eye. He roared, kicked, squirmed, tried to swing his left arm but someone had hold of that too. He let go his shield, was dragged back, off his horse and down, twisting into the shallows, rolling sideways and up onto his knees.

A young lad in a studded leather jacket was right next to him in the river, wet hair hanging round his face. He was staring down at something in his hand, something flat and glinting. Looked like an eye. The enamel that'd been in Shivers' face until a moment before. The boy looked up, and they stared at each other. Shivers felt something beside him, ducked, wind on his wet hair as his own shield swung past his head. He spun, axe following him in a great wide circle and thudding deep into someone's ribs, blood showering out. It bent him sideways and snatched him howling off his feet, flung him splashing down a stride or two away.

When he turned, the lad was coming at him with a knife. Shivers twisted sideways, managed to catch his forearm and hold it. They staggered, tangled together, went over, cold water clutching. The knife nicked Shivers' shoulder but he was far bigger, far stronger, rolled out on top. They wrestled and clawed, snorting in each other's faces. He let the axe shaft drop through his fist until he was gripping it right under the blade, the lad caught his wrist with his free hand, water washing around his head, but he didn't have the strength to stop it. Shivers gritted his teeth, twisted the axe until the heavy blade slid up across his neck.

"No," whispered the boy.

The time to say no was before the battle. Shivers pushed with all his weight, growling, moaning. The lad's eyes bulged as the metal bit slowly into his throat, deeper, deeper, the red wound opening wider and wider. Blood squirted out in sticky spurts, down Shivers' arm, over his shirt, into the river and washed away. The lad trembled for a moment, red mouth wide open, then he went limp, staring at the sky.

Shivers staggered up. His rag of a shirt was trapping him, heavy with blood and water. He tore it off, hand so clumsy from gripping his shield hard as murder that he clawed hair from his chest while he did it. He stared about, blinking into the ruthless sun. Men and horses thrashed in the glittering river, blurred and smeary. He bent down and jerked his axe from the boy's half-severed neck, leather twisted round the grip finding the grooves in his palm like a key finds its lock.

He sloshed on through the water on foot, looking for more. Looking for Murcatto.

The dizzy surge of strength the charge had given her was fading fast. Monza's throat was raw from screaming, her legs were aching from gripping her horse. Her right hand was a crooked mass of pain on the reins, her sword arm burned from fingers to shoulder, the blood pounded behind her eyes. She twisted about, not sure anymore which was east or west. It hardly mattered now.

In war, Verturio wrote, *there are no straight lines.*

There were no lines at all down in the ford, just horsemen and soldiers all tangled up into a hundred murderous, mindless little fights. You could hardly tell friend from enemy and, since no one was checking too closely, there wasn't much difference between the two. Your death could come from anywhere.

She saw the spear, but too late. Her horse shuddered as the point sank into its flank just beside her leg. Its head twisted, one eye rolling wild, foam on its bared teeth. Monza clung to the saddle-bow as it lurched sideways, spear rammed deeper, her leg hot with horse blood. She gave a helpless shriek as she went over, feet still in the stirrups, sword tumbling from her hand as she clutched at nothing. Water hit her in the side, the saddle dug her in the stomach and drove her breath out.

She was under, head full of light, bubbles rushing round her face. Cold clutched at her, and cold fear too. She thrashed her way up for a moment, out of the darkness and suddenly into the glare, the sound of battle crashing at her ears again. She gasped in a breath, shipped some water, coughed it out, gasped in another. She clawed at the saddle with her left hand, tried to drag herself free, but her leg was trapped under her horse's thrashing body.

Something cracked against her forehead and she was under for a moment, dizzy, floppy. Her lungs were burning, her arms were made of mud. Fought her way up again, but weaker this time, only far enough to snatch one breath. Blue sky reeling, shreds of white cloud, like the sky as she tumbled down from Fontezarmo.

The sun flickered at her, searing bright along with her whooping breath, then blurred and sparkling with muffled gurgles as the river washed over her face. No strength left to twist herself out of the water. Was this what Faithful's last moments had been like, drowned on the mill-wheel?

Here was justice.

A black shape blotted out the sun. Shivers, seeming ten feet tall as he stood over her. Something gleamed bright in the socket of his blinded eye. He lifted one boot slowly clear of the river, frowning hard, water trickling from the edges of the sole and into her face. For a moment she was sure he was going to plant that foot on her neck and push her under. Then it splashed down beside her. She heard him growling, straining at the corpse of her horse. She felt the weight across her leg release a little, then a little more. She squirmed, groaned, breathed in water and coughed it out, finally dragged her leg free and floundered up.

She trembled on hands and knees, up to her elbows in the river, babbling water sparkling and flickering in front of her, drips falling from her wet hair. "Shit," she whispered, every breath shuddering in her sore ribs. "Shit." She needed a smoke.

"They're coming," came Shivers' voice. She felt his hand rammed into her armpit, dragging her up. "Get a blade."

She staggered under the weight of wet clothes and wet armour to a bobbing corpse caught on a rock. A heavy mace with a metal shaft was still hanging by its strap from his wrist, and she dragged it free with fumbling fingers, pulled a long knife from his belt.

Just in time. An armoured man was bearing down on her, planting his feet carefully, peering at her with hard little eyes over the top of his shield, sword beaded with wet sticking out sideways. She backed off a step or two, pretending to be finished. Didn't take much pretending. As he took another step she came at him. Couldn't have called it a spring. More of a tired half-dive, hardly able to shove her feet through the water fast enough to keep up with the rest of her body.

She swung at him mindlessly with the mace and it clanged off his shield, made her arm sing to the shoulder. She grunted, wrestled with him, stabbed at him with her knife, but it caught the side of his breastplate and scraped off harmless. The shield barged into her and sent her stumbling. She saw one swing of his sword coming and just had the presence of mind to duck it. She flailed with the mace and caught air, reeled off balance, hardly any strength left, gulping for air. His sword went up again.

She saw Shivers' mad grin behind him, a flash as the red blade of his axe caught the sun. It split the man's armoured shoulder down to his chest with a heavy thud, sent blood spraying in Monza's face. She reeled away, ears full of his gargling shriek, nose full of his blood, trying to scrape her eyes clear on the back of one hand.

First thing she saw was another soldier, open helmet with a bearded face inside, stabbing with a spear. She tried to twist away but it caught her hard in the chest, point shrieked down her breastplate, sent her toppling, head snapping forwards. She was on her back in the ford and the soldier stumbled past, floundering into a crack in the river bed, sending water showering in her eyes. She fought her way up to one knee, bloody hair tangled across her face. He turned, lifting the spear to stab at her again. She twisted round and rammed the knife between two plates of armour, into the side of his knee right to the crosspiece.

He bent down over her, eyes bulging, opened his mouth wide to scream. She snarled as she jerked the mace up and smashed it into the bottom of his jaw. His head snapped back, blood and teeth and bits of teeth flew high. He seemed to stay there for a moment, hands dangling, then she clubbed his stretched-out throat with the mace, sprawled on top of him as he fell, rolled about in the river and came up spitting.

There were men around her still, but none of them fighting. Standing or sitting in their saddles, staring about. Shivers stood watching her, axe hanging from one hand. For some reason he was stripped half-naked, his white skin dashed and spattered with red. The enamel was gone from his eye and the bright metal ball behind it gleamed in the socket with the midday sun, dewy with beads of wet.

"Victory!" She heard someone scream. Blurry, quivering, wet-eyed, she saw a man on a brown horse, in the midst of the river, standing in his stirrups, shining sword held high. "Victory!"

She took a wobbling step towards Shivers and he dropped his scarred axe, caught her as she fell. She clung on to him, right arm around his shoulder, left dangling, still just gripping the mace, if only because she couldn't make the fingers open.

"We won," she whispered at him, and she felt herself smiling.

"We won," he said, squeezing her tight, half-lifting her off her feet. "We won."

Cosca lowered his eyeglass, blinked and rubbed his eyes, one half-blind from being shut for the best part of the hour, the other half-blind from being jammed into the eyepiece for the same period. "Well, there we are." He shifted uncomfortably in the captain general's chair. His trousers had become wedged in the sweaty crack of his arse and he wriggled as he tugged them free. "God smiles on results, do you Gurkish say?"

Silence. Ishri had melted away as swiftly as she had appeared. Cosca swivelled the other way, towards Friendly. "Quite the show, eh, Sergeant?"

The convict looked up from his dice, frowned down into the valley and said nothing. Duke Rogont's timely charge had plugged the gaping hole in his lines, crushed the Baolish, driven deep into the Talinese ranks and left them broken. Not at all what the Duke of Delay was known for. In fact, Cosca was oddly pleased to perceive the audacious hand, or perhaps the fist, of Monzcarro Murcatto all over it.

The Osprian infantry, the threat on their right wing extinguished, had blocked off the eastern bank of the lower ford entirely. Their new Sipanese allies had well and truly joined the fray, won a brief engagement with Foscar's surprised rearguard and were close to sealing off the western bank. A good half of Orso's army — or of those that were not now scattered dead on the slopes, on the banks downstream or floating face down out to sea — were trapped hopelessly in the shallows between the two, and were laying down their arms. The other half were fleeing, dark specks scattered across the green slopes on the valley's western side. The very slopes down which they had so proudly marched but a few short hours ago, confident of victory. Sipanese cavalry moved in clumps around their edges, armour gleaming in the fierce noon sun, rounding up the survivors.

"All done now, though, eh, Victus?"

"Looks that way."

"Everyone's favourite part of a battle. The rout." Unless you were in it, of course. Cosca watched the tiny figures spilling from the fords, spreading out across the trampled grass, and had to shake off a sweaty shiver at the memory of Afieri. He forced the carefree grin to stay on his face. "Nothing like a good rout, eh, Sesaria?"

"Who'd have thought it?" The big man slowly shook his head. "Rogont won."

"Grand Duke Rogont would appear to be a most unpredictable and resourceful gentleman." Cosca yawned, stretched, smacked his lips. "One after my own heart. I look forward to having him as an employer. Probably we should help with the mopping up." The searching of the dead. "Prisoners to be taken and ransomed." Or murdered and robbed, depending on social station. "Unguarded baggage that should be confiscated, lest it spoil in the open air." Lest it be plundered or burned before they could get their gauntlets on it.

Victus split a toothy grin. "I'll make arrangements to bring it all in from the cold."

"Do so, brave Captain Victus, do so. I declare the sun is on its way back down and it is past time the men were on the move. I would be ashamed if, in after times, the poets said the Thousand Swords were at the Battle of Ospria...and did nothing." Cosca smiled wide, and this time with feeling. "Lunch, perhaps?"

To the Victors...

Black Dow used to say the only thing better'n a battle was a battle then a fuck, and Shivers couldn't say he disagreed. Seemed she didn't either. She was waiting there for him, after all, when he stalked into the darkened room, bare as a baby, stretched out on the bed, her hands behind her head and one long, smooth leg pointing out towards him.

"What kept you?" she asked, rocking her hips from one side to the other.

Time was he'd reckoned himself a quick thinker but the only thing moving fast right then was his cock. "I was..." He was having trouble thinking much beyond the patch of dark hair between her legs, his anger all leaked away like beer from a broken jar. "I was...well..." He kicked the door shut and walked slowly to her. "Don't matter much, does it?"

"Not much." She slipped off the bed, started undoing his borrowed shirt, going about it as if it was something they'd arranged.

"Can't say I was expecting...this." He reached out, almost scared to touch her in case he found he was dreaming it. Ran his fingertips down her bare arms, skin rough with gooseflesh. "Not after last time we spoke."

She pushed her fingers into his hair and pulled his head down towards her, breath on his face. She kissed his neck, then his chin, then his mouth. "Shall I go?" She sucked gently at his lips again.

"Fuck, no," his voice hardly more'n a croak.

She had his belt open now, dug inside and pulled his cock free, started working at it with one hand while his trousers sagged slowly down, catching on his knees, belt buckle scraping on the floor.

Her lips were cool on his chest, on his stomach, her tongue tickled his belly. Her hand slid under his fruits, cold and ticklish, and he squirmed,

483

gave a womanly kind of a squeak. He heard a quiet slurp as she wrapped her lips around him and he stood there, bent over some, knees weak and trembling and his mouth hanging open. Her head started bobbing slowly in and out, and he moved his hips in time without thinking, grunting to himself like a pig got the swill.

Monza wiped her mouth on the back of her arm, squirmed her way onto the bed, pulling him after, kissing at her neck, at her breastbone, nipping at her chest, growling to himself like a dog got the bone.

She brought her knee up and flipped him over onto his back. He frowned, left side of his face all in darkness, right side full of shadows from the shifting lamplight, running his fingertips gently along the scars on her ribs. She slapped his hand away. "Told you. I fell down a mountain. Get your trousers off."

He wriggled eagerly free of them, got them tangled around his ankles. "Shit, damn, bastard—Ah!" He finally kicked them off and she shoved him down onto his back, clambered on top of him, one of his hands sliding up her thigh, wet fingers working between her legs. She stayed there a while, crouched over him, growling in his face and feeling his breath coming quick back at her, grinding her hips against his hand, feeling his prick rubbing up against the inside of her thigh—

"Ah, wait!" He wriggled away, sitting up, winced as he fiddled with the skin at the end of his cock. "Got it. Go!"

"I'll tell you when to go." She worked her way forwards on her knees, finding the spot and then nudging her cunt against him softly, gently, not in and not out, halfway between.

"Oh." He wriggled his way up onto his elbows, straining vainly up against her.

"Ah." She leaned down over him, her hair tickling his face, and he smiled, snapped his teeth at it.

"Oh-urgh." She pushed her thumb into his mouth, dragged his head sideways and he sucked at it, bit at it, catching her wrist, licking at her hand, then her chin, then her tongue.

"Ah." She started to push down on him, smiling herself, grunting in her throat and him grunting back at her.

"Oh."

* * *

She had the root of his cock in one hand, rubbing herself against the end
of it, not in and not out, always halfway between. She had the other round
the back of Shivers' head, holding his face against her tits while he gathered
them up, squeezed them, bit at them.

Her fingers worked under his jaw, thumb-tip sliding ever so gently onto
his ruined cheek, tickling, teasing, scratching. He felt a sudden stab of fury,
snatched hold of her wrist, hard, twisted it round, twisted her off him and
onto her knees, twisted her arm behind her, face pushed down into the
sheet, making her gasp.

He was grunting something in Northern and even he didn't know what.
He felt a burning need to hurt her. Hurt himself. He tangled his free hand
in her hair and shoved her head hard against the wall, growling and whimpering at her from behind while she groaned, gasped, mouth wide open,
hair across her face fluttering with her breath. He still had her arm twisted
behind her and her hand curled round, gripping his wrist hard while he
gripped hers, dragging him down over her.

Uh, uh, their mindless grunting. Creak, creak, the bed moaning along
with them. Squelch, squelch, his skin slapping hard against her arse.

Monza worked her hips against him a few more times, and with each
one he gave a little hoot, head back, veins standing from his stretched-out
neck. With each one she gave a snarl through gritted teeth, muscles all
clenched aching tight, then slowly going soft. She stayed there for a moment,
hunched over, limp as wet leaves, hard breath catching in the back of her
throat. She winced and he shivered as she ground herself against him one
last time. Then she slid off, gathered up a handful of sheet and wiped herself on it.

He lay there on his back, sweaty chest rising and falling fast, arms spread
out wide, staring at the gilded ceiling. "So this is what victory feels like. If
I'd known I'd have taken some gambles sooner."

"No, you wouldn't. You're the Duke of Delay, remember?"

He peered down at his wet cock, nudged it to one side, then the other.
"Well, some things it's best to take your time with..."

* * *

Shivers prised his fingers open, scuffed, scabbed, scratched and clicking from gripping his axe all the long day. They left white marks across her wrist, turning slowly pink. He rocked back on his haunches, body sagging, aching muscles loose, heaving in air. His lust all spent and his rage spent with it. For now.

Her necklace of red stones rattled as she rolled over towards him. Onto her back, tits flattened against her ribs, the knobbles of her hip bones sticking sharp from her stomach, of her collarbones sticking sharp from her shoulders. She winced, working her hand around, rubbing at her wrist.

"Didn't mean to hurt you," he grunted, lying badly, and not much caring either.

"Oh, I'm nothing like that delicate. And you can call me Carlot." She reached up and brushed his lips gently with a fingertip. "I think we know each other well enough for that..."

Monza clambered off the bed and walked to the desk, legs weak and aching, feet flapping against the cool marble. The husk lay on it, beside the lamp. The knife blade gleamed, the polished stem of the pipe shone. She sat down in front of it. Yesterday she wouldn't have been able to keep her trembling hands away from it. Today, even with a legion of fresh aches, cuts, grazes from the battle, it didn't call to her half so loud. She held her left hand up, knuckles starting to scab over, and frowned at it. It was firm.

"I never really thought I could do it," she muttered.

"Eh?"

"Beat Orso. I thought I might get three of them. Four, maybe, before they killed me. Never thought I'd live this long. Never thought I could actually do it."

"And now one would say the odds favour you. How quickly hope can flicker into life once more." Rogont drew himself up before the mirror. A tall one, crusted with coloured flowers of Visserine glass. She could hardly believe, watching him pose, that she'd once been every bit as vain. The hours she'd wasted preening before the mirror. The fortunes she and Benna had spent on clothes. A fall down a mountain, a body scarred, a hand ruined and six months living like a hunted dog seemed to have cured her of that, at least. Perhaps she should've suggested the same remedy to Rogont.

The duke lifted his chin in a regal gesture, chest inflated. He frowned, sagged, pressed at a long scratch just below his collarbone. "Damn it."

"Nick yourself on your nail-file, did you?"

"A savage sword-cut like this could easily have been the death of a lesser man, I'll have you know! But I braved it, without complaint, and fought on like a tiger, blood streaming, *streaming* I say, down my armour! I am beginning to suspect it could even leave a mark."

"No doubt you'll wear it with massive pride. You could have a hole cut in all your shirts to display it to the public."

"If I didn't know better I'd suspect I was being mocked. You do realise, if things unfold according to my plans — and they have so far, I might observe — you will soon be directing your sarcasm at the King of Styria. I have already, in fact, commissioned my crown, from Zoben Casoum, the world-famous master jeweller of Corontiz—"

"Cast from Gurkish gold, no doubt."

Rogont paused for a moment, frowning. "The world is not as simple as you think, General Murcatto. A great war rages."

She snorted. "You think I missed that? These are the Years of Blood."

He snorted back. "The Years of Blood are only the latest skirmish. This war began long before you or I were born. A struggle between the Gurkish and the Union. Or between the forces that control them, at least, the church of Gurkhul and the banks of the Union. Their battlefields are everywhere, and every man must pick his side. The middle ground contains only corpses. Orso stands with the Union. Orso has the backing of the banks. And so I have my...backers. Every man must kneel to someone."

"Perhaps you didn't notice. I'm not a man."

Rogont's smile broke out again. "Oh, I noticed. It was the second thing that attracted me to you."

"The first?"

"You can help me unite Styria."

"And why should I?"

"A united Styria...she could be as great as the Union, as great as the Empire of Gurkhul. Greater, even! She could free herself from their struggle, and stand alone. Free. We have never been closer! Nicante and Puranti fall over themselves to re-enter my good graces. Affoia never left them. Sotorius is my man, with certain trifling concessions to Sipani, no more than a few islands and the city of Borletta—"

"And what do the citizens of Borletta have to say to it?"

"Whatever I tell them to say. They are a changeable crowd, as you discovered when they scrambled to offer you their beloved Duke Cantain's head. Muris bowed to Sipani long ago, and Sipani now bows to me, in name at least. The power of Visserine is broken. As for Musselia, Etrea and Caprile, well. You and Orso between you, I suspect, have quite crushed their independent temper out of them."

"Westport?"

"Details, details. Part of the Union or of Kanta, depending on who you ask. No, it is Talins that concerns us now. Talins is the key in the lock, the hub of the wheel, the missing piece in my majestic jigsaw."

"You love to listen to your own voice, don't you?"

"I find it talks a lot of good sense. Orso's army is scattered, and with it his power is vanished, like smoke on the wind. He has ever resorted first to the sword, as certain others are wont to do, in fact..." He raised his brows significantly at her, and she waved him on. "He finds, now his sword is broken, that he has no friends to sustain him. But it will not be enough to destroy Orso. I need someone to replace him, someone to guide the troublesome citizens of Talins into my gracious fold."

"Let me know when you find the right shepherd."

"Oh, I already have. Someone of skill, cunning, matchless resilience and fearsome reputation. Someone loved in Talins far more than Orso himself. Someone he tried to kill, in fact...for stealing his throne..."

She narrowed her eyes at him. "I didn't want his throne then. I don't want it now."

"But since it is there for the taking...what comes once you have your revenge? You deserve to be remembered. You deserve to shape the age." Benna would have said so, and Monza had to admit that part of her was enjoying the flattery. Enjoying being so close to power again. She'd been used to both, and it had been a long time since she'd had a taste of either. "Besides, what better revenge could you have than making Orso's greatest fear come to pass?" That struck a fine note with her, and Rogont gave her a sly grin to show he knew it. "Let me be honest. I need you."

Let me be honest. I need you." That rested easily on Shivers' pride, and she gave him a sly smile to show she knew it. "I scarcely have a friend left in all the wide Circle of the World."

"Seems you've a knack for making new ones."

"It's harder than you'd think. To be always the outsider." He didn't need to be told that after the few months he'd had. She didn't lie, from what he could tell, just led the truth by the nose whichever way it suited her. "And sometimes it can be hard to tell your friends from your enemies."

"True enough." He didn't need to be told that either.

"I daresay where you come from loyalty is considered a noble quality. Down here in Styria, a man has to bend with the wind." Hard to believe anyone who smiled so sweetly could have anything dark in mind. But everything was dark to him now. Everything had a knife hidden in it. "Your friends and mine General Murcatto and Grand Duke Rogont, for example." Carlot's two eyes drifted up to his one. "I wonder what they're about, right now?"

"Fucking!" he barked at her, the fury boiling out of him so sharp she flinched away, like she was expecting him to smash her head into the wall. Maybe he nearly did. That or smash his own. But her face soon smoothed out and she smiled some more, like murderous rage was her favourite quality in a man.

"The Snake of Talins and the Worm of Ospria, all stickily entwined together. Well matched, that treacherous pair. Styria's greatest liar and Styria's greatest murderer." She gently traced the scar on his chest with one fingertip. "What comes once she has her revenge? Once Rogont has raised her up and dangled her like a child's toy for the people of Talins to stare at? Will you have a place when the Years of Blood are finally ended? When the war is over?"

"I don't have a place anywhere without a war. That much I've proved."

"Then I fear for you."

Shivers snorted. "I'm lucky to have you watching my back."

"I wish I could do more. But you know how the Butcher of Caprile solves her problems, and Duke Rogont has scant regard for honest men..."

* * *

I have nothing but the highest regard for honest men, but fighting stripped to the waist? It's so…" Rogont grimaced as though he'd tasted off milk. "Cliché. You wouldn't catch me doing it."

"What, fighting?"

"How dare you, woman, I am Stolicus reborn! You know what I mean. Your Northern accomplice, with the…" Rogont waved a lazy hand at the left side of his face. "Eye. Or lack thereof."

"Jealous, already?" she muttered, sick at even coming near the subject.

"A little. But it's his jealousy that concerns me. This is a man much prone to violence."

"It's what I took him on for."

"Perhaps the time has come to lay him off. Mad dogs savage their owner more often than their owner's enemies."

"And their owner's lovers first of all."

Rogont nervously cleared his throat. "We certainly would not want that. He seems firmly attached to you. When a barnacle is firmly attached to the hull of a ship, it is sometimes necessary to remove it with a sudden, unexpected and…decisive force."

"No!" Her voice stabbed out far sharper than she'd had in mind. "No. He's saved my life. More than once, and risked his life to do it. Just yesterday he did it, and today have him killed? No. I owe him." She remembered the smell as Langrier pushed the brand into his face, and she flinched. *It should've been you.* "No! I'll not have him touched."

"Think about it." Rogont padded slowly towards her. "I understand your reluctance, but you must see it's the safe thing to do."

"The prudent thing?" she sneered at him. "I'm warning you. Leave him be."

"Monzcarro, please understand, it's your safety I'm—Oooof!" She sprang up from the chair, kicking his foot away, caught his arm as he lurched onto his knees and twisted his wrist behind his shoulder blade, forced him down until she was squatting over his back, his face squashed against the cool marble.

"Didn't you hear me say no? If it's sudden, unexpected and decisive force I want…" She twisted his hand a little further and he squeaked, struggled helplessly. "I can manage it myself."

"Yes! Ah! Yes! I quite clearly see that!"

"Good. Don't bring him up again." She let go of his wrist and he lay there for a moment, breathing hard. He wriggled onto his back, rubbing gently at his hand, looking up with a hurt frown as she straddled his stomach.

"You didn't have to do that."

"Maybe I enjoyed doing it." She looked over her shoulder. His cock was half-hard, nudging at the back of her leg. "I'm not sure you didn't."

"Now that you mention it... I must confess I rather relish being looked down on by a strong woman." He brushed her knees with his fingertips, ran his hands slowly up the insides of her scarred thighs to the top, and then gently back down. "I don't suppose... you could be persuaded... to piss on me, at all?"

Monza frowned. "I don't need to go."

"Perhaps... some water, then? And afterwards—"

"I think I'll stick to the pot."

"Such a waste. The pot will not appreciate it."

"Once it's full you can do what you like with it, how's that?"

"Ugh. Not at all the same thing."

Monza slowly shook her head as she stepped off him. "A pretend grand duchess, pissing on a would-be king. You couldn't make it up."

Enough." Shivers was covered with bruises, grazes, scratches. A bastard of a gash across his back, just where it was hardest to scratch. Now his cock was going soft they were all niggling at him again in the sticky heat, stripping his patience. He was sick of talking round and round it, when it was lying between 'em, plain as a rotting corpse in the bed. "You want Murcatto dead, you can out and say it."

She paused, mouth half-open. "You're surprisingly blunt."

"No, I'm about as blunt as you'd expect for a one-eyed killer. Why?"

"Why what?"

"Why do you need her dead so bad? I'm an idiot, but not that big an idiot. I don't reckon a woman like you is drawn to my pretty face. Nor my sense of humour neither. Maybe you want yourself some revenge for what we did to you in Sipani. Everyone likes revenge. But that's just part of it."

"No small part..." She let one fingertip trail slowly up his leg. "As far as being drawn to you, I was always more interested in honest men than pretty faces, but I wonder... can I trust you?"

"No. If you could I wouldn't be much suited to the task, would I?" He caught hold of her trailing finger and twisted it towards him, dragged her wincing face close. "What's in it for you?"

"Ah! There's a man in the Union! The man I work for, the one who sent me to Styria in the first place, to spy on Orso!"

"The Cripple?" Vitari had said the name. The man who stood behind the King of the Union.

"Yes! Ah! Ah!" She squealed as he twisted her finger further, then he let it go and she snatched it back, holding it to her chest, bottom lip stuck out at him. "You didn't have to do that."

"Maybe I enjoyed doing it. Go on."

"When Murcatto made me betray Orso...she made me betray the Cripple too. Orso I can live with as an enemy, if I must —"

"But not this Cripple?"

She swallowed. "No. Not him."

"A worse enemy than the great Duke Orso, eh?"

"Far worse. Murcatto is his price. She threatens to rip apart all his carefully woven plans to bring Talins into the Union. He wants her dead." The smooth mask had slipped and she had this look, shoulders slumped, staring down wide-eyed at the sheet. Hungry, and sick, and very, very scared. Shivers liked seeing it. Might've been the first honest look he'd seen since he landed in Styria. "If I can find a way to kill her, I get my life," she whispered.

"And I'm your way."

She looked back up at him, and her eyes were hard. "Can you do it?"

"I could've done it today." He'd thought of splitting her head with his axe. He'd thought of planting his boot on her face and shoving her under the water. Then she'd have had to respect him. But instead he'd saved her. Because he'd been hoping. Maybe he still was...but hoping had made a fool of him. And Shivers was good and sick of looking the fool.

How many men had he killed? In all those battles, skirmishes, desperate fights up in the North? Just in the half-year since he came to Styria, even? At Cardotti's, in the smoke and the madness? Among the statues in Duke Salier's palace? In the battle just a few hours back? It might've been a score. More. And women among 'em. He was steeped in blood, deep as the Bloody-Nine himself. Didn't seem likely that adding one more to the tally would cost him a place among the righteous. His mouth twisted.

"I could do it." It was plain as the scar on his face that Monza cared nothing for him. Why should he care anything for her? "I could do it easily."

"Then do it." She crept forwards on her hands and knees, mouth half-open, pale tits hanging heavy, looking him right in his one eye. "For me." Her nipples brushed against his chest, one way then the other as she crawled over him. "For you." Her necklace of blood-red stones clicked gently against his chin. "For us."

"I'll need to pick my moment." He slid his hand down her back and up onto her arse. "Caution first, eh?"

"Of course. Nothing done well is ever…rushed."

His head was full of her scent, sweet smell of flowers mixed with the sharp smell of fucking. "She owes me money," he growled, the last objection.

"Ah, money. I used to be a merchant, you know. Buying. Selling." Her breath was hot on his neck, on his mouth, on his face. "And in my long experience, when people begin to talk prices, the deal is already done." She nuzzled at him, lips brushing the mass of scar down his cheek. "Do this thing for me, and I promise you'll get all you could ever spend." The cool tip of her tongue lapped gently at the raw flesh round his metal eye, sweet and soothing. "I have an arrangement…with the Banking House…of Valint and Balk…"

So Much for Nothing

Silver gleamed in the sunlight with that special, mouth-watering twinkle that somehow only money has. A whole strongbox full of it, stacked in plain sight, drawing the eyes of every man in the camp more surely than if a naked countess had been sprawled suggestively upon the table. Piles of sparking, sparkling coins, freshly minted. Some of the cleanest currency in Styria, pressed into some of its grubbiest hands. A pleasing irony. The coins carried the scales on one side, of course, traditional symbol of Styrian commerce since the time of the New Empire. On the other, the stern profile of Grand Duke Orso of Talins. An even more pleasing irony, to Cosca's mind, that he was paying the men of the Thousand Swords with the face of the man they had but lately betrayed.

In a pocked and spattered, squinting and scratching, coughing and slovenly line the soldiers and staff of the first company of the first regiment of the Thousand Swords passed by the makeshift table to receive their unjust deserts. They were closely supervised by the chief notary of the brigade and a dozen of its most reliable veterans, which was just as well, because during the course of the morning Cosca had witnessed every dispiriting trick imaginable.

Men approached the table on multiple occasions in different clothes, giving false names or those of dead comrades. They routinely exaggerated, embellished or flat-out lied in regards to rank or length of service. They wept for sick mothers, children or acquaintances. They delivered a devastating volley of complaints about food, drink, equipment, runny shits, superiors, the smell of other men, the weather, items stolen, injuries suffered, injuries given, perceived slights on non-existent honour and on, and on, and on. Had they demonstrated the same audacity and persistence in combat that they did in trying to prise the slightest dishonest pittance from their commander they would have been the greatest fighting force of all time.

But First Sergeant Friendly was watching. He had worked for years in the kitchens of Safety, where dozens of the world's most infamous swindlers vied daily with each other for enough bread to survive, and so he knew every low trick, con and stratagem practised this side of hell. There was no sliding around his basilisk gaze. The convict did not permit a single shining portrait of Duke Orso to be administered out of turn.

Cosca shook his head in deep dismay as he watched the last man trudge away, the unbearable limp for which he had demanded compensation miraculously healed. "By the Fates, you would have thought they'd be glad of the bonus! It isn't as if they had to fight for it! Or even steal it themselves! I swear, the more you give a man, the more he demands, and the less happy he becomes. No one ever appreciates what he gets for nothing. A pox on charity!" He slapped the notary on the shoulder, causing him to scrawl an untidy line across his carefully kept page.

"Mercenaries aren't all they used to be," grumbled the man as he sourly blotted it.

"No? To my eye they seem very much as violent-tempered and mean-spirited as ever. 'Things aren't what they used to be' is the rallying cry of small minds. When men say things used to be better, they invariably mean they were better for them, because they were young, and had all their hopes intact. The world is bound to look a darker place as you slide into the grave."

"So everything stays the same?" asked the notary, looking sadly up.

"Some men get better, some get worse." Cosca heaved a weighty sigh. "But on the grand scale, I have observed no significant changes. How many of our heroes have we paid now?"

"That's all of Squire's company, of Andiche's regiment. Well, Andiche's regiment that was."

Cosca put a hand over his eyes. "Please, don't speak of that brave heart. His loss still stabs at me. How many have we paid?"

The notary licked his fingers, flipped over a couple of crackling leaves of his ledger, started counting the entries. "One, two, three—"

"Four hundred and four," said Friendly.

"And how many persons in the Thousand Swords?"

The notary winced. "Counting all ancillaries, servants and tradesmen?"

"Absolutely."

"Whores too?"

"Counting them first, they're the hardest workers in the whole damned brigade!"

The lawyer squinted skywards. "Er..."

"Twelve thousand, eight hundred and nineteen," said Friendly.

Cosca stared at him. "I've heard it said a good sergeant is worth three generals, but you may well be worth three dozen, my friend! Thirteen thousand, though? We'll be here tomorrow night still!"

"Very likely," grumbled the notary, flipping over the page. "Crapstane's company of Andiche's regiment will be next. Andiche's regiment...as was...that is."

"Meh." Cosca unscrewed the cap of the flask Morveer had thrown at him in Sipani, raised it to his lips, shook it and realised it was empty. He frowned at the battered metal bottle, remembering with some discomfort the poisoner's sneering assertion that a man never changes. So much discomfort, in fact, that his need for a drink was sharply increased. "A brief interlude, while I obtain a refill. Get Crapstane's company lined up." He stood, grimacing as his aching knees crunched into life, then cracked a smile. A large man was walking steadily towards him through the mud, smoke, canvas and confusion of the camp.

"Why, Master Shivers, from the cold and bloody North!" The Northman had evidently given up on fine dressing, wearing a leather jack and rough-spun shirt with sleeves rolled to the elbows. His hair, neat as any Musselian dandy's when Cosca first laid eyes upon the man, had grown back to an unkempt tangle, heavy jaw fuzzed with a growth between beard and stubble. None of it did anything to disguise the mass of scar covering one side of his face. It would take more than hair to hide that. "My old partner in adventure!" Or murder, as was in fact the case. "You have a twinkle in your eye." Literally he did, for bright metal in the Northman's empty socket was catching the noon sun and shining with almost painful brightness. "You look well, my friend, most well!" Though he looked, in fact, a mutilated savage.

"Happy face, happy heart." The Northman showed a lopsided smile, burned flesh shifting only by the smallest margin.

"Quite so. Have a smile for breakfast, you'll be shitting joy by lunch. Were you in the battle?"

"That I was."

"I thought as much. You have never struck me as a man afraid to roll up his sleeves. Bloody, was it?"

"That it was."

"Some men thrive on blood, though, eh? I daresay you've known a few who were that way."

"That I have."

"And where is your employer, my infamous pupil, replacement and predecessor, General Murcatto?"

"Behind you," came a sharp voice.

He spun about. "God's teeth, woman, but you haven't lost the knack of creeping up on a man!" He pretended at shock to smother the sentimental welling-up that always accompanied her appearance, and threatened to make his voice crack with emotion. She had a long scratch down one cheek, some bruising on her face, but otherwise looked well. Very well. "My joy to see you alive knows no bounds, of course." He swept off his hat, feather drooping apologetically, and kneeled in the dirt in front of her. "Say you forgive me my theatrics. You see now I was thinking only of you all along. My fondness for you is undiminished."

She snorted at that. "Fondness, eh?" More than she could ever know, or he would ever tell her. "So this pantomime was for my benefit? I may swoon with gratitude."

"One of your most endearing features was always your readiness to swoon." He cranked himself back up to standing. "A consequence of your sensitive, womanly heart, I suppose. Walk with me, I have something to show you." He led her off through the trees towards the farmhouse, its whitewashed walls gleaming in the midday sun, Friendly and Shivers trailing them like bad memories. "I must confess that, as well as doing you a favour, and the sore temptation of placing my boot in Orso's arse at long last, there were some trifling issues of personal gain to consider."

"Some things never change."

"Nothing ever does, and why should it? A considerable quantity of Gurkish gold was on offer. Well, you know it was, you were the first to offer it. Oh, and Rogont was kind enough to promise me, in the now highly likely event that he is crowned King of Styria, the Grand Duchy of Visserine."

He was deeply satisfied by her gasp of surprise. "You? Grand fucking Duke of Visserine?"

"I probably won't use the word *fucking* on my decrees, but otherwise, correct. Grand Duke Nicomo sounds rather well, no? After all, Salier is dead."

"That much I know."

"He had no heirs, not even distant ones. The city was plundered, devastated by fire, its government collapsed, much of the populace fled, killed or otherwise taken advantage of. Visserine is in need of a strong and selfless leader to restore her to her glories."

"And instead they'll have you."

He allowed himself a chuckle. "But who better suited? Am I not a native of Visserine?"

"A lot of people are. You don't see them helping themselves to its dukedom."

"Well, there's only one, and it's mine."

"Why do you even want it? Commitments? Responsibilities? I thought you hated all that."

"I always thought so, but my wandering star led me only to the gutter. I have not had a productive life, Monzcarro."

"You don't say."

"I have frittered my gifts away on nothing. Self-pity and self-hatred have led me by unsavoury paths to self-neglect, self-injury and the very brink of self-destruction. The unifying theme?"

"Yourself?"

"Precisely so. Vanity, Monza. Self-obsession. The mark of infancy. I need, for my own sake and those of my fellow men, to be an adult. To turn my talents outwards. It is just as you always tried to tell me — the time comes when a man has to stick. What better way than to commit myself wholeheartedly to the service of the city of my birth?"

"Your wholehearted commitment. Alas for the poor city of Visserine."

"They'll do better than they did with that art-thieving gourmand."

"Now they'll have an all-thieving drunk."

"You misjudge me, Monzcarro. A man can change."

"I thought you just said nothing ever does?"

"Changed my mind. And why not? In one day I bagged myself a fortune, and one of the richest dukedoms in Styria too."

She shook her head in combined disgust and amazement. "And all you did was sit here."

"Therein lies the real trick. Anyone can *earn* rewards." Cosca tipped his head back, smiled up at the black branches and the blue sky beyond them. "Do you know, I think it highly unlikely that ever in history has one man gained so much for doing absolutely nothing. But I am hardly the only one to profit from yesterday's exploits. Grand Duke Rogont, I daresay, is happy with the outcome. And you are a great stride nearer to your grand revenge, are you not?" He leaned close to her. "Speaking of which, I have a gift for you."

She frowned at him, ever suspicious. "What gift?"

"I would hate to spoil the surprise. Sergeant Friendly, could you take your ex-employer and her Northern companion into the house, and show her what we found yesterday? For her to do with as she pleases, of course." He turned away with a smirk. "We're all friends now!"

In here." Friendly pushed the low door creaking open. Monza gave Shivers a look. He shrugged back. She ducked under the lintel and into a dim room, cool after the sun outside, with a ceiling of vaulted brick and patches of light across a dusty stone floor. As her eyes adjusted to the gloom she saw a figure wedged into the furthest corner. He shuffled forwards, chain between his ankles rattling faintly, and criss-cross shadows from the grubby window panes fell across one half of his face.

Prince Foscar, Duke Orso's younger son. Monza felt her whole body stiffen.

It seemed he'd finally grown up since she last saw him, running from his father's hall in Fontezarmo, wailing that he wanted no part in her murder. He'd lost the fluff on his top lip, gained a bloom of bruises ringing one eye and swapped the apologetic look for a fearful one. He stared at Shivers, then at Friendly as they stepped through into the room behind her. Not two men to give a prisoner hope, on the whole. He met Monza's eye, finally, reluctantly, with the haunted look of a man who knows what's coming.

"It's true then," he whispered. "You're alive."

"Unlike your brother. I stabbed him through his throat then threw him out of the window." The sharp knobble in Foscar's neck bobbed up and down as he swallowed. "I had Mauthis poisoned. Ganmark run through with a ton of bronze. Faithful's stabbed, slashed, drowned and hung from a waterwheel. Still turning on it, for all I know. Gobba was lucky. I only smashed his hands, and his knees, and his skull to bonemeal with a hammer." The list gave her grim nausea rather than grim satisfaction, but she forced her way through it. "Of the seven men who were in that room when they murdered Benna, there's just your father left." She slid the Calvez from its sheath, the gentle scraping of the blade as ugly as a child's scream. "Your father...and you."

The room was close, stale. Friendly's face was empty as a corpse's. Shivers leaned back against the wall beside her, arms folded, grinning.

"I understand." Foscar came closer. Small, unwilling steps, but towards her still. He stopped no more than a stride away, and sank to his knees. Awkwardly, since his hands were tied behind him. The whole time his eyes were on hers. "I'm sorry."

"You're fucking *sorry*?" she squeezed through gritted teeth.

"I didn't know what was going to happen! I loved Benna!" His lip trembled, a tear ran down the side of his face. Fear, or guilt, or both. "Your brother was like...a brother to me. I would never have wanted...that, for either of you. I'm sorry...for my part in it." He'd had no part in it. She knew that. "I just...I want to live!"

"So did Benna."

"Please." More tears trickled, leaving glistening trails down his cheeks. "I just want to live."

Her stomach churned, acid burning her throat and washing up into her watering mouth. Do it. She'd come all this way to do it, suffered all this and made all those others suffer just so she could do it. Her brother would have had no doubts, not then. She could almost hear his voice.

Do what you have to. Conscience is an excuse. Mercy and cowardice are the same.

It was time to do it. He had to die.

Do it now.

But her stiff arm seemed to weigh a thousand tons. She stared at Foscar's ashen face. His big, wide, helpless eyes. Something about him reminded her of Benna. When he was young. Before Caprile, before Sweet Pines, before they betrayed Cosca, before they joined up with the Thousand Swords, even. When she'd wanted just to make things grow. Long ago, that boy laughing in the wheat.

The point of the Calvez wobbled, dropped, tapped against the floor.

Foscar took a long, shuddering breath, closed his eyes, then opened them again, wet glistening in the corners. "Thank you. I always knew you had a heart...whatever they said. Thank—"

Shivers' big fist crunched into his face and knocked him on his back, blood bubbling from his broken nose. He got out a shocked splutter before the Northman was on top of him, hands closing tight around his throat.

"You want to fucking live, eh?" hissed Shivers, teeth bared in a snarling grin, the sinews squirming in his forearms as he squeezed tighter and tighter. Foscar kicked helplessly, struggled silently, twisted his shoulders, face turning pink, then red, then purple. Shivers dragged up Foscar's head with both his hands, lifted it towards him, close enough to kiss, almost, then rammed it down against the stone flags with a sharp crack. Foscar's boots jerked, the chain between them rattling. Shivers worked his head to one side then the other as he shifted his hands around Foscar's neck for a better grip, tendons standing stark from their scabbed backs. He dragged him up again, no hurry, and rammed his head back down with a dull crunch. Foscar's tongue lolled out, one eyelid flickering, black blood creeping down from his hairline.

Shivers growled something in Northern, words she couldn't understand, lifted Foscar's head, smashed it down with all the care of a stonemason getting the details right. Again, and again. Monza watched, her mouth half-open, still holding weakly onto her sword, doing nothing. Not sure what she could do, or should do. Whether to stop him or help him. Blood dashed the rendered walls and the stone flags in spots and spatters. Over the pop and crackle of shattering bone she could hear a voice. Benna's voice, she thought for a minute, still whispering at her to do it. Then she realised it was Friendly, calmly counting the number of times Foscar's skull had been smashed into the stones. He got up to eleven.

Shivers lifted the prince's mangled head once more, hair all matted glistening black, then he blinked, and let it drop.

"Reckon that's got it." He came slowly up to standing, one boot planted on either side of Foscar's corpse. "Heh." He looked at his hands, looked around for something to wipe them on, ended up rubbing them together, smearing black streaks of blood dry brown to his elbows. "One more to the good." He looked sideways at her with his one eye, corner of his mouth curled up in a sick smile. "Six out o' seven, eh, Monza?"

"Six and one," Friendly grunted to himself.

"All turning out just like you hoped."

She stared down at Foscar, flattened head twisted sideways, crossed eyes goggling up at the wall, blood spreading out across the stone floor in a black puddle from his broken skull. Her voice seemed to come from a long way off, reedy thin. "Why did you—"

"Why not?" whispered Shivers, coming close. She saw her own pale, scabbed, pinched-in face reflected, bent and twisted in that dead metal ball of an eye. "What we came here for, ain't it? What we fought for all the day, down in the mud? I thought you was all for never turning back? Mercy and cowardice the same and all that hard talk you gave me. By the dead, Chief." He grinned, the mass of scar across his face squirming and puckering, his good cheek all dotted with red. "I could almost swear you ain't half the evil bitch you pretend to be."

Shifting Sands

With the greatest of care not to attract undue attention, Morveer insinuated himself into the back of Duke Orso's great audience chamber. For such a vast and impressive room, it numbered but a few occupants. Perhaps a function of the difficult circumstances in which the great man found himself. Having catastrophically lost the most important battle in the history of Styria was bound to discourage visitors. Still, Morveer had always been drawn to employers in difficult circumstances. They tended to pay handsomely.

The Grand Duke of Talins was without doubt still a majestic presence. He sat upon a gilded chair, on a high dais, all in sable velvet trimmed with gold, and frowned down with regal fury over the shining helmets of half a dozen no less furious guardsmen. He was flanked by two men who could not have been more polar opposites. On the left a plump, ruddy-faced old fellow stood with a respectful but painful-looking bend to his hips, gold buttons about his chubby throat fastened to the point of uncomfortable tightness and, indeed, considerably beyond. He had ill-advisedly attempted to conceal his utter and obvious baldness by combing back and forth a few sad strands of wiry grey hair, cultivated to enormous length for this precise purpose. Orso's chamberlain. On the right, a curly-haired young man slouched with unexpected ease in travel-stained clothes, resting upon what appeared to be a long stick. Morveer had the frustrating sensation of having seen him somewhere before, but could not place him, and his relationship to the duke was, for now, a slightly worrying mystery.

The only other occupant of the chamber had his well-dressed back to Morveer, prostrate upon one knee on the strip of crimson carpet, clutching his hat in one hand. Even from the very back of the hall the gleaming sheen of sweat across his bald patch was most evident.

"What help from my son-in-law," Orso was demanding in stentorian tones, "the High King of the Union?"

The voice of the ambassador, for it appeared to be none other, had the whine of a well-whipped dog expecting further punishment. "Your son-in-law sends his earnest regrets—"

"Indeed? But no soldiers! What would he have me do? Shoot his regrets at my enemies?"

"His armies are all committed in our unfortunate Northern wars, and a revolt in the city of Rostod causes further difficulties. The nobles, meanwhile, are reluctant. The peasantry are again restless. The merchants—"

"The merchants are behind on their payments. I see. If excuses were soldiers he would have sent a mighty throng indeed."

"He is beset by troubles—"

"*He* is beset? He is? Are his sons murdered? Are his soldiers butchered? Are his hopes all in ruins?"

The ambassador wrung his hands. "Your Excellency, he is spread thin! His regrets have no end, but—"

"But his help has no beginning! High King of the Union! A fine talker, and a goodly smile when the sun is up, but when the clouds come in, look not for shelter in Adua, eh? My intervention on his behalf was timely, was it not? When the Gurkish horde clamoured at his gates! But now I need his help...forgive me, Father, I am spread *thin*. Out of my sight, bastard, before your master's regrets cost you your tongue! Out of my sight, and tell the Cripple that I see his hand in this! Tell him I will whip the price from his twisted hide!" The grand duke's furious screams echoed out over the hurried footsteps of the ambassador, edging backwards as quickly as he dared, bowing profusely and sweating even more. "Tell him I will be revenged!"

The ambassador genuflected his way past Morveer, and the double doors were heaved booming shut upon him.

"Who is that skulking at the back of the chamber?" Orso's voice was no more reassuring for its sudden calmness. Quite the reverse.

Morveer swallowed as he processed down the blood-red strip of carpet. Orso's eye held a look of the most withering command. It reminded Morveer unpleasantly of his meeting with the headmaster of the orphanage, when he was called to account for the dead birds. His ears burned with shame and horror at the memory of that interview, more even than his legs burned at the memory of his punishment. He swept out his lowest and most sycophantic bow, unfortunately spoiling the effect by rapping his knuckles against the floor in his nervousness.

"This is one Castor Morveer, your Excellency," intoned the chamberlain, peering down his bulbous nose.

Orso leaned forwards. "And what manner of a man is Castor Morveer?"

"A poisoner."

"*Master*... Poisoner," corrected Morveer. He could be as obsequious as the next man, when it was required, but he flatly insisted on his proper title. Had he not earned it, after all, with sweat, danger, deep wounds both physical and emotional, long study, short mercy and many, many painful reverses?

"Master, is it?" sneered Orso. "And what great notables have you poisoned to earn the prefix?"

Morveer permitted himself the faintest of smiles. "Grand Duchess Sefeline of Ospria, your Excellency. Count Binardi of Etrea, and both his sons, though their boat subsequently sank and they were never found. Ghassan Maz, Satrap of Kadir, and then, when further problems presented themselves, his successor Souvon-yin-Saul. Old Lord Isher, of Midderland, he was one of mine. Prince Amrit, who would have been heir to the throne of Muris—"

"I understood he died of natural causes."

"What could be a more natural death for a powerful man than a dose of Leopard Flower administered into the ear by a dangling thread? Then Admiral Brant, late of the Murisian fleet, and his wife. His cabin boy too, alas, who happened by, a young life cut regrettably short. I would hate to prevail upon your Excellency's valuable time, the list is long indeed, most distinguished and... entirely *dead*. With your permission I will add only the most recent name upon it."

Orso gave the most minute inclination of his head, sneering no longer, Morveer was pleased to note. "One Mauthis, head of the Westport office of the Banking House of Valint and Balk."

The duke's face had gone blank as a stone slab. "Who was your employer for that last?"

"I make it a point of professionalism never to mention the names of my employers...but I believe these are *exceptional* circumstances. I was hired by none other than Monzcarro Murcatto, the Butcher of Caprile." His blood was up now, and he could not resist a final flourish. "I believe you are acquainted."

"Some...what," whispered Orso. The duke's dozen guards stirred ominously as if controlled directly by their master's mood. Morveer became aware that he might have gone a flourish too far, felt his bladder weaken and was forced to press his knees together. "You infiltrated the offices of Valint and Balk in Westport?"

"Indeed," croaked Morveer.

Orso glanced sideways at the man with the curly hair. "I congratulate you on the achievement. Though it has been the cause of some considerable discomfort to me and my associates. Pray explain why I should not have you killed for it."

Morveer attempted to pass it off with a vivacious chuckle, but it died a slow death in the chilly vastness of the hall. "I...er...had no notion, of course, that you were in *any* way to be discomfited. None. Really, it was all due to a regrettable failing, or indeed a wilful oversight, deliberate dishonesty, *a lie*, even, on the part of my cursed assistant that I took the job in the first place. I should never have trusted that greedy bitch..." He realised he was doing himself no good by blaming the dead. Great men want living people to hold responsible, that they might have them tortured, hanged, beheaded and so forth. Corpses offer no recompense. He swiftly changed tack. "I was but the tool, your Excellency. Merely the weapon. A weapon I now offer for your own hand to wield, as you see fit." He bowed again, even lower this time, muscles in his rump, already sore from climbing the cursed mountainside to Fontezarmo, trembling in their efforts to prevent him from pitching on his face.

"You seek a new employer?"

"Murcatto proved as treacherous towards me as she did towards your illustrious Lordship. The woman is a snake indeed. Twisting, poisonous and...*scaly*," he finished lamely. "I was lucky to escape her toxic clutches with my life, and now seek redress. I am prepared to seek it *most* earnestly, and will not be denied!"

"Redress would be a fine thing for us all," murmured the man with the curly hair. "News of Murcatto's survival spreads through Talins like wildfire. Papers bearing her face on every wall." A fact, Morveer had seen them as he passed through the city. "They say you stabbed her through the heart but she lived, your Excellency."

The duke snorted. "Had I stabbed her, I would never have aimed for her heart. Without doubt her least vulnerable organ."

"They say you burned her, drowned her, cut her into quarters and tossed them from your balcony, but she was stitched back together and lived again. They say she killed two hundred men at the fords of the Sulva. That she charged alone into your ranks and scattered them like chaff on the wind."

"The stamp of Rogont's theatrics," hissed the duke through gritted teeth. "That bastard was born to be an author of cheap fantasies rather than a ruler of men. We will hear next that Murcatto has sprouted wings and given birth to the second coming of Euz!"

"I wouldn't be at all surprised. Bills are posted on every street corner proclaiming her an instrument of the Fates, sent to deliver Styria from your tyranny."

"Tyrant, now?" The duke barked a grim chuckle. "How quickly the wind shifts in the modern age!"

"They say she cannot be killed."

"Do...they...indeed?" Orso's red-rimmed eyes swivelled to Morveer. "What do you say, poisoner?"

"Your Excellency," and he plunged down into the lowest of bows once more, "I have fashioned a successful career upon the principle that there is *nothing* that lives that cannot be deprived of life. It is the remarkable ease of killing, rather than the impossibility of it, that has always caused me astonishment."

"Do you care to prove it?"

"Your Excellency, I humbly entreat only the *opportunity*." Morveer swept out another bow. It was his considered opinion that one could never bow too much to men of Orso's stamp, though he did reflect that persons of huge ego were a great drain on the patience of bystanders.

"Then here it is. Kill Monzcarro Murcatto. Kill Nicomo Cosca. Kill Countess Cotarda of Affoia. Kill Duke Lirozio of Puranti. Kill First Citizen Patine of Nicante. Kill Chancellor Sotorius of Sipani. Kill Grand Duke Rogont, before he can be crowned. Perhaps I will not have Styria, but I will have revenge. On that you can depend."

Morveer had been warmly smiling as the list began. By its end he was smiling no longer, unless one could count the fixed rictus he maintained across his trembling face only by the very greatest of efforts. It appeared his bold gambit had spectacularly oversucceeded. He was forcibly reminded of his attempt to discomfort four of his tormentors at the orphanage by placing Lankam salts in the water, which had ended, of course, with the untimely deaths of all the establishment's staff and most of the children too.

"Your Excellency," he croaked, "that is a significant quantity of murder."

"And some fine names for your little list, no? The rewards will be equally significant, on that you can rely, will they not, Master Sulfur?"

"They will." Sulfur's eyes moved from his fingernails to Morveer's face. Different-coloured eyes, Morveer now noticed, one green, one blue. "I represent, you see, the Banking House of Valint and Balk."

"Ah." Suddenly, and with profound discomfort, Morveer placed the man. He had seen him talking with Mauthis in the banking hall in Westport but a few short days before he had filled the place with corpses. "Ah. I really had not the *slightest* notion, you understand..." How he wished now that he had not killed Day. Then he could have noisily denounced her as the culprit and had something tangible with which to furnish the duke's dungeons. Fortunately, it seemed Master Sulfur was not seeking scapegoats. Yet.

"Oh, you were but the weapon, as you say. If you can cut as sharply on our behalf you have nothing to worry about. And besides, Mauthis was a terrible bore. Shall we say, if you are successful, the sum of one million scales?"

"One...million?" muttered Morveer.

"There is nothing that lives that cannot be deprived of life." Orso leaned forwards, eyes fixed on Morveer's face. "Now get about it!"

Night was falling when they came to the place, lamps lit in the grimy windows, stars spilled out across the soft night sky like diamonds on a jeweller's cloth. Shenkt had never liked Affoia. He had studied there, as a young man, before he ever knelt to his master and before he swore never to kneel again. He had fallen in love there, with a woman too rich, too old and far too beautiful for him, and been made a whining fool of. The streets were lined not only with old pillars and thirsty palms, but with the bitter remnants of his childish shame, jealousy, weeping injustice. Strange, that however tough one's skin becomes in later life, the wounds of youth never close.

Shenkt did not like Affoia, but the trail had led him here. It would take more than ugly memories to make him leave a job half-done.

"That is the house?" It was buried in the twisting backstreets of the city's oldest quarter, far from the thoroughfares where the names of men seeking public office were daubed on the walls along with their great qualities and other, less complimentary words and pictures. A small building, with slumping lintels and a slumping roof, squeezed between a warehouse and a leaning shed.

"That's the house." The beggar's voice was soft and stinking as rotten fruit.

"Good." Shenkt pressed five scales into his scabby palm. "This is for you." He closed the man's fist around the money then held it with his own. "Never come back here." He leaned closer, squeezed harder. "Not ever."

He slipped across the cobbled street, over the wall before the house. His heart was beating unusually fast, sweat prickling his scalp. He crept across the overgrown front garden, old boots finding the silent spaces between the weeds, and to the lighted window. Reluctant, almost afraid, he peered through. Three children sat on a worn red carpet beside a small fire. Two girls and a boy, all with the same orange hair. They were playing with a brightly painted wooden horse on wheels. Clambering onto it, pushing each other around on it, pushing each other off it, to faint squeals of amusement. He squatted there, fascinated, and watched them.

Innocent. Unformed. Full of possibilities. Before they began to make their choices, or had their choices made for them. Before the doors began to close, and sent them down the only remaining path. Before they knelt. Now, for this briefest spell, they could be anything.

"Well, well. What have we here?"

She was crouching above him on the low roof of the shed, her head on one side, a line of light from a window across the way cutting hard down her face, strip of spiky red hair, red eyebrow, narrowed eye, freckled skin, corner of a frowning mouth. A chain hung gleaming down from one fist, cross of sharpened metal swinging gently on the end of it.

Shenkt sighed. "It seems you have the better of me."

She slid from the wall, dropped to the dirt and thumped smoothly down on her haunches, chain rattling. She stood, tall and lean, and took a step towards him, raising her hand.

He breathed in, slow, slow.

He saw every detail of her face: lines, freckles, faint hairs on her top lip, sandy eyelashes crawling down as she blinked.

He could hear her heart beating, heavy as a ram at a gate.

Thump...thump...thump...

She slid her hand around his head, and they kissed. He wrapped his arms about her, pressed her thin body tight against him, she tangled her fingers in his hair, chain brushing against his shoulders, dangling metal knocking lightly against the backs of his legs. A long, gentle, lingering kiss that made his body tingle from his lips to his toes.

She broke away. "It's been a while, Cas."

"I know."

"Too long."

"I know."

She nodded towards the window. "They miss you."

"Can I..."

"You know you can."

She led him to the door, into the narrow hallway, unbuckling the chain from her wrist and slinging it over a hook, cross-shaped knife dangling. The oldest girl dashed out from the room, stopped dead when she saw him.

"It's me." He edged slowly towards her, his voice strangled. "It's me." The other two children came out from the room, peering around their sister. Shenkt feared no man, but before these children, he was a coward. "I have something for you." He reached into his coat with trembling fingers.

"Cas." He held out the carved dog, and the little boy with his name snatched it from his hand, grinning. "Kande." He put the bird in the cupped hands of the littlest girl, and she stared dumbly at it. "For you, Tee," and he offered the cat to the oldest girl.

She took it. "No one calls me that anymore."

"I'm sorry it's been so long." He touched the girl's hair and she flinched away, he jerked his hand back, awkward. He felt the weight of the butcher's sickle in his coat as he moved, and he stood sharply, took a step back. The three of them stared up at him, carved animals clutched in their hands.

"To bed now," said Shylo. "He'll still be here tomorrow." Her eyes were on him, hard lines across the freckled bridge of her nose. "Won't you, Cas?"

"Yes."

She brushed their complaints away, pointed to the stairs. "To bed." They filed up slowly, step by step, the boy yawning, the younger girl hanging her head, the other complaining that she wasn't tired. "I'll come sing to you later. If you're quiet until then, maybe your father will even hum the low parts." The youngest of the two girls smiled at him, between the banisters at the top of the stairs, until Shylo pushed him into the living room and shut the door.

"They got so big," he muttered.

"That's what they do. Why are you here?"

"Can't I just—"

"You know you can, and you know you haven't. Why are you…" She saw the ruby on his forefinger and frowned. "That's Murcatto's ring."

"She lost it in Puranti. I nearly caught her there."

"Caught her? Why?"

He paused. "She has become involved…in my revenge."

"You and your revenge. Did you ever think you might be happier forgetting it?"

"A rock might be happier if it was a bird, and could fly from the earth and be free. A rock is not a bird. Were you working for Murcatto?"

"Yes. So?"

"Where is she?"

"You came here for that?"

"That." He looked towards the ceiling. "And them." He looked her in the eye. "And you."

She grinned, little lines cutting into the skin at the corners of her eyes. It took him by surprise, how much he loved to see those lines. "Cas, Cas. For such a clever bastard you're a stupid bastard. You always look for all the wrong things in all the wrong places. Murcatto's in Ospria, with Rogont. She fought in the battle there. Any man with ears knows that."

"I didn't hear."

"You don't listen. She's tight with the Duke of Delay, now. My guess is he'll be putting her in Orso's place, keep the people of Talins alongside when he reaches for the crown."

"Then she'll be following him. Back to Talins."

"That's right."

"Then I will follow them. Back to Talins." Shenkt frowned. "I could have stayed there these past weeks, and simply waited for her."

"That's what happens if you're always chasing things. Works better if you wait for what you want to come to you."

"I was sure you'd have found another man by now."

"I found a couple. They didn't stick." She held out her hand to him. "You ready to hum?"

"Always." He took her hand, and she pulled him from the room, and through the door, and up the stairs.

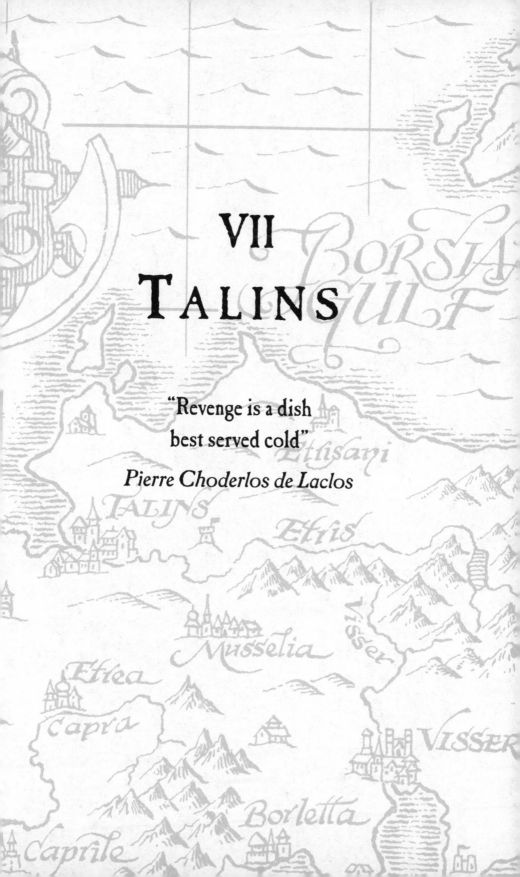

VII
TALINS

"Revenge is a dish
best served cold"

Pierre Choderlos de Laclos

Rogont of Ospria was late to the field at Sweet Pines, but Salier of Visserine still enjoyed the weight of numbers and was too proud to retreat. Especially when the enemy was commanded by a woman. He fought, he lost, he ended up retreating anyway, and left the city of Caprile defenceless. Rather than face a certain sack, the citizens opened their gates to the Serpent of Talins in the hope of mercy.

Monza rode in, but most of her men she left outside. Orso had made allies of the Baolish, convinced them to fight with the Thousand Swords under their ragged standards. Fierce fighters, but with a bloody reputation. Monza had a bloody reputation of her own, and that only made her trust them less.

"I love you."

"Of course you do."

"I love you, but keep the Baolish out of town, Benna."

"You can trust me."

"I do trust you. Keep the Baolish out of town."

She rode three hours as the sun went down, back to the rotting battlefield at Sweet Pines, to dine with Duke Orso and learn his plans for the close of the season.

"Mercy for the citizens of Caprile, if they yield to me entirely, pay indemnities and acknowledge me their rightful ruler."

"Mercy, your Excellency?"

"You know what it is, yes?" She knew what it was. She had not thought he did. "I want their land, not their lives. Dead men cannot obey. You have won a famous victory here. You shall have a great triumph, a procession through the streets of Talins."

That would please Benna, at least. "Your Excellency is too kind."

"Hah. Few would agree with that."

She laughed as she rode back in the cool dawn, and Faithful laughed beside her. They talked of how rich the soil was, on the banks of the Capra, watching the good wheat shift in the wind.

Then she saw the smoke above the city, and she knew.

The streets were full of dead. Men, women, children, young and old. Birds gathered on them. Flies swarmed. A confused dog limped along beside their horses. Nothing else living showed itself. Empty windows gaped, empty doorways yawned. Fires still burned, whole rows of houses nothing but ash and tottering chimney stacks.

Last night, a thriving city. This morning, Caprile was hell made real.

It seemed Benna had not been listening. The Baolish had begun it, but the rest of the Thousand Swords — drunk, angry, fearing they would miss out on the easy pickings — had eagerly joined in. Darkness and dark company make it easy for even half-decent men to behave like animals, and there were few half-decent men among the scum Monza commanded. The boundaries of civilisation are not the impregnable walls civilised men take them for. As easily as smoke on the wind, they can dissolve.

Monza flopped down from her horse and puked Duke Orso's fine breakfast over the rubbish-strewn cobbles.

"Not your fault," said Faithful, one big hand on her shoulder.

She shook him off. "I know that." But her rebellious guts thought otherwise.

"It's the Years of Blood, Monza. This is what we are."

Up the steps to the house they'd taken, tongue rough with sick. Benna lay on the bed, fast asleep, husk pipe near one hand. She dragged him up, made him squawk, cuffed him one way and the other.

"Keep them out of town, I told you!" And she forced him to the window, forced him to look down into the bloodstained street.

"I didn't know! I told Victus... I think..." He slid to the floor, and wept, and her anger leaked away and left her empty. Her fault, for leaving him in charge. She could not let him shoulder the blame. He was a good man, and sensitive, and would not have borne it well. There was nothing she could do but kneel beside him, and hold him, and whisper soothing words while the flies buzzed outside the window.

"Orso wants to give us a triumph..."

Soon afterwards the rumours spread. The Serpent of Talins had ordered the massacre that day. Had urged the Baolish on and screamed for more. The Butcher of Caprile, they called her, and she did not deny it. People would far rather believe a lurid lie than a sorry string of accidents. Would far rather believe the world is full of evil than full of bad luck, selfishness and stupidity. Besides, the rumours served a purpose. She was more feared than ever, and fear was useful.

In Ospria they denounced her. In Visserine they burned her image. In Affoia and Nicante they offered a fortune to any man who could kill her. All around the Azure Sea they rang out the bells to her shame. But in Etrisani they celebrated. In Talins they lined the streets to chant her name, to shower her with flower petals. In Cesale they raised a statue in her honour. A gaudy thing, smothered with gold leaf that soon peeled. She and Benna, as they never looked, seated on great horses, frowning boldly towards a noble future.

That was the difference between a hero and a villain, a soldier and a murderer, a victory and a crime. Which side of a river you called home.

Return of the Native

Monza was far from comfortable.

Her legs ached, her arse was chafed raw from riding, her shoulder had stiffened up again so she was constantly twisting her head to one side like a demented owl in a futile attempt to loosen it. Whenever one source of sweaty agony would ease for a moment, another would flare up to plug the gap. Her prodding joke of a little finger seemed attached to a cord of cold pain, tightening relentlessly right to her elbow if she tried to use the hand. The sun was merciless in the clear blue sky, making her squint, niggling at the headache leaking from the coins that held her skull together. Sweat tickled her scalp, ran down her neck, gathered in the scars Gobba's wire had left and made them itch like fury. Her crawling skin was prickly, clammy, sticky. She cooked in her armour like offal in a can.

Rogont had her dressed up like some simpleton's notion of the Goddess of War, an unhappy collision of shining steel and embroidered silk that offered the comfort of full plate and the protection of a nightgown. It might all have been made to measure by Rogont's own armourer, but there was a lot more room for chest in her gold-chased breastplate than there was a need for. This, according to the Duke of Delay, was what people wanted to see.

And enough of them had turned out for the purpose.

Crowds lined the narrow streets of Talins. They squashed into windows and onto roofs to catch a glimpse of her. They packed into the squares and gardens in dizzying throngs, throwing flowers, waving banners, boiling over with hope. They shouted, bellowed, roared, squealed, clapped, stamped, hooted, competing with each other to be the first to burst her skull with their clamour. Sets of musicians had formed at street corners, would strike up martial tunes as she came close, brassy and blaring, clanging away behind her, merging with the off-key offering of the next impromptu band to form a mindless, murderous, patriotic din.

It was like the triumph after her victory at Sweet Pines, only she was older and even more reluctant, her brother was rotting in the mud instead of basking in the glory and her old enemy Rogont was at her back rather than her old friend Orso. Perhaps that was what history came down to, in the end. Swapping one sharp bastard for another was the best you could hope for.

They crossed the Bridge of Tears, the Bridge of Coins, the Bridge of Gulls, looming carvings of seabirds glaring angrily down at the procession as it crawled past, brown waters of the Etris sluggishly churning beneath them. Each time she rounded a corner another wave of applause would break upon her. Another wave of nausea. Her heart was pounding. Every moment, she expected to be killed. Blades and arrows seemed more likely than flowers and kind words, and far more deserved. Agents of Duke Orso, or his Union allies, or a hundred others with a private grudge against her. Hell, if she'd been in the crowd and seen some woman ride past dressed like this, she'd have killed her on general principle. But Rogont must have spread his rumours well. The people of Talins loved her. Or loved the idea of her. Or had to look like they did.

They chanted her name, and her brother's name, and the names of her victories. Afieri. Caprile. Musselia. Sweet Pines. The High Bank. The fords of the Sulva too. She wondered if they knew what they were cheering for. Places she'd left trails of corpses behind her. Cantain's head rotting on the gates of Borletta. Her knife in Hermon's eye. Gobba, hacked to pieces, pulled apart by rats in the sewers beneath their feet. Mauthis and his clerks with their poisoned ledgers, poisoned fingers, poisoned tongues. Ario and all his butchered revellers at Cardotti's, Ganmark and his slaughtered guards, Faithful dangling from the wheel, Foscar's head broken open on the dusty floor. Corpses by the cartload. Some of it she didn't regret, some of it she did. But none of it seemed like anything to cheer about. She winced up towards the happy faces at the windows. Maybe that was where she and these folk differed.

Maybe they just liked corpses, so long as they weren't theirs.

She glanced over her shoulder at her so-called allies, but they hardly gave her comfort. Grand Duke Rogont, the king-in-waiting, smiling to the crowds from a knot of watchful guards, a man whose love would last exactly as long as she was useful. Shivers, steel eye glinting, a man who'd turned under her tender touch from likeable optimist to maimed murderer. Cosca winked back at her — the world's least reliable ally and most unpredictable enemy, and he could still prove to be either one. Friendly...who knew what went on behind those dead eyes?

Further back rode the other surviving leaders of the League of Eight. Or Nine. Lirozio of Puranti, fine moustaches bristling, who'd slipped nimbly back into Rogont's camp after the very briefest of alliances with Orso. Countess Cotarda, her watchful uncle never far behind. Patine, First Citizen of Nicante, with his emperor's bearing and his ragged peasant's clothes, who had declined to share in the battle at the fords but seemed more than happy to share in the victory. There were even representatives of cities she'd sacked on Orso's behalf — citizens of Musselia and Etrea, a sly-eyed young niece of Duke Cantain's who'd suddenly found herself Duchess of Borletta, and appeared to be greatly enjoying the experience.

People she'd thought of as her enemies for so long she was having trouble making the adjustment, and by the looks on their faces when her eyes met theirs, so were they. She was the spider they had to suffer in their larder to rid them of their flies. And once the flies are dealt with, who wants a spider in their salad?

She turned back, sweaty shoulders prickling, tried to fix her eyes ahead. They passed along the endless curve of the seafront, gulls sweeping, circling, calling above. All the way her nose was full of that rotten salt tang of Talins. Past the boatyards, the half-finished hulls of two great warships sitting on the rollers like the skeletons of two beached and rotted whales. Past the rope-makers and the sail-weavers, the lumber-yards and the wood-turners, the brass-workers and the chain-makers. Past the vast and reeking fish-market, its flaking stalls empty, its galleries quiet for the first time maybe since the victory at Sweet Pines last emptied the buildings and filled the streets with savagely happy crowds.

Behind the multicoloured splatters of humanity the buildings were smothered with bills, as they had been in Talins more or less since the invention of the press. Old victories, warnings, incitements, patriotic bluster, endlessly pasted over by the new. The latest set carried a woman's face — stern, guiltless, coldly beautiful. Monza realised with a sick turning of her guts that it was meant to be hers, and beneath it, boldly printed: *Strength, Courage, Glory.* Orso had once told her that the way to turn a lie into the truth was to shout it often enough, and here was her self-righteous face, repeated over and over, plastered torn and dog-eared across the salt-stained walls. On the side of the next crumbling façade another set of posters, badly drawn and smudgily printed, had her awkwardly holding high a sword, beneath the legend: *Never Surrender, Never Relent, Never Forgive.* Daubed across the bricks above them in letters of streaky red paint tall as a man was one simple word:

Vengeance.

Monza swallowed, less comfortable than ever. Past the endless docks where fishing vessels, pleasure vessels, merchant vessels of every shape and size, from every nation beneath the sun, stirred on the waves of the great bay, cobwebs of rigging spotted with sailors up to watch the Snake of Talins take the city for her own.

Just as Orso had feared she would.

Cosca was entirely comfortable.

It was hot, but there was a soothing breeze wafting off the glittering sea, and one of his ever-expanding legion of new hats was keeping his eyes well shaded. It was dangerous, the crowd very likely containing more than one eager assassin, but for once there were several more hated targets than himself within easy reach. A drink, a drink, a drink, of course, that drunkard's voice in his head would never be entirely silent. But it was less a desperate scream now than a grumpy murmur, and the cheering was very definitely helping to drown it out.

Aside from the vague smell of seaweed it was just as it had been in Ospria, after his famous victory at the Battle of the Isles. When he had stood tall in his stirrups at the head of the column, acknowledging the applause, holding his hands up and shouting, "Please, no!" when he meant, "More, more!" It was Grand Duchess Sefeline, Rogont's aunt, who had basked in his reflected glory then, mere days before she tried to have him poisoned. Mere months before the tide of battle turned against her and she was poisoned herself. That was Styrian politics for you. It made him wonder, just briefly, why he was getting into it.

"The settings change, the people age, the faces swap one with another, but the applause is just the same — vigorous, infectious and so very short-lived."

"Uh," grunted Shivers. It seemed to be most of the Northman's conversation, now, but that suited Cosca well enough. In spite of occasional efforts to change, he had always vastly preferred talking to listening.

"I always hated Orso, of course, but I find little pleasure in his fall." A towering statue of the fearsome Duke of Talins could be seen down a side street as they passed. Orso had ever been a keen patron to sculptors, provided they used him as their subject. Scaffolding had been built up its front, and now men clustered around the face, battering its stern features away gleefully with hammers. "So soon, yesterday's heroes are shuffled off. Just as I was shuffled off myself."

"Seems you've shuffled back."

"My point precisely! We all are washed with the tide. Listen to them cheer for Rogont and his allies, so recently the most despicable slime on the face of the world." He pointed out the fluttering papers pasted to the nearest wall, on which Duke Orso was displayed having his face pushed into a latrine. "Only peel back this latest layer of bills and I'll wager you'll find others denouncing half this procession in the filthiest ways imaginable. I recall one of Rogont shitting onto a plate and Duke Salier tucking into the results with a fork. Another of Duke Lirozio trying to mount his horse. And when I say 'mount'…"

"Heh," said Shivers.

"The horse was not impressed. Dig through a few layers more and — I blush to admit — you'll find some condemning me as the blackest-hearted rogue in the Circle of the World, but now…" Cosca blew an extravagant kiss towards some ladies on a balcony, and they smiled, pointed, showed every sign of regarding him as their delivering hero.

The Northman shrugged. "People got no weight to 'em down here. Wind blows 'em whatever way it pleases."

"I have travelled widely," if fleeing one war-torn mess after another qualified, "and in my experience people are no heavier elsewhere." He unscrewed the cap from his flask. "Men can have all manner of deeply held beliefs about the world in general that they find most inconvenient when called upon to apply to their own lives. Few people let morality get in the way of expediency. Or even convenience. A man who truly believes in a thing beyond the point where it costs him is a rare and dangerous thing."

"It's a special kind o' fool takes the hard path just 'cause it's the right one."

Cosca took a long swallow from his flask, winced and scraped his tongue against his front teeth. "It's a special kind of fool who can even tell the right path from the wrong. I've certainly never had that knack." He stood in his stirrups, swept off his hat and waved it wildly in the air, whooping like a boy of fifteen. The crowds roared their approval back. Just as if he was a man worth cheering for. And not Nicomo Cosca at all.

So quietly that no one could possibly have heard, so softly that the notes were almost entirely in his mind, Shenkt hummed.

"Here she is!"

The pregnant silence gave birth to a storm of applause. People danced, threw up their arms, cheered with hysterical enthusiasm. People laughed and wept, celebrated as if their own lives might be changed to any significant degree by Monzcarro Murcatto being given a stolen throne.

It was a tide Shenkt had often observed in politics. There is a brief spell after a new leader comes to power, however it is achieved, during which they can do no wrong. A golden period in which people are blinded by their own hopes for something better. Nothing lasts forever, of course. In time, and usually with alarming speed, the leader's flawless image grows tarnished with their subjects' own petty disappointments, failures, frustrations. Soon they can do no right. The people clamour for a new leader, that they might consider themselves reborn. Again.

But for now they cheered Murcatto to the heavens, so loud that, even though he had seen it all a dozen times before, Shenkt almost allowed himself to hope. Perhaps this would be a great day, the first of a great era, and he would be proud in after years to have had his part in it. Even if his part had been a dark one. Some men, after all, can only play dark parts.

"The Fates." Beside him, Shylo's lip curled up with scorn. "What does she look like? A fucking gold candlestick. A gaudy figurehead, gilded up to hide the rot."

"I think she looks well." Shenkt was glad to see her still alive, riding a black horse at the head of the sparkling column. Duke Orso might have been all but finished, his people hailing a new leader, his palace at Fontezarmo surrounded and under siege. None of that made the slightest difference. Shenkt had his work, and he would see it through to the end, however bitter. Just as he always did. Some stories, after all, are only suited to bitter endings.

Murcatto rode closer, eyes fixed ahead in an expression of the most bloody-minded resolve. Shenkt would have liked very much to step forwards, to brush the crowds aside, to smile, to hold out his hand to her. But there were altogether too many onlookers, altogether too many guards. The moment was coming when he would greet her, face to face.

For now he stood, as her horse passed by, and hummed.

So many people. Too many to count. If Friendly tried, it made him feel strange. Vitari's face jumped suddenly from the crowd, beside her a gaunt man with short, pale hair and a washed-out smile. Friendly stood in the stirrups but a waving banner swept across his sight and they were gone. A thousand other faces in a blinding tangle. He watched the procession instead.

If this had been Safety, and Murcatto and Shivers had been convicts, Friendly would have known without doubt from the look on the Northman's face that he wanted to kill her. But this was not Safety, more was the pity, and there were no rules here that Friendly understood. Especially once women entered the case, for they were a foreign people to him. Perhaps Shivers loved her, and that look of hungry rage was what love looked like. Friendly knew they had been fucking in Visserine, he had heard them at it enough, but then he thought she might have been fucking the Grand Duke of Ospria lately, and had no idea what difference that might make. Here was the problem.

Friendly had never really understood fucking, let alone love. When he came back to Talins, Sajaam had sometimes taken him to whores, and told him it was a reward. It seemed rude to turn down a reward, however little he wanted it. To begin with he had trouble keeping his prick hard. Even later, the most enjoyment he ever got from the messy business was counting the number of thrusts before it was all over.

He tried to settle his jangling nerves by counting the hoofbeats of his horse. It seemed best that he avoid embarrassing confusions, keep his worries to himself and let things take the course they would. If Shivers did kill her, after all, it meant little enough to Friendly. Probably lots of people wanted to kill her. That was what happened when you made yourself conspicuous.

Shivers was no monster. He'd just had enough.

Enough of being treated like a fool. Enough of his good intentions fucking him in the arse. Enough of minding his conscience. Enough worrying on other people's worries. And most of all enough of his face itching. He grimaced as he dug at his scars with his fingernails.

Monza was right. Mercy and cowardice were the same. There were no rewards for good behaviour. Not in the North, not here, not anywhere. Life was an evil bastard, and gave to those who took what they wanted. Right was on the side of the most ruthless, the most treacherous, the most bloody, and the way all these fools cheered for her now was the proof of it. He watched her riding slowly up at the front, on her black horse, black hair stirring in the breeze. She'd been right about everything, more or less.

And he was going to murder her, pretty much just for fucking someone else.

He thought of stabbing her, cutting her, carving her ten different ways. He thought of the marks on her ribs, of sliding a blade gently between them. He thought of the scars on her neck, and how his hands would fit just right against them to throttle her. He guessed it would be good to be close to her one last time. Strange, that he should've saved her life so often, risked his own to do it, and now be thinking out the best way to put an end on it. It was like the Bloody-Nine told him once — love and hate have just a knife's edge between 'em.

Shivers knew a hundred ways to kill a woman that'd all leave her just as dead. It was where and when that were the problems. She was watchful all the time, now, expecting knives. Not from him, maybe, but from somewhere. There were plenty of 'em aimed at her besides his, no doubt. Rogont knew it, and was careful with her as a miser with his hoard. He needed her to bring all these people over to his side, always had men watching. So Shivers would have to wait, and pick his time. But he could show some patience. It was like Carlot said. Nothing done well is ever... rushed.

"Keep closer to her."

"Eh?" None other than the great Duke Rogont, ridden up on his blind side. It took an effort for Shivers not to smash his fist right into the man's sneering, handsome face.

"Orso still has friends out there." Rogont's eyes jumped nervously over the crowds. "Agents. Assassins. There are dangers everywhere."

"Dangers? Everyone seems so happy, though."

"Are you trying to be funny?"

"Wouldn't know how to begin." Shivers kept his face so slack Rogont couldn't tell whether he was being mocked or not.

"Keep closer to her! You are supposed to be her bodyguard!"

"I know what I am." And Shivers gave Rogont his widest grin. "Don't worry yourself on that score." He dug his horse's flanks and urged on ahead. Closer to Monza, just like he'd been told. Close enough that he could see her jaw muscles clenched tight on the side of her face. Close enough, almost, that he could have pulled out his axe and split her skull.

"I know what I am," he whispered. He was no monster. He'd just had enough.

The procession finally came to an end in the heart of the city, the square before the ancient Senate House. The mighty building's roof had collapsed centuries ago, its marble steps cracked and rooted with weeds. The carvings of forgotten gods on the colossal pediment had faded to a tangle of blobs, perches for a legion of chattering gulls. The ten vast pillars that supported it looked alarmingly out of true, streaked with droppings, stuck with flapping fragments of old bills. But the mighty relic still dwarfed the meaner buildings that had flourished around it, proclaiming the lost majesty of the New Empire.

A platform of pitted blocks thrust out from the steps and into the sea of people crowding the square. At one corner stood the weathered statue of Scarpius, four times the height of a man, holding out hope to the world. His outstretched hand had broken off at the wrist several hundred years ago and, in what must have been the most blatant piece of imagery in Styria, no one had yet bothered to replace it. Guardsmen stood grimly before the statue, on the steps, at the pillars. They wore the cross of Talins on their coats but Monza knew well enough they were Rogont's men. Perhaps Styria was meant to be one family now, but soldiers in Osprian blue might not have been well received here.

She slid from her saddle, strode down the narrow valley through the crowds. People strained against the guardsmen, calling to her, begging for blessings. As though touching her might do them any good. It hadn't done much to anyone else. She kept her eyes ahead, always ahead, jaw aching from being clenched tight, waiting for the blade, the arrow, the dart that would be the end of her. She'd happily have killed for the sweet oblivion of a smoke, but she was trying to cut back, on the killing and the smoking both.

Scarpius towered over her as she started up the steps, peering down out of the corners of his lichen-crusted eyes as if to say, *Is this bitch the best they could do?* The monstrous pediment loomed behind him, and she wondered if the hundred tons of rock balanced on those pillars might finally choose that moment to crash down and obliterate the entire leadership of Styria, herself along with them. No small part of her hoped that it would, and bring this sticky ordeal to a swift end.

A gaggle of leading citizens — meaning the sharpest and the greediest — had clustered nervously in the centre of the platform, sweating in their most expensive clothes, looking hungrily towards her like geese at a bowl of crumbs. They bowed as she and Rogont came closer, heads bobbing together in a way that suggested they'd been rehearsing. That somehow made her more irritated than ever.

"Get up," she growled.

Rogont held his hand out. "Where is the circlet?" He snapped his fingers. "The circlet, the circlet!"

The foremost of the citizens looked like a bad caricature of wisdom — all hooked nose, snowy beard and creaky deep voice under a green felt hat like an upended chamber pot. "Madam, my name is Rubine, nominated to speak for the citizens."

"I am Scavier." A plump woman whose azure bodice exposed a terrifying immensity of cleavage.

"And I am Grulo." A tall, lean man, bald as an arse, not quite shouldering in front of Scavier but very nearly.

"Our two most senior merchants," explained Rubine.

It carried little weight with Rogont. "And?"

"And, with your permission, your Excellency, we were hoping to discuss some details of the arrangements —"

"Yes? Out with it!"

"As regards the title, we had hoped perhaps to steer away from nobility. Grand duchess smacks rather of Orso's tyranny."

"We hoped..." ventured Grulo, waving a vulgar finger-ring, "something to reflect the mandate of the common people."

Rogont winced at Monza, as though the phrase "common people" tasted of piss. "Mandate?"

"President elect, perhaps?" offered Scavier. "First citizen?"

"After all," added Rubine, "the previous grand duke is still, technically... alive."

Rogont ground his teeth. "He is besieged two dozen miles away in Fontezarmo like a rat in his hole! Only a matter of time before he is brought to justice."

"But you understand the legalities may prove troublesome—"

"Legalities?" Rogont spoke in a furious whisper. "I will soon be King of Styria, and I mean to have the Grand Duchess of Talins among those who crown me! I will be king, do you understand? Legalities are for other men to worry on!"

"But, your Excellency, it might not be seen as appropriate—"

For a man with a reputation for too much patience, Rogont's had grown very short over the last few weeks. "How appropriate would it be if I was to, say, have you hanged? Here. Now. Along with every other reluctant bastard in the city. You could argue the legalities to each other while you dangle."

The threat floated between them for a long, uncomfortable moment. Monza leaned towards Rogont, acutely aware of the vast numbers of eyes fixed upon them. "What we need here is a little unity, no? I've a feeling hangings might send the wrong message. Let's just get this done, shall we? Then we can all lie down in a dark room."

Grulo carefully cleared his throat. "Of course."

"A long conversation to end where we began!" snapped Rogont. "Give me the damn circlet!"

Scavier produced a thin golden band. Monza turned slowly to face the crowd.

"People of Styria!" Rogont roared behind her. "I give you the Grand Duchess Monzcarro of Talins!" There was a slight pressure as he lowered the circlet onto her head.

And that simply she was raised to the giddy heights of power.

With a faint rustling, everyone knelt. The square was left silent, enough that she could hear the birds flapping and squawking on the pediment above. Enough that she could hear the spatters as some droppings fell not far to her right, daubing the ancient stones with spots of white, black and grey.

"What are they waiting for?" she muttered to Rogont, doing her best not to move her lips.

"Words."

"Me?"

"Who else?"

A wave of dizzy horror broke over her. By the look of the crowd, she might easily have been outnumbered five thousand to one. But she had the feeling that, for her first action as head of state, fleeing the platform in terror might send the wrong message. So she stepped slowly forwards, as hard a step as she'd ever taken, struggling to get her tumbling thoughts in order, dig up words she didn't have in the splinter of time she did. She passed through Scarpius' great shadow and out into the daylight, and a sea of faces opened up before her, tilted up towards her, wide-eyed with hope. Their scattered muttering dropped to nervous whispering, then to eerie silence. She opened her mouth, still hardly knowing what might come out of it.

"I've never been one..." Her voice was a reedy squeak. She had to cough to clear it, spat the results over her shoulder then realised she definitely shouldn't have. "I've never been one for speeches!" That much was obvious. "Rather get right to it than talk about it! Born on a farm, I guess. We'll deal with Orso first! Rid ourselves of that bastard. Then...well...then the fighting's over." A strange kind of murmur went through the kneeling crowd. No smiles, exactly, but some faraway looks, misty eyes, a few heads nodding. She was surprised by a longing tug in her own chest. She'd never really thought before that she'd wanted the fighting to end. She'd never known much else.

"Peace." And that needy murmur rippled across the square again. "We'll have ourselves a king. All Styria, marching one way. An end to the Years of Blood." She thought of the wind in the wheat. "Try to make things grow, maybe. Can't promise you a better world because, well, it is what it is." She looked down awkwardly at her feet, shifted her weight from one leg to another. "I can promise to do my best at it, for what that's worth. Let's aim at enough for everyone to get by, and see how we go." She caught the eye of an old man, staring at her with teary-eyed emotion, lip quivering, hat clasped to his chest.

"That's all!" she snapped.

* * *

Any normal person would have been lightly dressed on a day so sticky warm, but Murcatto, with characteristic contrariness, had opted for full and, as it happened, ludicrously flamboyant armour. Morveer's only option, therefore, was to take aim at her exposed face. Still, a smaller target only presented the greater and more satisfying challenge for a marksman of his sublime skills. He took a deep breath.

To his horror she shifted at the crucial moment, looking down at the platform, and the dart missed her face by the barest whisker and glanced from one of the pillars of the ancient Senate House behind her.

"Damn it!" he hissed around the mouthpiece of his blowpipe, already fumbling in his pocket for another dart, removing its cap, sliding it gently into the chamber.

It was a stroke of ill fortune of the variety that had tormented Morveer since birth that, just as he was applying his lips to the pipe, Murcatto terminated her incompetent rhetoric with a perfunctory, "That's all!" The crowd broke into rapturous applause, and his elbow was jogged by the enthusiastic clapping of a peasant beside the deep doorway in which he had secreted himself.

The lethal missile went well wide of its target and vanished into the heaving throng beside the platform. The man whose wild gesticulations had been responsible for his wayward aim looked about, his broad, greasy face puckering with suspicion. He had the appearance of a labourer, hands like rocks, the flame of human intellect barely burning behind his piggy eyes.

"Here, what are you—"

Curse the proletariat, Morveer's attempt was now quite foiled. "My *profound* regrets, but could I prevail upon you to hold this for just a moment?"

"Eh?" The man stared down at the blowpipe pressed suddenly into his callused hands. "Ah!" As Morveer jabbed him in the wrist with a mounted needle. "What the hell?"

"Thank you *ever* so much." Morveer reclaimed the pipe and slid it into one of his myriad of concealed pockets along with the needle. It takes the vast majority of men a great deal of time to become truly incensed, usually following a predictable ritual of escalating threats, insults, posturing, jostling and so forth. Instantaneous action is entirely foreign to them. So the elbow-jogger was only now beginning to look truly angry.

"Here!" He seized Morveer by the lapel. "Here..." His eyes took on a faraway look. He wobbled, blinked, his tongue hung out. Morveer took him under the arms, gasped at the sudden dead weight as the man's knees collapsed, and wrestled him to the ground, suffering an unpleasant twinge in his back as he did so.

"He alright?" someone grunted. Morveer looked up to see a half-dozen not dissimilar men frowning down at him.

"*Altogether* too much beer!" Morveer shouted over the noise, adding a false little chuckle. "My companion here has become *quite* inebriated!"

"Inebri-what?" said one.

"Drunk!" Morveer leaned close. "He was so very, *very* proud to have the great Serpent of Talins as the mistress of our fates! Are not we all?"

"Aye," one muttered, utterly confused but partially mollified. "Course. Murcatto!" he finished lamely, to grunts of approval from his simian comrades.

"Born among us!" shouted another, shaking his fist.

"Oh, *absolutely* so. Murcatto! Freedom! Hope! Deliverance from coarse stupidity! Here we are, friend!" Morveer grunted with effort as he wriggled the big man, now a big corpse, into the shadows of the doorway. He winced as he arched his aching back. Then, since the others were no longer paying attention, he slid away into the crowds, boiling with resentment all the way. It really was insufferable that these imbeciles should cheer so very enthusiastically for a woman who, far from being born among them, had been born on a patch of scrub on the very edge of Talinese territory where the border was notoriously flexible. A ruthless, scheming, lying, apprentice-seducing, mass-murdering, noisily fornicating peasant thief without a filigree shred of conscience, whose only qualifications for command were a sulky manner, a few victories against incompetent opposition, the aforementioned propensity to swift action, a fall down a mountain and the accident of a highly attractive face.

He was forced to reflect once again, as he had so often, that life was rendered immeasurably easier for the comely.

The Lion's Skin

A lot had changed since Monza last rode up to Fontezarmo, laughing with her brother. Hard to believe it was only a year ago. The darkest, maddest, most bloody year in a life made of them. A year that had taken her from dead woman to duchess, and might well still shove her back the other way.

It was dusk instead of dawn, the sun sinking behind them in the west as they climbed the twisting track. To either side of it, wherever the ground was anything close to flat, men had pitched tents. They sat in front of them in lazy groups by the flickering light of campfires — eating, drinking, mending boots or polishing armour, staring slack-faced at Monza as she clattered past.

She'd had no honour guard a year ago. Now a dozen of Rogont's picked men followed eagerly as puppies wherever she went. It was a surprise they didn't all try to tramp into the latrine after her. The last thing the king-in-waiting wanted was for her to get pushed off a mountain again. Not before she'd had the chance to help crown him, anyway. It was Orso she'd been helping to his crown twelve months ago, and Rogont her bitter enemy. For a woman who liked to stick, she'd slid around some in four seasons.

Back then she'd had Benna beside her. Now it was Shivers. That meant no talk at all, let alone laughter. His face was just a hard black outline, blind eye gleaming with the last of the fading light. She knew he couldn't see a thing through it, but still she felt like it was always fixed right on her. Even though he scarcely spoke, still he was always saying, *It should've been you.*

There were fires burning at the summit. Specks of light on the slopes, a yellow glow behind the black shapes of walls and towers, smudges of smoke hanging in the deep evening sky. The road switched back once more, then petered away altogether at a barricade made from three upended carts. Victus sat there on a field chair, warming his hands at a campfire, his collection of stolen chains gleaming round his neck. He grinned as she reined up her horse, and flourished out an absurd salute.

"The Grand Duchess of Talins, here in our slovenly camp! Your Excellency, we're all shame! If we'd had more time to prepare for your royal visit, we'd have done something about all the dirt." And he spread his arms wide at the sea of churned-up mud, bare rock, broken bits of crate and wagon scattered around the mountainside.

"Victus. The embodiment of the mercenary spirit." She clambered down from her saddle, trying not to let the pain show. "Greedy as a duck, brave as a pigeon, loyal as a cuckoo."

"I always modelled myself on the nobler birds. Afraid you'll have to leave the horses, we'll be going by trench from here. Duke Orso's a most ungracious host — he's taken to shooting catapults at any of his guests who show themselves." He sprang up, slapping dust from the canvas he'd been sitting on, then holding one ring-encrusted hand out towards it. "Perhaps I could have some of the lads carry you up?"

"I'll walk."

He gave her a mocking leer. "And a fine figure you'll appear, I've no doubt, though I would've thought you could've stretched to silk, given your high station."

"Clothes don't make the person, Victus." She gave his jewellery a mocking leer of her own. "A piece of shit is still a piece of shit, however much gold you stick on it."

"Oh, how we've missed you, Murcatto. Follow on, then."

"Wait here," she snapped at Rogont's guards. Having them behind her all the time made her look weak. Made her look like she needed them.

Their sergeant winced. "His Excellency was most—"

"Piss on his Excellency. Wait here."

She creaked down some steps made of old boxes and into the hillside, Shivers at her shoulder. The trenches weren't much different from the ones they'd dug around Muris, years ago — walls of hard-packed earth held back by odds and ends of timber, with that same smell of sickness, mould, damp earth and boredom. The trenches they'd lived in for the best part of six months, like rats in a sewer. Where her feet had started to rot, and Benna got the running shits so bad he lost a quarter of his weight and all his sense of humour. She even saw a few familiar faces as they threaded their way through ditch, tunnel and dugout — veterans who'd been fighting with the Thousand Swords for years. She nodded to them just as she used to when she was in charge, and they nodded back.

"You sure Orso's inside?" she called to Victus.

"Oh, we're sure. Cosca spoke to him, first day."

Monza didn't draw much comfort from that idea. When Cosca started talking to an enemy he usually ended up richer and on the other side. "What did those two bastards have to say to each other?"

"Ask Cosca."

"I will."

"We've got the place surrounded, don't worry about that. Trenches on three sides." Victus slapped the earth beside them. "If you can trust a mercenary to do one thing, it's dig himself a damn good hole to hide in. Then there's pickets down in the woods at the bottom of the cliff." The woods where Monza had slid to a halt in the rubbish, broken to pulp, groaning like the dead in hell. "And a wide selection of Styria's finest soldiery further out. Osprians, Sipanese, Affoians, in numbers. All set on seeing our old employer dead. There ain't a rat getting out without our say-so. But then if Orso wanted to run, he could've run weeks ago. He didn't. You know him better than anyone, don't you? You reckon he'll try and run now?"

"No," she had to admit. He'd sooner die, which suited her fine. "How about us getting in?"

"Whoever designed the bastard place knew what they were doing. Ground around the inner ward's way too steep to try anything."

"I could've told you that. North side of the outer ward's your best chance at an assault, then try the inner wall from there."

"Our very thoughts, but there's a gulf between thinking and doing, specially when high walls are part of the case. No luck yet." Victus clambered up on a box and beckoned to her. Between two wicker screens, beyond a row of sharpened stakes pointing up the broken slope, she could see the nearest corner of the fortress. One of the towers was on fire, its tall roof fallen in leaving only a cone of naked beams wreathed in flames, notches of battlements picked out in red and yellow, black smoke belching into the dark blue sky. "We set that tower to burning," he pointed proudly towards it, "with a catapult."

"Beautiful. We can all go home."

"Something, ain't it?" He led them through a long dugout smelling of damp and sour sweat, men snoring on pallets down both sides. "'Wars are won not by one great action,'" intoning the words like a bad actor, "'but many small chances.' Weren't you always telling us that? Who was it? Stalicus?"

"Stolicus, you dunce."

"Some dead bastard. Anyway, Cosca's got a plan, but I'll let him tell you himself. You know how the old man loves to put on a show." Victus stopped at a hollow in the rock where four trenches came together, sheltered by a roof of gently flapping canvas and lit by a single rustling torch. "The captain general said he'd be along. Feel free to make use of the facilities while you wait." Facilities which amounted to dirt. "Unless there's anything else, your Excellency?"

"Just one more thing." He flinched in surprise as her spit spattered softly across his eye. "That's from Benna, you treacherous little fuck."

Victus wiped his face, eyes creeping shiftily to Shivers, then back to her. "I didn't do nothing you wouldn't have done. Nothing your brother wouldn't have done, that's certain. Nothing you didn't both do to Cosca, and you owed him more than I owed you—"

"That's why you're wiping your face instead of trying to hold your guts in."

"You ever think you might have brought this on yourself? Big ambitions mean big risks. All I've done is float with the current—"

Shivers took a sudden step forwards. "Off you float, then, 'fore you get your throat cut." Monza realised he had a knife out in one big fist. The one she'd given him the first day they met.

"Whoa there, big man." Victus held up his palms, rings glittering. "I'm on my way, don't worry." He made a big show of turning and strutting off into the night. "You two need to work on your tempers," wagging one finger over his shoulder. "No point getting riled up over every little thing. That'll only end in blood, believe me!"

It wasn't so hard for Monza to believe. Everything ended in blood, whatever she did. She realised she was left alone with Shivers, something she'd spent the last few weeks avoiding like the rot. She knew she should say something, take some sort of step towards making things square with him. They had their problems, but at least he was her man, rather than Rogont's. She might have need of someone to save her life in the coming days, and he was no monster, however he might look.

536

"Shivers." He turned to her, knife still clutched tight, steel blade and steel eye catching the torch flame and twinkling the colours of fire. "Listen—"

"No, you listen." He bared his teeth, taking a step towards her.

"Monza! You came!" Cosca emerged from one of the trenches, arms spread wide. "And with my favourite Northman!" He ignored the knife and shook Shivers warmly by his free hand, then grabbed Monza's shoulders and kissed her on both cheeks. "I haven't had a chance to congratulate you on your speech. Born on a farm. A nice touch. Humble. And talk of peace. From you? It was like seeing a farmer express his hopes for famine. Even this old cynic couldn't help but be moved."

"Fuck yourself, old man." But she was secretly glad she didn't have to find the hard words now.

Cosca raised his brows. "You try and say the right thing—"

"Some folk don't like the right thing," said Shivers in his gravelly whisper, sliding his knife away. "You ain't learned that yet?"

"Every day alive is a lesson. This way, comrades! Just up ahead we can get a fine view of the assault."

"You're attacking? Now?"

"We tried in daylight. Didn't work." It didn't look like darkness was working any better. There were wounded men lining the next trench— grimaces, groans, bloody bandages. "Wherever is my noble employer, his Excellency Duke Rogont?"

"In Talins." And Monza spat into the dirt. There was plenty of it for the purpose. "Preparing for his coronation."

"So soon? He is aware Orso's still alive, I suppose, and by all indications will be for some time yet? Isn't there a saying about selling the lion's skin before he's killed?"

"I've mentioned it. Many times."

"I can only imagine. The Serpent of Talins, counselling caution to the Duke of Delay. Sweet irony!"

"Some good it's done. He's got every carpenter, clothier and jeweller in the city busy at the Senate House, making it ready for the ceremony."

"Sure the bloody place won't fall in on him?"

"We can hope," muttered Shivers.

"It will bring to mind proud shadows of Styria's Imperial past, apparently," said Monza.

537

Cosca snorted. "That or the shameful collapse of Styria's last effort at unity."

"I've mentioned that too. Many times."

"Ignored?"

"Getting used to it."

"Ah, hubris! As a long-time sufferer myself I quickly recognise the symptoms."

"You'll like this one, then." Monza couldn't stop herself sneering. "He's importing a thousand white songbirds from distant Thond."

"Only a thousand?"

"Symbol of peace, apparently. They'll be released over the crowd when he rises to greet them as King of Styria. And admirers from all across the Circle of the World — counts, dukes, princes and the God of the fucking Gurkish too for all I know — will applaud his gigantic opinion of himself, and fall over themselves to lick his fat arse."

Cosca raised his brows. "Do I detect a souring of relations between Talins and Ospria?"

"There's something about crowns that makes men act like fools."

"One takes it you've mentioned that too?"

"Until my throat's sore, but surprisingly enough, he doesn't want to hear it."

"Sounds quite the event. Shame I won't be there."

Monza frowned. "You won't?"

"Me? No, no, no. I'd only lower the tone. There are concerns about some shady deal done for the Dukedom of Visserine, would you believe."

"Never."

"Who knows how these far-fetched rumours get started? Besides, some-one needs to keep Duke Orso company."

She worked her tongue sourly round her mouth and spat again. "I hear the two of you have been chatting already."

"No more than small talk. Weather, wine, women, his impending destruction, you know the sort of thing. He said he would have my head. I replied I quite understood his enthusiasm, as I find it hugely useful myself. I was firm yet amusing throughout, in fact, while he was, in all honesty, somewhat peevish." Cosca waved one long finger around. "The siege, pos-sibly, has him out of sorts."

"Nothing about you changing sides, then?"

"Perhaps that would have been his next topic, but we were somewhat interrupted by some flatbow fire and an abortive assault upon the walls. Perhaps it will come up when we next take tea together?"

The trench opened into a dugout mostly covered with a plank ceiling, almost too low to stand under. Ladders leaned against the right-hand wall, ready for men to climb and join the attack. A good three score of armed and armoured mercenaries knelt ready to do just that. Cosca went bent over between their ranks, slapping backs.

"Glory, boys, glory, and a decent pay-off!"

Their frowns turned to grins, they tapped their weapons against their shields, their helmets, their breastplates, sending up an approving rattle.

"General!"

"The captain general!"

"Cosca!"

"Boys, boys!" He chuckled, thumping arms, shaking hands, giving out lazy salutes. All as far from her style of command as could've been. She'd had to stay cold, hard, untouchable, or there would have been no respect. A woman can't afford the luxury of being friendly with the men. So she'd let Benna do the laughing for her. Probably why the laughter had been thin on the ground since Orso killed him.

"And up here is my little home from home." Cosca led them up a ladder and into a kind of shed built from heavy logs, lit by a pair of flickering lamps. There was a wide opening in one wall, the setting sun casting its last glare over the dark, flat country to the west. Narrow windows faced towards the fortress. A stack of crates took up one corner, the captain general's chair sat in another. Beside it a table was covered with a mess of scattered cards, half-eaten sweetmeats and bottles of varying colour and fullness. "How goes the fight?"

Friendly sat cross-legged, dice between his knees. "It goes."

Monza moved to one of the narrow windows. It was almost night, now, and she could barely see any sign of the assault. Perhaps the odd flicker of movement at the tiny battlements, the odd glint of metal in the light of the bonfires scattered across the rocky slopes. But she could hear it. Vague shouting, faint screaming, clattering metal, floating indistinctly on the breeze.

Cosca slid into the battered captain general's chair and rattled the bottles by putting his muddy boots up on the table. "We four, together again! Just like Cardotti's House of Leisure! Just like Salier's gallery! Happy times, eh?"

There was the creaking swoosh of a catapult released and a blazing missile sizzled overhead, shattered against the great foremost tower of the fortress, sending up a gout of flame, shooting out arcs of glittering embers. The dull flare illuminated ladders against the stonework, tiny figures crawling up them, steel glimmering briefly then fading back into the black.

"You sure this is the best time for jokes?" Monza muttered.

"Unhappy times are the best for levity. You don't light candles in the middle of the day, do you?"

Shivers was frowning up the slope towards Fontezarmo. "You really think you've a chance of carrying those walls?"

"Those? Are you mad? They're some of the strongest in Styria."

"Then why—"

"Bad form to just sit outside and do nothing. They have ample stocks of food, water, weapons and, worst of all, loyalty. They might last months in there. Months during which Orso's daughter, the Queen of the Union, might prevail upon her reluctant husband to send aid." Monza wondered whether the king learning that his wife preferred women would make any difference . . .

"How's watching your men fall off a wall going to help?" asked Shivers.

Cosca shrugged. "It will wear down the defenders, deny them rest, keep them guessing and distract them from any other efforts we might make."

"Lot of corpses for a distraction."

"Wouldn't be much of a distraction without them."

"How do you get men to climb the ladders for that?"

"Sazine's old method."

"Eh?"

Monza remembered Sazine displaying the money to the new boys, all laid out in sparkling stacks. "If the walls fall, a thousand scales to the first man on the battlements, a hundred each to the next ten who follow him."

"Provided they survive to collect the bounty," Cosca added. "If the task's impossible, they'll never collect, and if they do, well, you achieved the impossible for two thousand scales. It ensures a steady flow of willing bodies up the ladders, and has the added benefit of weeding the bravest men out of the company to boot."

Shivers looked even more baffled. "Why would you want to do that?"

"'Bravery is the dead man's virtue,'" Monza muttered. "'The wise commander never trusts it.'"

"Verturio!" Cosca slapped one leg. "I do love an author who can make death funny! Brave men have their uses but they're damned unpredictable. Worrying to the herd. Dangerous to bystanders."

"Not to mention potential rivals for command."

"Altogether safest to cream them off," and Cosca mimed the action with a careless flick of two fingers. "The moderately cowardly make infinitely better soldiers."

Shivers shook his head in disgust. "You people got a pretty fucking way of making war."

"There is no pretty way of making war, my friend."

"You said a distraction," cut in Monza.

"I did."

"From what?"

There was a sudden fizzing sound and Monza saw fire out of the corner of her eye. A moment later the heat of it washed across her cheek. She spun, the Calvez already part-drawn. Ishri was draped across the crates behind them, sprawled out lazily as an old cat in the sun, head back, one long, thin, bandaged leg dangling from the edge of the boxes and swinging gently back and forth.

"Can't you ever just say hello?" snapped Monza.

"Where would be the fun in that?"

"Do you have to answer every question with another?"

Ishri pressed one hand to her bandaged chest, black eyes opening wide. "Who? Me?" She rolled something between her long finger and thumb, a little black grain, and flicked it with uncanny accuracy into the lamp beside Shivers. It went up with a flash and sizzle, cracking the glass hood and spraying sparks. The Northman stumbled away, cursing, flicking embers off his shoulder.

"Some of the men have taken to calling it Gurkish sugar." Cosca smacked his lips. "Sounds sweeter, to my ear, than Gurkish fire."

"Two dozen barrels," murmured Ishri, "courtesy of the Prophet Khalul."

Monza frowned. "For a man I've never met he likes us a lot."

"Better yet..." The dark-skinned woman slithered from the boxes like a snake, waves running through her body from shoulders down to hips as if she had no bones in her, arms trailing after. "He hates your enemies."

"No better basis for an alliance than mutual loathing." Cosca watched her contortions with an expression stuck between distrust and fascination. "It's a brave new age, my friends. Time was you had to dig for months, hundreds of strides of mine, tons of wood for props, fill it up with straw and oil, set it on fire, run like merry hell, then half the time it wouldn't even bring the walls down. This way, all you need do is sink a shaft deep enough, pack the sugar in, strike a spark and—"

"Boom," sang Ishri, up on her toes and stretching to her fingertips.

"Ker-blow," returned Cosca. "It's how everyone's conducting sieges these days, apparently, and who am I to ignore a trend…" He flicked dust from his velvet jacket. "Sesaria's a genius at mining. He brought down the bell tower at Gancetta, you know. Somewhat before schedule, admittedly, and a few men did get caught in the collapse. Did I ever tell you—"

"If you bring the wall down?" asked Monza.

"Well, then our men pour through the breach, overwhelm the stunned defenders and the outer ward will be ours. From the gardens within we'll have level ground to work with and room to bring our numbers to bear. Carrying the inner wall should be a routine matter of ladders, blood and greed. Then storm the palace and, you know, keep it traditional. I'll get my plunder and you'll get—"

"My revenge." Monza narrowed her eyes at the jagged outline of the fortress. Orso was in there, somewhere. Only a few hundred strides away. Perhaps it was the night, the fire, the heady mixture of darkness and danger, but some of that old excitement was building in her now. That fierce fury she'd felt when she hobbled from the bone-thief's crumbling house and into the rain. "How long until the mine's ready?"

Friendly looked up from his dice. "Twenty-one days and six hours. At the rate they're going."

"A shame." Ishri pushed out her bottom lip. "I so love fireworks. But I must go back to the South."

"Tired of our company already?" asked Monza.

"My brother was killed." Her black eyes showed no sign of emotion. "By a woman seeking vengeance."

Monza frowned, not sure if she was being mocked or not. "Those bitches find a way of doing damage, don't they?"

"But always to the wrong people. My brother is the lucky one, he is with God. Or so they tell me. It is the rest of my family that suffer. We must work the harder now." She swung herself smoothly down onto the ladder, let her head fall sideways. Uncomfortably far, until it was resting on the top rung. "Try not to get yourselves killed. I do not intend that my hard work here be wasted."

"Your wasted work will be my first concern when they cut my throat." Nothing but silence. Ishri was gone.

"Looks like you've run out of brave men," came Shivers' croak.

Cosca sighed. "We didn't have many to begin with." The remnants of the assault were scrambling back down the rocky mountainside in the flickering light of the fires above. Monza could just make out the last ladder toppling down, perhaps a dot or two flailing as they fell from it. "But don't worry. Sesaria's still digging. Just a matter of time until Styria stands united." He slid a metal flask from his inside pocket and unscrewed the cap. "Or until Orso sees sense, and offers me enough to change sides again."

She didn't laugh. Perhaps she wasn't meant to. "Maybe you should try sticking to one side or the other."

"Why ever would anyone do that?" Cosca raised his flask, took a sip and smacked his lips in satisfaction. "It's a war. There is no right side."

Preparation

Regardless of the nature of a great event, the key to success is always preparation. For three weeks, all Talins had been preparing for the coronation of Grand Duke Rogont. Meanwhile, Morveer had been preparing for an attempt to murder him and his allies. So much work had been put into both schemes that, now the day for their consummation had finally arrived, Morveer almost regretted that the success of one could only mean the spectacular failure of the other.

In all honesty, he had been having little success achieving even the smallest part of Duke Orso's immensely ambitious commission to murder no fewer than six heads of state and a captain general. His abortive attempt on the life of Murcatto the day of her triumphant return to Talins, resulting in nothing more than at least one poisoned commoner and a sore back, had been but the first of several mishaps.

Gaining entrance to one of Talins' finest dressmakers through a loose rear window, he had secreted a lethal Amerind thorn within the bodice of an emerald-green gown meant for Countess Cotarda of Affoia. Alas, Morveer's expertise in dressmaking was most limited. Had Day been there she would no doubt have pointed out that the garment was twice too large for their waifish victim. The countess emerged resplendent at a soirée that very evening, her emerald-green gown a sensation. Morveer afterwards discovered, much to his chagrin, that the exceedingly large wife of one of Talins' leading merchants had also commissioned a green gown from that dressmaker, but was prevented from attending the event by a mysterious illness. She swiftly deteriorated and, alas, expired within hours.

Five nights later, after an uncomfortable afternoon spent hiding inside a heap of coal and breathing through a tube, he had succeeded in loading Duke Lirozio's oysters with spider venom. Had Day been with him in the kitchen she might have suggested they aim for a more basic foodstuff, but Morveer could not resist the most noteworthy dish. The duke, alas, had felt queasy after a heavy lunch and took only a little bread. The shellfish were administered to the kitchen cat, now deceased.

The following week, posing once more as the Purantine wine-merchant Rotsac Reevrom, he insinuated himself into a meeting to discuss trade levies chaired by Chancellor Sotorius of Sipani. During the meal he struck up lively conversation with one of the ancient statesman's aides on the subject of grapes and was able, much to his delight, deftly to brush the top of Sotorius' withered ear with a solution of Leopard Flower. He had sat back with great enthusiasm to observe the rest of the meeting, but the chancellor had steadfastly refused to die, showing, in fact, every sign of being in the most rude health. Morveer could only assume that Sotorius observed a morning routine not dissimilar to his own, and possessed immunities to who knew how many agents.

But Castor Morveer was not a man to be put off by a few reverses. He had suffered many in life, and saw no reason to alter his formula of commendable stoicism simply because the task seemed impossible. With the coronation almost upon him, he had therefore chosen to focus on the principal targets: Grand Duke Rogont and his lover, Morveer's hated ex-employer, now the Grand Duchess of Talins, Monzcarro Murcatto.

It would have been a rank understatement to say that no expense had been spared to ensure the coronation lived long in Styria's collective memory. The buildings enclosing the square had all been freshly painted. The stone platform where Murcatto had administered her fumbling speech, and where Rogont planned to soak up the adulation of his subjects as King of Styria, had been surfaced with gleaming new marble and adorned with a gilded rail. Workmen crawled on ropes and scaffolds across the looming frontage of the Senate House, garlanding the ancient stonework with fresh-cut white flowers, transforming the sullen edifice into a mighty temple to the Grand Duke of Ospria's vanity.

Working in dispiriting solitude, Morveer had appropriated the clothes, toolbox and documentation of a journeyman carpenter who had arrived in the city looking for piecework, and hence would be missed by nobody. Yesterday he had infiltrated the Senate House in this ingenious disguise to reconnoitre the scene and formulate a plan. While doing so, just as a bonus, he had carried out some challenging jointing work to a balustrade with almost conspicuous skill. Truly, he was a loss to carpentry, but he had in no way lost sight of the fact that his primary profession remained murder. Today he had returned to execute his audacious scheme. And to execute Grand Duke Rogont, both together.

"Afternoon," he grunted to one of the guards as he passed through the vast doorway along with the rest of the labourers returning from lunch, crunching carelessly at an apple with the surly manner he had often observed in common men on their way to labour. Caution first, always, but when attempting to fool someone, supreme confidence and simplicity was the approach that bore the ripest fruit. He excited, in fact, no attention whatsoever from the guards, either at the gate or at the far end of the vestibule. He stripped the core of his apple and tossed it into his workbox, with only the faintest maudlin moment spent reflecting on how much Day would have enjoyed it.

The Senate House was open to the sky, the great dome having collapsed long centuries ago. Three-quarters of the tremendous circular space was filled with concentric arcs of seating, enough for two thousand or more of the world's most honoured spectators. Each marble step was lower than the one behind, so that they formed a kind of theatre, with a space before them where the senators of old had once risen to make their grand addresses. A round platform had been built there now, of inlaid wood painted in meticulous detail with gilded wreaths of oak leaves about a gaudy golden chair.

Great banners of vividly coloured Suljuk silk hung down the full height of the walls, some thirty strides or more, at a cost Morveer hardly dared contemplate, one for each of the great cities of Styria. The azure cloth of Ospria, marked with the white tower, had pride of place, directly behind the central platform. The cross of Talins and the cockleshell of Sipani flanked it upon either side. Arranged evenly about the rest of the circumference were the bridge of Puranti, the red banner of Affoia, the three bees of Visserine, the six rings of Nicante, and the giant flags of Muris, Etrisani, Etrea, Borletta and Caprile besides. No one, it seemed, was to be excluded from the proud new order, whether they desired membership or not.

The whole space crawled with men and women hard at work. Tailors plucked at the hangings and the miles of white cushions provided for the comfort of the most honoured guests. Carpenters sawed and hammered at the platform and the stairways. Flower-sellers scattered the unused floor with a carpet of white blossom. Chandlers carefully positioned their waxen wares in endless rows, teetered on ladders to reach a hundred sconces. All overseen by a regiment of Osprian guardsmen, halberds and armour buffed to mirror brightness.

For Rogont to choose to be crowned here, in the ancient heart of the New Empire? The arrogance was incalculable, and if there was one quality Morveer could not abide, it was arrogance. Humility, after all, cost nothing. He concealed his profound disgust and made his way nonchalantly down the steps, affecting the self-satisfied swagger of the working commoner, weaving through the other tradesmen busy among the curving banks of seating.

At the back of the great chamber, perhaps ten strides above the ground, were two small balconies in which, he believed, scribes had once recorded the debates beneath. Now they were adorned by two immense portraits of Duke Rogont. One showed him stern and manful, heroically posed with sword and armour. The other depicted his Excellency in pensive mood, attired as a judge, holding book and compass. The master of peace and war. Morveer could not suppress a mocking smirk. Up there, in one of those two balconies, would be the fitting spot from which to shoot a dart lethal enough to deflate that idiot's swollen head and puncture his all-vaulting ambitions. They were reached by narrow stairways from a small, unused chamber, where records had been kept in ancient—

He frowned. Though it stood open, a heavy door, thick oak intricately bound and studded with polished steel, had been installed across the entrance of the anteroom. He in no way cared for such an alteration at this late stage. Indeed his first instinct was simply to place caution first and quietly depart, as he had often done before when circumstances appeared to shift. But men did not secure their place in history with caution alone. The venue, the challenge, the potential rewards were too great to let slip on account of a new door. History was breathing upon his neck. For tonight only his name would be audacity.

He strode past the platform, where a dozen decorators were busily applying gilt paint, and to the door. He swung it one way then the other, lips pursed discerningly as if checking the smooth workings of its hinges. Then, with the swiftest and least conspicuous of glances to ensure he was unobserved, he slipped through.

There were neither windows nor lamps within, the only light in the vaulted chamber crept through the door or down the two coiling stairways. Empty boxes and barrels were scattered in disorderly heaps about the walls. He was just deciding which balcony to choose as his shooting position when he heard voices approaching the door. He slid quickly on his side into the narrow space behind a stack of crates, squeaked as he picked up a painful splinter in his elbow, remembered his workbox just in time and fished it after him with one foot. A moment later the door squealed open and scraping boots entered the room, men groaning as though under a dolorous load.

"By the Fates, it's heavy!"

"Set it here!" A noisy clatter and squeal of metal on stone. "Bastard thing."

"Where's the key?"

"Here."

"Leave it in the lock."

"And what, pray, is the purpose of a lock with the key in it?"

"To present no obstacle, idiot. When we bring the damn case out there in front of three thousand people, and his Excellency tells us to open it up, I don't want to be looking at you and asking where the key is, and you find you dropped the fucker somewhere. See what I mean?"

"You've a point."

"It'll be safer in here, in a barred room with a dozen guards at the door, than in your dodgy pockets."

"I'm convinced." There was a gentle rattle of metal. "There. Satisfied?"

Several sets of footsteps clattered away. There was the heavy clunk of the door being swung shut, the clicking of locks turned, the squealing of a bar, then silence. Morveer was sealed into a room with a dozen guards outside. But that alone struck no fear into a man of his exceptional fortitude. When the vital moment came, he would lower a cord from one of the balconies and hope to slip away while every eye was focused on Rogont's spectacular demise. With the greatest of care to avoid any further splinters, he wriggled out from behind the crates.

A large case had been placed in the centre of the floor. A work of art in itself, fashioned from inlaid wood, bound with bands of filigree silver, glimmering in the gloom. Plainly it contained something of great importance to the coming ceremony. And since chance had provided him the key...

He knelt, turned it smoothly in the lock and with gentle fingers pushed back the lid. It took a great deal to impress a man of Morveer's experience, but now his eyes widened, his jaw dropped and sweat prickled at his scalp. The yellow sheen of gold almost warmed his skin, yet there was something more in his reaction than appreciation of the beauty, the symbolic significance or even the undoubted value of the object before him. Something teasing at the back of his mind...

Inspiration struck like lightning, making every hair upon his body suddenly stand tall. An idea of such scintillating brilliance, yet such penetrating simplicity, that he found himself almost in fear of it. The magnificent daring, the wonderful economy, the perfectly fitting irony. He only wished Day had lived to appreciate his genius.

Morveer triggered the hidden catch in his workman's box and removed the tray carrying the carpenter's equipment, revealing the carefully folded silken shirt and embroidered jacket in which he would make his escape. His true tools lay beneath. He carefully pulled on the gloves — lady's gloves of the finest calfskin, for they offered the least resistance to the dextrous operation of his fingers — and reached for the brown glass jar. He reached for it with some trepidation, for it contained a contact venom of his own devising which he called Preparation Number Twelve. There would be no repetition of his error with Chancellor Sotorius, for this was a poison so deadly that not even Morveer himself could develop the slightest immunity to it.

He carefully unscrewed the cap — caution first, always — and, taking up an artist's brush, began to work.

Rules of War

Cosca crept down the tunnel, knees and back aching fiercely from bending almost double, snatched breath echoing on the stale air. He had become far too accustomed to no greater exertions than sitting around and working his jaw over the last few weeks. He swore a silent oath to take exercise every morning, knowing full well he would never keep it even until tomorrow. Still, it was better to swear an oath and never follow through than not even to bother with the oath. Wasn't it?

His trailing sword scratched soil from the dirt walls with every step. Should have left the bloody thing behind. He peered down nervously at the glittering trail of black powder that snaked off into the shadows, holding his flickering lamp as far away as possible, for all it was made of thick glass and weighty cast iron. Naked flames and Gurkish sugar made unhappy companions in a confined space.

He saw flickering light ahead, heard the sounds of someone else's laboured breath, and the narrow passageway opened out into a chamber lit by a pair of guttering lamps. It was no bigger than a good-sized bed-room, walls and ceiling of scarred rock and hard-packed earth, held up by a web of suspect-looking timbers. More than half the room, or the cave, was taken up by large barrels. A single Gurkish word was painted on the side of each one. Cosca's Kantic did not extend far beyond ordering a drink, but he recognised the characters for fire. Sesaria was a great dark shape in the gloom, long ropes of grey hair hanging about his face, beads of sweat glistening on his black skin as he strained at a keg.

"It's time," said Cosca, his voice falling flat in the dead air under the mountain. He straightened up with great relief, was hit with a dizzy rush of blood to the head and stumbled sideways.

"Watch!" screeched Sesaria. "What you're doing with that lamp, Cosca! A spark in the wrong place and the pair of us'll be blown to heaven!"

"Don't let that worry you." He regained control of his feet. "I'm not a religious man, but I very much doubt anyone will be letting either of us near heaven."

"Blown to hell, then."

"A much stronger possibility."

Sesaria grunted as he ever so gingerly shifted the last of the barrels up tight to the rest. "All the others out?"

"They should be back in the trenches by now."

The big man wiped his hands on his grimy shirt. "Then we're ready, General."

"Excellent. These last few days have positively crawled. It's a crime, when you think about how little time we get, that a man should ever be bored. When you're lying on your deathbed, I expect you regret those weeks wasted more than your worst mistakes."

"You should have said if you had nothing pressing. We could have used your help digging."

"At my age? The only place I'll be moving soil is on the latrine. And even that's a lot more work than it used to be. What happens now?"

"I hear it only gets harder."

"Very good. I meant with the mine."

Sesaria pointed to the trail of black powder, grains gleaming in the lamp-light, stopping well short of the nearest keg. "That leads to the entrance to the mine." He patted a bag at his belt. "We join it up to the barrels, leave plenty of extra at the end to make sure it takes. We get to the mouth of the tunnel, we set a spark to one end, then—"

"The fire follows it all the way to the barrels and...how big will the explosion be?"

Sesaria shook his head. "Never seen a quarter as much powder used at one time. That and they keep mixing it stronger. This new stuff... I have a worry it might be too big."

"Better a grand gesture than a disappointing one."

"Unless it brings the whole mountain down on us."

"It could do that?"

"Who knows what it'll do?"

Cosca considered the thousands of tons of rock above their heads without enthusiasm. "It's a little late for second thoughts. Victus has his picked men ready for the assault. Rogont will be king tonight, and he's expecting to honour us with his majestic presence at dawn, and very much inside the fortress so he can order the final attack. I'm damned if I'm going to spend my morning listening to that fool whine at me. Especially with a crown on."

"You think he'll wear it, day to day?"

Cosca scratched thoughtfully at his neck. "Do you know, I've no idea. But it's somewhat beside the point."

"True." Sesaria frowned at the barrels. "Doesn't seem right, somehow. You dig a hole, you touch a torch to some dust, you run and—"

"Pop," said Cosca.

"No need for thinking. No need for courage. No way to fight, if you're asking me."

"The only good way to fight is the one that kills your enemy and leaves you with the breath to laugh. If science can simplify the process, well, so much the better. Everything else is flimflam. Let's get started."

"I hear my captain general and obey." Sesaria pulled the bag from his belt, bent down and started carefully tipping powder out, joining the trail up to the barrels. "Got to think about how you'd feel, though, haven't you?"

"Have you?"

"One moment you're going about your business, the next you're blasted to bits. Never get to even look your killer in his face."

"No different from giving others the orders. Is killing a man with powder any worse than getting someone else to stab him with a spear? When exactly did you last look a man in the face?" Not when he'd happily helped stab Cosca in the back at Afieri, that was sure.

Sesaria sighed, powder trickling out across the ground. "True, maybe. But sometimes I miss the old days, you know. Back when Sazine was in charge. Seemed like a different world, then. A more honest world."

Cosca snorted. "You know as well as I do there wasn't a dirty trick this side of hell Sazine would have balked at using. That old miser would have blown the world up if he thought a penny would fall out."

"Daresay you've the truth of it. Doesn't seem fair, though."

"I never realised you were such an enthusiast for fair."

"It's no deal-breaker, but I'd rather win a fair fight than an unfair one." He upended the bag, the last powder sliding out and leaving a glittering heap right against the side of the nearest barrel. "Leaves a better taste, somehow, fighting by some kind of rules."

"Huh." Cosca clubbed him across the back of the head with his lamp, sending up a shower of sparks and knocking Sesaria sprawling on his face. "This is war. There are no rules." The big man groaned, shifted, struggled weakly to push himself up. Cosca leaned down, raised the lamp high and bashed him on the skull again with a crunching of breaking glass, knocked him flat, embers sizzling in his hair. A little closer to the powder than was comfortable, perhaps, but Cosca had always loved to gamble.

He had always loved triumphant rhetoric too, but time was a factor. So he turned for the shadowy passageway and hurried down it. A dozen cramped strides and he was already breathing hard again. A dozen more and he thought he caught the faintest glimmer of daylight up the tunnel. He knelt down, chewing at his lip. He was far from sure how fast the trail would burn once it was lit.

"Good thing I always loved to gamble..." He carefully began to unscrew the broken cage around the lamp. It was stuck.

"Shit." He strained at it, fingers slipping, but it must have got bent when he clubbed Sesaria. "Bastard thing!" He shifted his grip, growled as he twisted with all his force. The top popped off suddenly, he fumbled both halves, the lamp dropped, he tried to catch it, missed, it hit the floor, bounced, guttered and went out, sinking the passageway into inky darkness.

"Fucking... shit!" His only option was to retrace his steps and get one of the lamps from the end of the tunnel. He took a few steps, one hand stretched out in front of him, fishing in the black. A beam caught him right in the face, snapped his head back, mouth buzzing, salty with blood. "Gah!"

He saw light, shook his throbbing head, strained into the darkness. Lamplight, catching the grain of the props, the stones and roots in the walls, making the snaking trail of powder glisten. Lamplight, and unless he had completely lost his bearings, it was coming from where he had left Sesaria.

Bringing his sword seemed suddenly to have been a stroke of genius. He slid it gently from its sheath with a reassuring ring of metal, had to work his elbow this way and that in the narrow space to get it pointing forwards, accidentally stuck the ceiling with the point and caused a long rivulet of soil to pour gently down onto his bald patch. All the while the light crept closer.

Sesaria appeared around the bend, lamp in one big fist, a line of blood creeping down his forehead. They faced one other for a moment, Cosca crouching, Sesaria bent double.

"Why?" grunted the big man.

"Because I make a point of never letting a man betray me twice."

"I thought you were all business."

"Men change."

"You killed Andiche."

"Best moment of the last ten years."

Sesaria shook his head, as much puzzled as angry and in pain. "Murcatto was the one took your chair, not us!"

"Entirely different matter. Women can betray me as often as they please."

"You always did have a blind spot for that mad bitch."

"I'm an incurable romantic. Or maybe I just never liked you."

Sesaria slid a heavy knife out in his free hand. "You should've stabbed me back there."

"I'm glad I didn't. Now I get to use another clever line."

"Don't suppose you'd consider putting that sword away and fighting knife to knife?"

Cosca gave a cackle. "You're the one who likes things fair. I tried to kill you by clubbing you from behind then blowing you up, remember? Stabbing you with a sword will give me no sleepless nights." And he lunged.

In such a confined space, being a big man was a profound disadvantage. Sesaria almost entirely filled the narrow tunnel, which made him, fortunately, more or less impossible to miss. He managed to steer the clumsy jab away with his knife, but it still pricked him in the shoulder. Cosca pulled back for another thrust, squawked as he caught his knuckles on the earth wall. Sesaria swung his heavy lamp at him and Cosca flopped away, slipped and went over on one knee. The big man scrambled forwards, raising the knife. His fist scraped on the ceiling, bringing down a shower of earth, his knife thudded deep into a beam above. He mouthed some curse in Kantic, wincing as he struggled to drag the blade free. Cosca righted himself and made another clumsy lunge. Sesaria's eyes bulged as the point punctured his shirt and slid smoothly through his chest.

"There!" Cosca snarled in his face. "Do you get...my point?"

Sesaria lurched forwards, groaning bloody drool, face locked in a desperate grimace, the blade sliding inexorably through him until the hilt got tangled with his sticky shirt. He seized hold of Cosca and toppled over, bearing him down on his back, the pommel of the sword digging savagely into his stomach and driving all his breath out in a creaking, "Ooooooof."

Sesaria curled back his lips to show red teeth. "You call...*that*...a clever line?" He smashed his lamp down into the trail of powder beside Cosca's face. Glass shattered, flame leaped up, there was a fizzling pop as the powder caught, the heat of it near to burning Cosca's cheek. He struggled with Sesaria's great limp body, struggled to untwist his fingers from the gilded basketwork of his sword, desperately tried to wrestle the big corpse sideways. His nose was full of the acrid reek of Gurkish sugar, snapping sparks moving off slowly down the passage.

He finally dragged himself free, clambered up and ran for the entrance, breath wheezing in his chest, one hand trailing along the dirt wall, knocking against the props. An oval of daylight appeared, wobbled steadily closer. He gave vent to a foolish giggle as he wondered whether it would be this moment or the next that saw the rock he was tottering through a mile in the sky. He burst out into open air.

"Run!" he screeched at no one, flinging his hands wildly around. "Run!" He pounded down the hillside, tripped, fell, rolled head over heels, bounced painfully from a rock, struggled up and carried on scrambling in a cloud of dust, loose stones clattering around him. The wicker shields that marked the nearest trench crept closer and he charged towards them, screaming madly at the top of his voice. He flung himself onto his face, slid along in the dirt, crashed between two screens and headlong down into the trench in a shower of loose soil.

Victus stared at him as he struggled to right himself. "What the—"

"Take cover!" wailed Cosca. All around him armour rattled as men shrank down into their trenches, raised their shields over their heads, clapped their gauntleted hands over their ears, squeezed their eyes tight shut in anticipation of an explosion to end the world. Cosca jammed himself back against the hard-packed earth, teeth squeezed together, clasping his hands around his skull.

The silent moments stretched out.

Cosca prised one eye open. A bright-blue butterfly fluttered heedlessly down, circled widdershins around the cowering mercenaries and came peacefully to rest on the blade of a spear. Victus himself had his helmet pushed right down over his face. Now he slowly tipped it back to display an expression of some confusion.

"What the hell happened? Is the fuse lit? Where's Sesaria?"

A sudden image formed in Cosca's mind of the trail of powder sputtering out, of Victus' men creeping into the murky darkness, lamps raised, their light falling across Sesaria's corpse, impaled on a sword with unmistakable gilded basketwork. "Erm..."

The very faintest of tremors touched the earth at Cosca's back. A moment later there was a thunderous detonation, so loud that it sent pain lancing through his head. The world went suddenly, entirely silent but for a faint, high-pitched whine. The earth shook. Wind ripped and eddied along the trench, tearing at his hair and nearly dragging him over. A cloud of choking dust filled the air, nipping at his lungs and making him cough. Gravel rained down from the sky, he gasped as he felt it sting at his arms, at his scalp. He cowered like a man caught out in a hurricane, every muscle tensed. For how long, he was not sure.

Cosca opened his eyes, dumbly uncurled his aching limbs and got weakly to his feet. The world was a ghost-place of silent fog. The land of the dead, surely, men and equipment no more than phantoms in the murk. The mist began to clear. He rubbed at his ears but the whining continued. Others got up, staring around, faces caked with grey dirt. Not far away someone lay still in a puddle in the bottom of a trench, his helmet stoved in by a chunk of rock, steered by the fickle Fates directly onto his head. Cosca peered over the lip of the trench, blinked up towards the summit of the mountain, straining through the gradually settling dust.

"Oh." The wall of Fontezarmo appeared undamaged, the outline of towers and battlements still very much present against the lead-white sky. A vast crater had been blown from the rock, but the great round tower directly above it still clung stubbornly to the edge, even slightly overhanging empty space. It seemed for a moment to be perhaps the most crushing anticlimax of Cosca's life, and there had been many.

Then, in dreamlike silence and with syrupy slowness, that central tower leaned, buckled, fell in on itself and collapsed into the yawning crater. A huge section of wall to either side of it was dragged after, all folding up and dissolving into rubble under its own weight. A man-made landslide of hundreds of tons of stone rolled, bounced, crashed down towards the trenches.

"Ah," said Cosca, silently.

For a second time men flung themselves on their faces, covered their heads, prayed to the Fates or whichever of a range of gods and spirits they did or did not believe in for deliverance. Cosca stayed standing, staring fascinated as a giant chunk of masonry perhaps ten tons in weight hurtled down the slope directly towards him, bouncing, spinning, flinging pieces of stone high into the air, all without the slightest sound but for perhaps a vague crunching, like footsteps on gravel. It came to an eventual stop no more than ten strides distant, rocked gently to one side and the other, and was still.

A second cloud of dust had plunged the trench into choking gloom, but as it gradually faded Cosca could see the vast breach left in the outer wall of Fontezarmo, no fewer than two hundred strides across, the crater beneath it now choked with settling rubble. A second tower at its edge leaned at an alarming angle, like a drunken man peering over a cliff, ready at any moment to topple into emptiness.

He saw Victus stand beside him, raise his sword and scream. The word didn't sound much louder than if he had spoken it.

"Charge."

Men clambered, somewhat dazed, from the trenches. One took a couple of wobbling steps and fell on his face. Others stood there, blinking. Still others began to head uncertainly uphill. More followed, and soon there were a few hundred men scrambling through the rubble towards the breach, weapons and armour shining dully in the watery sun.

Cosca was left alone in the trench with Victus, both of them coated with grey dust.

"Where's Sesaria?" The words thudding dully through the whine in Cosca's ears.

His own voice was a weird burble. "He wasn't behind me?"

"No. What happened?"

"An accident. An accident . . . as we came out." It wasn't difficult to force out a tear, Cosca was covered head to toe in knocks and bruises. "I dropped my lamp! Dropped it! Set off the trail of powder halfway down!" He seized Victus by his fluted breastplate. "I told him to run with me, but he stayed! Stayed . . . to put it out."

"He stayed?"

"He thought he could save us both!" Cosca put one hand over his face, voice choked with emotion. "My fault! All my fault. He truly was the best of us." He wailed it at the sky. "Why? Why? Why do the Fates always take the best?"

Victus' eyes flickered down to Cosca's empty scabbard, then back up to the great crater in the hillside, the yawning breach above it. "Dead, eh?"

"Blown to hell," whispered Cosca. "Baking with Gurkish sugar can be a dangerous business." The sun had come out. Above them, Victus' men were clambering up the sides of the crater and into the breach in a twinkling tide, apparently entirely unopposed. If any defenders had survived the blast, they were in no mood to fight. It seemed the outer ward of Fontezarmo was theirs. "Victory. At least Sesaria's sacrifice was not in vain."

"Oh, no." Victus looked sideways at him through narrowed eyes. "He'd have been proud."

One Nation

The echoing grumble of the crowd on the other side of the doors grew steadily louder, and the churning in Monza's guts grew with it. She tried to rub away the niggling tension under her jaw. It did no good.

But there was nothing to do except wait. Her entire role in tonight's grand performance was to stand there with a straight face and look like the highest of nobility, and Talins' best dressmakers had done all the hard work in making that ludicrous lie seem convincing. They'd given her long sleeves to cover the scars on her arms, a high collar to cover the scars on her neck, gloves to render her ruined hand presentable. They'd been greatly relieved they could keep her neckline low without horrifying Rogont's delicate guests. It was a wonder they hadn't cut a great hole out of the back to show her arse — it was about the only other patch of her skin without a mark across it.

Nothing could be seen that might spoil the perfection of Duke Rogont's moment of history. No sword, certainly, and she missed the weight of it like a missing limb. She wondered when was the last time she'd stepped out without a blade in easy reach. Not in the meeting of the Council of Talins she'd attended the day after being lifted to her new station.

Old Rubine had suggested she had no need to wear a sword in the chamber. She replied she'd worn one every day for twenty years. He'd politely pointed out that neither he nor his colleagues carried arms, though they were all men and hence better suited. She asked him what she'd use to stab him with if she left her sword behind. No one was sure whether she was joking or not. But they didn't ask again.

"Your Excellency." One of the attendants had oozed over and now offered her a silky bow. "Your Grace," and another to Countess Cotarda. "We are about to begin."

"Good," snapped Monza. She faced the double doors, shifted her shoulders back and her chin up. "Let's get this fucking pantomime over with."

She had no time to spare. Every waking moment of the last three weeks — and she'd scarcely slept since Rogont jammed the circlet on her head — she'd spent struggling to drag the state of Talins out of the cesspit she'd fought so hard to shove it into.

Keeping in mind Bialoveld's maxim — *any successful state is supported by pillars of steel and gold* — she'd dug out every cringing bureaucrat she could find who wasn't besieged in Fontezarmo along with their old master. There'd been discussions about the Talinese army. There wasn't one. Discussions about the treasury. It was empty. The system of taxation, the maintenance of public works, the preservation of security, the administration of justice, all dissolved like cake in a stream. Rogont's presence, or that of his soldiers anyway, was all that was keeping Talins from anarchy.

But Monza had never been put off by a wind in the wrong direction. She'd always had a knack for reckoning a man's qualities, and picking the right one for a given job. Old Rubine was pompous as a prophet, so she made him high magistrate. Grulo and Scavier were the two most ruthless merchants in the city. She didn't trust either, so she made them joint chancellors, and set each one to dream up new taxes, compete in their collection while keeping one jealous eye on the other.

Already they were wringing money from their unhappy colleagues, and already Monza had spent it on arms.

Three long days into her unpromising rule, an old sergeant called Volfier had arrived in the city, a man almost laughably hardbitten, and nearly as scarred as she was. Refusing to surrender, he'd led the twenty-three survivors of his regiment back from the rout at Ospria and all the way across Styria with arms and honour intact. She could always use a man that bloody-minded, and set him to rounding up every veteran in the city. Paying work was thin on the ground and he already had two companies of volunteers, their glorious charge to escort the tax collectors and make sure not a copper went missing.

She'd marked Duke Orso's lessons well. Gold, to steel, to more gold — such was the righteous spiral of politics. Resistance, apathy and scorn from all quarters only made her shove harder. She took a perverse satisfaction in the apparent impossibility of the task, the work pushed the pain to one side, and the husk with it, and kept her sharp. It had been a long, long time since she'd made anything grow.

"You look...very beautiful."

"What?" Cotarda had glided up silently beside her and was offering a nervous smile. "Oh. Likewise," grunted Monza, barely even looking.

"White suits you. They tell me I'm too pale for white." Monza winced. Just the kind of mindless twittering she had no stomach for tonight. "I wish I was like you."

"Some time in the sun would do it."

"No, no. Brave." Cotarda looked down at her pale fingers, twisting them together. "I wish I was brave. They tell me I'm powerful. One would have thought being powerful would mean one need not be scared of anything. But I'm afraid all the time. Especially at *events*." The words spilled out of her to Monza's mounting discomfort. "Sometimes I can't move for the weight of it. All the fear. I'm such a disappointment. What can I do about that? What would you do?"

Monza had no intention of discussing her own fears. That would only feed them. But Cotarda blathered on regardless.

"I've no character at all, but where does one get character from? Either you have it or you don't. You have. Everyone says you have. Where did you get it? Why don't I have any? Sometimes I think I'm cut out of paper, just acting like a person. They tell me I'm an utter coward. What can I do about that? Being an utter coward?"

They stared at each other for a long moment, then Monza shrugged. "Act like you're not."

The doors were pulled open.

Musicians somewhere out of sight struck up a stately refrain as she and Cotarda stepped out into the vast bowl of the Senate House. Though there was no roof, though the stars would soon show in the blue-black sky above, it was hot. Hot, and clammy as a tomb, and the perfumed stink of flowers caught at Monza's tight throat and made her want to retch. Thousands of candles burned in the darkness, filling the great arena with creeping shadows, making gilt glimmer, gems glitter, turning the hundreds upon hundreds of smiling faces that soared up on all sides into leering masks. Everything was outsize — the crowd, the rustling banners behind them, the venue itself. Everything was overdone, like a scene from a lurid fantasy.

A hell of a lot of effort just to watch one man put on a new hat.

The audience were a varied lot. Styrians made up the bulk, rich and powerful men and women, merchants and minor nobility from across the land. A smattering of famous artists, diplomats, poets, craftsmen, soldiers — Rogont wanted no one excluded who might reflect some extra glory onto him. Guests from abroad occupied most of the better seats, down near the front, come to pay their respects to the new King of Styria, or to try to wangle some advantage from his elevation, at least. There were merchant captains of the Thousand Isles with golden hoops through their ears. There were heavy-bearded Northmen, bright-eyed Baolish. There were natives of Suljuk in vivid silks, a pair of priestesses from Thond where they worshipped the sun, heads shaved to yellow stubble. There were three nervous-seeming Aldermen of Westport. The Union, unsurprisingly, was notable by its utter absence, but the Gurkish delegation had willingly spread out to fill their space. A dozen ambassadors from the Emperor Uthman-ul-Dosht, heavy with gold. A dozen priests from the Prophet Khalul, in sober white.

Monza walked through them all as if they weren't there, shoulders back, eyes fixed ahead, the cold sneer on her mouth she'd always worn when she was most terrified. Lirozio and Patine approached with equal pomposity down a walkway opposite. Sotorius waited by the chair that was the golden centrepiece of the entire event, leaning heavily on a staff. The old man had sworn he'd be consigned to hell before he walked down a ramp.

They reached the circular platform, gathering under the expectant gaze of several thousand pairs of eyes. The five great leaders of Styria who'd enjoy the honour of crowning Rogont, all dressed with a symbolism that a mushroom couldn't have missed. Monza was in pearly white, with the cross of Talins across her chest in sparkling fragments of black crystal. Cotarda wore Affoian scarlet. Sotorius had golden cockleshells around the hem of his black gown, Lirozio the bridge of Puranti on his gilded cape. They were like bad actors representing the cities of Styria in some cheap morality play, except at vast expense. Even Patine had shed any pretence at humility, and swapped his rough-spun peasant cloth for green silk, fur and sparkling jewels. Six rings were the symbol of Nicante, but he must have been sporting nine at the least, one with an emerald the size of Friendly's dice.

At close quarters, none of them looked particularly pleased with their role. Like a group who'd agreed, while blind drunk, to jump into the freezing sea in the morning but now, with the sober dawn, were thinking better of it.

"Well," grunted Monza, as the musicians brought their piece to an end and the last notes faded. "Here we are."

"Indeed." Sotorius swept the murmuring crowd with rheumy eyes. "Let us hope the crown is large. Here comes the biggest head in Styria."

An ear-splitting fanfare blasted out from behind. Cotarda flinched, stumbled, would've fallen if Monza hadn't seized her elbow on an instinct. The doors at the very back of the hall were opened, and as the blaring sound of trumpets faded a strange singing began, a pair of voices, high and pure, floating out over the audience. Rogont stepped smiling through into the Senate House, and his guests broke out into well-organised applause.

The king-in-waiting, all in Osprian blue, looked about him with humble surprise as he began to descend the steps. All this, for me? You shouldn't have! When of course he'd planned every detail himself. Monza wondered for a moment, and not for the first time, whether Rogont would turn out to be a far worse king than Orso might've been. No less ruthless, no more loyal, but a lot more vain, and less sense of humour every day. He pressed favoured hands in his, laying a generous palm on a lucky shoulder or two as he passed. The unearthly singing serenaded him as he came through the crowd.

"Can I hear spirits?" muttered Patine, with withering scorn.

"You can hear boys with no balls," replied Lirozio.

Four men in Osprian livery unlocked a heavy door behind the platform and passed inside, came out shortly afterwards struggling under the weight of an inlaid case. Rogont made a swift pass around the front row, pressing the hands of a few chosen ambassadors, paying particular attention to the Gurkish delegation and stretching the applause to breaking point. Finally he mounted the steps to the platform, smiling the way the winner of a vital hand of cards smiles at his ruined opponents. He held his arms out to the five of them. "My friends, my friends! The day is finally here!"

"It is," said Sotorius, simply.

"Happy day!" sang Lirozio.

"Long hoped for!" added Patine.

"Well done?" offered Cotarda.

"My thanks to you all." Rogont turned to face his guests, silenced their clapping with a gentle motion of his hands, swept his cloak out behind him, lowered himself into his chair and beckoned Monza over. "No congratulations from you, your Excellency?"

"Congratulations," she hissed.

"As graceful as always." He leaned closer, murmuring under his breath. "You did not come to me last night."

"Other commitments."

"Truly?" Rogont raised his brows as though amazed that anything could possibly be more important than fucking him. "I suppose a head of state has many demands upon her time. Well." He waved her scornfully away.

Monza ground her teeth. At that moment, she would've been more than willing to piss on him.

The four porters set down their burden behind the throne, one of them turned the key in the lock and lifted the lid with a showy flourish. A sigh went up from the crowd. The crown lay on purple velvet inside. A thick band of gold, set all around with a row of darkly gleaming sapphires. Five golden oak leaves sprouted from it, and at the front a larger sixth curled about a monstrous, flashing diamond, big as a chicken's egg. So large Monza felt a strange desire to laugh at it.

With the expression of a man about to clear a blocked latrine with his hand, Lirozio reached into the case and grasped one of the golden leaves. A resigned shrug of the shoulders and Patine did the same. Then Sotorius and Cotarda. Monza took hold of the last in her gloved right fist, poking little finger looking no better for being sheathed in white silk. She glanced across the faces of her supposed peers. Two forced smiles, a slight sneer and an outright scowl. She wondered how long it would take for these proud princes, so used to being their own masters, to tire of this less favourable arrangement.

By the look of things, the yoke was already starting to chafe.

Together, the five of them lifted the crown and took a few lurching steps forwards, Sotorius having to awkwardly negotiate the case, dragging each other clumsily about by the priceless symbol of majesty. They made it to the chair, and between them raised the crown high over Rogont's head. They paused there for a moment, as if by mutual agreement, perhaps wondering if there was still some way out of this. The whole great space was eerily silent, every man and woman holding their breath. Then Sotorius gave a resigned nod, and together the five of them lowered the crown, seated it carefully on Rogont's skull and stepped away.

Styria, it seemed, was one nation.

Its king rose slowly from the chair and spread his arms wide, palms open, staring straight ahead as though he could see right through the ancient walls of the Senate House and into a brilliant future.

"Our fellow Styrians!" he bellowed, voice ringing from the stones. "Our humble subjects! And our friends from abroad, all welcome here!" Mostly Gurkish friends, but since the Prophet had stretched to such a large diamond for his crown... "The Years of Blood are at an end!" Or they soon would be, once Monza had spilled Orso's. "No longer will the great cities of our proud land struggle one against the other!" That remained to be seen. "But will stand as brothers eternal, bound willingly by happy ties of friendship, of culture, of common heritage. Marching together!" In whatever direction Rogont dictated, presumably. "It is as if... Styria wakes from a nightmare. A nightmare nineteen years long. Some among us, I am sure, can scarcely remember a time without war." Monza frowned, thinking of her father's plough turning the black earth.

"But now... the wars are over! And all of us won! Every one of us." Some won more than others, it needed hardly to be said. "Now is the time for peace! For freedom! For healing!" Lirozio noisily cleared his throat, wincing as he tugged at his embroidered collar. "Now is the time for hope, for forgiveness, for unity!" And abject obedience, of course. Cotarda was staring at her hand. Her pale palm was mottled pink, almost deep enough to match her scarlet dress. "Now is the time for us to forge a great state that will be the envy of the world! Now is the time—" Lirozio had started to cough, beads of sweat showing on his ruddy face. Rogont frowned furiously sideways at him. "Now is the time for Styria to become—" Patine bent forwards and gave an anguished groan, lips curled back from his teeth.

"One nation..." Something was wrong, and everyone was beginning to see it. Cotarda lurched backwards, stumbled. She caught the gilded railing, chest heaving, and sank to the floor with a rustling of red silk. The audience gave a stunned collective gasp.

"One nation..." whispered Rogont. Chancellor Sotorius sank trembling to his knees, one pink-stained hand clutching at his withered throat. Patine was crouched on all fours now, face bright red, veins bulging from his neck. Lirozio toppled onto his side, back to Monza, his breath a faint wheeze. His right arm stretched out behind him, the twitching hand blotched pink. Cotarda's leg kicked faintly, then she was still. All the while the crowd stayed silent. Transfixed. Not sure if this was some demented part of the show. Some awful joke. Patine sagged onto his face. Sotorius fell backwards, spine arched, heels of his shoes squeaking against the polished wood, then flopped down limp.

Rogont stared at Monza and she stared back, as frozen and helpless as she had been when she watched Benna die. He opened his mouth, raised one hand towards her, but no breath moved. His forehead, beneath the fur-trimmed rim of the crown, had turned angry red.

The crown. They all had touched the crown. Her eyes rolled down to her gloved right hand. All except her.

Rogont's face twisted. He took one step, his ankle buckled and he pitched onto his face, bulging eyes staring sightlessly off to the side. The crown popped from his skull, bounced once, rolled across the inlaid platform to its edge and clattered to the floor below. Someone in the audience gave a single, ear-splitting scream.

There was the whoosh of a counterweight falling, a rattle of wood, and a thousand white songbirds were released from cages concealed around the edge of the chamber, rising up into the clear night air in a beautiful, twittering storm.

It was just as Rogont had planned.

Except that of the six men and women destined to unite Styria and bring an end to the Years of Blood, only Monza was still alive.

All Dust

Shivers took more'n a little satisfaction in the fact Grand Duke Rogont was dead. Maybe it should've been King Rogont, but it didn't matter much which you called him now, and that thought tickled Shivers' grin just a bit wider.

You can be as great a man as you please while you're alive. Makes not a straw of difference once you go back to the mud. And it only takes a little thing. Might happen in a silly moment. An old friend of Shivers' fought all seven days at the battle in the High Places and didn't get a nick. Scratched himself on a thorn leaving the valley next morning, got the rot in his hand, died babbling a few nights after. No point to it. No lesson. Except watch out for thorns, maybe.

But then a noble death like Rudd Threetrees won for himself, leading the charge, sword in his fist as the life left him — that was no better. Maybe men would sing a song about it, badly, when they were drunk, but for him who died, death was death, same for everyone. The Great Leveller, the hill-men called it. Lords and beggars made equal.

All of Rogont's grand ambitions were dirt. His power was mist, blown away on the dawn breeze. Shivers, no more'n a one-eyed killer, not fit to lick the king-in-waiting's boots clean yesterday, this morning was the better man by far. He was still casting a shadow. If there was a lesson, it was this — you have to take what you can while you still have breath. The earth holds no rewards but darkness.

They rode from the tunnel and into the outer ward of Fontezarmo, and Shivers gave a long, soft whistle.

"They done some building work."

Monza nodded. "Some knocking down, at least. Seems the Prophet's gift did the trick."

It was a fearsome weapon, this Gurkish sugar. A great stretch of the walls on their left had vanished, a tower tilted madly at the far end, cracks up its side, looking sure to follow the rest down the mountain any moment. A few leafless shrubs clung to the ragged cliff-edge where the walls had been, clawing at empty air. Shivers reckoned there'd been gardens, but the flaming shot the catapults had been lobbing in the last few weeks had turned 'em mostly to burned-up bramble, split tree-stump and scorched-out mud, all smeared down and puddle-pocked by last night's rain.

A cobbled way led through the midst of this mess, between a half-dozen stagnant fountains and up to a black gate, still sealed tight. A few twisted shapes lay round some wreckage, bristling with arrows. Dead men round a torched ram. Scanning along the battlements above, Shivers' practised eye picked out spears, bows, armour twinkling. Seemed the inner wall was still firm held, Duke Orso no doubt tucked in tight behind it.

They rode around a big heap of damp canvas weighted down with stones, patches of rainwater in the folds. As Shivers passed he saw there were boots sticking out of one end, a few pairs of dirty bare feet, all beaded up with wet.

Seemed one of Volfier's lads was a fresh recruit, went pale when he saw them dead men. Strange, but seeing him all broken up just made Shivers wonder when he got so comfortable around a corpse or two. To him they were just bits of the scenery now, no more meaning than the broken tree-stumps. It was going to take more'n a corpse or two to spoil his good mood that morning.

Monza reined her horse in and slid from the saddle. "Dismount," grunted Volfier, and the rest followed her.

"Why do some of 'em have bare feet?" The boy was still staring at the dead.

"Because they had good boots," said Shivers. The lad looked down at his own foot-leather, then back to those wet bare feet, then put one hand over his mouth.

Volfier clapped the boy on the back and made him start, gave Shivers a wink while he did it. Seemed baiting the new blood was the same the world over. "Boots or no boots, don't make no difference once they've killed you. Don't worry, boy, you get used to it."

"You do?"

"If you're lucky," said Shivers, "you'll live long enough."

"If you're lucky," said Monza, "you'll find another trade first. Wait here."

Volfier gave her a nod. "Your Excellency." And Shivers watched her pick her way around the wreckage and off.

"Get on top of things in Talins?" he muttered.

"Hope so," grunted the scarred sergeant. "Got the fires put out, in the end. Made us a deal with the criminals in the Old Quarter they'd keep an eye on things there for a week, and we wouldn't keep an eye for a month after."

"Coming to something when you're looking to thieves to keep order."

"It's a topsy-turvy world alright." Volfier narrowed his eyes at the inner wall. "My old master's on the other side o' that. A man I fought my whole life for. Never had any riots when he was in charge."

"Wish you were with him?"

Volfier frowned sideways. "I wish we'd won at Ospria, then the choice wouldn't have come up. But then I wish my wife hadn't fucked the baker while I was away in the Union on campaign three years ago. Wishing don't change nothing."

Shivers grinned, and tapped at his metal eye with a fingernail. "That there is a fact."

Cosca sat on his field chair, in the only part of the gardens that was still anything like intact, and watched his goat grazing on the wet grass. There was something oddly calming about her gradual, steady progress across the last remaining bit of lawn. The wriggling of her lips, the delicate nibbling of her teeth, the tiny movements that by patient repetition would soon shave that lawn down to stubble. He stuck a fingertip in his ear and waggled it around, trying to clear the faint ringing that still lurked at the edge of his hearing. It persisted. He sighed, raised his flask, heard footsteps crunching on gravel and stopped. Monza was walking towards him. She looked beyond tired, shoulders hunched, mouth twisted, eyes buried in dark pits.

"Why the hell do you have a goat?"

Cosca took a slow swig from his flask, grimaced and took another. "Noble beast, the goat. She reminds me, in your absence, to be tenacious, single-minded and hard-working. You have to stick at something in your life, Monzcarro." The goat looked up, and bleated in apparent agreement. "I hope you won't take offence if I say you look tired."

"Long night," she muttered, and Cosca judged it to be a tremendous understatement.

"I'm sure."

"The Osprians pulled out of Talins. There was a riot. Panic."

"Inevitable."

"Someone spread a rumour that the Union fleet was on its way."

"Rumours can do more damage than the ships themselves."

"The crown was poisoned," she muttered.

"The leaders of Styria, consumed by their own lust for power. There's a message in there, wouldn't you say? Murder and metaphor combined. The poisoner-poet responsible has managed to kill a chancellor, a duke, a countess, a first citizen and a king, and teach the world an invaluable lesson about life all in one evening. Your friend and mine, Morveer?"

She spat. "Maybe."

"I never thought that pedantic bastard had such a sense of humour."

"Forgive me if I don't laugh."

"Why did he spare you?"

"He didn't." Monza held up her gloved right hand. "My glove did."

Cosca could not help a snort of laughter. "Just think, one could say that by crushing your right hand, Duke Orso and his cohorts saved your life! The ironies pile one upon the other!"

"I might wait for a more settled moment to enjoy them."

"Oh, I'd enjoy them now. I've wasted years waiting for more settled moments. In my experience they never come. Only look around you. The Affoians almost all deserted before daybreak. The Sipanese are already splitting into factions, falling back south — to fight each other, would be my guess. The army of Puranti were so keen to get their civil war under way they actually started killing each other in the trenches. Victus had to break it up! Victus, *stopping* a fight, can you imagine? Some of the Osprians are still here, but only because they haven't a clue what else to do. The lot of them, running around like chickens with their heads cut off. Which I suppose they are. You know, I'm eternally amazed at just how quickly things can fall apart. Styria was united for perhaps the length of a minute and now is plunged into deeper chaos than ever. Who knows who'll seize power, and where, and how much?

It seems an end may have been called to the Years of Blood…" and Cosca stuck his chin out and gave his neck a scratch, "somewhat prematurely."

Monza's shoulders seemed to slump a little lower. "The ideal situation for a mercenary, no?"

"You'd have thought. But there's such a thing as too much chaos, even for a man like me. I swear, the Thousand Swords are the most coherent and orderly body of troops left up here. Which should give you some idea of the utter disorder that has struck your allies." He stretched his legs out in front of him, one boot crossed over the other. "I thought I might take the brigade down towards Visserine, and press my claims there. I very much doubt Rogont will be honouring our agreement now—"

"Stay," she said, and fixed her eyes on his.

"Stay?"

"Stay."

There was a long pause while they watched each other. "You've no right to ask me that."

"But I am asking. Help me."

"Help…you? It's coming to something when I'm anyone's best hope. What of your loyal subjects, the good people of Talins? Is there no help to be had there?"

"They aren't as keen for a battle as they were for a parade. They won't lift a finger in case they get Orso back in charge and he hangs every man of them."

"The fickle movements of power, eh? You've raised no soldiers while you had the throne? That hardly seems your style."

"I raised what I could, but I can't trust them here. Not against Orso. Who knows which way they'll jump?"

"Ah, divided loyalties. I have some experience with them. An unpredictable scenario." Cosca stuck his finger in his other ear, to no greater effect. "Have you considered the possibility of…perhaps…leaving it be?"

She looked at him as if he was speaking in a foreign tongue. "What?"

"I myself have left a thousand tasks unfinished, unstarted or outright failed across the whole breadth of the Circle of the World. In the end, they bother me considerably less than my successes."

"I'm not you."

"No doubt a cause of constant regret for us both. But still. You could forget about revenge. You could compromise. You could…be merciful."

"Mercy and cowardice are the same," she growled, narrow eyes fixed on the black gate at the far end of the blasted gardens.

Cosca gave a sad smile. "Are they indeed?"

"Conscience is an excuse not to do what needs doing."

"I see."

"No use weeping about it. That's how the world is."

"Ah."

"The good get nothing extra. When they die they turn to shit like the rest of us. You have to keep your eyes ahead, always ahead, fight one battle at a time. You can't hesitate, no matter the costs, no matter the—"

"Do you know why I always loved you, Monza?"

"Eh?" Her eyes flickered to him, surprised.

"Even after you betrayed me? More, after you betrayed me?" Cosca leaned slowly towards her. "Because I know you don't really believe any of that rubbish. Those are the lies you tell yourself so you can live with what you've done. What you've had to do."

There was a long pause. Then she swallowed as though she was about to puke. "You always said I had a devil in me."

"Did I? Well, so do we all." He waved a hand. "You're no saint, that much we know. A child of a bloody time. But you're nothing like as dark as you make out."

"No?"

"I pretend to care for the men, but in truth I don't give a damn whether they live or die. You always did care, but you pretend not to give a damn. I never saw you waste one man's life. And yet they like me better. Hah. There's justice. You always did the right thing by me, Monza. Even when you betrayed me, it was better than I deserved. I've never forgotten that time in Muris, after the siege, when you wouldn't let the slavers have those children. Everyone wanted to take the money. I did. Faithful did. Even Benna. Especially Benna. But not you."

"Only gave you a scratch," she muttered.

"Don't be modest, you were ready to kill me. These are ruthless times we live in, and in ruthless times, mercy and cowardice are *entire* opposites. We all turn to shit when we die, Monza, but not all of us are shit while we're alive. Most of us are." His eyes rolled to heaven. "God knows I am. But you never were."

She blinked at him for a moment. "Will you help me?"

Cosca raised his flask again, realised it was empty and screwed the cap back on. The damn thing needed filling far too often. "Of course I'll help you. There was never the slightest question in my mind. I have already organised the assault, in fact."

"Then—"

"I just wanted to hear you ask. I must say I am surprised you did, though. The mere idea that the Thousand Swords would do the hard work of a siege, have one of the richest palaces in Styria at their mercy and walk away without a scrap of booty? Have you lost your reason? I couldn't prise these greedy bastards away with a spade. We're attacking at dawn tomorrow, with or without you, and we'll be picking this place clean. More than likely my boys will have the lead off the roofs by lunchtime. Rule of Quarters, and all that."

"And Orso?"

"Orso is yesterday's man." Cosca sat back and patted his goat fondly on her flank. "Do as you please with him."

The Inevitable

The dice came up two and one.

Three years ago today, Sajaam bought Friendly's freedom from Safety. Three years he had been homeless. He had followed three people, two men and one woman, all across Styria and back. In that time, the place he had hated least was the Thousand Swords, and not just because it had a number in its name, though that was, of course, a good start.

There was order, here, up to a point. Men had given tasks with given times to do them, knew their places in the big machine. The company was all neatly quantified in the notary's three ledgers. Number of men under each captain, length of service, amount of pay, times reported, equipment hired. Everything could be counted. There were rules, up to a point, explicit and implied. Rules about drinking, gambling and fighting. Rules about use of whores. Rules about who sat where. Who could go where, and when. Who fought and who did not. And the all-important Rule of Quarters, controlling the declaration and assignment of booty, enforced with eagle-eyed discipline.

When rules were broken there were fixed punishments, understood by all. Usually a number of lashes of the whip. Friendly had watched a man whipped for pissing in the wrong place, yesterday. It did not seem such a crime, but Victus had explained to everyone, you start off pissing where you please, then you shit where you please, then everyone dies of the plague. So it had been three lashes. Two and one.

Friendly's favourite place was the mess. There was a comforting routine to mealtimes that put him in mind of Safety. The frowning cooks in their stained aprons. The steam from the great pots. The rattle and clatter of knives and spoons. The slurp and splutter of lips, teeth, tongues. The line of jostling men, all asking for more than their share and never getting it.

The men who would be in the scaling parties this morning got two extra meatballs and an extra spoon of soup. Two and one. Cosca had said it was one thing to get poked off a ladder with a spear, but he could not countenance a man falling off from hunger.

"We'll be attacking within the hour," he said now.

Friendly nodded.

Cosca took a long breath, pushed it out through his nose and frowned around him. "Ladders, mainly." Friendly had watched them being made, over the last few days. Twenty-one of them. Two and one. Each had thirty-one rungs, except for one, which had thirty-two. One, two, three. "Monza will be going with them. She wants to be the first to Orso. Entirely determined. She's set firm on vengeance."

Friendly shrugged. She always had been.

"In all honesty, I worry for her."

Friendly shrugged. He was indifferent.

"A battle is a dangerous place."

Friendly shrugged. That seemed obvious.

"My friend, I want you to stick near her, in the fighting. Make sure no harm comes to her."

"What about you?"

"Me?" Cosca slapped Friendly on his shoulder. "The only shield I need is the universally high regard in which men hold me."

"You sure?"

"No, but I'll be where I always am. Well behind the fighting with my flask for company. Something tells me she'll need you more. There are enemies still, out there. And Friendly..."

"Yes?"

"Watch closely and take great care. The fox is most dangerous when at bay — that Orso will have some deadly tricks in store, well..." and he puffed out his cheeks, "it's inevitable. Watch out, in particular... for Morveer."

"Alright." Murcatto would have him and Shivers watching her. A party of three, as it had been when they killed Gobba. Two watching one. He wrapped the dice up and slid them down into his pocket. He watched the steam rise as the food was ladled out. Listened to the men grumbling. Counted the complaints.

* * *

The washed-out grey of dawn was turning to golden daylight, sun creeping over the battlements at the top of the wall they'd all have to climb, its gap-toothed shadow slowly giving ground across the ruined gardens.

They'd be going soon. Shivers shut his eye and grinned into the sun. Tipped his head back and stuck his tongue out. It was getting colder as the year wore down. Felt almost like a fine summer morning in the North. Like mornings he'd fought great battles in. Mornings he'd done high deeds, and a few low ones too.

"You seem happy enough," came Monza's voice, "for a man about to risk his life."

Shivers opened his eye and turned his grin on her. "I've made peace with myself."

"Good for you. That's the hardest war of all to win."

"Didn't say I won. Just stopped fighting."

"I'm starting to think that's the only victory worth a shit," she muttered, almost to herself.

Ahead of them, the first wave of mercenaries were ready to go, stood about their ladders, big shields on their free arms, twitchy and nervous, which was no surprise. Shivers couldn't say he much fancied their job. They weren't making the least effort to hide what they had planned. Everyone knew what was coming, on both sides of the wall.

Close round Shivers, the second wave were getting ready too. Giving blades a last stroke with the whetstone, tightening straps on armour, telling a last couple of jokes and hoping they weren't the last they ever told. Shivers grinned, watching them at it. Rituals he'd seen a dozen times before and more. Felt almost like home.

"You ever have the feeling you were in the wrong place?" he asked. "That if you could just get over the next hill, cross the next river, look down into the next valley, it'd all . . . fit. Be right."

Monza narrowed her eyes at the inner walls. "All my life, more or less."

"All your life spent getting ready for the next thing. I climbed a lot of hills now. I crossed a lot of rivers. Crossed the sea even, left everything I knew and came to Styria. But there I was, waiting for me at the docks when I got off the boat, same man, same life. Next valley ain't no different from this one. No better anyway. Reckon I've learned . . . just to stick in the place I'm at. Just to be the man I am."

"And what are you?"

He looked down at the axe across his knees. "A killer, I reckon."

"That all?"

"Honestly? Pretty much." He shrugged. "That's why you took me on, ain't it?"

She frowned at the ground. "What happened to being an optimist?"

"Can't I be an optimistic killer? A man once told me — the man who killed my brother, as it goes — that good and evil are a matter of where you stand. We all got our reasons. Whether they're decent ones all depends on who you ask, don't it?"

"Does it?"

"I would've thought you'd say so, of all people."

"Maybe I would've, once. Now I'm not so sure. Maybe those are just the lies we tell ourselves, so we can live with what we've done."

Shivers couldn't help himself. He burst out laughing.

"What's funny?"

"I don't need excuses, Chief, that's what I'm trying to tell you. What's the name for it, when a thing's bound to happen? There's a word for it, ain't there, when there's no stopping something? No avoiding it, whatever you try to do?"

"Inevitable," said Monza.

"That's it. The inevitable." Shivers chewed happily on the word like a mouthful of good meat. "I'm happy with what's done. I'm happy with what's coming."

A shrill whistle cut through the air. All together, with a rattling of armour, the first wave knelt in parties of a dozen and took up their long ladders between them. They started to jog forwards, in piss-poor order if Shivers was honest, slipping and sliding across the slimy gardens. Others followed after, none too eager, sharpshooters with flatbows aiming to keep the archers on the walls busy. There were a few grunts, some calls of "steady" and the rest, but a quiet rush, on the whole. It wouldn't have seemed right, really, giving your war cry while you ran at a wall. What do you do when you get there? You can't keep shouting all the way up a ladder.

"There they go." Shivers stood, lifted his axe and shook it above his head. "Go on! Go on, you bastards!"

They made it halfway across the gardens before Shivers heard a floating shriek of, "Fire!" A moment later a clicking rattle from the walls. Bolts flitted down into the charging men. There were a couple of screams, sobs, a few boys dropped, but most kept pressing forwards, faster'n ever now. Mercenaries with bows of their own knelt, sent a volley back, pinging from battlements or flying right over.

The whistle went again and the next wave started forwards, the men who'd drawn the happy task of climbing. Light-armoured mostly, so they'd move nice and nimble. The first party had made it to the foot of the walls, were starting to raise their ladder. One of 'em dropped with a bolt in his neck, but the rest managed to push the thing the whole way. Shivers watched it swing over and clatter into the parapet. Other ladders started going up. More movement at the top of the walls, men leaning out with rocks and chucking them down. Bolts fell among the second wave, but most of 'em were getting close to the walls now, crowding round, starting to climb. There were six ladders up, then ten. The next one fell apart when it hit the battlements, bits of wood dropping on the shocked boys who'd raised it. Shivers had to chuckle.

More rocks dropped. A man tumbled from halfway up a ladder, his legs folding every which way underneath him, started shrieking away. There was plenty of shouting all round now, and no mistake. Some defenders on a tower roof upended a big vat of boiling water into the faces of a party trying to raise a ladder below. They made a hell of a noise, ladder toppling, running about clutching their heads like madmen.

Bolts and arrows hissed up and down each way. Stones tumbled, bounced. Men fell at the walls, or on their way to 'em. Others started crawling back through the mud, were dragged back, arms over the shoulders of comrades happy for an excuse to get clear. Mercenaries hacked about madly as they got to the top of the ladders, more'n one poked off by waiting spearmen, taking the quick way back down.

Shivers saw someone at the battlements upending a pot onto a ladder and the men climbing it. Someone else came up with a torch, set light to it, and the whole top half went up in flames. Oil, then. Shivers watched it burn, a couple of the men on it too. After a moment they toppled off, took some others with 'em, more screams. Shivers slid his axe through the loop over his shoulder. Best place for it when you're trying to climb. Unless you slip and it cuts your head off, of course. That thought made him chuckle again. Couple of men around him were frowning, he was chuckling that much, but he didn't care, the blood was pumping fast now. They just made him chuckle more.

Looked like some of the mercenaries had made it to the parapet over on the right. He saw blades twinkling at the battlements. More men pressed up behind. A ladder covered in soldiers was shoved away from the wall with poles. It teetered for a moment, upright, like the best stilt-show in the world. The poor bastards near the top wriggled, clutching at nothing, then it slowly toppled over and mashed them all into the cobbles.

They were up on the left too, just next to the gatehouse. Shivers saw men fighting their way up some steps onto the roof. Five or six of the ladders were down, two were still burning up against the wall, sending up plumes of dark smoke, but most of the rest were crawling with climbing soldiers from top to bottom. Couldn't have been too many men on the defence, and weight of numbers was starting to tell.

The whistle went again and the third wave started to move, heavier-armoured men who'd follow the first up the ladders and press on into the fortress.

"Let's go," said Monza.

"Right y'are, Chief." Shivers took a breath and started jogging.

The bows were more or less silenced now, only a few bolts still flitting from arrow-loops in the towers. So it was a happier journey than the folks before had taken, just a morning amble through the corpses scattered across the blasted gardens and over to one of the middle ladders. A couple of men and a sergeant were stood at the foot, boots up on the first rung, gripping it tight. The sergeant slapped each man as he began to climb.

"Up you go now, lads, up you go! Fast but steady! No loitering! Get up and kill those fuckers! You too, bastard — Oh. Sorry, your...er... Excellency?"

"Just hold it steady." And Monza started climbing.

Shivers followed, hands sliding on the rough uprights, boots scraping on the wood, breath hissing through his smile as his muscles worked up an ache. He kept his eyes fixed on the wall in front. No point looking anywhere else. If an arrow came? Nothing you could do. If some bastard dropped a rock on you, or a pot of boiling water? Nothing you could do. If they pushed the ladder off? Shitty luck, alright, but looking out for it would only slow you down and make it the more likely. So he kept on, breathing hard through his clenched teeth.

Soon enough he got to the top, hauled himself over. Monza was there on the walkway, sword already drawn, looking down into the inner ward. He could hear fighting, but not near. There were a few dead men scattered on the walkway, from both sides. A mercenary propped against the stonework had an arm off at the elbow, rope lashed around his shoulder to stop the blood, moaning, "It fell off the edge, it fell off the edge," over and over. Shivers didn't reckon he'd last 'til lunch, but he guessed that meant more lunch for everyone else. You have to look at the sunny side, don't you? That's what being an optimist is all about.

He swung his shield off his back and slid his arm through the straps. He pulled his axe out, spun the grip round in his fist. Felt good to do it. Like a smith getting his hammer out, ready for the good work to start. There were more gardens down below, planted on steps cut from the summit of the mountain, nowhere near so battered as the ones further out. Buildings towered over the greenery on three sides. A mass of twinkling windows and fancy stonework, domes and turrets sprouting from the top, crusted with statues and glinting prongs. Didn't take a great mind to spot Orso's palace, which was just as well, 'cause Shivers knew he didn't have a great mind. Just a bloody one.

"Let's go," said Monza.

Shivers grinned. "Right behind you, Chief."

The trenches that riddled the dusty mountainside were empty. The soldiers who had occupied them had dispersed, gone back to their homes, or to play their own small roles in the several power struggles set off by the untimely deaths of King Rogont and his allies. Only the Thousand Swords remained, swarming hungrily around Duke Orso's palace like maggots around a corpse. Shenkt had seen it all before. Loyalty, duty, pride — fleeting motivations on the whole, which kept men smugly happy in good weather but soon washed away when the storm came. Greed, though? On greed you can always rely.

He walked on up the winding track, across the battle-scarred ground before the walls, over the bridge, the looming gatehouse of Fontezarmo drawing steadily closer. A single mercenary sat slouched on a folding chair outside the open gate, spear leaning against the wall beside him.

"What's your business?" Asked with negligible interest.

"Duke Orso commissioned me to kill Monzcarro Murcatto, now the Grand Duchess of Talins."

"Hilarious." The guard pulled his collars up around his ears and settled back against the wall.

Often, the last thing men believe is the truth. Shenkt pondered that as he passed through the long tunnel and into the outer ward of the fortress. The rigidly ordered beauty of Duke Orso's formal gardens was entirely departed, along with half the north wall. The mercenaries had made a very great mess of the place. But that was war. There was much confusion. But that was war also.

The final assault was evidently well under way. Ladders stood against the inner wall, bodies scattered in the blasted gardens around their bases. Orderlies wandered among them, offering water, fumbling with splints or bandages, moving men onto stretchers. Shenkt knew few would survive who could not even crawl by themselves. Still, men always clung to the smallest sliver of hope. It was one of the few things to admire in them.

He came to a silent halt beside a ruined fountain and watched the wounded struggling against the inevitable. A man slipped suddenly from behind the broken stonework and almost ran straight into him. An unremarkable balding man, wearing a worn studded-leather jerkin.

"Gah! My most *profound* apologies!"

Shenkt said nothing.

"You are... are you... that is to say... here to participate in the assault?"

"In a way."

"As am I, as am I. In a way." Nothing could have been more natural than a mercenary fleeing the fighting, but something did not tally. He was dressed like a thug, this man, but he spoke like a bad writer. His nearest hand flapped around as though to distract attention from the other, which was clearly creeping towards a concealed weapon. Shenkt frowned. He had no desire to draw undue attention. So he gave this man a chance, just as he always did, wherever possible.

"We both have our work, then. Let us delay each other no longer."

The stranger brightened. "Absolutely so. To work."

*   *   *

Morveer gave a false chuckle, then realised he had accidentally strayed into using his accustomed voice. "To work," he grunted in an unconvincing commoner's baritone.

"To work," the man echoed, his bright eyes never wavering.

"Right. Well." Morveer sidestepped the stranger and walked on, allowing his hand to come free of his mounted needle and drop, inconspicuous, to his side. Without doubt the fellow had been possessed of an unusual manner, but had Morveer's mission been to poison every person with an unusual manner he would never have been halfway done. Fortunately his mission was only to poison seven of the most important persons in the nation, and it was one at which he had only lately achieved spectacular success.

He was still flushed by the sheer scale of his achievement, the sheer audacity of its execution, the unparalleled success of his plan. He was beyond doubt the greatest poisoner ever and had become, indisputably, a great man of history. How it galled him that he could never truly share his grand achievement with the world, never enjoy the adulation his triumph undoubtedly deserved. Oh, if the doubting headmaster at the orphanage could have only witnessed this happy day, he would have been forced to concede that Castor Morveer was indeed prize-winning material! If his wife could have seen it, she would have finally understood him, and never again complained about his unusual habits! If his infamous one-time teacher, Moumah-yin-Bek, could only have been there, he would have finally acknowledged that his pupil had forever eclipsed him. If Day had been alive, she would no doubt have given that silvery giggle in acknowledgement of his genius, smiled her innocent smile and perhaps touched him gently, perhaps even...But now was not the time for such fancies. There had been compelling reasons for poisoning all four of them, so Morveer would have to settle for his own congratulations.

It appeared that his murder of Rogont and his allies had quite eliminated any standards at the siege of Fontezarmo. It was not an overstatement to say that the outer ward of the fortress was scarcely guarded at all. He knew Nicomo Cosca for a bloated balloon of braggadocio, a committed drunkard and a rank incompetent to boot, but he had supposed the man would make some provision for security. This was almost disappointingly effortless.

Though the fighting upon the wall seemed largely to have ceased —

the gate to the inner ward was now in the hands of the mercenaries and stood wide — the sound of combat still emanated vaguely from the gardens beyond. An utterly distasteful business; he was pleased that he would have no occasion to stray near it. It appeared the Thousand Swords had captured the citadel and Duke Orso's doom was inevitable, but the thought gave Morveer no particular discomfort. Great men come and go, after all. He had a promise of payment from the Banking House of Valint and Balk, and that went beyond any one man, any one nation. That was deathless.

Some wounded had been laid out on a patch of scraggy grass, in the shadow of a tree to which a goat had, inexplicably, been tethered. Morveer grimaced, tiptoed between them, lip wrinkled at the sight of bloody bandages, of ripped and spattered clothing, of torn flesh —

"Water..." one of them whispered at him, clutching at his ankle.

"Always it's water!" Tearing his leg free. "Find your own!" He hurried through an open doorway and into the largest tower in the outer ward where, he was reliably informed, the constable of the fortress had once had his quarters, and Nicomo Cosca now had his.

He slipped through the gloom of narrow passageways, barely lit by arrow-loops. He crept up a spiral staircase, back hissing against the rough stone wall, tongue pressed into the roof of his mouth. The Thousand Swords were as slovenly and easily fooled as their commander, but he was fully aware that fickle chance might deflate his delight at any moment. Caution first, always.

The first floor had been made a storeroom, filled with shadowy boxes. Morveer crept on. The second floor held empty bunks, no doubt previously utilised by the defenders of the fortress. Twice more around the spiralling steps, he softly tweaked a door open with a finger and applied his eye to the crack.

The circular room beyond contained a large, curtained bed, shelves with many impressive-looking books, writing desk and chests for clothes, an armour stand with suit of polished plate upon it, a sword-rack with several blades, a table with four chairs and a deck of cards, and a large, inlaid cupboard with glasses upon the top. On a row of pegs beside the bed hung several outrageous hats, crystal pins gleaming, gilt bands glinting, a rainbow of different-coloured feathers fluttering in the breeze from an open window. This, without doubt, was the chamber Cosca had taken for his own. No other man would dare to affect such absurd headgear, but for the moment, there was no sign of the great drunkard. Morveer slid inside and eased the door shut behind him. He crossed on silent tiptoes to the cupboard, nimbly avoiding collision with a covered milking-bucket that sat beneath, and with gentle fingers teased open the doors.

Morveer allowed himself the smallest of smiles. Nicomo Cosca would, no doubt, have considered himself a wild and romantic maverick, unfettered by the bonds of routine. In fact he was predictable as the stars, as dully regular as the tide. Most men never change, and a drunk is always a drunk. The chief difficulty appeared to be the spectacular variety of bottles he had collected. There was no way to be certain from which he would drink next. Morveer had no alternative but to poison the entire collection.

He pulled his gloves on, carefully slid the Greenseed solution from his inside pocket. It was lethal only when swallowed, and the timing of its effect varied greatly with the victim, but it gave off only the very slightest fruity odour, entirely undetectable when mingled with wine or spirits. He took careful note of the position of each bottle, the degree to which the cork was inserted, then twisted each free, carefully let fall a drop from his pipette into the neck, replacing cork and bottle precisely as they had been prior to his arrival. He smiled as he poisoned bottles of varying sizes, shapes, colours. This was work as mundane as the poisoned crown had been inspired, but no less noble for that. He would blow through the room like a zephyr of death, undetected, and bring a fitting end to that repulsive drunkard. One more report of Nicomo Cosca's death, and one more only. Few people indeed would consider that anything other than an entirely righteous and public-spirited—

He froze in place. There were footsteps on the stairs. He swiftly pushed the cork back into the final bottle, slid it carefully into position and darted through a narrow doorway into the darkness of a small cell, some kind of—

He wrinkled his nose as he was assailed by a powerful reek of urine. Harsh Mistress Fortune never missed an opportunity to demean him. He might have known he would stumble into a latrine as his hiding place. He had now only to hope that Cosca was not taken with a sudden urge to void his bowels...

The battle on the walls appeared to have been settled, and with relatively little difficulty. No doubt the battle continued in the inner ward beyond, through the rich staterooms and echoing marble halls of Duke Orso's palace. But from Cosca's vantage point atop the constable's tower he could not see a blow of it. And even if he could have, what difference? When you've seen one fortress stormed . . .

"Victus, my friend!"

"Uh?" The last remaining senior captain of the Thousand Swords lowered his eyeglass and gave Cosca his usual suspicious squint.

"I rather suspect the day is ours."

"I rather suspect you're right."

"The two of us can do no more good up here, even if we could see anything."

"You speak true, as ever." Cosca took that for a joke. "It's all inevitable now. Nothing left but to divide the loot." Victus absently stroked the many chains around his neck. "My favourite part of any siege."

"Cards, then?"

"Why ever not?"

Cosca slapped his eyeglass closed and led the way back down the winding stair to the chamber he had taken for his own. He strode to the cabinet and snatched the inlaid doors open. The many-coloured bottles greeted him like a crowd of old friends. Ah, a drink, a drink, a drink. He took down a glass, pulled the cork from the nearest bottle with a gentle thwop.

"Drink, then?" he called over his shoulder.

"Why ever not?"

There was still fighting, but nothing you could call an organised defence. The mercenaries had swept the walls clean, driven the defenders out of the gardens and were even now breaking into the towers, into the buildings, into the palace. More of them boiled up the ladders every moment, desperate not to miss out on the plunder. No one fought harder or moved faster than the Thousand Swords when they could smell booty.

"This way." She hurried towards the main gate of the palace, retracing the steps she'd taken the day they killed her brother, past the circular pool, two bodies floating face down in the shadow of Scarpius' pillar. Shivers followed, that strange smile on his scarred face he'd been wearing all day. They passed an eager clump of men clustered around a doorway, eyes all shining with greed, a couple of them swinging axes at the lock, door wobbling with each blow. They scrambled over each other as it finally came open, scream-ing, shouting, elbowing to get past. Two of them wrestled each other to the ground, fighting over what they hadn't even stolen yet.

Further on a pair of mercenaries had a servant in a gold-trimmed jacket sitting on the side of a fountain, his shocked face smeared with blood. One would slap him and scream, "Where's the fucking money?" Then the other would do the same. Back and forth his head went. "Where's the fucking money, where's the fucking money, where's the fucking money…"

A window burst open in a shower of torn lead and broken glass and an antique cabinet tumbled out onto the cobbles, scattering splinters. A whooping mercenary ran past, arms heaped with glinting material. Cur-tains, maybe. Monza heard a scream, whipped about, saw someone plum-met from an upstairs window and headfirst into the garden, drop bonelessly over. She heard shrieking from somewhere. Sounded like a woman's voice, but it was hard to tell when it was that desperate. There was shouting, screaming, laughing everywhere. She swallowed her sickness, tried not to think that she'd made this happen. That this was where her vengeance had led. All she could do was keep her eyes ahead, hope to find Orso first.

Find him and make him pay.

The studded palace doors were still locked, but the mercenaries had found a way round, smashed through one of the great arched windows to one side. Someone must have cut himself in the rush to get in and get rich — there was blood smeared on the windowsill. Monza eased through, boots crunching on broken glass, dropped down into a grand dining room beyond. She'd eaten there once, she realised, Benna beside her, laughing, Faithful too. Orso, Ario, Foscar, Ganmark had all been there, a whole crowd of other officers. It occurred to her that pretty much every guest from that night was dead. The room hadn't fared much better.

It was like a field after the locusts come through. They'd carried off half the paintings, slashed up the rest for the sake of it. The two huge vases beside the fireplace were too big to lift, so they'd smashed them and taken the gilt handles. They'd torn the hangings down, stolen all the plates apart from the ones broken to fragments across the polished floor. Strange, how men are almost as happy to break a thing as steal it, at a time like that. They were still rooting around, ripping drawers from cupboards, chisel-ling sconces from the walls, dismantling the place for anything worth one bit. One fool had a chair balanced on the bare table and was straining up to reach the chandelier. Another was busy with a knife, trying to prise the crystal doorknobs loose.

A pock-faced mercenary grinned at her, fists bursting with gilded cutlery. "I got spoons!" he shouted. Monza shoved him out of the way and he tripped, his treasure scattering, other men pouncing on it like ducks on stray crumbs. She pushed through the open doorway, out into a marble hall, Shivers at her shoulder. Sounds of fighting echoed down it. Wails and yells, metal scraping, wood crashing, from everywhere and nowhere. She squinted both ways into the gloom, trying to get her bearings, sweat tickling at her scalp.

"This way." They passed a vast sitting room, men inside slashing the upholstery of some antique chairs, as if Orso kept his gold in his cushions. The next door was being kicked in by an eager crowd. One man took an arrow in his neck as they broke it open, others poured in past him, whooping, weapons clashed on the other side. Monza kept her eyes ahead, thoughts fixed on Orso. She pushed on up a flight of steps, teeth gritted, hardly feeling the ache in her legs.

Onto a dim gallery at one end of a high, vaulted chamber, its barrelled ceiling crusted with gilded leaves. The whole wall was a great organ, a range of polished pipes sprouting from carved wood, a stool drawn up before the keyboard for the player. Down below, beyond a delicately worked wooden rail, there was a music room. Mercenaries shrieked with laughter, battering a demented symphony from the instruments as they broke them apart.

"We're close," she whispered over her shoulder.

"Good. Time to get this over with, I reckon."

Her very thoughts. She crept towards the tall door in the far wall. "Orso's chambers are up this way."

"No, no." She frowned over her shoulder. Shivers stood there, grinning, his metal eye shining in the half-light. "Not that."

She felt a cold feeling creeping up her back. "What, then?"

"You know what." His smile widened, scars twisting, and he stretched his neck out one way, then the other.

She dropped into a fighting crouch just in time. He snarled as he came at her, axe flashing across. She lurched into the stool and upended it, nearly fell, mind still catching up. His axe thudded into the organ pipes, struck a mad clanging note from them. He wrenched the blade free, leaving a great wound behind in the thin metal. He sprang at her again but the shock had faded now and cold anger leaked in to fill the gap.

"You one-eyed cocksucker!" Not clever, perhaps, but from the heart. She lunged at him but he caught the Calvez on his shield, swung his axe, and she only just hopped away in time, the heavy blade crashing into the organ's surround and sending splinters flying. She dropped back, watchful, keeping her distance. She'd about as much chance of parrying that weight of steel as she did of playing sweet music on that organ.

"Why?" she snarled at him, point of the Calvez moving in little circles. She didn't care a shit about his reasons, really. Just playing for time, looking for an opening.

"Maybe I got sick o' your scorn." He nudged forwards behind his shield and she backed off again. "Or maybe Eider offered me more'n you."

"Eider?" She spat laughter in his face. "There's your problem! You're a fucking idiot!" She lunged on the last word, trying to catch him off guard, but he wasn't fooled, knocked her jabs calmly away with his shield.

"I'm the idiot? I saved you how many times? I gave up my eye! So you could sneer at me with that empty bastard Rogont? You treat me like a fucking fool and still expect my loyalty, and *I'm* the idiot?" Hard to argue with most of that, now it was stuck under her nose. She should've listened to Rogont, let him put Shivers down, but she'd let guilt get in the way. Mercy might be brave, like Cosca said, but it seemed it wasn't always clever. Shivers shuffled at her and she gave ground again, fast running out of it.

"You should've seen this coming," he whispered, and she reckoned he had a point. It had been coming a long time. Since she fucked Rogont. Since she turned her back on Shivers. Since he lost his eye in the cells under Salier's palace. Maybe it had been coming from the first moment they met. Before, even. Always.

Some things are inevitable.

Thus the Whirligig...

Shivers' axe clanged into the pipes again. He didn't know what the hell they were for but they made a bastard of a racket. Monza had already dodged away though, weighing her sword, narrowed eyes fixed on his. More'n likely he should've just axed her in the back of the skull and put an end to it. But he wanted her to know who'd done it, and why. Needed her to know.

"You don't have to do this," she hissed at him. "You could still walk away."

"I thought the dead could do the forgiving," he said, circling to cut off her space.

"I'm offering you a chance, Shivers. Back to the North, no one would chase you."

"They're free to fucking try, but I reckon I'll stay a little longer. A man has to stick at something, don't he? I've got my pride, still."

"Shit on your pride! You'd be selling your arse in the alleys of Talins if it wasn't for me!" True, more'n likely. "You knew the risks. You chose to take my money." True too. "I made no promises to you and I broke none!" True and all. "That bitch Eider won't give you a scale!"

Hard to argue with most of that, maybe, but it was too late to go back now, and besides, an axe in the head is the last word in any argument. "We'll see." Shivers eased towards her, shield leading the way. "But this ain't about money. This is about... vengeance. Thought you'd understand that."

"Shit on your vengeance!" She snatched up the stool and flung it at him, underhand. He got his shield in the way and knocked it spinning over the balcony, but she pressed in fast behind it. He managed to catch her sword on the haft of his axe, blade scraping down and just holding on the studs in

589

the wood. She ended up close, pressed against him almost, snarling, point of her sword waving near his good eye.

She spat in his face, made him flinch, threw an elbow and caught him under the jaw, knocked his head sideways. She pulled her sword back for a thrust but he lashed at her first. She dodged, the axe hacked into the railing and broke a great chunk of wood from it. He twisted away, knowing her sword would be coming, felt the steel slide through his shirt and leave a line of hot pain across his stomach as it whipped out. She stumbled towards him, off balance. He shifted his weight, growled as he swung his shield round with all his strength and all his rage behind it. It hit her square in the face, snapped her head about and sent her reeling into the pipes with a dull clang, back of her skull leaving a great dent. She bounced off and pitched over on her back on the wooden floor, sword clattering from her hand.

He stared at her for a moment, blood whacking at his skull, sweat tickling his scarred face. A muscle twitched in her neck. Not a thick neck. He could've stepped up and cut her head off easy as chopping logs. His fingers worked nervously round the grip of his axe at the thought. She coughed out blood, groaned, shook her head. She started to roll over, eyes glassy, dragged herself up onto hands and knees. She reached out woozily for the grip of her sword.

"No, no." He stepped up close and kicked it into the corner.

She flinched, turned her head away from him, started crawling slowly after the blade, breathing hard, blood from her nose pit-pattering on the wooden floor. He followed, standing over her, talking. Strange, that. The Bloody-Nine had told him once — if you mean to kill, you kill, you don't talk about it — and it was advice he'd always tried to stick to. He could've killed her easily as crushing a beetle, but he didn't. He wasn't sure if he was talking to stretch the moment out or talking to put the moment off. But he was talking, still.

"Let's not pretend like you're the injured party in all this! You've killed half o' Styria so you could get your way! You're a scheming, lying, poisoning, murdering, treacherous, brother-fucking cunt. Aren't you! I'm doing the right thing. S'all about where you stand and that. I'm no monster. So maybe my reasons ain't the noblest. Everyone's got their reasons. The world'll still be better for one less o' you!" He wished his voice hadn't been down to a croak, because that was a fact. "I'm doing the right thing!" A fact, and he wanted her to admit it. She owed him that. "Better for one less o' you!" He leaned down over her, lips curling back, heard footsteps hammering up to his side, turned—

Friendly rammed into him full-tilt and took him off his feet. Shivers snarled, caught him round the back with his shield arm, but the best he could do was drag the convict with him. They plunged through the railing with a snapping of wood and went tumbling out into empty air.

Nicomo Cosca came into view, whipping off his hat and flinging it theatrically across the room, where it presumably missed its intended peg since Morveer saw it tumble to the floor not far from the latrine door behind which he had concealed himself. His mouth twisted into a triumphant sneer in the pungent darkness. The old mercenary held in his hand a metal flask. The very one Morveer himself had tossed at Cosca as an offhand insult in Sipani. The wretched old drunk must have gone back and collected it afterwards, no doubt hoping to lick out the barest trickle of grog. How hollow now did his promise seem never to drink again? So much for man's ability to change. Morveer had expected little better, of course, from the world's leading expert on empty bravado, but Cosca's almost pitiable level of debasement surprised even him.

The sound of the cabinet being opened reached his ear. "Just must fill this up." Cosca's voice, though he was out of sight. Metal clinked.

Morveer could just observe the weasel-like visage of his companion. "How can you drink that piss?"

"I have to drink something, don't I? It was recommended to me by an old friend, now, alas, dead."

"Do you have any old friends who aren't dead?"

"Only you, Victus. Only you."

A rattling of glass and Cosca swaggered through the narrow strip to which Morveer's vision was reduced, his flask in one hand, a glass and bottle in the other. It was a distinctive purple vessel, which Morveer clearly remembered poisoning but a few moments ago. It seemed he had engineered another fatal irony. Cosca would be responsible for his own destruction, as he had been so often before. But this time with a fitting finality. He heard the rustling, snapping sound of cards being shuffled.

"Five scales a hand?" came Cosca's voice. "Or shall we play for honour?"

Both men burst out laughing. "Let's make it ten."

"Ten it is." Further shuffling. "Well, this is civilised. Nothing like cards while other men fight, eh? Just like old times."

"Except no Andiche, no Sesaria and no Sazine."

"Aside from that," conceded Cosca. "Now then. Will you deal, or shall I?"

Friendly growled as he dragged himself clear of the wreckage. Shivers was a few strides away, on the other side of the heap of broken wood and ivory, twisted brass and tangled wire that was all that remained of Duke Orso's harpsichord. The Northman rolled onto his knees, shield still on his arm, axe still gripped in his other fist, blood running down the side of his face from a cut just above his gleaming metal eye.

"You counting fuck! I was going to say my quarrel ain't with you. But now it is."

They slowly stood, together, watching each other. Friendly slid his knife from its sheath, his cleaver out from his jacket, the worn grips smooth and familiar in his palms. He could forget about all the chaos in the gardens, now, all the madness in the palace. One man against one man, the way it used to be, in Safety. One and one. The plainest arithmetic he could ask for.

"Right, then," said Friendly, and he grinned.

"Right, then," hissed Shivers through gritted teeth.

One of the mercenaries who had been breaking the room apart took a half-step towards them. "What the hell is—"

Shivers leaped the wreckage in one bound, axe a shining arc. Friendly dropped away to the right, ducking underneath it, the wind of it snatching at his hair. His cleaver caught the edge of Shivers' shield, the corner of the blade squealed off and dug into the Northman's shoulder. Not hard enough to do more than cut him, though. Shivers twisted round fast, axe flashing down. Friendly slid around it, heard it crash into the wreckage beside him. He stabbed with his knife but the Northman already had his shield in the way, twisted it, jerking the blade out of Friendly's fist, sending it clattering across the polished floor. He hacked with his cleaver but Shivers pressed close and caught Friendly's elbow against his shoulder, the blade flapping at the blind side of his face and leaving him a bloody nick under his ear.

Friendly took a half-step back, cleaver going out for a sideways sweep, not giving Shivers room to use his axe. He charged forwards behind his shield instead, caught Friendly's flailing cleaver against it and lifted him, growling like a mad dog. Friendly punched at his side, struggling to get a good fist around that big circle of wood, but Shivers had more weight and all the momentum. Friendly was bundled through the door, frame thudding against his shoulder, shield digging into his chest, gaining pace all the time. His boots kicked at the floor, then the floor was gone and he was falling. The back of his head hit stone, he jolted, bounced, tumbling over and over, grunting and wheezing, light and darkness spinning round him. Stairs. Falling down stairs, and the worst of it was he couldn't even count them.

He growled again as he slowly picked himself up at the bottom. He was in a long kitchen, a vaulted cellar lit by small windows, high up. Left leg, right shoulder, back of his head all throbbing, blood on his cheek, one sleeve torn back and a long raw scrape down his forearm, blood on his trouser leg where he must have cut himself on his own cleaver as he fell. But everything still moved.

Shivers stood at the top of a flight of fourteen steps, two times seven, a big black shape with light twinkling from one eye. Friendly beckoned to him.

"Down you come."

She kept crawling. That was all she could do. Drag herself one stride at a time. Keep both eyes ahead, on the hilt of the Calvez in the corner. Crawl, and spit blood, and will the room to stay still. All the slow way her back was itching, tingling, waiting for Shivers' axe to hack into it and give her the ugly ending she deserved.

At least the one-eyed bastard had stopped talking now.

Monza's hand closed around the hilt and she rolled over, snarling, waving the blade out in front of her like a coward might wave a torch into the night. There was no one there. Only a ragged gap in the railing at the edge of the gallery.

She wiped her bloody nose on her gloved hand, came up slowly to her knees. The dizziness was fading now, the roar in her ears had quieted to a steady thump, her face a throbbing mass, everything feeling twice the size it should have. She shuffled to the shattered balustrade and peered down. The three mercenaries who'd been busy destroying the room were still at it, stood staring down at a shattered harpsichord under the gallery. Still no sign of Shivers, still no clue what had happened. But there were other things on Monza's mind.

Orso.

She clenched her aching jaw, crossed to the far door and heaved it open. Down a gloomy corridor, the noise of fighting steadily growing louder. She edged out onto a wide balcony. Above her the great dome was painted with a sky touched by a rising sun, seven winged women brandishing swords. Aropella's grand fresco of the Fates bearing destinies to earth. Below her the two great staircases swept upwards, carved from three different colours of marble. At their top were the double doors, inlaid with rare woods in the pattern of lions' faces. There, in front of those doors, she'd stood beside Benna for the last time, and told him she loved him.

Safe to say things had changed.

On the round mosaic floor of the hall below, and on the wide marble steps, and on the balcony above, a furious battle was being fought. Men from the Thousand Swords struggled to the death with Orso's guards, three score or more of them, a boiling, flailing mass. Swords crashed on shields, maces staved in armour, axes rose and fell, spears jabbed and thrust. Men roared with fury, blubbered with pain, fought and died, hacked down where they stood. The mercenaries were mad on the promise of plunder and the defenders had nowhere to run to. Mercy looked in short supply on both sides. A couple of men in Talinese uniform were kneeling on the balcony not far from her, cranking flatbows. As one of them stood to shoot he caught an arrow in his chest, fell back, coughing, eyes wide with surprise, spattering blood over a fine statue behind him.

Never fight your own battles, Verturio wrote, *if someone else is willing to fight them for you.* Monza eased carefully back into the shadows.

The cork came out with that sucking pop that was Cosca's favourite noise in all the world. He leaned across the table with the bottle and sloshed some of the syrupy contents into Victus' glass.

"Thanks," he grunted. "I think."

To put it politely, Gurkish grape spirit was not to everyone's taste. Cosca had developed if not a love for it then certainly a tolerance, when employed to defend Dagoska. In fact he had developed a powerful tolerance for anything containing alcohol, and Gurkish grape spirit contained a very great deal at a most reasonable cost. The very thought of that gloriously repulsive burned-vomit taste was making his mouth flood with saliva. A drink, a drink, a drink.

He unscrewed the cap of his own flask, shifted in the captain general's chair, fondly stroking the battered wood of one of its arms. "Well?"

Victus' thin face radiated suspicion, causing Cosca to reflect that no man he had ever met had a shiftier look to his eyes. They slid to his cards, to Cosca's cards, to the money between them, then slithered back to Cosca. "Alright. Doubles it is." He tossed some coins into the centre of the table with that delightful jingle that somehow only hard currency can make. "What are you carrying, old man?"

"Earth!" Cosca smugly spread his cards out.

Victus flung his own hand down. "Bloody earth! You always did have the luck of a demon."

"And you the loyalty of one." Cosca showed his teeth as he swept the coins towards him. "I shouldn't worry, the boys will be bringing us plenty more silver in due course. Rule of Quarters, and all that."

"At this rate I'll have lost all my share to you before they get here."

"We can hope." Cosca took a sip from his flask and grimaced. For some reason it tasted even more sour than usual. He wrinkled his lips, sucked his gums, then forced another acrid mouthful down and half-screwed the cap back on. "Now! I am deeply in need of a shit." He slapped the table with one hand and stood. "No tampering with the deck while I'm away, you hear?"

"Me?" Victus was all injured innocence. "You can trust me, General."

"Of course I can." Cosca began to walk, his eyes fixed on the dark crack down the edge of the doorway to the latrine, judging the distances, back prickling as he pictured where Victus was sitting. He twisted his wrist, felt his throwing-knife drop into his waiting palm. "Just like I could trust you at Afieri—" He spun about, and froze. "Ah."

Victus had somehow produced a small flatbow, loaded, and now aimed with impressive steadiness at Cosca's heart. "Andiche took a *sword-thrust* for you?" he sneered. "Sesaria *sacrificed* himself? I *knew* those two bastards, remember! What kind of a fucking idiot do you take me for?"

Shenkt sprang through the shattered window and dropped silently down into the hall beyond. An hour ago it must have been a grand dining room indeed, but the Thousand Swords had already stripped it of anything that might raise a penny. Only fragments of glass and plate, slashed canvases in shattered frames and the shells of some furniture too big to move remained. Three little flies chased each other in geometric patterns through the air above the stripped table. Near them two men were arguing while a boy perhaps fourteen years old watched nervously.

"I told you I had the fucking spoons!" a pock-faced man screamed at one with a tarnished breastplate. "But that bitch knocked me down and I lost 'em! Why didn't you get nothing?"

"'Cause I was watching the door while you got something, you fucking—"

The boy raised a silent finger to point at Shenkt. The other two abandoned their argument to stare at him. "Who the hell are you?" demanded the spoon-thief.

"The woman who made you lose your cutlery," asked Shenkt. "Murcatto?"

"Who the hell are you, I asked?"

"No one. Only passing through."

"That so?" He grinned at his fellows as he drew his sword. "Well, this room's ours, and there's a toll."

"There's a toll," hissed the one with the breastplate, in a tone no doubt meant to be intimidating.

The two of them spread out, the boy reluctantly following their lead. "What have you got for us?" asked the first.

Shenkt looked him in the eye as he came close, and gave him a chance. "Nothing you want."

"I'll be the judge of that." His gaze settled on the ruby ring on Shenkt's forefinger. "What about that?"

"It isn't mine to give."

"Then it's ours to take." They closed in, the one with the pocked face prodding at Shenkt with his sword. "Hands behind your head, bastard, and get on your knees."

Shenkt frowned. "I do not kneel."

The three zipping flies slowed, drifting lazily, then hanging almost still.

Slowly, slowly, the spoon-thief's hungry leer turned into a snarl.

Slowly, slowly, his arm drifted back for a thrust.

Shenkt stepped around his sword, the edge of his hand sank deep into the thief's chest then tore back out. A great chunk of rib and breastbone was ripped out with it, flew spinning through the air to embed itself deep in the ceiling.

Shenkt brushed the sword aside, seized the next man by his breastplate and flung him across the room, his head crumpling against the far wall, blood showering out under such pressure it made a great star of spatters across the gilded wallpaper from floor to ceiling. The flies were sucked from

their places by the wind of his passing, dragged through the air in mad spi-
rals. The ear-splitting bang of his skull exploding joined the hiss of blood
spraying from his friend's caved-in chest and all over the gaping boy as time
resumed its normal flow.

"The woman who made your friend lose his cutlery." Shenkt flicked the
few drops of blood from his hand. "Murcatto?"

The boy nodded dumbly.

"Which way did she go?"

His wide eyes rolled towards the far door.

"Good." Shenkt would have liked to be kind. But then this boy might
have run and brought more men, and there would have been further entan-
glements. Sometimes you must take one life to spare more, and when those
times come, sentiment helps nobody. One of his old master's lessons that
Shenkt had never forgotten. "I am sorry for this."

With a sharp crack, his forefinger sank up to the knuckle in the boy's
forehead.

They smashed their way through the kitchens, both doing their level worst
to kill each other. Shivers hadn't planned on this but his blood was boiling
now. Friendly was in his fucking way, and had to be got out of it, simple as
that. It had become a point of pride. Shivers was better armed, he had the
reach, he had the shield. But Friendly was slippery as an eel and patient as
winter. Backing off, dropping away, forcing nothing, giving no openings.
All he had was his cleaver, but Shivers knew he'd killed enough men with
that alone, and didn't plan on adding his name to the list.

They tangled again, Friendly weaving round an axe-blow and darting
in close, hacking with the cleaver. Shivers stepped into it, caught it on his
shield then charged on, sent Friendly stumbling back against a table, metal
rattling. Shivers grinned, until he saw the table was covered with knives.
Friendly snatched up a blade, arm going back to throw. Shivers dropped
down behind his shield, felt the thud as the knife buried itself in the wood.
He peered over the edge, saw another spinning at him. It bounced from
the metal rim and flashed up into Shivers' face, left him a burning scratch
across the cheek. Friendly whipped up another knife.

Shivers weren't about to crouch there and be target practice. He roared
as he rushed forwards, shield leading the way. Friendly leaped back, rolled

across the table, Shivers' axe just missed him, leaving a great wound in the wood and sending knives jumping in the air. He followed while the convict was off balance, punching away with the edge of his shield, swinging wild with his axe, skin burning, sweat tickling, one eye bulging wild, growling through gritted teeth. Plates shattered, pans scattered, bottles broke, splinters flew, a jar of flour burst open and filled the air with blinding dust.

Shivers left a trail of waste through that kitchen the Bloody-Nine himself might've been proud to make, but the convict dodged and danced, nipped and slashed with knife and cleaver, always just out of reach. All Shivers had to show for his fury by the time they'd done their ugly dance the length of the long room was a bleeding cut on his own arm and a reddening mark on the side of Friendly's face where he'd caught him with his shield.

The convict stood ready and waiting, a couple of steps up the flight leading out, knife and cleaver hanging by his sides, sheen of sweat across his flat chunk of face, skin bloody and battered from a dozen different little cuts and kicks, plus a fall off a balcony and a tumble down some stairs, of course. But Shivers hadn't landed nothing telling on him yet. He didn't look halfway to being finished.

"Come 'ere, you tricky fucker!" Shivers hissed, arm aching shoulder to fingers from swinging his axe. "Let's put an end to you."

"You come here," Friendly grunted back at him. "Let's put an end to you."

Shivers shrugged his shoulders, shook out his arms, wiped blood off his forehead on the back of his sleeve, twisted his neck one way then the other. "Right… you…*fucking* are!" And he came on again. He didn't need asking twice.

Cosca frowned down at his knife. "If I said I was just going to peel an orange with it, any chance you'd believe me?"

Victus grinned, causing Cosca to reflect that no man he had ever met had a shiftier smile. "Doubt I'll believe another word you say. But don't worry. You won't be saying many more."

"Why is it that men pointing loaded flatbows always feel the need to gloat, rather than simply letting fly?"

"Gloating's fun." Victus reached for his glass, smirking eyes never leaving Cosca, glinting point of the flatbow bolt steady as stone, and quickly tossed back his spirit in one swallow. "Yeuch." He stuck his tongue out. "Damn, that stuff is sour."

"Sweeter than my situation," muttered Cosca. "I suppose now the captain general's chair will be yours." A shame. He'd only just got used to sitting in it again himself.

Victus snorted. "Why would I want the fucking thing? Hasn't done much good for the arses on it up to now, has it? Sazine, you, the Murcattos, Faithful Carpi, and you again. Each one ended up dead or close to it, and all the while I've stood behind, and got a lot richer than a nasty little bastard like me deserves." He winced, put one hand on his stomach. "No, I'll find some new idiot to sit there, I think, and make me richer'n ever." He grimaced again. "Ah, shit on that stuff. Ah!" He staggered up from his chair, clutching the edge of the table, a thick vein bulging from his forehead. "What've you done to me, you old bastard?" He squinted over, flatbow suddenly wobbling.

Cosca flung himself forwards. The trigger clicked, the bowstring twanged, the bolt clattered against the plaster just to his left. He rolled up beside the table with a whoop of triumph, raising his knife. "Hah *hah*—"

Victus' bow bashed him in the face, just above his eye. "Gurgh!" Cosca's vision was suddenly filled with light, his knees wobbling wildly. He clutched at the table, waved his knife at nothing. "Sfup." Hands closed around his throat. Hands crusted with heavy rings. Victus' pink face loomed up before his, spit spluttering from his twisted mouth.

Cosca's boots went out from under him, the room flipped over, his head crashed into the table. And all was dark.

The battle under the dome was over, and between the two sides they'd made quite a mess of Orso's cherished rotunda. The glittering mosaic floor and the sweeping steps above it were strewn with corpses, scattered with fallen weapons, dashed and spattered, pooled and puddled with dark blood.

The mercenaries had won — if a dozen of them left standing counted as a victory. "Help me!" one of the wounded was screeching. "Help me!" But his fellows had other things on their minds.

"Get these fucking things open!" The one taking charge was Secco, the corporal who'd been on guard when she rode into the Thousand Swords' camp only to find Cosca there ahead of her. He dragged a dead Talinese soldier out of the way of the lion-head doors and dumped the corpse down the stairs. "You! Find an axe!"

Monza frowned. "Orso'll have more men in there for sure. We'd better wait for help."

"Wait? And split the takings?" Secco gave her a withering sneer. "Fuck yourself, Murcatto, you don't give us orders no more! Get it open!" Two men started battering away with axes, splinters of veneer flying. The rest of the survivors jostled dangerously close behind them, breathless with greed. It seemed the doors had been made to impress guests, not keep out armies. They shuddered, loosening on their hinges. A few more blows and one axe broke clean through, a great chunk of wood splintering away. Secco whooped in triumph as he rammed his spear into the gap, levering the bar on the other side out of its brackets. He fumbled with the ragged edge, pulling the doors wide.

Squealing like children on a feast day, tangled up with each other, drunk on blood and avarice, the mercenaries spilled through into the bright hall where Benna died. Monza knew it was a bad idea to follow. She knew Orso might not even be in there, and if he was, he'd be ready.

But sometimes you have to grasp the nettle.

She dashed round the doorframe after them, keeping low. An instant later she heard the rattling of flatbows. The mercenary in front of her fell and she had to duck around him. Another tumbled backwards, clutching at a bolt in his chest. Boots hammered, men bellowed, the grand room with its great windows and its paintings of history's winners wobbled around her as she ran. She saw figures in full armour, glimpses of steel shining. Orso's closest guards.

She saw Secco jabbing away at one with his spear, the blade scraping uselessly off heavy plate. She heard a loud bonk as a mercenary smashed in a helmet with a big mace, then a scream as he was cut down himself, chopped near in half across the back with a two-handed sword, blood jumping. Another bolt snatched a man from his feet as he charged in and sent him sprawling backwards. Monza crouched, setting her shoulder under the edge of a marble table and heaved it over, a vase that had been on top shattering across the floor. She ducked down behind it, flinched as a flatbow bolt glanced off the stone and clattered away.

"No!" she heard someone shout. "No!" A mercenary flashed past her, running for the door he'd burst through with such enthusiasm a moment before. There was the sound of a bowstring and he stumbled, a bolt sticking from his back, tottered another step and fell, slid along on his face. He tried to push himself up, coughed blood, then sagged down. He died looking right at her.

This was what you got for being greedy. And here she was, wedged in behind a table and all out of friends, more than likely next.

"Grasp the fucking nettle," she cursed at herself.

Friendly backed up the last of the steps, his boots suddenly striking echoes as a wide space opened up behind him. A great round room under a dome painted with winged women, seven lofty archways leading in. Statues looked down from the walls, sculptures in relief, hundreds of pairs of eyes following him as he moved. The defenders must have made a stand here, there were bodies scattered across the floor and up the two curving staircases. Cosca's mercenaries and Orso's guards mixed up together. All on the same side, now. Friendly thought he could hear fighting echoing from somewhere above, but there was still plenty of fight for him down here.

Shivers stepped out from the archway. His hair was dark with blood on one side, plastered to his skull, scarred face streaked red. He was covered with nicks and grazes, right sleeve ripped wide, blood running down his arm. But Friendly hadn't been able to put in that final blow. The Northman still had his axe in one fist, ready to fight, shield criss-crossed with gouges. He nodded as his one eye moved slowly around the room.

"Lot o' corpses," he whispered.

"Forty-nine," said Friendly. "Seven times seven."

"Fancy that. We add you, we'll make fifty."

He threw himself forwards, feinting high then swinging his axe in a great low, ankle-chopping sweep. Friendly jumped it, cleaver coming down towards the Northman's head. Shivers jerked his shield up in time and the blade clanged from its dented boss, sending a jolt up Friendly's arm right to his shoulder. He stabbed at Shivers' side as he passed, got his arm tangled with the haft of the axe as it swung back, but still left the Northman a long cut down his ribs. Friendly spun, raising his cleaver to finish the job, got Shivers' elbow in his throat before he could bring it down, staggered back, near tripping over a corpse.

They faced each other again, Shivers bent over, teeth bared, arm pressed to his wounded side, Friendly coughing as he fought to get his breath and his balance back both at once.

"Another?" whispered Shivers.

"One more," croaked Friendly.

They went at each other again, their snatched breath, squeaking boots, grunting and growling, the scrape of metal on metal, the clang of metal on stone, all echoing from the marble walls and the painted ceiling, as though men were fighting to the death all around them. They chopped, hacked, spat, kicked, stabbed at each other, jumping over bodies, stumbling over weapons, boots slipping and squeaking in black blood on polished stone.

Friendly jerked away from a clumsy axe-swing that hit the wall and sent chips of marble spinning, found he was backing up the steps. They were both tiring now, slowing. A man can only fight, sweat, bleed for so long. Shivers came after him, breathing hard, shield up in front.

Backing up steps is a bad enough idea when they're not scattered with bodies. Friendly was so busy watching Shivers he put his boot down on a corpse's hand, twisted his ankle. Shivers saw it, jabbed with his axe. Friendly couldn't get his leg out of the way in time and the blade tore a gash out of his calf, half-dragged him over. Shivers growled as he lifted his axe high. Friendly lurched forwards, slashed Shivers' forearm with his knife, left a red-black wound, blood running. The Northman grunted, fumbled his axe, the heavy weapon clattering down beside them. Friendly chopped at his skull with the cleaver but Shivers got his shield arm in the way, the two of them getting tangled, the blade only slitting Shivers' scalp, blood bubbling from the wound, pattering over them both. The Northman grabbed Friendly's shoulder with his bloody hand, dragging him close, good eye bulging with crazy rage, steel eye spattered shining red, lips twisted in a mad snarl as he tipped his head backwards.

Friendly drove his knife into Shivers' thigh, felt the metal slide in to the hilt. Shivers gave a kind of squeal, pain and fury together. His forehead smashed into Friendly's mouth with a sick crunch. The hall reeled around, the steps hit Friendly in the back, his skull cracked against marble. He saw Shivers loom over him, thought it would be a good idea to bring the cleaver up. Before he could do it, Shivers rammed his shield down, metal rim clanging against stone. Friendly felt the two bones in his forearm break, cleaver dropping from his numb fingers and clattering down the steps.

Shivers reached down, specks of pink spit flicking from his clenched teeth with each moaning breath, fist closing around the grip of his axe. Friendly watched him do it, feeling no more than a mild curiosity. Everything was bright and blurry, now. He saw the scar on the Northman's thick wrist, in the shape of a number seven. Seven was a good number, today, just as it had been the first day they met. Just as it always was.

"Excuse me." Shivers froze for a moment, his one eye sliding sideways. He reeled around, axe coming after. A man stood behind him, a lean man with pale hair. It was hard to see what happened. The axe missed, Shivers' shield shattered in a tangle of flying wood, he was snatched off his feet and sent tumbling across the chamber. He crashed into the far wall with a gurgle, bounced off and rolled slowly down the opposite set of steps, flopping over once, twice, three times, and lying still at the bottom.

"Three times," gurgled Friendly through his split lips.

"Stay," said the pale man, stepping around him and off up the stairway. It was not so difficult to obey. Friendly had no other plans. He spat a lump of tooth out of his numb mouth, and that was all. He lay there, blinking slowly, staring up at the winged women on the ceiling.

Seven of them, with seven swords.

A rapid spectrum of emotions had swept over Morveer during the past few moments. Triumphant delight, as he had seen Cosca drink from his flask and all unknowing doom himself. Horror and a pointless search for a hiding place as the old mercenary declared his intention to visit the latrine. Curiosity, as he then saw Victus produce a loaded flatbow from beneath the table and train it on his general's back. Triumph once again as he watched Victus consume his own fatal measure of spirit. Finally he was forced to clamp one hand over his mouth to smother his amusement as the poisoned Cosca flung himself clumsily at his poisoned opponent and the two men wrestled, fell to the floor and lay still in a final embrace.

The ironies positively piled one upon the next. Most earnestly they had attempted to kill each other, never realising that Morveer had already done both their jobs for them.

With the smile still on his face he slid his mounted needle from its hidden pocket within the lining of his mercenary's jerkin. Caution first, always. In case any trace of life remained in either of the two murderous old mercenaries, the lightest prick with this shining splinter of metal, coated with his own Preparation Number Twelve, would extinguish it for good and to the general benefit of the world. Morveer carefully eased the latrine door open with the gentlest of creaks, and on pointed toes crept out into the room beyond.

The table was tipped over on its side, coins and cards widely scattered. Cosca lay on his back beside it, left hand hanging nerveless, his flask not far away. Victus was draped on top of him, small flatbow still gripped in one fist, the clasp at its end spotted with red blood. Morveer knelt beside the deceased, hooked his free hand under Victus' corpse and with a grunting effort rolled it off.

Cosca's eyes were closed, his mouth open, blood streaked his cheek from a wound on his forehead. His skin was waxy pale with the unmistakable sheen of death.

"A man can *change*, eh?" sneered Morveer. "So much for *your* promises!"

To his tremendous shock, Cosca's eyes snapped suddenly open.

To his even more tremendous shock, an indescribably awful pain lanced up through his stomach. He took in a great shuddering breath and gave vent to an unearthly howl. Looking down, he perceived that the old mercenary had driven a knife into his groin. Morveer's breath whooped in again. Desperately he raised his arm.

There was a faint slapping sound as Cosca seized his wrist and wrenched it sharply sideways, causing the needle to sink into Morveer's neck. There was a pregnant pause. They remained frozen, a human sculpture, the knife still in Morveer's groin, the needle in his neck, gripped by his hand, gripped by Cosca's hand. Cosca frowned up. Morveer stared down. His eyes bulged. His body trembled. He said nothing. What could one possibly say? The implications were crushingly obvious. Already the most potent poison of which he was aware, carried swiftly from neck to brain, was causing his extremities to become numb.

"Poisoned the grape spirit, eh?" hissed Cosca.

"Fuh," gurgled Morveer, unable now to form words.

"Did you forget I promised you never to drink again?" The old mercenary released the knife, reached across the floor with his bloody hand, retrieved his flask, spun the cap off with a practised motion and tipped it up. White liquid splashed out across the floor. "Goat's milk. I hear it's good for the digestion. The strongest thing I've had since we left Sipani, but it would hardly do to let everyone know it. I have a certain reputation to uphold here. Hence all the bottles."

Cosca shoved Morveer over. The strength was rapidly fading from his limbs and he was powerless to resist. He flopped limp across Victus' corpse. He could scarcely feel his neck. The agony in his groin had faded to a dull throb. Cosca looked down at him.

"Didn't I promise you I'd stop? What kind of a man do you take me for, that I'd break my word?"

Morveer had no breath left to speak, let alone scream. The pain was fading in any case. He wondered, as he often had, how his life might have differed had he not poisoned his mother, and doomed himself to life in the orphanage. His vision was clouding, blurring, growing dark.

"I need to thank you. You see, Morveer, a man *can* change, given the proper encouragement. And your scorn was the very spur I needed."

Killed by his own agent. It was the way so many great practitioners of his profession ended their lives. And on the eve of his retirement, too. He was sure there was an irony there somewhere...

"Do you know the best thing about all this?" Cosca's voice boomed in his ears, Cosca's grin swam above him. "Now I can start drinking again."

One of the mercenaries was pleading, blubbering, begging for his life. Monza sat against the cold marble slab of the tabletop and listened to him, breathing hard, sweating hard, weighing the Calvez in her hand. It would be little better than useless against the heavy armour of Orso's guards, even if she'd fancied taking on that many at once. She heard the damp squelch of a blade rammed into flesh and the pleading was cut off in a long scream and a short gurgle.

Not really a sound to give anyone confidence.

She peered round the edge of the table. She counted seven guards still standing, one ripping his spear free of a dead mercenary's chest, two turning towards her, heavy swords ready, one working an axe from Secco's split skull. Three were kneeling, busily cranking flatbows. Behind them stood the big round table on which the map of Styria was still unrolled. On the map was a crown, a ring of sparkling gold sprouting with gem-encrusted oak leaves, not unlike the one that had killed Rogont and his dream of Styria united. Beside the crown, dressed in black and with his iron-shot black hair and beard as neatly groomed as ever, stood Grand Duke Orso.

He saw her, and she saw him, and the anger boiled up, hot and comforting. One of his guards slipped a bolt into his flatbow and levelled it at her. She was about to duck behind the slab of marble when Orso held out one arm.

"Wait! Stop." That same voice that she had never disobeyed in eight hard years. "Is that you, Monzcarro?"

"Damn right it is!" she snarled back. "Get ready to fucking die!" Though it looked as if she might be going first.

"I've been ready for some time," he called out softly. "You've seen to that. Well done! My hopes are all in ruins, thanks to you."

"You needn't thank me!" she called. "It was Benna I did it for!"

"Ario is dead."

"Hah!" she barked back. "That's what happens when I stab a worthless cunt in the neck and throw him from a window!" A flurry of twitches crawled up Orso's cheek. "But why pick him out? There was Gobba, and Mauthis, and Ganmark, and Faithful — I've slaughtered the whole crowd! Everyone who was in this room when you murdered my brother!"

"And Foscar? I've heard no word since the defeat at the fords."

"You can stop listening!" Said with a glee she hardly felt. "Skull smashed to pulp on a farmhouse floor!"

The anger had all gone from Orso's face and it hung terribly slack. "You must be happy."

"I'm not fucking sad, I'll tell you that!"

"Grand Duchess Monzcarro of Talins." Orso tapped two fingers slowly against his palm, the sharp snaps echoing off the high ceiling. "I congratulate you on your victory. You have what you wanted after all!"

"What I wanted?" For a moment she could hardly believe what she was hearing. "You think I wanted *this*? After the battles I fought for you? The victories I won for you?" She was near shrieking, spitting with fury. She ripped her glove off with her teeth and shook her mutilated hand at him. "I fucking wanted *this*? What reason did we give you to betray us? We were loyal to you! Always!"

"Loyal?" Orso gave a disbelieving gasp of his own. "Crow your victory if you must, but don't crow your innocence to me! We both know better!"

All three flatbows were loaded and levelled now. "We were loyal!" she screamed again, voice cracking.

"Can you deny it? That Benna met with malcontents, revolutionaries, traitors among my ungrateful subjects? That he promised them weapons?

That he promised you would lead them to glory? Claim my place? Usurp me! Did you think I would not learn of it? Did you think I would stand idly by?"

"What the...you fucking *liar!*"

"Still you deny it? I would not believe it myself when they told me! My Monza? Closer to me than my own children? My Monza, betray me? With my own eyes I saw him! With my own eyes!" The echoes of his voice slowly faded, and left the hall almost silent. Only the gentle clanking of the four armoured men as they edged ever so slowly towards her. She could only stare, the realisation creeping slowly through her.

We could have our own city, Benna had said. *You could be the Duchess Monzcarro of... wherever.* Of Talins, had been his thought. *We deserve to be remembered.* He'd planned it himself, alone, and given her no choice. Just as he had when he betrayed Cosca. *It's better this way.* Just as he had when he took Hermon's gold. *This is for us.*

He'd always been the one with the big plans.

"Benna," she mouthed. "You fool."

"You didn't know," said Orso quietly. "You didn't know, and now we are come to this. Your brother doomed himself, and both of us, and half of Styria besides." A sad little chuckle bubbled out of him. "Just when I think I know it all, life always finds a way to surprise me. You're late, Shenkt." His eyes flicked to the side. "Kill her."

Monza felt a shadow fall across her, lurched around. A man had stolen up while they spoke, his soft work boots making not the slightest sound. Now he stood over her, close enough to touch. He held out his hand. There was a ring in his palm. Benna's ruby ring.

"I believe this is yours," he said.

A pale, lean face. Not old, but deeply lined, with harsh cheekbones and eyes hungry bright in bruised sockets. Monza's eyes went wide, the chill shock of recognition washing over her like ice water.

"Kill her!" shouted Orso.

The newcomer smiled, but it was like a skull's smile, never touching his eyes. "Kill her? After all the effort I went to keeping her alive?"

The colour had drained from her face. Indeed she looked almost as pale as she had done when he first found her, broken amongst the rubbish on the slopes of Fontezarmo. Or when she'd first woken after he pulled the stitches, and stared down in horror at her own scarred body.

"Kill her?" he asked again. "After I carried her from the mountain? After I mended her bones and stitched her back together? After I protected her from your hirelings in Puranti?"

Shenkt turned his hand over and let the ring fall, and it bounced once and tinkled down spinning on the floor beside her twisted right hand. She did not thank him, but he had not expected thanks. It was not for her thanks that he had done it.

"Kill them both!" screamed Orso.

Shenkt was always surprised by how treacherous men could be over trifles, yet how loyal they could be when their lives were forfeit. These last few guards still fought to the death for Orso, even though his day was clearly done. Perhaps they could not comprehend that a man so great as the Grand Duke of Talins might die like any other, and all his power so easily turn to dust. Perhaps for some men obedience became a habit they could not question. Or perhaps they came to define themselves by their service to a master, and chose to take the short step into death as part of something great, rather than walk the long, hard road of life in insignificance.

If so, then Shenkt would not deny them. Slowly, slowly, he breathed in.

The drawn-out twang of the flatbow string throbbed deep in his ears. He stepped out of the path of the first bolt, let it drift under his raised arm. The aim of the next was good, right for Murcatto's throat. He plucked it from the air between finger and thumb as it crawled past, set it carefully down on a polished table as he crossed the room. He took up an idealised bust of one of Orso's forebears from beside it — his grandfather, Shenkt suspected, the one who had himself been a mercenary. He flung it at the nearest flatbowman, just in the process of lowering his bow, puzzled. It caught him in the stomach, sank deep into his armour, folded him in half in a cloud of stone chips and tore him off his feet towards the far wall, legs and arms stretched out in front of him, his bow spinning high into the air.

Shenkt hit the nearest man on the helmet and stove it deep into his shoulders, blood spraying from the crumpled visor, axe dropping slowly from his twisting hand. The next had an open helm, the look of surprise just forming as Shenkt's fist drove a dent into his breastplate so deep that it bent his backplate out with a groan of twisted metal. He sprang to the table, marble floor splitting under his boots as he came down. The nearest

of the two remaining archers slowly raised his flatbow as though to use it as
a shield. Shenkt's hand split it in half, string flailing, tore the man's helmet
off and sent it hurtling up into the ceiling, his body tumbling sideways,
spraying blood, to crumple against the wall in a shower of plaster. Shenkt
seized hold of the other archer and tossed him out of one of the high windows, sparkling fragments tumbling down, bouncing, spinning, breaking
apart, deep clangour of shattering glass making the air hum.

The last but one had his sword raised, flecks of spit floating from his
twisted lips as he gave his war cry. Shenkt caught him by the wrist, hurled
him upside-down across the room and into his final comrade. They were
mangled together, a tangle of dented armour, crashed into a set of shelves,
gilded books ripped open, loose papers spewing into the air, gently fluttering down as Shenkt breathed out, and let time find its course again.

The spinning flatbow fell, bounced from the tiles and clattered away
into a corner. Grand Duke Orso stood just where he had before, beside the
round table with its map of Styria, the sparkling crown sitting in its centre.
His mouth fell open.

"I never leave a job half-done," said Shenkt. "But I was never working
for you."

Monza got to her feet, staring at the bodies tangled, scattered, twisted
about the far end of the hall. Papers fluttered down like autumn leaves,
from a bookcase shattered around a mass of bloody armour, cracks lancing
out through the marble walls all about it.

She stepped around the upended table. Past the bodies of mercenaries
and guards. Over Secco's corpse, his smeared brains gleaming in one of the
long stripes of sunlight from the high windows.

Orso watched her come in silence, the great painting of him proudly
claiming victory at the Battle of Etrea looming ten strides high over his
shoulder. The little man and his outsized myth.

The bone-thief stood back, hands spattered with blood to the elbow,
watching them. She didn't know what he had done, or how, or why. It
didn't matter now.

Her boots crunched on broken glass, on splintered wood, ripped paper,
shattered pottery. Everywhere black spots of blood were scattered and her
soles soaked them up and left bloody footprints behind her. Like the bloody

trail she'd left across Styria, to come here. To stand on the spot where they killed her brother.

She stopped, a sword's length away from Orso. Waiting, she hardly knew what for. Now the moment had come, the moment she'd strained for with every muscle, endured so much pain, spent so much money, wasted so many lives to reach, she found it hard to move. What would come after?

Orso raised his brows. He picked up the crown from the table with exaggerated care, the way a mother might pick up a newborn baby. "This was to be mine. This almost was mine. This is what you fought for, all those years. And this is what you kept from me, in the end." He turned it slowly around in his hands, the jewels sparkling. "When you build your life around only one thing, love only one person, dream only one dream, you risk losing everything at a stroke. You built your life around your brother. I built mine around a crown." He gave a heavy sigh, pursed his lips, then tossed the circle of gold aside and watched it rattle round and round on the map of Styria. "Now look at us. Both equally wretched."

"Not equally." She lifted the scuffed, notched, hard-used blade of the Calvez. The blade she'd had made for Benna. "I still have you."

"And when you have killed me, what will you live for then?" His eyes moved from the sword to hers. "Monza, Monza...what will you do without me?"

"I'll think of something."

The point punctured his jacket with a faint pop, slid effortlessly through his chest and out of his back. He gave a gentle grunt, eyes widening, and she slid the blade free. They stood there, opposite each other, for a moment.

"Oh." He touched one finger to dark cloth and it came away red. "Is that all?" He looked up at her, puzzled. "I was expecting...more."

He crumpled all at once, knees dropping against the polished floor, then he toppled forwards and the side of his face thumped damply against the marble beside her boot. The one eye she could see rolled slowly towards her, and the corner of his mouth twitched into a smile. Then he was still.

Seven out of seven. It was done.

Seeds

It was a winter's morning, cold and clear, and Monza's breath smoked on the air.

She stood outside the chamber where they killed her brother. On the terrace they threw her from. Her hands resting on the parapet they'd rolled her off. Above the mountainside that had broken her apart. She felt that nagging ache still up the bones of her legs, across the back of her gloved hand, down the side of her skull. She felt that prickling need for the husk-pipe that she knew would never quite fade. It was far from comfortable, staring down that long drop towards the tiny trees that had snatched at her as she fell. That was why she came here every morning.

A good leader should never be comfortable, Stolicus wrote.

The sun was climbing, now, and the bright world was full of colour. The blood had drained from the sky and left it a vivid blue, white clouds crawling high above. To the east, the forest crumbled away into a patchwork of fields — squares of fallow green, rich black earth, golden-brown stubble. Her fields. Further still and the river met the grey sea, branching out in a wide delta, choked with islands. Monza could just make out the suggestion of tiny towers there, buildings, bridges, walls. Great Talins, no bigger than her thumbnail. Her city.

That idea still seemed a madman's ranting.

"Your Excellency." Monza's chamberlain lurked in one of the high doorways, bowing so low he almost tongued the stone. The same man who'd served Orso for fifteen years, had somehow come through the sack of Fontezarmo unscathed, and now had made the transition from master to mistress with admirable smoothness. Monza had stolen Orso's city, after all, his palace, some of his clothes, even, with a few adjustments. Why not his retainers too? Who knew their jobs better?

"What is it?"

"Your ministers are here. Lord Rubine, Chancellor Grulo, Chancellor Scavier, Colonel Volfier and... Mistress Vitari." He cleared his throat, looking somewhat pained. "Might I enquire whether Mistress Vitari has a specific title yet?"

"She handles those things no one with a specific title can."

"Of course, your Excellency."

"Bring them in."

The heavy doors were swung open, faced with beaten copper engraved with twisting serpents. Not the works of art Orso's lion-face veneers had been, perhaps, but a great deal stronger. Monza had made sure of that. Her five visitors strutted, strode, bustled and shuffled through, their footsteps echoing around the chill marble of Orso's private audience hall. Two months in, and still she couldn't think of it as hers.

Vitari came first, with much the same dark clothes and smirk she'd worn when Monza first met her in Sipani. Volfier was next, walking stiffly in his braided uniform. Scavier and Grulo competed with each other to follow him. Old Rubine laboured along at the rear, bent under his chain of office, taking his time getting to the point, as always.

"So you still haven't got rid of it." Vitari frowned at the vast portrait of Orso gazing down from the far wall.

"Why would I? Reminds me of my victories, and my defeats. Reminds me where I came from. And that I have no intention of going back."

"And it is a fine painting," observed Rubine, looking sadly about. "Precious few remain."

"The Thousand Swords are nothing if not thorough." The room had lost almost everything not nailed down or carved into the mountainside. Orso's vast desk still crouched grimly at the far end, if somewhat wounded by an axe as someone had searched in vain for hidden compartments. The towering fireplace, held up by monstrous marble figures of Juvens and Kanedias, had proved impossible to remove and now contained a few flaming logs, failing utterly to warm the cavernous interior. The great round table too was still in place, the same map unrolled across it. As it had been the last day that Benna lived, but stained now in one corner with a few brown spots of Orso's blood.

Monza walked to it, wincing at a niggle through her hip, and her ministers gathered around the table in a ring just as Orso's ministers had. They say history moves in circles. "The news?"

"Good," said Vitari, "if you love bad news. I hear the Baolish have crossed the river ten thousand strong and invaded Osprian territory. Muris has declared independence and gone to war with Sipani, again, while Sotorius' sons fight each other in the streets of the city." Her finger waved over the map, carelessly spreading chaos across the continent. "Visserine remains leaderless, a plundered shadow of her former glory. There are rumours of plague in Affoia, of a great fire in Nicante. Puranti is in uproar. Musselia is in turmoil."

Rubine tugged unhappily at his beard. "Woe is Styria! They say Rogont was right. The Years of Blood are at an end. The Years of Fire are just beginning. In Westport, the holy men are proclaiming the end of the world."

Monza snorted. "Those bastards proclaim the end of the world whenever a bird shits. Anywhere without calamities?"

"Talins?" Vitari glanced around the room. "Though I hear the palace at Fontezarmo did suffer some light looting recently. And Borletta."

"Borletta?" It wasn't much more than a year since Monza had told Orso, in this very hall, how she'd thoroughly looted that very city. Not to mention spiked its ruler's head above the gates.

"Duke Cantain's young niece foiled a plot by the nobles of the city to depose her. Apparently, she made such a fine speech they all threw aside their swords, fell to their knees and swore undying fealty to her on the spot. Or that's the story they're telling, at any rate."

"Making armed men fall to their knees is a neat trick, however she managed it." Monza remembered how Rogont won his great victory. *Blades can kill men, but only words can move them, and good neighbours are the surest shelter in a storm.* "Do we have such a thing as an ambassador?"

Rubine looked around the table. "I daresay one could be produced."

"Produce one and send him to Borletta, with a suitable gift for the persuasive duchess and...offers of our sisterly affection."

"Sisterly...affection?" Vitari looked like she'd found a turd in her bed. "I didn't think that was your style."

"My style is whatever works. I hear good neighbours are the surest shelter in a storm."

"Them and good swords."

"Good swords go without saying."

Rubine was looking deeply apologetic. "Your Excellency, your reputation is not...all it might be."

"It never has been."

"But you are widely blamed for the death of King Rogont, Chancellor Sotorius and their comrades in the League of Nine. Your lone survival was…"

Vitari smirked at her. "Damnably suspicious."

"In Talins that only makes you better loved, of course. But elsewhere… if Styria were not so deeply divided, it would undoubtedly be united against you."

Grulo frowned across at Scavier. "We need someone to blame."

"Let's put the blame where it belongs," said Monza, "this once. Castor Morveer poisoned the crown, on Orso's instructions, no doubt. Let it be known. As widely as possible."

"But, your Excellency…" Rubine had moved from apologetic to abject. "No one knows the name. For great crimes, people must blame great figures."

Monza's eyes rolled up. Duke Orso smirked triumphantly at her from the painting of a battle he was never at. She found herself smirking back. Fine lies beat tedious truths every time.

"Inflate him, then. Castor Morveer, death without a face, most infamous of Master Poisoners. The greatest and most subtle murderer in history. A poisoner-poet. A man who could slip into the best-guarded building in Styria, murder its monarch and four of its greatest leaders and away unnoticed like a night breeze. Who is safe from the very King of Poisons? Why, I was lucky to escape with my life."

"Poor innocent that you are." Vitari slowly shook her head. "Rubs me wrong to heap fame on that slime of a man."

"I daresay you live with worse."

"Dead men make poor scapegoats."

"Oh, come now, you can breathe some life into him. Bills at every corner, proclaiming his guilt in this heinous crime and offering, let's say, a hundred thousand scales for his head."

Volfier was looking more worried by the moment. "But...he is dead, isn't he?"

"Buried with the rest when we filled in the trenches. Which means we'll never have to pay. Hell, make it two hundred thousand, then we look rich at the same time."

"And looking rich is almost as useful as being it," said Scavier, frowning at Grulo.

"With the tale I'll get told, the name of Morveer will be spoken with hushed awe when we're long dead and gone." Vitari smiled. "Mothers will scare their children with it."

"No doubt he's grinning in his grave at the thought," said Monza. "I hear you unpicked a little revolt, by the way."

"I wouldn't insult the term by applying it to those amateurs. The fools put up bills advertising their meetings! We knew already, but bills? In plain sight? You ask me, they deserve the death penalty just for stupidity."

"Or there is exile," offered Rubine. "A little mercy makes you look just, virtuous and powerful."

"And I could do with a touch of all three, eh?" She thought about it for a moment. "Fine them heavily, publish their names, parade them naked before the Senate House, then...set them free."

"Free?" Rubine raised his thick white eyebrows.

"Free?" Vitari raised her thin orange ones.

"How just, virtuous and powerful does that make me? Punish them harshly, we give their friends a wrong to avenge. Spare them, we make resistance seem absurd. Watch them. You said yourself they're stupid. If they plan more treason they'll lead us to it. We can hang them then."

Rubine cleared his throat. "As your Excellency commands. I will have bills printed detailing your mercy to these men. The Serpent of Talins forbears to use her fangs."

"For now. How are the markets?"

A hard smile crossed Scavier's soft face. "Busy, busy, morning until night. Traders have come to us fleeing the chaos in Sipani, in Ospria, in Affoia, all more than willing to pay our dues if they can bring in their cargoes unmolested."

"The granaries?"

"The harvest was good enough to see us through the winter without riots, I hope." Grulo clicked his tongue. "But much of the land towards Musselia still lies fallow. Farmers driven out when Rogont's conquering forces moved through, foraging. Then the Thousand Swords left a sweep of devastation almost all the way to the banks of the Etris. The farmers are always the first to suffer in hard times."

A lesson Monza hardly needed to be taught. "The city is full of beggars, yes?"

"Beggars and refugees." Rubine tugged his beard again. He'd tug the bastard out if he told many more sad tales. "A sign of the times—"

"Give the land away, then, to anyone who can yield a crop, and pay us tax. Farmland without farmers is nothing more than mud."

Grulo inclined his head. "I will see to it."

"You're quiet, Volfier." The old veteran stood there, glaring at the map and grinding his teeth.

"Fucking Etrisani!" he burst out, bashing his sword-hilt with one big fist. "I mean, sorry, that is, my apologies, your Excellency, but...those bastards!"

Monza grinned. "More trouble on the border?"

"Three farms burned out." Her grin faded. "The farmers missing. Then the patrol who went looking for them was shot at from the woods, one man killed, two wounded. The rest pursued, but mindful of your orders left off at the border."

"They're testing you," said Vitari. "Angry because they were Orso's first allies."

Grulo nodded. "They gave up everything in his cause and hoped to reap a golden harvest when he became king."

Volfier slapped angrily at the table's edge. "Bastards think we're too weak to stop 'em!"

"Are we?" asked Monza.

"We've three thousand foot and a thousand horse, all armed, drilled, all good men seen action before."

"Ready to fight?"

"Only give the word, they'll prove it!"

"What about the Etrisanese?"

"All bluster," sneered Vitari. "A second-rate power at the best of times, and their best was long ago."

"We have the advantage in numbers and quality," growled Volfier.

"Undeniably, we have just cause," said Rubine. "A brief sortie across the border to teach a sharp lesson—"

"We have the funds for a more significant campaign," said Scavier. "I already have some ideas for financial demands that might leave us considerably enriched—"

"The people will support you," cut in Grulo. "And indemnities will more than cover the expense!"

Monza frowned at the map, frowned in particular at those spots of blood in the corner. Benna would have counselled caution. Would have asked for time to think out a plan . . . but Benna was a long time dead, and Monza's taste had always been to move fast, strike hard and worry about the plans afterwards. "Get your men ready to march, Colonel Volfier. I've a mind to take Etrisani under siege."

"Siege?" muttered Rubine.

Vitari grinned sideways. "It's when you surround a city and force its surrender."

"I am aware of the definition!" snapped the old man. "But caution, your Excellency, Talins has but lately come through the most painful of upheavals—"

"I have only the greatest respect for your knowledge of the law, Rubine," said Monza, "but war is my department, and believe me, once you go to war, there is nothing worse than half measures."

"But what of making allies—"

"No one wants an ally who can't protect what's theirs. We need to demonstrate our resolve, or the wolves will all be sniffing round our carcass. We need to bring these dogs in Etrisani to heel."

"Make them pay," hissed Scavier.

"Crush them," growled Grulo.

Volfier was grinning wide as he saluted. "I'll have the men mustered and ready within the week."

"I'll polish up my armour," she said, though she kept it polished anyway. "Anything else?" The five of them stayed silent. "My thanks, then."

"Your Excellency." They bowed each in their own ways, Rubine with the frown of weighty doubts, Vitari with the slightest, lingering smirk.

Monza watched them file out. She might have liked to put aside the sword and make things grow. The way she'd wanted to long ago, after her father died. Before the Years of Blood began. But she'd seen enough to know that no battle is ever the last, whatever people might want to believe. Life goes on. Every war carries within it the seeds of the next, and she planned to be good and ready for the harvest.

Get out your plough, by all means, Farans wrote, *but keep a dagger handy, just in case.*

She frowned at the map, left hand straying down to rest on her stomach. It was starting to swell. Three months, now, since her blood had come. That meant it was Rogont's child. Or maybe Shivers'. A dead man's child or a killer's, a king's or a beggar's. All that really mattered was that it was hers.

She walked slowly to the desk, dropped into the chair, pulled the chain from her shirt and turned the key in the lock. She took out Orso's crown, the reassuring weight between her palms, the reassuring pain in her right hand as she lifted it and placed it carefully on the papers scattered across the scuffed leather top. Gold gleamed in the winter sun. The jewels she'd had prised out, sold to pay for weapons. Gold, to steel, to more gold, just as Orso always told her. Yet she found she couldn't part with the crown itself.

Rogont had died unmarried, without heirs. His child, even his bastard, would have a good claim on his titles. Grand Duke of Ospria. King of Styria, even. Rogont had worn the crown, after all, even if it had been a poisoned one, and only for a vainglorious instant. She felt the slightest smile at the corner of her mouth. When you lose all you have, you can always seek revenge. But if you get it, what then? Orso had spoken that much truth. Life goes on. You need new dreams to look to.

She shook herself, snatched the crown up and slid it back inside the desk. Staring at it wasn't much better than staring at her husk-pipe, wondering whether or not to put the fire to it. She was just turning the key in the lock as the doors were swung open and her chamberlain grazed the floor again with his face.

"And this time?"

"A representative of the Banking House of Valint and Balk, your Excellency."

Monza had known they were coming, of course, but they were no more welcome for that. "Send him in."

For a man from an institution that could buy and sell nations, he didn't look like much. Younger than she'd expected, with a curly head of hair, a pleasant manner and an easy grin. That worried her more than ever.

The bitterest enemies come with the sweetest smiles. Verturio. Who else?

"Your Excellency." He bowed almost as low as her chamberlain, which took some doing.

"Master...?"

"Sulfur. Yoru Sulfur, at your service." He had different-coloured eyes, she noticed as he drew closer to the desk — one blue, one green.

"From the Banking House of Valint and Balk."

"I have the honour of representing that proud institution."

"Lucky you." She glanced around the great chamber. "I'm afraid a lot of damage was done in the assault. Things are more...functional than they were in Orso's day."

His smile only widened. "I noticed a little damage to the walls on my way in. But functional suits me perfectly, your Excellency. I am here to discuss business. To offer you, in fact, the full backing of my employers."

"I understand you came often to my predecessor, Grand Duke Orso, to offer him your full backing."

"Quite so."

"And now I have murdered him and stolen his place, you come to me."

Sulfur did not even blink. "Quite so."

"Your backing moulds easily to new situations."

"We are a bank. Every change must be an opportunity."

"And what do you offer?"

"Money," he said brightly. "Money to fund armies. Money to fund public works. Money to return glory to Talins, and to Styria. Perhaps even money to render your palace less...functional."

Monza had left a fortune in gold buried near the farm where she was born. She preferred to leave it there still. Just in case. "And if I like it sparse?"

"I feel confident that we could lend political assistance also. Good neighbours, you know, are the surest shelter in a storm." She did not like his choice of words, so soon after she'd used them herself, but he went smoothly on. "Valint and Balk have deep roots in the Union. Extremely deep. I do not doubt we could arrange an alliance between you and their High King."

"An alliance?" She didn't mention that she'd very nearly consummated an alliance of a different kind with the King of the Union, in a gaudy bedchamber at Cardotti's House of Leisure. "Even though he's married to Orso's daughter? Even though his sons may have a claim on my dukedom? A better claim than mine, many would say."

"We strive always to work with what we find, before we strive to change it. For the right leader, with the right backing, Styria is there for the taking. Valint and Balk wish to stand with the victor."

"Even though I broke into your offices in Westport and murdered your man Mauthis?"

"Your success in that venture only demonstrates your great resourcefulness." Sulfur shrugged. "Men are easily replaced. The world is full of them."

She tapped thoughtfully at the top of her desk. "Strange that you should come here, making such an offer."

"How so?"

"Only yesterday I had a very similar visit from a representative of the Prophet of Gurkhul, offering his...backing."

That gave him a moment's pause. "Whom did he send?"

"A woman called Ishri."

Sulfur's eyes narrowed by the smallest fraction. "You cannot trust her."

"But I can trust you, because you smile so sweetly? So did my brother, and he lied with every breath."

Sulfur only smiled the more. "The truth, then. Perhaps you are aware that the Prophet and my employers stand on opposite sides of a great struggle."

"I've heard it mentioned."

"Believe me when I say you would not wish to find yourself on the wrong side."

"I'm not sure I wish to find myself on either side." She slowly settled back into her chair, faking comfort when she felt like a fraud at a stolen desk. "But never fear. I told Ishri the price of her support was too high. Tell me, Master Sulfur, what price will Valint and Balk ask for their help?"

"No more than what is fair. Interest on their loans. Preference in their business dealings and those of their partners and associates. That you refuse to deal with the Gurkish and their allies. That you act, when my employers request, in concert with the forces of the Union—"

"Only whenever your employers request?"

"Perhaps once or twice in your lifetime."

"Or perhaps more, as you see fit. You want me to sell Talins to you and thank you for the privilege. You want me to kneel at your vault door and beg for favours."

"You over-dramatise—"

"I do not kneel, Master Sulfur."

It was his turn to pause at her choice of words. But only for a moment. "May I be candid, your Excellency?"

"I'd like to see you try."

"You are new to the ways of power. Everyone must kneel to someone. If you are too proud to take our hand of friendship, others will."

Monza snorted, though behind her scorn her heart was pounding. "Good luck, to them and to you. May your hand of friendship bring them happier results than it brought to Orso. I believe Ishri was going to start looking for friends in Puranti. Perhaps you should go to Ospria first, or Sipani, or Affoia. I'm sure you'll find someone in Styria to take your money. We're famous for our whores."

Sulfur's grin twitched even wider. "Talins owes great debts to my employers."

"Orso owes great debts to them, you can ask him for your money back. I believe he was thrown out with the kitchen waste, but you should find him if you dig, down there at the bottom of the cliff. I'll happily lend you a trowel for the purpose."

Still he smiled, but there was no missing his threat. "It would be a shame if you left us no choice but to yield to the rage of Queen Terez, and let her seek vengeance for her father's death."

"Ah, vengeance, vengeance." Monza gave him a smile of her own. "I don't startle at shadows, Master Sulfur. I'm sure Terez talks a grand war, but the Union is spread thin. They have enemies both North and South and inside their borders too. If your High King's wife wants my little chair, well, she can come and fight me for it. But I rather suspect his August Majesty has other worries."

"I do not think you realise the dangers that fill the dark corners of the world." There was no good humour in Sulfur's huge grin now. "Why, even as we speak you sit here...alone." It had become a hungry leer, filled with sharp, white teeth. "So very, very fragile."

She blinked, as if baffled. "Alone?"

"You are mistaken." Shenkt had walked up in utter silence until he stood, unobserved, right at Sulfur's shoulder, close as his shadow. Valint and Balk's representative spun about, took a shocked step back and stood frozen, as though he'd turned to see the dead breathing in his ear.

"You," he whispered.

"Yes."

"I thought—"

"No."

"Then...this is your doing?"

"I have had my hand in it." Shenkt shrugged. "But chaos is the natural state of things, for men pull always in their own directions. It is those who want the world to march all the same way that give themselves the challenge."

The different-coloured eyes swivelled to Monza, and back. "Our master will not—"

"*Your* master," said Shenkt. "I have none, anymore, remember? I told him I was done. I always give a warning when I can, and here is yours. Get you gone. Return, you will not find me in a warning mood. Go back, and tell him you serve. Tell him I used to serve. We do not kneel."

Sulfur slowly nodded, then his mouth slipped back into the smirk he wore when he came in. "Die standing, then." He turned to Monza, gave his graceful bow once more. "You will hear from us." And he strutted easily from the room.

Shenkt raised his brows as Sulfur disappeared from sight. "He took it well."

She didn't feel like laughing. "There's a lot you're not telling me."

"Yes."

"Who are you, really?"

"I have been many things. An apprentice. An ambassador. A solver of stubborn problems, and a maker of them. Today, it seems, I am a man who settles other people's scores."

"Cryptic shit. If I want riddles I can visit a fortune-teller."

"You're a grand duchess. You could probably get one to come to you."

She nodded towards the doors. "You knew him."

"I did."

"You had the same master?"

"Once. Long ago."

"You worked for a bank?"

He gave his empty smile. "In a manner of speaking. They do far more than count coins."

"So I'm beginning to see. And now?"

"Now, I do not kneel."

"Why have you helped me?"

"Because they made Orso, and I break whatever they have made."

"Revenge," she murmured.

"Not the best of motives, but good outcomes can flow from evil motives, still."

"And the other way about."

"Of course. You brought the Duke of Talins all his victories, and so I had been watching you, thinking to weaken him by killing you. As it happened, Orso tried to do it himself. So I mended you instead, thinking to persuade you to kill Orso and take his place. But I underestimated your determination, and you slipped away. As it happened, you set about trying to kill Orso..."

She shifted, somewhat uncomfortably, in her ex-employer's chair. "And took his place."

"Why dam a river that already flows your way? Let us say we have helped each other." And he gave his skull's grin one more time. "We all of us have our scores to settle."

"In settling yours, it seems you have made me some powerful enemies."

"In settling yours, it seems you have plunged Styria into chaos."

That was true enough. "Not quite my intention."

"Once you choose to open the box, your intentions mean nothing. And the box is yawning wide as a grave now. I wonder what will spill from it? Will righteous leaders rise from the madness to light the way to a brighter, fairer Styria, a beacon for all the world? Or will we get ruthless shadows of old tyrants, treading circles in the bloody footsteps of the past?" Shenkt's bright eyes did not leave hers. "Which will you be?"

"I suppose we'll see."

"I suppose we will." He turned, his footfalls making not the slightest sound, and pulled the doors silently shut behind him, leaving her alone.

All Change

Y ou need not do this, you know."

"I know." But Friendly wanted to do it.

Cosca squirmed in his saddle with frustration. "If only I could make you see how the world out here . . . swarms with infinite possibilities!" He had been trying to make Friendly see it the entire way from the unfortunate village where the Thousand Swords were camped. He had failed to realise that Friendly saw it with perfect, painful clarity already. And he hated it. As far as he was concerned, fewer possibilities was better. And that meant infinite was far, far too many for comfort.

"The world changes, alters, is born anew and presents a different face each day! A man never knows what each moment will bring!"

Friendly hated change. The only thing he hated more was not knowing what each moment might bring.

"There are all manner of pleasures to sample out here."

Different men take pleasure in different things.

"To lock yourself away from life is . . . to admit defeat!"

Friendly shrugged. Defeat had never scared him. He had no pride.

"I need you. Desperately. A good sergeant is worth three generals."

There was a long moment of silence while their horses' hooves crunched on the dry track.

"Well, damn it!" Cosca took a swig from his flask. "I have made every effort."

"I appreciate it."

"But you are resolved?"

"I am."

Friendly's worst fear had been that they might not let him back in. Until Murcatto had given him a document with a great seal for the authorities of the city of Musselia. It detailed his convictions as an accomplice in the murders of Gobba, Mauthis, Prince Ario, General Ganmark, Faithful Carpi, Prince Foscar and Grand Duke Orso of Talins, and sentenced him to imprisonment for life. Or until such time as he desired to be released. Friendly was confident that would be never. It was the only payment he had asked for, the best gift he had ever been given, and sat now neatly folded in his inside pocket, just beside his dice.

"I will miss you, my friend, I will miss you."

"And I you."

"But not so much I can persuade you to remain in my company?"

"No."

For Friendly, this was a homecoming long anticipated. He knew the number of trees on the road leading to the gate, the warmth welling up in his chest as he counted them off. He stood eagerly in his stirrups, caught a tingling glimpse of the gatehouse, a looming corner of dark brickwork above the greenery. Hardly architecture to fill most convicted men with joy, but Friendly's heart leaped at the sight of it. He knew the number of bricks in the archway, had been waiting for them, longing for them, dreaming of them for so long. He knew the number of iron studs on the great doors, he knew—

Friendly frowned as the track curved about to face the gate. The doors stood open. A terrible foreboding crowded his joy away. What could be more wrong in a prison than that its doors should stand open and unlocked? That was not part of the grand routine.

He slid from his horse, wincing at the pain in his stiff right arm, still healing even though the splints were off. He walked slowly to the gate, almost scared to look inside. A ragged-looking man sat on the steps of the hut where the guards should have been watching, all alone.

"I've done nothing!" He held up his hands. "I swear!"

"I have a letter signed by the Grand Duchess of Talins." Friendly unfolded the treasured document and held it out, still hoping. "I am to be taken into custody at once."

The man stared at him for a moment. "I'm no guard, friend. Just using the hut to sleep in."

"Where are the guards?"

"Gone."

"Gone?"

"With riots in Musselia I reckon no one was paying 'em, so…they up and left."

Friendly felt a cold prickle of horror on the back of his neck. "The prisoners?"

"They got free. Most of 'em ran right off. Some of 'em waited. Shut 'emselves into their own cells at night, only imagine that!"

"Only imagine," said Friendly, with deep longing.

"Didn't know where to run to, I guess. But they got hungry, in the end. Now they've gone too. There's no one here."

"No one?"

"Only me."

Friendly looked up the narrow track to the archway in the rocky hillside. All empty. The halls were silent. The circle of sky still looked down into the old quarry, maybe, but there was no rattling of bars as the prisoners were locked up safe and sound each night. No comforting routine, enfolding their lives as tightly as a mother holds her child. No more would each day, each month, each year be measured out into neat little parcels. The great clock had stopped.

"All change," whispered Friendly.

He felt Cosca's hand on his shoulder. "The world is all change, my friend. We all would like to go back, but the past is done. We must look forwards. We must change ourselves, however painful it may be, or be left behind."

So it seemed. Friendly turned his back on Safety, clambered dumbly up onto his horse. "Look forwards." But to what? Infinite possibilities? He felt panic gripping him. "Forwards all depends on which way you face. Which way should I face now?"

Cosca grinned as he turned his own mount about. "Making that choice is what life is. But if I may make a suggestion?"

"Please."

"I will be taking the Thousand Swords — or those who have not retired on the plunder of Fontezarmo, at least, or found regular employment with the Duchess Monzcarro — down towards Visserine to help me press my claims on Salier's old throne." He unscrewed the cap of his flask. "My entirely righteous claims." He took a swig and burped, blasting Friendly with an overpowering reek of strong spirits. "A title promised me by the

King of Styria, after all. The city is in chaos, and those bastards need someone to show them the way."

"You?"

"And you, my friend, and you! Nothing is more valuable to the ruler of a
great city than an honest man who can count."

Friendly took one last longing look back, the gatehouse already disap-
pearing into the trees. "Perhaps they'll start it up again, one day."

"Perhaps they will. But in the meantime I can make noble use of your
talents in Visserine. I have entirely rightful claims. Born in the city, you
know. There'll be work there. Lots of... work."

Friendly frowned sideways. "Are you drunk?"

"Ludicrously, my friend, quite ludicrously so. This is the good stuff. The
old grape spirit." Cosca took another swig and smacked his lips. "Change,
Friendly... change is a funny thing. Sometimes men change for the better.
Sometimes men change for the worse. And often, very often, given time and
opportunity..." He waved his flask around for a moment, then shrugged.
"They change back."

Happy Endings

Few days after they'd thrown him in there, they'd set up a gallows just outside. He could see it from the little window in his cell, if he climbed up on the pallet and pressed his face to the bars. A man might wonder why a prisoner would go to all that trouble to taunt himself, but somehow he had to. Maybe that was the point. It was a big wooden platform with a crossbeam and four neat nooses. Trapdoors in the floor so they only had to kick a lever to snap four necks at a go, easy as snapping twigs. Quite a thing. They had machines for planting crops, and machines for printing paper, and it seemed they had machines for killing folk too. Maybe that's what Morveer had meant when he spouted off about science, all those months ago.

They'd hanged a few men right after the fortress fell. Some who'd worked for Orso, given some offence someone needed vengeance for. A couple of the Thousand Swords as well, must've stepped onto some dark ground indeed, since there weren't many rules to break during a sack. But no one had swung for a long time now. Seven weeks, or eight. Maybe he should've counted the days, but what difference would counting 'em have made? It was coming, of that much he was sure.

Every morning when the first light crept into the cell and Shivers woke, he wondered if that would be the morning they'd hang him.

Sometimes he wished he hadn't turned on Monza. But only because it had come out the way it had. Not because he regretted any part of what he'd done. Probably his father wouldn't have approved of it. Probably his brother would've sneered and said he expected no better. No doubt Rudd Threetrees would've shook his head, and said justice would come for it.

But Threetrees was dead, and justice with him. Shivers' brother had been a bastard with a hero's face, and his sneers meant nothing no more. And his father had gone back to the mud and left him to work out his own way of doing things. So much for the good men, and the right thing too.

From time to time he wondered whether Carlot dan Eider got away from the mess his failure must've left her in, or whether the Cripple caught up with her. He wondered whether Monza got to kill Orso, and whether it had been all she hoped for. He wondered who that bastard had been who came out of nowhere and knocked him across the hall. Didn't seem likely he'd ever find out the answers now. But that's how life is. You don't always get all the answers.

He was up at the window when he heard keys rattling down the corridor, and he almost smiled at the relief of knowing it was time. He hopped down from his pallet, right leg still stiff where Friendly had stuck his knife in it, stood up tall and faced the metal gate.

He hadn't thought she'd come herself, but he was glad she had. Glad for the chance to look her in the eye one more time, even if they had the jailer and a half-dozen guards for company. She looked well, no doubt of that, not so gaunt as she used to, nor so hard. Clean, smooth, sleek and rich. Like royalty. Hard to believe she ever had aught to do with him.

"Well, look at you," he said. "Grand Duchess Monzcarro. How the hell did you come out o' this mess so fine?"

"Luck."

"There you go. Never had much myself." The jailer unlocked the gate and pushed it squealing open. Two of the guards came in, snapped manacles shut round Shivers' wrists. He didn't see much purpose in making a fight of it. Would've been just an embarrassment all round. They marched him out into the corridor to face her.

"Quite the trip we've been on, ain't it, Monza, you and I?"

"Quite the trip," she said. "You lost yourself, Shivers."

"No. I found myself. You going to hang me now?" He didn't feel much joy at the thought, but not much sorrow either. Better'n rotting in that cell, he reckoned.

She watched him for a long moment. Blue eyes, and cold. Looked at him like she did the first time they met. Like nothing he could do would surprise her. "No."

"Eh?" Hadn't been expecting that. Left him disappointed, almost. "What, then?"

"You can go."

He blinked. "I can what?"

"Go. You're free."

"Didn't think you still cared."

"Who says I ever did? This is for me, not you. I've had enough vengeance."

Shivers snorted. "Well, who'd have fucking thought it? The Butcher of Caprile. The Snake of Talins. The good woman, all along. I thought you didn't have much use for the right thing. I thought mercy and cowardice were the same."

"Mark me down a coward, then. That I can live with. Just don't ever come back here. My cowardice has limits." She twisted the ring off her finger. The one with the big, blood-red ruby in it, and tossed it in the dirty straw at his feet. "Take it."

"Alright." He bent down and dug it out of the muck, wiped it on his shirt. "I ain't proud." Monza turned and walked away, towards the stairway, towards the lamplight spilling from it. "So that's how this ends, is it?" he called after her. "That's the ending?"

"You think you deserve something better?" And she was gone.

He slid the ring onto his little finger and watched it sparkle. "Something worse."

"Move, then, bastard," snarled one of the guards, waving a drawn sword.

Shivers grinned back. "Oh, I'm gone, don't you worry on that score. I've had my fill of Styria."

He smiled as he stepped out of the darkness of the tunnel and onto the bridge that led away from Fontezarmo. He scratched at his itching face, took in a long breath of cold, free air. All things considered, and well against the run of luck, he reckoned he'd come out alright. Might be he'd lost an eye down here in Styria. Might be he was leaving no richer than when he'd stepped off the boat. But he was a better man, of that he'd no doubt. A wiser man. Used to be he was his own worst enemy. Now he was everyone else's.

He was looking forward to getting back to the North, finding some work that suited him. Maybe he'd make a stop in Uffrith, pay his old friend Vossula a little visit. He set off down the mountain, away from the fortress, boots crunching in the grey dust.

Behind him, the sunrise was the colour of bad blood.

Acknowledgments

As always, four people without whom:
Bren Abercrombie, whose eyes are sore from reading it.
Nick Abercrombie, whose ears are sore from hearing about it.
Rob Abercrombie, whose fingers are sore from turning the pages.
Lou Abercrombie, whose arms are sore from holding me up.

Then, my heartfelt thanks:
To all the lovely and talented folks at my UK Publisher, Gollancz, and their parent Orion, particularly Simon Spanton, Jo Fletcher, Jon Weir, Mark Stay and Jon Wood. Then, of course, all those who've helped make, publish, publicise, translate and above all *sell* my books wherever they may be around the world.

To the artists responsible for somehow making me look classy: Didier Graffet, Dave Senior and Laura Brett.

To editors across the Pond: Devi Pillai and Lou Anders.

To other hard-bitten professionals who've provided various mysterious services: Robert Kirby, Darren Turpin, Matthew Amos, Lionel Bolton.

To all the writers whose paths have crossed mine either electronically or in the actual flesh, and who've provided help, laughs and a few ideas worth stealing, including but by no means limited to: James Barclay, Alex Bell, David Devereux, Roger Levy, Tom Lloyd, Joe Mallozzi, John Meaney, Richard Morgan, Adam Roberts, Pat Rothfuss, Marcus Sakey, Wim Stolk and Chris Wooding.

And lastly, yet firstly:
For unstinting support, advice, food, drink and, you know, *editing* above and beyond the call of duty, my editor, Gillian Redfearn. Long may it continue. I mean, I'm not going to write these damn things on my own...

extras

orbit

meet the author

Photo Credit: Lou Abercrombie

JOE ABERCROMBIE is the *New York Times* bestselling author of the First Law series and the Shattered Sea trilogy. He is a full-time writer, and occasional freelance film editor, who lives in Bath, England, with his wife and three children. Find out more about Joe Abercrombie at www.joeabercrombie.com.

interview

Did you find the experience of writing **BEST SERVED COLD,** *a standalone novel, to be more challenging than writing the First Law Trilogy?*

I did find it more challenging. I think mostly because I had the ideas and characters for the First Law Trilogy cooking in my head for a very long time—right back to childhood in some cases—so when I started writing, a lot came out quite easily, and more and more easily as I went along. Also, when I started writing *The Blade Itself,* I was doing it purely for the fun of it, as a hobby, with no pressure at all, so I was free to take as much time as I wanted and to experiment with what worked. For *Best Served Cold,* I had to come up with new characters and settings and implement them on a much tighter schedule, with some level of expectation from readers and publishers, which is a very different challenge. Although the plot was, in a way, much more straightforward than with the First Law, it took a long time for me to really get a feel for the characters in *Best Served Cold.* It wasn't until I'd pretty much finished the first draft that I felt I'd gotten the voice for some of them, particularly Monza, anywhere near right. Then it was a case of revising the rest of the book to match.

How did you develop the idea for the novel?

Seven villains for Monza to wreak vengeance on felt like a good number, and so it seemed like a good idea as well that there should be seven heroes (and I'm using "hero" and "villain" in their loosest possible senses, of course). I filled as many of those roles as I thought was reasonable with characters readers might already have met in the First Law because, although I wanted the book to stand alone, I also wanted there to be some reward and feeling of continuation for people who'd read the trilogy. The book split naturally into seven parts, in each of which Monza and her motley group of helpers visits a different city and tries to kill the next man on the list. I tried to make each effort different in nature, and in some way to reflect the character both of the target and the city that the events takes place in, and also for the scale of the plots and the numbers of people involved to steadily grow, so that hopefully the tone of each part is different enough to keep the reader interested. I then approached each part separately, planning it in detail before writing it, and to some degree letting the overall story develop as it seemed appropriate in each part. I try to plan pretty carefully in advance, but at the same time, you have to give the plot a bit of room to squirm around as new ideas come to you and the characters take on firmer personalities.

Monza Murcatto is a brilliantly intriguing character. Who or what were your inspirations in creating her?
It's always difficult to say exactly where the ideas for characters come from, since often the basic idea will just seem to be there in your head when you begin but the details only develop as you write the book and get a sense of how they talk, think, and behave. The First Law had been a very male set of books, and so I wanted to try my hand at a female main character. I'd always been fascinated by renaissance Italy, the complex and treacherous politics of feuding city-states, the mixture of terrible destruction and wild creativity, the poisonous popes, the intriguing merchants, the rampaging mercenaries, and so I took that as my inspiration for setting. The book was intended to be a fantasy thriller, and I wanted my central character to have one foot in

the underworld but the other in the political world. A mercenary general seemed perfect—as well as having the ideal skill set for a revenger. I also felt that, since the leadership of mercenary companies tended to be pretty fluid and more based on merit than birth or tradition, a female mercenary leader was believable, and not without historical precedent. Then it was a case of thinking about what characteristics such a woman would need to have to succeed in such a male-dominated sphere as war. Some personal capacity for violence was clearly important, but ruthlessness, intelligence, dedication, and superhuman single-mindedness seemed even more so. An acid sense of humor wouldn't hurt either. Then it was a question of seeing whether I could make such a character in any way sympathetic to the reader.

As one of the main progenitors of the subgenre known as "scoundrel lit," how do you feel about the direction the genre is moving in?

I tend to think of it as "unheroic fantasy," but certainly there seems to be a real current within epic fantasy lately toward darker, grittier, more morally ambiguous, more character-centered writing. I heartily approve of it because it's to my personal taste, but also because I feel that epic fantasy had become a bit repetitive and predictable and variety has got to be a good thing. George R.R. Martin, I think, was very important in demonstrating that this kind of work could be commercially successful, that you could produce books that were recognizably epic fantasy—and gave readers everything they hoped for from the form—but at the same time were unpredictable, challenging, and unapologetically adult in every sense of the word. But guys like Fritz Leiber and Jack Vance were writing morally questionable heroes and seedy settings long before I was born, so I'm not sure I regard myself as any kind of progenitor, just a humble practitioner in a long and proud tradition.

Alright, not so humble.

extras

Your books are often compared to films. How does your film editing background influence your books?

I spent ten years or so as a freelance editor, mostly working on live music (concerts, festivals, and awards shows) and documentaries. Certainly, that was important experience. I think it gave me a good idea of timing, of how to come into and get out of a scene, of how you can cut between different strands of action to get the most drama out of both. I was also lucky to see some really skilled producers work on scripts for documentary, where the aim is often to tell the story in the most economical number of words. But above all, I think it taught me how to get on with people and the value of listening to others' opinions and making changes. As an editor, you can't be too precious—you do your best with the material, but if a director, producer, or client wants something different, you have to make changes. You might resent that to begin with, but often you find that looking again with the benefit of a new viewpoint allows you to make improvements. The same is true of a writer. You need to be able to listen to your editor, listen to the opinions of readers, and not necessarily do exactly what they tell you, but always be looking for ways to improve what you're doing.

Will we see previous characters returning in your next novel? Maybe even Murcatto?

Having finished the First Law, I really wanted to write some standalone books set in the same world, which could be accessible to new readers and serve as a jumping-in point but that hopefully, at the same time, would serve as some kind of continuation of the life of the world for readers who had read the trilogy. So I wanted there to be plenty of characters in common—for major characters from the trilogy to appear in the background of the standalones while minor characters took center stage. I enjoy the sense of threads coming in and out of the narrative, of the nods and references that long-term readers might pick up on and the sense it gives of a complete, interconnected world. The next novel takes place in the North, so we'll see a lot of the Northman characters from the First Law making an appearance—Black Dow, Caul Shivers, Princes Calder, and Scale, among others, as well as quite a few Union soldiers—Kroy, Jalenhorm, Bremer dan Gorst. Even a certain Magus makes an appearance. Most of the characters from *Best Served Cold* are sitting this one out, but they'll be there on the bench in case I need them in the future.

What can you tell us about your next novel?

It's called *The Heroes* and it is the story of one battle for control of the North, most of the book taking place in the same location and over the course of three days. It follows six characters as they variously take part in the fighting or try to avoid it, as their paths cross and interweave throughout the course of the battle. On the Union side, we have the most disreputable corporal in His Majesty's whole army, the venomously ambitious daughter of the Marshal in command, and a depressive master swordsman who once served as the king's bodyguard. With the Northmen, we have a hard-bitten veteran who's losing his nerve, a young lad eager to prove himself a warrior, and a disinherited prince eager to reclaim his father's throne by any means necessary, apart from fighting. So where *Best Served Cold* was a fantasy thriller, *The Heroes* is a fantasy war story that attempts to investigate the whole notion of heroism. My five-second pitch is *Lord of the Rings* meets a *Bridge Too Far*.

introducing

THE HEROES

by Joe Abercrombie

*They say Black Dow's killed more men than winter,
and clawed his way to the throne of the North up a hill of skulls.
The King of the Union, ever a jealous neighbor, is not about to
stand smiling by while he claws his way any higher. The orders
have been given and the armies are toiling through the northern
mud. Thousands of men are converging on a forgotten ring of
stones, on a worthless hill, in an unimportant valley,
and they've brought a lot of sharpened metal with them.*

"Too old for this shit," muttered Craw, wincing at the pain in his
dodgy knee with every other step. High time he retired. Long past
high time. Sat on the porch behind his house with a pipe, smiling
at the water as the sun sank down, a day's honest work behind him.
Not that he had a house. But when he got one, it'd be a good one.

He found his way through a gap in the tumble-down wall, heart
banging like a joiner's mallet. From the long climb up the steep
slope, and the wild grass clutching at his boots, and the bullying
wind trying to bundle him over. But mostly, if he was honest, from
the fear he'd end up getting killed at the top. He'd never laid claim
to being a brave man and he'd only got more cowardly with age.

Strange thing, that – the fewer years you have to lose the more you fear the losing of 'em. Maybe a man just gets a stock of courage when he's born, and wears it down with each scrape he gets into.

Craw had been through a lot of scrapes. And it looked like he was about to snag himself on another.

He snatched a breather as he finally got to level ground, bent over, rubbing the wind-stung tears from his eyes. Trying to muffle his coughing which only made it louder. The Heroes loomed from the dark ahead, great holes in the night sky where no stars shone, four times man-height or more. Forgotten giants, marooned on their hilltop in the scouring wind. Standing stubborn guard over nothing.

Craw found himself wondering how much each of those great slabs of rock weighed. Only the dead knew how they'd dragged the bastard things up here. Or who had. Or why. The dead weren't telling, though, and Craw had no plans on joining 'em just to find out.

He saw the faintest glow of firelight now, at the stones' rough edges. Heard the chatter of men's voices over the wind's low growl. That brought back the risk he was taking, and a fresh wave of fear washed up with it. But fear's a healthy thing, long as it makes you think. Rudd Threetrees told him that, long time ago. He'd thought it through, and this was the right thing to do. Or the least wrong thing, anyway. Sometimes that's the best you can hope for.

So he took a deep breath, trying to remember how he'd felt when he was young and had no dodgy joints and didn't care a shit for nothing, picked out a likely gap between two of those big old rocks and strolled through.

Maybe this had been a sacred place, once upon an ancient day, high magic in these stones, the worst of crimes to wander into the circle uninvited. But if any old Gods took offence they'd no way of showing it. The wind dropped away to a mournful sighing and that was all. Magic was in scarce supply and there wasn't much sacred either. Those were the times.

The light shifted on the inside faces of the Heroes, faint orange on pitted stone, splattered with moss, tangled with old bramble and nettle and seeding grass. One was broken off half way up, a couple more had toppled over the centuries, left gaps like missing teeth in a skull's grin.

Craw counted eight men, huddled around their wind-whipped campfire with patched cloaks and worn coats and tattered blankets wrapped tight. Firelight flickered on gaunt, scarred, stubbled and bearded faces. Glinted on the rims of their shields, the blades of their weapons. Lots of weapons. Fair bit younger, in the main, but they didn't look much different to Craw's own crew of a night. Probably they weren't much different. He even thought for a moment one man with his face side-on was Jutlan. Felt that jolt of recognition, the eager greeting ready on his lips. Then he remembered Jutlan was twelve years in the ground, and he'd said the words over his grave.

Maybe there are only so many faces in the world. You get old enough, you start seeing 'em used again.

Craw lifted his open hands high, palms forward, doing his best to stop 'em shaking any. "Nice evening!"

The faces snapped around. Hands jerked to weapons. One man snatched up a bow and Craw felt his guts drop, but before he got close to drawing the string the man beside him stuck out an arm and pushed it down.

"Whoa there, Redcrow." The one who spoke was a big old lad, with a heavy tangle of grey beard and a drawn sword sitting bright and ready across his knees. Craw found a rare grin, 'cause he knew the face, and his chances were looking better.

Hardbread he was called, a Named Man from way back. Craw had been on the same side as him in a few battles down the years, and the other side from him in a few more. But he'd a solid reputation. A long-seasoned hand, likely to think things over, not kill then ask the questions, which was getting to be the more popular way of doing business. Looked like he was Chief of this lot too, 'cause the lad called Redcrow sulkily let his bow drop, much to Craw's relief. He didn't want anyone getting killed tonight, and wasn't ashamed to say that counted double for his self.

There were still a fair few hours of darkness to get through, though, and a lot of sharpened steel about.

"By the dead." Hardbread sat still as the Heroes themselves, but his mind was no doubt doing a sprint. " 'Less I'm much mistaken, Curnden Craw just wandered out o' the night."

"You ain't." Craw took a few slow paces forwards, hands still high, doing his best to look light-hearted with eight sets of unfriendly eyes weighing him down.

"You're looking a little greyer, Craw."

"So are you, Hardbread."

"Well, you know. There's a war on." The old warrior patted his stomach. "Plays havoc with my nerves."

"All honesty, mine too."

"Who'd be a soldier?"

"Hell of a job. But they say old horses can't jump new fences."

"I try not to jump at all these days," said Hardbread. "Heard you was fighting for Black Dow. You and your dozen."

"Trying to keep the fighting to a minimum, but as far as who I'm doing it for, you're right. Dow buys my porridge."

"I love porridge." Hardbread's eyes rolled down to the fire and he poked thoughtfully at it with a twig. "The Union pays for mine now." His lads were twitchy – tongues licking at lips, fingers tickling at weapons, eyes shining in the firelight. Like the audience at a duel, watching the opening moves, trying to suss who had the upper hand. Hardbread's eyes came up again. "That seems to put us on opposite sides."

"We going to let a little thing like sides spoil a polite conversation?" asked Craw.

As though the very word "polite" was an insult, Redcrow had another rush of blood. "Let's just kill this fucker!"

Hardbread turned slowly to him, face squeezed up with scorn. "If the impossible happens and I feel the need for your contribution, I'll tell you what it is. 'Til then keep it shut, halfhead. Man o' Curnden Craw's experience don't just wander up here to get killed by the likes o' you." His eyes flicked around the stones, then back to Craw. "Why'd you come, all by your lone self? Don't want to fight for that bastard Black Dow no more, and you've come over to join the Dogman?"

"Can't say I have. Fighting for the Union ain't really my style, no disrespect to those that do. We all got our reasons."

"I try not to damn a man on his choice o' friends alone."

"There's always good men on both sides of a good question," said Craw. "Thing is, Black Dow asked me to stroll on down to the Heroes, stand a watch for a while, see if the Union are coming up this way. But maybe you can spare me the bother. Are the Union coming up this way?"

"Dunno."

"You're here, though."

"I wouldn't pay much mind to that." Hardbread glanced at the lads around the fire without great joy. "As you can see, they more or less sent me on my own. The Dogman asked me to stroll up to the Heroes, stand a watch, see if Black Dow or any of his lot showed up." He raised his brows. "You think they will?"

Craw grinned. "Dunno."

"You're here, though."

"Wouldn't pay much mind to that. It's just me and my dozen. 'Cept for Brydian Flood, he broke his leg a few months ago, had to leave him behind to mend."

Hardbread gave a rueful smile, prodded the fire with his twig and sent up a dusting of sparks. "Yours always was a tight crew. I daresay they're scattered around the Heroes now, bows to hand."

"Something like that." Hardbread's lads all twitched to the side, mouths gaping. Shocked at the voice coming from nowhere, shocked on top that it was a woman's. Wonderful stood with her arms crossed, sword sheathed and bow over her shoulder, leaning up against one of the Heroes as careless as she might lean on a tavern wall. "Hey, hey, Hardbread."

The old warrior winced. "Couldn't you even nock an arrow, make it look like you take us serious?"

She jerked her head into the darkness. "There's some boys back there, ready to put a shaft through your face if one o' you looks at us wrong. That make you feel better?"

Hardbread winced even more. "Yes and no," he said, his lads staring into the gaps between the stones, the night suddenly heavy with threat. "Still acting Second to this article, are you?"

Wonderful scratched at the long scar through her shaved-stubble hair. "No better offers. We've got to be like an old married couple who haven't fucked for years, just argue."

"Me and my wife were like that, 'til she died." Hardbread's finger tapped at his drawn sword. "Miss her now, though. Thought you'd have company from the first moment I saw you, Craw. But since you're still jawing and I'm still breathing, I reckon you're set on giving us a chance to talk this out."

"Then you've reckoned the shit out o' me," said Craw. "That's exactly the plan."

"My sentries alive?"

Wonderful turned her head and gave one of her whistles, and Scorry Tiptoe slid out from behind one of the stones. Had his arm around a man with a big pink birthmark on his cheek. Looked almost like two old mates, 'til you saw Scorry's hand had a blade in it, edge tickling at Birthmark's throat.

"Sorry, Chief," said the prisoner to Hardbread. "Caught me off guard."

"It happens."

A scrawny lad came stumbling into the firelight like he'd been shoved hard, tripped over his own feet and sprawled in the long grass with a squawk. Jolly Yon stalked from the darkness behind him, axe held loose in one fist, heavy blade gleaming down by his boot, heavy frown on his bearded face.

"Thank the dead for that." Hardbread waved his twig at the lad, just clambering up. "My sister's son. Promised I'd keep an eye out. If you'd killed him I'd never have heard the end of it."

"He was asleep," growled Yon. "Weren't looking out too careful, were you?"

Hardbread shrugged. "Weren't expecting anyone. If there's two things we've got too much of in the North it's hills and rocks. Didn't reckon a hill with rocks on it would be a big draw."

"It ain't to me," said Craw, "but Black Dow said come down here—"

"And when Black Dow says a thing..." Brack-i-Dayn half-sang the words, that way the hillmen tend to. He stepped into the wide circle of grass, tattooed side of his great big face turned towards the firelight, shadows gathered in the hollows of the other.

Redcrow made to jump up but Hardbread weighed him down with a pat on the shoulder. "My, my. You lot just keep popping up." His eyes slid from Jolly Yon's axe, to Wonderful's grin, to Brack's belly, to Scorry's knife still at his man's throat. Judging the odds, no doubt, just the way Craw would've done. "You got Whirrun of Bligh with you?"

Craw slowly nodded. "I don't know why, but he insists on following me around."

Right on cue, Whirrun's strange valley accent floated from the dark. "Shoglig said... I would be shown my destiny... by a man choking on a bone." It echoed off the stones, seeming to come from everywhere at once. He'd quite the sense of theatre, Whirrun. Every real hero needs one. "And Shoglig is old as these stones. Hell won't take her, some say. Blade won't cut her. Saw the world born, some say, and will see it die. That's a woman a man has to listen to, ain't it? Or so some say."

Whirrun strolled through the gap one of the missing Heroes had left and into the firelight, tall and lean, face in shadow from his hood, patient as winter. He had the Father of Swords across his shoulders like a milkmaid's yoke, dull grey metal of the hilt all agleam, arms slung over the sheathed blade and his long hands dangling. "Shoglig told me the time, and the place, and the manner of my death. She whispered it, and made me swear to keep it secret, for magic shared is no magic at all. So I cannot tell you where it will be, or when, but it is not here, and it is not now." He stopped a few paces from the fire. "You boys, on the other hand..." Whirrun's hooded head tipped to one side, only the end of his sharp nose, and the line of his sharp jaw, and his thin mouth showing. "Shoglig didn't say when you'd be going." He didn't move. He didn't have to. Wonderful looked at Craw, and rolled her eyes towards the starry sky.

But Hardbread's lads hadn't heard it all a hundred times before. "That Whirrun?" one muttered to his neighbour. "Cracknut Whirrun? That's him?"

His neighbour said nothing, just the lump on the front of his throat moving as he swallowed.

"Well, my old arse if I'm fighting my way out o' this," said Hardbread, brightly. "Any chance you'd let us clear out?"

"I've a mind to insist on it," said Craw.

"We can take our gear?"

"I'm not looking to embarrass you. I just want your hill."

"Or Black Dow does, at any rate."

"Same difference."

"Then you're welcome to it." Hardbread slowly got to his feet, wincing as he straightened his legs, no doubt cursed with some sticky joints of his own. "Windy as anything up here. Rather be down in Osrung, feet near a fire." Craw had to admit he'd a point there. Made him wonder who'd got the better end of the deal. Hardbread sheathed his sword, thoughtful, while his lads gathered their gear. "This is right decent o' you, Craw. You're a straight edge, just like they say. Nice that men on different sides can still talk things through, in the midst of all this. Decent behaviour... it's out o' fashion."

"Those are the times." Craw jerked his head at Scorry and he slipped his knife away from Birthmark's throat, gave this little bow and held his open hand out towards the fire. Birthmark backed off, rubbing at the new-shaved patch on his stubbly neck, and started rolling up a blanket. Craw hooked his thumbs in his sword-belt and kept his eyes on Hardbread's crew as they made ready to go, just in case anyone had a mind to play hero.

Redcrow looked most likely. He'd slung his bow over his shoulder and now he was standing there with a black look, an axe in one white-knuckled fist and a shield on his other arm, a red bird painted on it. If he'd been for killing Craw before, didn't seem the last few minutes had changed his mind. "A few old shits and some fucking woman," he snarled. "We're backing down to the likes o' these without a fight?"

"No, no." Hardbread slung his own scarred shield onto his back. "I'm backing down, and these fellows here. You're going to stay, and fight Whirrun of Bligh on your own."

"I'm what?" Redcrow frowned at Whirrun, twitchy, and Whirrun looked back, what showed of his face still stony as the Heroes themselves.

"That's right," said Hardbread, "since you're itching for a brawl. Then I'm going to cart your hacked-up corpse back to your mummy and tell her not to worry 'cause this is the way you wanted it. You loved this fucking hill so much you just had to die here."

Redcrow's hand worked nervously around his axe handle. "Eh?"

"Or maybe you'd rather come down with the rest of us, blessing the name o' Curnden Craw for giving us a fair warning and letting us go without any arrows in our arses."

"Right," said Redcrow, and turned away, sullen.

Hardbread puffed his cheeks at Craw. "Young ones these days, eh? Were we ever so stupid?"

Craw shrugged. "More'n likely."

"Can't say I felt the need for blood like they seem to, though."

Craw shrugged again. "Those are the times."

"True, true, and three times true. We'll leave you the fire, eh? Come on, boys." They made for the south side of the hill, still stowing the last of their gear, and one by one faded into the night between the stones.

Hardbread's nephew turned in the gap and gave Craw the fuck yourself finger. "We'll be back here, you sneaking bastards!" His uncle cuffed him across the top of his scratty head. "Ow! What?"

"Some respect."

"Ain't we fighting a war?"

Hardbread cuffed him again and made him squeal. "No reason to be rude, you little shit."

Craw stood there as the lad's complaints faded into the wind beyond the stones, swallowed sour spit, and eased his thumbs out from his belt. His hands were trembling, had to rub 'em together to hide it, pretending he was cold. But it was done, and everyone involved still drawing breath, so he guessed it had worked out as well as anyone could've hoped.

Jolly Yon didn't agree. He stepped up beside Craw frowning like thunder and spat into the fire. "Time might come we regret not killing those folks there."

"Not killing don't tend to weigh as heavy on my conscience as the alternative."

Brack tut-tutted from Craw's other side. "A warrior shouldn't carry too much conscience."

"A warrior shouldn't carry too much belly either." Whirrun had shrugged the Father of Swords off his shoulders and stood it on end, the pommel coming up to his neck, watching how the light moved on the crosspiece as he turned it round and round. "We all got our weights to heft."

"I've got just the right amount, you stringy bastard." And the hillman gave his great gut a proud pat like a father might give his son's head.

"Chief." Agrick strode into the firelight, bow loose in his hand and an arrow dangling between two fingers.

"They away?" asked Craw.

"Watched 'em down past the Children. They're crossing the river now, heading towards Osrung. Athroc's keeping a watch on 'em, though. We'll know if they double back."

"You reckon they will?" asked Wonderful. "Hardbread's cut from the old cloth. He might smile, but he won't have liked this any. You trust that old bastard?"

Craw frowned into the night. "'Bout as much as I'd trust anyone these days."

"Little as that? Best post guards."

"Aye," said Brack. "And make sure ours stay awake."

Craw thumped his arm. "Nice o' you to volunteer for first shift."

"Your belly can keep you company," said Yon.

Craw thumped his arm next. "Glad you're in favour, you can go second."

"Shit!"

"Drofd!"

You could tell the curly lad was the newest of the crew 'cause he actually hurried up with some snap. "Aye, Chief?"

"Take the saddle horse and head back up the Yaws Road. Not sure whose lads you'll meet first – Ironhead's most likely, or maybe Tenways'. Let 'em know we ran into one of the Dogman's dozens at the Heroes. More'n likely just scouting, but..."

"Just scouting." Wonderful nibbled some scab off one knuckle and spat it from the tip of her tongue. "The Union are miles away, split up and spread out, trying to make straight lines out of a country with none."

"More'n likely. But hop on the horse and pass on the message anyway."

"Now?" Drofd's face was all dismay. "In the dark?"

"No, next summer'll be fine," snapped Wonderful. "Yes, now, fool, all you've got to do is follow a road."

Drofd heaved a sigh. "Hero's work."

"All war work is hero's work, boy," said Craw. He'd rather have sent someone else, but then they'd have been arguing 'til dawn over why the new lad wasn't going. There are right ways of doing things a man can't just step around.

"Right y'are, Chief. See you in a few days, I reckon. And with a sore arse, no doubt."

"Why?" And Wonderful gave a few thrusts of her hips. "Tenways a special friend o' yours is he?" That got some laughs. Brack's big rumble, Scorry's little chuckle, even Yon's frown got a touch softer which meant he had to be rightly tickled.

"Ha, bloody ha." And Drofd stalked off into the night to find the horse and make a start.

"I hear chicken fat can ease the passage!" Wonderful called after him, Whirrun's cackle echoing around the Heroes and off into the empty dark.

With the excitement over Craw was starting to feel all burned out. He dropped down beside the fire, wincing as his knees bent low, the earth still warm from Hardbread's rump. Scorry had found a place on the far side, sharpening his knife, the scraping of metal marking the rhythm to his soft, high singing. A song of Skarling Hoodless, greatest hero of the North, who brought the clans together long ago to drive the Union out. Craw sat and listened, chewed at the painful skin around his fingernails and thought about how he really had to stop doing it.

Whirrun set the Father of Swords down, squatted on his haunches and pulled out the old bag he kept his runes in. "Best do a reading, eh?"

"You have to?" muttered Yon.

"Why? Scared o' what the signs might tell you?"

"Scared you'll spout a stack of nonsense and I'll lie awake half the night trying to make sense of it."

"Guess we'll see." Whirrun emptied his runes into his cupped hand, spat on 'em then tossed 'em down by the fire.

Craw couldn't help craning over to see, though he couldn't read the damn things for any money. "What do the runes say, Cracknut?"

"The runes say..." Whirrun squinted down like he was trying to pick out something a long way off. "There's going to be blood."

Wonderful snorted. "They always say that."

"Aye." Whirrun wrapped himself in his coat, nuzzled up against the hilt of his sword like a lover, eyes already shut. "But lately they're right more often than not."

Craw frowned around at the Heroes, forgotten giants, standing stubborn guard over nothing. "Those are the times," he muttered.

651

introducing

If you enjoyed
BEST SERVED COLD,
look out for

PROMISE OF BLOOD

The Powder Mage Trilogy: Book One

by Brian McClellan

Field Marshal Tamas's coup against his king sent corrupt aristocrats to the guillotine and brought bread to the starving. But it also provoked war with the Nine Nations, internal attacks by royalist fanatics, and the greedy to scramble for money and power by Tamas's supposed allies: the Church, workers unions, and mercenary forces.

Stretched to his limit, Tamas is relying heavily on his few remaining powder mages, including the embittered Taniel, a brilliant marksman who also happens to be his estranged son, and Adamat, a retired police inspector whose loyalty is being tested by blackmail.

Now, as attacks batter them from within and without, the credulous are whispering about omens of death and destruction. Just old peasant legends about the gods waking to walk the earth. No modern educated man believes that sort of thing. But they should…

Adamat wore his coat tight, top buttons fastened against a wet night air that seemed to want to drown him. He tugged at his sleeves, trying to coax more length, and picked at the front of the jacket where it was too close by far around the waist. It'd been half a decade since he'd even seen this jacket, but when summons came from the king at this hour, there was no time to get his good one from the tailor. Yet this summer coat provided no defense against the chill snaking through the carriage window.

The morning was not far off but dawn would have a hard time scattering the fog. Adamat could feel it. It was humid even for early spring in Adopest, and chillier than Novi's frozen toes. The soothsayers in Noman's Alley said it was a bad omen. Yet who listened to soothsayers these days? Adamat reasoned it would give him a cold and wondered why he had been summoned out on a pit-made night like this.

The carriage approached the front gate of Skyline and moved on without a stop. Adamat clutched at his pantlegs and peered out the window. The guards were not at their posts. Odder still, as they continued along the wide path amid the fountains, there were no lights. Skyline had so many lanterns, it could be seen all the way from the city even on the cloudiest night. Tonight the gardens were dark.

Adamat was fine with this. Manhouch used enough of their taxes for his personal amusement. Adamat stared out into the gardens at the black maws where the hedge mazes began and imagined shapes flitting back and forth in the lawn. What was...ah, just a sculpture. Adamat sat back, took a deep breath. He could hear his heart beating, thumping, frightened, his stomach tightening. Perhaps they *should* light the garden lanterns...

A little part of him, the part that had once been a police inspector, prowling nights such as these for the thieves and pickpockets in dark alleys, laughed out from inside. *Still your heart, old man*, he said to himself. *You were once the eyes staring back from the darkness.*

The carriage jerked to a stop. Adamat waited for the coachman to open the door. He might have waited all night. The driver rapped on the roof. "You're here," a gruff voice said.

Rude.

Adamat stepped from the coach, just having time to snatch his hat and cane before the driver flicked the reins and was off, clattering into the night. Adamat uttered a quiet curse after the man and turned around, looking up at Skyline.

The nobility called Skyline Palace "the Jewel of Adro." It rested on a high hill east of Adopest so that the sun rose above it every morning. One particularly bold newspaper had compared it to a starving pauper wearing a diamond ring. It was an apt comparison in these lean times. A king's pride doesn't fill the people's bellies.

He was at the main entrance. By day, it was a grand avenue of marbled walks and fountains, all leading to a pair of giant, silver-plated doors, themselves dwarfed by the sheer façade of the biggest single building in Adro. Adamat listened for the soft footfalls of patrolling Hielmen. It was said the king's personal guard were everywhere in these gardens, watching every secluded corner, muskets always loaded, bayonets fixed, their gray-and-white sashes somber among the green-and-gold splendor. But there were no footfalls, nor were the fountains running. He'd heard once that the fountains only stopped for the death of the king. Surely he'd not have been summoned here if Manhouch were dead. He smoothed the front of his jacket. Here, next to the building, a few of the lanterns were lit.

A figure emerged from the darkness. Adamat tightened his grip on his cane, ready to draw the hidden sword inside at a moment's notice.

It was a man in uniform, but little could be discerned in such ill light. He held a rifle or a musket, trained loosely on Adamat, and wore a flat-topped forage cap with a stiff visor. Only one thing could be certain... he was not a Hielman. Their tall, plumed hats were easy to recognize, and they never went without them.

"You're alone?" a voice asked.

"Yes," Adamat said. He held up both hands and turned around.

"All right. Come on."

The soldier edged forward and yanked on one of the mighty silver doors. It rolled outward slowly, ponderously, despite the man putting his weight into it. Adamat moved closer and examined the soldier's jacket. It was dark blue with silver braiding. Adran military. In theory, the military reported to the king. In practice, one man held their leash: Field Marshal Tamas.

"Step back, friend," the soldier said. There was a note of impatience in his voice, some unseen stress—but that could have been the weight of the door. Adamat did as he was told, only coming forward again to slip through the entrance when the soldier gestured.

"Go ahead," the soldier directed. "Take a right at the diadem and head through the Diamond Hall. Keep walking until you find yourself in the Answering Room." The door inched shut behind him and closed with a muffled thump.

Adamat was alone in the palace vestibule. Adran military, he mused. Why would a soldier be here, on the grounds, without any sign of the Hielmen? The most frightening answer sprang to mind first. A power struggle. Had the military been called in to deal with a rebellion? There were a number of powerful factions within Adro: the Wings of Adom mercenaries, the royal cabal, the Mountainwatch, and the great noble families. Any one of them could have been giving Manhouch trouble. None of it made sense, though. If there had been a power struggle, the palace grounds would be a battlefield, or destroyed outright by the royal cabal.

Adamat passed the diadem—a giant facsimile of the Adran crown—and noted it was in as bad taste as rumor had it. He entered the Diamond Hall, where the walls and floor were of scarlet, accented in gold leaf, and thousands of tiny gems, which gave the room its name, glittered from the ceiling in the light of a single lit candelabra. The tiny flames of the candelabra flickered as if in the wind, and the room was cold.

Adamat's sense of unease deepened as he neared the far end of the gallery. Not a sign of life, and the only sound came from his own echoing footfalls on the marble floor. A window had been shattered, explaining the chill. The result of one of the king's famous temper tantrums? Or something else? He could hear his heart beating in his ears. There. Behind a curtain, a pair of boots? Adamat passed his hand before his eyes. A trick of the light. He stepped over to reassure himself and pulled back the curtain.

A body lay in the shadows. Adamat bent over it, touched the skin. It was warm, but the man was most certainly dead. He wore gray pants with a white stripe down the side and a matching jacket. A tall hat with a white plume lay on the floor some ways away. A Hielman. The shadows played on a young, clean-shaven face, peaceful except for a single hole in the side of his skull and the dark, wet stain on the floor.

He'd been right. A struggle of some kind. Had the Hielmen rebelled, and the military been brought in to deal with them? Again, it didn't make any sense. The Hielmen were fanatically loyal to the king, and any matters within Skyline Palace would have been dealt with by the royal cabal.

Adamat cursed silently. Every question compounded itself. He suspected he'd find some answers soon enough.

Adamat left the body behind the curtain. He lifted his cane and twisted, bared a few inches of steel, and approached a tall doorway flanked by two hooded, scepter-wielding sculptures. He paused between the ancient statues and took a deep breath, letting his eyes wander over a set of arcane script scrawled into the portal. He entered.

The Answering Room made the Hall of Diamonds look small. A pair of staircases, one to either side of him and each as wide across as three coaches, led to a high gallery that ran the length of the room on both sides. Few outside the king and his cabal of Privileged sorcerers ever entered this room.

In the center of the room was a single chair, on a dais a handbreadth off the floor, facing a collection of knee pillows, where the cabal acknowledged their liege. The room was well lit, though from no discernible source of light.

A man sat on the stairs to Adamat's right. He was older than Adamat, just into his sixtieth year with silver hair and a neatly trimmed mustache that still retained a hint of black. He had a strong but not overly large jaw and his cheekbones were well defined. His skin was darkened by the sun, and there were deep lines at the corners of his mouth and eyes. He wore a dark-blue soldier's uniform with a silver representation of a powder keg pinned above the heart and nine gold service stripes sewn on the right breast, one for every five years in the Adran military. His uniform lacked an officer's epaulettes, but the weary experience in the man's brown eyes left no question that he'd led armies on the battlefield. There was a single pistol, hammer cocked, on the stair next to him. He leaned on a sheathed small sword and watched as a stream of blood slowly trickled down each step, a dark line on the yellow-and-white marble.

"Field Marshal Tamas," Adamat said. He sheathed his cane sword and twisted until it clicked shut.

The man looked up. "I don't believe we've ever met."

"We have," Adamat said. "Fourteen years ago. A charity ball thrown by Lord Aumen."

"I have a terrible time with faces," the field marshal said. "I apologize."

Adamat couldn't take his eyes off the rivulet of blood. "Sir. I was summoned here. I wasn't told by whom, or for what reason."

"Yes," Tamas said. "I summoned you. On the recommendation of one of my Marked. Cenka. He said you served together on the police force in the twelfth district."

Adamat pictured Cenka in his mind. He was a short man with an unruly beard and a penchant for wines and fine food. He'd seen him last seven years ago. "I didn't know he was a powder mage."

"We try to find anyone with an affinity for it as soon as possible," Tamas said, "but Cenka was a late bloomer. In any case"—he waved a hand—"we've come upon a problem."

Adamat blinked. "You . . . want my help?"

The field marshal raised an eyebrow. "Is that such an unusual request? You were once a fine police investigator, a good servant of Adro, and Cenka tells me that you have a perfect memory."

"Still, sir."

"Eh?"

"I'm still an investigator. Not with the police, sir, but I still take jobs."

"Excellent. Then it's not so odd for me to seek your services?"

"Well, no," Adamat said, "but sir, this is Skyline Palace. There's a dead Hielman in the Diamond Hall and..." He pointed at the stream of blood on the stairs. "Where's the king?"

Tamas tilted his head to the side. "He's locked himself in the chapel."

"You've staged a coup," Adamat said. He caught a glimpse of movement with the corner of his eye, saw a soldier appear at the top of the stairs. The man was a Deliv, a dark-skinned northerner. He wore the same uniform as Tamas, with eight golden stripes on the right breast. The left breast of his uniform displayed a silver powder keg, the sign of a Marked. Another powder mage.

"We have a lot of bodies to move," the Deliv said.

Tamas gave his subordinate a glance. "I know, Sabon."

"Who's this?" Sabon asked.

"The inspector that Cenka requested."

"I don't like him being here," Sabon said. "It could compromise everything."

"Cenka trusted him."

"You've staged a coup," Adamat said again with certainty.

"I'll help with the bodies in a moment," Tamas said. "I'm old, I need some rest now and then." The Deliv gave a sharp nod and disappeared.

"Sir!" Adamat said. "What have you done?" He tightened his grip on his cane sword.

Tamas pursed his lips. "Some say the Adran royal cabal had the most powerful Privileged sorcerers in all the Nine Nations, second only to Kez," he said quietly. "Yet I've just slaughtered every one of them. Do you think I'd have trouble with an old inspector and his cane sword?"

Adamat loosened his grip. He felt ill. "I suppose not."

"Cenka led me to believe that you were pragmatic. If that is the case, I would like to employ your services. If not, I'll kill you now and look for a solution elsewhere."

"You've staged a coup," Adamat said again.

Tamas sighed. "Must we keep coming back to that? Is it so shocking? Tell me, can you think of any fewer than a dozen factions within Adro with reason to dethrone the king?"

"I didn't think any of them had the skill," Adamat said. "Or the daring." His eyes returned to the blood on the stairs, before his mind traveled to his wife and children, asleep in their beds. He looked at the field marshal. His hair was tousled; there were drops of blood on his jacket—a lot, now that he thought to look. Tamas might as well have been sprayed with it. There were dark circles under his eyes and a weariness that spoke of more than just age.

"I will not agree to a job blindly," Adamat said. "Tell me what you want."

"We killed them in their sleep," Tamas said without preamble. "There's no easy way to kill a Privileged, but that's the best. A mistake was made and we had a fight on our hands." Tamas looked pained for a moment, and Adamat suspected that the fight had not gone as well as Tamas would have liked. "We prevailed. Yet upon the lips of the dying was one phrase."

Adamat waited.

" 'You can't break Kresimir's Promise,' " Tamas said. "That's what the dying sorcerers said to me. Does it mean anything to you?"

Adamat smoothed the front of his coat and sought to recall old memories. "No. 'Kresimir's Promise'... 'Break'... 'Broken'... Wait—'Kresimir's Broken Promise.' " He looked up. "It was the name of a street gang. Twenty...twenty-two years ago. Cenka couldn't remember that?"

Tamas continued. "Cenka thought it sounded familiar. He was certain you'd remember it."

"I don't forget things," Adamat said. "Kresimir's Broken Promise was a street gang with forty-three members. They were all young, some of them no more than children, the oldest not yet twenty. We were trying to round up some of the leaders to put a stop to a string of thefts. They were an odd lot—they broke into churches and robbed priests."

"What happened to them?"

Adamat couldn't help but look at the blood on the stairs. "One day they disappeared, every one of them—including our informants. We found the whole lot a few days later, forty-three bodies jammed into a drain culvert like pickled pigs' feet. They'd been massacred by powerful sorceries, with excessive brutality. The marks of the king's royal cabal. The investigation ended there." Adamat suppressed a shiver. He'd not once seen a thing like that, not before or since. He'd witnessed executions and riots and murder scenes that filled him with less dread.

The Deliv soldier appeared again at the top of the stairs. "We need you," he said to Tamas.

"Find out why these mages would utter those words with their final breath," Tamas said. "It may be connected to your street gang. Maybe not. Either way, find me an answer. I don't like the riddles of the dead." He got to his feet quickly, moving like a man twenty years younger, and jogged up the stairs after the Deliv. His boot splashed in the blood, leaving behind red prints. "Also," he called over his shoulder, "keep silent about what you have seen here until the execution. It will begin at noon."

"But..." Adamat said. "Where do I start? Can I speak with Cenka?"

Tamas paused near the top of the stairs and turned. "If you can speak with the dead, you're welcome to."

Adamat ground his teeth. "How did they say the words?" he said. "Was it a command, or a statement, or...?"

Tamas frowned. "An entreaty. As if the blood draining from their bodies was not their primary concern. I must go now."

"One more thing," Adamat said.

Tamas looked to be near the end of his patience.

"If I'm to help you, tell me why all of this?" He gestured to the blood on the stairs.

"I have things that require my attention," Tamas warned.

Adamat felt his jaw tighten. "Did you do this for power?"

"I did this for me," Tamas said. "And I did this for Adro. So that Manhouch wouldn't sign us all into slavery to the Kez with the Accords. I did it because those grumbling students of philosophy at the university only play at rebellion. The age of kings is dead, Adamat, and I have killed it."

Adamat examined Tamas's face. The Accords was a treaty to be signed with the king of Kez that would absolve all Adran debt but impose strict tax and regulation on Adro, making it little more than a Kez vassal. The field marshal had been outspoken about the Accords. But then, that was expected. The Kez had executed Tamas's late wife.

"It is," Adamat said.

"Then get me some bloody answers." The field marshal whirled and disappeared into the hallway above.

Adamat remembered the bodies of that street gang as they were being pulled from the drain in the wet and mud, remembered the horror etched upon their dead faces. *The answers may very well be bloody.*